Chasing Infinity

Aria Harding

Cover Design by: Graziana with Chris Covers

First Edition published 2023

ISBN Paperback: 979-8-9883784-0-2

ISBN Ebook: 979-8-9883784-1-9

Dear Reader

To my Loyal Readers,

It has always been my dream to write an <u>Epic Love Story</u> that tells the whole story, not just the bits and pieces. That is "Chasing Infinity." This is an *epic* love story that spans decades. This book is long, and detailed, but it is *everything*. This book is focused more on the journey, so it may seem slow at times, but everything has been crafted meticulously.

I hope you read this book and fall in love with Addison and Noah just as I have. I wouldn't be here, writing this epigraph without the support of everyone who put time and dedication into this book. Thank you to all my lovely readers on Inkitt who stood by me while this book was being written. Without you all, I would have nothing.

Love,

Aria

Foreword

Some of the material in this novel may be triggering. This novel contains traumatic material such as mention of physical abuse by a parent, death of a parents to a fire, and themes referencing human trafficking. This is not a dark romance, but if any of these themes may make you uncomfortable, please read with discretion.

Chasing Infinity is a long novel, purposefully designed that way. It aims to tell the entire story between Noah and Addison, the good, the bad, and everything in between. With that in mind, I hope you enjoy this epic love story!

Contents

Part One
Now

I love her, and that is the beginning and end of everything.

- F. Scott Fitzgerald

* * *

Chapter 1
Noah

Thunder rattles outside, making the frame of my car shake. The rain bombards the windows and I groan, pulling the edges of my flimsy pillow across my ears to drown it out. Shifting around in the backseat of the pathetic run-down car, I try to get comfortable. It takes great effort not to let my situation weigh me down too far.

My life is a shit show. Nothing about where I am right now would have been on my plan for my life. I never imagined the catalyst to bring me back to this godforsaken town would be my mother's funeral. But here we are. Life has a funny way of turning the tables around on you.

Almost ten years have passed since the last time I set foot in this town. While the threat of knowing I'd have to return at some point lingered in my mind like a foul odor, I generally did a fair job of keeping myself distracted. I was living in a happy little fantasy outside this picturesque place. Unfortunately, now that I'm back, the bubble has burst.

Willow Heights is where I was born, where I grew up, and where I crashed and burned. The residents of this town probably still walk around whispering my name like a legend. This place elicits too many memories for me to be comfortable hanging around for too long. But it's home. This is why I begrudgingly parked in front of Monty's Market & Pharmacy when I rolled up to the city limits last night. As I slowed to a stop, I attempted to deter myself from recalling when old Monty caught me buying a pack of condoms at fourteen. I was mortified.

Throughout the rest of the night, the memories of growing up in this town flood my brain as I attempt to get some sleep. I keep tossing and turning, trying to get comfortable, but it's pointless. There is nothing left for me in this town, and reliving all those years here is a stark reminder.

I sit up in the car with a groan and lean my head against the window. Rain is pelting down on the frame of my vehicle. The clatter of the raindrops on the metal soothes me. Usually, it would lull me to sleep, but I've concluded that it likely won't be happening at this point. I peer out the window at the giant clock tower looming like a beacon on the Main Street square. I squint my eyes, trying to read the hands. Six-thirty. The heavy clouds hanging over the town give the morning an ominous air.

I weigh my options: I could stay in my car and hope that sleep comes to me for another few hours, or I could leave my car and brave the rain. I'm camped out a few storefronts down from a cozy-looking café. The lights are on, and I see people walking in and out holding coffees and bagels. They're all much too cheery for it being six-thirty on a Thursday. I can't blame them; their world hasn't tilted on its axis like mine.

I sigh and reach for my wallet, throwing the worn leather open and peering inside. I have fifty bucks sitting in there. A coffee and a muffin would be what, seven? I estimate no more than ten dollars. It's not all I have to my name, but contributing to Willow Heights's economy makes me want to barf. But my stomach growls in a pathetic pleading noise, and I concede. I need to get something to eat.

With a wince at my aching back, I open the door of my car and clamber out into the rain. I pull the hood of my sweatshirt up to cover my head. My feet slosh in the puddles on the street, and I grimace. The puddle water will seep through the holes in my boots and ruin my entire day.

I schlep down the sidewalk to the diner, keeping my head low and hoping no one will recognize me. The last time I was here, I was a teenager, now I'm a man. I hope the maturity is considerable enough that identification won't be too quick.

In such a small town as Willow Heights, it's impossible not to know everything and everyone. Not to mention, my father's been the mayor since I was fifteen. Makes me kind of a small-town name, despite my utter reluctance. It wasn't much later that I realized that having a name associated with the mayor of Willow Heights wasn't all it cracked up to be.

I pull open the door to the diner and step in. Immediately, the warmth from the little restaurant seeps inside of me. My muscles relax as the atmosphere warms me to the bones. The scent of fresh omelets and greasy bacon hits my nose. My stomach rumbles again, begging me for something to eat. I peruse the layout, looking for the best place to sit, but the diner is packed. I finally settle on the last seat at the bar. It's off to the side, so hopefully, I'll stay out of everyone's way.

As I head towards my targeted seat, a flash of red and brown flies into my line of drive. Her toe catches on the tip of my boot, and she stumbles. My arms reach out instinctively to steady her.

"Oh my gosh, I'm so sorry!" she exclaims, looking down and trying to straighten the food she has on her tray. It doesn't take much to put together that she works here and was mid-stride to delivering some-one's breakfast when she tripped.

I let her go, frowning at the now-occupied seat I was aiming for. Someone else snagged it right from under me during the fiasco. I exhale, frustrated as I say, "All good, sorry for getting in your way. I was trying to find a seat."

"I think there's one over in that corner if you want," the woman says, finally satisfied with the tray. "I'll be over to take your order in just a moment—" her sentence cuts off with a gasp. I drag my glare from the douche who took my seat. My own breath catches in my throat when I glance down at her.

"Noah," she gasps, now gazing directly at me, her plump lips falling open on my name. Her eyes flutter across my face as she appraises me standing in front of her. She studies me as if she's re-committing me to memory. Or upgrading her old memory of me to the newer version, filling in the pieces that have changed.

"Parks," I say back with an edge of surprise. Her name on my tongue recalls the memories of her I've held at bay for so long. They come rushing into my brain like a tsunami, triggered by the famil-iarity of her hazel eyes on me once more. Those hazel eyes have haunted my dreams all these years. Always hazel, with flecks of gold flaring from the pupil and a dark freckle on the left iris. So familiar after all this time, but yet unfamiliar.

"Long time no see." I recompose myself as best as possible. I slide my hands into my pocket and grip my fingers into tight fists, my eyes never leaving her.

Parks stares at me, shell-shocked. Her silence draws out the moment before she shakes herself out of it and shifts the tray around to settle on her hip. "You're back."

"So it would seem," I mutter, my eyes still roving her. Out of all the people, I figured I would run into here, she was not one of them. She is supposed to be far, far away from here. She should have left and never looked back. "As are you."

Parks has the decency to blush a little bit at my blunt statement. "Yeah, I am. Um," she looks back at the table in the corner, taking her bottom lip between her teeth and worrying at it. "If you want to grab that seat, I'll bring you a coffee or something in just a minute."

The corners of my lips pull up into a smirk, and I dip my chin at her. "Sure thing, Parks."

Parks inhales, her chest rising with a deep breath, and she nods. Her eyes peek at me for a second longer before she hurries off to deliver the food so it doesn't get cold.

My eyes follow after her for a second too long, then I saunter over to the lonely table in the corner. I pull out the chair and make myself comfortable, flipping through the menu sitting in front of me. I only manage to peruse the menu's first page before she comes over. She's holding a pot of coffee and an empty white ceramic mug.

"Cream and sugar are on the table. Have you had a chance to look at the menu?" she asks, giving me a tight smile as she pours a cup of coffee for me. Parks' expression develops into a more professional demeanor. She can pretend it's not just her and me, but I don't know how long that will work.

"Yeah, I'll have the French toast with a side of sausage," I tell her, folding up the plastic menu and sliding it away from me.

A smile plays on her lips as she sets the now full mug of coffee in front of me. The steam swirling from it hits my chin, and the aroma of the coffee is enough to make up for my missing hours of sleep. My brain is already re-energizing from the scent of it.

"I'll get that right in for you," she says briskly. She spins on her heel and heads to the back. With her exit, she leaves me to my own devices. As she walks away, I watch her go, a familiar constriction forming around my heart. My hand unconsciously rubs on my sternum to ease some of the ache.

Addison Parks was the greatest thing to happen and not happen to me. We could have had it all together, but it wasn't the right time. I ended up leaving Willow Heights, and she was supposed to pursue her dreams elsewhere. Yet here she is, standing in front of me.

My eyes roam around the quaint little diner, and as I look around, my memory jogs. I remember that this was the exact storefront that used to be Parks' parents' café once upon a time. My deductive skills fill in the blanks, and I determine she must have bought out the space and made it her own.

It's small, but there are enough tables to keep the staff busy. It has that classy hometown atmosphere. The employees look energetic and happy to be there. They greet every customer by name as they walk through the door.

One of the other workers delivers my breakfast a few minutes later. I thank them before digging in, not remembering when I last had a serving of French Toast this delicious. Addison comes over again as I finish up, bracing a black square bucket on her hip that's half full of dirty dishes. I raise an eyebrow at her as she stares at me.

"I was sorry to hear about your mom," Addison says carefully after an awkward moment of ogling at me as if she can't believe I'm truly right in front of her. I can tell she's uncomfortable at how distant we are, not sure how to approach the conversation. Well, that makes two of us, sweetheart. "I didn't even realize that she was...."

"Suicidal?" I fill in for her, chuckling humorlessly under my breath. "Me neither, but I can't say it's out of character, given who she was married to."

Addison's dark eyebrows pull in at the middle as she frowns, unsure how to respond. "But even so, I know your mom means a lot to you."

"She does."

"Charlie told me," she informs me. "He was the one who got called onto the scene first. He said he tried everything to resuscitate her but—"

"Yeah," I reply and shift in my seat, the wooden chair putting uncomfortable pressure on my low back.

Jesus H. Christ, get me out of this conversation.

I glance around the diner, searching for something to comment on to move off this topic. I clear my throat when I find nothing worth talking about. "Well, this has been... I'm not sure. But I need to go. Maybe we can catch up another time."

I don't mean to brush her off, but I know it is likely how my brusque tone translates for her. God, that's the last thing I'd ever want to do, but distance is my friend now. I have to keep my mind on my reason for being here. I can't let myself fall back into old habits. If I did, I'd never leave this diner again—or her.

"Oh," Addison says, the brightness in her eyes dimming slightly.

"I have a meeting with Sullivan to talk about—you know," I inform her, surveying her.

The brightness slowly returns when she realizes that I'm not trying to jump ship on her again. "Are you going to be staying long?"

"I'm not sure. I haven't decided yet." I sigh and rub the back of my neck, meeting her eyes and shrugging a shoulder.

"Okay," she responds, clearly unsure what else to say, her eyes tracking my every movement as I ball up my napkin and drop it on the empty plate. "Can I get you anything else before you go?"

"I'm good, Parks. Thank you, though." I stand up and brush off my jeans, reaching into my back pocket for my wallet. "How much do I owe you?"

Parks is still staring at me with her wide hazel eyes as she waves her hand in a blow-off manner. "It's fine. It's on me today."

"You don't have to do that," I argue.

"We're friends, Noah. And this is my diner. I can do what I want."

"Thank you," I shoot her a grin as I head toward the door. I raise my hand in her direction before I leave. "I'll see you around, yeah?"

Addison presses her lips together, narrowing her eyes and tilting her head at me. "Yeah, I'll see you around. Bye, Noah."

* * *

"Sully!" I shout as I throw open the front door to the Sheriff's department. "Get your ass out here."

I hear a scuffle in the other room. Charlie fucking Sullivan walks out holding—and I'm not even making this shit up—a glazed chocolate doughnut and a to-go cup of what I'm assuming was coffee. The coffee has the *Sunny Side Up Diner* logo pasted on the side, and I realize he got it from Addison's diner. I try to school my features as best as possible, remaining impassive. Still, despite my best efforts,

I'm sure my upper lip curls into the signature sneer I reserve just for Charlie Sullivan.

Sullivan raises his eyebrows in surprise and struggles to gulp down his massive bite of doughnut. "Lockwood, you're here."

I hold up the folded business card in my hand. "You rang?"

Sully sets his coffee down on a neighboring desk and gently places his doughnut on top. "Yeah, but I didn't think you'd be here that quickly."

I roll my eyes and take a few steps towards him, noticing the shiny new badge under his nameplate: Sheriff. "Whoa, man, congrats on the promotion. Dear old Dad, finally hand over the reins?"

Charlie grimaces and shakes his head. "Ah, no. He passed away last year heart attack."

I press my lips together and freeze for a brief second before regaining my mojo. "Well, shit, man. I'm sorry to hear that."

"It was pretty sudden, like someone just pointed their finger at him and muttered a curse or something. One second he was here, and then he was gone. Kind of like what happened with your mom, I guess," he says sheepishly, looking up at me like he's afraid I'm going to punch him in the throat. "I'm sorry, by the way."

I cross my arms over my chest and hold his gaze. "Thanks, it was a bit of a shock."

"Understandable. I was the one who arrived on the scene first, you know?"

I know, I say to myself, my mind darting back to Addison this morning. "Well, I'm glad you were there."

"Me too," he says, his eyes locked on mine.

"I'm not really sure how to do this." As I stare at my old schoolmate, I stay quiet for another moment. I clear my throat and he glances back at me with an eyebrow raised.

Charlie laughs humorlessly. "It's okay. I'm not looking for a hug or anything."

"Okay, good," I say with a sigh of relief. "Now, can we get to business?"

"By all means, my office is this way."

He leads us back past all the desks belonging to his deputies into an office. His workspace is spotless, of course. I follow him in, and he shuts the door behind me, reaching over to pull the blinds closed.

"First things first, thanks for the note; you know I love a cryptic message," I shoot at him. He opens his mouth to retort, but I hold up a hand, not finished. "Second, would you care to explain to me why I ran into Parks? Here in Willow Heights, of all places?"

Charlie grimaces again and moves around to sit in his chair, taking a moment to answer me. "I was hoping to talk to you before you ran into her."

"So this is a thing then," I speculate. "She's actually still here. After you told me you'd convince her to leave?"

"Noah, listen, it's not that—"

"You gave me your word, Charlie," I growl back at him. "How the fuck are we supposed to do this when she's still here, still at risk? My dad knows about her and isn't afraid to risk her life again to prove a point. Especially with me being back here."

"She wouldn't leave."

"Well, then, you did a shitty job of convincing her."

"It's more complicated than that. Look, I'll be the first to admit I could have done more, but she wouldn't leave. Not after she saw you in New York a few years back. She was set to go, but I dunno, man, that gave her hope or something."

"Is that it? That's the story you're sticking to?"

He hesitates a moment too long. "Yep."

"I can tell you're hiding something, Sullivan. You're a shit liar, and you always have been. What, has she found someone else?"

By his expression, I already know the answer. That's fine. I told her not to wait for me. Honestly, I'd be surprised if she didn't have another man. Parks is a catch. "Who is it?"

"Don't ask me that."

"Okay, you've just narrowed it down to about five people. Go ahead and just rip the bandaid off."

He holds up a single finger. "I want to make it known for the record that I didn't want to tell you this, but you basically forced it out of me." I roll my eyes, and he continues, "It's Eli."

Mother fucker.

I bark out a laugh and grip the back of my neck. "You've got to be fucking kidding me. This guy again?"

"Things are a little more complicated than that."

"This is a small town, Charlie. Of course, things are complicated. Spill it, then we can get to the real reason I'm here," I order. I choose to ignore that we resemble a pair of two old ladies gossiping about the town's juicy business right now.

He sighs loudly, as if this is the last thing he wants to do, but concedes, "They're not dating per se, but just seeing each other. They both have different ideas of how they want their relationship to progress. You know Eli, he's been in love with her since he first saw her."

"I'm aware," I say through gritted teeth.

"But Addie is more just looking for a friends-with-benefits deal, I think. Something to take the edge off when she has a bad day." I grit my teeth at his phrasing, not liking the mental image that gives me. "I can't imagine she sees herself settling down with him. She's always had eyes for someone else, you know? And as history has shown, Eli doesn't live up to that for her."

I scrub my hand over my face, trying not to dwell too hard on the fact that I want to throw up at this recent development. "Okay."

"That's it? Okay?"

I scowl at my not-so-much friend. "I don't know what else you want me to do. Your bestie and his incessant puppy-love isn't my problem."

"What about Addie?"

"Parks is a grown woman." And a fucking beautiful woman at that. The image of her plump lips falling open when she ran into me this morning pops into my brain, and I shake my head, trying to clear it, focusing on where I am. "She can handle herself."

I've spent way too long daydreaming about Addison Parks, and I know that despite it all, I'll spend much more time continuing to do just that. Later tonight, when I'm alone, I'll break apart every second of our interaction today, analyzing all aspects of what we said to each other. But, for now, I shove it to the back of my mind so I can focus on the task at hand.

"So, about this nice card you sent me," I begin. About a week and a half ago, I received a plain white envelope with my name and address written on it. I found a Willow Heights City Hall business card when I opened it. Nothing was written on the card. It was enough to send a message and confirm that my coming back for my mother's funeral was not the only reason I was supposed to be back here.

Sullivan steeples his fingers and looks at me, his green eyes turning severe. I realize I'm now talking to the Sheriff of Willow Heights, the Charlie I grew up with, now pushed to the sidelines. "I think I have him."

"You think? What does that mean?" I ask him, praying to whatever God is up there that I didn't come back to this godforsaken town for a hunch.

"I had someone undercover at the right place at the right time, and I think we have a lead."

"Again, with the 'you think' bit. Charlie, drop the façade and just tell me what the hell you got."

"My guy heard Mayor McCoy talking about delivery to someone named Orville Marks. I haven't heard of anyone in that town, but I'm looking into it. We'll check databases for neighboring towns and go larger if we have to. I think this might be our way in."

I frown. I guess there might be something here. It's not much to go on, but something, at least. "Did he allude to anything illegal? Or literally, anything else that could get us a warrant?"

Charlie looks contrite as he shakes his head. "Unfortunately, no, but I'm hoping that now you're back in town, we'll be able to smoke him out a little. Hopefully, he'll think we're onto him—which we are —and he'll trip himself up."

I fall into the chair in front of his desk. My hand rubs at the back of my neck to soothe the tension. "He'll definitely know we're onto something."

"Why's that?"

"Because I basically said as much," I mutter, looking out the window at a squirrel climbing a tree. I try to dampen the white-hot fiery anger that boils in my chest whenever my father crosses my mind, but it's no use. "He might believe that my mother's death gives him a free pass, which, sure. I'll give him that one. But I told him he'd be in cuffs the next time he'd see me."

"Well, that might be a little extreme. We still have a long way to go before we get there. We don't have any solid proof yet."

"So, what's the plan then, Chief?" I say, turning back to him.

"Just lie low for now. I have my guys out there with their ears peeled, just in case he slips up again. I want you to re-acclimatize yourself here in town, maybe rattle him up a bit, but don't pursue anything. Then he'll let his guard down, and we'll get him."

"Do you want me to—" I shrug my shoulders, unsure, "Make him think I'm not after him or what? That I've given up?"

Charlie's eyebrows pull in. "No, I don't think that would be the best course of action. You two have always been at each other's throats. If you pulled a full one-eighty on him, he would know something was up. I think you should just go back to how it was before."

"Before?" I scoff. "Sorry, man, with all due respect, but that's a bullshit plan. Not only am I a completely different man than I was then, but now my mother's gone. Before is nonexistent."

"That's all I got right now, Noah. Don't make it obvious that we're trying to nab him, and we'll be fine."

"And not to mention if I go back to 'before' as you say," I twitch my fingers into quotations, still on a roll, "I'm knowingly putting Addison back in danger. Or have you forgotten what happened to her parents when my father thought I was onto him the last time?"

He narrows his eyes at me. "I haven't forgotten."

I lean back into the chair. "My point. I don't want anything to happen to her. She's suffered enough because of me."

"We'll just have to play it a certain way. Like I told you, Addie is in some sort of weird arrangement with Eli. Let's just let that come to a head, so you don't have to worry about that. Just stay away from her. If your father doesn't think she means anything to you anymore, there won't be a problem."

My chest squeezes tightly. Visuals of wide hazel eyes come to mind, and I frown. "I'm not sure if I can promise that."

"You can't just stay away from her for a little longer? I thought that wouldn't be much to ask of you." I glare at him at his unspoken words, and his eyebrows heighten.

"It's asking a lot for me to pretend that she's not everything to me, Charlie," I growl.

"You're hung up on her still, then?" I remain silent, which is answer enough. "Okay, whatever. Just try," he pleads with me. "I don't want to see Addie hurt any more than you do. She's my best friend."

"Why do I feel like I'm just a pawn in your game here?"

"Because that's what I need you to be right now," Charlie says bluntly, holding my eyes with a heavy stare. "We'll get him, Noah. We will. I promise you that."

Chapter 2
Addison

"Good morning, Jack!" I say as I bound down the stairs into the diner. My opening manager looks at me as soon as I step out on the floor with a grin and a nod of his head.

"Good morning. Going out for a run?"

"Yeah," I acknowledge, walking over to the register and popping it open to check the on-hand cash. "Think you can handle everything here for about an hour or so? I'll just do a quick one, and then I'll come back and get cleaned up to help you with the morning rush."

"It's fine, Addie. I've been running this shift for the last year. I think I got it covered," Jack says, his expression telling me that he has everything under control. I do my best to keep the micromanager part of myself hidden, but he can see right through me. I'm grateful that Jack is proficient at managing me just as much as he can manage the diner.

I opened this diner about five years ago once everything finally got back in order after the fire which burned it down. The building used to be my parents' café. Given the history, it took me a while to be comfortable setting foot in the place. This wasn't what I had ever imagined my life would turn out to be: Addison Parks, Small Town Diner Owner—but here we are. I know my parents would have been proud to see what I've accomplished if they were still alive, and that's all that matters to me.

It took a few months for business to steadily pick up around here, but my best friend Grace and I worked our asses off to build it to what it is today. And now, it's hard for me to release the reigns sometimes to let my capable staff take over.

"Okay, okay," I concede with an amused smile. "I'll be back in an hour. I have my phone if anything happens, so you can call—"

"Leave, Addison," Jack orders me with a chuckle. I close the register and hold my hands up in surrender. "Fine, I'm leaving. Call me if you need me."

As I head out, a familiar older woman walks into the diner and gives me a wide smile. "Good morning Addison."

"Good morning, Mrs. Hawley," I greet her with a grin before turning back to Jack, who's standing behind the counter watching our exchange. "Jack, make sure you don't forget Mrs. Hawley's favorite scone this morning on the house!"

"Oh, thank you, dear," Mrs. Hawley pats my shoulder. "You're always too kind to me."

"My pleasure," I say, smiling back at her. "Enjoy your breakfast."

With that, I finally make it out of the diner. I stand on the sidewalk and fiddle with the watch on my wrist, programming it to start tracking my workout. I pull up my favorite playlist and take off as soon as the beat hits my ears. My feet thrum against the pavement as the scenery flashes by. I wave every once in a while at some of my regular customers when they see me. I make my rounds, keeping pace with the music. My morning run is my favorite way to ensure that my day starts on the right foot—no pun intended.

The sun is slower to come up around this time of the year. This means I get to see the full glory of the sunrise in person rather than behind the front windows of my diner. Watching the sun rise is something that I value as part of my regular routine. Days that I actually get to see it are generally better than days that I don't. I try not to think about the more significant meaning of it now that Noah's back in town, forcing my brain to focus on other things.

Unfortunately, though, a thin blanket of clouds covers the sky this morning. The sun reflects off them as it peeks over the horizon, emitting a warm golden-pink glow. As the sun rises a little higher, its rays bounce off the trees illuminating the changing colors of the leaves. Everything in the fall is cozy and comforting despite the ever-constant loom of winter around the corner.

My watch vibrates against my wrist as I round my last block and come to a stop in front of Monty's Market. I slow my pace to catch my breath as I sync my watch to my activity log. A sheen of sweat is playing across my forehead, and I wipe it off with my long sleeve running shirt. Movement in my peripheral vision snags my attention, and I frown. Next to me, parked against the curb, is a shoddy old beater of a car. I usually wouldn't pay it any mind, but I'm positive I saw something move in the back seat.

I pause for a second, debating what I should do. Making up my mind, I take a deep breath and step closer, noting that someone is sleeping in the back of this car. Curious now, I get close enough to peer into the window. My jaw hinges open as soon as I do, the muscles in my face going slack.

There's Noah, curled up in the back seat of his car, a pathetic torn-up blanket thrown over his shoulders that doesn't reach past his knees. He's bent at an odd angle, his height clearly not allowing him to find a comfortable position in such a compact space.

My mind races as I work to piece together why he's sleeping in his car like a homeless person when his dad still sits as the mayor of this town. I know he's not best friends with his father after all that happened between the two of them—and given everything he's done, I can't say I'm shocked Noah wouldn't want Declan's help. But I still would have hoped that Noah would be well enough to find a place to stay that was a tad bit more comfortable than squishing himself into a car.

I stand there gaping at him like a fool for a few moments,

pondering it all, before I snap out of it and turn on my heel, walking away as if I saw nothing. It's none of my business. I haven't heard a single peep out of the man since we last connected in New York over five years ago. Despite our history, I don't know what he's got going on in his life, so if he wants to sleep in his car, that is fine by me.

I still can't ignore the constriction of my chest as I walk away, and I find myself peeking over my shoulder once more, looking at the old car. Letting out a frustrated sigh, I shake my head to clear it and hurry back into the diner.

It's not my business.

The front door jingles as I step in, and I wave at Jack as I bound up the stairs to my flat. I hop in the shower and rinse all the sweat off before drying my hair and finding something presentable to wear for the rest of the day.

My diner is open every day of the week, from six to ten. I try to give myself ample time off during the long daily hours, and I have rotating shifts of people who can cover the front for me when I have to run out. Not to mention my business partner-slash-best friend, Grace, is usually here to help take some of the strain off. However, she's out of town until tomorrow, visiting her family, which means I've been working overtime.

I filter through my closet, pursing my lips as I search to find something to wear. My usual attire consists of jeans or leggings and a variety of long-sleeve shirts. I prefer to keep the diner atmosphere comfortable and laid back, and my wardrobe reflects that.

Settling on a red flannel and boot-cut jeans, I change and throw some makeup on to cover up my cheeks which are still rosy red from my run and the steamy shower. As soon as I'm satisfied with my appearance, I head downstairs.

I jump into the middle of madness with the brunt of the morning rush. People circulate in and out of the diner. Some sit for breakfast while others head straight to the counter to pick up a coffee-to-go and a pastry item of their choice.

I step behind the counter and tap Jack on the shoulder. "How's it going?"

"Just splendid," he chirps back, using a pair of silver tongs to pick up a blueberry scone and drop it into a paper bag. "Do you want to pour Sadie a cup of coffee to go? This scone is for her."

"Of course," I say and set to my task. As soon as Sadie, who runs the florist shop across the town square, heads out the door with her breakfast, I pour myself a cup of coffee and take a sip, leaning the edge of my hip against the counter. I nearly groan when the warmth of the brew hits my stomach, warming me from the inside out. No morning is complete without a good cup of coffee, which is why I'm so grateful for my staff who can make it.

"Jack, you make a mean pot of coffee. What would I do without you?"

My friend looks at me with a dryly amused expression. "Probably go out of business. What kind of diner owner doesn't know how to make coffee?"

I laugh and take another sip. "It's not that I don't know how to. I'm just not very good at it."

Jack waves me off and mutters under his breath, "Basically, the same thing." I roll my eyes, still laughing to myself, and pick up some of the slack from the morning rush.

As soon as eight-thirty hits, the craziness starts to calm down— just as it does every morning once the working class has finished their hustle-and-bustle. With a sigh of contentedness, I pour myself another cup of coffee and reach for a muffin when the door flies open, yanking my attention away from my own breakfast.

A loud and boisterous "There's my girl!" echoes throughout the diner. I look up right as Eli struts in, his arms splayed wide in a grand show. Charlie follows behind him rolling his eyes at our mutual friend's obnoxious display of his deep appreciation for me.

As much as I try to fight it, a slight smile tugs on the corner of my lips as Eli circles the counter and wraps his arm around my waist. He pulls my body into his and presses a kiss to my hair. "How are you today, gorgeous?"

I wiggle out of Eli's grip and step further away from him. I see Jack shake his head out of the corner of my eye at the events unfolding—just your average Friday morning around here. "I'm fine. How are you?"

"I'm great!" he exclaims, moving to the right side of the counter and leaning over on his elbows. He's receiving a few sideways glances from my customers, and I exhale, equally flattered and annoyed that he feels the need to showboat this way. "It's Friday. I get to see my girl tonight. There's nothing that could bring my mood down today."

Charlie and I meet eyes, and I press my lips together. I instantly register that we're thinking of the same thing—about someone's return to town—that would very much bring down Eli's mood. And it's someone I just so happened to catch passed out in the backseat of his car this morning. I make a split decision to save that topic for a little later, aware that there are more pressing matters to discuss.

"Um, I was actually going to talk to you about that," I say, rubbing away a few crumbs resting on the counter. "I have a few things I was hoping to get finished tonight since Grace won't be back until Sunday. Do you think we could move date night to tomorrow?"

Eli has always worn his feelings for me on his sleeve. My stomach clenches when his expression falls at my request. He hits me with those bright blue puppy dog eyes and I want to immediately apologize for hurting his feelings, but I refrain. "Oh, yeah, that's fine."

I'm aware it's probably not *fine* to him, but frankly, I don't have time to see him tonight. With Grace being out of town, I have to pick up her back-office duties with the diner—such as payroll, so I can get my employees' checks to them on time. In my mind, that takes priority over a date night with Eli, where all we'll do is eat shitty food, fall into bed, and have mediocre sex.

Sue me.

"Thanks for understanding," I say simply. I rub my hands

together and look at my favorite guys, plastering a smile on my face. "Can I get you two anything to eat?"

"I'll take a ham and cheese omelet with peppers in it," Eli says, his mood bouncing back like a springboard.

"I'll just do an everything bagel with cream cheese and a coffee," Charlie requests. "Thanks, Addie."

"Oh, a coffee for me too! Thanks, Addie!" Eli chimes in, and I shake my head in amusement as I plug in their orders.

Once they both have plates in front of them and are happily sipping on coffee, I can finally sit down to eat my breakfast. I place a blueberry muffin on a small plate and sit next to my friends. Eli is jabbering away about how they have to do inventory at the market this weekend and how much he will dread it when his face goes blank. His expression stays that way for just a moment and then relights with mischief.

"I just remembered; you will never guess who I saw back in town last night. I wasn't sure if I was going crazy, but it was definitely him." I look over at Charlie, raising an eyebrow at him as he shifts in his seat uncomfortably. Uncertainty clouds his face as to where this conversation is going. This is fine, though, if Eli already knows, Charlie and I don't have to be the ones to tell him that Noah's back.

"Who?" I ask, playing dumb.

Eli looks around dramatically and then leans towards Charlie and me, lowering his voice. "Noah McCoy."

"It's actually Lockwood," Charlie supplies without missing a beat.

I dart my gaze over to him again, curious. "What?"

"He changed his name after he left. He goes by Noah Lockwood. It was his mother's name."

"Really?" I question and chew on the inside of my lip, digesting this new information. "That's—"

"Weird," Eli supplies for me. "His dad's the mayor. Why would he want to change his name? As much as I hate to admit it, that last name has sway around here."

Charlie and I meet eyes again, silently sharing the same wavelength about the integrity of the name *McCoy*, but neither of us is brave enough to bring it up. "I'm not surprised he's back, though," I say instead. "You know his mother passed away, right?"

"Oh yeah, that's right," Eli says unenthusiastically, stabbing at a piece of omelet with his fork. "It's just kind of a bummer. I thought I was done dealing with him for good."

I look down at the counter, noticing a piece where the laminate is starting to pull up. I mindlessly pick at it, making a note to find some superglue and fix it later. A tingle on the back of my neck tells me that Charlie's watchful green eyes are on me. Charlie knows me better than anyone in the world, except for maybe Noah. At least Noah *used* to know me better. I'm not sure where we stand with each other anymore.

"Well, I should probably head to the station," Charlie says, breaking the awkward silence.

"Let me get you a to-go cup," I say, spinning around and pouring him more coffee to take to work.

"Thanks," he says and turns to his best friend. "You coming, Eli? Or are you going to hang around for a while?"

"I'll go with you. Get out of Addie's hair for a while. I'm sure she has lots of diner things to do."

I wince at the weird compliment but don't acknowledge it, crossing my arms over my chest and watching the boys with an amused smile.

"Right," Charlie replies with a laugh. "Alright, we'll see you around, Addison. Let me know if you need anything." He gives me a lingering look that informs me his comment had a lot to do with the mysterious Noah Lockwood—who has made an abrupt comeback in our little town. I nod my head at him, pursing my lips to the side. I get his message.

Charlie is more aware of everything that went down between Noah and me than Eli is, and I'd prefer to keep it that way. Eli and Charlie head out of the diner, and I take a deep breath as soon as they leave. I love both of them more than life, but they have a habit of distracting me from my tasks when they're around.

My friendship with Charlie has always been just that—he's been my best friend since day one. And Eli?

Well, he's Eli.

Our relationship has been a roller coaster from the moment I met him—we've been hot and cold for each other and every possible temperature in between. I've resigned myself to the fact that I will likely end up marrying Eli one day and to be honest, I'm still coming to terms with that. He's not the epic love of my lifetime, but he's good to me, really. Given our history, it would make the most sense to end up with him, except…

That epic love was in my grasp, but I let it slip away. I've seen it and experienced how consuming it can be. I have first-hand knowledge of what it means to fully connect and understand another person, and if I end up with Eli, that will always be in the back of my mind. Those thoughts will forever be there with a bold NOAH stamped across them in red letters.

With a sigh, I grab a rag and wipe down the crumbs from their breakfast as one of my other workers clears the plates and silverware. Things are quieting down now; most of my morning regulars have come and gone. My employees take the chance to catch their breath and focus on some of their slow-time tasks: wiping down menus, filling condiment bottles, etc. I work on a few chores of my own, falling into the comfort and muscle memory of my job.

I'm in the middle of a phone call when I see him. Noah's sauntering down the sidewalk, his attention trained on the ground, his face suggesting he's lost deep in his own thoughts. I watch him stride to the front door and walk in. His striking blue eyes search the room until he finds me and gives me a full look over, his gaze trailing the length of my body.

Shivers crawl down my spine at the weight of his appreciative gaze on me. I hold up one finger to let him know I'll be with him in a minute, and he dips his chin in acknowledgment. After wrapping up my phone call, I head over to where he's still standing by the front door.

"Back again, huh?" I ask him playfully. I motion with my head for him to follow me and seat him at the counter, right on the end.

Noah appears slightly uncomfortable and shifts around on his stool. "Oh yeah, I guess. Can I just get a coffee and a muffin?"

"No French Toast today?" Finally, a smirk hints on his lips, and I congratulate myself on the minuscule victory.

"Not today, Parks. Thanks, though."

I nod once and step over to the glass display where the muffins are. "Cinnamon Apple or blueberry?"

"Apple, definitely," he says, his steely silver eyes watching as I reach for the muffin from the tray.

"I should have known," I reply, fighting off a grin. Apples always were his favorite.

Noah watches me, resting his chin on his fist and smiling slyly. "You should have."

"Eli was just in here gossiping about your return," I tell him. "You just missed him."

Noah looks down at the muffin that I place in front of him. "I bet Monty is all hot and bothered that I'm back in his town."

"Oh, he is," I say with a laugh at Noah's old nickname for Eli—a play off his last name—but I sober up right after. I'm not sure what possesses me to say the following sentence that comes from my mouth. Maybe it's the fact that Noah's just sitting there, joking with me, as if no time has passed at all. Or how the broadness of his shoulders makes me yearn for him to wrap me in his arms in a strong hug. Regardless, it's like word vomit when I blurt out as if I'm admitting a heinous crime, "I'm dating Eli."

The best part is that it's not even really true. Yes, Eli Montgomery and I do go on dates every week. Yes, he might someday be my husband, for lack of other contenders. But for now? I have no significant complaints about our arranged Friday night dinners and convenient hookups. But for whatever reason, I am interested in how Noah will respond.

Noah eyes me curiously, and then he plucks a piece of muffin and pops it into his mouth. He continues to watch me as he chews, collecting his thoughts. I twist my fingers nervously, waiting for him to say something, *anything*.

It's not that I care what he thinks. Really.

"Sully informed me of your ah...current relationship status," he says after a drawn-out pause to finish chewing. "It sounds like it's serious."

I shrug my shoulder noncommittally. "Well, I don't know about that, but—"

"I'm happy for you, Parks. What? Don't look at me like that. I am," he says with a laugh under his breath when my face displays the surprise that I'm feeling internally. I do my best to dampen the twinge of disappointment to prevent it from making an appearance.

"Thank you. That means—well, just thank you," I stutter out, unsure how to respond. I might be going into shock, my heart is palpitating, and my palms are sweaty.

Noah would take every chance he could to irritate Eli when we were growing up and vice versa. It only became worse when Noah and I took our friendship into more romantic territory. When Noah left, he said he wanted me to move on, but I never imagined he would be so...complacent about it if he returned to find that I had taken his advice.

"Do you know when your mom's funeral will be?" I ask carefully, wanting to switch the subject off me. I'm aware this isn't the most fun topic to bring up, but my curiosity for the details is getting the best of me.

Noah's long fingers run across the plate's edge in front of him before moving his hand to run it down his face. "I don't know, actually. I planned to talk to my father about it today."

"Oh," I respond, stunned. "I bet you're looking forward to that."

Noah hits me with such a doleful stare that I can't help but giggle under my breath. "You have no idea, Parks. I'm leaping with joy."

I shake my head in exasperation at the man sitting in front of me. "You'll have to tell me what he tells you, though. I'd like to attend...if that's okay with you."

Noah's silver-blue eyes scour my face, the heaviness of his gaze crushing down on me. "Of course, Parks. It would mean a lot to me if you were there."

A bubble of warmth blooms in my chest, though I suspect it's from my coffee, and not something else. "Good."

"What's on your agenda for today?" he asks me, taking me off guard at his attempt at small talk.

I motion with my hand around the diner. "This is it."

"That sounds...invigorating."

"I have no complaints. I'm happy with how my life has turned out."

His eyes narrow slightly, his lips pulling at the corner on one side. "I'm glad to hear that."

I'm sure we look like a straight-up riot, the two of us having an intense stare-down in the middle of my diner. Still, I can't pull my eyes away from him, and he doesn't seem to be in a hurry to look elsewhere, either.

"Noah," I start softly. His pupils flare at my name on his lips, but he doesn't respond, waiting for me to continue. I lose my train of thought, the intensity of his blue eyes distracting me. I make a fool of myself, staring at him for another moment, trying to come up with something...anything I can say to him.

"Yes, Parks?" he verbally nudges me, looking like he's anticipating whatever I'm about to say. Noah leans towards me across the counter as he waits for me to speak my mind.

"You should stop in the bar down the road," I blurt out. A flash of disappointment streaks across his face so quickly that I almost miss it.

Then he leans back, the moment broken. I hadn't realized how close we'd gotten to each other until he moved away. His fingers drum against the laminate at a nervous pace. "Why?"

"I just think you might enjoy catching up with the owners. They've missed you too, you know."

"Who owns it?" he asks, his dark eyebrows arching, his intrigue piqued.

"You don't want to wait and be surprised?" I tease him.

"No. I hate surprises, you know that."

"Fine, spoilsport. It's Jordan and Caleb's bar. They opened it a few years back. I'm sure they're both there today if you want to pop in," I explain, knowing that the names of his best friends from growing up might be enough to convince him to say hi.

"Really," he says, rubbing his finger along his jaw in contemplation. "Maybe I will."

"You won't regret it. They're still just the same as you left them, Trouble with a capital T."

Noah laughs—a deep noise from his chest which makes my lower abdomen flutter. "Well, that's a relief. I guess I'll put that onto my list of things to do today."

"What time do you have to go meet your dad?"

"Whenever," he says with a noncommittal shrug. "I didn't tell him I was coming, so I'll just go by whenever I get the chance. What do I owe you?"

"It's okay—" I start to say. I let him eat free yesterday simply because I hadn't seen him in a while. But the image of him sleeping in his car this morning burns in the back of my head, and I press my lips together, feeling bad for him.

"No, let me pay you. You're going to go out of business if you just keep giving free meals away," he says teasingly, but the edge to his tone tells me he's not playing around.

"Fine," I respond begrudgingly and pull out his ticket from the pocket of the apron tied at my waist. He takes it from me, shoots me a wry smirk, and places a shiny blue credit card on top of it. I scowl back at him but go off to run his payment.

When I return, I hand it to him and tell him sheepishly, "I put the friend's discount on it, and there's no going back now."

Noah's eyebrows raise, and he chuckles under his breath and stands up, sliding his wallet into his back pocket. "You're impossible."

As he stands, shock courses my thoughts again at how tall he is. Growing up, he was always taller than me, but his profile is now more built since the last time I saw him—broader, developed shoulders now lead down into a lean tapered waist. His sharp jawline is alluring, as is his heightened gaze as he takes me in.

"That's kind of my MO around here," I reply breathlessly.

"Why am I not surprised? I suppose I better go," he says, still studying me. I can see a hint of what he's not quite willing to say right behind his eyes.

"Yeah," I whisper in agreement, my chest threatening to cave in from a lack of oxygen in his presence.

My heart aches to take another step closer to him. Just a brush of my hand against his would be enough. The magnetic pull to him is nearly too much for me to ignore. It's a revelation that it hasn't waned in intensity even after all these years. Everything about him lures me in.

But I hold my ground and give him a kind smile instead of throwing myself at him like I want to. "I better get back to work. And you have two rowdy bar owners to go tend to." I take a few steps toward the back room, still not tearing my eyes away from him. "But let me know what your dad says. I really would like to go to the funeral."

Noah nods, watching me back away from him with amusement lighting up his eyes. He knows. He always knows. "I will."

"Okay, good."

"Just go back to work, Parks. I can see myself out," he says with a chuckle, shaking his head at me.

"Right. Bye then!" I toss an embarrassing wave at him and spin around, hurrying back to the stockroom, ignoring the pointed looks Jack and my staff are giving me.

I step into the storeroom and close the door behind me, not bothering to switch the light on. When I'm alone, I turn my back and lean against the cool paneled door, covering my face with my hands and taking a few deep breaths.

I need to get a grip. It's only Noah. But therein lies the issue, doesn't it?

It's only Noah.

Chapter 3
Noah

"Well, well, look what the cat dragged in," Jordan calls as I step into the little dive bar. He's standing behind the bar wiping a few tumblers with a white towel. "Yo, Caleb! Get your ass out here."

With the ruckus, I receive a few curious glares from the guys sitting at the bar. I narrow my eyes at them. Caleb walks out from the back, stopping abruptly when he sees me standing there.

"As my eyes deceive me. I know that isn't Noah McCoy standing here in my bar."

I cross my arms over my chest and hit my two best friends with a solid glare. "It's Lockwood now. Noah Lockwood."

Jordan whistles lowly and shares a cheeky grin with Caleb. "Sticking it to the man, huh? Wasn't that your mother's—?"

"Maiden name. Yes."

"Well, that's cute," Caleb jokes with me, his face taking on a more serious expression. "But I get it, man."

I stare at my friends for a moment, my eyes darting back and forth between the pair of them. I shake my head and laugh. "So this is what you two shitheads have been up to since I left?"

"That, among other things," Jordan says as he steps around the edge of the bar to give me a hug. His arms wrap around my upper back, giving me a few solid claps on my shoulders. I hug him back. I haven't seen either of them since I left.

"Missed you, brother," I mutter. Jordan's arms tighten around my shoulders.

"Hey, let me in on this love fest," Caleb protests, walking toward us and enveloping us in a group hug.

These guys have been my best friends for as long as I can remember. We've been with each other through it all. They know me as well as I know myself—all the secrets I've kept and the skeletons hidden deep in the closets of the McCoy mansion.

When we're finished being mushy with each other, I take a step back and stick my hands in my pockets, my eyes dancing around the bar. "I like it. It definitely suits the two of you."

"Thanks, man," Jordan responds, turning and heading back behind the bar. He sets to work filling up three glasses of beer from a tap. Caleb wanders over to the stools at the bar and settles in one, taking the glass Jordan offers him. I follow suit and take a deep swig, not minding that it's barely noon.

"Fill me in on everything. What have I missed?" I ask.

"Jordan married Rose!" Caleb blurts out. I don't miss the annoyed look Jordan gives our other friend.

I raise my eyebrows in surprise. "For real?"

"Yeah, they eloped last summer. Pissed off their parents *real* bad."

Jordan leans over and slaps Caleb upside the head. "Would you maybe mind letting *me* tell my best mate about my marriage to his ex-girlfriend? I don't like being thrown under the bus."

I laugh and shake my head. "She was barely my girlfriend, and you know it."

"Oh, I know, you were too busy making puppy dog eyes at Addison Parks to even pretend to care about Rose."

I take another swig of beer and frown. "I was not."

"We're still doing this then, eh?" Caleb teases me. "It's gonna be the whole, 'I don't like her' game again. How'd that work out for you last time? Just be honest with yourself, Noah, for once in your damn life."

"Noted," I glower at him. "But my feelings for Parks have no place in her life anymore. And that's on me, and I realize that. It's just time for me to move on."

"That's right, she's still with Monty, isn't she?"

Another swig. "Apparently."

Jordan laughs next to me. "I bet that really gets your gears grinding."

"Can we not talk about Parks and Monty right now?" I shoot back, ignoring the jab from my friend. "Go on and tell me how you got lucky enough to elope with Rose."

Jordan dives into a long story explaining how he ended up marrying his now-wife, leaving out no details. It's not surprising to hear that he and Rose initially reconnected soon after I left Willow Heights.

I could argue that one of the best and worst parts about being in a small town is that the kids I grew up with became my second family during those vital years. Given that Jordan, Caleb, myself, *and* Rose also came from the town's founding families, we formed a pretty tightly-knit circle right from the start.

"And there's actually something else that I need to tell you both," Jordan says after he's done sharing their story. He looks between Caleb and me with a grin forming on his face. "Rose is expecting."

"Holy shit," I mutter, my mouth falling open. "A baby?"

"I'm gonna be an uncle!" Caleb yells, reaching over and grasping Jordan into a headlock. "This is the greatest day ever!"

"A baby," I repeat, still digesting the news. I'm a little shell-shocked, honestly.

Hearing that he's going to be a dad doesn't surprise me, given that we're all nearing thirty, but it will take some getting used to. I grew up with Jordan Coldwell, and that transition in my mind from friend to *dad* isn't as smooth as I'd like it to be.

"Congratulations, man!" Caleb is reeling about the announcement.

I am happy for him and Rose, but their news reminds me of where my life is at compared to everyone else. I'm still chasing my demons while my friends are settling down and getting on with their lives. An uncomfortable tightness in my stomach tells me I need to take some time once everything is said and done and figure my shit out.

But for now, I plaster on a wide grin and hold up my glass of beer. "A toast! To Jordan and Rose and the terror they're about to unleash on Willow Heights."

"Here, here!" Caleb joins in, and Jordan rolls his eyes but plays along, raising his glass and clinking the others.

We shoot the shit together for another hour before I manage to excuse myself, explaining my next task for the day. When I tell them I have to visit my father, I receive a series of apologies, making me laugh. They both are fully aware of exactly how he can be. Jordan and Caleb have seen the numerous masks of the esteemed mayor of Willow Heights. After another round of hugs and congratulations to Jordan, I finally leave the little bar.

Instead of driving my car across town towards my father's office, I decide to walk. With my hands in my pockets, I stroll down the sidewalk. Thankfully the town is quiet at this hour of the day, aside from a few meandering people. My feet shuffle along the pavement as I let the memories of the years spent here fill my mind.

The place is charming. I'll give it that.

The heart of Willow Heights exists around a pocket park that serves as the focal point for the historic downtown. In the middle of it stands a courtyard that is the destination for various season-themed festivals that occur throughout the year. The location is the home to the annual Willow Heights Easter egg hunt and trunk-or-treat at Halloween. When Christmastime rolls around, it's ground zero for the giant Christmas tree and the light-lighting festival. That's the annual event where the Christmas lights are flipped on, and the massive golden star is placed on top of the tree.

In addition to all the events, the park acted as a home base for Jordan, Caleb, and myself when we were still in school. I remember sitting on the old wooden bridge over the pond and watching townspeople come and go to Addison's parents' café. At that time, I spent most of my energy plotting ways to ruin her week. We were each other's bane of our existence before we were ever cordial towards one another. Though my feelings for her gradually grew into something significantly different than my disdain for her initially.

Addison's diner is on the South end of the town center, where her parents' café used to be, along with a few other smaller storefronts that line the park's perimeter. City Hall stands on the north end, the massive old brick building with a white shingled roof looming tall over the rest of the business district.

I walk briskly, noting the hay bales and fall-themed decorations lingering in the town center. As soon as I arrive at City Hall, I bound up the white alabaster stairs to the giant wooden doors and head towards where my father's office is. I push open the door to the waiting area, and his secretary looks up, her eyes going wide when she sees me. "Can I help you?"

"Yes, I'd like to speak with the mayor," I tell her, walking close until I'm standing right in front of her desk. I push my hands into my pockets as I wait for her.

"I'm sorry, he's not doing open hours right now. I could make you an appointment for later, though," she explains, pulling up the scheduling application on her computer.

"He'll have time for me. My name is Noah. I'm his son," I say, ignoring the bitter taste the words leave in my mouth.

Her eyes widen at this new information and her teeth sink into her bottom lip. She's notably pretty, and I determine that my father *must* be sleeping with her on the side. He's simply the kind of person who would do something like that. "Oh, I'm so sorry. Of course, I'll let him know you're here."

The secretary taps her fingers on the keyboard, clearly sending a message to my father. Her nails are long, clicking as they fly across the keys. After she hits send, she brings one thumb up to her lip and nibbles on the nail, waiting for a response.

While I wait on her, I wander around and observe all of the frames adorning the walls in the lobby. There are awards and certifications, as well as pictures highlighting my father's endeavors as mayor. One photo specifically catches my eye. As I study it, I determine it must be from the latest meeting of the Founding Family Council. I step closer and examine the familiar faces in the picture, almost chuckling when I notice how uncomfortable everyone looks at having to be that close to each other.

Seven families founded Willow Heights: McCoy, Sullivan, Montgomery, Bradford, Lauder, Coldwell, and Abbot. Over the years, Willow Heights grew to what it is now—a quaint Vermont town with a population of just under ten thousand. Still, to this day, the founding families have a heavy presence in the infrastructure and politics, working with the elected mayor to make sure everything runs smoothly.

Though the families work together on a lot of the major decisions, they're not always friendly with each other. That was part of the reason Eli Montgomery and I never managed to get along growing up —his father and my father weren't the biggest fans of each other either. Sins of the father and all of that nonsense.

"You can go in. He said he'll see you," the secretary informs me.

"Wonderful, thank you," I reply, turning back to her and shooting her a smile. I see her cheeks flare bright pink, and I fight the urge to roll my eyes as I walk toward the door leading into my father's office. Yeah, he's for sure sleeping with her.

As I walk to the door, I reach behind my head and pull my shoulder length hair into a ponytail at the nape of my neck, securing it with the green hair tie around my wrist. I always used to keep my hair cropped short, but I've worn it longer recently—it fits the appearance I'm trying to achieve.

My fist raps against the wood door, and from behind it, I hear, "Come in." Pushing the door open, I'm met with the sight of my father sitting in his chair at his desk, flipping through some papers. He glances up when I walk in and gives me a tight smile as if he's unsure how to react to my presence. It's been a long time since I've seen him, noted by how different he looks from the last time we were in each other's presence.

He's still the same old Declan McCoy. His dark demeanor hasn't changed much other than the specks of white now peppering his hair and beard. I can see crinkles around his eyes as he watches me with a narrowed stare. His stern gaze rakes over me, much like I appraise him, and I'm aware he's sizing me up.

As little as he's changed, I've changed a lot. I'm no longer his lanky teenage son who didn't have the balls *or* the wherewithal to stand up with him. My father has always been the built type—as a young kid, I used to think he was invincible—but now I rival him in stature and stance, and I know for a *fact* that he isn't invincible. My shoulders are broad, just like his now, and I stand a little taller than him.

He stares at me with his deep dark eyes, taking me in. His gaze pauses on my face looking straight into my eyes, and I know he's seeing my mother's striking blues reflecting back at him. I hold my expression firm, not giving away the slight nervousness I have at being face-to-face with him for the first time in nearly a decade.

"Noah."

"Declan," I say back.

He pushes away from his desk and strides around the edge. My body involuntarily tenses up as he comes closer to me. Still, I let myself relax a little when he extends a hand for me to shake rather than the uncomfortable hug I was anticipating. I take the offering, gripping his hand tight enough to convey that I won't be intimidated by him.

"Sorry we have to meet again under these circumstances," my

father says to me as he drops my hand and watches me closely. "I was wondering if you'd show up."

"For my mother's funeral?" I ask him incredulously. "Of course, I'd be here."

He turns away from me. "How was I supposed to know that? I haven't heard from you in years. No form of communication, not even a peep."

"And you're blaming that on *me?*"

He looks at me over his shoulder and laughs snidely under his breath. "Glad to see you're still living your martyr fantasy. You're not blameless in everything, Son. I thought you'd be mature enough now to take responsibility for your actions."

"My actions?" I ask him, raising my voice slightly. "You're really gonna sit there and—" I catch myself before I lose control of this conversation. I close my eyes and breathe heavily, pinching the bridge of my nose. I've been here barely two minutes, and I'm already allowing him to get under my skin. I need to get a grip.

"I don't want to argue with you," I tell him after I have a handle on my irritation.

"Likewise," Declan responds. He's watching me curiously from behind his desk again, as if he's updating his inner file on me, gauging my weaknesses or how he can rile me up. My father is a seasoned predator, always observing his prey for the slightest chink in their armor in an attempt to take them down with the least amount of effort. "So, what can I do for you today, Noah?"

"I'm stopping by out of courtesy," I explain. "I don't want anything from you other than the details for Mom."

"I see. Well, please, sit down, and we can chat. Can I get you anything to drink?" He motions over to a mini cart that houses a bottle or two of what looks like expensive bourbon. I hesitate, rapidly weighing the pros and cons of having a drink with my father.

"I'll take what you're having."

My father gives me a brisk nod and sets to work, pouring two glasses with a finger of amber liquid. I seat myself in one of the sumptuous leather chairs he has positioned in front of his desk. I watch him, crossing one of my ankles over my knee as I wait. When he's finished pouring, he hands me a glass and sits in the chair across from mine.

"It was somewhat of a shock to find her," he says, settling into his seat. "I didn't know she had been dealing with such demons."

"Maybe if you would have paid her one ounce of attention, you would have known," I glower down at my drink.

My father barks out a laugh, but I don't give him the satisfaction of looking up. "You've always been so quick to judge me, Noah. Maybe you should look in the mirror before you start placing all of the blame on me."

I give him a grunt as a response, not taking the bait, and continue to examine my glass. I still haven't taken a sip.

"It's not poisoned, you know," my father says when he catches me swirling the tumbler and observing the top layer of the brandy. He chuckles when I don't deign to look up at him. "Trust me, if I were planning to off you, I'd pick a more...effective measure. A fire, perhaps. Arson seems to always do the trick."

I finally snap my eyes up to him and give him a sharp glare. I know he's taunting me, trying to get my attention, and I hate that it managed to work. He laughs again at my expression and takes a sip of his brandy, showing me it's safe to drink. "Relax, Son, I'm only teasing."

"Yeah? Well, it's not funny."

"Honestly, though, maybe it was for the better. Your girl has proven to be much more successful in that storefront than her parents' silly little café ever was. That diner has been raking in revenue ever since it opened. She should be happy the place was burned down. Sure was a shame but it allowed her to be a successful business owner. Gave her the chance to make her place in our little town."

"Addison lost everything in that fire. It's an insult to pretend otherwise. And she's not my girl."

My father laughs again and takes another sip. "Sure."

I clench my teeth and finally take a sip, letting the brandy burn down my throat. "Can we please discuss what I came here for?"

"By all means. There will be a visitation for your mother on Sunday at one after church services are finished, with the funeral on Monday at eleven. There should be an online obituary somewhere."

I nod my head, making a mental note. "Do you need anything from me?"

"No, Noah, I've been handling things without you for quite some time, if you've forgotten. I just need you to show up and not cause any trouble. I assume you'll take off again once everything is said and done?"

"I'm not sure."

"I see. Well, just stay out of my way while you're here," my father says, throwing back the rest of his drink and standing. "We both remember what happened the last time you crossed me. I don't believe you'd like a repeat of events."

I stand up as well, following his lead. I roll my shoulders back and tilt my head up, pretending that his words do not affect me. "Is that a threat?"

"Oh no, Son." Slowly, his lips pull up into a sinister smirk that has goosebumps forming on the back of my neck. His expression screams danger and every instinct in me tells me to run far away from him. But I stay steady. "It's a promise."

Chapter 4
Addison

Saturday morning kicks off like any other. I stick to my same routine, going for a jog first to get my blood pumping, then cleaning up before heading down to help Jack open the diner up. Weekends are typically busier than weekdays since more people have time to have a leisurely breakfast instead of eating on the go. The regulars come in, happy to see us and receive their breakfasts. Everything runs smoothly, like a well-oiled machine.

It's a typical morning until it isn't.

The chime above the diner door rings. I look up initially with a welcoming smile. It leaves my face as soon as I set eyes on my newest patron, my spine straightening and my stomach sinking as he walks closer. "Mr. Mayor," I say in surprise. "What can I do for you?"

Declan McCoy struts into my diner as if he owns the place, his unmistakable air of confidence following him like a storm cloud. "Ms. Parks, so lovely to see you. It's been a while since I've visited your... quaint little diner. I just thought I'd pop in and say hello."

"I'm so happy you did," I say, making sure that outwardly I sound much more thrilled about my newest guest than I do on the inside. "Is there anything I can get you?"

"I'll take a coffee. Black, if you wouldn't mind."

Like your soul, Declan. "Of course, sir. Coming right up."

I turn on my heel and grab a to-go cup to fill with coffee. No way am I giving this guy a dine-in mug so he can stick around and torment me any longer than he needs to. All of my previous experiences with the mayor have been less than favorable. We have a quiet agreement that I stay out of his way, and he doesn't bother me. It's no secret that he's aware of my history with his son; how could it be? But he has never brought it up in the years that Noah's been gone. Until he does, I certainly won't either.

As soon as the cup is full of hot coffee, I find a sleeve, slide it on, and secure a lid on top. I gently push the cup across the counter to the mayor. "Here you are, have a nice day."

"Actually, Ms. Parks, there was something else I was hoping to discuss with you. Business-related. Is there somewhere we could go that would be more, eh—" he looks around the diner and crinkles his nose in mock disgust. "Professional to talk?"

I can't help but cross my arms over my chest and narrow my eyes at him, getting a little defensive. This man is something else, walking into *my* diner with an arsenal full of back-handed compliments. "This will be fine. What did you want to discuss?"

He purses his lips in displeasure before dipping his chin and sliding into what must be his business mode. Though, to be fair, I wouldn't know the difference. As I said, I tried to stay far away from him. "As you know, my late wife's funeral is Monday, and I was—Oh, you didn't know."

I must have appeared taken off guard, which I was. I hadn't heard any of Mrs. McCoy's funeral arrangement plans yet. I swiftly school my facial expression.

"I thought for sure my son would have told you," he hums to himself while watching me with slightly amused eyes. This man was a sly fox. "Well, that's neither here nor there. As I was saying, her funeral is Monday at eleven. I was hoping to speak with you to see if you'd be willing to prepare and serve a meal here afterward."

"Me?"

Declan raises an eyebrow and looks around the diner. "I don't see any other small restaurant owner around here. Yes, you have the space and the menu. I thought you might be interested in doing your civic duty and helping your poor, grieving mayor. It certainly would be one less thing I'd have to worry about while burying my wife."

His words leave a sour taste in my mouth, but I force myself to swallow it away. I'm tempted to inquire what game he's playing at, but I refrain, fully aware that's exactly what he wants. Declan McCoy is a snake who enjoys the chase. Instead, I nod my head and plaster on a smile. "I think I can do that. Is there anything, in particular, you'd like me to serve? And are you hoping for a buffet-style or full service?"

"My, my, you are quite the businesswoman, aren't you?" he observes, a smile playing at the corners of his mouth. "I'll leave the decisions on the menu to your discretion, but I think I would prefer having buffet style. That way, people can come and pay their respects to me, get some food, and then leave."

"Okay, I can definitely do that."

"Thank you, Ms. Parks, and thank you for the coffee on the house. It really means a lot to me," he says snidely, raising his cup in the air at me in a mock toast before turning on his heel and strutting out of my diner.

I scowl in his wake, feeling the aftermath of his presence crawl over my skin. Jack comes up next to me and clicks his tongue. "That man is a real piece of work. I have no idea how he keeps getting reelected."

"Because the people in this town buy right into his stupid charade. They don't actually know him or know what he's capable of," I mutter as I stomp over to the register and grab a notepad. "Well, now my day just got a lot more hectic. Did you hear everything he said?"

"I did," Jack replies warily. "I hope he's planning to pay you."

I look up at him and raise my eyebrows. "Oh shit, I didn't even think to discuss payment."

"I'm sure that's what he was banking on."

I groan and scribble a few notes down on the pad. "I'll just send the bill to his office and keep sending it until I get a check."

"Have you ever done catering before, Addie?"

"Nope," I say, my lips popping over the word. I shoot Jack a fake smile. "But there is a first for everything, isn't there? Now let's get to work. We have a lot to do."

The rest of the day passes like organized chaos and moves into Sunday. Sundays are usually busy for the diner anyway, as many of the townsfolk like to come in for brunch after church. Add planning the meal for tomorrow on top of that?

Organized Chaos.

Sometimes I wonder what I would do if I didn't have Jack there to help me run the place. My life would be infinitely more chaotic without him. I'm hoping that Grace can pick up some slack tomorrow since she'll be home this evening. I'm overly thankful that I have my dream team to help keep everything afloat.

As night falls, the diner traffic slows by the hour. By eight o'clock, the place looks like a ghost town, and I've sent everyone home for the evening. I don't usually lock the door until nine. Still, I'll take the quiet as an opportunity to finish organizing everything for tomorrow.

Grabbing my notepad, a menu, and a cup of coffee, I sit at one of the tables by the window so I can work and spread out all that I need. I have the majority of the menu for the repast all planned out. I aim to keep things as simple as possible so I don't work myself into the ground, ensuring all the guests are fed and content. I dive into my work for an hour or two, crossing items off my to-do list as I go in hopes of polishing my plan for tomorrow.

The night drags on, and I work until my upper back and neck cramp up. I try to massage a knot in my shoulder, but when that doesn't work, I put my pen down on the table and raise my arms above my head. My middle back bends over the back edge of the chair as I stretch out my spine. The movement is a relief, and I take a deep breath in and out, allowing the extra oxygen to help my muscles relax. I am not used to being hunched at a table for so long, and I am paying the price with my protesting body.

In the middle of my stretch, I catch movement outside in my peripheral vision, and I turn my head to see Noah trekking down the sidewalk. His hands are shoved in his pockets, his gaze straight on the pavement in front of him. My heart rate picks up, and part of me hopes he'll come in and say hi. But disappointment sets in when he walks by without even looking up.

Noah continues to stroll down the sidewalk, unaware I'm sitting a few measly yards from him. With his head bowed and slow pace, I wonder if he is troubled by something—I mean, the man has *lots* going on in his life right now. I wish I could talk to him to see if I could help, but I'm not confident he would welcome that. Before, I wouldn't have hesitated. We were always that person for each other. Looking back, Noah's troubles ultimately changed the tides between us in the first place. I happened to be in the right place at the right time, and he accepted my help. Noah let his guard down, allowing himself to be vulnerable, trusting that I wouldn't take advantage of him when he couldn't fight back.

Up to that point, we had consistently been each other's rivals, taking turns on who would have the last word. It was him versus me, no questions asked—until that day. After that, there was an unspoken treaty between us, and we quietly and quickly became each other's confidants. I had no doubt that I could turn to Noah for anything and everything and that he could do the same. The tides changed from that moment on, and our friendship developed, gradually taking on a more romantic air as the years passed. Still, the foundation of our relationship remained the same.

The way Noah and I are skirting around each other now is a stark contrast to how close we were at one point. I secretly wonder if those versions of ourselves are lost forever or if we can find them again. From my perch inside the diner, I can see his set expression and furrowed eyebrows illuminated by the street lamps. He meanders until he stops in front of Monty's market and pulls out a set of keys from his pocket.

Noah unlocks his car and opens the back door, crawling in the rear seat. I watch him close the door again, disappearing into his makeshift bed. I grip my coffee cup in both hands, still staring at where he was last standing, and frown into my drink. I don't like that he's sleeping in there. Not that Willow Heights is riddled with crime, but he should have someplace comfortable and warm to rest.

I pick up my notepad and menu with a frustrated sigh and pour out the remainder of my coffee. I fear that if I sit here any longer, I'll look up at Noah's car every few minutes, and I won't finish what I need to do tonight. Giving one last forlorn glance out the window, I lock the front door and shut the place down.

As soon as I'm upstairs in my apartment, I change out of my jeans and find some lounge pants so I can finish working comfortably.

Another hour passes, and I make it to the point where I'm satisfied with my progress when I hear a loud call from the entrance to my apartment. "'Darling, I'm home!'"

A door closes, and I hear a thump of a purse and a set of keys. I'm sitting on my bed, running expense numbers on my laptop, but I can't help the grin that crosses my face. I roll off my bed and pad out of my bedroom into the living room.

In front of me stands the refreshing sight of my best friend. Her hands are on her hips, and she greets me with a blinding smile. "Did ya miss me?" she asks playfully.

I bound over to her and wrap my arms around her thin frame in a hug. Grace was out of town for only a week, but it felt like ages to me. "Of course I missed you! Thank you for coming over! How was your trip?"

"It was good overall. I'm glad I was able to go. How have things been here?" Grace asks me, pulling away and grabbing both of my hands in her own, contrasting my pale skin with her dark ebony. "I see everything is still standing."

I drop my shoulders with a sigh. "Barely. Gosh, so much has happened in the last week. I—"

"Tell me everything. Right now. Where's the wine?"

"It's in the fridge," I say with a laugh. Grace bolts over to my refrigerator, yanking it open and giving a great sigh of relief.

"Ah, you're an angel; you got Merlot!"

"I know it's your favorite," I reply, going over to the china cabinet and reaching for two long-stemmed wine glasses. I stroll into the living room to my couch, where Grace has set up camp and is working on uncorking the bottle. She pulls it out with a *pop* and pours us each a generous serving.

We pick our glasses up and clink them together before Grace hits me with a look that instantly makes me feel guilty for something, though I don't know what. Her warm eyes display mischief as she waits for me to spill my guts expectantly. I take another deep sip of my wine, pretending not to notice.

"Time's ticking, babe. I have jet lag. I want to go home to my own bed, but I can't when you're withholding the deets from me!"

I look over at my best friend with a smirk. Grace is one of the kindest, pushiest, most gorgeous people I have the pleasure of knowing. And since she's been in my life for nearly sixteen years, I'm fully aware that she will not back down until I give her what she wants.

"Fine. Well, for starters, Hailey has decided to put her two weeks in, so we'll have to start the hiring process again," I say.

Grace waves it off. "I'll put an ad up tomorrow. Now give me the good stuff! I know something crazy has to have happened in this town since I've been gone."

I take in a deep breath and decide to dive right in. "Mrs. McCoy passed away this past week, which means Noah's back in town, and I don't know, it's weird."

Grace is staring at me wide-eyed, her entire face the picture of shock. She definitely was not expecting that. "Excuse me?"

"What?"

"Noah's back in town, and that wasn't the first thing that came out of your mouth? You're wasting time telling me about Hailey, who we've *known* has had one foot out the door since the day she started?"

I laugh, trying to play it off. "It's not like Noah and I are…together or anything, Grace. Those days are long gone."

"Right, and that's why you still get a lady boner anytime anyone brings him up!"

My mouth drops open, and I shove her shoulder. "I do NOT!"

"You do too, babe, and it's fine. I mean, he was hella handsome in high school, and based on how the mayor is aging like a fine wine, I can imagine he's pretty easy on the eyes these days. Just don't pretend to kid yourself. Noah's always taken priority in your mind, and that's okay. You two are," she shakes her head and shrugs at me, "like written in the stars or some shit like that."

I frown down at my wine glass. Grace has a point about Noah being easy on the eyes, though he could use a haircut. I'm still trying to decide if I like his long-haired look on him. "Well, he missed that memo. In fact, he missed it almost ten years ago."

"Honey, when it comes to true love, there really is no timeline."

"Maybe. Or maybe we just aren't meant to be," I say, sloshing the wine around in my glass. I change the subject to something other than Noah and me, "Oh, also, I agreed to host Mrs. McCoy's repast tomorrow after the funeral. The Mayor kind of bullied me into it without actually bullying me."

Grace presses her lips together, pondering my statement. "Yeah, he does have a way of doing that. What do you need me to do?"

I shrug and take a sip of wine. "I'm not sure yet. I think I'm going to play it safe with the menu, but I'll have to be up early tomorrow to make sure everything is in order. The service is at eleven, and I'd like to go to that to support Noah, so if you could take the helm while I'm there, that would be incredible."

"Of course, I'll do whatever you need me to do. Put me to work, oh, fearless leader!"

Her words make me laugh, and I steer the conversation toward her trip. Grace tells me about her time in Maine, visiting her extended family. Her grandmother has been ill for the last few months, so it was an important trip. She would be kicking herself if she couldn't get there before it was too late. Her tone takes on a hint of dolefulness as she fills me in about everything, but I can tell her heart is at peace as she explains how she spent this last visit with her grandma.

After she's done sharing her experience, she flips the switch and bounces on the couch cushions, her curly hair springing up and down with her. "Okay, now tell me everything about Noah. What is he looking like these days? Was I right in that he's pretty handsome? I'm not into white guys like that but girl, I can still appreciate good genes when I see them."

I roll my eyes and take a sip, trying to be coy about the whole Noah topic. "I mean... he's not *bad* looking."

Grace makes a noise that I can only attribute to a scoff. "Sure. Does he still have those striking blue eyes like his mother?"

"I mean, he can't exactly change his eye color, Grace." My friend shrugs as if it could be a possibility. "Yes, his eyes are still just as breathtaking," I admit, remembering how his silver-blue gaze froze me in my place the first time I ran into him this week. "His hair is absolutely out of control, though. It's down to his shoulders."

"Mmm, okay, go on. He's rocking the nomad-y type hipster look, got it."

"And he's sleeping in his *car*, Grace."

Grace pauses with this new information. "Okay, so maybe not nomad but more...homeless?"

"No, I'm sure he could afford something if he had to. I just don't think he wants to. I kind of get the feeling that he's hoping to bail as soon as possible."

"That can't be right. You're here," my friend says as if it's the most clear-cut explanation in the world. "He can't leave again 'cause you're here."

I look down, my lips pulling into a frown. The familiar swell of abandonment settles in my stomach, and I take another gulp of wine in an attempt to numb it. "Well, that didn't stop Noah before, did it?"

Grace sighs empathetically and reaches over to take my hand. "I'm sorry, Addie. I just have to hope that things will work out for you two one way or the other. I can't believe he's sleeping in his car, though. What happened to that stuck-up kid he used to be. That version of Noah wouldn't *dream* of sleeping in a car."

"I wish there was something I could do."

She pauses and looks down at the cushions we're sitting on. "Doesn't this couch pull out? Like it's got a bed inside of it?"

I stare at her warily as I reply, "Yes."

"Solution found," Grace says with a wink, and I gape at her.

"You want me to let Noah sleep *here*?"

"Why not?"

"You know why not! He's my ex-whatever. I can't share an apartment with him!" I'm still going back and forth on what to call Noah. My ex-lover, maybe? He was my boyfriend for maybe five minutes before everything went to shit, and he jumped town. It took us a long time to even get to "almost." I had a hard time letting go of the friendship we had developed, even though every part of me wanted more with him. Noah might've been the one for me, but it was just the wrong timing.

"I think that's all the more reason *to* offer him the place to stay," Grace says compassionately. "You never know what it might lead to."

I frown at my friend. "Noah was clear when he left me that note in New York. He told me that we couldn't be together. It couldn't be him, not yet."

"Well then, maybe you just need to show him that he was wrong, hm? Or show him that the time is now."

I get the idea that she's going to argue about any other point I bring up, so I turn away and take a sip out of my wine glass. "I'll think about it. It doesn't seem like a good idea, though."

"Babes, trust me. I've seen how you perk up every time his name comes up in conversation or how your cheeks have been bright red the entire time we've discussed him—and no, I don't think it's from the wine. You and Noah are supposed to be together. I know it, he knows it, you know it. We just have to get the ball rolling."

"If I offer him a place to stay, that's not what my intention is going to be," I protest. "I'm with Eli, and I'm happy with him."

"Are you?"

"Grace!" I snap at her. "Please, stop meddling. Listen, if I let myself get attached to Noah again while he's here—for his mom's funeral, I might add, nothing permanent—and then he leaves me again, I don't think I could survive it. So please, just *hear me* when I say I need to keep a safe distance from him."

"Fine, fine. I hear you. I won't meddle—too much, at least. I've always had to meddle a little bit when it comes to you two."

I roll my eyes and take another sip.

"You could let him sleep here, though. I'm sure he'd rather sleep on your couch than in a car," Grace says softly.

"He has other friends, you know. What about Jordan or Caleb? I'm sure they have couches."

"Maybe, but do you really think Noah would willingly impose himself on his friends? You told me *you* saw *him* sleeping in his car."

I turn my gaze back to her and purse my lips. "Yeah, that's true. But to be fair, I'm not sure if I even know Noah anymore."

"But you did know him once. And I've never known you not to help someone who's important to you and in need."

She's right. My best friend has me pegged. Generally speaking, I'm about as hospitable as they come. I guess that's partly to blame for the homey feeling my diner took on since day one. I love helping people. It's what I do best. "You're not going to let this go easily, are you?" I ask her, swirling my wine around in my glass.

"Probably not," Grace responds with a wink.

I place my wine on the table with a sigh, then cover my face with my hands. "I just really don't think it's a good idea. Noah's probably only going to be in town for the funeral tomorrow, and then he'll leave again."

Grace raises one hand in surrender. "Hey, it was just a sugges-tion. If you don't want to do it, don't do it."

"I hate you, you know that?"

My friend throws her head back with a laugh and scoots closer to me, wrapping her arm around my shoulder, pulling me into her, and pressing a kiss to my cheek. "Well, I love you!"

I laugh under my breath and hug her back, glad that my best friend is home. Grace has been my rock and stronghold through some of the most challenging moments in my life. Despite her pushing and insisting, Willow Heights is always a little darker when Grace is not here.

Chapter 5
Noah

"Well, you look put together," my father observes as I walk toward him. I have my hands in the pocket of my black slacks, and I tighten up one fist where he can't see it—resisting the urge to punch him in the nose. His compliment is a slight dig at my attire the last time I saw him. In his opinion, this suit would be a significant improvement from my tattered old jeans.

"Thank you," I reply dryly.

"You could use a haircut, though," he says, as his eyes scan me head to toe. I've worn my hair down today, knowing that he wouldn't be able to resist making some side comment about it.

"I'll think about it," I tell him, biting back a laugh. I have no intention of cutting my hair, especially now that he's indicated he disapproves.

"Where's your ring?" Father asks, eyeing my hands in my pockets. "I noticed you weren't wearing it the other night either."

I give him a blank look. He's really going all-in on the attire appraisal today. "I pawned it."

"Real nice, Noah," he sneers at me.

I shrug a shoulder noncommittally. "I needed the cash."

My father doesn't respond, though I hope he's fuming on the inside. He turns away from me and glances out the window, straightening his tie in the reflection of the glass. The expensive McCoy signet ring I was gifted on my eighteenth birthday is currently in a safe deposit box in New York. Still, he doesn't need to know that. He has a deep sense of family loyalty. I'm sure the fact that I'd sold my signet ring and changed my surname is eating him from the inside out.

"Should have a good turnout today. Almost everyone who came to the visiting hours yesterday said they planned to be at the service this morning," my father speculates in a strained attempt to save face. He tilts his chin up to glance over my shoulder. I follow his gaze, looking out the window at the cars lining up along the roads in front of the church. "It was a shame that the funeral home said we couldn't do open-casket yesterday. I imagine people would have liked to see her one last time."

I don't bother mentioning that I called the funeral home and arranged for the casket to be shut on my way into town. As far as anyone else is concerned, it is closed due to her cause of death. If my mother would've had her say in the whole matter, she wouldn't want people gawking at her while my father puts on a theatrical performance.

"A lot of people really love Mom," I say fondly as I watch people dressed in black walk up towards the church.

My father's eyes snap back to me, and his expression hardens. "Of course, she was an extraordinary woman. Impossible not to love."

"That's a lot coming from you."

"For the love of Christ, Noah. This is for your mother. Could you at least make an attempt not to be little shit today? Stop acting like a prick and put on a good face. I raised you better than that."

Clearly, my father has had enough of our little verbal spar and effectively chose to end it. His version of closing a subject is to lash out and get nasty. And if we're being honest, he's full of it, assuming he can stand here and soak up the town's love for my mother and pretend like he's a grieving widower. I wish he'd admit that he has less to worry about with her out of the way.

I scowl at him and turn on my heel, heading toward the bathroom. Stalking away, I throw open the bathroom door and lock it behind me. It's a multi-stall bathroom, but I need a moment to myself to get my head in order. I stride over to the sinks, gripping the edge of the white porcelain so tightly that my knuckles pale. I focus on taking a few deep breaths in and out until my frustration with my father dissipates slightly.

As soon as my heart rate settles, I release the sink, turn on the water, and splash the coolness over my face for good measure. Bracing my elbows against the edge of the sink, I bury my hands in my hair, tugging on the strands. The sharp tug helps me to regain a sense of balance, and I remind myself why I'm here. Once I catch my breath, I lift my gaze and stare at my reflection in the dirty mirror—my eyes look wild, and my hair is a mess. Straightening my spine, I try to smooth out my hair and compose myself.

All I have to do is make it through today. Attending a funeral for my mother is not my first choice of how I'd like to be spending a Monday morning, but there's no avoiding it at this point. All the memories spent together with my parents circulate around me like a foul odor, never dissipating but effectively suffocating me.

Growing up, I linked my parents together as an unbeatable force for the longest time. I understood that I could always talk to my mother, and she would try her best to protect me from him. Still, it wasn't until right before I left town that it became clear to me that she and I had been on the same team the whole time.

My father loved my mother, though he had a backward way of showing it sometimes. This circus he is putting on today in "her honor" would embarrass her. Despite being married to an attention-hungry politician, my mother always preferred the more muted events. She wasn't one to put herself out into the spotlight if she could help it. As the wife of the mayor, she was there to support my father when he needed it and offered a refined strength that he could lean back on when he was losing his grip on control. If my father was running rampant, she would come up behind him, placing a gentle hand on his shoulder and whispering something that would completely disarm him.

It intrigues me to see how he will take advantage of his newfound freedom now that she's not here to balance him out. This could work in my favor, or it could be catastrophic. Time will tell.

I concentrate on taking a few deep breaths until my world isn't spinning out of control and my vision settles into focus. My reflection looks back at me as if mocking me, but I stand straight, square my shoulders and leave the bathroom to brave my father again. He observes me walking toward him with an amused expression on his face.

"Are you done with your tantrum?"

"Fuck off."

He laughs in response to my vulgarity and shoots me a withering glare before sauntering off to greet guests. Across the foyer, I see Parks and her posse walk in through the large doors. Addison's eyes scan the room, and I realize she's looking for me. I take a slight step forward, landing myself in her line of sight. Her hazel eyes spot me after a moment of searching, and her expression softens, a sympathetic smile crossing her face. She lifts her hand in a small wave. Some of the tension in my shoulders dissipates as I dip my chin toward her in acknowledgment. A sense of calm settles in my chest, knowing she's here. For me.

Charlie and Eli stand on either side of her, unaware of our silent interaction. Eli mutters something to Addison, and she looks at him before rolling her eyes and swatting his arm with the program. I step back into my previous position, observing the trio as they head into the church to find a seat for the service.

I stay where I am until my father comes to usher me into the church, informing me that the service is about to start. He directs me to the first row of pews, where I take my seat, and he slides in next to me, much to my great displeasure.

His fake attempts at grief throughout the funeral service distract me to the point where all I notice is what he's doing. I find myself gritting my teeth so hard my jaw aches. He nods his head, making a show of being moved with emotion by what the preacher says about the processes of life and death.

When they speak of my mother's character and her devotion to her passions, he dramatically lifts his hand to wipe away an invisible tear.

I need to get out of this church and away from him. I need to get a grip before I do anything stupid. With that in mind, as soon as the service concludes, I locate the one person in this town who I can trust to keep me in line when I feel like I'm out of control.

Addison is standing with Charlie in the entryway to the church. She's wearing a black long-sleeved dress that swoops across her chest in a respectable but flattering style, covering her arms all the way down to her wrists. Her honey-brown hair falls in soft layers of curls around her frame, and they bounce lightly as she turns and looks at me. I swallow thickly as I walk up to her, the weight of the situation weighing heavily on my shoulders.

She gives me a tender smile as I walk up to her, but I don't waste time with formalities. "Parks, can I ride with you?" I ask her bluntly. "To the gravesite."

Addison's eyebrows raise a fraction, not expecting my question, but she nods her affirmation. "Of course, you can, but don't you want to ride with—"

"No. I can't be near him right now."

"I understand," she replies, turning to Charlie standing by her side. "Do you think you can get Eli to go with you?"

"No problem," Charlie tells her with a nod of his head and eyeballs me warily. "You doing okay, man?"

"I'll be honest, Sully, I don't really have the capability of pretending to be your friend right now," I tell him tersely. Charlie has the decency to look amused. "I'm about two more fake shows of grief away from strangling my father, and I need to get out of here."

"Let's go then," Parks says abruptly. "I'll see you guys there. Come on, Noah."

She reaches for my hand, and I take it gratefully, a sense of relief flooding through me at her touch, washing away my spiking irritation. I follow her as she leads me to her car, a black midsize SUV.

Parks unlocks the car and releases my hand, striding to her side and hopping into the driver's seat. I follow suit, sliding in and settling into my own seat. My head falls back against the headrest, and I close my eyes, taking a few long deep breaths.

Thankfully, Addison doesn't say much right away, giving me a chance to collect myself before she bombards me with the questions. I let the movement of the car lull all the edges of my temper as we drive. I can smell her perfume—a blend of lavender and vanilla—which swirls around me as I sit there. The fragrance is warm and smooth but not too overpowering in the small cabin of the car. It's Addison, and it's comforting to me.

When at last, it appears she's had enough of the silence, she glances over at me. We're sitting at a red light, not moving. I roll my head on the seat towards her to meet her eyes. She's studying me as if trying to solve a tricky puzzle. It's an expression on her that I know well, and I brace myself for the interrogation that's likely to happen.

"Do you want to talk about it?" she asks me, simply.

I turn my head to look out the windshield at the passing scenery when the light turns green. "I don't know if there is really anything to talk about. Declan is who he is. There's no changing that. He snags any opportunity he can find to make things about him."

"Still, though, I know it must be hard for you. Trust me, I know. And to watch him take something special for your mom and turn the attention onto himself?" Addison questions softly. Her hands tighten on the steering wheel. "It doesn't excuse him to act that way just because you're used to his behavior."

"I suppose you're right," I mumble. "He can't seem to help himself. He always has to be the star of the show."

"I'm sorry, Noah." I turn and look at Parks again when she apologizes. She looks at me briefly before securing her eyes back on the road. "That you have to deal with him. You deserve better."

"Maybe, but it's all I've known," I snicker humorlessly. "Turns out your observation of my father all those years ago still rings true—he's not a very nice man."

Addison gives a single laugh, not about what I said but recalling the conversation that changed our entire dynamic. A similar moment to now, me regaling how awful my father is, dealing with the aftermath, and Addison offering her strength in silent support. I couldn't see it then, but Addison is much like my mother in that sense. She always seems to know the right things to say at the right moments. It's a skill that makes her invaluable to have around in moments of crisis.

"I didn't want to be right about him, you know," she whispers so softly I almost miss it.

"You're always right. One of the most annoying things about you," I say as I look at her fondly and smirk.

She rolls her eyes at me but offers a kind smile. "Is there anything I can do for you?"

"You're doing it, Parks," I tell her. "I don't think I could've made it through this day if you weren't here."

I can see my words affect her as soon as she puts the car in park at the cemetery and turns her body to face mine. She reaches to take my hand, twining our fingers together. Her hand feels warm and comforting as if she's sending me strength through our connection. Her hazel eyes glitter and I wonder if she can feel it too.

"There is nowhere I'd rather be today, Noah."

I trace her delicate features with my gaze as she holds my hand tightly in her own. I take in her round eyes as they observe me, the sharp angle of her freckled-covered nose and the swell of her lips meeting in a subtle Cupid's Bow, and my heart skips a beat.

Addison Parks is beautiful—in every possible aspect of the word. She's the kindest, most tender-hearted person I've had the pleasure of having in my life. Trying to grasp that she can't be mine in the way I yearn for her has been one of the most painful realizations I've lived through. If we were together again, I'd spend hours worshipping every part of her stunning body, not leaving an inch of her untouched. She deserves to be adored, and, in a perfect world, I would be the man to do it.

But we don't live in a perfect world. At least not right now. Addison's involvement with me would sign her fate for something terrible. She's already suffered enough at the hands of my father. It would kill me if anything else happened to her. My father is excellent at spotting his opponents' weaknesses, and Addison is mine. He made an example out of her before, and I know he would have no qualms about doing it again.

That is something I'm just not willing to risk. Which means I need to keep my distance for now.

With that in mind, I pull my hand away, ignoring how her expression falls, and look out at the cemetery in front of us. "Guess we better go."

Without waiting for her response, I push open my door and step into the soft grass. My shoes squish through the dirt as I make the trek to my mother's grave. The funeral directors have set up a large blue canopy next to where they're holding the last bit of the service. Underneath the tent are three rows of chairs, but I find a spot near the outer edge instead of sitting. I'd rather not take a seat from someone else who needs it. A few people have gathered around the gravesite, softly talking amongst themselves and shooting me sympathetic glances when they think I'm not looking. Unlike my father, I'm not interested in using this event to attract attention. In fact, I'd rather they'd ignore me altogether.

I stand on the outskirts of the tent, my arms crossed over my chest, and stare at the hole in the ground where they'll place the casket. Addison catches up to me, stepping into the space to my right. Still, despite my hesitation to give in to my desire for her, her presence next to me is comforting.

It isn't long before the rest of the guests from the funeral start arriving, my father right along with them. I watch him walk up to the tent with a scowl on my face. He's milking the attention again, making a big show of accepting hugs and handshakes, taking on the part of the grieving widower. Watching him makes me sick to my stomach. The anger that Addison helped qualm quickly takes root again. I turn away from him, unable to watch it any longer. I'm counting down every minute of every day until he is out of my life forever. It will be a relief when he's held accountable for everything resting on his shoulders.

The graveside service begins soon and proceeds without a hitch— another brief message and a prayer. Most of the guests leave before they set about with the last step of the ceremony, lowering the casket into the ground. Still, I stay, my eyes glued to the workers as they get into position. The creaking of the contraption echoes in my ears as the wooden box disappears under the earth.

As soon as the casket is out of sight and they have the plot covered up, I turn to leave. I'm ready for this whole event to be over with. It's not something I want to prolong, so I glare at the ground, trying my best to compartmentalize the events of the day in my head.

"Noah, wait up," I hear Parks call my name as I drift away. I clench my jaw but stop and turn back. She's walking towards me, the skirt of her dress splaying in the wind giving me a peek at her toned thighs, her curls flutter over her face, and she brushes them away with her hand. "I have a question for you."

I rub the back of my neck as she comes closer, feeling the tightly corded muscles protest at the pressure. I could use a nap, but the thought of scrunching into my car deters me from the idea. Doing so would only make my neck hurt worse.

When Addison's standing right in front of me at last, I look down at her expectantly. "Go on."

"Would you—well...." Addison pauses, gearing herself up to ask what's on her mind. Her chest is heaving, slightly breathless from chasing me. I'm fully aware it is only her lungs attempting to refill with air, but it's distracting; the swell of her breasts rising and falling entices me. "I know you've been sleeping in your car, and I was wondering if you would want to come stay with me? I don't have an extra bedroom, but I have a comfy couch, and I would like to think it might be a little more comfortable than sleeping in the back of your car."

I look at her in surprise. I certainly wasn't expecting that to be her question.

Addison takes my quiet shock as an excuse to continue babbling. "I mean if you want to. You don't have to. I know things between us are kind of," she waves her hand as if that is the perfect way to describe our situation. "Anyway. I promise I won't jump you or anything. I know you're not interested in me like that anymore, and I've moved on. I'm with Eli, kind of, as you know, and—"

"Parks."

She stops abruptly and takes a deep breath. I stare at her, my eyebrows pulling in towards the middle. I study her face, taking in every beautiful feature of hers, from her show-stopping hazel eyes to the freckles that dot her nose. I still remember the moment I fell in love with those freckles...I wish I could spend hours counting each and every one.

"What?" Parks exhales, bringing me back to the present.

"That wasn't the reason," I tell her, my voice low, my confession falling between the two of us like dead weight. My feelings for her press against the barriers of my heart almost painfully. Unspoken words are on the tip of my tongue. I want to tell her everything, but now isn't the time. "My being interested in you was never the problem. Trust me, you shouldn't ever doubt how I felt about you."

"Oh," her lips fall open on the word.

"There are several reasons why I left, but it wasn't because I didn't want you," I say firmly. I hope that if Parks retains anything at all from this conversation, it's that. "So I'd appreciate it if you'd just wipe that thought process out of that pretty little head of yours, okay?" Addison stares at me and nods her head like a robot. "What does your boyfriend think about this? I can't imagine he'd be okay with another man, namely me, sharing a space with you." She darts her eyes away from me, and I instantly have my answer—she hasn't talked to him about it. "I see. I'll think about your offer. I'm not sure how long I'll be in town yet, and I don't want to inconvenience you."

Her proposition intrigues me. Staying with her provides the ideal excuse to be close to her without being *too* close. As much as either of us might deny it—or, in my case, fight it—her soul calls to mine, mine to hers. I often used to think that she was the missing piece to me. If today is any indication, that is still the case. Addison brings a sense of peace I have yet to find with anyone else. But before I agree to anything, I need to do a complete risk analysis. My first reaction is to say yes, simply because I want to be near her, but I can't rush into something that might bite me in the ass later. I would hate to put us through all I have to keep her out of danger only to return and bring that same risk upon her with my recklessness. It was bad enough that I ran to her today when I needed her, but to move in with her? That might take things just a tad too far, though the offer is enticing.

"Of course," she replies. Her fingers tighten around the handle of the black clutch purse she's holding. "Well, just let me know."

"I will," I tell her.

"Good. I should get back to the diner before guests start arriving. I think your father has headed that way already. Do you want to ride with me?"

"Actually, I think I'll walk," I say with a shrug. "I need some time to myself to clear my mind."

"I understand. I'll see you back at the diner then," Addison quips before reaching and squeezing the muscle at the top of my arm in a comforting gesture. I'm suspicious about what my father's game plan was asking her to host today. He looked far too amused when he informed me of the matter. But I squash that thought process and go for gratefulness that she'll be around for the rest of this shitty day.

I offer her a smile, "Okay, thank you, Parks."

"Sure," she grins back, her eyes lighting up. "I'll see you soon."

Chapter 6
Addison

"This was a mistake," I mutter to Jack. Since the funeral ended, the diner has had a non-stop flow of guests coming to pay their respects to the Mayor and Noah. I do not have enough staff to sustain the buffet I spent all last night and this morning preparing. I don't know what I was thinking about agreeing to host Noah's mother's repast.

Jack looks at me with sweat dotting his forehead and tries to offer me what I can only assume is a sympathetic smile. "Just hang in there, Addie. It won't be much longer. You're doing great. We just gotta keep things rolling for a little while longer."

"Jack, I have no idea what I would do without you."

Jack pauses from his task of piling dishes into the bin to be washed and shrugs his shoulders cheekily. "Probably sink into a pit of despair. I do have a way of making things brighter."

I laugh, feeling my shoulders release their tension a bit, and then run to the back to grab another tin of mashed potatoes. Once I have them, I hurry back out to the floor and nearly run Noah over. "*Shit!*" I swear as I start to wobble, the heavy container of potatoes setting me slightly off balance.

Noah's hands reach out and grip my elbows, steadying me. My

skin warms where his hands touch and I look up at him with a grateful smile. This is the first time I've seen him since the cemetery. I understand why he wanted to walk independently, but I'm glad he's here now. As quickly as he reaches to touch me, his hands fall away from my arms.

"Well," He rumbles in a deep voice. "That was a close one. Can't let you spill the mashed potatoes everywhere. That would be a catastrophe."

"It definitely would have been something," I reply, slightly breathless. "Thank you. I have to go put these out."

"Do you need any help?" he inquires, following after me as I head towards the buffet line.

As soon as the potatoes are where they need to be, I brush my hands on the apron tied around my waist. I shoot Noah a wary glance and then shake my head. "No, it's fine. You'd just be in the way."

Noah barks out an amused laugh. "Tell me how you really feel, then Parks."

"I'm sorry, I didn't mean it that way. I just mean that we have everything covered." I squeeze my eyes shut and dampen a groan.

Noah leans forward slightly until his face is right in front of mine. By the mischievous twinkle in his eye, I know he's about to say something particularly witty, and I brace myself to be amazed.

Only he doesn't get the chance. His phone starts blaring from his back pocket, and his eyebrows furrow on his forehead as he registers that the noise is coming from him. Noah straightens up, frowning as he pulls the device from his pocket. He glances at the screen and then looking at me helplessly. "Sorry, I gotta take this."

"No problem," I wave him off. "By all means."

I watch Noah briskly exit the diner by the front door, putting the phone to his ear. As he does, his face takes on a completely different expression, one I've not seen on him before. He looks like he's suddenly aged five years, his features growing stern and severe. I watch him for a minute out the front window as he talks. A deep frown covers his face, and a tight ball of worry starts to form in my belly as if alerting me that something's not right.

Before I can eavesdrop on his conversation, Grace rounds around the buffet table and gives me an exasperated look. "If you're done ogling at Noah, the refreshment pitchers could be refilled."

My cheeks heat up with embarrassment at being caught, and I nod, deciding that I'll worry about checking in on Noah once things settle down here.

Of course, that moment doesn't come for another few hours when the last few guests finally leave the diner. Grace and I wave at them as they go, and then we both collapse into the nearest booth, each letting out a collective groan.

"You are never, ever doing this to us again," Grace grumbles.

"Agreed. I didn't think there would be that many people here. I feel like we just fed the five thousand."

"Try ten-thousand. I didn't even know that many people lived in this stupid town," she mutters and then reaches her hand under the table to pull her shoes off. "God, my feet are killing me. I don't think I've sat down all day."

"Me either," I agree. "At least you didn't have to wear heels to the funeral on top of all of this too."

My friend shoots me an apologetic look. "Touché. How was it, by the way? I haven't had a chance to talk to you at all since this morning."

"It was nice," I reply, turning my head over my shoulder to where Noah and his dad are still standing. They're having a conversation, and it doesn't look entirely hostile for once. Maybe Declan has run out of his bullshit for the day.

"And how's Noah?"

"I'm not sure, honestly." I look back at her for a moment and then down at my fingernails. I have mashed potato stuck under one, and I focus on dislodging it.

"Really?" Grace asks, surprise lacing her tone. "I thought you two had some weird witchy connection where you could always tell what the other was feeling."

"What?" I retort incredulously. "Where on earth did you come up with that?"

"No idea, but am I wrong?" she presses.

I frown. "I don't know. Yesterday I would've said you were wrong, but now I don't know."

"There's a story in there somewhere, and I best be hearing it in the next thirty seconds."

I chuckle at my friend but explain to her how Noah sought me out after the service, asking for a ride. It had made my stomach do all sorts of happy somersaults—the feeling of being sought after by a man like Noah is empowering. Especially when he came to me for help. He made it clear by his actions that he had needed me with him today, and I did my best to be present so I could help in any way I could.

I also told Grace about the ride back to the diner from the cemetery. Eli claimed my front seat again rather than going with Charlie and was particularly vocal about how he felt of Noah riding with me today. I had given Eli a firm stare and made a point that not only had the day been about Noah's mother, he was also one of my oldest friends. Eli had grumbled about it, clearly not appeased, but had let it lie. Eli knows better than to push disagreements with me too hard. History has shown I've always won when it comes down to it.

"You better be careful with that," Grace says. "I know you're not interested in Eli long term, but he definitely is interested in you. And we're both fully aware of how Eli feels about Noah."

"I know. But I would hope that Eli knows that Noah's still important to me and won't push it too far," I explain.

"You give him a lot more credit than you should, babe. He's still a man, who happens to hold you on a very high pedestal. Just be aware of that. Also side-note, the mayor is coming this way. Look alive; he preys on the weak," she whispers to me. At her words, my spine straightens, and my shoulders roll back. I can feel every muscle in my upper body come to attention to avoid getting caught off guard.

Declan McCoy steps into my view seconds later, a sly grin painting his face. I glance to his right and see Noah a few paces away, watching the interaction with observant eyes. His body is coiled tight as if he's ready to intervene at a moment's notice.

"Ms. Parks," Declan begins. "I just wanted to give you my gratitude before I left. Thank you for making such a remarkable effort today. We had a great turnout, and it seemed everyone was pleased with the service."

"I'm glad to hear that," I reply to him honestly.

Declan hums and nods before looking towards Noah. "You've got a good one here, Son. I'd keep an eye on her if I were you, wouldn't want somebody to steal her right from under your nose again, hm?"

I look at Noah just in time to see the full effect of his scowl towards his father. It only spurs Declan on, as he lets out an amused laugh and then excuses himself with another muttered thank you. Noah takes a few steps after his father before stopping and turning towards me. Where Declan's eyes displayed strategy as if I was a little pawn in his game, Noah's gaze exhibits sincerity.

"Thank you, Addison," he says in his low voice.

I raise my eyebrows at the sound of my first name coming from his lips. I can probably count on one hand the number of times he's outright called me Addison. Usually, in moments where he wants to get across how he's feeling without actually saying it. Though my attention is entirely on Noah standing in front of me, I can see Grace bounce giddily in her seat in my peripheral vision.

"You're welcome. It was my pleasure. Really."

"I'm glad you were—" he pauses and considers his words carefully before saying them. "Thank you for being there today. I don't know if I could have done it without you."

"You could have," I whisper. "You're stronger than you think."

A kind of softness that I've never seen crosses his face. My heart rate skyrockets and my stomach flips as I feel the full weight of his appreciation on me. Noah gazes at me for a moment too long before remembering himself. He takes a deep breath and squares his shoulders the cool mask of indifference sliding onto his features muting the affection in his eyes. He dips his chin in my direction before heading towards the door. I manage to hop to my feet, trailing after him not quite ready for him to leave.

"Wait." He stops. I glance back at Grace, who's watching the events play out as if we were a bad soap opera. When I speak to him again, I lower my voice so only he can hear me. "Maybe it's not my business, but when you took that phone call earlier today you looked really troubled about something. Is everything okay?"

Noah blinks at me before looking away and tightening his jaw, the muscles ticking methodically. "Yeah, Parks. As okay as it can be. I better go."

"Oh," I reply, deflating. Throughout today, I felt like we were making headway, getting back to the way things used to be. It felt good, as if the world was finally back on its correct axis, but I guess I was wrong. "Okay. Well if you ever need to talk, you know where to find me."

Noah doesn't reply. He just dips his chin and turns on his heel, leaving my diner and me in his wake. I watch after him as he goes. His broad shoulders are tight and he walks with purpose, his feet striking the ground with every step. I press my lips together, suddenly regretting not pushing a little harder. Noah's struggling, and I wish I could do more to help, but I suppose it's not my place. With a resigned sigh I head back to the booth were Grace is sitting smugly.

"What?" I snap at her when I get close enough. She's observing me like the cat who got the cream—her lips pulling up on one side in a smirk, dark eyes gleaming.

"That man is really putting up the good fight."

"What does that mean?" I ask her, exasperated. "I'm way too exhausted for your riddles."

"Oh, it doesn't mean anything," she says with a flick of her hand.

"Just know that I'm fully invested in seeing where this leads over the next few days."

"*Grace*," I groan, dropping my head in my hands.

"Did you ask him if he wanted to stay on your couch?"

I peek over my fingers at her and then drop my arms onto the table with a dull *thud*. "Yes."

"And?"

"And he said he'd think about it. It didn't sound too promising. Noah is as independent as they come. No way he would accept a handout like that, especially from me."

"On the contrary, my dear friend," Grace says, pointing at me. "I think that if he were to accept a handout like that from anyone, it would *only* be from you."

"You give me way too much credit."

Grace shrugs and then pushes herself into a standing position. "That's what best friends are for! Unless you need me to do anything else, I am out of here. I feel like I need to sleep for a week."

"Same here. You're good to go. Jack said he'd help get everything cleaned up."

Grace gives a big sigh of relief and then pulls me up to stand, too, and wraps her arms around me in a hug. I hug her right back, grateful that she was here today to help. I'm not sure how today would have gone without her being at the helm.

As soon as Grace leaves, I set to work helping the crew with the cleanup. Jack and the staff have finished most of it already, but I hop in where I can, and we get everything sorted. Once we're finished, I send everyone home for the evening, despite it still being early. We've had a full day, and the majority of the town has been in and out of here already today that I doubt we'll have much of a dinner rush.

I shut the diner down, ensuring the door is locked and the lights are off, then go up to my apartment. After my parents' original shop burned down and I expressed an interest in refacing the building, I got the architect to build it specifically for what I needed. My dual real estate layout is peculiar, but it works for me.

My apartment is located right above the diner so that I can get to and from work easily. The stairwell from the diner up to my home opens into a hallway. I also have another exit built into the side alley for visitors, mailmen, or package deliveries. This way, they don't have to go through the diner to get to my front door.

As soon as I'm inside my apartment, I kick off my shoes and head straight to the fridge to get a glass of wine. Today was an emotionally charged, crazy busy day. Now I plan to sit on my couch, watch a terrible movie, and have some wine until I can't keep my eyes open any longer.

Self-care.

I settle on a cheesy romance movie I find on a streaming service and queue it up before padding into my bedroom to put on a pajama shirt and lounge pants. After I've changed, I settle into my couch and cuddle up under a blanket, ready to dive into this cliche love story.

The movie is halfway through when I hear a knock on the door. I frown as I reach for the remote, pausing the movie. Grabbing my wine glass by the stem, I pad over to the front door and switch the deadlock open before swinging it open. I feel my jaw drop when I see Noah standing on the other side of the threshold, a green rucksack thrown over his shoulder and his hands stuffed in his jean pockets.

His eyes scan me up and down, pausing for only a moment when he registers that I'm in my pajamas. When he meets my gaze, I see a wry smirk start to form on his lips. "I heard you might have a couch that's available for rent."

I stare at him silently for a moment, surprised that he actually showed up. Noah and I staying in the same apartment screams bad idea—I know it, and I'm sure he knows it. But I can't in good conscience let him sleep in the back of his car any longer. The image of this large man scrunched up in his backseat burns in the back of my head and my heart aches.

Without a word, I open my front door wider and step back, allowing him to enter my home. He offers me a smile as if he knows the internal warfare I just went through and strides past me. Noah's eyes dart all around my apartment. His gaze lands on the couch where I was sitting, taking in the abandoned popcorn bowl and a half-empty bottle of white wine.

"Did I interrupt something?" he asks me teasingly, his steely blue eyes looking back at me.

"Only self-care," I tell him, crossing my arms over my chest. "Today was a little draining."

He rubs the back of his neck with his free hand and nods in agreement. "You can say that again. Are you sure you're okay with my staying here? It won't be too...."

"Weird? Uncomfortable?"

"Yeah," he agrees, his cheeks tinting pink. An unusual look for Noah. "All those things."

"It's not weird unless you make it weird, Noah. We both are adults now, I think we can manage to stay under the same roof. Or at least I can."

As soon as I say that, I'm reminded of his words from earlier in the day, *"My interest in you was never the problem."*

Now it's my turn for my cheeks to heat up. Maybe this wasn't such a great idea.

"If you want me to go, I can," Noah offers in the kindest way he can.

I shake my head and offer him as significant of a smile as I can muster and spread my arms out. "Welcome to my humble abode. Mi casa es su casa."

An amused smile appears on his lips as he looks around. "It's cute. Very quaint."

"It's not much," I agree, chewing on my lip. "But it's only me here 100% of the time, so it works."

"I like it," he tells me, and I know he means it. "So where do you want me to—"

"Oh, over here," I say, hustling around the couch to grab the remote and shut down the movie. "Sorry, I was just watching a movie."

"Don't stop on my behalf."

"Trust me, you don't want to watch this," I inform him with a laugh. "I don't even want to watch the rest of it."

I exit the stream, turn off the TV for good measure and then move to straighten out the blanket I was huddled under. "So this is my couch. I know, I know, it's extremely chic. But anyway, it will pull out into a bed if you want. Or you can just sleep on it the way it is too. It's really comfortable either way."

Noah's eyes are on me as I babble on like some deranged tour-guide Barbie.

"That's the kitchen over there. I've got an oven, a refrigerator, and a microwave. Oh, and an air fryer if you're feeling frisky."

"Impressive," he says, and I can hear the amusement in his inflection, but I ignore it.

"Bathroom is over there, and that's my room. And I think that's it," I clap my hands together and look at him wryly. "Any questions?"

"Do you have a tip jar?"

"Ha ha."

"Thank you, Parks," he says, no hint of joking in his tone now. "It really means a lot. I didn't particularly care to sleep in my car another night."

My curiosity flares, and I tilt my head at him. "Why were you sleeping in your car? Surely you could've gotten a hotel or a B&B or something."

Noah shrugs, almost as if he's not really sure himself. "I didn't know how long I was staying. I also didn't really want to make a scene of my arrival, so my car seemed like the best bet."

I cross my arms over my chest. "Do you know how long you're planning on staying now?"

He presses his lips together and shakes his head. "I don't."

Looking away and taking a deep breath, I nod my head towards the couch. "Well, feel free to stay as long as you need. You won't bother me."

"Thank you."

"I'll leave you to it then. Towels are in the bathroom closet if you want to shower. I have extra toiletries in there too. Help yourself," I rack my brain to make sure I do not forget anything. When I'm satisfied that I'm not, I look back at my newest house guest. "Goodnight, Noah."

I turn to leave when I'm halted in my tracks.

"Parks," he calls and catches my left hand. I spin around and look at him in question, wondering if I did forget to mention something else, but his eyes are on my arm. Discomfort tingles across my skin, but I don't say a word. I just let him look. It's not the first time he's seen the scar, the remnants of the horrible night I lost everything. Though it has been a while since he's laid eyes on it. He traces his thumb across the mangled, bubbled skin with a gentle reverence that makes my chest hurt. In that moment, I'm reminded of just how well Noah knows me. Or knew me.

"You always wear long sleeves," he notes. "It's because of this?"

I pull my hand away from his and wrap my arm around my middle, my right hand coming to hide the bubbly keloid scar covering the expanse of my forearm. "Of course. No one wants to come to a diner to get a good meal and have to come face to face with a horrible scar like this."

"I think you're giving people far too little credit."

He had a point. The fire that took my parents' café wasn't a secret to the townspeople. They all probably remembered it as vividly as I did. "Maybe, maybe not. But wearing the sleeves makes me feel better about myself. "

Noah's face is unreadable at my confession. Noah was there when I got the burn which lead to my scar. In fact, he's the reason I walked away from that ordeal with *only* a scar. But despite all of that, the heat of his gaze still makes me want to jump ship. It's been a long time since anyone's looked at me that way. Even Eli prefers that I keep the scar covered. It makes him sad to see it, and while he would never complain if I didn't keep it hidden, I do so to prevent the pitying glances and the sympathetic apologies for the tragedy.

"Why are you hiding? You survived, you should wear it with pride."

"Why should I wear it with pride when the very thing that caused it took away all I had?" I shoot back at him, and he takes a step back. He might see the mark as a battle scar, but all I see every day is a reminder of the fire that caused it—the fire that took everything from me in on way or another. I take a deep breath, trying to ease my trembling muscles. "Just leave it. I like my sleeves, and I'll continue to wear them."

He raises his hands in surrender, his expression softening. "I just don't want you to ever feel embarrassed for something like that. Not with me."

I run my hands over my face, feeling my irritation growing. Today has been too long of a day for a serious conversation like this. "Goodnight, Noah."

I turn away from him and head towards my bedroom. I can hear him exhale a disappointed sigh before muttering back, "Goodnight, Parks."

As I settle into bed, I pray for patience because thinking that nothing could go wrong with this setup has got to be one of my craziest ideas yet.

Chapter 7
Noah

"Noah," a singsong voice calls my name. I groan, rolling over on the lumpy pillow and squeeze my eyes shut tighter. My nose is hit with the warm vanilla and lavender scent, trademarked to Addison Parks. She does this every morning, and it has yet to lose its ability to grate on my nerves.

"Go *away*, Parks. I'm sleeping."

"It's a nice day out. You should get up and stop being a lazy bum."

I roll back over and open my eyes wide enough so she can catch the full force of my glare. Instead of scaring her off as I'd intended, she giggles like a schoolgirl, causing me to scowl at her even more.

"What is so funny?"

"Your hair is a disaster. Come on, get up. There's coffee and breakfast downstairs. I want to see you in five minutes, chop chop!"

I groan again, listening for the tell-tale sound of the door closing and her feet bounding down the stairs to the diner. As soon as she's gone, I push myself up into a seated position and stretch my arms up and back over my head, hearing the *pop* of both of my shoulder joints as I stretch. I've officially been roommates with Addison for almost a week now, and every moment has been just as irritating as this one.

She is impossible to live with, but I've secretly enjoyed it—early mornings and all. At the very least, it's a massive improvement from sleeping in the back of my car. Maybe she'll even make me an early riser one of these days, though I doubt it.

I push off the blanket and get up, locating a t-shirt and jeans and shucking them on before heading to the bathroom to straighten my hair out. I startle when I catch my reflection in the mirror. Addison was right; my hair is a wreck. What the hell was I doing in my sleep last night?

I comb my fingers through the long strands, thinking, begrudgingly, that I might need to schedule a haircut. This mess is getting out of control. Giving up, I undress and hop in the shower, rinsing off and wetting my hair to help tame it. When I'm done, I get dressed again and pull my wet hair back into a bun with my green hair tie on the back of my head. I'll worry about it more once I've got some coffee in my system.

I head down to the diner to see Addison pouring two mugs of coffee. When she spots me, she makes a show of checking an invisible watch on her wrist and clucking her tongue. She told me five minutes, and I definitely took longer than that, but she just grins and hands me a mug full of coffee.

"Looks like you've made it just in time."

I accept the steaming drink from her gratefully and raise it to my lips, taking a deep gulp of the brew. Immediately my eyes go wide, and I spit it right back into the cup. It tastes like lukewarm bean water. "What the fuck?"

"Oh shoot, Noah. I'm so sorry," Parks apologizes profusely, embarrassment coloring her features. "Usually Grace or Jack makes the coffee, but they're both running late today, which left me to be the one to start it. I'll admit, I'm not very good at it. I was hoping that I had the right measurements, but I guess I didn't."

I watch her incredulously, cocking an eyebrow and trying to fight the smirk that's threatening to take hold of my lips. "So you're telling me that you, Addison Parks, owner extraordinaire of a delightful little diner, can't brew a cup of coffee?"

Addison groans and drops her head into her palms. "I don't want to talk about it."

I can't help but toss my head back with a laugh as I scoot my butt out of my chair and round the counter towards where she is. I raise my eyebrows, silently asking her permission before I cross the invisible line behind the register. Addison waves her hand in a *whatever* type of way.

I'm still laughing as I make my way to her coffee machine, pulling out the carafe and putting on a big show of pouring it down the drain in the sink right next to it. Addison huffs and then crosses her arms.

"Am I supposed to thank you for coming to my rescue or something?"

I shoot her a grin over my shoulder as I start measuring out coffee grounds *the right way*. "If you must."

"You're a pain in the ass."

"That's why you love me." The words slip out before I can stop them, and an awkward silence falls over the two of us. I let it linger for a little too long, not really knowing how to get rid of it.

Finally, I clear my throat uncomfortably and look over at her again. "See, this is how you measure out coffee. I usually stick to about a scoop to scoop-and-a-half per cup. It doesn't make it too strong but still gives you that kick."

Parks takes my fumble in stride and walks over to me, making gallant effort of observing my instructions. "I see. I guess that's where I go wrong. I can never get the right measurements."

I glance at her out of the corner of my eye and smile. "For someone who used to love chemistry, that's a pretty big admission."

"Yeah, maybe. Look where I ended up, though," Parks turns and sweeps her arm in front of her at the empty diner. "I think I still came out on top."

"Why didn't you go?" I ask her, honestly curious. We've been living together for better or for worse for the last week, but she's been so busy. I feel like we haven't had a chance to talk much, and questions are burning a hole in my mind begging to be asked.

When I left, her plan was to get into a prestigious university on a scholarship, major in science, and then continue in grad school to become a researcher. Diner-owner was never on the agenda at that time. Addison's one of the most intelligent people I've ever met. The sky would've been the limit had she wanted to go that route.

Addison exhales and looks at me, unsure. "I don't know, I guess I —" she purses her lips, contemplating, and then shrugs. "It just wasn't what I was meant to do, I guess. After everything, the thought of leaving here just made me sick. I was all ready to go but then you...."

When she trails off, I know what she didn't mean to silently admit. "But then I left, and you felt—"

"Lost," she says, looking at me with sad eyes. "I don't want to drudge up old wounds, but you asked."

"It's okay," I tell her, and I mean it. "I want to hear it."

"I suddenly didn't know which way was up anymore. The only thing I had that felt familiar was Charlie and Eli. My parents were gone, my home was gone, *you* were gone. So I stayed where I felt safe. I think I just was reaching and grasping at any sense of belongingness, and I found it here. Even after I saw you in New York, it wasn't enough to set me back on that path," she explains. "I don't regret a thing, you know? I'm happy here. I'm happy with how my life turned out."

"Good," I reply, taking a deep breath and looking deep into her eyes. "That's all I wanted for you."

"Yeah," she trails off, her warm hazel eyes holding mine, a mixture of unsaid words swirling in their depths. Finally, she shakes whatever was sitting on her mind off and smiles widely. My pulse picks up a beat or two at the way her face lights up with mischief. "Look at us, just falling right back into what we do best."

I bark out a laugh. "I think what we do best is push each other's buttons. Or have you completely blocked out those early years?"

Parks dismissively waves her hand. "It's a blip on the radar.

When I think back to that time, all I remember is you being the one person I could always count on to listen to me. Always there, having my back. And now here you are, listening to me babble on just like it's old times."

"I like listening to you babble," I admit fondly. Addison holds her smile a while longer. In comfortable quiet, I take the opportunity to pour myself a good cup of coffee and swing back around to sit on the stool I've claimed as my own, so I can talk to her more.

As the morning starts to roll, the rest of the staff arrives and a few customers come into the diner. Addison hurries off to get their orders as soon as they walk in, leaving me with my coffee and my thoughts. She'll come and go over the next hour or two in between taking care of tables or putting out fires with her employees. She'll toss me a smile or stick her tongue out at me as she passes where I sit. Grace is in the backroom checking inventory and taking care of other back office duties, and Jack handles the register out front.

After getting the opportunity to spend some time in the diner, I've realized that Addison has built her own little legacy here, and I love it. The respect and familiarity the town has for her are apparent. People come in and greet her as if she's a part of their family. As much as I would have loved for her *not* to be in Willow Heights anymore, I can recognize why it would be difficult for her to leave now.

"Morning, Lockwood," a deep voice mutters, pulling me out of my musings. I look to my left as a body fills the seat next to me. I lift my cup to my lips and take another swig of coffee.

"Sully, good morning. Looking as sharp as ever," I heckle the sheriff. "Here for your morning doughnut?"

"Actually, I was thinking a breakfast burrito today," Charlie Sullivan replies, not skipping a beat.

"Where's Tweedle Dumbass?" I question.

He barks out a laugh despite himself. "Eli? I haven't seen him, sorry to disappoint." Thankfully, I've been able to avoid Eli Montgomery relatively efficiently since moving into Addison's apartment, and I'd like to keep it that way for as long as possible. "Where's Addie?" he asks.

"She ran to the back to get more butter for table seven," I reply. I can feel Charlie's incredulous stare on me, and I glare right back at him. "What?"

"Table seven, huh? Seems like you're getting pretty comfortable with diner life."

I narrow my eyes at the sheriff, not wanting to get into this right now. "Is there something I can help you with, Sullivan?"

"Just thought I'd check-in. We haven't talked in a few weeks."

"Really? You want to do this here?" I ask him quizzically.

Charlie looks around and presses his lips together. "Do what? I'm just checking in on a grieving friend."

Now I roll my eyes. This is precisely why we *aren't* friends. Charlie is annoying as hell. "Sure. Why don't you tell me why you're really here?"

Charlie rounds his shoulders and leans towards me. "I wanted to talk to you about Orville Marks."

"Have you found anything?"

"I've found two people with that name in the ten neighboring towns. I've reached out to the departments in those jurisdictions to keep an eye out to see if anything suspicious is delivered to their home residences. But other than that, I don't have much. We'll just have to keep looking."

"Well, that is disappointing. And here I thought you had good news to share with me over breakfast."

Charlie snickers as Addison comes flying out of the back storeroom and zooms over to table seven, waving at us on the way, effectively shutting down any further conversation on the matter. "Morning, Charlie!"

He waves back at her, a cheeky grin on his face, and I resist the urge to groan in annoyance. Charlie and Addison have always had the strangest relationship. Even weirder than our relationship. They're like two peas in a pod. As far as I know, Charlie has never thought of Addison in any sort of way other than a sister. Charlie has left the bragging rights of crossing that line to Eli, the town idiot. But as far as him and Parks go? Nothing but best buddies.

I am slightly curious, though, and I look at him over the rim of my cup. "So, Charlie."

He raises a suspicious eyebrow at me, not liking my tone of voice. "What do you want?"

"Oh, you know, I was just wondering if you've got a special someone."

The expression that crosses Charlie's face is priceless—it's a mix of abject horror and severe confusion. "Are you propositioning me, Lockwood?"

"Nope," I reply, reaching for a doughnut sitting on a display holder and taking a bite out of it. "I was just curious if you've settled down or if you're still a bachelor at large."

He's still looking at me like he doesn't trust me, but then he sighs and rubs his fingers over his eyebrows.

"Sometimes, I forget that you haven't been here for the last decade. Yeah, I'm married." Charlie points to his left hand, where I see a gold band glinting on his fourth finger.

"Oh nice, who is it?" I ask after swallowing my doughnut thickly. I guess I could've just checked his hand for myself instead of subjecting us to this painful conversation.

"He's married to Wyatt," Addison chimes in, sweeping across the counter with a wet rag, capturing all the crumbs I've left from the pastry. "Bradford. Another case of high school sweethearts."

My eyebrows raise for a second with the new information before I remember myself and look back at the sheriff, who's watching me expectantly as if to see how I'll react. "I'm not surprised. You always did have the hots for him."

Charlie rolls his eyes and shakes his head at me. "Addie, can I get that omelet to go? I don't think I can be around Lockwood here much longer. He's getting weird."

I chuckle and reach for another doughnut. Addison slaps my

hand away from the display, and I smirk at her as an idea pops into my head. I've wanted to spend more time with her, but I know I won't be able to do that while she's here running the show.

"Do you think you could get out of here today?" I ask her hopefully, leaning forward on my elbows.

Addison looks at me warily and then glances around the diner. Before she can respond, Grace pops over her shoulder and interrupts. "She can. What do you have in mind?"

I have to bite back a laugh when Parks shoots her best friend the dirtiest glare.

"I saw in the paper that Huck's Farm has all their apples ready to pick. I was wondering if you'd like to go do that with me today," I offer.

Addison fumbles with her long sleeves, something I've noticed she does when she's nervous. "I don't know if that's a good idea, Noah."

"Oh, she'll go with you. You were just saying the other day that you wished you had time to go get some apples for some pies, weren't you, Addie?" Charlie interjects and receives another irritated look from Addison.

"She was. I heard her!" Grace chimes in.

Parks' cheeks are now a bright red, and she's frowning at her friends. "You guys are the worst." Then with a resigned sigh, she meets my waiting gaze. "Yes, I could probably make that happen. When would you want to go?"

"Whenever works best for you. You tell me."

Two hours later, we find ourselves wandering the rows of apple trees at Huck's Family Farm. During our car ride out here, we got the chance to catch up a little. I mostly asked her questions about what she's done the last few years, steering the conversation away from any inquiries about my life or career. There will be a time where I can tell her everything about what I've been up to in the past few years. It's just not now. Not when I get to spend the whole afternoon with her. I don't want the gloomy cloud of my past hovering over us today.

"It looks like all the good apples have been picked over," Parks observes as we walk down the row of trees. I glance around and note that she's right. The majority of reachable apples have been picked. The few that linger on the trees are bruised or rotten through.

"What about the ones up there?" I ask, pointing out a bunch of perfect-looking apples up at the tops of the trees.

Addison follows my finger but then sighs, frustrated. "They're too tall for me to reach."

"Luckily for you, I happen to be quite tall," I smirk at her and step closer to a tree, extending my arm and reaching towards the bundle of apples at the very top. The branches are in the way, but I maneuver around them as best as possible.

"Noah, you're going to scratch your whole body up if you keep doing that," Addison says with a laugh when I reach up again, jump, and grunt when a branch digs into my stomach. I do manage to grab one apple on my way down.

I hold it out to her as an offering, and her hazel eyes twinkle with a grin that crosses her whole face as she takes it from me. Parks twists the fruit around in her hand, checking every side to ensure it's not bruised or rotten. "This one is perfect, thank you."

"Of course," I say, then look back up at the trees. All the good ones are all the way at the top. I've dragged her all the way out here today to get apples for her desserts, and I'm not going to give up until we get what we came for.

"Here, I have a better idea," I tell her. "Get on my back."

"What? Noah, no, I'm too heavy."

"I promise that you're not. Just get on."

Parks mumbles under her breath but does as I ask her, hopping onto my back and wrapping her legs around my waist. She secures her ankles together at my middle ensuring she doesn't fall. I shiver when her hands circle my shoulders. Her fingers trail across my muscles, triggering every last one of my nerve endings. Her legs grip the sides of my waist tightly as I stand up to my full height. Her body is rigid on my back, trying to hold on. I snake my hands around the backs of her thighs to give her a little more support.

"Ready to get the good ones now?"

Addison squeaks in response when I step close to a tree and lift her up a little by her thighs. My fingers press into the supple muscle of her leg as her torso stretches against my back so she can reach for a few apples.

"Just a little closer," she mutters.

I oblige her, stepping further into the tree, ignoring the dull sounds of apples hitting the grass beneath us. The branches scratch up my arms a little bit as she collects the fruit from this tree, but I don't say anything. They'll heal.

"Okay, I think I got them all from this tree."

"Onto the next one then?" I ask, and she agrees. We continue this way until Addison's plastic bag bursts full of perfect apples to make into pies. I admit I'm intrigued by the prospect of a freshly made apple pie.

Her hand taps my shoulder, and I look back at her. "Can I help you?"

She giggles and leans forward a little on my back, her chin resting against my shoulder. Her cheek is right next to mine, and I can feel her warm breath on my face when she says, "I think I've got enough. You can let me down now."

A sly grin pulls on my lips, and I shake my head. "What if I don't want to?"

"Noah!"

"Parks!" I shout back at her, still grinning as I walk towards where the tractor loads to take us back to the central part of the farm. "I kind of like you up there. I can actually keep an eye on you this way."

"You're so annoying."

"I learned it from you, sweetheart."

Addison stiffens on my back slightly and then laughs nervously but doesn't press the issue any further. She behaves like a good passenger until we get to the tractor when I finally let her down. I crouch into a squat, feeling the burn from the extra weight in my thighs. Addison slides off of my back in a delicious way that has my heart stuttering and a tightness forming low in my gut.

Once she's on the ground again, Parks brushes her hands on her jeans and then runs her fingers through her hair—nervous movements accentuated by the light pink blush that is forming on her freckled cheeks. Her hands grip tightly to the handles of the apple bag, holding it right in front of her body. She doesn't meet my eyes fully, glancing away every time she looks at me.

"Do you want me to hold that for you?" I ask, stepping closer to her. Now that she's further away from me, I immediately want to rectify that. The magnetic pull that I've always felt around her is in full force, urging me toward her.

Parks takes a step back as I come closer to her, her hazel eyes flashing with an unspoken warning for me to keep my distance. I stop in my tracks, waiting. "I think I can handle it until we get to the car, thank you."

"Okay," I concede, taking a step back and giving her the space she's indicating she needs right now.

When the tractor comes, we load up our apples and make the trek back from the orchard. Addison seems lost in her thoughts as we pay for the fruit and head back to the car.

She stays quiet the whole drive to the diner, and I'm starting to worry she's feeling embarrassed or mad at me about the entire piggy-back ride thing. I put the car into park right in front of the diner and sigh. Shifting my hips towards her, I reach for her hand on her lap and thread my fingers through hers. She startles and turns her head to look at me, eyes wide with apprehension.

"Hey," I say on a breath. "Is everything okay?"

"Please don't, Noah."

"Just let me—"

"No." She pulls her hand out of mine and rubs at her forehead with her fingers. "I think we need to talk about some things. You've been living in my house, and we've been doing fine, but I think we need to straighten a few things out. Set some boundaries so lines don't get blurred."

"Is this just because I let you ride on my back so you could get the good apples off the tree? If you think that was a form of foreplay, then Eli really needs to step up his game," I grit through my teeth. Wincing to myself when it comes out a little harsher than I intended.

"That was uncalled for," she says back, now looking at me, her lips pulled thin.

I deflate and lean back against the window. "Sorry."

"Noah, I need you to be honest with me. Do you think you can do that?"

I pause before answering her, unsure of where she's going with this. "I can try."

"What do you want?"

"In what capacity?" I try to clarify, still unsure where the direction of this conversation is headed.

"I think you know what I'm asking. It's not fair of you to come here and derail my life only if you're planning on leaving again," she says. "How am I supposed to know that you won't disappear into the night?"

I blink at her, "Look, I'm sorry if I gave you the wrong impression. I just thought that—"

"Don't do that," Parks cuts me off. "You and I both know exactly what you were doing. It's *me*, Noah. It's you and me. There is no other way for us."

"And? What's your point?" I prod her even though I know exactly what she's trying to say. My defenses are rising despite that I'm the one who's being selfish. It's selfish of me to sit here, attempting to force us back to the way we were before when I can't offer her anything in return. At least not yet.

"My point is that all this flirting and joking around is great. It's just like old times. But you know how that went the last time and I need to know if you have any intention for it to be something more. I don't want to put myself on the line just for you to leave me behind again. I have someone who actually wants me. Who wants to be with me and build a life with me."

"Eli?" I snarl at her, completely bypassing the whole point of her little speech. "You can't be serious."

"He was here when you weren't," Parks whispers, her eyes cutting me like daggers. "And he hasn't left."

"Lovely, then go be with your Prince Charming if you want him so much. I won't stop you. I hope you have a happy life together."

I immediately know I've said the wrong thing by the hurt expression that covers her face. Regret seeps into me, and I open my mouth to try and fix the situation when movement catches out of the corner of my eye, and I glance at the sidewalk. Eli's standing in front of the diner watching the two of us, his arms crossed over his chest and a thunderous scowl on his face. What perfect fucking timing, as usual.

Addison also notices him and then she turns to me. I can't read what's going on in her mind, but register that she's done talking with me for now. "Okay. I think we should take a rain check on this conversation. If we don't, we're just going to hurt each other more. I'll see you later."

Without another word on the matter, she swivels in her seat and throws the passenger door open, getting out of my car. When she's on the sidewalk, Eli walks up to her, his face taking on a much more affectionate appearance. I glower out the window as he wraps an arm around her shoulder, pulling her into his side. As he leads her into the diner, he looks back at my car and shoots me a spiteful glare lifting his free hand and giving me the middle finger. As soon as she's inside, I drop my forehead against the steering wheel and let out a low irritated groan, jealousy knotting in my gut.

Why am I such a fucking idiot?

Chapter 8
Addison

"Hey, Addie," Grace calls my name, and I glance up, startled. My friend is looking at me, concerned. We're taking a long lunch together while Jack and Noah hold down the fort at the diner. Noah has been helping out here and there since he claims he doesn't have much else to do these days. I've assigned him easy tasks such as bussing and restocking. "Is everything okay? I've said your name like five times."

I close the catalog I'm reading and sigh before running my fingers through my hair in a frustrated manner. "Oh, sorry. I guess I'm just lost in my thoughts."

"Want to tell me what's going on?"

"It's just this thing with Noah the other day that I can't shake," I admit honestly, remembering our disagreement in his car after going to the apple orchard. I haven't been able to stop thinking about it since it happened. I tell Grace about the whole afternoon as best as I can, not leaving any bit out, especially about what was said in the car afterward. "Maybe I shouldn't have pushed him, I don't know," I say. "It was just so confusing to me at the moment that I felt like I had to talk it out. I think that might have been a mistake."

"You feel like it was a mistake to ask him what his intentions are?" She asks incredulously, not as if she's making fun of me, but to clarify that she understands correctly.

"I don't know," I say honestly. Grace looks at me with soft eyes as if she can see my inner turmoil about all of this. "Things had been going so well ever since he moved in. Too well. It's like we slipped right back into the way we used to be when we were best friends."

"That's good, though, isn't it?"

"It is. It's been great, really. But the other day, he was so...flirty, and I don't know. I panicked. I was getting some seriously mixed signals. I guess I was feeling hopeful that there might be more there, but I think I just scared him away. He has a tendency of shutting down when he gets cornered," I explain.

Since that conversation, Noah and I have been walking on eggshells around each other. There's no doubt in my mind that he witnessed the exchange between Eli and me in front of the diner. Since then, he's retreated significantly. And to be honest, I'm not sure how I feel about it. On the one hand, it's a relief not to be questioning every interaction we have with one another. But on the other hand, I miss him. It sucks missing a person who's standing right in front of you most days.

Grace is looking at me with wide eyes. I know where she stands when it comes to Noah and me. She'd bend over to backward see us together, but she also knows when it's the right time to meddle and when it's the wrong time.

"What do *you* want, Addie?" she inquires, echoing the question I asked Noah the other day.

"I don't know."

"Is it Noah?"

I let out an exasperated sigh. "It will always be Noah. And that's the problem. It's like when he left, he blew a hole in my heart, and it's still a gaping wound that has never closed. It's always there as if a piece of me is missing at all times."

"Even now? After he's been gone for so long?"

"Yes. Even more now, honestly. I'd be lying if I said otherwise." I laugh humorlessly, running my finger over the rim of my glass of iced tea.

"Well, I guess some love never dies, you know?" Grace says gently.

"What do I do?" I plead with her, hoping that she'll be able to give me the answer to this question that's been burning in my mind ever since I ran into Noah for the first time at the diner. I've been trying my hardest to keep everything in order. But whenever Noah's around, all my plans get blown to bits.

"What do you want to do?" she tosses back at me. I note the sparkle in her eye, proving that she had some sort of inkling that we'd be having this conversation eventually.

"I don't know. I think that's part of the problem. Noah doesn't know what he wants either," I laugh humorlessly. "Eli knows what he wants, though, so at least I always have that option."

"Do you have a date with him tonight?" Grace asks. It's Friday, and she knows Fridays I typically spend hanging out with Eli.

I lean my head down on the counter and groan. "Yes." She chuckles and stands next to me, rubbing her hand over my back.

"I'm sure you'll figure out the best way to handle things. You always do."

"I'm glad you believe that," I say and check the time on my phone. "We should probably get back to the diner to let the others have a break."

We pay our checks and head back, taking our time strolling down the sidewalk. We arrive just as the lunch rush is winding down. The diner has only a few customers seated at tables. Jack is behind the counter, showing Noah how to use the milkshake machine. I can't help the amused grin that takes over my face as I watch Noah listening intently to Jack's instructions. Noah's got his hands on his waist with his head bent slightly towards the machine, where Jack points out the different buttons and contraptions, teaching him the process.

"Am I going to have to put you on the payroll?" Grace asks Noah as we walk up to the counter. Noah turns his head and glances between me and Grace, an amused grin forming.

"I'm not sure how valuable an employee I'd be. I don't think I'll ever figure out how to work this thing."

"It's okay; none of us really know how to do it," I tell him. Noah darts his gaze back over to me, his lips press into a thin line, and he nods his head at me but doesn't say anything else. A sick feeling settles in my stomach at the distance that is still so apparent between us.

Grace raises her eyebrows at me, questioning the apparent snub from Noah. I grind my teeth together but leave it. If Noah wants to be crabby, then that's on him. When he's ready to talk, I'll be waiting.

Deciding that I will not waste any more energy on this situation, I go into the back and grab my apron. I plan to focus on work to pass the time until my date with Eli this evening. I keep my head down and fall into the routine of my job.

Before I know it, the clock above the door reads five o'clock, and my date is arriving. The chimes ring as Eli walks in, exclaiming, "Hey, beautiful! Ready to go?"

I look up and smile at him, feeling Noah's heavy gaze from across the room. He's ignored me all day, but now his full attention is on me.

"Yes, just give me a moment!" I say as I untie my apron around my waist and rush it back to the stock room. When I turn around, Noah stands right in front of me, arms crossed. I mirror his positioning and glower at him. "You're in my way."

"You've barely talked to me in days, Parks. That's what you're going to start with?"

"I've barely talked to *you*? I've been here all day with you, and you haven't said a word. You're the one who's been treating me like a stranger!" I huff at him and mentally decide I'm not doing this right now. "I'm kind of in a hurry, Noah. Could you please move?"

He frowns at me. "No, we need to clear things up from our disagreement the other day."

"Not now," I mutter as I try and push past him, but he's too big for me to manhandle.

"Parks," he says my name in his deep voice, his hands grabbing hold of my arms and stopping me in my tracks. Electricity travels through my body from the point of contact. "Would you just look at me?"

With a notable sigh, I do as he asks. "What?"

Noah traces my face with his gaze as he restrains me in front of him. His eyes hold something behind them that I just don't have the time to decipher. "Don't go with him. We need to talk."

"So now you want to talk? When I'm trying to leave? No, we can talk tomorrow, though I'm not sure we even have anything to talk about anymore."

"I didn't mean to ruin everything," he says, and I'm shocked at the brutal honesty coming from him. Of all the times he could have chosen to be honest with me, it's when I'm supposed to be out the door on a date with another man. "Is there a way we can just rewind and forget what happened after the apple orchard? So we can be friends again?"

I wiggle out of his grasp and take a step back. "What if I don't want to do that? We've never been that good at being friends."

It's a lie, we both know it.

"I thought we were doing okay."

I run my fingers over my brow, trying to massage away the nasty headache threatening to hit me with full force. "We'll talk later, okay? I promise. But I really need to go right now."

To my surprise, he sidesteps out of the way. As he moves, I give him a lingering glare, and then I brush past him back into the diner. I can hear his footsteps behind me. Eli is leaning against the counter, talking to Grace when I go up to him. He greets me with a wide cheeky grin that quickly falls when he sees Noah follow me from the back. He narrows his eyes at the man behind me and his jaw ticks.

"Ready to go, Addie?"

"As I'll ever be, what do you have planned for tonight?" I ask him, feeling hopeful that he might have come up with something new or exciting.

"Oh, the usual," he says, a smile taking hold of his features. "Thought we could get some take-out and finish the movie we started last week. We got a little distracted halfway through," he says to Grace with an exaggerated wink.

My friend gives him a tight-lipped smile, getting his innuendo, and I suddenly have a great desire to sink into the ground underneath me. From behind me, I hear a scoff from Noah. It shouldn't bother me, but it does. I can't help but glance over my shoulder at him. He's watching the interaction with a stormy expression on his face, his eyes dark and lips set into a deep frown. My stomach flips, and I turn back to Eli.

"Let's go," I tell him.

His face lights up, and he leans forward, pressing his lips to my cheek. Eli takes my hand and leads me toward the door. I feel Noah's pointed stare on my back as I walk out. We both get into Eli's car, and he speeds away from the diner. Eli keeps glancing over at me as we drive like he's trying to make up his mind about something.

"Is everything okay?" I ask him, finally.

He clears his throat and then chuckles nervously. "McCoy looked like he was ready to punch me back there. Not to mention you coming out of the storeroom with him hot on your heels. Want to tell me what that was all about?"

I grip the handle of my purse tightly, registering his jealous tone. "Nothing. Noah's just been helping out at the diner, and I think he was hoping I could show him a few more things before I left."

"You sure that was all?" he presses. "Cause to me, it looks like he wants you back."

"He doesn't," I tell him, though I'm fully aware that might be a flat-out lie. "It was nothing, Eli. Can we just drop it? I'm here with you now, aren't I? Let's just have a nice evening together."

"Fine," he mutters though I can tell he's not happy. To my relief, he doesn't bring it up again.

Eli decides on Thai food take-out, and then we end up back at his place, just like we do every Friday date night. I do my best to dampen my disappointment at the unoriginality and focus on spending quality time with Eli. I settle on the couch with the brown paper take-out bag, setting my jacket and purse off to the side while he grabs plates and utensils.

The smell of Thai food immediately surrounds his small living room, and I feel warm—too warm. I'm tempted to pull off the long-sleeved flannel shirt I'm wearing, as I have a short sleeve underneath it. Still, I remember that my scar makes Eli uncomfortable, so I decide against it, settling on using my hand to fan my neck in an attempt to cool down.

Eli returns to the living room, notices what I'm doing, and frowns at me. "Do you want me to turn down the heat in here?"

"Would you?" I ask him. "I could take off this flannel, but I—"

"I'll turn it down," he cuts me off, disappearing down the hallway where I hear him punch a few buttons on his thermostat. When he returns, he rubs his hands together, a boyish grin on his face. "I'm starved. Let's eat!"

We dig into the food and start to watch our movie. We are laughing within minutes, and I look at Eli, amused when he chokes on a noodle. These moments are what I love best about our "Date nights."

Eli has been one of my best friends since I came to this town. Charlie was my first, but by default, Eli followed shortly behind. Charlie and Eli generally come as a package deal. The three of us have built a lot of great memories over the years. I love to spend time with Eli, but as I peek over at him throughout the rest of the movie, I conclude that there's no spark. At least not the way there should be.

I don't break out in full-body shivers whenever he comes close to me or brushes my hand with his. Not like when Noah put his hands on me earlier in the stockroom. It's not fair to Eli, I know he loves me more than anyone, but I'm starting to realize I don't feel the same towards him.

As the movie finishes, I decide that this will likely be our last date night. Technically speaking, we're not in a relationship. I know he is hopeful that it will lead to more someday, but I don't see that happening. Even if it means I end up being single for the rest of my life, it is what it is. Eli just isn't the one for me, and he needs to know.

The movie's credits begin to roll, and Eli turns his body towards mine. I look at him and offer him a timid smile—already knowing where this is headed. Eli cups my jaw with his hand and tilts my chin up before claiming my lips. His kiss is forward, his warm lips pressing against mine as he takes what he wants.

It's a fast process from there. Eli maneuvers his body over mine until I'm stretched out on the couch, and he's hovering above me. His fingers leave my face and make quick work of the jeans I'm wearing, unbuttoning them and pushing them down and off my legs. Once my jeans are off Eli yanks his shirt over his head, removes his pants, and crawls above me. His hand goes to the hem of my shirt and bunches it up to the cups of my bra. As soon as my stomach is exposed, he leans down and kisses me. He does this for a few minutes, his tongue tickling the sensitive skin of my belly before his hand dips between my legs, working me quickly.

Before I know what's happening, Eli is positioned at my center and pushing into me. I bend my legs to change the angle slightly to accommodate him, and his hand grips my hip as he begins to move in me. I toss my head back at the full sensation when he bottoms out, and Eli groans into my neck.

"God, you're incredible," Eli says, his eyes watching me as he takes me. I arch my back, still trying to find that perfect angle for him to hit. I finally find the right position and start working towards what I need. Eli leans over me, his arms supporting the arch in my spine as he snaps his hips back and forth.

"Keep going," I urge him, feeling my body start to climb towards my peak. Eli continues to thrust into me, his movements becoming erratic, and it dawns on me that he's not going to last as long as I need him to.

I snake my hand down my belly, resorting to using my fingers to get myself there as he continues moving against me. I'm still not fast enough. Eli groans and buries himself deep inside of me before stilling. His head rests against my shoulder, his sweaty forehead sticking to my skin.

Immediately the fuse is dampened, and I know I'm not going to get my turn tonight with him, not that I'm surprised. Sex with Eli can be great, but there have been more times than I can count that I've had to finish myself off after the fact. My head drops back against the pillow, and I exhale, my breath ruffling Eli's dark hair.

"That was amazing," he whispers, pushing himself up on his hands, so he's hovering over me. His eyes glitter at me, and I offer him a small smile in response. "You're amazing. Did you finish?"

I know he knows I didn't, so I don't bother lying. "No, but that's okay. You know I don't always."

Apprehension clouds his eyes. "Do you want to stay the night? I could run us a bath or a shower, and then maybe we could go for round two in a little."

I press my hand against his chest, silently telling him to get off of me. My stomach is hurting from the knot of built-up pressure, and I feel too warm still. "I think I'm going to head home, actually. I'm pretty tired."

Eli's face falls in disappointment, but he masks it right away. "No problem, I get it."

I find my jeans across the room and pull them on. He watches me as I do so. I look back at him and purse my lips before deciding that I'll talk to him about everything tomorrow. I'm not that cruel. I'll just let tonight be tonight and end things later when he's not in post-coital bliss.

"Do you want me to drive you home? It's kind of late," he says, standing up, still stark naked but not ashamed. I chuckle and find his jeans on the floor, holding them up in front of him and shaking my head.

"No, I can get home. It's not too far of a walk. Thank you,

though," I tell him. The walk in the brisk night air might do me some good, actually. It might help dissipate the deep ache that I'm feeling due to my lack of release.

Eli steps towards me and cups my face with both hands, bringing my lips to his in a kiss. I kiss him back, but it does nothing for me. When he pulls away, his lips are in a thin line, his eyes studying me intently. Eli isn't stupid, and I see the wheels turning in his head, trying to piece together the motives behind my actions. Usually, I would stay the night with him. But I'm not feeling it tonight.

"Goodnight, Addie."

"Night," I offer him a smile before leaving.

The night is cold, winter just around the corner. My boots crunch against old brown leaves scattered across the sidewalk, giving off a satisfying sound. The town is quiet. The only noises are the occasional car driving past or the rustle of wind in the trees. I look up at the sky, noting it's clear, the bright stars twinkling against their black background. I exhale into the night, noting I can see my breath swirling in front of me, and start my trek home.

When I finally get there, the apartment is dark, and I assume Noah's sleeping already. I close the front door as quietly as possible and then tiptoe into my bedroom. The cool air did nothing to soothe the ache that still lingers. Need courses through my body. My lower belly is wound up so tightly that as soon as I'm in my room, I close and lock the door, turning on the fan by my bed to the highest setting to drown out any noise.

I shuck off my pants and crawl underneath my covers, reaching for my vibrator in my bedside drawer. My hand slips under the band of my panties, and I let out a breathy moan as my finger brushes the most sensitive part of my body. Dipping my fingers through my wetness, I know it won't be long until I find release. I need this so bad. I use my fingers at first, letting the pressure build until they're just not enough to push me over the edge. When I get to that point, I grab my vibrator, turn it on, and shove it under the covers. I sigh, relieved when the vibrations course through my body right where I need them.

My eyes squeeze shut as I get closer and closer, small whimpers leaving my lips despite my best efforts to contain them. I'm right there, right at the edge, and I gasp for breath, feeling beads of sweat form on my forehead as I chase it. Right at the last moment before I crash over the precipice, Noah's steely silver eyes pop into my mind.

The pleasure floods over me like a tsunami, and I groan out Noah's name as I feel everything crumble around me. I can practically feel his hands on me as I come harder than I have in a long time, as if he's right there next to me, coaxing me and encouraging me. The dirty words he would say to me echo in my ears, making me quiver, prolonging the pleasure.

When the contractions from my orgasm wane, I open my eyes and stare at my ceiling, even though I can't see anything in the darkness. Rolling onto my side, I drop my vibrator onto the bedside table and take a deep breath, trying to calm my racing heart.

I've only had sex with Noah once, but it was good enough that I've never forgotten it. No one has ever lived up to my experience with Noah, and now he's right outside my bedroom door, and my heart is begging me to throw all reason out the window. A part of me burns with embarrassment at the fact that I just got off to the image of my house guest. The other part yearns for me to go to him and let him take care of me like I know he would.

I close my eyes and settle into my pillow, letting my mind imagine what would happen if I did go out to the living room to see Noah. Would he push me away? Or would he push all rationality aside and take me in his arms, kissing me until I see stars?

I shiver, thinking about the way Noah knows how to kiss me. It's been years since our lips have touched, but I can still feel the intensity and weight of his mouth on mine. He would wrap his hands around my waist, pulling me into his lap until we were flush together. His hard length would press against me, and— *Stop it*, I tell myself with a groan, burying my face into my pillow.

Desire coils tightly in my belly again, and I try and take a few deep breaths to dissipate it. There's no way I will get any sleep tonight if I keep thinking about him like that. I roll over onto my back and pull my covers up to my chin. It's going to be a long night.

When morning finally does come—after a night of endless tossing and turning—I roll out of bed with a few muttered curses. I stumble out of my room and into the kitchen, where I grab a mug and fill it with water, sticking it in the microwave to heat up. I find my favorite tea out of the cupboard and pull out a bag right as my water is done warming up.

"How was your date last night?" I hear a low rumble from across the room.

His voice startles me, and I jump, splashing water onto the counter. I give Noah a quick glance and then look back at my cup of tea, dunking the teabag in and out.

"It was good."

"Yeah? Is that why I heard you getting yourself off with your vibrator last night?"

My jaw falls open as I turn and blink at him, dumbfounded. He fixes me with a solid stare, raising a challenging eyebrow in my direction. We face each other silently for a few moments, him waiting on me to admit something and me not willing to cave.

Finally, Noah stands up from his spot on the couch and walks over to the kitchen. I try my hardest to keep my eyes to myself. Still, I feel my cheeks heating up at the sight of him sauntering across the living room in only a pair of sweatpants, his torso completely bare.

I notice a tattoo depicting a map covering his entire left shoulder that travels down into his pectoral. He's been living here for two weeks, but up until this point, I haven't seen him shirtless. My eyes are glued to the ink as he walks toward me, taking in the finer details.He has an old-style compass tattooed on his chest, the north arrow pointing at the illustration of land. Circling around the compass is a rope looping into a knot right over his heart. My mouth goes dry when I recognize the infinity symbol hidden in plain sight.

Noah is quiet as he walks toward me, watching me watch him. He comes to stand behind me, the warmth of his skin seeps into my back through my thin t-shirt, and I suppress a shiver. One large hand snakes up my side and rests on my hip. Fire burns my skin underneath his touch, and I bite my tongue so I don't make a sound. The desire from last night flares brightly inside me and I bite back a moan.

Noah bends down so his lips are close to my ear, his fingers brushing my hair away from my shoulder. His breath is warm on my skin, and I clench my thighs together, easing the ache that is readily forming within me. "A woman like you should never be left wanting after a date. If you were mine, you might as well throw that thing away. But you already know that don't you?"

He steps back, and I'm hit with a chill. With my heart beating in my ears, I turn around and look at him, breathless. He gives me that signature smirk and shrugs a shoulder.

"Just food for thought, Parks. I'm gonna go shower. Looking forward to having that little chat with you later."

I gape after him, my cheeks pink and my brain still not fully awake enough to comprehend the encounter.

What the hell just happened?

Chapter 9
Noah

Sunlight streams through the blinds, hitting my face and alerting me that morning is here. With a sigh, I roll onto my side on the couch, turning my face away from the bright light. I blink my eyes a few times, trying to focus. After I've laid there, dawdling for longer than I should, I push myself up into a seated position. I stretch my arms over my head before getting up and heading to the kitchen to make a pot of coffee.

As I get up and move around, I'm surprised to see Addison's bedroom door still closed. Usually, she's up before me, hustling about and getting ready for the day. She'll usually go on a run before the sun comes up and then come back to shower before I've even started to stir. Maybe she decided to sleep in this morning.

Despite living under the same roof, I haven't seen her much in the last few days. She has avoided me since I called her out on her date with her vibrator a few nights ago. If I had to guess based on how her cheeks flamed when I brought it up, I embarrassed the shit out of her. We still haven't had the chance to talk things through since then.

I pour myself a cup of coffee and sit at the kitchen table. Today, I need to get back on track with my purpose of being here. I'll probably run down to the sheriff's station later today. I need to talk to Charlie to see if he has any more leads on the Orville Marks situation or has anything further on my father.

My fingers drum against the ceramic mug as I try and organize everything that's bouncing around in my head. We don't have much to go on when it comes to nabbing my father for all his crimes. Still, if this Orville Marks turns out to be a solid lead, I could quickly get a warrant and move things forward significantly. All I need is something to get the ball rolling, and the rest should fall into place with little effort.

"Noah," I hear her croak from inside Addison's bedroom, pulling me from my thoughts.

I frown, staring at her bedroom door, unmoving. Her voice sounds scratchy when she calls for me again, and I stride over, rapping my fingers against the wood of her door. From behind it, I hear a weak, "Come in."

I twist the knob and push the door open, peeking my head inside. "Parks?"

She's just a lump buried under pillows and blankets, and I see her hazel eyes peeking at me from underneath. Before she can say anything, a god-awful cough emits from her lungs. It sounds heavy and productive. I take a step further into the room, my eyebrows pulling together. "Are you okay?"

"No," she squeaks. "I'm sick."

"I can hear that," I mutter, walking in until I'm closer to her bed.

"No, Noah, don't come any closer. I don't want you to get sick too," Parks protests shooting a hand out from under the covers. "I just wanted to make sure you knew I wasn't feeling well."

"What do you need me to do?" In rebellion, I sit down on the edge of her bed, reaching for her comforter and pulling it down so I can see her face. I frown even harder.

She turns her head away to cough again, and I wince at the sound. "Can you call Grace and tell her I won't be down there this morning? She and Jack can handle it."

"I can do that," I tell her, reaching up and resting the back of my fingers against her forehead. She groans at my cool touch and closes her eyes. "God, sweetheart, you're burning up."

"I feel like death."

"Do you have any cold medicine here?" Parks shakes her head no at my question. "I'll run down to Monty's today and get you a few things. Just wait here. I know we have some juice in the fridge; I'll get you some."

Parks moans when I get up, getting jostled by my movement. "Could you make me some tea?"

I nod my head at her before returning to the kitchen and making her some tea. I heat up the water and pull out her favorite kind of tea before steeping it. Bringing it back into her bedroom, I retake a seat on the edge of her bed.

"Here you are, Parks," I nudge her gently and hand the cup over to her.

Addison pushes herself up from where she's become one with her pillows and takes it from me, bringing the steaming cup of hot leaf water up to her lips and taking a sip. "Thank you."

"Of course. Is there anything else I can get you?"

She shakes her head and leans over to set the cup on her night-stand before hunkering under the covers again. I spot her cell phone on the charger and reach for it, holding out for her to unlock it when I come to the passcode screen. I punch my phone number into a new contact, aware that I might regret doing this down the road.

"You have my number now in case you need anything. I'm going to head downstairs and get everything sorted with the diner, and then I'll get you a few things from Monty's. Call me if something comes up, or you need me back up here, okay?" I instruct her. She nods, grunting to let me know she got the message.

I head down to the diner, tossing one more look at her door before leaving. When I get down to the main floor, Jack has already opened things up, and a few customers linger in front of the counter, waiting for their breakfast and coffee.

Jack's standing at the coffee machine, his back facing the

customers. I sidle up next to him and mutter, "Addison's sick. She asked me to talk to you and Grace about handling things down here today. I can help out where needed too. Just tell me what to do."

Jack nods his head. "That's no problem. I got it covered. Do you want to go back to the kitchen and see if they need anything?"

I do as he asks, and the cook informs me he's all set. Grace arrives fifteen minutes later and sashays into the back office to drop off her personal items. I follow her in to let her know what's going on.

Grace startles when she turns around and finds me standing in the doorway. She places a hand over her heart. "Jesus, Noah. Gotta give a girl some warning before you sneak upon them."

"Sorry," I say sheepishly. "I'm efficient at stealth mode."

Grace rolls her eyes and asks why I'm bothering her, to which I laugh under my breath and inform her that her business partner is ill. Grace doesn't miss a beat and steps into Addison's shoes right away, calling in Jack and delegating jobs to him and also—to my surprise— me. I expected to be more of a busboy again today, picking up the slack where I could, but Grace put me on front counter duty for the morning so Jack could help her with more of the big tasks.

To my complete and utter amazement, the morning goes by smoothly. The regulars came in and got their breakfast, only a few commenting on my presence behind the counter. I stay there until the lunch rush is over, signaled when the steady stream of customers starts to slow. As soon as things slow down enough, Grace peeks her head out of the office and tells me to take a break. I take the opportunity to zip over to Monty's Market to pick up some supplies for Addison: cold medicine, soup, tissues, and some popsicles just in case her throat hurts.

Once I have what I need, I come home and bound up the stairs to the apartment, unlocking the door and going straight to her room. I knock on the door once before going in and find her in precisely the same position I left her in. She's curled up under her blankets in the fetal position, an arm outstretched off the edge of the bed with a tissue bunched up in her fingers.

"Did you bring me drugs?" Addison asks. Her nose is all stuffy, making her voice muffled.

"Just some cough syrup and soup. Hope that will suffice."

"How's everything going down there?" she questions me further, trying to sit up and reaching a hand out for the cold medicine. "Are Grace and Jack doing okay?"

"Everything's perfect, Parks. All you need to worry about is getting better. You picked a good team. They've got everything under control."

Parks rips open the packaging on the medicine and pours herself a dose, downing it quickly and then hacking a little at the taste. She looks down at the bottle and scowls at it. "Gross."

"Is there anything else I can get you? I told Grace I'd be back as soon as I checked on you." I sit down on the edge of her bed.

"Are they putting you to work?" Parks asks, settling back down into her pillows.

"Yeah, I hope that's okay. They're all so worried about you. I think Jack is two seconds away from coming up here himself."

She groans into her pillow. "Oh God, please don't let anyone up here. I look like a snot goblin."

I chuckle. "Don't worry, I'll make sure no one bothers you. You sure you're okay with me helping out downstairs?"

"Of course, thank you. It—" Addison takes a break to cough into her arm. "It means a lot to me."

I ask Addison again if there's anything else I can do for her before I go back downstairs. She declines my offer, her eyes already drooping. I restate her blanket for her before stepping out of her room, closing her door behind me. After ensuring everything in the apartment is in order, I return to the diner to help.

I spot a few stragglers from lunch still hanging out in the diner and finishing their meals, but overall the place is empty. I grab a washrag from the bucket and start wiping down the counter and tables. Just as I complete my task, the bell above the door rings, and an angry voice fills the room. I look up, an unamused expression on my face.

"What are you doing back there?" Eli snarls at me as soon as he walks in the door, Charlie tailing right after him.

I stare at him deadpan until he's got smoke coming out his ears, and then I look back down at what I'm doing. "Parks is feeling under the weather today, so I told her I'd handle things here today."

"She's sick?" he asks, his tone taking on a more worrying approach. "Where is she? Is she upstairs?"

Eli makes a beeline for the door leading up to Addison's apartment. Still, I'm faster than him, and I move swiftly, reaching my arm across and blocking the doorframe. "What do you think you're doing?"

"I'm going up to check on her. Now *move*, McCoy, before I move you myself."

"I don't think so. Parks is sleeping right now, and she needs her rest."

"You don't get to tell me what to do. Addison's my girlfriend, so I have to check on her."

I hear a cough behind him, and I pull my attention away from the menace in front of me to see Sullivan standing behind him. He's rolling his eyes at the apparent pissing match that's about to take place. I look back at Eli. "All I'm telling you is that she's resting and doesn't want visitors. Trust me once she's feeling better you can hang out with her all you want, but until then, give her her space."

"Block this door all you want, McCoy. I'll just use the other entrance," he scowls at me. "You don't get to tell me that I can't see my best friend! You're the one who abandoned her when she needed you!"

"Okay, okay." Charlie decides to intervene, pulling Eli off me by the collar and situating space between us.

I glower at them and cross my arms over my chest. "Parks told me not to let anyone up there. Are you trying to go against her wishes?"

"Is she well enough to make decisions like that?" Eli snarls back at me. "What if she's passed out in the shower or burned herself trying to make soup or something."

I hit Eli with a level stare. "She's fine. I was up there not even an hour ago, and she was sleeping. She probably is still sleeping."

"Okay, there you go, Eli. Maybe you should back down now, I'm sure Noah—" Charlie tries to interject.

"You're trusting him? What if this is all just a ruse, and he has her bound and gagged somewhere—"

"That's enough!" I shout at him, unwilling to listen to his bullshit anymore.

Eli can spout his mouth all he wants but not about something like *that*. The idea that he could think of me capable of something like that hits deeply. Still, I plaster on an impassive expression. Charlie is now glaring at his buddy, knowing all too well the severity of the implication.

"We'll get out of your hair," Charlie says, his eyebrows still pulled tightly as he frowns.

"What? We haven't even gotten lunch yet," Eli protests.

"Then we'll go somewhere else. Come on. We'll chat later, Lock-wood," Charlie grabs Eli by the collar and then practically pulls him out of the diner, Eli protesting and questioning him the whole way. As they leave the diner, I glower after them.

"You're protective of her," Grace observes as she comes to stand by me. My mouth feels dry and I swallow thickly.

"Of course I am. Someone needs to be."

Addison's best friend hums at me and turns to face me fully. "Let me ask you a question, Noah."

Here we go.

"Go for it," I tell her, rising to her challenge.

"Do you believe in soul mates?" she asks me, her dark eyes studying me intently.

I must admit, I'm taken off guard by her question. I regain my footing swiftly, though, and respond back. "That depends."

"Really. So would you say that you and Addie are soul mates?"

My teeth grind together so hard that the muscles in my jaw begin to ache. "Grace," I warn.

She holds up her hands but still fixes me with a heady stare. "I'm asking out of curiosity. Love isn't random, you know. There's a reason why you've always been drawn to her and her to you. All I'm looking for is your opinion on the matter. Surely you must have one."

"Of course I do, but my opinion on whether or not Parks is my *soulmate* really doesn't concern you, does it?"

"On the contrary," she says, pointing her finger at me, "it does. Addie is my best friend. I watched the two of you skirt around each other since we were teenagers and her struggle over your connection since the moment you set foot back in this town."

"Cut to the chase, please. I don't have time for this," I growl at her. "I'm getting tired of having this conversation all the damn time."

"Listen, I just want you to think long and hard about who you're stringing along. I think the phrase 'right person wrong time' was written with you two in mind. So now that begs the question, when is the right time? Or is there a right time?"

"How would Parks feel if I told her you were meddling like this?" I shoot back at her, my patience running thin. This is part of the reason why I never truly missed living in a small town—in a big city like New York or DC, my business stayed my business. At least as much as it could, given my line of work.

"I'm just saying, Noah. You're both too old to be playing games with each other. So figure it out." With that, she saunters off and doesn't bother me for the rest of the day.

As the hours tick by, her words nag at me, and a part of me knows she's right. I need to figure everything out, which needs to start with having that conversation that Parks promised me we would have. I need her to be well enough for that first, though. I continue with my course for the day, picking up the odds and ends of tasks that need to be done.

As soon as I'm back in the apartment at the end of the day, I yank my shirt off over my head, feeling like I've got the essence of bacon following me everywhere from learning to work the grill. I hop in the shower, quickly rinsing. Once I'm done, I pull on a pair of sweatpants and grab a beer from the fridge. I pop open the top and wander over to the living room, collapsing onto the couch. I reach for the remote and scan channels until I find some trivia gameshow I can watch without too much effort.

"Noah?" A meek voice calls out my name from the bedroom not long after I get settled. "Are you home?"

"I'm on the couch. Come on out."

"I don't want to get you sick," she protests, but I hear her feet pad against the floor, indicating her presence.

As soon as Parks steps into my line of sight, I have to fight back a pitiful laugh. "You look like death warmed over."

Parks sniffles as she comes a tad bit closer to me, and I see the tip of her sharp nose is chapped. She's standing there with a blanket wrapped around her shoulders and covering her head. Her eyes are red with deep purple pockets underneath as if she hasn't had decent rest in days. I conclude she was probably tossing and turning while trying to sleep today.

Parks scowls at me and then sniffles again, a pathetic sound that tugs on my heart. I raise my left arm up onto the back of the couch and then pat the spot next to me. "Come here, Parks."

She doesn't waste time crossing the living room and hopping onto the couch, curling up to my left side. I help her situate her blanket so that it's fully covering her and she nestles her face against my chest. I smooth a hand over her wild honey-brown hair that could really use a brush. My left arm falls into the dip of her waist, and I hold her close to me.

"I think your fever broke," I speculate as I gauge the temperature of her cheek on my chest. She doesn't feel as wildly hot as she did this morning. "How are you feeling?"

"Tired."

"Did you not sleep today?" I question.

"Some. Not really good sleep, though. This flu, or whatever it is, sucks." She sniffles again and then asks, "How did everything go at the diner today?"

"Flawlessly," I respond, reaching for the remote and turning down the TV before grabbing my beer and taking a sip. "You've got a good team. I just helped where I could."

"Thank you for that."

"My pleasure. I'm glad I could help."

She sighs and snuggles in impossibly closer, and I tighten my arm around her hips. We lay together for a while. She stays snuggled up to me, and my eyes remain on the television, watching but not hearing the show on the screen.

The sensation of her fingers dancing across my skin prompts me to glance down. She's tracing the outline of my tattoo, running her finger over the dark lines. She circles the compass before tracing the shape of the twined rope over my heart.

"Infinity," Addison whispers. I close my eyes and hold her tighter. *Infinity*. It would look like a rope looping around in a knot to everyone else, but she sees it for what it is. Addison has always been good at that—seeing past surface level. "It's really a nice tattoo."

"Thank you."

"Did it hurt?" she asks, and I chuckle at her question.

"It didn't feel good, but it wasn't the worst pain I've ever been through."

"Yeah," she agrees and then yawns.

"You should go back to bed," I mutter, resting my nose in her hair and inhaling her lavender and vanilla scent—fresh and sweet.

"I don't have the energy to walk," she mewls. "Can you carry me?"

I chuckle against her hair and then move her so she's in my lap. Parks struggles a little bit, her bony knee hitting somewhere it shouldn't, and I grunt in discomfort. "Yep, just jam your knee right up my crotch, why don't ya, Parks. Thanks for that."

To my relief, she giggles softly and gives me a quiet apology. I scoop her up in my arms, carrying her from the couch back to her bedroom. I deposit her on the bed and readjust her comforter so she's all tucked in.

"I'm so glad you were here today," Parks says as I move to my knees so we're at face level. Her hazel eyes settle on my face, and a tender smile curls on her lips. My heart constricts, and I feel a tug toward her deep in my soul. My thoughts jump back to Grace's question today, but I squash it down, not ready to address that situation just yet.

"You shouldn't look at me like that," I say breathlessly.

"Like what?"

"Like I'm your knight in shining armor. Your hero." I admit, brushing a few strands of hair away from her face. "I'm far from that."

"Well, you were today," she whispers, nuzzling into her pillow and closing her eyes.

I exhale through my nose, stroking my hand over her hair a few more times until her breathing evens out, and I realize she's fallen asleep. As I stand up, I can't help but lean forward and press a kiss to her cheek, my lips lingering on her soft skin. She sighs happily in her sleep at the contact, and the tightness grows in my chest.

"Goodnight, Parks."

Chapter 10
Addison

"Well, well," Grace calls to me as I walk into the diner. She's standing behind the counter with Jack, the two of them grinning at me from ear to ear. "If it isn't Addison Parks, risen from the dead!"

I roll my eyes and walk toward my friends, accepting their hugs and well wishes.

"How are you feeling, Addie?" Jack asks me. "That was a nasty cold you had."

I was out for almost the whole week. Yesterday was the first time I felt like I had the energy to get up and move around. I'm still not quite up to snuff, but I'm functional at least. Noah gave me strict instructions that I shouldn't be working yet, and as he's the one who's put his life on hold the past few days for me, I figured the least I could do was listen to his suggestion.

I had to come down and check and see how everyone was doing, though. The Type-A personality in me could not just let everything lie. I try my hardest not to micromanage my team. I trust my employees and give them the freedom to make suggestions about making the business more successful. Still, at the end of the day, the diner is mine, and I want to ensure it's all running smoothly. Especially now that I've been out for almost a week.

Grace and Jack give me the paraphrased version of the events over the last few days. To my relief, it sounds like there was nothing out of the ordinary. Though my jaw nearly hits the ground when I hear about Noah and Eli almost getting into a brawl over me.

"Thankfully, Charlie was able to mediate the whole ordeal, and he had to physically remove Eli from the premises," Grace tells me. "Gotta admit, though, the whole thing was kind of hot."

"Can concur," Jack chimes in. "Your man's kinda badass."

"Eli?" I ask incredulously, tapping my finger against the countertop.

Jack drops his head back and barks out a laugh. "No. Noah."

I chuckle nervously, feeling my cheeks heat up. "Oh, right. Well, thank you guys for keeping everything afloat. I'll try my best not to get sick again soon."

"If you do, just send Noah in your place," Jack says, and I look at him in surprise. "What? He was actually really helpful. He kept his head down and did what we needed him to. He was better than some of those new hires we've had recently. Maybe you should offer him an official position."

I feel my blush deepen at the prospect of hiring Noah. I don't know what it is, but the thought of being his boss rubs me the wrong way—or maybe the right way, in the wrong way. "I'll ask him. But again, thank you guys for covering. I'll get out of your way, and hopefully, I'll see you tomorrow."

They wave goodbye to me as I leave, and I have to force myself to walk all the way out. After Noah's strong recommendation that I not work today, I decided that I'd take a stroll around the town square to keep me busy. I think fresh air in my lungs and some old-fashioned vitamin D from the sun will do me good.

It's a gorgeous day outside, a little warm for early November. I smile as soon as I step out onto the sidewalk, pull my jacket tighter around my shoulders, and begin my walk. Fall is on its way out, and winter threatens to appear soon. Most of the colorful leaves are still up on the trees, but the ground is covered by those who couldn't hold out much longer. I shuffle along the sidewalk, kicking at small piles of discarded leaves as I go, smiling to myself.

As I walk, I get a few hellos and questions from a few friendly faces, wondering if I'm feeling better. I smile, nod, and answer their questions, telling them I'll see them for breakfast tomorrow. My favorite part of the job is getting to know everyone personally and being part of daily routines. *Sunny-Side Up Diner* is just that. It's a favorite stop in the mornings, a favorite lunch location for meetings or breaks, and a favorite place to have dinner when you don't feel like cooking.

Somehow, I've successfully created a place where people feel safe and welcome, which is invaluable. I wouldn't trade it for the world.

"Addie!" I hear a deep voice call my name just as I'm about to head back into the diner from my walk. I turn around in time to get a glimpse of Eli as he barrels toward me, wrapping me up in a huge hug that almost suffocates me. I laugh and pat him on the back.

"I was so worried about you. Are you feeling better?" he asks, releasing me and encircling my cheeks with his hands so he can look me over. His baby blue eyes roam my face.

I try to pull out of his grasp, but he's got me in a weird position. His fingers rest heavily on my cheekbones, not wanting to let me wiggle away from him. "I'm feeling a lot better, Eli. Thank you."

"I tried to come to see you," he grumbles. "But that bastard McCoy wouldn't let me come up, and then Charlie got involved and—"

"I heard about that. It was probably for the best, you know? I was pretty sick, and I would've felt terrible if you caught whatever I had."

"You didn't seem to care if Noah got sick, though," he says pointedly.

I shift uncomfortably. "Noah's staying in my apartment, Eli. If I was that contagious, he would've already gotten it."

"Yeah, I guess. I still think letting him stay with you was a bad idea. I don't trust him one bit."

I contain my desire to roll my eyes at him. "Well, there haven't been any issues so far."

"Yeah, I guess. You're feeling better, though, now, right? Like back to normal?"

"Mostly," I reply with a shrug. "I think it might take a few days to —*oomph*."

Eli cuts my sentence off by grabbing me around the waist and pulling me into him before claiming my lips with his in an aggressive kiss. As we're lip-locked, I stare wide-eyed at him, my brain slow on the uptake to what's happening right now. I push him away from me and wipe at my mouth, frowning at him.

"What was that?"

"I just haven't seen you in so long. I needed to kiss you," Eli says sheepishly, his cheeks turning pink as if that will excuse his brash behavior.

"You could've been a little gentler about it. And as I was saying before you interrupted me, Eli is that I'm feeling *mostly* better. But, I still have a few lingering symptoms, so I hope you didn't just infect yourself," I retort.

Eli shrugs his shoulders and gives me a grin. "It would have been worth it. Do you think you'll be up for date night this week?"

I sigh and look down at my hands. I know I need to talk to Eli about our situation. I don't love the dynamic anymore, and it's not fair to him to pretend that I do. "Yeah, I thought we could get together at the end of the week. There are a few things I wanted to talk to you about."

He nods, "Okay, I'll text you later, and we can work out the details." Eli steps forward and presses a kiss on my cheek. "I really am glad you're feeling better, Addie. I missed seeing you around here."

I give him an appreciative smile back. He's acting like I was gone for months rather than a week. But as much as Eli grinds my gears sometimes, he is one of my oldest and dearest friends. We've been through thick and thin together, and I hope he'll be understanding about what I need to tell him. He says his goodbyes and offers me a wave before heading back to the Market where he works with his dad. I reciprocate the motion and turn around, walking up the few stairs back into the diner.

The door jingles as I walk in, and I'm immediately barraged with a blank look from Noah, standing behind the counter.

"That was cute," Noah remarks when I step through the door. He's staring at me, a plate in his hand that he's drying with a rag. I raise an eyebrow at him, challenging him to continue. "The little reunion you had out front. You'd almost think you were on your death bed the way Monty just mauled you."

I roll my eyes. *These men.* "He was just glad I'm feeling better."

"I am also glad you're feeling better, Parks. That doesn't mean I'm going to try to eat you the first chance I get."

My eyes flare at his unintentional innuendo, my stomach coiling tight and thighs clenching at the thought. Noah has the decency to look a little embarrassed, but he just clears his throat, moving on without addressing the blunder.

"Anyway, now that you're almost fully recovered, I was wondering if we could talk?" he asks hesitantly. "You know that conversation we've been putting off?"

Instead of arousal being the culprit of my impending stomach ache, now anxiety takes root. How did I get to this point in my life where all I seem to do is schedule important conversations? Things shouldn't be this complicated. "Of course. This evening after you get finished helping out here? We could talk over dinner somewhere."

He presses his lips into a thin line before saying, "Could we just stay in? I think I'd like to duke this out just the two of us without an audience."

I nod, trying to ignore the rising anxiety taking over, "Sure."

"Great, I'll bring up some food once I'm done here," he says, his eyes falling away from my face and looking anywhere but at me.

It takes a moment, but I realize Noah appears as nervous as I feel.

Suddenly I'm not sure that talking is the best thing we can do. Noah and I have fallen into a kind of understanding. Do we really want to stir the pot?

There are a lot of words left unsaid between the two of us, and I don't know which direction this conversation will go. It's not like any more damage could be done, but it's strange seeing Noah look uncomfortable. I always remembered him being the stronghold during challenging situations. Maybe he's lost his edge.

I shake my head right after that thought comes across. There's no way Noah's lost his edge. He's Noah—one of the strongest men I know who exercises control like it's a daily workout. And despite us being apart for the last eight or nine years, I know he hasn't changed fundamentally. At least not *that* much.

When Noah's done with the plates, he gets me a white ceramic mug of hot water and places it in front of me. I take a seat at the bar dunking the teabag he chose in and out of the water. He and I don't exchange any more words. I just nod to him, grateful for my tea, and he gives me a sideways grin before walking to the back and disappearing from sight.

Grace wanders out from the office and spots me at the bar, immediately coming over. She starts rattling about certain things that I need to approve tomorrow and fills me in on more of the nitty-gritty details of the last few days. Overall I'm pleased to hear that everything has gone smoothly, and I'm grateful I have such good partners.

After returning to the apartment, I spend about an hour cleaning and sanitizing. I toss my bedsheets and comforter into the wash and wipe down all the countertops with disinfectant. I'm thankful Noah was here while I was sick, but my apartment clearly displayed that fact. He's not the tidiest housemate. Once everything's sparkling and spotless, I settle myself on the couch.

Checking the time on my phone, I determine I have a little over an hour before Noah will finish up downstairs. I scroll through one of my streaming services and pick a movie to watch in the meantime.

Not long later, Noah enters the apartment carrying a large paper bag. I'm curled up on the couch under a fuzzy blanket, pausing my movie, when he walks in. I offer to help, but he declines immediately, setting the bag on the little table in front of the couch.

"What are you watching?" he asks, glancing at my paused movie.

I shrug sheepishly and tell him, "*50 First Dates*. I know it's old, but it's one of my favorites."

"Is there much left?"

"I think I'm a little more than halfway, maybe."

"That's great. We can finish watching while we eat. I got Chinese food," Noah says, rubbing the back of his neck. "I guess I should've checked to see if you're feeling up to that. I didn't get anything too spicy, just some sesame beef and sweet and sour chicken and then rice."

My stomach growls as he explains his haul, indicating that I'm more than up for it. I've been surviving off chicken noodle soup and toast for the last week, so any type of real food sounds fantastic to me. I nod my head, my stomach still rumbling, and sit back down on the couch, opening up the paper bag and pulling out the familiar white and red boxes.

"It's probably not the best idea to eat this, but it smells so good," I say.

Noah chuckles and takes a seat next to me. "Actually, I think this is just what you need to get back into the groove of things before going back to work tomorrow. You'll need all the extra calories to jumpstart."

I agree with him with a laugh and then start the movie again.

"Here, I got you these," Noah says, digging around in the bag until he finds what he's looking for, then offering it to me. I hold my hand out. Not sure what he's giving me when I see a pair of chopsticks. I grin from ear to ear, my heart skipping a beat.

"You remembered!"

Noah rolls his eyes at me. "It's not as novel as you think it is to use chopsticks to eat Chinese food. I'm just no good at it, so I always go with the good old-fashioned fork."

I'm still grinning as I situate the chopsticks in my hand and start picking at the food. I've had Chinese takeout with Eli more times than I can count. Every time, without fail, he always forgot to get me chopsticks even though he knows I prefer to eat all Asian food with them. Yet here is Noah, remembering the little detail about me when we have Chinese for the first time in years.

The two of us dig into our food, not saying a word to each other. The movie continues, but I find it difficult to focus, knowing that Noah and I will have this dreaded conversation as soon as it's over. I try my hardest to watch the unfolding of the love story on the TV. Still, all I can think about is what I'm going to say to him, making up fake responses to what he'll lay on the table. It's a pointless waste of energy, but the longer he sits next to me, not saying anything, the more nervous I get.

Noah gathers the containers and throws everything away when we finish our food. I try not to notice how he looks at me when he saunters back towards the couch, falling down next to me and landing a little too closely. The heat from his body radiates into mine, triggering the butterflies in my stomach to start flipping out again. I tighten my hands into fists, trying to simultaneously watch the rest of the move and get my head back in the game.

It's no use, though. I'm glad I've seen this movie hundreds of times; otherwise, I wouldn't have any clue how it ends. As soon as the end credits start to roll, I brace myself for the impending conversation we're about to have. It takes a few moments, but I finally drag up the courage to start.

"Noah," I say hesitantly as I turn to him. He's reclined against the couch. His arms are draped across the back on either side, his knees splayed a little—the picture of ease. His silver blues watch me warily as I address him. Though he's good at hiding it, I think he's still as nervous as I am. "We should probably talk now."

"There's still a few minutes of credits rolling," he teases, nodding his head towards the TV. Then, resignedly he sighs, sitting forward out of his relaxed position and turning off the TV. I'm facing him fully now, my legs crisscrossed in front of me, and I watch him expectantly. "Where do you want to start?" he asks.

I shrug my shoulders. "Maybe we should start with you cornering me in the backroom before I went on my date last week. Want to tell me what that was about? It was pretty aggressive."

Noah's got his elbows resting on his knees, his hands clasped together. His eyes are trained on the ground as he collects his thoughts. When he finally looks at me, his eyes are steeled. "Alright then, I guess we'll dive right in—I don't like seeing you with Eli. He's not right for you. In fact, in my opinion, he's absolutely *wrong* for you. Not that thats new information for you. You know I've never liked him for you."

I frown at him. "That's not fair."

"I *know*. This is why I'm having such a difficult time with this, Parks. I know it's unfair to leave and then come back and say things like this and expect you to rearrange your life for me. But that's just how I'm feeling." He runs his hand through his long hair, laughing humorlessly. "God, it's just, even earlier today when I saw him kiss you, I thought I was going to see red. You deserve better than him."

"Eli cares about me."

"Oh, I bet he does. He's probably a flawless boyfriend. Plays everything right out of the book."

At this point, he stands up and starts pacing, agitated. I think about informing him that he's wrong, but I don't get the chance. Everything that he's trying not to say is bottling up. I can see the pressure increasing tenfold with every second that passes. His hands run through his long hair, and he shakes his head before he can't hold it anymore, and the words start spilling out.

"Good old Eli Montgomery, right? He probably says all the right things at the right times, brings you gifts, and tells you lovely things while you're together, how you're the stars that light up his sky when there's no hope for anything else. Well, that's great, except that's not what you need, is it?" He stops and looks at me dead on, the severity of his gaze cutting me deep. "You need someone who will have real conversations with you. Put that gorgeous brain to work. Someone to challenge you, push you, infuriate you. Push you out of your comfort zone but at the same time offer you comfort. Someone who knows when to let you take control but isn't afraid to take back the reigns when you need them to—so you don't always have to carry the burden and responsibility on your shoulders alone. You need a partner who knows the ins and outs of what makes you *you*."

"Someone like you?" I interrupt breathlessly, pushing off the couch to stand right in front of him. My heart is threatening to go into cardiac arrest at his words, every single one striking my soul like a mallet hitting a bell.

He's taken off guard and pauses abruptly, his eyes flaring with silver flames as his gaze devours me. He steps closer to me, our chests nearly touching now. Noah bends his neck until his forehead is pressed against mine. He hesitates for only another moment before exhaling and closing his eyes, taking me in. I follow his lead and let my eyelids fall shut, too, leaning into the weight of his head against mine. He's breathing hard as if he's trying to catch his breath, his body trembling.

"Noah—" I trail off when he shakes his head. I pull away from him and look at him, worried. He's got his eyes closed, neck bent low.

"I'm sorry."

"You told me to find someone else. You told me not to wait," I whisper to him.

"Yes, and I'm not telling you that you have to stop being with him if that's what you want. You just wanted to talk, and so we're talking. I'm not going to hide how I'm feeling about you. I did that once, and all it accomplished was wasting time we could've spent together."

"What are you trying to tell me, Noah? Just tell me how you're feeling. Trust me, like I trust you." I plead with him.

Noah turns his head to look at me, the full brunt of his metallic blue eyes hitting me squarely. "I'm sorry. I never wanted to make things difficult. I just didn't imagine being back here with you would affect me as much as it has. If anything, it's reinforced my opinion why leaving in the first place was the right decision."

I recoil as if he'd slapped me, a gasp falling from my lips. Noah's eyes go wide, and then he grimaces. "I didn't mean it like—"

"No," I interrupt him, pushing myself to a standing position. "I think you did. If you're going to break my heart again, Noah, just do it. I can't go through this again. I can't fall in love with you again just for you to rip me to shreds."

Noah follows me, standing up as well. His hands reach out to grab mine, halting me in my attempt to turn away from him. His grip isn't hard, just enough to stop me from running. "Would you stop trying to run away during our conversations? We're not done here."

"Let me go."

Instead, he holds me tighter, pulling me around and closer to him until we're standing face to face. I turn my head away from him, suddenly interested in a stain on the carpet below me. "Addison, look at me."

When I don't oblige, he lets go of one of my hands, his fingers coming up to cup my chin so gently that I barely feel it, though it's enough pressure to bring my face up to meet his gaze.

"Look, I can't tell you very much about why I'm back," he whispers, holding my eyes with his. His stare is so magnetic that I can't get myself to pull away. "I want to, so bad, I do. And I will. But I can't right now. It's important that I'm able to focus on what I need to do. And what I meant with my earlier statement is that you have a way of derailing everything in my life—in the best way. Parks, you could take me down with just a look from those gorgeous hazel eyes if you wanted to. You are my biggest weakness, the only person who has that kind of power over me. So yes, I meant what I said, but only because you become my biggest priority if I'm around you. Everything else just flits away."

"Are you leaving again?" The corners of my eyes start to burn at his words, and I swallow thickly. Fear grips my heart, the familiar feelings of abandonment sinking into my system. When I'm with

Noah, everything feels right and whole. It's a feeling that sinks into my soul and fills all the gaps that have been for so long I forgot they existed. Now that I know what it's like to have him back in my life, I'm terrified for him to leave again.

Noah's eyes trace my face, and his expression softens. His hand moves from my chin to my cheek, his thumb stroking against my cheekbone. I tilt my head into his palm, closing my eyes and letting the warmth from his hand seep into my skin. When he touches me, everything in my world feels right, back on track.

"No, I'm not leaving. I don't know if I'm strong enough to leave you again." He exhales before reaching to tuck some hair behind my ear.

Relief floods through my system, and my muscles relax. "I still don't know where we stand."

Noah's eyes narrow slightly, and he considers how to respond. "I don't either, but I hope we can figure it out together."

"Do you regret leaving?"

His thumb stills for a second on my cheek but then resumes its motion. "Every day, but I thought it was the right decision at the time. I was young and all I wanted to do was keep you from getting hurt more than you already had been by then. I just didn't realize that I was hurting you most by leaving when you needed me."

"I wish things were different for us," I whisper, looking into his eyes. "All I wanted was you."

"I know, Parks. I feel the same way."

I'm hesitant as I mutter the words on the tip of my tongue. "After New York, you said that someday we could be together. Is it someday yet?"

I think back to the scrawled out note Noah left me after I found him in New York all those years ago. The words I've read so many times they linger in the back of my mind. I've read them more times than I can count.

There is nothing I want more than for you to have everything you want, but that can't be me. Not yet.

Noah looks deep in thought as he brings his hand and rests it in the crook of my neck, his large thumb resting on the angle of my jaw where he moves it in small circles. His fingers leave a warm trail across my skin, and I wet my lips, feeling my heart rate pick up slightly in anticipation of what he'll say next. Hope tingles in the back of my neck and my breath catches.

You are everything to me. Never forget that. I'll never forget you. That's all I can promise, for now.

He leans forward and presses a kiss to my forehead, then pulls away and rests his head on mine, his gaze smoldering until I feel like I might incinerate. Underneath his gaze I come alive. My soul flares and for the first time in what feels like forever, I feel *seen*. Noah knows me, he knows how I'm feeling because we're one and the same.

"Soon, Parks. I promise."

Chapter 11
Noah

"Morning, Noah," Addison chirps when I make it down from the apartment in the morning. She's looking especially chipper today. I wonder if it's due to our conversation last night. I know she still has questions, and we still have a ways to go before everything is smoothed out, but it felt nice to just *talk* to her last night.

I give her a sideways grin, take the mug of coffee she offers me, and slide into the last seat at the counter. "Good morning. Sleep well?"

Addison nods. Her eyes are bright as she gazes at me. "Better than I have in a while."

Grace is watching our interaction from the other end of the counter, looking suspiciously between the two of us and our cheeky grins. "What the hell is up with you two this morning?"

I smirk into my coffee mug but leave Addison to talk her friend down. "Nothing. We just had a good talk last night."

Despite it being the whole truth, it doesn't ease Grace's suspicions in the slightest. She looks put out as she goes back to her task. "Sure. If that's the story you want to go with."

Addison places a plate of sausage, scrambled eggs, and an English

Muffin in front of me. After giving her an appreciative smile that makes her blush, I watch proudly as she hurries around, taking care of business. She runs this place like a pro, managing multiple tasks simultaneously and never missing a beat. Parks has definitely built herself her own legacy here with this little diner.

I observe her as she takes care of her customers, greeting everyone by name. She's got the small-town diner aesthetic on lock, hitting every one of the checkboxes that make a place like this successful. Everyone who walks in that door is happy to see her, and she reflects that energy without flaw, her face lighting up with a grin that makes her eyes sparkle.

The stool next to me screeches against the flooring as it's pulled away from the counter. I look over my shoulder and find Charlie Sullivan sliding into the seat beside me. I bite my muffin and frown at him as I realize this is becoming a regular occurrence. He says good morning to Addison and Grace and orders his breakfast before turning to look at me.

"Morning, Lockwood."

"Sullivan," I greet him. "To what do I owe the pleasure?"

He shoots me an annoyed look. "I can't just sit here for breakfast?"

"Nope," I reply, my lips popping around the word. "You must have ulterior motives for being this close to me."

He laughs but doesn't deny it. "Eli and I were going to go to the range today. I need to get some practice in, and Eli's tagging along just because, but I wondered if you might want to join. Figured you could probably use the practice too."

I blink at Sullivan a few times, contemplating his offer a minute before nodding. "Yeah, I do actually need to get down there. What time are you all going?"

Charlie glances down at the watch on his wrist. "Say an hour or two? I'll finish my breakfast and then get Eli and swing back around here."

"Perfect," I nod again and brush the crumbs off my hands. "I'll need to get a few things from the apartment, then I'll be ready."

Addison arrives and places a plate down in front of Charlie, offering him a friendly smile. "One order of biscuits and gravy."

Sullivan tips his head gratefully and then starts into his breakfast. I stay in my seat next to him, finishing up my coffee and muffin, running through my mental file of our mission.

"So, Sully, any news from the home front?" I ask him. Since Addison got sick, I haven't had the chance to check in with him. I could use a progress report.

Charlie looks at me out of the side of his eye and then shakes his head. "Not much. Your dad is a professional at keeping things under lock and key. It seems like I've got ears everywhere, but I haven't heard a thing. Not even a whisper."

"Anything else on our friend Orville?"

He presses his lips together and shakes his head briskly. "Nada."

I exhale, frustrated. This is proving to be a wild goose chase. How the hell am I going to get what I need when every lead we find turns out to be a dead-end? I glare down at my coffee mug, trying to think of something that I can do to edge things along. It's like this whole operation is at a standstill right now—either my father is waiting for us to make the first move, or we're too busy grasping at straws trying to find something that isn't there.

My father is intelligent, and I conclude that I'll have to get three, if not five, steps ahead of him if I'm going to win this game—it's simply a matter of how to get ahead.

"I can hear your mind working from over here, dude," Charlie mutters in between bites. "You'll give yourself a brain hemorrhage if you keep that up."

"There's gotta be something that we're missing. Something that we haven't considered yet that's the key to all of this."

"We'll get there. Don't rush it. Things will fall into place."

I frown at him. "I'm not sure I like your can-do attitude about this. There may not be an official deadline but I'd like to get this wrapped up sooner than later. There are actual lives at stake here, you realize that?"

I've been back in Willow Heights for nearly a month now at this point, which in the grand scheme of things, is hardly any time at all. And yet in that month we've hardly made any headway.

Charlie puts down his fork and turns to face me fully. "I'm well aware, Noah. I had the same debriefing as you, you know. But us rushing into things and making sloppy mistakes is only going to hurt us in the long run. You know this."

I look behind the counter to ensure Addison isn't nearby hearing all of this. I'm not ready for her to be in the thick of it, not just yet. "I think we need to take some risks to start the ball rolling."

"I think you're wrong."

"We'll agree to disagree then, Sully," I growl. "But this is my case."

"And this is my town," he protests back, his face taking on a severe expression, informing me he's not playing around. "You brought me into this because you wanted my help. So maybe just take a walk and cool off, and we'll reconvene later. I'm trying to eat here, and my biscuits are getting cold listening to your bullshit."

I turn away from him and grab my coffee mug, glaring into the brown liquid, fuming.

"What are you boys up to today?" Addison asks in a singsong tone, sauntering over with a coffee pot in her hand. She looks between the two of us expectantly as she refills our drinks.

"Noah's going to come with Eli and me to the shooting range," Charlie informs her. Addison gives me a smile that lights up her hazel eyes, and I fight off a groan at how excited she is that I'm spending time with her boy toys.

"That's great! I think that will be a lot of fun. You've been cooped up in here for the last week covering for me, so you could use a break. You've earned it," Addison implores me, leaning across the counter in my direction.

Charlie is watching his friend, his brows pulled in at the center. I can see he's trying to piece together what's changed in our dynamic with each other, similarly to how Grace was earlier. There's no hiding that Addison and I are on better terms today after our discussion yesterday, especially from observant people like Charlie or Grace. They seem to have a personal interest in what goes on between us.

"Right," I say, scooting away from her and trying to deter Charlie's knowing gaze. "Well, Sully, enjoy your cold biscuits. I'm just going to run upstairs and change and get my stuff together. Shoot me a text when you're ready to head that way."

Charlie nods, still looking between Addison and me as if he's trying to fill in the blanks or put the pieces together on a puzzle. I grimace internally. Nothing happened last night other than words, but Grace and Charlie are looking at us as if we've been caught red-handed for something much worse. I excuse myself from their questionable gazes and go upstairs to shower.

About an hour and a half later, I get the text message that Charlie and Eli are ready to go. I rifle through my old bag, looking for my gun, and secure it in my waistband, not bothering with a holster. When I go downstairs, I see Eli has claimed the front seat of Charlie's patrol car, which means I have the privilege of sitting in the back like a criminal. There are a few hellos from the two men up front as I situate myself on the hard plastic seats before we take off.

"You ever been to the range before, McCoy?" Eli sneers at me over his shoulder from the front seat. "Or was daddy too busy showing you how to hit clay pigeons out of the sky to show you how to really use a gun? Clay pigeons your only expertise?"

Charlie shifts, and I can see him getting ready to inform Eli of my *actual* expertise, but I cut him off and let Eli run his mouth. It makes no difference to me. "Yeah, I guess. Something like that."

I notice Charlie eyeing me in the rearview mirror, one brow raised, silently questioning what the hell I'm doing. I smirk and shrug a shoulder back at him. We'll see where this goes. It could be fun jerking Eli along.

We have to travel to the next town from Willow Heights to get to the range. It's about a thirty-minute drive, and not even five minutes in, I feel like banging my head against the window listening to Eli talk. He's muttering this and that about plans for his date with Addison now that she's feeling better. They're all terrible ideas, and I wonder if he even knows her at all, despite being one of her oldest friends.

It's not my place to bring up the conversation I had with her last night. The ball is in Addison's court now. And I must admit, it's weird not knowing what she's going to do with that. From what I've gathered, she's still weighing pros and cons, which she happens to be a professional at. I'm sure she's got a written list stashed somewhere to effectively make an informed decision.

Still, I'm anxious to see how everything will play out. I don't want her to stay with Eli, but it's not my place to say otherwise if that's what she chooses. I look out the window as we drive, watching the scenery pass by, trying not to fall into a rabbit hole of unwanted thoughts.

We get onto the highway, and something off in the distance catches my attention.

"That place is still empty?" I ask Charlie as we drive past the old, worn-down Witch House. Growing up, the place was the source of countless cheesy horror stories told with a flashlight under your chin at parties.

"The Witch House?" Charlie asks, looking out the window at what I'm referencing. "Yep, still empty. I always assign some guys to stand guard around Halloween, so kids don't get too ambitious with their dares. The place should be condemned. It's a safety hazard— practically falling apart."

"Do people still believe it's haunted?"

Charlie laughs and nods his head. "The officers I assign usually prefer to stay in their cars when they have to post there. The guy this year swore up and down that he could hear ghosts when he was up there."

I frown, the gears in my brain working with the new information, and continue to stare out the window. "Is it still for sale?"

Eli laughs at my question, jumping into the conversation with full force. "Why are you looking to invest in real estate? Find a cute little house to build a family in?" I glare at him but don't design a response. He's on a roll, though, and continues to run his mouth. "I'm sure the future Mrs. Noah McCoy would love nothing more than to realize her hero of a husband bought her a broken-down shack for her wedding present."

"Eli," Charlie warns his buddy, and I grit my teeth together.

Eli chuckles again and taps his knuckles against the window. "I'm just messing around, Charlie. No one would want to marry Noah anyway. He looks like a homeless person."

I roll my eyes at the jab and pull out my phone, sending a few quick texts and opening my email. I've decided I need to find out more about that Witch House. I had completely forgotten about its existence, but now, it's raising a few red alerts in my head. I type out an email to a realtor in Willow Heights, asking if I could set up a time to look at the old house in the next week. It couldn't hurt to do some sleuthing.

When we get to the range, Eli, for some reason, attaches himself to my side, insisting that he wants to shoot with me in my lane. Charlie sends me an apologetic shrug but strides down the aisle to his own lane without further fussing. I grit my teeth and walk with Eli to our assigned space.

Eli jumps right into "instructor mode" without missing a beat and starts running me through each tiny detail of shooting a weapon at the range. I fight the urge to roll my eyes with every word that comes out of his mouth but let him do his thing.

"Okay, so you're going to want to make sure that you reset every time you fire a round," Eli tells me as if I don't already know this. "So instead of rapid firing, after each shot, just line up again and hit it. You'll be more likely to get your target each time you do that." I nod my head along as if his instructions are really sinking in.

I sure wish Charlie was near our booth to see the ass whooping I'm about to give Eli Montgomery.

"Okay, I think I got it," I respond, playing along. I set up my stance, doing it wrong on purpose and grinning to myself when Eli corrects me.

"There, that's better, nice stance, good form. Go ahead and give it a try."

I nod and then look toward where the target is down the lane. I line up my sights, move my finger to the trigger and take a deep breath in and out, sinking into the hold before firing the shot. I know I hit dead center, but I line up again, tuning out Eli's praises from beside me. I do this four more times, firing five shots in total before relaxing my stance and hitting the button to bring back the target.

As it's coming up the track, I hear Eli clapping his hands slowly, patronizing me. "Not too shabby, McCoy. You look like you could be a natural. All you gotta do is keep practicing it. I bet you got at least one on the target."

I don't bother responding. I just look down the lane as the target paper gets closer and closer. As soon as I can see the results, I smirk. When it's close enough that Eli can see it, too, he goes suspiciously silent. I look at him, the sly grin still pulling at my lips.

"Not too shabby, eh, Monty?"

Eli's staring at the target, his jaw slack and eyes wide, where I managed to hit not one but all five of my rounds right in the center. "Nope," he says after a beat, then mutters more to himself than me, "What the hell?"

Charlie walks to our bay and whistles lowly when he sees my target. "Damn, Lockwood, you still got it."

Eli looks accusingly at Sully. "You knew he could shoot like that? Why the hell didn't you tell me?"

Charlie laughs and nudges Eli with his elbow. "You were on a roll, man. I didn't want to get in your way."

"Honestly, though, you'd make a good instructor," I tell Eli with a smirk. "You ever thought about giving private lessons?"

Eli groans and drops his head back. "Thanks, guys, real nice."

We go for another hour or so. Eli grumbles every time my target returns with each shot perfectly placed, but he doesn't give me any more shit. When our time is up, we head back to the lobby. As I'm about to step through the door behind Eli, I feel a hand clasp my shoulder. I turn and come face-to-face with Charlie, who's giving me a severe look.

"I just wanted to have a word with you," he says at my questioning stare. "It's no secret that you and Addison have some history, and I saw how she was looking at you this morning." I frown and open my mouth to retort, but he holds up his hand. "Let me finish. I know things are changing between the two of you again, and I just thought we needed to have a heart-to-heart."

"God, please don't do this." I squeeze my eyes shut and let my head fall back. I should've known this was coming by the way he was watching us so curiously this morning.

"I should have done this the last time you two were getting together, but I just let you two have at it, and maybe that was a mistake, but... I won't let you hurt her again, Lockwood." Charlie fixes me with a hard stare. His *sheriff* stare.

I let his statement sink in before I respond. "That's a nice sentiment, Sullivan, but what happens between Parks and me is really none of your—"

"No," he cuts me off firmly. "It is my business. Addison is like a sister to me. She's one of my favorite people in the whole world. And frankly, she's the best thing to ever happen to you if you get so lucky. I know her better than anyone, and she'll take you back in a heartbeat if you decide that's what's best for you. But I swear to everything, Noah, don't hurt her again."

"I won't."

"Good," he claps me on the shoulder, appeased for now. "I might not be as good a shot as you are, but I can certainly hold my own. I'm not playing here. I hope you know that."

"I do." I fix him with a nod. "You're a good friend to her, Charlie."

"Yeah, I try to be. We're all she has left, you know? I'm her family; she's mine," he exhales and then presses his lips together in resignation. "And I'm not an idiot. I realize there's a good chance that someday you may take that position, but she'll always be important to me."

"I know," I admit. Though I've never fully understood it, their relationship doesn't bother me now as much as it used to.

"Thanks. We better go find Eli," Charlie says and starts heading to the waiting area.

"Wait, one more thing," I say. Charlie pauses and glances back at me, an eyebrow raised. "I set up a time to look at the Witch House."

Surprise takes over Charlie's features and then morphs into uncertainty. "Noah, I don't know if that's really necessary. Like I said earlier, the place is a safety hazard. There's no way there's anything of value in there. I have guys stationed there various times throughout the year, and nothing has ever come up."

"I hear you. I just have a hunch," I implore him. "The realtor said she wouldn't be able to take me out there until Friday of next week, and I was hoping you'd be able to go with me out there. You know, as backup."

Charlie rubs his neck, clearly considering what I'm saying to him. "You really think there's something there?"

I shrug. "I don't know, but I think it's worth checking out."

"Fine, I'll see if I can work that out, and I'll let you know."

"Thanks, Sully. I appreciate it."

He exhales in resignation, and I'm glad to see there's no hard feelings from our little tiff earlier at the diner. "You're the lead here, Noah. If you say you gotta hunch, then we have to follow through with it."

We head out to where Eli is waiting for us. He's at the counter looking at a new gun but hands it back when he sees us walking towards him. "You two done canoodling back there?"

Charlie rolls his eyes, and I have to wonder again why they're as good of friends as they are. My buddies rib me plenty, but not on the level that Eli does, Charlie. Eli has an abrasive attitude and a hot head. He always has. That's part of why he and I have never gotten along since day one. But for some reason that I'll probably never understand, he and Charlie are the best of friends.

I watch the two of them converse as we drive home. They're talking about nothing important, so I ignore the subject matter and focus more on their tones and facial expressions. It's clear to me as I observe them that they're on the same page. Even when Eli is being a dipshit—which, to be blunt, is more often than not—Charlie never gets irritated with him. He might roll his eyes at his friend's nonsense, but I have yet to see Charlie not take Eli's side on things.

When we make it back to the diner, Charlie thanks me for coming, and Eli dips his chin at me. I have to mask my surprise at his almost cordial goodbye. As soon as I'm out of the car, they drive off. I watch the car drive away for a minute, thinking about how I actually had a decent time with the dynamic duo today. At that thought, I wonder if I might finally be coming down with Addison's illness.

I turn and walk into the diner with a shake of my head. It's pretty dead, with only one older customer hanging out at a table with a cup of coffee and a muffin, his attention focused solely on the Sudoku puzzle in front of him. It seems like Addison is the only one at the helm, and she smiles at me when I walk in, tucking a piece of hair behind her ear.

"You guys have fun?" Addison asks me when I walk up to the counter.

I settle into a stool and cross my arms over each other, leaning towards her. "Your boyfriends might not actually be that bad of company to keep."

She laughs and purses her lips at me teasingly. "I've only been telling you that for years."

"Yeah, yeah. I'm not saying we're all besties now, but I didn't have the worst time today."

A wry grin tugs on the corners of her mouth. "You don't know how happy that makes me."

I run my hands over my face and groan. "Don't go getting too many ideas. I have a maximum limit of how much I can handle those two in a day."

"You seem to get along with Charlie better now," she says, narrowing her eyes. "You used to hate him as much as you did, Eli."

I could tell her that Charlie and I have a similar outlook on life these days or are working together to end the tyrannical reign of my father. But instead, I offer her a shrug and look down at the counter. I absently brush away a few lingering crumbs before saying, "Yeah, I guess it was about time that we put our differences aside. There are more important things."

"Like what?" she prods, and I suddenly get the sense that Addison is savvy about what goes on around her much more than I give her credit. She must've seen the heated discussion between Charlie and me this morning.

I shrug again and give her a wry smile. "Like you. You're important to Charlie, and you're important to me. Make love, not war, right?"

"You're making love with Charlie?" She teases.

"Well, maybe not. But you understand what I'm saying, right?" I ask her.

"Yeah," she whispers, her gorgeous hazel eyes tracing the features of my face as if she's trying to read a hidden message. "I think I do."

"Well, I'm going to head home and take a nap. I'm wiped out from dealing with Tweedle Dee and Tweedle Dumber all morning," I tell her, pushing away from the counter and heading towards the doorway that leads upstairs.

"You'll tell me the truth one day, right?" she asks, stopping me in my tracks. I turn around slowly, looking at her with the unspoken question in my eyes. Addison is staring right back at me, her arms crossed over her chest. "You'll tell me why you're really here and what you're really doing with Charlie one day, won't you?"

I hesitate, trying to find the right words, but finally settle on replying, "Of course, Parks. You know I can't keep secrets from you."

Her lips thin but she nods. I've appeased her for now. I take a moment to appreciate the woman she is. I know it's killing her not being in the know, but she's putting her trust in me that I'm doing what's best. And I am.

I love Addison Parks with everything in me, and the thought of something terrible happening to her makes me sick to my stomach. It's what drove me to leave in the first place, and it's what's leading me in every decision I make regarding how I deal with this case. If keeping this secret from her is what keeps her safe, there's no limit to how long I'll be willing to hold my tongue. Like I told her last night, she's my top priority—despite my desire to take down my father and his shady business, I want to keep her safe. And if keeping secrets is how I do that, then so be it.

Chapter 12
Addison

My fingers drum against the wooden table as I wait for Eli to show up. I told him to meet me at this café at a specific time, and as I glance at my watch, I realize he's ten minutes late. It's right in character for him to be pushing the clock, so I'm not worried. He'll be here eventually. In the meantime, I rehearse what I will say to him.

After much contemplation over the last week, I've decided that I need to break things off with him for good. His request for a date night the other day provided me with the perfect opportunity to get him alone, so we could have this talk just the two of us.

After thinking about it long and hard and running through different scenarios, I realized it would be a good idea to meet in a more public place. Eli has a bad habit of letting his emotions get the best of him, and the worry was that if we were alone, he would be more likely to explode at what I have to tell him. He would never hurt me, but I knew there would be a good chance for a lot of yelling.

Not that there won't be now, but the chances go down significantly if other people are around.

Finally, fifteen minutes after we agreed to meet, Eli comes rushing into the restaurant like a whirlwind. His eyes scour the room until he sees me sitting off to one side, and I wave one hand at him. He strides over, giving me a sheepish shrug and an apologetic smile.

"Sorry I'm a little late, things were wild over at the market today, and I couldn't get away."

"It's okay." I give him a tight-lipped smile—this is one of his favorite excuses. I've heard it more times than I can count throughout our friendship. He's not the only one who has responsibilities. Still, somehow it never seems to affect my schedule when I say I'm going to be somewhere at a specific time.

Eli opens his menu and reads it over, glancing up at me. "Do you know what you're going to get to eat?"

I nod my head. "I'm just going to do some broccoli cheddar soup and a turkey sandwich."

"Great, I'll go up and order it then," Eli says, standing from his seat and leaning forward to press a chaste kiss to my cheek. "Be right back."

I offer him another smile and pick at my nails while he's gone, running over my script in my head. It doesn't take long before he sets down a plate in front of me with a steaming bowl of soup and half a sandwich on it. I look over at the meal he placed in front of himself and realize he ordered the same thing as me.

"Eli, you hate turkey," I remind him, raising a confused eyebrow.

He looks at me and shrugs a shoulder. "You always order this when you come here, so I figure it must be good. I just wanted to try it."

I sigh at the man in front of me and shake my head, this hopeless romantic fool. He means well, but I never asked for that. We eat our lunches in silence, Eli attempts to make small talk here and there, but I don't engage. We'll talk when we're done, and I have to admit, now that he's sitting in front of me, I'm growing increasingly nervous.

I don't want to hurt Eli, but I'm afraid it's inevitable. I have to do this to get back on track in the best way for our relationship. It'll be like ripping a band-aid off.

As soon as I take the last bite of my soup, I set my spoon down and look at Eli from across the table. He's been finished long before me, though a few bites of his turkey sandwich remain—he still mustn't like turkey. I'm not surprised.

"Eli," I begin and grip my hands together under the table. He eyes me for a second, his gaze tracing over my face like he's searching for clues. Then he sighs, his shoulders slumping.

"You're ending things between us, right?" Eli asks me sadly, his face looking like someone just kicked his puppy.

"Wh—how did you know that's what I wanted to talk to you about?" I ask him, taken off guard.

"I could tell after you left after our last date night that you weren't happy. I'm going to lose you, aren't I?"

I brace myself and look down at my lap, my cheeks heating. "Eli, I was never yours, to begin with. You know how I felt going into this deal with you, and I still feel the same way now."

"Addie," he pleads. "Is there no chance for me to prove that you're making a mistake with this?"

"I love you, Eli, but not how I think you want me to. We don't work well as a couple. We never really have."

"Why not? I can try harder. I'll be better."

"No, that's the thing. I don't *want* you to try harder; you're my *friend*. You'll always be my friend. But I don't want to be with you like this anymore."

"Addie," he says again, then drops his head in his hands, groaning into his palms. "Throw me a line here, please."

"I'm sorry," I say despite it all.

Eli sighs, dropping his hands from his face and hitting me with a suspicious glare. I square my shoulders up, knowing that the civility of our conversation might take a turn.

"This is because of McCoy, isn't it? It's because he's back in town again that you're dumping me. Even though we're perfect together, you're going to throw it all away for someone like him."

I take a deep breath in through my nose. There's a lot to unpack there. "It's partly about him, yes. But Eli, it's more than that. You and

I are *not* perfect for each other. It might be hard for you to see that now, but I promise you, you'll find someone who is that perfect person for you someday, and then you'll see the difference."

"And you think Noah McCoy is somehow that 'perfect' person?" he uses air quotes, mocking my phrasing.

I press my lips together, unsure how to respond without hurting him more than I have to. There's no denying that Noah and I have something in a completely different ballpark. Still, I don't know how that will come across to Eli, so instead, I stay quiet, which is likely answer enough.

"I think you're making a mistake," Eli says harshly, his eyes holding mine, silently imploring me to reconsider.

"I don't think I am," I retort.

"That Noah is a psychopath. You're better off without him."

"That's unnecessary, Eli. Noah isn't a psychopath."

"I'm just saying, he's hiding shit. You should've seen what he did at the range when we were there. Something's not right there. I don't trust him, and you shouldn't either."

"I actually trust him more than anyone."

I'm fully aware that Noah's keeping things from me, from everyone, but I have to trust that he knows what he's doing. After our discussion the other night, I understand Noah would never intentionally hurt me without a good reason, and I have to believe he's doing what's best.

"Really? You're going to sit here and tell me that you're picking him over me?"

I blink at him. "I'm not *picking* him over you, Eli. I'm just trying to tell you that I don't want to be in this relationship or whatever it is with you anymore."

"Because of him, though. We were happy until he showed up."

"Maybe *you* were happy. I was..." I pause, trying to think of the best way to say what I want to say. When the word doesn't come, I shake my head. "I don't know. I think I was comfortable, and I don't want to just be *comfortable*. Noah challenges me in a way that I'm not sure you could ever manage, and I think he needed to come back for me to remember that. That doesn't necessarily mean that he's the reason, though."

It's a harsh thing to say, and I can see its effect on Eli. His face pulls into a frown, his eyes narrowing at me even more. "One of the greatest mysteries of the earth is why you've always been so obsessed with him. I'll never understand."

"I'm not asking you to understand. Just respect my decision. Can you do that?"

"Is there any chance I can change your mind on this?" he asks me.

I shake my head. "No, I'm sorry."

"So you're going back to him?" he questions me further. I avert my eyes, looking down at the table, brushing a crumb off onto the floor. Again my silence gives him his answer, and he exhales, frustrated. "Can we still be friends?"

I snap my eyes back up to him. "Eli, of *course*. That's what I've been trying to say."

"Fine. If it means that I get to still have you in my life in some capacity, I can do that. I'm not happy about this, Addie. But I know when you make up your mind about things, no one can tell you otherwise."

I offer Eli a smile, relieved that he finally acquiesced. "Thank you, Eli. And I promise we'll always be friends. I couldn't imagine a world where you aren't in my life."

"I just want to be clear, when he hurts you again—and *he will*—I'm not going to be the guy who picks you up and puts you back together again. Do you understand that?"

"Yes, and I don't think I would want you to." Again the bitter truth, but there's no point in sugar-coating anything anymore.

He drops his head back and groans again. "Well, this sucks. I've just been permanently friend-zoned, haven't I?"

I can't help the small, humorless laugh that escapes me, and I cover my mouth with my hand. Eli snaps his head back up and glares at me for a second before he relaxes and laughs too. Overall this whole conversation went so much better than if I had written it out myself.

"I'm sorry, Eli," I tell him again.

He stands and pulls his jacket off the chair, slipping his arms through the sleeves. I follow suit, and then we walk out of the café side-by-side. As soon as we're on the sidewalk, Eli turns to me and puts his hands on my shoulders. He exhales, disappointment written all over his face before he pulls me into him and wraps me in a big hug. I wrap my arms around his middle, hugging him back, breathing in the familiar scent of his coat. Eli smells like home, like friendship. It doesn't trigger a response in my body other than contentedness and affection. There is no spark that would indicate that he and I should be anything further than what we are, and I know I've made the right decision today.

After a quiet moment between us, Eli pulls away and gives me a tight-lipped smile. "I guess I'll see you around, Addie."

"Breakfast as always?" I ask him hopefully. I'm crossing my fingers that his ego didn't take too hard of a hit this afternoon, and he'll still want to be around for the usual routines.

A genuine grin takes root on his face as he walks away and points at me. "You can bet on it."

I laugh, waving at him as he turns and heads back to the market. Sticking my hands in my jacket pockets, I walk across the town square towards the diner. I stop in and check to ensure everything is running smoothly before heading upstairs.

I push open the door to the apartment, dropping my keys in the dish on the counter. Noah catches my eye across the room on the couch. He's got a bowl of chips and a half-drunken beer on the table, a cheesy game show on the TV. I've learned that those are his favorite programs to watch because he doesn't have to follow a storyline. He glances at me when I walk in and tilts his chin up.

As I stare at him, my breath catches in my throat, my body tensing with desire as I observe him. He's lounging in a pair of dark wash jeans and a white t-shirt. His long dark hair is down, falling to his shoulders and messy as if he's been running his hands through it nervously. Noah knew I was meeting Eli this afternoon, and I'm sure he's been worrying about it. I haven't indicated to him that I would be breaking things off with Eli. As far as Noah's aware, I heard what he said the other night but haven't made any life-changing decisions yet.

That will be changing tonight, though.

After I hang up my coat, I grab a beer from the fridge and pad over to sit next to him, folding my legs underneath me as I settle into the couch. I'm hit with the scent of Noah's body wash. The mahogany and apple blend. I take a deep breath, the smell traveling through my body and igniting every one of my nerve endings until I'm thrumming with pent-up energy.

"How was your lunch date?" he asks gruffly.

"It was fine," I tell him hoping my voice doesn't come out as shaky as I feel.

"Glad to hear it." His tone is deadpan, informing me that he's actually not glad about it at all. I smile to myself and stretch out my legs, landing them in Noah's lap.

He glances over at me out of the corner of his eye. Despite the brusque attitude he's displaying, his lips pull up into a sideways smirk. Noah rests his hands on my ankles and looks back at the TV. We sit there watching the show together. His strong fingers have taken to rubbing the soles of my feet, kneading out the tight muscles in the arches.

When his thumb hits a sweet spot, I groan, and his eyes flash to me. My cheeks heat up as I look back at him, but neither of us breaks the silence. His hands start to get bold, sneaking up my ankles to my calves and rubbing the muscles.

Having his hands on my legs is doing things to me. Everywhere his fingers touch leaves a tingly path over my skin as if my activated nerve endings are now erupting like fireworks. As his hands move over the length of my legs, I feel a heat bloom in my core as his touch travels higher and higher. The desire to clench my legs together to relieve the ache grows as he mindlessly runs his hands over me.

I try my hardest to watch the show with him, but the deep need continues to grow as the minutes tick by and his fingers get closer to my most sensitive areas. I try to enjoy the sensations, but it's starting to ache, and I need to do something about it. At the next commercial break, I finally build up the courage, sitting up and swiftly crawling across the couch and on his lap, straddling his legs.

I settle my core against him, noting that he's hardened beneath me. I undulate my hips against him, biting my tongue at the pleasurable sensation that courses through my body. Noah's eyes widen, his pupils dilated, making his silver blues appear darkened. His large hands rest on the curves of my hips, a few of his fingers slipping under my shirt hem and searing my skin with heat.

"Can I *help you*, Parks?"

Instead of answering him with words, I do so with actions. My arms wrap around his shoulders, my fingers tangling into the hair at the back of his neck. Leaning forward, our breaths mix until his lips brush against mine. I can taste the beer lingering on his breath as I finally put us both out of our misery and close the distance.

Noah lets out a strangled groan when I press my lips against his again. His hands wrap around my hips and pull me closer to him, tilting my hips so our bodies collide in the most delicious way. Our tongues tangle as I kiss him deeply. We kiss as if our lives depend on it. Noah's hands trace up and down my back, finally settling on my rear end, where he grips tightly.

I break away from him, both of us gasping. "Noah," I breathe, desire coursing through my veins. "Noah, I need you."

Another tortured sound comes out of his lips, and before I can comprehend what's happening, Noah's flipped me, so my back is on the couch, and he's hovering above me. He sinks his weight down onto me as he claims my lips again, his lower half settling between my legs. I nearly groan at the delightful feel of his weight on me, and I subconsciously tilt my pelvis up, trying to find that perfect friction against him.

Noah pulls away from me again, his wild gaze searing mine. His lips are just as swollen as I assume mine are. "If we do this, Parks, you and Eli are done, do you understand? I'm not going to share you with anyone else."

"I'm yours, Noah, only yours," I tell him. I can see the last bit of resistance flit away, and I gasp as he moves to kiss my neck, his tongue laving against my skin and causing my body to shiver. "I broke it off with him today. For good."

Noah's lips and tongue freeze, and then he pulls away. His eyes travel my face as he stares down at me, looking for something. "You did what?"

My chest is heaving, still trying to catch my breath from his earlier ministrations. "I broke it off with Eli. We're done. I'm all yours."

He stares at me as if he's waiting for me to drop the punchline. When he realizes I'm not joking, he drops his head into the crook of my neck and breathes out heavily in relief. "Thank God," he mutters before he's on me again, kissing my neck.

While his tongue works against my skin, his hand trails down my side until he finds the waistband of my jeans. His fingers locate the button, and he swiftly unhooks it, moving to the zipper and sliding it down. As soon as he pulls his lips away from me and sits back, I lift my hips, inviting him to take the jeans off.

Noah watches me, heat flaring in his eyes, as he slowly peels the jeans down my legs, revealing the light blue thong underneath. His gaze devours the sight of my legs. He licks his lips before tossing the jeans to the side.

"Parks," He murmurs as he bends down to press kisses against my belly. I wriggle underneath him, willing him to go lower where I need his touch the most right now. "I'm thinking we should move this to the bedroom before I lose control and take you right here." Noah trails kisses down from my belly button to my core as he says that. Dropping one kiss right over my panties and I jerk.

"Yes!" I cry out when he does it again and again.

Noah chuckles breathlessly and then slides his hands under me, sweeping me into his arms so he can relocate us. I giggle, wrapping my arms around his neck as he carries me. Noah pushes past the door to my room, kicking it closed behind him before dropping me right into the middle of the mattress. I bounce twice as he crawls on top of me, his eyes hungry.

Noah kisses me deeply once more before putting space between us again. He holds my gaze as he unbuckles his belt, the clattering noise sending shivers of anticipation down my spine. He kicks off his jeans and boxers, then his arm reaches behind his head, pulling his white t-shirt over his shoulders. My mouth waters as soon as he's naked. He's the sexiest man I think I've ever seen.

Noah once again climbs onto the mattress, closing the distance between us until I can feel the heat of his body seeping into mine. Gently, I trace the outline of his tattoo on his shoulder with my fingers, loving the way his smooth skin feels under mine.

"I love this tattoo," I whisper.

Noah offers me an appreciative smile and then leans towards me again. "I love these lips," he says gruffly as he kisses me. "I've missed these lips." He pulls away from me and kisses lower until he hovers over my core. He presses a kiss against the fabric of my panties again and raises an eyebrow at me, a smirk forming. "And I've missed these lips."

My cheeks flare as I gasp when he kisses me over my panties again. I hook my thumbs into the waistband of my underwear and push them down. Noah pulls them the rest of the way off, tossing them over the edge of the bed. He wraps his big hands behind my back, gently pulling me up until I sit right in front of him. His fingers play with the hem of my shirt before he swiftly lifts it up and off of me, leaving me almost bare in just my bra.

His eyes travel over my body, taking me in. I feel a tingle of discomfort at being so exposed. My eyes fall to the deep scar on my left arm, and I fight the urge to cover and hide it from him. Noah follows my gaze and reaches for my left hand, linking our fingers together and pulling my arm towards him. With his other hand, he traces the bubbled edges of my scar. His touch feels warm and comforting.

"You're perfect, Parks," he whispers to me, holding my eyes with his in a heavy stare that speaks volumes.

I sink my teeth into my bottom lip, pulling my arm away from him. He raises a questioning eyebrow but lets me go. My fingers go to the back clasp of my bra and unhook it. I toss it onto the floor to join my underwear. Noah takes a deep breath, his eyes glued to my chest. My hand wraps around his neck, and I lay back, pulling him with me.

Noah kisses my lips once before traveling down my neck. He presses open-mouthed kisses across each of my clavicles and then explores downward towards the length of my sternum. My stomach clenches when he pulls back slightly, and I moan as his lips close over my left nipple. His hand moves to grasp my other breast, kneading it as his tongue flicks my nipple back and forth. I writhe underneath his hands.

"Oh my God," I gasp as he switches, moving to give my right side the same amount of attention with his mouth. I can feel his hardness pressing into the side of my thigh, promising me what's to come. My breasts are swollen and heavy as he works them, spending equal time on both. I feel myself getting wetter between my legs as he kisses and kneads my chest. My whole body feels coiled tight as if I could detonate any second.

I whine when he finally pulls away, leaning back to sit on his legs, looking down on me. His big hands wrap around my thighs, spreading them apart so he can see all of me. His breath hitches, and he bends his neck to press a kiss right under my belly button. He looks at me from under his eyelashes, and I bite my lip.

I wriggle my hips against him, silently indicating that I'm ready to move things along. Noah chuckles under his breath and moves his hand to my core, sliding his fingers through my wetness. A satisfied sound rumbles in his chest as his fingers explore my most sensitive area. He teases me until I'm writhing on the bed, my hips lifting and begging for more. He slowly inserts a finger deep within me, agonizingly, and I moan at the feeling. He works his finger in and out before adding a second one. I toss my head back with pleasure.

"Yeah? Does that feel good?" Noah asks, a cheeky grin forming on his lips. I catch my breath long enough to glare at him.

"Noah, stop teasing me and fuck me already," I whine, my eyes squeezing shut. His fingers slide out of me, and he moves away. I whimper when he disappears, not liking the sudden emptiness that consumes me. "Noah!" I protest as my hips thrust up against nothing, desperate for him, for friction, for anything.

"Shh, don't worry, love, I'm here," he whispers into my ear, rolling on top of me. His weight is a comforting pressure, and I wrap my legs around his hips. Noah's blue eyes flare when the lower halves of our bodies line up just perfectly. I throw my head back against my pillow with a wanton groan, quickly becoming addicted to the feel of his body against mine.

"Please," I whisper again, gasping.

"I've got you, Parks. You are so fucking beautiful," Noah says, his eyes reverent on mine before he kisses my throat and slides deep inside me.

Chapter 13

Noah

I bury my face into Addison's neck as soon as I'm deep within her, wondering if I might be having an out-of-body experience. *Fuck.* She feels incredible against me, so tight and warm, I'm not sure I've felt anything this good since—well, since her, I guess.

Addison's fingernails claw at my back as I start to move within her, and she moans a sweet delectable sound that pulls at something deep inside me. I suddenly want to hear her make that sound again, and again, and again. I move away from her slightly, bracing myself with one arm against the mattress. Using my other hand, I push open one of her legs wrapped around me, spreading her wider for me. Watching with heated eyes as she tilts her hips to meet me, searching for that perfect friction.

"So good, Parks," I grunt, and she gasps when I hit the spot deeper inside of her, her hazel eyes flashing at me. "There you go, love."

Addison whimpers my name over and over, begging me not to stop. I can feel her walls fluttering, her muscles clenching around me so tight that I can hardly move. I know she's close.

"That's it, you're doing so well. Come for me," my hand moves from her leg to her core, where I circle her clit slowly and deliberately. Addison's cheeks are turning pink, her chest gasping for breath as she's right on the precipice of pleasure. "Let it go now, Parks, come on."

"Oh god, Noah, I'm going to—I'm gonna come."

"Yeah?" I grunt out, keeping my pace for her. "You gonna come for me, Parks? So good for me, that's my good girl."

Addison's body contracts, her hands reaching up for me and pulling me into her for a kiss as she comes apart around me. I groan against her lips, feeling her fall apart as I continue to slide in and out of her, coaxing her through it. Her inner walls contract around my length, pulling me deeper inside her body. It feels too good, being with her like this again that I know I'm not going to last much longer.

"*Fuuuckkk*," I moan, pulling away and burying my face in her neck as I thrust deep inside her. I never want this to end. "Parks, are you on birth control?"

Addison nods her head, her lips falling open and her fingers tangling into my hair, pulling at the roots. With a low groan, I push as deep inside of her as I can, feeling my release through the length of my spine. Addison tosses her head back, her hands gripping at my shoulders as I finish inside of her. My body collapses against hers as my muscles shudder from the force of the pleasure coursing through me.

We lay like that for a few minutes, our slick bodies pressed together. I feel her chest heaving underneath me, and I push myself off of her a little, taking off some of my weight. Her hazel eyes find mine right away, and they light up as she smiles at me.

"Hi," she whispers. I take a moment to appreciate how beautiful she looks right now. Her honey-brown hair is splayed all across her satin pillowcase, her freckled cheeks rosy from the exertion, and her lips so swollen I just want to kiss them again.

I run my fingers over her forehead, catching a few stray hairs and pushing them out of her face. "Hi."

"That was—" Parks closes her eyes and sighs happily.

"It was," I agree, grinning at her. I lean down and kiss her. "You're amazing."

She wiggles underneath me where we're still connected and blushes when she meets my eye. "You're still inside me."

I smirk at her and peck her lips again. "Is that a problem?" She shakes her head rapidly, and I move my kisses down from her lips to her neck, where I suck on the small space above her collarbone, knowing I'll leave a slight mark against her skin.

It's been too long since we've been connected in this way. I'm not in any rush to move. Instead, I wrap my arms around her and turn onto my side, bringing her with me so that she's now facing me. I hook her thigh across my hip so that she's still open to me. I roll my hips gently into her again, not trying to start anything quite yet, but enough to let her know that she's still mine. I'm half hard and could go for round two whenever, but honestly, I'm loving just being inside her. In this moment in time, I have zero complaints.

"Somehow, that was just as good as I remembered it being," she whispers, closing her eyes and sighing dreamily.

I let out a breathy laugh and tighten my arms, bringing her closer to me. "I agree. You are incredible, you know?"

She peeks open one eye at me and smiles. "I know."

I chuckle again, my fingers brushing over the bare skin of her shoulder. "So you and Eli, you're really done?"

"Yes, I told him today over lunch that I think we are better off as friends."

"Ouch," I say, though secretly I'm living for this drama. "How did he take it?"

Addison shifts her shoulders slightly, so we're more face to face. She opens her eyes fully now. "Surprisingly well. I mean he wasn't thrilled about the whole thing. He said he knew I wasn't happy after the last time we were together, so I think he might have been expecting it."

"Did he blame me?" I ask her, moving my hand from where it's tracing patterns on her shoulder, up into her hair.

She gives me an amused look. "Of course he did."

"That's fine, let him blame me if he needs to. I can handle his wrath."

Addison exhales, "I know, but you shouldn't have to, at least not for me."

Her words take me by surprise. She might be right, but Eli and I have been arch-nemeses for as long as I can remember, and that fact was only exacerbated when Addison came along. As much as she's the center of my world, I know she's just that for Eli's world as well.

"Mm, that feels good," Addison purrs as my fingers run through her hair as I mull over what she was saying. I apply a little bit of pressure on her scalp, rubbing the tension away.

"I don't have to be inside you to make you feel good, you know?" I tease her.

"You're dirty."

"You have no idea," I murmur to her, leaning forward and rubbing the length of my nose against hers. I finally unhook her leg from around my waist and slide out of her. She whimpers at the sensation and snuggles closer to me. "Let's get you cleaned up, Parks."

I untangle myself from the bedsheets and wander into the bathroom, grabbing a washcloth and wetting it with warm water. Back in the bedroom, Addison's splayed out flat on her back, her legs spread most gloriously. I lick my lips, hardening again just at the sight of her. Crawling up on the bed, I gently wipe between her legs, getting rid of the evidence of our sex before tossing the washcloth towards the door and snuggling back in next to her.

"How is it that you can leave for almost ten years, but it feels like no time has passed at all?" Addison whispers to me as I gather her up in my arms again.

"I think that's just who we are," I say back. "There's no limit to how much time passes. I know I'll always feel the same way about you. Never stopped for a second."

"Did you ever find someone else?" she asks. "When you were gone."

"No," I tell her the truth. "There were others that I was with, but no one came close to what you mean to me. Not by a landslide. More to just take the edge off."

Addison goes quiet, and I wonder if I've said the wrong thing. It would be a lie for me to tell her that there was no one else. I'd love nothing more to tell her that she's the only one I've ever been with in this capacity, but that's unrealistic. I'm a man with a challenging career. There were nights that I just didn't want to be alone. I couldn't be alone.

But as far as connections go, I have yet to be with anyone who has come close to the type of connection that I have with Addison. Making love with her tonight solidified that for me. She can reach parts of my soul that I didn't even know were there.

She nestles close to me, her cheek rubbing against my chest. "I missed you, Noah. More than you could ever possibly know."

I press a kiss to her forehead, tightening my hold on her. "I probably know more than you think. I missed you too."

Addison turns her head up to face me. "Really?"

"Every minute of every day."

She looks pleased with my answer and then leans back on my chest, her fingers tracing the outline of my pecs and down to my stomach. My muscles clench as she continues her exploration lower, and she laughs, looking up at me with twinkling eyes.

"Ticklish?"

My lips twitch. "A little."

"I feel like there's so much I don't know about you, still. All these years that we could've had together, just...gone."

I turn my eyes up to the ceiling at her admission, trying to think of a way that I can respond. Thankfully my body chooses that time to react to its baser needs—my stomach growls obnoxiously loud.

"Are you hungry?" Addison asks me, amusement twinkling in her eye now.

"I did just expend an insane amount of calories. A man's gotta recharge," I tease her, thankful for the redirection of conversation. "Do you have any frozen pizzas?"

"Luckily for you, I just might." She pushes off of me, moving to sit up. Her fingers tangle in her hair, and she pulls it up into a bun on top of her head. Grabbing the comforter off the bed, she wraps it around her body and pads out of the bedroom into the kitchen.

I hear her rustling around in the freezer, and I reach for a pair of sweatpants, pulling them on over my hips so I can go join her. When I walk out to the kitchen, Addison's got a thin crust supreme pizza in her hands, and she's preheating the oven. I move behind her, my hands coming to rest on her hips over the comforter, and I lean down, pressing a kiss to the juncture of her neck and shoulder. Her body shivers against me, and I grin devilishly.

"I have never seen anything quite as sexy as you standing here wrapped in a blanket and making me a pizza. Like something out of a wet dream."

Addison gasps and whips around to face me, her cheeks blushing bright pink. "Noah!"

"Just telling it how it is, Parks."

She wiggles out of my grip and opens the oven door, tossing the pizza in without waiting for the appliance to preheat. Then she turns back to face me, her hands letting go of the blanket wrapped around her body and traveling up to circle around my neck. I can't help but let my eyes fall to her body, taking in her standing naked before me.

When my gaze finally returns to hers, she's blushing again, her teeth nibbling on her bottom lip. "How about you have me for a snack while we wait?"

"How long do we have?"

"Sixteen to twenty minutes."

I bend down and scoop her underneath her ass in a swift movement, lifting her by the thighs. She wraps her legs around me and presses her body close to mine. Her teeth find my ear lobe, and she bites gently, just like she was doing to her bottom lip only moments ago.

"The clock's ticking, Lockwood," she whispers. "Are you up to the challenge?"

"I was made to serve you, my queen," I mutter to her before capturing her lips in a kiss. I walk us back to her bedroom, tossing her onto the mattress and crawling up her body. Addison wriggles underneath me, jutting her hips up against mine, searching for friction.

A wry smirk crosses my face as I pull away from her. Her eyes flare at me as I press a kiss to both of her clavicles, then kiss my way to her belly button, my tongue dipping into the divot of her belly. I raise an eyebrow at her, silently asking permission to explore lower. Addison bites her bottom lip and nods her head fervently at me, her pelvis rising slightly in invitation. I smile to myself and resume kissing her, not wasting any more time.

Exactly seventeen minutes later, we're camped out on her bed underneath the covers. Addison is sated, her cheeks flushed a gorgeous pink indicating our recent activities, and I'm shoving pizza into my face. The way I see it, we're both perfectly satisfied. I glance over at Addison in between slices and see she's still working on her first one, her eyes glazed. Scooting closer to her, I place a finger under her chin and tilt her face up to meet me.

"You alright there?" I inquire.

Her eyes refocus on me, and she smiles. "I've never been better. Just worn out in the best way."

I smirk back at her, feeling the pride well in my chest. "So I guess you won't be needing your vibrator tonight?"

Addison laughs lightly. "No, definitely not. I should take your advice and just throw that thing away, I suppose."

I let go of her chin and reach for another slice of pizza, watching her out of the corner of my eye. "Well, I don't know if you need to go to that extreme. We could probably find a good use for it together."

As I expect, Addison's already flushed cheeks flushing at my suggestion. "Noah!"

"Just a thought, I don't know about you, but I like other flavors besides just vanilla," I say with a chuckle and bite into my pizza.

Addison looks down at her fingers, picking at the cuticle. "I might like other flavors too. Nothing like...outrageous though."

"Well, we'll have to explore that, hm?" I murmur to her, leaning over and pressing a kiss to her cheek. "I'll never do anything you're not comfortable with."

Her hazel eyes meet mine, and they sparkle with trust and something else I can't quite name. "I like that idea."

I shoot her a grin and reach for the last slice of pizza. Not long after, we find ourselves snuggled up together in her bed. Her head is resting on my chest, tracing the outline of my tattoo. I start to run my fingers through her long hair again, loving the way her silky strands feel.

"Do you miss your mom?" she asks me out of the blue.

I still my hand in her hair, frowning. "That was random."

"Sorry, I was just thinking about how great it's been having you back in town, but then I remembered what brought you here in the first place. We haven't really talked about it much since the funeral."

I start stroking her hair again, turning my eyes up towards the ceiling. "Yeah, I miss her. She was another woman I let down in my life. I didn't really stay in touch for a while after I left."

"Did you talk to her at all?"

"A few times," I admit. "More recently, I'd say in the last year or so."

"Did you know that she—?"

"No," I tell her abruptly, wishing we could change the subject. "It never came up."

"She was a kind woman," Parks says wistfully. "She was always nice to me whenever our paths crossed. Even after you left, if I ran into her, she would make a point to speak with me, as if she was checking up."

I smile to myself. I didn't know she had been doing that, but it doesn't surprise me. "She knew how important you were to me."

"Were?" Addison teases me, tilting her head up to look at me.

I glance down at her and smirk. "How important you *are.*"

Her plump lips pull apart in a broad smile, but it quickly falls, and she starts retracing my tattoo, heavier topics still weighing on her mind. "Have you cried?"

Despite my best attempts to keep it in, I chuckle slightly. "No, I don't cry."

"We both know that's not true," she pokes me. "I think it would help. When my parents died, I didn't feel like I was ready to move forward until I cried about it. Like really cried."

"You had a lot going on at that time," I recall, moving my hand from her head down to her back and soothing my touch along her spine.

"And you don't have a lot going on right now?" she questions. "You're still in the middle of whatever you're trying to do, holding the weight of the world on your shoulders. All by yourself."

I don't respond, letting her words linger. I know she's right, and if I could manage to get myself to cry and grieve, I would. But that's simply not necessary right now. Addison's fingers are light on my skin as she travels the spans of the ink on my chest. I close my eyes, letting her touch calm me.

"What was your favorite thing about her?"

Her question settles over me, and I open my eyes again, trying to think of all the good qualities that made up Catherine McCoy. There are too many to choose from, but one in particular needles at me more than the others.

"She is—*was* protective."

Addison hums in approval. "That must be where you get it from."

My lips twitch, and I glance down at her, warmth blooming in my chest. "It must be."

"I like that," she whispers and then falls silent.

We lay together for a while, neither of us saying anything. There's something to be said about simply *being* with the person that means so much to you. There were more times than I could count when I would be lying in my apartment in New York, all alone, wishing that I had her there with me. I would close my eyes and imagine this exact moment.

I've spent so long running from this, running from her. Though my intentions were admirable, I can't help but accept that I prevented us from having and sharing moments like these together. Just like Parks said a few hours ago, all those years that we could've had together, memories, and quiet moments like these are simply...gone.

Though I'd never openly admit it to anyone, imagining a life with her was always my fallback for when I needed to escape reality. It wasn't hard to imagine nights together, like this one, where we'd be snuggled up together in a blanket, our body heat keeping us warm. Or spending mornings together drinking coffee.

And now that I've actually lived it, seen what a life with her could be, I make the decision that I'll never leave her again. I don't know what will happen in the near future, but I know that at the end of the day she's what I want. What I've always wanted. Addison is the stars that light up my sky, and without her, I'm in darkness.

I think back to my conversation with Grace a few days ago about whether or not I thought Addison was my soulmate. Though our start was rocky, there's no denying that Addison and I were meant to find each other. Meant to balance each other out.

"Noah?" she says my name, pulling me out of my thoughts. Her voice is so soft that I almost miss it.

I glance down at her resting on my chest and run my fingers through her hair. "Hm?"

Addison doesn't respond right away, and for a moment, I think she's fallen asleep, but finally, she mutters three words that gut me so deeply but also fill me with a joy I haven't experienced before. "I love you."

I squeeze my eyes closed as my heart threatens to jump right out of my chest. Those three little words that we've skirted around for so long are finally out in the open. It was no secret how we felt about each other when we were younger, but I told her to wait. Wait until there would be no obstacles, and we could love each other freely and passionately as we both desired to do. And while now isn't—shouldn't be—that time, there's no going back.

For years I've known I've loved her, and now finally, I have verbal confirmation that she loves me back. I'm still not sure if I believe in Soulmates, but Addison Parks is undoubtedly a part of me that I've been missing. And now that I have her again, I'm never letting her go.

"I love you," I whisper back to her, feeling as if I've never spoken truer words in my lifetime. Her only response is a gentle snore, indicating that she's actually fallen asleep this time.

I smile to myself and wrap my arms around her, pulling her feminine body into mine. Addison nestles her cheek against my chest in her sleep, and I bury my nose in her hair, finding comfort in her warm lavender scent. I hold her close to me throughout the night, feeling like everything is right in the world for the first time in as long as I can remember.

Chapter 14
Addison

"Stop! Noah, stop! You're getting soap in my eye!" I screech, batting my hands at the man in front of me. He's got his muscular arms wrapped around my naked body, holding me close to his chest as he rubs his wet hair all over my face.

He finally stops and throws his head back. His deep laugh sends desire straight through my body, and I laugh along with him, rubbing at my eyes, trying to swipe away the soap. I can't remember who had the great idea to shower together this morning, but it's becoming a disaster. A soapy, wet, delightful disaster.

"Come on, Parks," he says between laughter, "Let me wash your hair out."

I turn around, giving him access to my hair. His big hands roam down my arms and my sides, resting on the swell of my hips before landing a sharp smack to my rear end. I yelp in surprise and look back at him over my shoulder, a blush forming on my cheeks. He smirks at me darkly, desire flaring in his blue eyes.

"Aren't you going to wash my hair?" I ask him, the corners of my lips pulling up.

His fingers go to my hips, and he pulls me back into his body. I shiver as I feel his hard length against my rear end. "Is that what you want?" he questions me.

Warm desire blooms in my belly and travels throughout my body. I turn around to face Noah, my arms raising to wrap across his shoulders. I tilt my chin up towards him, feeling the weight of his heavy gaze roaming my body. I run my tongue over my lower lip, and his eyes track the movement. I feel emboldened when I'm with him in this way as if I have all the confidence in the world. It's something I've only experienced with him. He makes me powerful in my own skin.

"I want you."

Noah bends down, closing the distance between us until our lips are locked together. His hand cups the back of my neck, maneuvering me how he wants me so he can devour me. I moan into his mouth, my body arching against his, bending to his will. I'm obsessed with the feel of his bare skin on mine. A part of me never wants us to have to put clothes on again. He scoops me up in his arms, his hands gripping me by the thighs and pressing my back into the cool tile wall.

"Luckily for you," he murmurs huskily against my lips. "That's exactly what I want too."

I lean my head back against the wall as his lips assault my neck. My eyes close as I let him take me to heights I never knew I could reach until him. At that moment, all I know is Noah and the pleasure that he's giving.

When we're finally sated and rinsed off, we leave the bathroom, get dressed and start working on breakfast. Noah makes the coffee, and I throw some eggs and sausage in a pan on the stove. I pull a package of tortillas out of the pantry and get the fixings for breakfast burritos.

A knock at the door has us both pausing in our tasks and turning towards the sound. I frown and walk over to the door, peeking through the eye hole to see who it is. My heart constricts uncomfortably as Eli's discouraged face comes into view. I step back, squeezing my eyes shut, and groan.

"Everything okay?" Noah asks, walking towards me, concern etched on his features. His shoulders square up as he comes closer as if he's getting ready to fight off a threat, and his hand rests on my hip, his fingers strong against me.

"Yeah, it's Eli," I tell him before turning back to the door. "I have no idea what he wants."

I unlock the deadbolt and open up the door. Eli perks up, turning towards me, his face hopeful. His expression falls immediately as he notices his arch-nemesis standing protectively behind me, and his eye drops to Noah's hand on my hip.

"Eli, what's up?" I ask him, ignoring the pointed glare Eli is sending Noah.

He turns back to me, his face softening slightly. "I wanted to talk to you."

"It couldn't wait until later? I figured I would see you for breakfast down at the diner this morning."

He rubs at his neck sheepishly. "Ah, no. I kind of wanted to talk to you in private." His eyes dart between Noah and me uncomfortably. Noah's shoulders square up behind me, but he doesn't say anything, waiting to take my lead. I glance at him over my shoulder and nod my head slightly.

"It will just be a minute," I tell him.

Noah exhales irritably but remains silent, turning away, going into my bedroom, and shutting the door behind him. I face Eli again and force a smile. This whole interaction is incredibly uncomfortable already, and I know it's likely only going to get worse. Nothing with Eli can ever be straightforward.

Despite my better judgment, I open the door further and invite him inside. "Want to come in?"

Eli follows me to the kitchen, where he pulls out a seat at the breakfast bar. He eyes the breakfast burritos Noah and I were in the process of making and frowns again but doesn't comment on it. I know he's thinking about how in the past, up until this point, I would eat my breakfast with him and Charlie on mornings they would come into the diner. I start to form a mental rebuttal if he decides to bring it up. But until then, I clear my throat awkwardly, his attention back to me.

"You look tired," I observe and walk towards the coffee maker where Noah has already got my daily fix brewing.

"Yeah? Well, you look disgustingly happy," Eli mutters snidely.

I try my hardest to fight off the grin that threatens to show on my lips, but it's futile. Even thinking of Noah has me blushing like a schoolgirl. "I am happy."

He barks a miserable sounding laugh and runs his hands over his face. I narrow my eyes at him, catching sight of the dark purple pockets underneath his eyes. "Have you been sleeping?"

"Not really."

"I'm sorry, maybe you should take a break from the market. I know your dad is working you hard."

Eli scoffs and gives me an incredulous scowl. "Really? That's how you're going to play this? That's not the reason I look like shit Addison, and you know it." I press my lips together and pour him a cup of coffee, offering it to him over the counter. He takes a sip and then scowls down at the brew. "*He* made this, didn't he? There's not a chance in hell you've learned how to make coffee this good."

I look anywhere but at him. This isn't going well. I can tell Eli is about one lousy utterance from me away from a full-blown meltdown."I'm not sure what to say, Eli."

"That's it then, huh? You're gonna end things with me and get back together with Noah just like that? That kinda makes me feel a little shitty, you know?"

I sigh, trying to think of the best way to explain this to Eli without hurting his feelings. Could I have handled this situation better? Absolutely. But at this point it's too late. What's done is done. "I know, I'm sorry."

"You said it wasn't because of him. I came here today to try and convince you that I think we made a mistake. I still think we're meant to be together."

"Eli—" I start, but he cuts me off.

"No just listen to me, Addie. He *left* you! I don't understand how you can just forget that whole thing. I didn't! Do you want to know why? Because I was the one who held you while you cried for days over him. I'm the one who was there, not him. He didn't think you were enough."

I wince, knowing that he's right, but that was then. It won't do any good for me to try and convince him at this moment that things have changed. "Eli, it's more than just that. I don't think this is a black-and-white situation. There's more to the story."

"So you're just giving him the benefit of the doubt? Over me, when I'm the one who has proven to be more loyal than he is?"

"But you haven't been all that loyal the whole time, have you?" I shoot back at him, getting aggravated with his aggressive approach. Eli can sit here and throw hurtful words at me but he isn't all that perfect either. "I remember a time when all I wanted was to be with you, but you were too interested in the other girls in our year. The prettier, thinner, cheerleader type. And do *you* know who was there when you ditched me for those girls? *Noah.*"

Eli recoils from me and narrows his eyes. "That's not fair. That was a long time ago."

"It was about the same length of time from when Noah left me too. Those events happened in the same year, remember?"

Eli leans against the backrest of the stool. "How can I convince you that you're wrong here? Do I need to get Charlie involved? I'm sure he would take my side."

I shake my head at him. "No, I'm not sure he would. But if you feel like you need to, then so be it. But I've made my mind up, Eli. Even if Noah leaves again, he's what I want right now. He'll always be what I want."

"I don't understand why this keeps happening!" he shouts.

"Some things are just above our understanding. And maybe what I have with Noah is one of those things. It will always be him. I'm sorry."

"I really think you're going to regret this. After today I'm done, Addison. I've said my piece, and I'm not going to wait around for you anymore."

"I never asked you to," I tell him softly, trying to reign this conversation back into control. Eli is out of line, we weren't in a serious relationship, by any means. We were spending time together to see if it could go anywhere. And it didn't.

"Well, I mean it. I'm going to find someone else, and when he leaves you again, it will be too late."

The bedroom door clicks open across the room, and I close my eyes, knowing Noah's coming to investigate the loud voices. He swaggers out of my bedroom, hands stuck into his jean pockets, eyes critical of Eli and me. He doesn't say anything, walking towards me and positioning himself protectively behind me. Eli gets out of his chair and stands with his arms crossed over his chest, watching Noah like he's a predator.

"Everything okay out here?" Noah asks in a deep voice that causes goosebumps to rise on my arms.

Eli glares at him. "It's none of your business. I'm here to talk to Addie, not you."

"Anything that has to do with her *is* my business now," he says firmly as his hands come to rest possessively on my shoulders. I close my eyes and sigh, equal parts comforted by his presence and irritated that he likely just made things worse.

"Addie, are you safe? Do you need me to get you out of here?" Eli asks. "If he's hurting you—" Noah's fingers tighten on my shoulders.

I snap my eyes open and look at him incredulously. "What? Why in the world would you ask me that? Noah would never hurt me."

"You don't know that. You barely even know the guy."

"I think she knows me a lot better than you could possibly imagine," Noah mutters under his breath, and I fight the urge to roll my eyes. Male pride.

Before I know what's happening, Noah is pulled off of me and thrown up against the wall. I yelp in surprise as Eli presses his forearm against Noah's throat. Noah grimaces only a little and glares at Eli, his face not giving away anything he's thinking inside. Deep in his silver-blue eyes, I can see a fire starting to rage.

Eli growls at him. "Do *not* talk about Addie that way. She's not just someone you can use and throw away. I won't let you do that to her."

Noah struggles to push him away. "You don't know what you're talking about, Montgomery. Maybe take a step back and realize you're the one hurting her right now, not me."

Eli growls at him and brings his arm back before clocking Noah square across the jaw. Noah's head snaps to the side with the force of the blow.

I shout at Eli, running towards him and jumping on his arm right before he throws the next punch. Noah grabs my waist and spins me around, so I'm standing behind him, his back pressing me into the wall. Only a moment later, Eli recoils his arm and thrusts it forward, catching Noah again in a direct hit. Noah staggers a few steps, grunting with the impact, his hand coming to cradle his cheekbone just below his eye.

"Stop it!" I shout at Eli, running towards him with my hands outstretched, blocking his next attack. "Get out, Eli!"

As if a switch is flipped, the anger clears off Eli's face, and he darts his eyes between me and Noah, who's straightening his body up behind me. Regret immediately takes hold of Eli, and his eyebrows raise.

"Addie, I'm sorry. He was just—"

"You need to leave," I tell him sharply, my heart hammering in my ears. "Get out."

Eli stares at me a moment longer before his shoulders drop, and he shuffles to the door. I watch as he leaves, not wanting to take my eyes off him just in case he loses his mind again. Right before he steps out, he turns back to me. Remorse is written all over his face.

"I'm sorry."

I'm so wound up from what just happened that his apology

means nothing to me at this moment. I know at some point I'll be able to forgive him, but not yet. Not now. "Goodbye, Eli."

He dips his chin at me and leaves.

I wait for a second or two to make sure he doesn't come back, and then my muscles sag. I press my hand to my forehead, trying to catch my breath and reorient myself. I'm supposed to be down at the diner in less than half an hour, but my whole morning has been derailed. I turn to Noah, who's observing me carefully.

"Are you okay?" he asks, his hand rising to cup my jaw.

"Why are you asking me that? I'm not the one who got clocked twice this morning. Are *you* okay?"

He shrugs a shoulder nonchalantly and tries to smirk, but his swollen lip prevents him. "I've had worse."

I scoff and roll my eyes. "I'm sure you have. Come on, let's get you cleaned up."

Taking his hand, I drag him into the bathroom. I position him on top of the toilet, giving him a once-over. His lower lip is split right open, blood pooling on the cut. He's got a bruise forming underneath his eye from the second attack. Feeling sick to my stomach, I grab one of my darker washcloths and wet it with cool water, pressing it to his split lip. He winces as the cloth touches the wound, and I jerk back, worried I've hurt him.

"It's fine, Parks," Noah says, catching my concern. "Just stings a little bit."

"I feel like I should apologize that this happened to you."

"Why? You're not the one who threw the punch."

"Yeah, but he's my friend," I argue back. "He can be hotheaded sometimes. I just can't believe he actually hit you. Why didn't you fight back?"

Noah pauses, then looks up at me through his dark eyelashes, his blue eyes smoldering me. "You know I wouldn't be opposed to handing Eli's ass to him on a silver platter, but I figured he could have this one."

"Why?"

"Because I have something that he doesn't now. He feels like I took something from him."

"Did you?"

"You tell me."

I press my lips together in a thin line, considering the question. The truth is clear, but I'm not sure how he'll respond to it. Drawing back on the confidence I felt this morning in the shower with him, I blurt it out. "You know I've always been yours, Noah."

His pupils dilate as he stares at me, his breath catching in his throat. "And that's why I let him take the win today. It won't happen again, though, that's for damn sure. He's got one hell of a right hook."

"Well, it's stopped bleeding," I tell him, pulling the cloth back and dropping it in the bathtub. "Do you want to stay up here today? Just rest it off?"

"Hell no," he shoots back. "I've got a lot of pent-up energy now, and staying up here by myself is only going to make it worse. I'll go down with you still."

Together we finish getting ready for the day and then go downstairs to the diner. Grace has already got everything opened and running. A few customers linger up at the counter, waiting for their breakfasts.

"Hey, babes," Grace says, looking up and glancing between Noah and me before frowning. "What the hell happened to you?"

Noah scowls but walks straight past her. "I'll be on the grill today, don't feel like facing any more of the loonies in this town."

I press my lips together, watching him disappear, then I turn to Grace. "Eli came by this morning in a tizzy and ended up punching Noah *twice.*"

Grace's dark eyes widen in shock. "And Noah just let him?" I shrug, and her jaw falls open before she regains her composure. "Well shit. Here I was thinking you two were getting up to something kinky."

Her response takes me off guard, and I bust out laughing. "No, nothing like that."

"No judgment, if you were...but man, I don't know why you'd want to mess up a pretty face like his."

I laugh again with her and shake my head before wandering back to my office to get started...

Thankfully, the rest of the day passes smoothly. Noah keeps to his word on not wanting to deal with customers today and sticks to the kitchen area. I see him pop out every once in a while, but he mostly keeps to himself. Grace, Jack, and I run the show like normal. I'm forever grateful that I have the two of them to help me. I don't know what I'd do without either of them.

After the dinner rush slows down, I go back to my office to finish a few things before leaving for the night. Jack's on closing duty this evening which means the diner is in good hands, so I can take off. I decide to run next door to Monty's Market to grab a few things for dinner and head out with a wave.

When I get back from the market, I head straight to the kitchen, dropping my bags on the counter, and set to work pulling out what I'll need for dinner. I'm not in the mood to cook up anything fancy, so I'm sticking to tacos. The recognizable sound of the shower running hits my ears, alerting me that Noah's home too. He always likes to shower after working the grill at the diner.

As soon as my supplies are set out on the counter, I put my favorite playlist on, link it to the Bluetooth speaker in my living room, and start chopping the onions, tomatoes, and lettuce.

The knife slides smoothly through the tomato, cutting it into tiny pieces. I press my lips together, focusing on my task. I can hear the shower turn off right as the next song picks up from my playlist. The familiar few opening notes and beat of the melody have me closing my eyes and exhaling a long breath, taking me back to a different time, a different night, the same song.

I lean my hips against the counter, my fingers gripping the edge as I let the music wash over me, the knife forgotten on the cutting board. The sound of bare footsteps pad behind me, and suddenly I'm swept around and up. A breath escapes me as I open my eyes to come face to face with Noah, fresh from his shower. The smell of his body wash assaults my senses, apple and mahogany, a blend of both sweet and spice, just like Noah. His silver-blue eyes are steely as he scours my face, the past haunting him as much as me.

First, I feel his large hands rest on my shoulders. Slowly he turns me around to face him. I find him staring down at me, eyes heated with unspoken words, and my mouth goes dry. Noah's arms wrap around my waist, pulling me closer towards him until we're flush together. My breasts press up against the hard planes of his chest, and I wonder if he can feel my rapidly beating heart. One of his hands finds mine, and he lifts and holds our hands together. We sway together to the music.

"I wasn't sure you'd remember," I whisper to him, keeping my voice low so that the moment isn't broken.

Noah's lips twitch, and he pulls me impossibly tighter, his hand splaying flat against my low back to bring me closer to him. "How could I forget? You were beautiful that night."

My heart flutters, butterflies setting loose and making me feel tingly as if we're back dancing together for the first time. I watch the man in front of me carefully as I ask him my next question, testing the waters to see how he's feeling. There's still so much I don't know about Noah-the-Man. I thought I knew all there was to know about Noah-the-Boy, and I ended up getting burned in the end—both literally and figuratively.

"Would you do anything differently? If you could go back?"

Noah's eyes are hard on me for a moment as he ponders my question. We step lightly across the kitchen floor, dancing our way back into the past. "Yes, there are things I'd change."

"Like what?" I prod him gently, loving the feel of his warmth underneath the pads of my fingertips. I can feel his heartbeat steady under where my palm rests against his chest, a contrast to my quickening heart rate.

"For starters, I actually would punch Eli in the throat for calling you a string bean instead of just thinking about it. You were the most gorgeous girl in that room, and he knew it," he tells me, a wry smirk pulling on his mouth. His smile is a little distorted still from the swelling of his lip. I know the desire to get back at Eli for this morning is pulling strongly at him.

My cheeks are warm, and I look down at the floor, not wanting to meet his eyes. "Green was your favorite color."

The memory of my silky green prom dress floats into my mind. The way Noah's eyes scoured me when I walked into his line of vision will forever be engrained into my brain. I've never felt more beautiful in my entire life. He was the exact reason why I picked out that dress, and the expression on his face was worth every penny. His eyes tracked me as if he was afraid I would disappear if he looked away. Like I was the moon that lit up his sky.

"It was, still is," he says, his voice a low rumble as his grip tightens around me.

The song's bridge hits, and I look back up with him, questions still on my mind. "What else?"

"I would probably make sure that I had enough balls to ask you to dance for more than just a few songs at the end of the night. If I could go back, I would've spent the whole night with you."

"We weren't together yet," I breathe, my chest feeling tight. "People would've talked."

"I would've let them. If Eli was dumb enough to go chasing after someone else when you were right there looking the way you were, he never deserved you." Noah hits me with the full force of his stare.

"And you did?"

"No. I still don't."

I raise an eyebrow at his honest admission. The song changes, but Noah's grip on me doesn't ease. He's still holding me close to him, swaying, dancing. I don't say anything as I wait for him to fill in on his thought process.

"What if I say you do?" I ask him, tilting my chin up and offering my lips to him. He takes my offering, leaning down and kissing me.

When he pulls away, he rests his forehead against mine, still swaying us gently to the next song.

"A man like me could never deserve a woman like you. You're too good, too kind, too *you*," Noah says under his breath, but there's no humor behind it. His gaze travels deep into my soul as he speaks. "Someone worthy of your love wouldn't leave you when you needed him most."

My heart constricts at his words, the hurt from when he left still fresh in my muscle memory. It felt like I was split in two that day. I watched him walk away without looking back, and I don't know if the damage has ever fully recovered. Now that he's back, the edges have started to seam back together, I can feel him making me whole again, but the wound is still there. Not fresh, but scarred over, still fragile from the trauma.

"You had your reasons," I whisper back the truth that I know, that he's told me, even though it hasn't fully taken root in my reality.

"Yes, and every minute of every day, I wished that I was back here with you."

"Then why weren't you?"

"Because you are the most important thing in my life. I don't think I could live with myself if something were to happen to you, so I had no choice."

"Nothing's going to happen to me, Noah," I try to soothe him, but he closes his eyes tightly and shakes his head.

"You can't know that. If someone wanted to get to me, the easiest way would be through you. That's why I stayed away for so long."

"But you're back now, so can't we just let the past go?" I prod him.

"There is nothing I'd like more, Parks, but unfortunately, that can't happen just quite yet."

"When will you tell me what's going on? I don't like being left in the dark."

He chuckles and tightens his hand around my waist. "I know, but trust me, when it comes to this, the less you know, the better."

I lean my head back away from him. "You keep saying that, but I'm not sure how my being left out helps anything. I could help you know? Whatever it is, I want to help you."

"You can't, not with this. I swear, Parks, I'll tell you everything, but right now, I need you to listen and trust that I've got everything under control. I'd never let anything happen to you if I can help it."

I sigh, frustrated. "That's not what I'm worried about. Who's protecting *you* while you're so busy protecting everyone else?" Noah blinks at me, my question taking him off guard. "I had to fight you to let me in once before, and I don't want to have to do it again, but I will if that's what it takes."

"I don't want you to fight me," he says softly.

"I don't want to fight you either, but don't think I won't," I threaten him, my voice taking on a teasing edge though we both know I'd see my threat through if I had to.

"You're a force to be reckoned with, Addison Parks," Noah says to me, a wry smile forming on his lips. "But I wouldn't have you any other way."

I grin up at him. "Well, good, cause I don't have any plans to let you off the hook."

"You wouldn't be you if you did."

"Just promise me that if things get worse, you'll tell me. I want to be with you, Noah, but that means you need to let me help you when you need it. This is what we do. We protect each other. But you need to let me protect you too."

"I hear you. I'll try my best."

"I know you will," I say, tilting my chin up and brushing the length of his nose with mine.

Noah's gaze is heavy as he looks down at me, his eyes warm and open. I reach up and run my fingers through his long hair. It's still weird for me to come to terms with the fact that he's here. With me. Right now.

Sometimes I still find myself worried that if I blink too long, he'll be gone. "Take me to bed, Noah," I whisper to him.

"What about dinner?"

I smirk at him, standing up on my tiptoes and pressing my lips to his, being careful of his still swollen lower lip. He kisses me back with fervor, apparently not caring about his injury, his tongue tangling with mine and his hands tightening on my hips. When I pull away, our lips are swollen, his still from being punched this morning, and mine from being kissed so deeply. Desire flares in Noah's eyes, and I know I've convinced him.

"Dinner can wait," he mutters, bending down and scooping me up into his arms, crossing the apartment until we're in my bedroom.

Later, when we're sweaty and sated, Noah rolls off me onto his back. He stretches his arm out, inviting me to curl up next to him. I snuggle into his side, pressing my cheek into his pectoral. His skin is damp from the exertion of our lovemaking, but I still turn my nose closer, feeling the tickle of the coarse hair on his chest and breathe him in.

He smells like sex, and Noah, and home.

His hand curls around my hip, pulling me into him. I drape one of my legs over his body and take a deep cleansing breath, my muscles relaxing against him. Noah tilts his head, so his cheek rests against my forehead.

"I hope you know how much you mean to me, Parks," he mumbles. His voice is coming out in a deep masculine tone that I can feel rumble against my cheek on his chest.

I press myself tighter to him and smile into his skin. For the first time in longer than I can remember, the part I always thought was missing feels whole again, and the seams holding me together grow stronger.

Chapter 15
Noah

Tap, tap, tap.

My eyes scrunch shut at the interruption to my sleep. I growl low in my chest, my arms tightening around the thin body next to me. The incessant tapping against my shoulder continues, and I finally open my eyes, narrowly glaring at the woman lying next to me. Golden-hazel eyes stare back at me, wide awake and up to no good. I groan and roll onto my back, bringing her with me.

Addison giggles, restating herself atop of me. "Will you wake up already? You've been sleeping for a million years."

"And it still isn't enough," I grumble. "What time is it anyway? I feel like it's way too early for this."

"It's seven o'clock," she chirps, and I groan again.

"I was right, way too early. Let me get my sleep, woman."

"No-ahh," she whines. I smile to myself, remembering the way she moaned my name precisely like that last night as I kissed her from head to toe relentlessly. Thankfully my split lip has healed quickly from when Eli punched me, and it doesn't hurt to ravish my girl like she deserves. All that lingers from that altercation is a minor discoloration and a slightly wounded ego. "It's time to get up so we can have breakfast and start our day."

"I'd rather just stay here with you," I mutter to her. She's peering down at me from atop my chest, and I can see the shift in her, telling me that she isn't going to put up with any excuses anymore.

"You're with me practically all the time now, aren't you tired of me yet?"

I roll her over, so now I'm the one on top. I give her a grin as I hover above her. "Never."

I lean my head down, capturing her lips in mine and kissing her deeply. Her fingers thread through my hair as she holds me closely, her legs wrapping around my hips and digging her heels into my back. When I pull away, we're both panting, out of breath. I grin at her. Addison's legs are still wrapped tightly around me, causing our lower halves to be pressed together rather intimately.

Testing the waters out, I thrust my hips forward slightly, wondering if she's feeling as frisky as I am. Her eyes shut blissfully, and she lets out a breathy moan at my movements. I lean down to kiss her again when I'm interrupted by the loud ringing of my phone.

It startles me, and I snap my head towards where it's sitting on the nightstand and give the device a scowl. I begrudgingly pull away from Addison, rolling onto my back and reaching for the phone. When I see my father's name flash across the screen, I growl and have half a mind to decline the call, but curiosity wins out, and I answer despite my better judgment.

"What do you want?"

"Noah," my father replies, and I can hear the condescending amusement in his tone. "What a lovely way to greet your father."

I sit up and run my hand over my face, adjusting my body until I'm sitting back against the headboard of Addison's bed. She's watching me, still nestled under the covers, her face wary. "Can I help you?"

"I was wondering if you had dinner plans this evening. I know you're still in town, but I haven't seen you in a while. Thought it might be good to catch up?"

I stare at the wall for a moment as his request sinks in. Alarm bells ring in my brain; why the hell does he want me to come over? I run through a few scenarios in my head rapidly before responding, "I'll have to check my schedule, but it should be fine."

My father laughs on the other end of the line like I just told the funniest joke. "What could you possibly be doing instead? You're still a visitor here, if I remember. I'll see you at seven tonight, Noah. Don't be late."

He doesn't allow me to respond before he hangs up once he finishes his instructions. Pulling the phone away from my ear, I scowl at the device. Bastard.

"What was that about?"

"Just Declan playing mind games. He wants me to go over for dinner tonight."

"Oh," Addison worries at her bottom lip. "Do you want me to go with you?"

I look at her sharply and shake my head. "Absolutely not."

"Don't need to be rude about it," she huffs at me, frowning.

"That came out wrong. I didn't mean it that way. I just don't want you to subject yourself to an evening of misery and psychological warfare with my father."

"It's fine, Noah," she says, her tone indicating that it's definitely *not* fine. Addison rolls away from me and out of bed. Finding a pair of sweatpants on the floor and my t-shirt from last night, she dresses quickly and starts to walk out of the bedroom.

I grumble to myself, following right after her to the bathroom, not caring to pull on any clothes. "Are you mad at me?"

Addison's reflection in the mirror stares at me as she puts tooth-paste on her toothbrush. "No."

"You are," I argue back, my arms sliding around her waist and pulling her into my body. Addison starts brushing her teeth but closes her eyes at our close contact, relaxing against my chest. "I'm sorry. It's not that I don't want you with me. I do. Always. I just don't want you around *him* if I can help it. He's dangerous, Parks."

She opens her eyes and stares at me, still brushing her teeth. I can see the wheels spinning in her head as she ponders what I've said. Finally, she spits out all the excess toothpaste into the sink and then turns to face me. Her arms wrap around my neck, and she leans up to kiss me. Her breath tastes minty.

When she pulls away, she gives me a small smile. "I get it. Just... I'm getting tired of being left out of the loop. You know how I like to know things. And it's not that I don't trust you, but I feel like you don't trust me."

I inhale deeply, staring down at her. We've had this conversation on what feels like a non-stop loop, I'm growing tired of it, but I know she won't let up until I tell her what she's wanting to know. Or she might go searching for answers on her own, and if she were to come across the wrong person, that could be catastrophic. I make the decision that I'll finally tell her everything like she's been bugging me to.

"Okay," I tell her, tightening my hold on her waist. "How about after I get back from dinner this evening, you and I sit down, and I'll tell you everything."

"Really?" she asks, her eyes brightening. "Everything?"

I nod my head, fighting off the sick feeling in my gut telling me this is a huge mistake. Knowledge is power, but ignorance can be bliss. The deep-seated fear that knowledge of this might lead to consequences we can't come back from lingers deep in my mind. I don't want Addison privy to this dark side of my story. Yet despite feeling ill, I know this is what I need to do if we're going to keep moving forward together. And more than anything else, I want that with her.

"Every last detail. Tonight."

A grin takes hold of her face, and she stands up on her tiptoes to kiss me again. When she pulls away, she presses forward and wraps me in a hug. "Thank you, Noah. Now go put some clothes on."

I laugh as I release her from the hug and look at her teasingly. "I thought you liked me naked."

"Oh, I do. But when you're naked, *I* want to be naked too, and we've got to get going."

"Fair enough. Only there's one problem."

"What?" she asks suspiciously.

I smirk down at her, my fingers tugging on the hem of the t-shirt she's wearing. "You've stolen my clothes."

Addison bats my hands away and laughs, turning back to the mirror. "I'm sure you have more, now leave me alone."

"But this is my *favorite* shirt."

"I think the mayor would have an issue if you showed up to his dinner tonight wearing this ratty old thing. Please tell me you have something nicer to wear," she retorts.

I step back, smiling at her. "I do. Don't worry, I know how to play my father's game."

She looks up at me, her hazel eyes scouring my face as if she's searching for something. "Will you be okay? What do you think he wants?"

My teasing expression drops, and I take a deep breath, a ball of tension settling in my stomach. "I'm not sure. But I'll find out."

"Is there anything I can do?"

"I need to stop by and see Charlie," I tell her as I rub the back of my neck nervously. Maybe if I stop in and do a quick debrief with the sheriff, I'll feel better. At the very least, it wouldn't hurt to have him know where I will be tonight just in case this spontaneous dinner party goes sideways.

Addison and I finish getting ready for the day and then head downstairs to her diner. I settle in on one of the stools at the counter as she situates herself for the day. I pull out my phone and send a few quick texts to the powers that be, letting them know what's going down tonight. A fail-safe.

The more I think about it, the more my suspicion grows that my father is up to something. Even when I lived in his home, we never had the kind of relationship where I would just casually have dinner with him.

No. There's something else going on, and I need to be on my A-game.

Addison stops in front of me, holding a plate with eggs and toast on it. "You need to eat something; you're looking pale. Are you feeling okay?"

I stare at her blankly for a moment, her words not making sense. "What?"

Her expression displays concern as she looks at me. "Noah, is everything okay?"

"Fine, thanks for breakfast," I tell her, forcing a smile on my face and reaching for the fork she hands me. "I gotta run out of here soon, and I probably won't be back until after this whole thing."

She still looks apprehensive but nods her head once. "Okay, promise me you'll call me if something happens."

"I will."

I quickly scarf down the eggs and toast, finishing off my coffee with it. Before I leave, I step around the counter and place my hand on Addison's waist, pulling her close to me. She looks up in surprise but doesn't push me away.

"I'll see you tonight, Parks," I murmur to her, bending my neck so I can kiss her soundly on the mouth. When I pull away, her eyebrows are knitted together, displaying the same uneasiness I'm feeling on the inside.

"Noah, you're worrying me," she whispers.

"Everything will be fine. I'll see what he wants, and then I'll get right out of there, okay?"

She nods her head. "Okay."

I kiss her once more before letting her go and striding out of the diner. The ball of anxiety in my stomach steadily growing as I walk towards the police station. I do my best to talk myself out of my worry, but there's something niggling in the back of my mind telling me my paranoia is warranted.

"Hey," I say, knocking on the door to Sheriff Sullivan's office. He looks up from his computer; his eyes are wide and bloodshot. Charlie's staring at me like he's not actually looking at me. I frown and step into the office, concern taking root. "Whoa, man. Everything okay? Did I just walk into something?"

Charlie shakes it off and runs his hands over his face, groaning. "Sorry. Things have been crazy around here today."

"What's going on? Did my father—"

"No, actually nothing to do with him. Well," Charlie pauses and rubs at the scruff forming on his chin. "At least I didn't think so. But who the hell knows in this town anymore?"

"What happened?"

"We got an alert about a missing woman a few hours ago. Apparently, she went missing from a rest stop off US 7 just outside Manchester. No one has any idea who took her or which direction they went. We've been on it all day. I've got my crews hovering over the highways and nearby gas stations, but the camera footage from the rest stop was unhelpful. There were no witnesses—I've got nothing."

"So it could be my father."

"I don't know, Noah. Do you really think he would instigate something of this measure while you're back in his town?" Charlie asks me. "If he did, that would be the biggest *fuck you* I've ever heard of. No, my gut tells me that this was someone else, someone unrelated."

"Just don't scratch him off as a suspect. This whole thing is right up his alley," I tell him. "He could be toying with us."

Charlie narrows his eyes at me. "Maybe—that's actually why I wanted to talk to you today before everything went batshit around here. Your father came to see me this morning."

"That—" I pause, letting this new information sink in, "is not good." My anxiety kicks up a notch, and I inhale a deep breath, dampening it further, shoving it down, so it doesn't take over.

"No," Charlie agrees with me, scowling down at his desk. "Definitely not. Apparently, I have a mole on my squad who thinks it's more beneficial to report to the mayor than me."

"What does that mean?"

"It means that Mayor McCoy is fully aware of our investigation into Orville Marks. This morning, he came here and informed me that an officer came to him to alert him that we were using department resources for an external investigation. The mayor was not too pleased."

"Department resources?" I laugh. "That's a stretch."

"Well stretch nonetheless, the mayor is cracking down on the department and funding. He's onto us."

I press my lips into a thin line, the pieces of this whole ordeal slowly starting to come together. "He asked me to come to dinner tonight."

Charlie's eyes widen. "Shit. I don't like that at all. Be careful, Noah."

"So I'm not crazy to think that he's got some ulterior motive behind all this façade?"

"Definitely not," Charlie affirms. "He's your father. You probably know his tricks. Not to mention you're a seasoned professional at this kind of shit, and if you have a bad feeling, then there's probably some merit to that."

"I wanted to make sure you knew what was going on before I went over there, just in case something bad were to happen," I tell him, grateful for the first time in my entire damn life that I have Charlie Sullivan on my team.

"Thanks for telling me. I'll stay late tonight, just in case shit blows up. Does Addie know?"

"She just knows I'm going over there this evening. I told her I would fill her in on everything else after I got back," I tell him. When he frowns at me, I continue, "It's time. I can't keep her in the dark forever. If we're going to be anything more than what we are right now, we need to be on even footing."

"Is that what you want? More with her?"

"Man, if I could have everything with her, I'd take it in a heartbeat. I'd travel to the ends of the world for her, you know that. But as it were, I'm kind of wrapped up in the middle of all this mess. So for now, I'll take what I can get."

"For now?"

"For now," I say firmly. He doesn't need to be privy to everything in my world. It's not necessary to tell him that I've started thinking through another obstacle standing between Parks and me—the fact that I don't actually live here anymore. It's a work in progress, one that set up camp in the back of my mind since my return, especially now that we've changed the dynamic so significantly. My moving here would involve a lot more than just a handful of boxes, and that might take some finagling on my end.

"Did you see if you could come with me to check out the Witch House next Friday?" I ask Charlie, changing the subject back to the case. I had heard back from the realtor about checking out the shoddy worn-down shack next week, and I was hoping Charlie would be able to go with me as a backup and a second pair of eyes.

"Yeah, I did. That should work for me. Are you sure you still want to do that, though?" he replies, his hand running over the line of his jaw. "I still don't think there's going to be anything there."

"I'm sure. I just have a weird feeling about it."

"You're the boss, man. You tell me when and I'll be there."

"Will do. Hey, do you mind if I camp out here for a while? I don't want to go back to Parks' place cause she'll just worry, but I need to do some work before going tonight."

Charlie gets me set up at a spare desk in the back. I settle in and pull up the browser. I can't get to all of my files on this computer since it's not secure, but I can access my email account; that will be enough for now. I make a few phone calls and send a few emails over the next few hours, ensuring that everything is set for this meeting and that I'm not walking into anything blind. I'll still be going on my own. However, it's probably a good call to have people know what the hell is going on tonight just in case.

The morning flies by and goes straight into the afternoon. I do what I need to do and assist Charlie in this missing woman case, but there's not much I can do on that front, given that there have been no leads on her. Though it's right in line with my area of expertise, I've got bigger things to worry about right now.

Three o'clock rolls around, and I stand from my makeshift desk. I need to get out of here before I go crazy. My hands are twitching with the energy building up in my body, and I decide to take a walk around the square to try and alleviate it. I still have a handful of hours before I'm expected at my father's house. It's not really a surprise that I find myself on the old wooden bridge overlooking the pond in the center of town. It always used to be home base—glad to see that hasn't changed. I lean against the railing and look down into the murky water, willing my fight-or-flight response to settle a bit.

"Noah!"

I look up from the pond and recognize Jordan Coldwell running towards me. I straighten my stance, waiting for him to catch up. "What's up, man?" I ask him.

When he's close enough, he claps me on the shoulder, his hand firm. "I haven't seen you around in a while. Whoa, you alright? You look like someone kicked your puppy."

I fight the desire to roll my eyes at my friend and instead give him a blank look. Jordan narrows his dark eyes at me, waiting for me to continue, obviously able to tell something is going on.

"Yeah, listen, Jordan. Things might start getting wild around here. I've been waiting to catch my father in on some of his more heinous activity, and I think I'm getting closer."

"What does that mean?"

"It means that if he knows I've got him, he's going to make sure to do everything in his power to prevent himself from falling. He won't go easily."

"Does he know that you're onto him?"

"He might. I'm actually going to see him this evening. I'm glad I ran into you," I tell him, rubbing the back of my neck. "I need you to keep an eye on Addison. The sherriff is in on everything I'm doing. And yeah, he's her best friend, but he's also Charlie Sullivan."

Jordan throws his head back and laughs. "Heard, brother. Yeah, I'll keep an eye on your girl. I don't know how receptive she'll be towards me, though. I don't think we've spoken more than ten words to each other this year."

"I don't need you to be best buddies with her or anything, just keep an eye out. Tell Caleb too. If my father is going to get to me, the easiest way would be through her."

Jordan's face takes on a more severe expression. "Like last time."

"*Exactly* like last time," I confirm. "But I don't know to what extent he would be willing to go. If I'm successful, he'll be behind bars for the rest of his life at a minimum."

"I'm sure he wouldn't be too happy about that."

"No, he most certainly wouldn't. So you understand?"

"I understand, Noah. I've got your back."

I reach over and clap him on the shoulder. "Thank you. This might be the beginning of the end of this whole ordeal."

"It's about time," he replies. "You've only been working up to this moment for the last ten years."

"Precisely. I'm ready for this shit to be over so we all can get on with our lives."

"Whatever you need, Noah. I've got you."

"Thank you, Jordan."

"Any time, man. Oh hey, anyway, I was glad I caught you. Rose and I are having a little co-ed baby shower deal in a few weeks, and I wanted to invite you and Addison. It'll just be at the bar probably and pretty low-key."

I reach up and rub the back of my neck, still not comfortable with the fact that my shit-head best friend will be a father in a handful of months. "Yeah, that sounds great. Do you want to just text me the date and time, and I'll run it by Parks? I'm sure we'll be able to make it."

My heart skips a beat when I realize that this is the first time I've made conjoined plans for the two of us—as if we're a couple.

"Sure thing. Also, we are waiting to find out if it's a boy or girl, so if Addison wants to buy something, tell her to keep it to elephants and duckies."

I raise one eyebrow at him. "Duckies?"

Jordan raises his palms. "Don't look at me, bro. That's just how Rose has been saying it, so I'm sticking to it. Word to the wise if you and Addison ever get to this point, her word is *a law,* man. You know how fierce Rose is normally. These pregnancy hormones have just made her worse."

"Noted," I say with a laugh, trying to ignore my skipping heart at the thought of Addison and me being pregnant. That's a dream for another time.

"Alright, well, I'll let you go. Let me know how dinner with your dad goes tonight, yeah?" Jordan offers me his hand to shake and then pats me on the back.

I watch him go, rubbing at my jaw, then shake my head and turn on my heel towards home. When I make it to the apartment, I bound up the stairs and collapsed on the couch, groaning into one of the throw pillows. I still have a little time before I need to head over, so I stretch out and try my best to relax, but my brain is running a thousand miles per minute. I'm tempted to go downstairs to the diner and spend time with Addison. However, I squash that idea, figuring she's busy working. So instead, I lay there and watch the minutes tick by.

When enough time has passed that I can justify getting ready, I drag myself off the couch and into the shower, turning it as high as I can tolerate it. I let the hot water cascade over me in an attempt to soothe some of the pent-up tension in my shoulders, but it's no use. I can't fight off this feeling that something will happen tonight.

There's no going back now.

When I'm ready, I go downstairs, not bothering to check in with Addison. I told her I'd see her right after, and I don't want to worry her with my apparent nerves. Instead, I go straight to my car, taking a deep breath before starting it up and driving off towards my father's house. I'm not sure what I will be walking into tonight, but I'll be on guard. He won't get one over on me that easily. This showdown has been coming for years, and if he wants to up the ante, I'll be ready.

Chapter 16
Addison

A knock on my office door has me looking up from the inventory reports I'm going over. I've been trying my best to distract myself from thinking about Noah today. He was visibly shaken before he left the diner this morning, and I'd be lying if I said I wasn't worried.

Grace standing in front of me, a sheepish smile on her face. Her knuckles are poised to knock on the door again.

"Sorry, am I interrupting anything? I was hoping I could talk to you about something, but if you're busy—"

I blink at her and then set the report down on my desk. "Of course not, come in." Grace steps into the office and closes the door behind her. I frown, immediately picking up on the vibe that this isn't going to be one of our girly chats—this is business. "Is everything okay?"

"Well, I guess that depends on how you take what I'm about to tell you." Grace sits down in the spare chair I have and pulls it closer towards my desk, so we're facing one another.

"Is it your grandma? Or someone else?"

"No, nothing like that. I um—" Grace pauses and presses her lips together as if she's trying to think of the best words.

"Whatever it is, you can tell me, Grace. You know I'll always be here for you."

"You might hate me after this," she says hesitantly. "But I'll just get it over with, like ripping a bandaid off."

I purse my lips together, waiting for her to continue. She takes a deep breath and then squares her shoulders, looking me straight in the eyes.

"Addison, I want to start my own business, which means I'm leaving."

I'm not sure what I expected to come out of my best friend's mouth, but it certainly wasn't that. I blink at her once, twice, then nod my head slipping my business woman mask on. "How soon will you leave?" I ask her, my heart constricting at the thought of not getting to see my best friend at work every day.

Grace's eyes hold mine as she hesitates for a moment but then chalks up the courage to drop the bomb. "This is my two-week notice."

I'm struck speechless for a moment. I was hoping for more time. "Oh."

"I'm sorry, Addie."

"Don't be. You need to do what's best for you. I'm just surprised, is all," I say, looking down, shuffling the papers on my desk, and trying to reign in all my emotions. I need to be the boss right now, not just Addison.

"I'm sorry," she says again. "I've just had this dream for a while now, and I've been trying to squash it and convince myself that I'm in the best place possible—which I am, don't get me wrong, I love working with you."

"I'm sensing a *but* coming...." I say softly.

Grace's face falls, and she looks down at her lap. "But I want to be successful in my own right. I want to build something like you have, something to be proud of. And the opportunity just kind of fell in my lap."

"How so?"

She looks up at me again, her warm brown eyes sad. "There's a little shop a few blocks down that just went up for lease. Newly renovated, exactly what I wanted, so I jumped on it. Signed the papers last night."

"Well, congratulations," I tell her, forcing a smile on my face. I'm happy for her, really, but sad at the same time that I'm losing my partner. "What kind of business are you going to open?"

"I want to make it into a cozy coffee shop, but more than that. It will have a variety of other drinks like herbal teas and specialty coffees. And I might add in a little sales part that's more homemade goods."

"That sounds lovely, Grace," I say, and I mean it.

"You think?"

"Definitely. Is there anything I can do to help with this?"

My friend presses her lips together. "No, I think I've got almost everything covered. I took out a business loan, so now I just need to get things moving. That's why I'm here. I'll still see out the two weeks while you find someone to replace me."

I offer her a resigned smile. "You know I could *never* replace you."

Grace reaches her hand across my desk, an offering. I take it, squeezing her fingers with mine. "I love you, Addie."

"I love you too, Grace. I'm not sure what I'm going to do without you, but I'll find a way."

"You always do," she says fondly. "I'll get out of your hair. Let me know if I can do anything to help with the transition. If you need me to train or whatever or do reports while you interview."

My stomach sinks with the thought of everything that I'm going to have to do to find a replacement. It's been a long time since I've done hiring for management—not since I hired Jack five years ago when I first opened the place.

Jack.

Maybe I can move him up into Grace's position and find someone to take his spot. That might be a solution.

I smile at Grace and wave her off with that thought in mind. "We'll be fine, Grace. Focus on being excited for this new chapter of yours. I know you'll be amazing at it. And please, *let me* know if I can do anything to help you."

My friend grins at me. "I will. Thanks, Addie."

Then she walks out of the office, leaving me alone. I groan and drop my head into my hands, dreading the shit storm that just landed on my plate. I take a few minutes and let myself be upset and frustrated at this new development. When my few minutes are over, I tuck it into the back of my mind and start focusing on the next task.

After a while, I start to feel a little claustrophobic sitting in my office, so I head back out to the floor. As soon as I step out, I see Eli seated at the counter, staring expectantly at me like he's a stray waiting for handouts. I nearly turn around as soon as I see him.

"Addie," Eli pleads with me the moment he catches me trying to walk away.

I squeeze my eyes shut, not entirely sure I can handle this today. With the stress of whatever's going on with Noah and Grace leaving me, I can't deal with Eli's shenanigans. Not right now. But I turn towards him anyway and plant my hands on my hips.

"Please don't, Eli. I can't deal with this today," I tell him, my voice cracking.

Eli frowns, pauses for a second, and then rushes towards me, his hands resting on my shoulders so he can hold me and look me over. "What did he do?"

"What? Who?"

"Fucking McCoy, what did he do to you?" Eli growls at me.

I rip myself out of his grip and glared at him. "*Noah* didn't do anything. And last I checked, I'm still mad at you, so what the hell do you think you're doing, barging in here and acting all high and mighty?"

"I wanted to talk to you. You said we'd talk, but it's been days since—"

"Since you lost your mind and attacked my boyfriend?" I nearly snarl at him.

Eli glowers at me, the accidental endearment not slipping past him. I feel my cheeks heat up, but I hold my ground. "Yeah, that."

I let out a frustrated groan and squeeze my eyes shut. "Look, I really can't deal with this right now."

"Will you just tell me what happened that's got you all wrecked, Addie? You're worrying me."

I sigh, drop the rag on the counter, and glance to make sure Grace isn't around. "Grace turned in her two weeks today."

Eli rears back in shock. "What? Why?"

"She's starting up her own business. I'm happy for her, but it's just put a lot onto my plate all of a sudden, so when I say that I don't have time to deal with your hissy fits, I actually mean it."

Eli raises his hands in surrender. "Okay, okay. I'll back off. Just... let me know if I can do anything to help. I know Grace pulls a lot of weight around here, so if you need me to step in or anything, just say the word."

"Thank you," I tell him quietly, though, on the inside, I'm confirming with myself that that will never happen. Eli might be good at working at his father's market, but he wouldn't know the first thing about how I run things here. That would just be a recipe for disaster.

"Okay, well...I guess I'll try and come by at a better time so we can talk. I'm really sorry about the other day. I don't know what came over me."

I cross my arms over my chest. "You were acting like a jealous idiot. That's what came over you. I don't care about the history between you and Noah, but I won't have you coming into my home and attacking him. Is that clear?"

"Yes, I messed up, I know. I just want things to go back to how they were."

"That's impossible, Eli. I'm with Noah now."

"I mean as friends. I want to be your friend again."

I sigh, running my hand through my hair. "We'll talk later, okay? Maybe we should get Charlie to mediate, but I promise we'll duke it out at some point."

"I guess that's all I can ask for."

"That's all you *better* ask for right now, Eli," I tell him warningly. He's still my best friend, but I've had it up to here with him for the time being.

"Okay, I got it. We'll talk soon," he scoots out of his chair and heads towards the door, throwing me one last glance over his shoulder. His expression falls when he notices I haven't moved from my position, then he tosses me an awkward wave and leaves.

I nearly slump with exhaustion as soon as he's gone. I'm going to need a big glass of wine and a hot bubble bath at the end of this ridiculous day. Rubbing at my forehead, I turn away from the front, deciding I need to spend the rest of the day in my office after all. I give a brisk nod at one of my workers, who's staring at me like I've grown two heads.

Just another day.

When I walk towards the back, I hear a pair of voices discussing something back and forth. I step closer, catching sight of Jack talking to one of our other newer employees. I stop before I get too close, my mind darting to my thought process from earlier as I listen and gauge how he's handling whatever he's handling.

"Maybe next time, just try it how I just taught you. I promise you'll have better results, okay?"

"Okay," the young girl says sheepishly. "Thanks, Jack."

"Anytime. Now get back to work," he teases. She scurries off, and then Jack turns around, startling when he sees me standing there. A wry grin settles on his face. "Were you spying on me, boss?"

"Maybe a little," I say with a laugh. "I need to talk to you about something."

"Is it about Grace?" he beats me to the punch.

I raise my eyebrows in surprise. "Yes, I guess she told you?" He nods his head, and I exhale sharply. "Well, then I guess you know what kind of pickle we're in. I need a new assistant manager."

"Do you want me to write up an ad that we can put out?"

"Actually, I was wondering if you would want it?"

Jack pauses as if he's registering my words, and then his eyes light up as he grins widely at me. "I'll take it. No need to ask twice. When do I start?"

"How about ten minutes ago? I know you basically know everything already but get together with Grace a few times over the next few weeks and make sure we're not missing anything. I'll get your raise in for you as of today."

"A raise?" he asks hopefully.

I step up and put my hand on his arm. "Of course, Jack. You've saved my ass more times than I can count, and this is a huge step up for you. You deserve it."

My new assistant manager wraps me in a tight hug. "Thank you, Addie. I won't let you down."

"I know you won't. Now, if you'll excuse me, I have to go to the back and bang my head against the wall."

* * *

The rest of the day passes in a chaotic blur. I spend hours putting out the subsequent fires that come with my partner leaving. In some consolation, it's helpful knowing that I still have two weeks left with her to smooth out the rest of the kinks.

But still, my heart feels heavy as I leave the diner for the day. Jack offers to close for me tonight, and I take him up on the offer immediately, knowing that I need to go home and decompress before Noah gets home. The apartment is quiet when I step in. I glance at the clock on the microwave and see that it's just past six-thirty. I've probably just missed him. It's almost too quiet with him not here.

Now that Noah's been living here with me, I'm not used to being alone. I'll admit that it's nice knowing that there's someone else in the house. Especially now that he's been sleeping with me in my room for the last few nights, the sense of loneliness that I had grown so accustomed to is long gone, and I hope it stays that way.

Noah and I haven't really had the chance to sit down and talk about what this looks like for us long term. To be honest, I'm a little worried about how he'll respond when I bring it up. I know Noah feels just as strongly about me as I do about him, but he's got so much on his plate that I'm unsure where I fall on the hierarchy of priorities. I'm important to him, I know that, but important enough for him to stay?

He said tonight he'll tell me about everything going on with this mess about his father. I am curious to see if that involves him divulging his plan for what happens after. If not, I'll have to pull on my big girl jeans and force him to tell me what his goal is. For now, I'm pleased living in this little romantic bubble we've created. Still, the thought of losing him again makes me sick to my stomach, and that's only going to get worse the closer we become to each other.

I tangle my fingers together, the worry returning and knotting low in my belly, thinking about why Noah's father wanted to see him tonight. Noah's kept me out of the loop regarding his father for the entirety of our friendship-slash-relationship. All I know is that Mayor McCoy has some pretty significant skeletons in his closet. With that in mind, it can't be for a good reason that the mayor has summoned his son.

My eyes glance at the clock again. It's only been a few minutes since I've set foot in the door, but it feels like hours. I've had one hell of a day. Making a decision, I go to the refrigerator and pull out my chilled bottle of wine. I pour myself a healthy glass and then strut towards the bathroom to run myself a bath, bottle and drink in hand. I'm sure Noah will be gone for the better part of the evening, so I have time.

I turn my favorite playlist on my phone and settle into the warm water once it's drawn. I let the heat pull out the tension of the day as I lay back and try and relax, sipping on my wine. I stay in the tub until the water grows cold, then I get out, feeling like a significant weight has been lifted off my shoulders.

After getting dressed in my favorite pair of pajama pants and Noah's t-shirt from yesterday, I glance around the apartment, looking for something to do to keep myself busy. I take another sip of wine as my eyes fall on Noah's old duffle bag that is still sitting by the couch. My mind comes up with a plan, and I grin.

He's been sleeping with me in my bed the last few nights. I have no desire to kick him out anytime soon—I might as well move his stuff into my bedroom, so he doesn't have to wander all the way out here whenever he needs anything. I can clear out some space in my drawers for his things.

Plan set in stone, I get to work.

First, I clear out a space for him in my dresser, and then I go back out to the living room, aiming for his stuff. I wrap my arms around the large duffle bag, struggling to pick it up. It's awkward to carry, and all of his clothes start spilling out of the top.

"Shit," I mutter, losing my grip and dropping it all. His clothes fall all over the living room floor. I grumble to myself as I get down on my knees and shove them back into the duffel bag.

I really should throw everything in the washing machine before I store them in his very own drawer that I cleaned out. I think about it for a second and then decide that I'll just put everything away so Noah can be surprised, and then I can wash things as he uses them.

My fingers wrap around a pair of his jeans, and I pull them towards me when I notice a black leather wallet underneath. I frown, reaching for it. Did Noah forget his wallet when he went to his father's? When I pick it up, the weight feels uneven. I sit back on my heels and press my lips together.

Curiosity wins out, and I flip the wallet open, my eyes going wide as I take in the contents, my stomach starting to churn. It's not a wallet, not at all. As I hold it in my hand the light from the ceiling glints off of the gold badge. I should've known what it was upon first glance since my father always used to carry one around. I just never expected Noah to follow in his footsteps. All these years, this is what he's been doing, and I had no clue.

"Oh, Noah," I whisper to no one in particular. "What in the world have you gotten yourself into?"

Chapter 17
Noah

The tires of my car crunch against the gravel of the driveway leading up to my father's house. He's still living at the property that I grew up in, but it's been a *long* time since that place has been my home. It's located more on the outskirts of Willow Heights rather than being right at the heart of the small town. The house is a grand colonial-style manor, built on such a large plot of land that it has a private driveway barricaded by a black iron fence.

I pull up to the gate and hit the call button. Not a moment later, the iron gate creaks and opens, allowing me entrance into the grounds. As I direct my beat-up car down the long drive, it's hard for me to grasp that I actually grew up here. My life is not nearly as privileged as it was when I was a child, and to be honest, I'm better off for it.

I park my car on the circle drive and then walk up the stairs to the front door. I give a tug to the bottom of my suit jacket, making sure it's straight. Now that I'm here, I regret not bringing along my badge and weapon just in case this night takes a turn for the worse, but it's too late now. I dampen my nerves as best as I can before taking a deep breath and bracing myself to knock on the door. I wait for a minute or two until the front door is pulled open by one of my father's house-maids. She bows her head to me, holding the door open so I can enter.

"Mr. McCoy is expecting you," she says, reaching for my coat as I shrug it off, and I grimace at the formality of the encounter. "He's waiting in the sitting room. Dinner should be served shortly."

"Thank you," I tell her, and she dips her chin and then scurries away to go back to her work.

I stick my hands in the pockets of my slacks and stand in the entryway, looking around uncomfortably. Steeling myself, I walk further into the house towards the sitting room, which is just off to the left of the foyer. My father is lounging on one of the couches reading the newspaper. He looks up when I enter and folds the paper upon his lap. His beady brown eyes appraise me as he offers me a sardonic smile.

"Welcome home, Son."

I grit my teeth but manage to stay polite. "Thank you, it's been a long time."

"That it has," he says with a dark chuckle and then stands up, stepping towards me and extending his hand as a peace offering. I ruefully shake it. "Shall we head into the dining room? I've got the chef searing up some filets."

"Sure, lead the way."

My father steps around me and crosses the foyer into the large formal dining room. Memories of the many dinners I had to endure in the room flood my mind. My father always sitting at the head, as regal and untouchable as ever. My mother would sit to his right, and me to the left, his loyal subjects. How many nights did I have to sit there and listen to him sing his own praises?

Too many.

Not to my surprise, he takes his usual seat at the head and motions me towards his left, with a spark in his eye. "Just like old times, huh?"

I press my lips into a line, knowing he's trying to taunt me, but I don't respond as I settle into my seat. The house staff comes out of the kitchen carrying plates and covered dishes, setting them in front of us and quickly disappearing.

My father doesn't waste any time and serves himself. I follow his lead, wishing the time would speed up so I could find out what he wants and get the hell out of here.

"So, Noah, how's work been?" my father questions me, breaking the silence. He watches me with his beady brown eyes as he stabs a piece of his steak with his fork and raises it to his lips. I get the uncomfortable feeling that I'm being set up so I make the decision to proceed with caution. "You *do* have a job, right?"

"Yes, and it's been fine," I reply simply, not offering any type of embellishment.

"What is it you're doing these days? I don't recall receiving a graduation announcement from you. Did you even get a degree?"

"I did. I'm just doing freelance work—little of this, little of that."

"In what field?"

I run my tongue over my teeth. I'm definitely being set up. "Communications."

My father observes me with a gleam in his eye as if he knows more than he's letting on. I clench my jaw. "I see."

Dinner continues with awkward bouts of silence in between a few prodding questions. My father is trying to get me to open up and talk to him, but that's the last thing I'll do. He's not attempting to disguise his goal of getting answers out of me, which makes me more uncomfortable with the whole evening.

My father wipes at his mouth with the white cloth napkin when we're both finished. He then pushes his chair away from the table, glancing over at his staff as they immediately flood in to start clearing dishes.

"I thought we could head to my study and discuss a few things. Do you have anywhere else to be this evening?" he asks me in feign interest.

Anywhere but here, I think to myself as I stand but offer him the answer he's looking for.

As we walk down the hallway towards my father's office, his phone begins to ring. My father pulls his device out of his pocket, glances at the screen, and then waves me forward.

"You go ahead, Noah. I'll just be a moment."

I dip my chin as he turns and paces away from me, answering his phone with a brisk, "Speak."

His office is the third door on the left, and I find myself standing alone in the room, surrounded by all the ghosts of my childhood. It's not a large space, but I remember it felt like walking into a throne room when I was young. The big looming oak desk the throne my father sat behind right before delivering his judgments.

I step towards the desk, running my hand along the smooth wood. His workspace is clear, with no wayward notes or documents lying around for me to sift through. Taking a glance at the door and deciding I have enough time, I settle myself in his chair and run my hands down each drawer, giving them a slight tug as I pass over.

All locked.

I skim my hands along the bottom side of the desk on the off chance—*there.*

My jaw nearly drops as my fingers run over the edge of a piece of paper taped up against the bottom of his desk. I shoot another look at the door, straining my ears to see if I can hear his deep voice coming closer. Swiftly I duck beneath the desk and turn on the flashlight of my phone, aiming it towards what I've found.

Scrawled on a scrap of paper are two series of numbers. Nine digits, then twelve. Bank information.

My eyebrows knit together as I process what I've found. This could easily be a misdirect planted by my father specifically for me to find. It wouldn't be a stretch if he's suspecting that I've been onto him. Or it could actually be something beneficial. It might be a long shot, but at this point I need to follow every lead I can get.

I hear the volume of my father's voice increasing, alerting me that he's heading back to the study. I quickly take a picture of the scratch paper and text it to Charlie before rolling out from underneath his desk and standing up straight, righting my clothes. I turn around and pretend to be observing his collection of books as he opens the door and steps in.

"Looking for some light reading?" my father sneers, and I instantly know that he's onto me.

I turn around and stick my hands in my pockets trying to play cool. "Always looking for something to read, have any recommendations?"

"Cut the shit, Noah. I'm getting tired of your games," he says darkly, taking this conversation into a whole new territory.

I glare back at him, squaring my shoulders and walking around from behind the desk. "I could say the same to you."

He chuckles under his breath and strides over to the minibar, looking at me out of the corner of his eye. "Bourbon or Scotch?"

I narrow my eyes at him. "What are you having?"

"Still think I'm trying to poison you?" he asks with a laugh, then shakes his head. "You always were one for dramatics."

I remain silent and he laughs again before pouring amber liquid from a crystal decanter into two glasses. He crosses the room and hands one to me. I'm struck with a sense of déjà vu as I observe the liquor in my tumbler, looking for any type of film over the top that could indicate lacing. I wouldn't trust him if he was holding my life in his hands. My father sips his bourbon and watches me in amusement. I finally take a drink, feeling the alcohol warm my stomach.

My father clears his throat and sets me with a heady stare. "Now, let's get to the point of why I asked you here. I know what you're doing."

A sick feeling settles in my stomach, and my pulse picks up. I need to keep control of this situation. "I'm not sure what you mean."

"You think you can go around to the other organizations in New England, sticking your nose into business that shouldn't pertain to you, and I wouldn't *know*?" he questions darkly, his tone low and ominous, making me feel more on edge. "Do you think I'm an idiot? I might not have been privy to your sneaking around while you were in the middle of it, but I'm very capable of putting pieces together when they're laid right out in front of me."

I cross my arms across my chest, gripping my hands into fists where he can't see it. "How did you find out?"

"You think management doesn't talk?" He laughs humorlessly and hits me with a steely-eyed glare. "Word of a freelancer asking too many questions travels quick. And you bouncing back and forth between operations made you intriguing. Of course, I didn't realize it was *you* until you showed up back in town and started digging into my business. You've been going behind my back for the last few years, it would seem, snooping around in matters that should really be of no interest to you. After all, you said you didn't want any part of my work. So I decided I needed to figure out what you were up to."

"I'm sure you did."

"You know your mother had a habit of sticking her nose into business that wasn't hers, too," my father says. He shakes his head in mock fondness as if to derail our conversation, release the tension. Then as he raises his tumbler to his lips, his eyes cut over to me, "You're very much like her in that aspect."

I let his backward compliment roll off me, my face remaining impassive. When I was younger, I'd allow his words to cut deep like he wanted, but not now. I know he's trying to get a rise out of me— trick me into admitting something I shouldn't.

It's true. Over the last three or four years, I've been working the other organizations in the region, attempting to get a handle on just how far my father's reach is when it comes to his business. I wasn't trying to keep it a secret. I chose my undercover alias specifically, banking on his ability to instantly recognize it was me. Jackson, the middle name that he gave me. Lockwood, my mother's maiden name.

My goal was to rattle him, maybe shake his solid footing by realizing that I was lurking around. If my father wants to believe that I'm trying to get a piece of the reward, let him.

"I would prefer that you keep my mother out of this. She's not here to defend herself."

"Are you worried I'll sully her good name?" he asks. He's toying with me, I know. "She was not as innocent as you think she was."

I'm well aware of my mother's role in my father's shady business, but that isn't important. What's important is that she's not involved anymore, quite the opposite, in fact. So I let that conversation piece die out, sipping at my drink and waiting for him to move on. This whole evening is a test of wills.

"Aren't you going to ask what I found?" he asks, baiting me. I don't respond, staring at him with a blank expression. When he recognizes that I won't give him the satisfaction of playing along, my father tilts his chin up at me. "When you're a man with the level of influence I have, red tape doesn't really get in the way, you know? Your files might have been sealed to the average man, but I had no problem getting access."

"And? Are you going to actually tell me or keep playing this game?"

My father looks at me smugly from his position in his chair. He waits a dramatic beat before drawling, "FBI Special Agent, Noah Lockwood."

I swallow thickly. It would be impossible for my father to never figure out my occupation. Still, hearing him say it out loud is unsettling. I was hoping he'd be in cuffs before the truth came out.

"You look uncomfortable, Son. Did you think I wouldn't find out?" He chuckles darkly. "You should've known better. I wasn't surprised, really, when I saw the file. You've always had this cute fantasy that you would be able to bring me down. I'll tell you right again, Noah, it won't work."

"We'll see."

"No, we won't. You're going to let this go. Go back to your little FBI and tell them that you hit a dead end. Chasing after me is a fool's errand, and I know you're not willing to risk what it takes to see it through. Remember Noah, I know all your weak spots, and I know where she lives. This is my town, my business. I call the shots here—not you."

I narrow my eyes at him, my pulse stammering. "Are you threatening Parks? You've already taken enough from her."

He swirls his drink, looking down his nose at me. "Then that should be motivation enough. I'm telling you blatantly now, Noah, so you don't get lost in the subtext. Back. Down. You will not win this fight against me. You've tried before, and you failed. And you're not the first to attempt it either. This time will not be any different, I assure you."

"That's where you're wrong," I tell him, setting my glass down. "It already is different. I have proof of what you're doing, and one little slip up on your part is all it will take for me to cash it in."

"There's no way," he bites back, but his voice wavers slightly. I see the curiosity in his dark eyes—he wants to know what I have on him. Good. "And besides, whatever you have wouldn't be enough to hold up in court."

"Is that what you think?" Now I laugh at him. "I'm very good at my job, Father. I've taken down several operations—to be fair, they weren't as far-reaching as yours—but I know what I need to do to succeed. Your organization will crumble, and I will be the one standing there holding the sledgehammer. Your days are numbered, *I* assure *you*."

My father sneers at me. "Get out."

"Gladly," I deadpan. "Thanks for dinner. It was...insightful."

As I turn to leave, he hits me with one more blow. "You're going to regret this. If I were you, I'd keep a close eye on that diner girl of yours. I'm not above ruining her again if that's what it takes to send you a message you won't forget."

I don't turn around, but my throat feels tight. "You'll have to go through me first, and I'd like to see you try."

I know my father is not bluffing. After this showdown, I must get Addison out of here. I'll take her somewhere where he can't find her, somewhere she's safe—I know exactly where. I throw open the door to his study and storm through the halls towards the front entrance. The maid is standing there holding my coat, and I snatch it from her, remembering my manners at the last second and muttering a thank you right before I leave.

The night is chilly, and I grip my coat tight around my shoulders as I make a run for my car. I don't bother putting on the seat belt as I fire the old car up and tear it out of the driveway. As soon as I've cleared the gates, I press the button on the side of my phone, activating the voice command.

"Call Addison Parks," I grit out between clenched teeth, fully on edge. Maybe hearing her voice will help settle my nerves, until I can be with her at home.

The phone starts dialing. My other hand grips onto the steering wheel. As the call rings, I see a pair of headlights flick on down the road. I narrow my eyes, my foot increasing pressure on the gas pedal.

The headlights in front of me pull onto the road, driving in my direction. He swerves into my lane right as he passes me, but I was expecting that, and I yank the steering wheel, moving my car out of the way all the while cursing to myself.

I hear Addison's voice on the phone, but her words are not registering in my mind. I have no idea what she's saying. My focus is solely on ditching this car. In the rearview mirror, I see the car bust a u-turn, then speeding up, trailing my vehicle. I hit the gas again.

"Noah?" I register Addison asking. "Noah, are you there?"

"Parks," I gasp. "Parks, I need you to—*fuck!*" The sound of screeching tires cuts me off, and I swerve the steering wheel to the right out of pure reflexive instinct. Another car has come out of nowhere off a side street, colliding with the passenger side of my car.

The momentum from the collision is enough to push me off my course. It feels as if time is suspended, then the car twists and turns, the roof smashing against the concrete of the road and rolling twice. The car's velocity propels off the road's edge and down over the side. I roll a few more times, crashing through bushes and trees, the movements violent and out of control. My head jolts and hits the window sharply, my arms raise above to brace myself, and I hear a sickening snap come from my wrist.

When everything settles, I'm barely conscious. My vision is spinning, and my ears are ringing. My head is throbbing, and I can feel the slide of blood trickling down my cheek. It takes a minute or two, but I can vaguely make out Addison's voice calling my name, crying, and asking what happened and if I can hear her. I can picture her in my mind, her delicate eyebrows furrowed in concern, her lips pursed. I try to respond, but the pain is too much; blackness plays on the edges of my eyes.

My nervous system kicks my body into action again when I spot headlights coming to a stop on the hill right above me. I grunt and groan, wiggling myself out of my seat, feeling a flash of pain shoot through my wrist as I try to grip the headrest. I look down, and though it's dark, I can see the limb sitting at an angle it's not supposed to be—definitely broken. With my free hand, I grab my phone.

"Parks," I rasp, feeling nausea start to settle in my stomach from the sight of my injuries. I swallow it back down, attempting to get a grip of myself.

"Noah!" Addison screeches. "What happened? Are you okay?"

I don't respond right away as I try to figure out a way out of the car. The vehicle lies sideways after rolling down the hillside, with the driver's side down. I push into a crouched position and elbow the passenger side window with my good arm. It takes a few tries, but I'm able to smash the window so I can pull myself out.

Addison calls my name again, and I mutter out a quick response. "I got driven off the side of the road. I think my wrist is broken, and I hit my head pretty hard, so I'm sure I'll have a concussion at the least."

"Where are you?"

Again it takes me a minute to pull myself out of the car with only one arm. I feel the shards of broken glass catching on my suit coat, a few of them digging deep into my skin. Gritting my teeth against the sharp pain, I manage to stumble over the edge of the car towards the ground. My eyes glance towards where the other vehicle is, and I quickly decide that I need to get the hell out of here. Before I have the chance, someone steps around the car and starts firing gunshots towards the wreckage. I jump behind my car, using it as a shield until they stop their attack.

"*Fuck, fuck, fuck,*" I mutter out loud. My heart is beating so rapidly I can hear it thrumming in my ears. When they stop firing, I don't wait around any longer.

I start running.

I'm not sure which direction I'm headed, but I keep going, pushing my injured body as hard as I possibly can. If I slow down, they might catch up to me, and I can't risk that happening.

"I'm about a block past my father's property line," I pant as I run. "I need you to call Charlie and tell him what happened. I need him to call Vincent and have them ping my phone. I'm not sure where I'll end up, but Vincent should be able to track my phone as long as I have service."

I was hoping to keep Vin out of it, but I'm out of other options at this point. Charlie won't have the necessary clearance to ping my phone, so we'll have to get the higher-ups involved. I'm sure there will be consequences, but if I'm choosing between getting out of this alive and getting a slap on the wrist? I'll take the latter any day.

"Who's Vincent?" Parks questions. "I don't know—"

"Parks now is not the time for questions. Charlie knows, that's enough," I say breathlessly.

I hear voices behind me a little ways away, confirming my suspicions that they were instructed to follow me. Gunfire echoes through the woods again, and I make it over over a small bluff, my eyes spotting a fallen tree right in a cutout. This will have to do.

I scramble behind it, involuntary grunting in pain as I land on my broken wrist. White-hot pain shoots up my arm towards my shoulder. I bite my tongue in an attempt to keep myself from shouting as I crouch low so I won't be easily spotted. I'm hoping I still have a far enough lead on them that they'll give up before making it this far, but I can't bank on it.

"Noah?" she asks.

"I'm here," I whisper back. Now that I'm not moving, the pain starts to really sink in. My vision blurs, and my head starts pounding. "Please, Addison, call Charlie. I think I'm about to blackout."

"I'll call him right now. We'll come get you."

"Thanks," I murmur. The blackness around my eyes starts to close in, my body trembles uncontrollably, and I know I'm about to pass the fuck out.

"Noah, I love you. You're going to be fine."

My lips turn up at her words, and I lean my head back against the trunk of the tree I'm resting against. For a moment, panic takes over my body. What if they can't find me? What if this is it? Memories of my years with Addison flash behind my eyes, and regret for all the time that we've lost lingers deep in my bones. Before I completely lose consciousness, I helplessly whisper her name one more time, like a prayer.

"Parks—"

I love you.

Part Two
Then

I wish I'd done everything on earth with you.
- F. Scott Fitzgerald

* * *

Chapter 18
Noah & Addison

Noah - Age -12

"Parks?" the teacher calls out to the room. "Addison Parks?"

I look up from the piece of math homework I've been working on. I'm right in the middle of trying to solve one of those stupid multiplication problems with different steps. No matter how much I practice or study, math is never my best subject. I still get good grades, but I'm not as confident in that class as I am in others.

I turn away from my homework to look at my friend, Caleb Lauder, sitting at the table next to me. He raises his eyebrow in a silent question. Who the heck is our teacher talking about? There is no one at this school named Parks. Caleb shrugs his shoulders, dark eyes just as confused as mine.

"Here!" a girly voice chirps from the back of the room. The whole class turns in their seats to investigate the newcomer, including me.

She's sitting in the back at a table with Eli Montgomery, who's looking at her as if she's one of his dumb comic book heroes, here to save the day. His puppy-dog gaze locks on the new girl. Her arm is straight up in the air, a wide toothy grin on her face.

I can't keep my upper lip from curling at the sight of her. Her mousy-brown hair looks like it was an after thought, piled up into some kind of bird's nest on top of her head. She looks like she walked here straight from an orphanage.

"Where did she come from?" I mutter to Caleb, not at all impressed with our new classmate.

"Beats me," Caleb replies, his eyes still on the new girl. "I've never seen her before now."

I stare at her for a second or two longer, watching as she drops her hand down from the roll-call. I frown as she turns back to Eli, giving him her full attention and talking enthusiastically about something or another.

"Looks like Monty's got a new girlfriend, though. Hopefully, he won't scare this one away," Jordan Coldwell whispers with a laugh as he leans back in his chair from the position in front of Caleb and me. We both nod our heads in agreement.

"They look like they're soulmates—a match made in heaven. I'm sure Eli's already planning out the wedding," I add in a jab. "Won't that be the event of the century?"

"Maybe we should throw them a ceremony out at recess today," Jordan says. "We could probably force one of the sixth graders to be the pastor."

I roll my eyes at my friend's dumb idea. "Don't be an idiot, Jordan. We don't have time for that. Recess today is already booked, remember?"

"What's going on today?" Caleb asks.

"We have that HORSE tournament that we have to finish against Charlie and Wyatt. We're going to pummel them into the ground. Show them that they can't challenge us and get away with it."

"Aren't they winning, technically?" Jordan asks hesitantly.

I scowl at him, and he snaps his mouth shut. "They're only one point ahead. We can still beat them."

"Okay, whatever you say, Noah," Jordan replies, picking up my pencil and going to fill out the rest of my math homework for me. I give him an appreciative nod and then recline in my chair, stretching my back out against the plastic. As our homeroom teacher continues to take the roll, I find myself getting curious about our newest classmate again. So while the other guys are still working on homework, I turn around slightly to get another glimpse.

As inconspicuously as possible, I give her a good look over. She really is quite frumpy. Her hair is an absolute rat's nest as if it hasn't been brushed in weeks and her clothes are wrinkled like they were left in the wash for too long.

"She's kind of cute, in a weird way, though, don't you think?" Jordan asks next to me. I jolt at being caught observing her, and I look back at Jordan. His eyes are glued to Addison Parks, too, just as mine had been. I resist the urge to punch him in the shoulder and instead sneer at him.

"No, definitely not. She looks poor."

The boys laugh at my comment and return to whatever task our teacher goes to assign us next. While I feel the power of their amusement rolling off of me, I can't help but throw my eyes back to her one more time. Jordan might have a point. Underneath all the mess, she's not *terrible* to look at. I could even say she was kind of cute, but I already have a thing in the works with Rose. I don't have time to worry about Addison Parks, despite how cute she *could* be—if she ever learned what a hairbrush is.

Despite it all, though, I get more and more curious as I watch her at the back of the room. Her expression lights up animatedly as she talks to Sullivan and Monty, a big grin crossing her face that reaches up to her eyes. At that moment, I decide that I'll have to further investigate what's going on with this new girl. Perhaps inform her that she should make better decisions regarding friends.

My curiosity increases later in the week when I finally get the chance to interact with her face-to-face. I'd been forced to watch her raise her hand up in the air for every question all week. And as soon as she was called on, she'd rattle off the answer like an utter *know-it-all*. I was thoroughly annoyed with her by the end of the first day.

When I run across her sitting at *our* table during lunch, I finally take full advantage to let all the irritation with her out.

"What do you think you're doing here?" I growl as I stomp up to the table.

Addison looks up, startled from the book she was getting absorbed into. Her wide hazel eyes show surprise for only a moment before they narrow at me in response to the attack. "I'm reading a book, obviously. What are you doing?"

"I'm trying to sit at my table and eat my lunch," I tell her bluntly. "Except it appears a washed-up street rat is sitting there instead."

"Oh, I'm sorry. I didn't see your name on the table," she says back with feigned concern, attitude laces her tone, and a frown forms on her freckled face. "In fact, what did you say your name was again?"

Now I know for a fact we hadn't been properly introduced at this time. I'd been avoiding her all week, not really willing to associate myself with the likes of her or her new best friends. Eli Montgomery and Charlie Sullivan had firmly attached themselves to her after that first day. Wherever she was, they weren't far behind. I grew up with Eli and Charlie, and they were up there on my list of least favorite people. Out of all of the kids of the Founding Families in my class, they're the ones I avoid the most. My father despises their fathers, so it only makes sense to follow his lead.

"You don't know who I am?" I ask her, laying the arrogance on thick. I cross my arms over my chest, gripping the lunch box handle in my hand. Jordan and Caleb will likely be coming along soon, so I need to get this wrapped up quickly.

"Must not be that important," she replies with a shrug. Then she leans off the bench she's sitting on, extending her hand toward me. "I'm Addison Parks."

"I know."

"Well, *clearly*, you found *me* important enough to learn my name," she says smugly, triumphantly. She takes her hand back when I refuse to accept the offering.

"No, I just remember you nearly falling out of your chair from raising your hand so high each morning during roll call," I grind out in a nasty tone. "I've never seen someone *that* excited to be at school."

"Well, now you have."

"Look, are you going to move or what?" I ask her, getting impatient with this back and forth. "My friends will be coming soon, and I'd like to eat my lunch before we have to go back inside."

"I'm actually sitting at this one right now, but I think there's an open table across the field there."

"Listen, Parks," I growl at her, taking a few steps and closing the distance until I'm right in front of her. Addison is still sitting, so she comes face-to-face with my stomach until she looks up to meet my eyes. Her face is an equal display of the annoyance I feel roiling inside. "This is *my* table. I *always* sit here. So you need to move."

Addison turns her nose up at me. "I don't think so. I'm not going to move, so unless you'd like to have lunch with me, I'd suggest finding a new place to sit." She waves her hand at me as if in a show of dismissal before diving back into the book sitting on the table.

"You're going to regret this."

"I doubt it," she chirps. "See you later!"

I stand there for another moment, feeling like a complete idiot. She dismisses me and goes right back to reading her book as if our entire encounter never happened. Nothing will come to mind quickly enough so I can have the last word on the matter. Finally, thoroughly irritated now, I turn around and stomp off towards the other table that she pointed out.

From behind me, I hear her call out, "Have a nice lunch, Noah!"

I pause mid-stride and turn around to stare at her, my mouth falling open slightly in disbelief. So she *does* know my name. She looks up at me right at that moment and meets my eyes. She flutters her fingers at me in a girly manner, meanwhile, shooting me one of those smiles which seems to light up her whole face before taking a bite of her sandwich and going back to her book. My blood starts to boil.

I spin around and grumble to myself, "Who's not important now? Stupid little—"

"What's going on?" Jordan's voice questions as he comes to stand next to me. "Are we not sitting at our usual table today?"

"Apparently not," I reply between my teeth. "Come on, we'll just sit over here."

"What the heck was that about? I could hear you two yelling at each other from all the way across the field." Caleb asks.

I tighten my fists at my sides as we walk the remaining distance to our new table. "Addison Parks just made a big mistake."

I can't deny it, though; as much as I'm annoyed with the whole ordeal, a part of me is slightly impressed that she had the gall to stand up to me. No one else in this school would have dared. That was *my* table. I always sat there, which meant that no one else did. It was as simple as that. I could've given her the benefit of the doubt with being a new student or whatever, but now. She had to go and dig her heels in *deep* and wouldn't back down even when I blatantly informed her to her face.

Impressive.

Or stupid.

But I meant what I said when I told Caleb that Parks made a mistake. She wouldn't live this down that easily. No one makes a McCoy look like a fool. It's a lesson she will learn, and she'll learn it fast.

Addison Parks has my full attention now, and she likely won't lose it after that little fiasco over a lunch table.

Addison - Age 12

"Are you okay?" a soft voice asks. For the second time during that lunch hour, I'm interrupted from this chapter I'm trying to get through in my book about Greek mythology. Suppressing a frustrated sigh, I find Charlie Sullivan standing in front of me, wearing an unsure expression on his face.

"I'm fine."

"Noah McCoy can be a jerk sometimes." He pauses and thinks about it some more. "No, actually, he's a jerk about ninety-nine percent of the time."

I brush a few wild stray hairs out of my face as I look at Charlie. It's windy out today. I'm immensely grateful that my mom had tamed my hair enough to pull it into a bun before school; otherwise, I'm sure I'd be left with a bigger disaster of a hair day than usual. "Clearly. What is his problem?"

Charlie motions to the bench next to me, silently asking if he can sit. I nod my head, and he slides into his seat, resting his elbows on the table. He observes me with his kind green eyes. "Noah's just not used to not getting his way. His parents are rich, and they spoil him by giving him whatever he wants, so when that doesn't happen...."

"He turns into a jerk?"

"Exactly."

"Well, I don't like him. How was I supposed to know that this was his table?" I ask incredulously. "And besides, I'm already sitting here. Did he just expect me to move?"

Charlie laughs, "Probably. I bet he's not sure what to do with you now. You've probably just made yourself Public Enemy number one."

I frown at him, thinking back to my recent face off with Noah. "He told me I'd regret it."

"Yeah, you probably will." My eyes go wide at my friend's blunt response. Charlie laughs and shrugs his shoulders. "What? It's the truth. Noah's got a lot of pull around here."

"We're in middle school. What does he think he can do to me?"

"We're in middle school," Charlie repeats my statement as if that is answer enough. "Probably a lot."

I sigh and reach for a baby carrot from my lunch box, popping it into my mouth and biting down, appreciating the crunching sound between my teeth. "Well, that's unfortunate."

Charlie chuckles again and pats my shoulder in mock comfort. "I think you'll live. You seem to be pretty tough. Are your parents like professional wrestlers or something?"

I laugh now and shake my head. "No, my dad is a cop, and my mom likes to bake. She's probably the most non-threatening person around."

As soon as my sentence leaves my mouth, alarm bells sound off in my head, and I glance up at my friend in panic. Charlie notes the stress now written all over my face and frowns. "What's wrong?"

I set my half-eaten carrot down on the wooden table and bite my lower lip. "I wasn't supposed to tell you that," I mutter. "I wasn't supposed to tell anyone."

"What, that your dad's a cop? Mine's a cop too. Maybe they work together."

I shake my head and look at Charlie with wide, alarmed eyes. "He's not working as a cop here. At least not officially. I'm supposed to say that they're both just a chef and a baker, so we moved here so they could open up their own café."

My heart thuds in my chest as Charlie scans my face. I can almost see the wheels turning in his head, attempting to put the pieces together. I pray silently that he doesn't decide to go and tell their teacher that she's making up wild stories for attention. My parents would be so mad at me. They gave me one explicit instruction, *do not tell anyone.*

We've barely been in Willow Heights for a week, and I'm already doing the exact opposite of what they told me to do.

Finally, after searching my face for what feels like ages, Charlie shrugs and reaches for the other half of my carrot. He pops it in his mouth and gets an equally satisfying crunch, not caring that I'd already taken a bite out of it. "My dad's the sheriff. Don't worry, I won't say anything."

I breathe out a sigh of relief and open my mouth to thank him when my attention is pulled by the sound of my name. I turn to the right to see the third of my new little trio of friends. Eli bounds over with his Spider-Man lunch box dangling from his hands.

"Hey, guys!" he exclaims far too loudly as he sits across from them at the table. "What are you talking about?"

I glance at Charlie right as he abruptly responds, "Nothing."

I decide then, at this moment, that Charlie is going to be an irreplaceable friend. Though I've only known him for a few days, this solidifies my trust in him. He effortlessly could have filled Eli in on our conversation, but he doesn't. He promised me he wouldn't tell anyone, and I know he meant it.

Eli frowns for a second, feeling left out, but he smoothly replaces it with a big grin. "Oh, okay. So anyway, I just overheard Noah complaining to his friends that Addison bullied him out of this table. She's been here for, what, four days, and she's already a legend?"

I scrunch my nose at this new development. "I don't think I *bullied* him."

Eli shakes his head. "No, it's fine. It's great, actually. Noah's been walking around here for years, acting like he's better than us. He deserved to be put in his place. And I'm glad you were the one to do it."

"Why me?"

"Because you're new. You don't have any history like the rest of us do. I think it was a good rude awakening for him. Hopefully, he realized that he's not the untouchable king he thought he was," Eli observes as he unzips his lunch box. He pulls out a sandwich with a groan. "Bologna again? I told my mom I *hate* bologna."

"Why does it matter if I don't have any history here?" I ask him, trying to get Eli back on topic. I close my mythology book, already knowing that I'm not going to get back to it during this lunch break.

"Because Noah likes to think that he's the top dog. But that doesn't mean anything if he can't extend it to people outside the little 'Founding Families' circle," Charlie fills in, reaching into *my* lunch box for another carrot. "He's powerless against you, and I'm sure that will really start to bother him."

"He's going to self-combust," Eli adds, his mouth full of his gross bologna sandwich. "And I personally can't wait till that happens. I've been dreaming of it since kindergarten."

"I think you need a new hobby," I tell him softly. Charlie snickers next to me, and Eli frowns, not fully understanding the joke, but shrugs anyway and pretends to laugh along.

"I'm so glad you came here, Addie. You will be the greatest thing that happened to this little town. I already know it," Eli tells me, his eyes warm and round as they gaze at me adoringly.

I register my cheeks starting to heat up underneath Eli's stare. Still, I manage to smile back at him despite feeling shy under all this newfound attention. No one ever seemed to give me a second thought at my old school, especially boys. I was just Addie—nerdy Addie—who only wanted to read and always got the highest scores on homework. If I was getting any attention, it was because the kids in my class wanted me to give them the answers.

But now? Now, my only two friends were these two boys, and I'm still unsure what to make of this change in events.

From that first week on, though, we are inseparable. It doesn't take long for me to realize that being the new kid in a new town isn't quite so bad with them by my side. Charlie and Eli continue to surprise me throughout my first year here by being some of the best friends that I could've ever dreamed of having.

As the year passes by, I manage to get the best grades in my class —of course—followed closely by Noah, who never seems to want to let me forget it. He hardly lets up on his threatening promise from the showdown over the lunch table. Noah seizes any chance he can get to throw a snide comment or a mean remark my way. He always takes the easy way out and makes his strikes at my curly, unruly hair or that my parents are trying to open a little café.

His ammunition is weak, and I never let him forget it.

As much as Noah pushes me that first year, I push back. For the first few months, we're constantly at each other's throats, picking on one another and tossing insults back and forth. It quickly becomes the new normal.

After we return from Christmas break, the intensity of our rivalry seems to calm down. However, it still lingers behind every interaction we have. At the end of the school year, Noah slides by me, bumping my shoulder with his once the final bell rings, releasing us into our summer vacations. He tilts his head around to glare at me.

"Watch where you're going, Parks."

"Maybe you should open your eyes when you walk instead of expecting everyone just to get out of the way for you."

He stops and turns to face me fully. He's grown over the spans of the year, now a few inches taller than me. I tilt my chin up to meet his glare. His eyes study me before his expression relaxes, and a wicked smirk takes hold of his face.

"Have a good summer, Parks. Maybe I'll see you around."

Trepidation settles in my stomach. Willow Heights is a small town. There's no way he's *not* going to see me around. As I head home, I steel myself for the worst. I don't regret standing up to Noah; bullies need to be put in their place. But I have the feeling that Noah and my story is just beginning. If this first year has been any indication of what the future will be like, I better prepare for whatever storm he will unleash.

Chapter 19
Noah

Noah - Age 13

"Mooommmm, can we please go somewhere else? I don't want to go in there," I whine. I'm following closely behind my parents as they walk down the sidewalk towards the corner café that I typically try my hardest to avoid at all costs.

"Quit acting like a child," I hear my father bark at me in his deep, firm voice. I immediately straighten my back as if it is an instinctive response to the authoritative man. "You're going to embarrass us."

"Sorry, Father," I mutter sullenly. My mother glances over her shoulder at me, the corners of her lips turning downwards. She's likely just as displeased with my behavior as my father is, but what am I supposed to do? I really *don't want to go in there.*

Somehow, I haven't seen much interaction with Addison Parks this school year. We were placed into different homerooms, so now we only run across each other during lunch and recess breaks. Surprisingly, Parks and her little posse relinquished their hold on my lunch table this year, and we haven't been forced to have a showdown just yet. However, I know it's probably inevitable.

Up to this point, I don't think I've said but a few words to Parks since school started for the semester. Honestly, that's fine with me, if not a little boring. After spending all summer coming up with good pranks to pull on her, I can't help but be a little disappointed. Aside from Parks, there was hardly anyone worth wasting the energy to pick on. My usual go-to's were Charlie and Eli, but it seems Parks is not far behind wherever they are.

But now, here I am, being forced against my will into the Parks' Family café. It's named some dumb French thing that I don't know how to pronounce, much less what it means. Though if I had to guess, the English translation would be something like "Gross Baked Goods."

"I can't believe we haven't had a chance to visit yet," my mother says absentmindedly to my father as we get closer to the café. "It was such a big deal that they could get the corner property. I heard they had a big open house a few weeks ago for their grand opening."

They did. Parks had brought both eighth-grade homerooms these cupcakes that her mom made during the first week of school. She made a big show of passing them out to everyone during lunch. They were chocolate cakes with bright yellow icing on them with little colorful sprinkles on top. I didn't give her the pleasure of watching me or my friends enjoy them, even though she tried to give us some.

It was a stand-off—a battle of wills.

She kept offering them to Jordan and Caleb, and my poor friends were almost tempted beyond what they could handle, but they held firm. It was a proud moment for me when they could resist the pull that Addison Parks' cupcakes presented. How was I to know that they weren't poisoned?

Truth be told, though, after classes that day, I found a lone cupcake sitting on a napkin in my locker. I never bothered to put a lock on the thing because no one at that school would be brave enough to get into my stuff without my explicit permission.

No one except *her*, of course.

That disgustingly perfect-looking cupcake was sitting there, placed daintily on a white napkin. The guys had already taken the bus home, so I was alone.

If anyone asks, I didn't eat it. But *damn*, it was good.

I'll take that truth with me to the grave.

Now with that in mind, as my family steps into the Parks' café, I try my hardest not to look intrigued by the sweets and goodies on display behind the glass case. I know it's a failed attempt, though, when my mother leans down close to me and whispers, "Everything looks so good, doesn't it?"

Before I can retort, a man approaches the front counter with a broad smile plastered on his face. I've never seen him before, but I guess that this might be Addison's father. He has the same goody-two-shoes appearance around him. "Can I help you?" he asks kindly, looking between the three of us.

My father steps up towards the counter and extends his hand. "I'm not sure if we've officially met. My name is Declan McCoy. I'm on the city council, hoping to get my name in the hat for mayor in a few years, so I thought I'd stop in and introduce myself. This is my wife, Catherine, and my son, Noah."

Mr. Parks eyes my father's hand hesitantly but shakes it nonetheless and then glances over at my mother and me with a nod of his head. He looks back at me, and a broad smile takes over once more. "You look to be about my daughter's age, Noah. What grade are you in?"

I scowl at him and start furiously working to find something rude to say about Mr. Parks' daughter when she beats me to the punch. Addison comes flouncing out of the back, holding a notebook and a water bottle as though she were summoned.

"He's in my grade, Dad. He's pretty shy though, doesn't say much," she chirps, not missing a beat as she wiggles herself into the conversation. Then she leans in closer to her father as if she's going to tell him a secret but speaks in a normal voice, "He still wets the bed, doesn't want anyone to know."

My eyes go wide, and my jaw falls open at the blatant disrespect.

Mr. Parks' eyes dart from his daughter to me, then to my father with a sheepish smile. At least *he* has the decency to appear embarrassed that his daughter's a deviant. "I'm so sorry, Mr. McCoy, this is my daughter Addison, but I must apologize for her behavior. I don't know what came over her."

"I'm sure it's just playground talk," my mother says with a chuckle, doing what she does best and diffusing the situation.

"Certainly," my father's hand lands on my shoulder and squeezes too tightly. I grind my teeth together, attempting not to wince as he looks down at me. He is *not* happy with this change of events. Anyone standing within thirty feet of him could see the thunderous expression and sharp glint in his eye. "Noah, why don't you stand up for yourself and stop making us look bad?"

"Uh—I don't—" I stammer, unsure what to say being put on the spot like this. I'm equally embarrassed by what Parks said about me and at how my father managed the fallout. I bet if my father wasn't in public, he'd kick me into next year for this.

"Noah," my father prompts sternly, his deep voice like nails on a chalkboard. Panic courses down my spine and I freeze.

My mother takes that moment to finally step in, putting her hand on my father's forearm. His hand still grips my shoulder tightly, and I attempt to wiggle away, feeling the muscles in my shoulder protesting his rough grip. "Declan, let's just order and sit down. We're trying to have a nice day, *remember?*"

My father releases his death hold on me at my mother's insistence, turning towards his wife and plastering a fake smile on his face. One I've come to know well. As soon as his hand is off of me my muscles cave in and relief floods me. "Of course, dear, go ahead and order."

My mother steps toward Mr. Parks, who is waiting behind the register and trying not to watch the McCoy Family Circus, and puts in an order for a few donuts and coffee. I stand close to my mother's side, my head down low as I try not to meet Addison's penetrating stare. She's still standing next to her father. Where Mr. Parks was doing his best not to intrude, Addison watched the interaction with sharp, observant eyes.

I grit my teeth and glare at her, but she doesn't back down. *Great, just what I needed.*

The rest of our visit goes smoothly. We get our donuts and coffee, and sit at a small table in the corner. I remain quiet as my parents talk, picking at the donut in front of me. I take small bites, not really having an appetite anymore, but I can't help myself—the donut is *delicious.* As much as I want to finish it off, my stomach is churning in knots, and I can't get myself to eat it.

My father clears his throat, and my attention snaps to him. I swallow thickly when I notice the thunderous expression on his face. "Are you done, Son?"

I dip my chin and nod my head quietly.

My father scoots his chair back as my mom goes to throw away our trash. I follow my father's lead, standing up next to him.

"Stand up tall, Noah. Quit looking like you've been defeated. You're a McCoy. *No one* defeats you."

"Yes, Father," I murmur and straighten up my spine. Maybe if I show him I'm making an effort, he won't be so mad when we get home. I haven't seen Addison since we sat down, but I can still feel her watchful eyes on me.

"We'll discuss what happened here today at home, do you understand?"

I nod, my hopes falling. My response must be good enough for my father as he grunts at me and then takes long, powerful strides out of the café, my mother and I following closely behind him. I try to keep to myself the rest of the afternoon. My goal is to avoid my father at all costs and hope my mother will be able to talk him out of whatever punishment he's coming up with.

Declan McCoy's directions were clear, don't be an embarrassment.

Then Addison Parks had to come in and start running her mouth, and now I'm the one in hot water. She doesn't even know what kind of damage she's done.

When we get home, my father sends me to my room right away, saying we'll discuss things later. I sullenly shuffle up the stairs to my bedroom and close the door behind me. Sighing, I flop onto my bed and reach for a comic book. There's nothing else I can do than wait the day out and hope my father forgets about the whole thing. But I'm not naive enough to think that my father will let this mishap go unpunished.

* * *

The following day at school, Parks surprises me by sneaking up behind my locker door. When I go to shut it, there she is, frizzy hair and all, nearly scaring the life out of me. I startle but quickly morph my features to glare at her. "What do you want?" I expect a witty comment right back, but I'm surprised when I find her looking at me as if she's trying to solve a 1000-piece puzzle. I drop my head back with an irritated groan. "*What, Parks?*"

She takes a moment to respond, but eventually, she says softly, "Your dad is kind of mean to you, isn't he?" I register that she's talking about the fiasco at her family's café yesterday. I frown and shut the locker the rest of the way, letting it slam closed before narrowing my eyes at her.

"Why would you say something like that? My dad isn't mean to me."

She gives me a look that obviously says *Nice Try* but instead of verbalizing what she wants to say, she just presses her lips together. "I'm sorry he treats you like that." Then she turns on her heel and skips away.

I stare after her, shifting my backpack up on my shoulder and trying not to wince at the bruising that my father left from his firm grip yesterday. It took a few hours after we got home, but my father eventually came knocking at my door, leather belt in hand. To be honest, it wasn't as bad as it could have been, especially given my behavior. But Addison never needed to know any of that. I try my hardest to make sense of what just went down with her just now. Parks acting like she was concerned about me? I must be in a fever dream.

I finally shake my head and roll my eyes, deciding that I'll never be able to fully understand what goes on in that girl's head. I don't know what type of game she's trying to play this time around, but I'm not going to get involved.

My dad isn't *mean* to me. He's just *strict*.

Right?

As much as Addison Parks would like to think so, she doesn't know everything, and I don't need her opinion. She's barely been in Willow Heights for a year, so where does she get off, acting like she knows what goes on in my life at home?

"What was that all about?" Jordan asks as he comes to stand next to me, following my gaze and looking down the hallway

I glower after Addison's retreating form. "Nothing. Just Parks and her stupid mind games."

"I heard her say something about your dad," Jordan keeps prodding.

"Yeah, just leave it. It's nothing," I try to brush him off. When he continues to stare at me, I glare right back before snapping, "Fine, my parents made me go into her family's little café or whatever yesterday. She got to see Declan McCoy in all his freaking glory, okay? That's it."

"Okay, Noah, don't bite my head off," Jordan held his hands up in surrender. "I was just curious."

"Well, don't be. It's none of your damn business."

"Jeez, you're touchy today."

"Shut up. Let's just go to class so we can get today over with. I'm tired of being here already."

Jordan, thankfully doesn't push me any further than that. We walk down the hallway to our homeroom, and I take my seat between

Jordan and Caleb. I don't say a word as I pull out my history book to get ready for our first class. I hate starting my day with an interaction with Parks. Messing with her was fun most of the time, but this morning was different.

I would never outwardly admit it to anyone, but she hit a nerve today. I don't need her sniffing around in something that doesn't concern her. The more I sit here and think about it, the more irritated I get. I decide that I need to make sure that she knows my business is just that—my business. I don't have time to put up with her fake attempt at concern. Not if she's just going to turn around and use it against me. I need to make sure she knows she doesn't know what she's talking about.

Later, when I make it to the cafeteria for lunch, I spot Parks across the room, and I frown in her direction. Of course, she's talking to Charlie and Eli, sitting at a small table in the corner out of the way. I make my mind up then and there that we need to discuss what happened this morning with her. I had to put her in her place.

"Hey, do you want to go find a table, and I'll catch up with you guys in a minute?" I ask Caleb and Jordan. They exchange a glance with each other but saunter off to find a table without any protest.

As soon as they're gone, I stomp off towards where Parks and her boyfriends are sitting. She notices me coming and sits up straighter as I get closer. Her bushy eyebrows pull in tightly together, and she asks me outright, "What do you want, Noah?"

"I need to talk to you."

"Right now?"

"Yes, right now, Parks. Why else would I be over here?"

She rolls her eyes but looks at Charlie and Eli. "I'll be right back, guys."

Eli frowns. "Why are you going with him? What if he hurts you?"

I resist the urge to laugh out loud. Addison presses her lips together at her friend. "He's not going to hurt me. We just have to talk about something."

Pleased that she doesn't put up a fight, I stalk out of the cafeteria and into the closest hallway, making sure there's no one around who could eavesdrop on our conversation. I hear her light footsteps following me, and as soon as we're far enough away from everyone else, I turn on her. Addison must've been expecting the attack. When I turn towards her, she's got her arms crossed over her chest, looking at me as if she's not the slightest bit impressed.

"What the heck was that this morning?"

"I don't know what you're talking about, Noah. I didn't do anything to you."

"Yes, you did! You can't just pretend like you know me or my family cause you don't. So I'd appreciate it if you didn't go around just assuming things."

Her eyebrows raise, and it suddenly all clicks together for her. "Noah, I was trying to be *nice*. I didn't mean anything—"

"Well, don't. We're not nice to each other. We have everything figured out, so don't go and ruin it by being nice. You mind your business, I'll mind mine, and we'll go back to not liking each other. Got it?"

"I don't know what your problem is."

"My problem is that I like the way things are! I'm mean to you; you give it right back. I don't want you to think that we're friends or anything just because my parents forced me to eat a donut from your stupid little café."

Addison drops her arms to her sides and glares at me. "Fine."

"Fine," I sneer back at her and turn on my toe, walking away from her.

"I hate you, Noah!" she hollers after me, not caring how her voice echoes off the lockers.

"Yeah, yeah," I mutter to myself, not giving her the satisfaction of turning around. "Join the club."

* * *

I wish I could say that that had been the end of it—and to my vast surprise, it is, regarding Addison. She leaves me alone for the better part of the year. However, with my father's need to chase the campaign trail growing exponentially, so does his need to make sure that I stay in line. He watches me like a hawk at all hours of the day, making sure that I don't do anything that might jeopardize his future career.

At school, I walk around worried that Addison might exact her revenge at some point. I'm constantly walking on glass at home to ensure I don't do anything that could land a solid punch to my stomach in retribution, or another few hidings with his belt.

As things with my father grew worse, I wish that I could take the edge off by going back and forth with Addison. Though I would never admit it to anyone, I miss our banter. Where it was all a game before, now it feels like a necessity. I have all this pent-up energy from toeing the line with my father so religiously that I need to get it out one way or the other. But it never really works. Parks quickly picks up on my need to fight with her, so her guard is up anytime she is in my vicinity. She doesn't engage with me like she had the year before. We slip right back into ignoring each other as much as possible.

It's a double-edged sword. As much as I'm glad she's staying out of my business and my life, sometimes I wonder if I made a mistake in running her off the way I did. But at this point, it doesn't matter. What's done is done. When at the crossroads, I made my decision, and now I've got to stick to it.

Chapter 20

Addison

Addison - Age 14

"Thank you again for showing our new student around," Principal Mabee says to me as we step out of her office. "I'm sure she'll be in good hands with you. It wasn't that long ago you were the one getting the grand tour."

"I remember," I reply, trying my hardest not to think about my first days at this school and how quickly I made friends and enemies.

Principal Mabee and I make it to the waiting area, where I see a girl and her mom waiting patiently for us. They both stand up as soon as we walk towards them.

"Ms. Turner, Grace, this is Addison. She's in the same grade as Grace and will be showing her around today."

The girl my age steps towards us and holds her hand out, offering a big smile. Her warm brown eyes are welcoming, and I find myself grinning back at her right away. She's got dark skin and magnificent curly hair pulled into two ponytails on either side of her head. "Hi, I'm Grace."

"I'm Addison, but you can call me Addie."

"Thanks for letting me follow you around today. I already know we're going to be good friends," Grace says hopefully, clasping her hands together in front of her body. She gives a quick goodbye to her mom, and then we step out of the principal's office into the hallways.

I do my best to give her the tour, showing Grace our homeroom and her locker. It's the middle of the fall semester, so already, there are flyers up announcing the homecoming game and dance that Grace looks longingly at every time we pass one.

"Are you going to the homecoming dance?" she asks me as we walk down the hall side-by-side

I press my lips together. "I'm not sure. No one's asked me yet, but I might go with some of my friends anyway."

"What are your friends like?"

"Charlie and Eli?" I smile. "They're the two best friends anyone could ask for. We clicked right away on my first day here, and we haven't separated since. We'll catch up with them at lunchtime, and you can meet them."

"That sounds great. I was friends with mostly boys at my old school too. I'm glad they put me with you today, though. I've been needing a good girl best friend in my life."

I grin at Grace and nod my head in agreement. I feel the same way. Charlie and Eli are great friends, but they *are* boys. And there are just some things I can't talk with them about.

Soon, the bell in the hallways buzzes to let everyone out for a lunch break. Students flood into the halls and Grace reaches for my hand, gripping it tightly, so she doesn't get lost in the sea of our peers. We walk together towards the cafeteria, passing the courtyard on our way.

"Who are they?" Grace asks, pointing to someone. I follow her gaze across the courtyard to the bench she's indicating. I try not to vomit. Of course, I should have known that Noah would catch Grace's attention. He currently has Rose Abbot in a solid lip lock, his hand cupping the back of her hair as he moves her face to meet his perfectly.

I roll my eyes and tug Grace away towards the cafeteria. "That's

Noah and his girlfriend Rose. They're both in our class. They've been together officially since the start of the semester, and they're literally *always* making out."

"Can't say I blame her. He's kind of cute. Or at least from what I've seen," she speculates. I crinkle my nose up and make a dramatic gagging noise. Grace laughs, "What? Is he not?"

"Definitely not. He's disgusting. If you listen to any piece of advice all day, stay away from Noah McCoy."

Grace stops walking, and I turn around to face her. She's looking at me with an eyebrow raised, her dark eyes sparkling with something I can't place since I've only known her for a few hours. "Do you like him?"

"Ew. No."

"Really? Cause it seems like you've got jealousy written all over your face right now. But hey, what do I know? I'm new here."

I frown at her. "I definitely don't like Noah. We've been enemies since my very first day here. He can be really mean. Last year he yelled at me just for being concerned about him."

"You know what they say; it's a fine line between love and hate."

I purse my lips, not loving the direction this conversation is going. I have never given anyone any indication that I liked Noah even the slightest bit. In fact, quite the opposite. But here's Grace now, making me wonder if I'm putting off some weird vibe towards him. She's been at this school for practically two minutes and already making assumptions.

"How about lunch?" I ask her in an attempt to thwart Grace from traveling further down this rabbit hole?

She looks at me knowingly, a sideways grin settling on her face, but she tags along anyway. I walk her through the lunch line process—how to determine which food would be good and which food to avoid at all costs. We each grab a tray and load it up. I settle for my favorite mac and cheese, and Grace goes for the special of the day, a brave move. As soon as we exit the line, I scan the room to find Charlie and Eli.

I spot them all the way at the back, sitting at a table that's already full, but I notice there's one close to them still that has a few seats left. Grace follows me as we weave through all the tables in the lunchroom, arriving at our table without injury.

I tap Charlie on the shoulder, and he turns around, Eli following suit. "Hey guys, this is Grace. She's just starting here, and I wanted to introduce you all."

The boys sound a chorus of hellos and scoot over on the bench to make room for us. I sit next to Eli, and Grace takes the seat across from me, next to Charlie.

"So, has Addie been giving you the inside scoop on the place?" Charlie asks her before taking a bite out of his sandwich.

Grace nods her head, giving me a bright smile. "Yes, she's an excellent tour guide. She pointed out the cleanest bathrooms and ensured I know which vending machines are always stocked."

Eli nods his head. "Good, all the stuff that matters."

"Pretty much," Grace agrees. I feel a sense of pride swelling in my belly as she continues to tell the boys everything we did during her tour. "She's even told me who the nicest people here are, don't worry, you two were at the top of the list."

I fight off a chuckle as Charlie and Eli glance at each other, each with an arrogant smirk on their faces. "I can't say she's wrong. We're about as nice as they get," Eli says with a grin.

"Pretty much everyone here is nice, save for maybe a few people. Just make sure to stay out of Noah's way. He can be a real asshole sometimes," Charlie warns her. Grace nods her head, probably recalling our conversation about our resident bully just an hour or so ago.

"Yeah, just the other day, he and Charlie got into it over a stupid dodgeball game cause Charlie tagged him out," Eli contributes. "I thought for sure he would deck you, Charlie."

"Me too," my other friend says sheepishly. "He is bad news all around."

"I've tried telling her, but she has this fixation that I like—" I protest.

"Oh, speak of the devil, here he comes," Grace chimes in cheekily, pointing with her fork at the figure of Noah McCoy striding towards us. He has a cocky smirk on his face as if he can't wait to deliver the snide remarks he's likely been thinking of all morning.

Right after our altercation last year, the dynamic between Noah and me became even more strained. It will go in waves—he'll leave me alone for most of the week. Then, suddenly, hellfire rains down, and he's taking every opportunity he can to ruin my day. As much as I try not to be, I'm always on edge when he's around because I'm unsure which version of him I will get—the aloof Noah or the aggressive one.

"Who's your new girlfriend, Parks?" Noah taunts me as he gets closer to where we're sitting. "Get tired of Monty making passes at you and decided to swing for the other team?" he asks, shooting a pointed glare at Eli. Eli's face heats up red, but he doesn't take the bait for once. Noah braces himself with one hand on our table, extending the other out to Grace. He offers her the biggest cheesiest grin I think I've ever seen him plaster on his face. "I'm Noah McCoy. Welcome to my school."

"Grace Turner," Grace introduces herself, flashing her brown eyes at Noah as if she can see right through his "cool kid" façade. A smile plays on her lips as she takes his extended hand. Next to her, I grit my teeth together as I prepare to watch this mess unfold. "Nice to meet you, Noah. Addison has told me *all* about you."

Surprise crosses his face for a split second before he masks it. "Has she?" he questions, shooting his silver gaze towards me, a suspicious smirk now appearing. "Well, be careful what you believe. Parks here has a habit of embellishing the truth. Sometimes I think she's got it out for me."

"I do not," I chime in, defending my honor and glaring at him. "And I definitely wouldn't waste my breath trying to list all your flaws to her. We'd be here all day."

"Easy there, Parks. Don't get too riled up," Noah says with a sneer, thoroughly enjoying the game he's just started.

"Noah, could you please just leave? I was about to explain to Grace what the rest of our day will look like, and you're scaring her."

"Actually, I'm fine," Grace announces, watching us go at each other with amusement. "Don't stop on my account."

"See, Parks, *you're* really the problem here. No one else seems to have an issue with me. Only you and your two boy-wonders."

"And why do you think that is?" I shoot back, standing up and taking a step towards him. "Maybe because I've barely had *two seconds* of peace and quiet ever since I've been here because of you? Because you're so obsessed with me that you can't just leave me alone?"

Noah frowns, his eyes narrowing, "What? I'm not obsess—"

"Oh really? When was the last time you went a week without giving me crap about something? What I'm wearing or how my hair looks, or the fact that my parents aren't rich? I try and stay out of your way like you ordered me to last year, yet you always find a way to weasel your way and attack. You're a jerk, Noah. There is no other way to put it. And I'm counting down the days until we graduate, so I'll never have to see your selfish ass again!"

Noah stares open-mouthed at me during my outburst, clearly struggling to find a comeback. Finally, he gives a half-hearted laugh and rolls his eyes. "Okay, I'm done here. I don't have time for you when you're PMSing so hard." I glare at him as he turns back to Grace and gives her a fake smile. "Later, New Girl. Hit me up if you ever get tired of Ms. Goody-Two-Shoes here. I'm sure I can show you around a lot better than she can."

"Don't you have to stick your tongue down Rose's throat or something?" I say darkly, ready for him to be gone.

He shoots me a withering glare and turns on his heel, walking away from us. I fold my arms over my chest and watch him cross the cafeteria. He takes his seat next to his girlfriend again. His eyes flash to mine before he smirks and bends down to kiss Rose. I scowl even harder and fall back into my seat.

"You weren't kidding. He really is an ass," Grace observes, reaching for another French fry.

"See?" I reply, "I told you."

"Yep, but he definitely likes you."

I stare incredulously at her. "What part of that confrontation gave you any idea that he *likes* me?"

"I'm just saying. There's definitely something there."

"Well, you're wrong."

She turns to me and grins. "I don't know. Yeah, you two have this weird enemy thing going on but based on how his eyes lit up when he saw us sitting here, I'd say it only goes so deep. He definitely doesn't hate you the way he says he does. Otherwise, he wouldn't be engaging at all."

"His eyes light up with the spirit of Satan, that's all. Sorry, Grace. You're wrong on this one."

Grace shrugs her shoulders with a smirk as if she knows something I don't. "We'll see."

* * *

Thankfully, Noah seems to leave us alone for the next few weeks, aside from a few sinister smiles here and there. Grace is under the impression that he's letting her get acclimated to her new school, but I know better. I figure Noah's just biding his time until the opportune moment when he can strike.

I'm right.

The Friday before Halloween, Noah makes his move.

"What's up, New Girl?" he jeers, sidling up to Grace and me after school. He dips his chin at me. "Parks."

Grace looks at him coolly and cocks her hip to the side. "The sky. What do you want?"

"Just thought I'd check and make sure Parks here told you about the Halloween traditions this weekend."

I nearly groan when Grace looks at me accusingly, eyebrow raised with intrigue. "She didn't, but I'm sure you're about to," Grace says back to Noah.

His lips twist in amusement as he leans forward and looks around as if he's telling a secret he shouldn't be. "Tomorrow night. Witch House. Nine o'clock."

"Witch House? What the heck is that?"

I roll my eyes and enter the conversation. "This ancient creepy house on the outskirts of town that everyone thinks is haunted."

"It is haunted," Noah says deadpan. "Legend has it that you can still hear the screams of the witches being tortured in there from back during the witch hunt."

"It's ridiculous," I say. "There's no such thing as ghosts or hauntings or whatever. It's scientifically unproven."

"You and your science-bull crap again," Noah says. "There's more to life than just evidence and research."

I cross my arms and scowl. "Fine, then how about I point out that Vermont only had one known witch hunt, and it was about an hour south of here."

Noah glares at me, his eyes taking on a sharp edge. "You *would* know that."

I flip my hair over my shoulder and hit him back with a satisfied smirk. "I'm surprised you don't. And besides, that was hundreds of years ago. Do you think a random house would've survived without any upkeep? I don't think so."

"You're ruining the fun, Parks. Maybe stop using your brain for one second and just enjoy the experience."

"What about all those screams that people hear then?" Grace asks me.

I shrug and look down at my fingernails, picking at a cuticle. "I'm sure there's a perfectly logical explanation for that. Probably the wind hitting a hole in the roof just right."

Noah groans loudly. "Oh my *God*, Parks, would you shut up?"

He looks to Grace. "If you can get whatever stick is up her ass out, we'll be at the Witch House tomorrow. There will be a bonfire and games and such."

Grace looks at me with a smile and a gleam in her eye. "We're going."

I cross my arms over my chest and press my lips together. It seems I'm losing this battle. Which is how I find myself standing in the middle of a field the next evening. The sky is dark overhead, just the twinkling of stars and the light of the moon illuminating the area.

"The game is 'ghost in the graveyard,'" Noah instructs everyone. I side-eye Grace and plant my hands on my hips, trying to appear unimpressed. "Think of it as backward hide-and-seek. I'll assign two groups: one to be groundsman and the other ghosts."

Noah continued on to explain the objective of the game. The groundsmen count down from one o'clock to midnight while the ghosts scatter and hide. If a groundsman locates a ghost, they have to yell out, *'ghost in the graveyard!'* Then all the groundsmen have to run back to home base while the ghost chases them, trying to tag them. If you get tagged by a ghost, you become a ghost too.

In my opinion, the whole game sounds trivial, and I would much rather be at home. There's supposed to be a special on haunted houses across America on the History Channel tonight, but Grace insisted we come.

Noah informs everyone that to split into the two groups, he's going to flip a coin, and we're supposed to call out what we think will fall: if we're right, we get to be groundsmen, wrong, and we're ghosts. He gets his quarter ready and then flips it up into the air, catching it and slapping it over onto the back of his hand. Everyone calls out their prediction right as his eyes lock on mine expectantly.

Grace calls heads out beside me, and I follow her lead. "Heads."

A sardonic smirk forms on his face, and his eyes are still on mine as he mutters, "Tails." Then he takes his hand off the coin and observes the result. "Heads it is. Those who said tails are with me as ghosts."

We split into the two teams, and the ghosts go off and hide. One of Noah's friends, I think it's Caleb, starts the countdown from one o'clock, and we begin our hunt for ghosts. Since the idea of the game is to *not* get tagged when a ghost is found, Grace scampers off, and I find myself alone in the middle of the Witch House property.

I trek carefully, my eyes darting every which way trying to locate a ghost if they're nearby. Someone across the field yells, *"Ghost in the graveyard!"* And I turn to run back to the designated home base when someone jumps in front of me.

"Gotcha!"

I scream so loudly that I wonder if maybe *this* is the source of the questionable wailing coming from the Witch House.

Once all my breath has left my body, I bend over, my hands resting on my knees. I take short breaths in and out, hyperventilating. My heart rate is way too high, and though it's dark out, my vision swirls.

"Whoa, whoa," a male voice whispers as arms wrap around my shoulders, holding me steady and straightening me up. "Calm down, Parks."

Only one person calls me by my last name.

I spin around to face Noah. His face is hidden in the shadows, but even that can't hide the concern on his face. I wonder if I'm hallucinating. He frowns as I put my hand to my chest, taking big gulps of air.

"That's it, you're okay," he mutters softly, his hands running down my arms. "Deep breaths."

When I've finally managed to calm my heartbeat to a regular rate, all sense comes back to me. I reach out and shove Noah away from me. "You *scared* me!"

"Isn't that the point of Halloween?" he asks, though his expression doesn't match his tone. If I look close enough, I might see a hint of worry still playing on his features.

"No, and I wouldn't even be here tonight if it weren't for you. Go find someone else to bother." I start stomping away, but he reaches out and grabs my hand, halting my escape.

"Hey, hold on just a second." I turn and glare at his hand holding mine, and he promptly let's go. "Seriously, are you okay? You really freaked out there for a second. You were white as a ghost. Even though I think that's *my* role in the game."

"I—I'm fine, thank you. You just startled me."

Noah's eyes soften to my complete and utter shock, and he steps forward. I observe him, waiting for the floor to fall from underneath me. He looks like he's about to say something when he's cut off by the sound of his name being called by a feminine voice from the darkness.

Rose.

The interruption breaks whatever spell that came over the two of us. I shake my head and distance between us, wrapping my arms around my middle. "I think your girlfriend is looking for you."

Noah's eyes narrow, and again he looks like he wants to say something else when Rose calls for him once more. He glances off in her direction, clenching his teeth together. I take advantage of his divided attention and skitter off, not looking back at him.

I find Grace standing on top of the hill at the home base, hands on her hips. She lets out a large, relieved sigh when she sees me coming toward her. "Where the heck have you been, Addie? Did you get tagged?"

I hesitate before answering. "Nowhere. Are you ready to leave? I don't want to play anymore."

"I wouldn't be opposed to it. This place is creepy."

I link our arms together, and we head back down the hill towards the main road. On our way, we pass Noah and Rose. Rose has her hands on her hips, an angry expression on her face, while Noah stands there and takes whatever heat she's throwing at him.

"Wonder what's going on there?" Grace muses. "Weren't they just in la-la-land yesterday?"

I press my lips together, knowing that while Rose was searching for her boyfriend, he had been with me, trying to calm me down from almost having a panic attack. "Yeah, who knows. Noah's always starting trouble."

Grace hums but lets it lie as we continue our escape from the Witch House. On the way home, I try my hardest not to think about the strange moment with Noah tonight. For a second, he almost seemed...concerned? But that couldn't be. It must have been a trick of the light or the enhanced nerves of Halloween Night. Noah made it clear that we aren't concerned with each other. He wouldn't change his mind on that.

It was just a one-off. Monday, I'll get to school, and everything will be back to normal. Noah will be his regular snotty self, and I'll go back to hating him.

"Oh, there you two are," Charlie says, relieved when we walk up to him and Eli by the road. "You disappeared during the game, and I thought something bad had happened."

"Afraid the ghosts were going to get me?" I tease him, unsettled by the truth in my statement.

He makes a face. "More like you'd run into someone you wouldn't want to run into during the witching hour."

I know immediately he's talking about Noah and his buddies. I consider telling him about what happened with Noah just moments ago, but I don't get the chance to.

"Tapping out already, Sullivan? The night's barely begun," Noah sneers, sauntering up to us. Rose is in his wake, scowling hard at him. She turns her head and shoots me a glare as soon as they reach us. I narrow my eyes at her, confused. What the heck did I do to her?

"Just tired of your games, McCoy," Charlie counters back, squaring his shoulders towards Noah. My friend takes a few steps closer, so Grace and I are slightly behind him.

Noah notices this and raises a mocking eyebrow at me. "Nice guard dog. Where's the other one? Off to get his rabies shot? I did notice he was foaming at the mouth a little yesterday." He pauses and raises his eyebrows as if he's had an epiphany. "Nope, no, that was just because Parks was in his vicinity, wasn't it?"

"Noah," Rose grumbles at her boyfriend. He barely glances at her over his shoulder before his attention is on the three of us again.

"Well, go on then. If you want to leave the fun, help yourself." Noah drapes his arm over Rose's shoulders, and the couple turns to walk away. As he's leaving, he turns towards me once more, his eyes still narrowed but the malice not meeting the rest of his features. Though it's dark, I can still see the silver-blue hue of his eyes as they travel over my body. He presses his lips into a thin line. A confused expression crosses his face for brief moment before he turns away from me completely.

Charlie leads us to where we stashed our bicycles, riding with us the whole way home to ensure we make it back safely. I can't help but smile to myself at Noah calling Charlie our guard dog. Though he said it with negative connotations, it wasn't far off from the truth. Out of our little friend group, Charlie is always the one looking out for everyone else.

We ride in silence, the three of us stewing over our last encounter with Noah. The cool air helps me clear my head so I can think about the events of the evening with a little more clarity. I got to see a side of Noah I never knew existed before tonight. The image of his eyes going soft when I nearly had a panic attack will forever be ingrained in my mind.

It was weird, but in a good way. Usually, Noah has an edge, sharp as a serrated knife, but tonight? No, tonight, I think I might have gotten a view of the real Noah McCoy underneath all the armor. Nice looked good on him, and I wish he would display that side of him more often.

As we ride home, I let my imagination run wild and think of how different my life might look if Noah catered to the good instead of the bad, as he did more often than not.

Chapter 21
Noah

Noah - Age 15

"Ow! Hey, watch it," I exclaim as I run face-first into another student walking through the hallways. To be fair, I was looking down at my science binder, trying to find the lab assignment I'm supposed to work on today. Still, that fact doesn't make me any less irritated. When I look up, I see Charlie Sullivan bending down to pick up all the papers he dropped from our collision. I scowl down at him, and he glares back at me.

"You were the one who wasn't watching where they were walking. Maybe if you could get your head out of your ass for two seconds."

I raise my eyebrows at Sullivan's abrupt comeback and snap my binder shut. "Wow, look who's finally decided to grow a pair. Feeling brave enough to stand up to me now, Sully?"

Sullivan stands up now to face me. We're both around the same height now. I may have an inch on him, but not much more. He scrutinizes me with his green eyes. "I don't need to stand up to you. You're not worth the energy."

"Remember who you're talking to, Sully," I sneer at him. "I'm the son of the future mayor of this town."

"And?" he prompts me. "I'm the son of the sheriff. As I have been literally since I was born. Are we really going to waste time doing this?"

"As a matter of fact, your father will be answering to Mayor McCoy soon," I rib Charlie, ignoring his question. To my extreme irritation, his face remains expressionless, as if he's bored. I take another stab. "Will the honorable sheriff of Willow Heights be able to handle taking orders from someone as sophisticated as my father?"

"Are you finished?"

I hesitate. Usually, Charlie would've taken the bait by now, but he is really over this conversation. I grip my green binder to my chest and glare at him. He looks off down the hallway and then sighs tiredly before turning back at me.

"My father told me that the problem with people who hunt for power is that they're never satisfied. Nothing will ever be able to make them happy. There will always be something more and something bigger that they will strive for. And the biggest problem? They don't care who they have to destroy to get it."

"What's your point, Sullivan?" I growl at him.

"Just something you might want to keep in mind. If your father is one of those people, you might want to stay on his good side." He turns to walk away but thinks of something else and faces me again. "Don't worry about my father. I think he knows how to handle a bully like Declan McCoy. Just like I know how to handle the younger version."

"You say that now," I spit at him.

Sullivan shrugs. "I guess only time will tell. But us common folks of Willow Heights won't be the only ones affected by your father getting a higher rank. Just a thought. I'll be interested to see what side you choose when all is said and done. Don't pick the wrong one, McCoy."

Anger boils in my gut, and I fight back the urge to punch Charlie Sullivan across his stupid smug face. "Get out of my sight, Sullivan. I'm done talking to you."

"With pleasure," he mumbles, hands gripping the straps of his backpack as he walks off.

I do my best to let the altercation with Sullivan not phase me as I stalk toward the science wing. Of all the days that I have to spend extra time working on a project at school. Not to mention my project *partner* is none other than Hurricane Addison herself. It was a cruel, cruel day when our science teacher paired the two of us up for our big term project. I grit my teeth when I get to the closed door to the science lab and breathe deeply through my nose. This is a really shitty day.

"Well, well, what do we have here?" I say out loud, laying on the snark, as I step into the chemistry lab. Addison looks up from her lab notebook and glowers when she sees me walking toward her. I can't help the amused laugh that comes out of my throat at her appearance. She looks ridiculous with the gray school-issued lab coat and lab goggles that are much too big for her face. Addison is clearly taking this science class way too seriously.

"You're late, Noah. I don't want to do this whole thing by myself."

"Aw, Parks," I say as I walk closer to the workbench, she's chosen for us. I don't bother telling her that I'm late because her bestie, Charlie, is a pain in the ass. "You already know you're doing most of it by yourself. I'm just here for moral support."

"Why do you do that?" she shoots back at me.

"Do what?"

"Pretend that you're not good at school. I've seen your tests that you've gotten back, and I know—"

"Why are you peeking at my scores, Parks?" I question her, my defenses going up. Where does Parks get off being so nosy?

I catch her off guard with my tone, her eyes going wide as she attempts to backtrack. "Well, it's not like I did it on purpose. We're lab partners, we sit at the same table, and I just happened to see your score on the last exam. It was good, Noah. *Really* good."

"I'm aware," I say through gritted teeth. "I am the one who took the test after all."

"My point is, I don't get why you pretend that you're above doing well in school. Like it's a bad thing if your friends were to find out that you get good grades."

"I don't act that way."

Addison stares at me like I'm stupid, and I don't like it. Not one bit. "Yes, you do," she argues back. "You act all high and mighty and make fun of me for getting good grades when you're scoring *higher* than me on some of the exams. Like—I don't get it, Noah."

"You don't have to 'get it,'" I snarl back at her, making air quotations with my fingers. "There's nothing for you to 'get.' I literally don't know why we're having this conversation for the millionth time. Stay the hell out of my business, Parks."

"Fine!" she shouts, holding her hands up in exasperation. "God, Noah, you drive me crazy. Why is it so hard for you to just have a regular conversation with someone?"

I glare at her. "I am fully capable of having conversations with people. I just prefer not to have them with people who piss me the hell off."

"Real mature."

"Shut up, Parks, and just tell me what to do so I can get out of here."

To my complete and utter shock, Parks does what I ask of her and puts me to work without another word. Every few minutes, she gives me instructions on what to do to accomplish the next section of our experiment, but as far as communication goes? She keeps it to a minimum.

At first, I think it's glorious not having to listen to her nag at me or say things that make me want to strangle her. But after a while, it starts to become unnerving. I've known Parks for three—give or take—years at this point, and never once have I seen her this quiet before. Usually, she's too busy being a know-it-all or picking fights with me over the littlest topics. But not today.

I find myself saying things as the morning goes on, trying to goad her into snapping back, but she doesn't crack. She remains dutiful to the task at hand, filling out our lab notebook and doing the calculations for the experiment. I continue to get more frustrated with the lack of response and keep trying to trigger a reaction out of her. When I finally say something particularly nasty, Addison slams the notebook down, hitting me with a heavy glare.

I gear myself up for a fight at the thunderous expression on her face. *Finally*.

"By all means, Noah, keep playing this game where you say mean things and try to make me feel terrible all the time," Parks says, looking down at the table as she piles her assignments into a folder and shuts it. Her hazel eyes find mine as she looks sideways at me. "But your words don't hurt me because I have people who love me for exactly the way I am, and I can't help but wonder if—"

"If what?" I snarl at her when she stops short, already knowing that I'm not going to like where she's taking this. I realize I might have pushed her just a little too far this time.

Parks turns towards me fully, and instead of seeing my irritation reflected back at me in her eyes, I see exhaustion and a calculative sadness as if she's worried that her suspicions are right. "I can't help but wonder if you even know what it feels like. To have someone love you without expecting anything back."

My jaw goes slack, a proper response failing to come forward. Addison studies me for another moment before she breathes through her nose and gathers up her school things.

"I think that's enough for today. We can finish the rest tomorrow."

"Tomorrow's Saturday," I complain. It's the only thing I can manage to respond right now.

Her eyes flash at me, and my stomach clenches with unease. She definitely is irritated with me. "And you've been putting off our project all week even though I've tried to get it finished earlier. It's due Monday, Noah. So we have to finish it this weekend."

I groan and drop my head into my arms on the workbench. I recall her pestering me all week, trying to get me to stay late so we could get this done, but I just ignored her. Now I'm going to pay the price. "You're going to kill me. I can't do it tomorrow. My dad has this thing tonight, and I'm sure it's going to go late—"

"Noah," she cuts me off, and I look at her. Her expression is shut-off, her eyes cold. "I literally don't give two shits about what you have going on tonight or what your perfect family is up to. We have a project due Monday, and you've been procrastinating, so now you have to step up and do your part. And frankly, you better come tomorrow with a better attitude. I'm getting real tired of dealing with your shit."

I can't help but be surprised at the forcefulness of her tone. Where the hell is all *this* attitude coming from? "Damn, Parks."

Addison shrugs off her lab coat, hangs it on the racks in the room, and then grabs her backpack, swinging it around her shoulders. "I'll be here at nine tomorrow. If you don't show up, I will tell Mr. Reese that you didn't participate at all in the project and that he should give you a zero. I'm not playing around here, Noah."

"Clearly," I mutter, annoyed. "Fine, I'll do my best to be here tomorrow."

Appeased, she lowers her weapons slightly. "Thank you. I'll see you tomorrow." And she heads towards the door. Before leaving, she pauses and then glances at me over her shoulder. "I hope you have fun at your family thing tonight."

Taken aback at the quick change in tone, I gape at her, feeling like I just got whiplash from her swift shift in approach. She sighs at my lack of prompt response and then steps out of the lab. I balk at the door for a second more, finally saying the "Thanks" that was stuck on the tip of my tongue.

Once I get my bearings back, I collect my things and leave. I'm running a little bit later than I would like. Still, hopefully, I'll be able to get home and sneak upstairs before my father realizes I'm running late.

I pull my skateboard out of my locker and speed home, throwing the door open and bounding inside. My eyes are set on my room upstairs, but I'm not fast enough.

"Where have you been, Noah?" my father interrogates, stepping out of the dining room into the foyer. He shoots me an icy cold glare and turns slightly away to straighten his tie in the mirror on the wall.

I freeze mid-stride and look at him like a deer in the headlights. "I was at school late. We have a project due."

"You know tonight is important for me, don't you?" he asks me snidely, his gray eyes burning a hole into me like gunmetal. "Are you trying to ensure I don't get elected?"

"No, Father, I'm sorry."

"I would hope you're sorry. How does it look for the future mayor of this town to have his son MIA on one of the most important nights of the campaign? If they think I'm incapable of managing my own family, why would they elect me? Voting day is next week, so everything that happens tonight matters. Now get your ass upstairs and go change. You look like a mess. That's not how I raised you. I can't have you embarrassing me tonight, do you understand?"

"Yes, sir," I mutter, thoroughly reprimanded as I head towards the stairs.

"You have thirty minutes, Noah," he calls after me.

I jump in the shower right away to rinse off and wash my hair. I do it in record time, toweling off most of the way before tracking down the suit I laid out for tonight and pulling it on. My heart is racing as the imaginary clock in my head ticks down. I only have a few minutes before my father comes knocking, and I absolutely do *not* want to deal with him any more than I have to tonight. Not to mention the fallout if I run any later than I am already.

Once dressed, I start messing with my shaggy hair, taming it back into something the Future Mayor will find presentable. As I comb the product through my hair, I hear a soft knock on my door.

"I'm almost done!" I yell in defense.

"Are you okay, sweetheart?" the sound of my mother's soft voice has me looking over my shoulder. My muscles sag as she comes up behind me, her hand resting on my upper back.

"He's mad at me," I say softly, showing rare vulnerability. Something I'm only ever comfortable doing around her. "I don't want to go tonight and do something wrong and make it worse."

"Oh honey, you won't. Your father is just concerned about how tonight will play in his campaign. It's nothing you've done."

"You always say that," I say to her, slowly turning around. "And yet he's always mad at me about something. Why am I not good enough for him?"

When I meet my mother's eyes, my stomach clenches. She's looking at me with *pity* in her blue eyes, silently confirming to me that my feelings are valid. My mother places her hand on my shoulder again, an attempt at comfort, but I shrug her off. "Noah, just listen to me. Your father is under a lot of stress, and he just wants everything to be perfect."

"And I'm not perfect enough for him. I get it."

"No, that's not what I'm saying at all."

"It's fine, Mom. Just tell him I'll be down in a few minutes and that I'll try my best to be *perfect* tonight."

"Noah."

I turn away from her and stride into my en suite bathroom, closing the door behind me. As soon as I'm in private, I lean against the counter, breathing a shaky sigh. I squeeze my eyes shut, feeling the tears burn, but I don't give in, not willing to let myself cry over him. I stopped doing that years ago.

This stupid campaign of my father's has ruined everything. Not that my family was super tight-knit, to begin with, but now things are frayed more than ever. My father's goals always come first, and my mother and I get dragged into it to put on a good show.

My mother always makes an effort when things with my father get tough, though it doesn't always work out in my favor. I will tell my mother how I'm feeling, and while she'll always listen, I know she'll never be on my side completely at the end of the day. Catherine McCoy is the perfect politician's wife, though sometimes I wonder if she's forgotten how to be a mother in the process.

I inhale a few deep breaths, taking a second to splash cold water on my face in an attempt to get a grip of myself. When I feel like I'm finally put together enough to face my father, I straighten my tie, square my shoulders, and go downstairs to where I know my parents are waiting.

"That's better," my father says when he walks into the room. His eyes appraise my appearance with a satisfactory gleam. "Now you look the part." He turns to my mother and takes her hand, bringing it to his lips to press a kiss against the back. "Shall we, my love? The car is waiting for us outside."

My mother provides her husband with a smile that barely reaches her eyes and then looks at me, giving me a slight nod of her head, her eyes flashing at me in question. I dip my chin back at her, telling her I'm okay even though I'm not. I'm really not.

The evening progresses flawlessly; at least, I hope it does. My father practically ignores me all night in favor of schmoozing everyone who shows up for him. I stand dutifully by my parents' side and remain quiet unless I'm spoken to directly. I don't want to risk *embarrassing* my father again.

Dinner is served, and then the band starts playing as people mingle. I take the opportunity to slip away. Jordan and Caleb are in attendance this evening, and so is my girlfriend, Rose. Still, I try my best to avoid them, knowing that they'll expect me to be the person my father has prohibited me from being tonight. I head over to the bar and ask for beer, but I settle on a Coke when the tender refuses me.

Fine, whatever.

I stand off on the sidelines for a while. My friends spot me and come to stand next to me. Jordan and Caleb start right away with the jokes about the suits they're in and how the group of us look like we're mafia bosses.

"Not tonight, guys," I mutter to them. "My father is on red alert, and I don't feel like getting an ass-beating later for appearing to have too much fun."

My friends sober up, knowing that my father doesn't mess around when he says he means business. So, we stand together quietly in solidarity, watching the night unfold.

"Hey, baby," Rose says as she joins our little group. Her eyes are trained on my parents making their rounds. "Maybe that will be us one day," she whispers in my ear as she sidles closer to me. She laces her arm through mine and presses her body close.

My father is the picture of power, smiling widely and shaking the hands of everyone in attendance. If someone had a baby around here, I'm sure he would kiss the hell out of it just for the photo-op. Of course, my mother's standing next to him, playing her part and looking so proud and honored to be by his side.

I swirl the ice in my soda as I watch them, thinking over Rose's statement. I can see it all playing out like that. Me, ten, twenty years in the future, walking around an elegant ballroom with a fake smile plastered on my face while Rose takes compliments left and right. The image makes me sick to my stomach.

Finally, I turn to her and frown. "I really, really hope not."

Surprise colors her face, but I don't wait to hear her response. I have my eyes on the door, and nothing will stop me now. Pushing Rose off of me I stride away without looking back. I need to get the hell out of here. I can hear Rose calling my name behind me, but I don't stop.

As soon as I'm outside, I take a big deep gulp of air, reaching to loosen the tie around my neck.

The thought of becoming a man like my father and having Rose by my side as a complacent wife like my mother? No. I don't want that. I don't want my life to be anything like that.

I make the resolve right then and there. I will do anything and everything to *not* be like him. Not now. Not ever.

Chapter 22
Addison

Addison - Age 15

As I exit the classroom, I exclaim to my classmates, "I'll see you all at the game tonight!" They sound off a round of responses as I leave. Still smiling, I head towards the library to return some books I borrowed last week. My footsteps echo down the lonely hallways. By this time of day, the school has emptied for the day. Students have headed home or are busy taking part in extracurricular activities.

Students will flood the campus again in a few hours despite the hallways being empty right now. Tonight is the annual football game against one of our biggest rival schools. No one wants to miss out on the biggest game of the fall. My plan until then? I have to study and finish my homework for the week.

I run through the checklist in my head of things that I'd like to accomplish before the game as I walk down the empty halls. When something catches my eye, I stop mid-stride.

A student is sitting all alone down the hall from me. His back is against the wall, and his knees are bent. I take a step closer and nearly stumble when I realize who it is.

"Noah?" I ask in a whisper, though my voice travels down the empty hall.

He turns his head towards me and grimaces before looking back out the window. "Go away, Parks. I don't have the energy to fight with you right now."

I hesitantly walk up to him as if I would a wounded animal. At this moment, I was unsure if there was a vast difference between the two. Noah looks defeated. I've never seen him this way before, and I'd be lying if I said it isn't a bit disconcerting. I know Noah for his playful arrogance and the confidence he exudes in everything he does.

But now? It's not there. Not at all. In fact, that confidence hasn't been there for a few weeks.

Things between him and me have been...weird, too. I was pretty harsh on him that night in the science lab when we were trying to finish our chemistry project. I felt terrible about it for the rest of the evening. I intended to apologize the next Saturday when he came in, but I never got the chance.

Noah did show up the following morning, but he was out of sorts. I wasn't brave enough to bring up our argument because he was acting so out of the ordinary. I didn't want to make things even more awkward by making him talk about something he didn't want to. But things haven't been the same since. He's been dealing with something, and I can't hold my curiosity back any longer. I need to find out what's happening with him.

"What's wrong?" I ask him, unsure.

"Go *away*, Parks," he repeats with a growl. Then, as if that takes too much energy, he lets his head fall back against the wall. His eyes squeeze shut, crinkles forming in his eyelids with the effort. "Please."

My jaw falls open at the request. I'm positive that something is going on with him now. So I do the opposite of what he asks—of course—and walk closer to him. I set my backpack a few feet away and lean against the wall, sliding down until I'm sitting right next to him. Noah stiffens when I get in his space, but he doesn't fight me on it.

As I settle on the floor beside him, I can't help but notice he smells good. Clean. A mix of cologne and a fresh apple scent. Until this point, I haven't been close enough to catch it. But I like it.

We sit in silence for a few minutes. Noah's emotions are radiating off of him in waves, but I can't place my finger on what it is. I can't identify if it's anger, sadness, or a mixture of both. But I let my intuition guide me and just sit there in silence with him. I stare out the hallway windows and notice there are birds in the trees. I find different things to focus on as Noah stews on whatever's bothering him.

As time goes on, I become less and less sure that I'm doing what's right. Noah still hasn't said a word. Every few minutes, I peek over at him to see if he's moved, but nothing. He's still sitting there, head against the wall and eyes closed, breathing in air deep into his lungs. Though he outwardly appears relaxed, I notice his muscles are taut, like he's getting ready to recoil at the first hint of danger.

I weigh my options and decide that this was a mistake. I'm not positive about what I thought this would lead to, but I was obviously wrong. Just as I'm about to call it quits and get up to leave, he speaks.

"He won the election," Noah murmurs, softly enough that I almost don't hear him.

"Your dad?" I whisper back, even though I know the answer. I saw the results last night.

"Yup."

"And that's not a good thing?" I ask, trying to fill in the missing pieces. I'm not familiar with Noah in this capacity. I am in uncharted territory. All I know regarding Noah and his family is that it's complicated, and I should stay out of it. The McCoys put on a good show from the outside, making everyone think they are one of the perfect Founding Families. Given what I've witnessed in the past, and now sitting here with Noah, I'm starting to think that's the exact opposite of his reality.

"No, Parks," he replies. "It's definitely not a good thing."

"I'm sorry," I tell him, unsure what else I can offer in words of comfort.

"Yeah."

I reach down and find his hand resting between us on the cold tile floor. Gauging his reaction out of the corner of my eye, I lace my fingers through his, not saying a word. To my complete and utter amazement, Noah doesn't fight me on this. He allows me to wrap his hand in mine.

We sit there, hand in hand, for a few minutes, neither of us saying anything. It's a pleasant contrast to how our interactions typically go. I continue to watch him, and my heartbeat seems to pick up with every minute. Noah's staring out the hallway windows, barely blinking, almost as if he's numb. I wonder if he's looking at the birds now too.

On a day-to-day basis, his dark brown hair is neatly arranged. Today as I look at him, I notice his hair is unruly as if he's been running his hands through it incessantly. A few strands fall across his forehead and into his eyes, but it doesn't seem to bother him at this moment.

After a few minutes pass, Noah lets his head rotate against the wall until he's looking at me. Those same blue eyes which have haunted the last few years of my life bore into me. "What are we doing?" he asks into the silence.

"Sitting?"

"No, I mean—" he pauses and shifts his position, so he's more comfortable against the wall but doesn't move his hand out of mine, his eyes still heavy on me. "Why do we always argue with each other?"

"I'm not sure," I say with a shrug. "That's just how it's always been. You started it, by the way."

Noah chuckles under his breath, but it sounds defeated. "Yeah. I know. And now I'm ending it. We don't have to be friends, but I'm done. I'm tired of this. I'm tired of fighting with you for no good reason, and now I'm done."

"Noah, are you okay?" I ask him again, hoping I can find out what's bothering him. The way he's talking has me worried, and right now, our past aside, I just want to help him.

"No, I don't think so," he mumbles, casting his eyes towards our hands. He gives my fingers a light squeeze, gently enough for me to wonder if I imagined it. "My dad is...you were right." I frown at him in confusion. I usually am right about things, but I'm not sure what it was this time. And I'm not sure if I should want to be right about this one. "He's not very—" Noah falters with his words before finishing his thought, "Not very nice."

"Oh." That's all I can say, remembering Noah's reference to what I said the day after he and his family visited our café for the first time a few years ago.

"And now that he's the mayor, he will have more sway, more pull over just about everything that goes on in this town. And it won't be good for any of us."

I stare at him for a beat, still not knowing now to navigate this situation. Finally, I settle on, "I'm sorry."

Noah sighs and looks at me. "Yeah, Parks. Me too."

I'm struck then by this side of Noah that I'm meeting for the very first time. I've known Noah for three years, but all this time, he's been the stuck-up mean kid. Aside from that one-off moment on Halloween last year, I haven't seen this side of him. In that instance, I wondered what he might be like if he was that way more often, and now I realize I'm experiencing that right now. I struggle to string together a response as I stare at him.

"Better close your mouth, or you might catch flies," he says to me with a slight smirk and an eyebrow arched.

I snap my mouth shut, unaware that I was gaping at him. "Sorry. I just don't really know what's happening right now."

"Me either, but I'm going with it."

"Okay."

We sit together in the empty hallway for a bit longer, then he breaks the silence again. "You were pretty brutal last week, you know, back in the lab? Kinda harsh."

I look down at my hands. "Yeah, about that. I mean to apologize, but I wasn't sure if you would—"

"You were right about that, too," he says with a sigh and leans back. "You always seem to be right. You're very observant, Parks."

"I'm sorry."

He snickers under his breath. "Don't be. It just is what it is. I broke up with Rose."

I raise my eyebrows. "Oh, I'm sorry."

Now Noah laughs. "Would you stop apologizing?"

"Sorry, I—" I laugh too and place my palm on my forehead. "I can't seem to stop."

"I see that. Overall, I think this will be a good thing. I need to figure some things out."

I pause, unsure if he wants me to take the bait. "Like what?"

He looks at me, his eyes narrowing slightly, and I brace for his offensive attack. But it doesn't come. Instead, his expression relaxes, and he exhales. "I just... don't like the path I'm heading down. And I want to change that."

Surprise sears through my body. I can't recall hearing Noah be that open and honest before, with anyone, much less me. "Wow, that's... that's great, Noah."

He snorts. "I guess. Woo-hoo, give me a gold star for not wanting to turn into a shit bag like my father."

"That's not what I meant."

"I know, Parks. But that's how it is."

I stare at him, tracing over his features and registering how subdued he is in front of me. "He's really not a good guy, is he?"

"No, he's not. I don't want to be like that, Parks. I won't."

I swallow. "Noah, did something happen? You seem upset."

"Yeah, I looked in a mirror and saw my dad staring back, and it scared the shit out of me," he surprises me again with his honesty.

"Well, if you ever need someone to talk to, I'll always be willing to listen, even given our history. You shouldn't have to keep everything to yourself, you know? Bottling up what's bothering you won't do you any good."

"I'm talking to you now, aren't I?"

"Yeah, I guess you are."

He laughs again, his shoulders shaking. "You're ridiculous. Don't push too much, Parks."

"Sorry—I, shoot, I did it again," I mimic his movements with a chuckle of my own.

Noah tilts his head towards me and grins, like actually grins at me. He says nothing right away and just looks at me. His expression takes on a more confused state as time passes. "You—you have beautiful eyes, Parks," he mutters, his silver-blue gaze holding mine steady. "I can't believe I haven't noticed them before. They've got these golden flares in the middle like—"

He cuts himself off and swallows thickly. My cheeks heat and a flutter of something erupts in my belly. I curse myself. Why is Noah McCoy, of all people, making me blush? It's the most absurd thing I've ever heard.

As if he's had a similar train of thought, Noah pushes off the wall and stands. "Well, thanks for the talk, Parks. It was... enlightening. Don't go spreading my shit around to everyone, yeah? I'm trusting you to not bite me in the ass."

Standing up with him, I nod my head. "I won't, promise."

"Good." Noah crosses his arms over his chest and looks at me as if debating what to say next. He surprises me again and asks me, "Are you going to the football game tonight?"

"I was thinking about it," I lie, knowing that I'm going but curious to see what he says.

Noah looks at me for another beat and then sticks his hands in the pockets of his jeans. "Maybe I'll see you there then."

"Yeah, maybe," I whisper back.

His gaze holds mine again before he dips his chin and saunters off. I'm left standing in the middle of an empty hallway, my brain spinning, trying to catch up with the events that just transpired.

I took a chance and approached the wounded animal. And instead of getting my head bitten off, I might have—made a friend?

I'm not sure what that was, other than an awkward encounter with my arch-nemesis, who may or may not have called a permanent truce? I will be replaying each moment of this conversation back in my head later, trying to decipher what happened.

I do this even later in the evening at the football game. The team is on the field running through their plays in the attempt to score a touchdown. Meanwhile, my mind is replaying every second of my conversation with Noah from earlier. Each time I run through it again, more questions pop up, and I stash them away to mull over later.

It's a game against a rival school, so most of the student body showed up dressed in school spirit wear. I'm standing up on the bleachers next to Grace. Eli and Charlie are right in front of us. Eli is dunking pieces of a soft pretzel into hot, melty cheese, and Charlie is cupping his hands around his mouth, shouting at our quarterback, Wyatt. I want to tell Charlie that Wyatt can't hear him yelling from all the way over here, but I'm too distracted.

My eyes keep sliding over towards where Noah is standing, leaning against the brick wall of the snack bar. I observe him, darting my gaze away whenever he looks over at me. My cheeks heat again, thinking about how we were holding hands earlier in the day. I try not to worry too much about the butterflies rapidly forming in my stomach.

We nearly ran into each other on our way into the stadium before the game. I had been coming from the library, lost in thought, and he was coming from the other way, also not paying attention. We rammed into each other, and his hands had found my shoulders to steady me. Hot sparks of electricity instantly traveled through my body at his touch, and even moreso when I looked up and found him staring down at me.

Noah's lips were pulled into a thin line, and his eyes narrowed. But instead of yelling at me for not watching where I was going, he asked, "Are you okay?"

My lips had fallen open as I blinked at him stupidly. "Fine. You?"

"Great."

"Okay."

At that moment, Noah realized that his hands were still on my shoulders, and he let them fall right away. One of his hands traveled to the back of his neck, and he rubbed nervously. "I'll let you get back to your friends."

He bolted off like a horse out of the gate, not giving me a chance to say anything else. I watched him walk away from me, still shell-shocked. Not long after that, I found my friends in the bleachers. They waved me down, and I joined them.

After the game started, I spotted Noah standing by the snack bar, where he's still perched against the building, his eyes locked on a target in the stands: me. As soon as I suspect that he's not gazing at me, I glance at him again, immediately regretting it. He hasn't looked away at all. No, now he's staring right at me, his brows pulled together. He watches me, his hand coming up to rub the back of his neck. He looks puzzled, as if he is trying to work out a riddle in his head. Finally, he looks away. I can see his jaw clench tight from where I'm sitting.

"Why does Noah keep staring at you?" Grace asks me, suspicion clouding her tone.

I glance at her and then back towards where Noah is. His attention is now wholly on the game playing out on the field. "He and I kind of had a weird moment earlier today." Grace doesn't respond right away, so I look back and find her staring at me in shock. "What?"

"You're going to say that and not expect me to want the whole story?"

I shrug one shoulder. "There's nothing to tell. He was pretty upset about the election, and I sat with him and talked a little. That's it."

"That's it, huh? And he didn't attack you verbally, pull on your hair, or drop a raw egg on your head?"

"No, of course not."

"You say that like it's outside the realm of possibility. Addison, this is huge! I can't believe you're acting so level-headed about this," she protests. "Didn't he shove you into a locker just last week?"

I press my lips into a thin line, knowing I still have a sore shoulder from that event, and begrudgingly admit. "Yes, but to be fair, I was in front of his locker."

"So you're making excuses for him now, huh?" she asks, though there's a ring of amusement to her tone. If I know Grace, she's eating every second of this up.

"Making excuses up for who?" Charlie asks, turning around and looking at me with unasked questions written all over his face. Eli turns around to face me too, a frown playing on the corner of his mouth.

Grace smirks at Charlie victoriously. "Noah. They had a moment in the hallway earlier."

Another blush takes over my cheeks, and I wish I could slap my hand right over her mouth. "We did not. He was just—" I pause, not wanting to air his business to more people than I need to. "We didn't have a moment."

"Good," Charlie says, looking at me strangely. "That would just be...I don't know, weird?"

"Believe me, I'm aware."

Thankfully, my friends leave it, not pressing the issue any further. The game continues, and we end up winning with an extra touchdown. Charlie goes wild when Wyatt is the one to make the last touchdown at the last minute, and I grin, clapping along with him.

As soon as the teams leave the field, the stands begin to empty. Grace and I grab our bags and glue ourselves to the boys' sides, so we don't get lost in the crowd. As we walk to our cars, I can't help but shiver as a chill comes over me. Eli is right by my side, wrapping his arm around my shoulder and pulling me close to him.

"You cold?" he asks lowly.

I look up at him, embarrassment flooding my belly, and nod, saying nothing. I snuggle into his side closer, risking another glance up at him. Eli's got a massive goofy grin all over his face as his arm tightens on my shoulder. A ball of nervous energy is now sitting inside me at being this close to him. Eli and I have been skirting around each other recently. Both of us are unsure about what to do about these rising feelings for each other.

Grace pretends to make a gagging noise next to us, but I do my best to ignore her. I'm aware she's not a massive fan of Eli and me being together, but to be honest, I'm not a fan of her choice for me. She's still on the Noah-Addie train, believing that we are secretly in love with each other, but there's just no way.

Not with the way being this close to Eli makes my body thrum with anticipation.

I'm not sure what it's supposed to feel like to be in love, but I know that being with Eli makes me happy. He makes me laugh and always tries to ensure that I'm having a good time with whatever we're doing. When he does things like this, wrapping his arm around me or holding my hand underneath the lunch table, it makes my stomach flip with anticipation.

Even as I walk with Eli, I think about how Noah opened up to me earlier, and I feel content warmth spread through my body despite the chill of the fall night. Before that thought can grow to be anything more than it needs to, I shake my head. I'm only feeling warm now because Eli's got his arm around me—nothing more. I'm not sure if Noah could ever come close to how I feel around Eli. Eli is safe. He's always liked me for who I am. And we all know that's not the case when it comes to Noah.

Yet, my thoughts keep straying back to Noah despite my best attempts to avoid it. I replay our interaction in the hallway this afternoon once more, analyzing it for clues or nuances that I might have missed. Overall, he seemed down about the whole thing, and I'm not sure what I'm supposed to do with that. I don't know if there's any way that I can help him with what's going on in his home life. All I know is that deep in my soul, I feel things will shift after this. I don't know if it's intuition or delusion, but the tides changed today, and I hope it will all be for the better.

Chapter 23
Noah

Noah - Age 16

"Noah!" I hear my name being called, and I shrug my backpack up further on my shoulder as I look around for the source. From across the quad, I see Jordan waving his hand, Caleb grins at me right next to him. "Over here!"

I wander over to them. "What's up?"

"Where have you been, man? We've barely seen you all summer!" Caleb complains as he takes my hand and pulls me in for a hug.

"My mom and I went down to our house in Florida for the summer. Chance to get away from it all, you know?"

My father had been on a rampage ever since the year started, going after my mom and me for every little thing imaginable. We had to act a certain way and say the right words at the right time. Thankfully, my mother was just as sick of it as I was, and the minute school let out for the summer, she packed up my bags and shoved me in a car.

Instead of listening to my father rag on me for merely existing the entire summer, I got to listen to waves crashing against the shore. A pretty good trade-off, in my opinion.

"That sounds better than being stuck in this shitty town for three months," Jordan says.

"Oh, speaking of summer excursions, you know who else went away for the summer and came back an absolute smoke show?" Caleb asks me. His face screams mischief.

"Who?" I ask, carefully.

"None other than *the* Addison Parks."

I eye my friend. "Why do you say it that way?"

He and Jordan share a conspiratorial look, but Caleb shrugs. "No reason."

It shocked the two of them when I told them about Parks' and my little "moment" in the hallway last year, and they've been ribbing me about it ever since. There were irritating comments here and there or a nudge to the shoulder whenever she showed up at school wearing a cute outfit or something.

Irritating as hell.

Despite our insignificant moment in the hallway, nothing has changed other than me not making her life miserable at every opportunity. No, if anything, it leads to a truce at best and an understanding at worst.

I roll my eyes, choosing not to linger on the subject. Instead, I walk into the school to stick my stuff in my locker. It doesn't even matter. As far as I can tell, Parks is still hung up on Eli Montgomery. Not that I'd be interested in her anyway, but it makes my friends' efforts moot. She's part of the light side, and I'm over here firmly rooted in the dark. As long as Declan McCoy is mayor, I'm not sure I'll ever get the chance to be seen as anything other than his son. Which means all the negative connotations that come with that title.

I am a McCoy, after all. There's really no getting around that. Addison Parks can do a lot better than me, even if it is with stupid Eli.

I hear a commotion down the hallway, and I look up from what I'm doing, and my mouth goes dry. *Holy shit*, Caleb was right. It's as if Addison Parks left at the end of last summer as ugly a duckling as ever but came back a swan. She's down the hall catching up with Grace. She tosses her head back with a laugh, and I blink at her as if I'm not sure what I'm seeing.

Her normally mousy brown hair has a tint of gold in it from the hours spent in the sun. It catches in the light as she tosses it over her shoulders. I can see those freckles over her nose, more pronounced even from where I'm standing a few yards away from her. Her skin looks soft, now tan from the summer, accentuated by the white tank top she wears. I avert my eyes when I notice the jean shorts, displaying her toned legs.

Something tightens in my chest, and I absently rub at it as I stare at her, taking her in entirely for the first time. Addison Parks looks —*wow*.

Grace closes her locker, and then the two of them walk down the hallway toward where I'm standing like I just got struck by lightening. Addison's walking on the side closest to me, and as she gets closer, panic sets in. I turn around and focus on my task at my locker, trying not to make it obvious that I was watching her.

Still, I can't help but peek as she walks by me. My heart is beating so fast I can hear it in my ears. Parks glances over at me as she passes, her lips pulling up slightly as she gives me a small wave. I do nothing to respond, but I turn and watch her as she walks toward her classroom. The scent of vanilla and lavender follows in her wake and overwhelms my senses.

As soon as she's out of my vicinity, my heart rate calms to a healthier pace. However, my stomach is left in knots. I wonder if something that I ate for breakfast wasn't fresh or maybe the smell of her perfume was too strong. That's the only thing I allow myself to think as explanation for the weird visceral reaction I just had.

It happens again the next day, and this time, I conclude it has nothing to do with what I've eaten. I'm standing outside in the school's courtyard, polishing off a bagel I snatched from the breakfast menu. She sneaks up and startles me enough, making me drop my bagel onto the grass. I turn to her and arch a brow, waiting.

"Hi Noah," she says softly, unsure where we stand with each other. I can't really blame her. It's like we're in limbo right now. I wouldn't call us friends, but we're no longer enemies.

"Parks," I say back. I must have grown another inch or two over the summer. She seems so much shorter than me than a few months ago. "Good summer?"

Addison looks down at the grass and then bends to pick up my poor discarded bagel. She hands it back to me. "Yes, you? I didn't see you around town much."

Something flutters in my chest, but I suppress it and clear my throat. "We were in Florida for the summer. My mom wanted to get us away from my father."

"Oh," her eyes find mine again, and she searches my face. "Is everything... are you okay?"

"As good as I can be when your father's the mayor," I say, trying to come off as jovial, but I know she can see right through it. The scent of her perfume lingers around me again, lavender and vanilla. Now that I'm getting more of a whiff, I realize that I *really* like it.

The bell rings, and Parks looks away from me towards the school. "I better go. Charlie and Eli will probably wonder where I am. I'll... see you around?"

"Sure. Later, Parks."

She offers me a soft smile and then turns away from me to walk into the school. My stomach twists almost painfully as I stare after her. I look down at the bagel in my hand. It's covered in dirt with a few pieces of grass plastered to the top. I scowl before walking over to the trash can and chucking it in. I head to class and try not to think about the lavender and vanilla essence surrounding me.

The year continues uneventfully. I do my best to keep my good grades and maintain my GPA, but I always come in right behind Parks no matter how hard I try. It may be one of the few things I admire about her—her ability to keep her head down and do what she needs to do to succeed.

Fall rolls around, and the posters go up to remind everyone to purchase tickets for the homecoming game and dance the following night. The minute word about a dance gets out, everyone acts like absolute fools. All the girls come to school dressed up as if they're trying to attract the attention of a male to take them to the dance. And the guys? Well, most of them buy right into it.

Thankfully, for the second year in a row, I'm single. That means I don't have to waste my money buying the limo and the special dinner or stress myself out trying to find a tie that matches her dress perfectly. Not having a girlfriend has turned into a blessing in disguise.

As the dance gets closer and closer, I'm forced to witness and listen to more homecoming proposals than I ever care to hear. But the most annoying one of all comes on a random Thursday at lunch hour.

"Can I have everyone's attention?" Eli Montgomery's annoying ass announces to the cafeteria. I look up from where I'm leaning against the wall and see him standing up on a table bench. My nose crinkles at him, and I know I will not like whatever he's about to do. Jordan and Caleb look at me, silently asking if they should put a stop to it. I shake my head, curious to see how this will play out.

Eli hops down off the bench and then turns towards Parks, reaching down to take her hand so he can help her stand up too. Addison looks between him and her other friends, still sitting at the table. I notice the blush forming on her cheeks from across the room, and I narrow my eyes. She doesn't like attention, it seems.

"What are you doing?" she asks Eli.

Eli leans in and whispers something in her ear before turning towards the rest of the student body in the cafeteria and looking at them victoriously. He turns back to Parks and takes her other hand.

"Addison Parks, will you go to homecoming with me?" Eli asks her in a voice loud enough that everyone can hear. He puffs his chest out, standing straight. A vast, confident smile takes root on his face, and it suddenly occurs to me that there's no doubt in his mind that she'll say yes.

I'm not sure why, but that bugs me. A lot.

I suddenly decide I don't want to watch this entire exchange anymore, and I turn to leave out of the cafeteria. I decide to eat somewhere else, not sure I can stomach the sight of Eli and Parks canoodling across the cafeteria while I try to eat a ham sandwich. Jordan and Caleb trail after me, snickering.

"You've kinda got a thing for her, don't ya, buddy?" Jordan nudges me with his elbow as we walk.

I glower at him and shove his shoulder away from me. "I don't know what you're talking about."

"I can't blame you. I mean, you two have always had this weird vibe going on. And she's gorgeous now. It only makes sense that you'd be interested."

Something about the way he says that rubs me the wrong way. As if I'd only be interested in her since she's hot now. I scowl even harder at him, my blood pressure rising.

"Well, I'm not, so drop it. I wouldn't touch her with a ten-foot pole," I sneer. "Pretty or not, she's still Hurricane Addison. Nothing will ever change that."

I can tell Jordan believes me just about as much as I believe myself, which is minimal, to say the least. A smirk takes over his features, and he looks at me with amusement. "Whatever you gotta tell yourself to sleep at night, brother."

"Shut the hell up, Jordan." He snickers as I turn and walk away from him, seething.

I do my best to stay out of everyone's way for the rest of the day. I limit my attendance to my classes; as soon as the bell rings, I'm gone. I skateboard to the park and make my way to the old wooden bridge.

Setting my book bag down on the fraying wood, I settle in and try my best to get comfortable.

This bridge in this little park is one of my favorite places in town. People are often too busy running errands in the town square to remember that it's here, which typically means it's vacant. I lean my head against one post, closing my eyes. I listen to the sound of the water trickling in the creek below. After a while, I hear footsteps on the wood, but I don't look to see who it is, guessing they'll just go on with their day.

I'm wrong, of course.

"Hi."

The sound of a feminine voice breaks through the silence. I look up from where I'm resting to find Addison Parks standing over me, a stack of books in one arm and a water bottle in the other. I narrow my eyes against the sun and shift a bit. "Parks, to what do I owe the pleasure?"

"I saw you sitting out here, and I was wondering if I could join you? Things are busy in the café, and I want to get some homework done."

"Careful, Parks. Someone might see you sitting with me and think we're friends or something," I say, but motion for her to sit next to me anyway, and she does without hesitation. I watch her warily. This is different.

She laughs. "That would be just terrible for you, wouldn't it?"

I grin at her, and she smiles back, one of those lovely smiles that makes her hazel eyes gleam. With the afternoon sun shining on her face, I can distinguish the golden streaks in her eyes. They flare out from her pupil and make her iris appear as if it is a thousand leagues deep. Parks feels my heavy gaze on her, and then she glances away quickly and opens up her book, thumbing to a page with a bookmark.

"What are you studying?" I ask her with a lazy voice.

"I have an exam coming up in my zoology-botany class," she murmurs.

"Nerd," I muffle with a cough, and she rolls her eyes at me but doesn't engage any further, quickly getting sucked into her reading.

I lean back again and close my eyes to relax, but I'm hyperaware of her sitting just a few feet from me. Finally, unable to take the silence any longer, I sit up straighter, my fingers finding a little twig on the bridge next to me, and muster the courage to say something to her.

"I saw Monty asked you to homecoming," I say, twisting the twig between my fingers.

Addison looks up at me from her textbook, an eyebrow raised. "He did."

"And you said yes?" I inquire, even though I already know the answer. I was right there, for God's sake.

"I did?" she says it like a question.

I lean back against the wooden frame of the bridge, closing my eyes and letting the sun hit my face. "That's good. Wouldn't want Monty to get his feelings hurt. You two make a good pair."

Parks is silent for a moment, and I hear a page turning. "He asked me to be his girlfriend, too."

I open my eyes and look at her, intrigued by her motive in telling me this tidbit of information. She's staring back at me, her cheeks pink, but her expression unsure, as if she wants me to reassure her she did the right thing. "Did you say yes to that, too?" She nods her head slowly. "Well, well, I'm happy for you, Parks."

She ties her fingers together on top of the book in her lap. "Yeah, I guess it's good. I'm not really sure... I'm not good at this kind of stuff, Noah. What if he wants something more—"

I narrow my eyes at her, not liking the direction our conversation is leaning. "More like...?"

"Just *more* than what I want to give. It's not really a secret about what's supposed to happen after homecoming, and I am not sure if I'm ready. I'm worried he might have asked me simply because of that, which is stupid. But it's just a thought lingering in my mind. I don't even know why I'm talking to you about this, of all people. I just," she pauses and takes a deep breath, looking at me hesitantly. "I'm not sure what to do and you always seem so confident with stuff like this, I mean you dated Rose for *forever*."

I sit up straight and hold her gaze steady. My blood thrums in my ears as I get more and more agitated at the thought of Monty trying to take it too far with her. "You tell him no. If he does something you don't want him to do, you tell him no, and you call someone—Sullivan or your dad or... me."

"Wouldn't that be weird?" she asks, her nose wrinkling. "If I called you for something like that? I didn't realize we were friends in that way. Or at all."

"It doesn't matter if we're friends or not. No girl should be put in a situation like that, and they need to have people they can call. I'd do the same for any other girl in our school," I tell her forcefully. "Don't go feeling like you're special or anything."

Her cheeks turn a light shade of pink, and she looks down at her book again, a smile playing on the corner of her lips. "Thanks, Noah."

I grumble something unintelligible under my breath and lean back again, closing my eyes. I listen to the sound of the creek underneath the bridge and the birds chirping in the trees. It's a perfect day outside. Fall in Willow Heights is always my favorite because of days like this.

As much as I try to fight it, I can feel her heavy gaze on me. I peek at her with one eye and frown. "Why are you staring at me like that?"

She blushes as if I just caught her doing something she wasn't supposed to be. She thinks about her response for a second, too long, before looking me in the eye. "You're just different from what I always thought you were."

I sigh, tossing my head back. "Yeah, yeah. Don't go getting any wild ideas. I can't have you tarnishing my reputation with rumors that I'm *nice* or something."

"You are nice. Underneath it all, I think you have a good heart."

"Don't mistake my being a decent human for something it's not, Parks. You know who I am. Who my father is."

"I don't think that has to mean what you think it means. You don't have to be that way."

"Is this turning into a nature versus nurture conversation? Because I hate to break it to you, but I've got a shitty deal on both accounts."

Parks squints her eyes at me as if she's trying to see something more clearly. "Don't sell yourself short, Noah. You've got a lot of life yet to live."

"Don't go getting all mushy on me now. We've barely been cordial with each other for two minutes. Should I be expecting a homecoming proposal from you next?" I tease her, and she laughs.

"Highly unlikely. I don't think you're my type," Parks replies and sticks her tongue out at me.

"Likewise," I say with a crinkle of my nose, but I can't help but notice the uncomfortable tightness that settles in my chest. I cough to clear it, but it doesn't work. It's still there, reminding me that I just lied through my teeth.

We fall into another slightly awkward, slightly comfortable silence. Parks continues with her homework, jotting a note down here and there. Meanwhile, I peel the bark off of the stick I found to pass the time. Finally, I can't take it anymore, and I push up into a standing position, making a show of stretching my back.

"Well, I better get home before the mayor finds out I'm late for dinner," I tell her. "Wouldn't want him to put me in jail or something."

"I think that's more Charlie's dad you'd have to worry about," she says, looking up at me.

"Good point. Well anyway, I'll see you around. And seriously, Parks, if something happens with Monty, you kick him in the nuts and go find someone you trust. Someone who can give him the real beat down."

Her cheeks blush, and she fights a smile. "I will, thanks, Noah."

I wave her off as if it's nothing and head home without another word on the matter, but truth be told, it bothers me incessantly for the next few weeks. I'm tempted to bring it up to her, tell her I don't think she should go to the dance if she's worried that he'll try something. I get a lot of opportunities. For some reason, she's taken to joining me at the bridge almost every afternoon. We don't always talk much, but it's nice just sitting with her.

But at the end of the day, I just leave it. I'm not her keeper. It's not my responsibility to protect her against Monty getting too handsy—even if the thought of it makes me want to throw up.

Parks is old enough to handle her own, And besides, from my limited knowledge of her, she's not the type to want a knight in shining armor, anyway. If I had to pick a type for her, it would be someone who would challenge her and make her question her very existence. Parks is bookish—academic—not so much the roses and rainbows type.

Hopefully, Eli Montgomery is wise enough to realize that because I sure as hell won't be telling him. I don't know what she even sees in him, anyway. He's too clingy and pathetic. Definitely not someone I would pair her with. Not for a thousand years.

And yet the Monday after homecoming, I see them walking together hand-in-hand. Parks looks happy with that post-dance glow, so I can't be too upset. I think back to our conversation a few weeks ago and wonder what happened with that. Did she end up giving it up to Monty? The thought makes my blood burn and bile rise in my throat. Not that it's any of my business, but the idea of her and Monty in the sack makes me want to barf. She deserves someone way better than him.

Someone like you?

I shake my head and turn back to my locker. Not me. Never me. Not after the way I treated her all those years.

Still, as the days move on, I can't help but paying attention to all the little things about her. I notice how she twirls one of the front pieces of her hair around one finger while listening to a lecture. I pick up on the scrunch of her nose when trying to solve a difficult math problem, her tongue darting out in concentration.

I even notice days later when Eli leans over to say something to her and she tosses her head back with a laugh. Her hazel eyes light up with mirth, and she smiles from ear to ear. My heart constricts, but I quickly dampen whatever feelings I'm deluding myself into having.

Parks is way out of my league, and I'd be stupid for ever thinking otherwise.

Chapter 24

Addison

Addison - Age 16

"You're in my spot," a deep voice says above me.

I remove my head from my hands and look up. An exhale escapes through my nose when I realize it's Noah. Of *course*, it's Noah at this moment. After looking at him, I put my head back in my hands.

The sound of something thumping on the floor echoes through the hallways. And then Noah's presence is next to me as he slides down against the wall. The smell of his body wash floods my senses, and I take a deep breath, appreciating the now familiar smell. I don't look up at him, but I know we're mirroring last fall when I found him in this same hallway after his father won the election. I guess that's why he said I'm in his spot.

And now he's in mine.

"What's wrong?" he asks, his voice low.

I wait a minute before answering. Before I do, I wonder if I'm making a horrible decision to confide in Noah. "Eli and I broke up today," I tell him, taking my time before looking up so I can gauge his reaction.

Noah keeps his face impassive, but I notice the slight twitch of his eyebrow attempting to furrow. "What did he do to you? Do you want me to go punch him in the throat?"

"He did nothing, so no. Don't get too excited to beat him up."

Noah turns his head away from me and leans it against the lockers. "So what happened?"

I shrug a shoulder and look at the wall. "It just wasn't working."

A beat passes. "Are you sad?"

"Maybe? I'm not sure. It was kind of my idea. Being together like that was too different. I missed the version of Eli that was my friend. He didn't seem like the idea was out of the blue, though, so I think he was feeling the same way." I think about it a bit more. "I guess I am a little sad, but maybe just more sad that it wasn't what I thought it would be."

Noah shifts next to me, trying to get comfortable, and then questions, "He didn't—he didn't pressure you into something, did he?" I don't answer, and Noah shifts again. "Don't answer that. I shouldn't have even asked. It's not my business," he mutters with a sullen tone.

"He didn't," I offer with a whisper, watching Noah out of the corner of my eye. "I set the boundary, and he didn't push it."

I leave it at that, not bothering to fill in the rest of the blanks. Somehow, I feel like Noah knows I'm not telling the whole truth, but he doesn't press further. He gives a brisk nod and says, "Good." Then leaves the topic be.

Like the last time we were in this hallway together, Noah lets the silence fall over us like a blanket. It doesn't feel awkward this time, though.

"How's everything with you?" I ask.

Noah shrugs next to me. "Same old shit, different day."

"Is your dad still giving you trouble?"

"Always," he grumbles, then turns to look at me. His eyes then travel to my hands resting in my lap. He holds out his hand, asking me a question without his voice. I place my hand on his large one, and he laces our fingers together.

Again, I'm hit with the sense of déjà vu as I think of the last time we sat in this hallway together. Holding hands.

"You know what they say. What goes around comes around. And I can't wait for the day when he finally gets what's coming to him. I hope I'm there to see it," Noah says, his attention now on our entwined hands.

"Just promise me you won't let your hatred for him ruin your life," I say to Noah, barely above a whisper. "You have such potential, Noah. I'd hate to see him take that from you."

His eyes flash up to mine, and he studies my face. There's something hidden behind that blue gaze I can't place, but it intrigues me. "I'll try not to if you promise me you won't let this breakup with Eli Montgomery hold you back."

My lips twitch, and I give his hand a squeeze. "I promise."

Noah squeezes my hand back. "Great, it's a deal then."

The next few weeks fly by. I do what I promised and do my best to focus on getting my life as back to normal as I can. Grace and I wander into the library during the study hall hour and claim a table to work at. I reach for my laptop and set up a makeshift workstation so I can attempt to knock out some of my outstanding assignments. Grace settles into the chair across from me and starts playing on her phone.

We've only been sitting for a few minutes when Eli and Monica St. Cloud walk in holding hands. They find a couch nearby and sit close together. I watch them out of the corner of my eye. Eli leans close to Monica and tucks a piece of hair behind her ear. I'm not surprised when I don't feel any jealousy or anything else. My lips press together in a thin line, and I shake my head to clear it and focus on the assignment I'm working on. Over the last month, Eli and I have fallen back into our general routine. He's back to being my best friend, and honestly, I'm happy with that.

"Ugh, I literally can't believe him," Grace sneers over at Eli and his new girlfriend. I roll my eyes and hit the backspace on my laptop. I've got to finish this essay before tomorrow, so I don't have time for distractions. "It's barely even been a month since you two split up, and he's already trying to hook up with *her*? You're way prettier than her, anyway."

"It's fine, Grace," I tell my friend, not interested in this conversation. "We broke up mutually. I'm not really upset that he's found someone else."

"Well, I am," Grace huffs, crossing her arms over her chest. "He could at least give you the courtesy to not date anyone for the rest of the year."

"The year?" I ask her incredulously, even though the school year is only a few weeks from being over. It's April now, and school lets out in mid-May. "That's a little extreme. Especially since I really don't care. I told him I thought we weren't working as a couple right now, and he agreed. That's all there is to it. Neither of us was feeling the relationship."

"I know, but still."

I shake my head at my friend and peek toward where Eli is sitting again. He's leaning even closer to Monica now, his heart on his sleeve as beams at her. He seems happy, and honestly, that's all I care about.

It's not that I'm *not* still interested in him in that way. I could still see myself dating Eli again at some point. He was a decent boyfriend —or at least I think he was. He's my best friend, so he knows me on a level that other guys might not. But also, in some ways, I felt like he didn't know me at all.

Eli didn't pressure me into anything. He respected my limits, but he wasn't happy about them. Eli and I did some handsy stuff, just testing the waters and experimenting. However, I still felt unsure about it, and I wasn't comfortable taking things further with him. That's also why I'm not too upset about being single once more.

If I'm single, I don't have to worry about falling short of meeting expectations.

"Ugh, I can't sit here any longer and watch this. I don't know how you can stomach it," Grace mutters, bringing me back to the present. "Come find me whenever you're done with your paper."

She grabs her water bottle and leaves me sitting there alone. I'm not too sad to see her go because I still need to finish this essay. I narrow my eyes and try to find that deep level of focus, so I can power through my assignment.

"Careful, Parks. If you frown for long, your face will get stuck in that position."

I groan at the interruption. My eyes flick up to see Noah standing before me with his arms crossed over his chest. I lean away from my computer and stare up at him. "I don't think that's true."

He leans towards me and grins devilishly. "Would you like to test the theory? I'll leave you to it to frown at your computer all you want —for research."

I roll my eyes. "What do you want, Noah?"

"I was just overhearing Grace's frustration at your lover boy across the room there. That really doesn't bother you?"

I groan in frustration and toss my head back. "No, why is everyone so concerned with how I'm coping with Eli having a new girlfriend? We agreed to break up *mutually*. You know this. Grace knows this. Everyone knows this. Do I need to shout it off a mountain? I really don't care who he wants to kiss now."

"Monty's an idiot."

"What did he do now?" I ask, feeling exasperated.

Noah smirks at me again and shuffles around until he's sitting next to me. His shoulder presses against mine, and I raise my eyebrow at him, wondering if he notices the contact. He doesn't move away from me but continues, "Oh, it's mostly just because of his mere existence. But no, if he thinks Monica will ever live up to you? The poor guy really is an idiot."

"It's fine, Noah. Why does it feel like no one is listening to me when I keep saying that repeatedly?"

Noah leans back in his chair in a relaxed manner. "Because it sounds like a little mosquito buzzing in my ear when you talk."

"Thanks for that."

"I live to please, Parks."

"Will you please leave me alone now? I really need to finish this assignment."

"Sure, sure. I'll see you later. Go be a perfect student, get those straight A's."

I stick my tongue at him as he walks away, both of us aware that Noah gets just as good of grades as I do. Noah extends his hand and slaps Eli upside the head as he walks past him. Eli makes a strangled noise of protest and swings around to glare at Noah. In response, Noah just flips him the middle finger and struts away.

Eli looks over at me like I'm supposed to do something about it, and I bend my head to let a curtain of hair cover my face to obscure the amused grin on my lips. I'll give it to Noah; as much as he can press my buttons sometimes, he has an incredible skill of amusing me.

The same thing happens later when I run into him right before lunch. He's with his friends, but they scatter when they see me. They each give Noah a cheesy look and then walk into the cafeteria.

"Hey," I say. "Why did you hit Eli on the head earlier?"

Noah grips the straps of his backpack and shrugs his shoulders. "He probably deserved it."

"You need to be nicer to him," I tell him.

He just gives me a wry grin. "Why?"

"Because he's my friend."

"And? I'm your friend too, aren't I?"

I think back to all the moments Noah and I have had together over the last year, ever since we've called our truce, and I reluctantly agree. "I suppose so."

"So? I get a free pass then."

"How does that work?"

"You extend Monty and Sully an unlimited number of free passes every day, but you can't give me one just this once?" he teases me, his bright blue eyes sparkling.

"I think you probably get more free passes than you think. You're always up to something you shouldn't be."

He shrugs his shoulders again. "Maybe so. It's part of my charm."

Am I going crazy, or is Noah *flirting* with me? That can't be right, so I shake my head and squash that notion. "Is that what they're calling being a pain in the ass these days?"

"Absolutely." He winks at me, and then his lips pull into a smirk as he says, "I'll catch you later, Parks."

Despite my best efforts, I feel the corners of my mouth twitch with a smile at him. He makes it a few paces away before stopping and turning back to me. "You gonna be at the bridge later today?" he asks, a strain of hope lingering in his tone.

"Oh." Surprise courses through me. "I'm not sure. I'll need to check-in at the café first to ensure they don't need help, but I might be."

He watches me for a moment and then dips his chin. "Well, maybe I'll see you there, then."

"Maybe," I respond, a smile forming on my lips. Noah raises a hand in a wave, then leaves for class.

I'm still smiling when I walk over to the table my friends are sitting at. They all look at me as if I'm from outer space when I approach.

"What?" I ask. "Is there something on my shirt?" My eyes rove over my clothing but I don't notice any stain.

"What's up with you and Noah?" Charlie gets the gall to ask. Eli frowns at his food, but I notice a familiar vein in his neck twitch.

"Nothing," I respond too quickly. "What do you mean?"

"It's just you two have been almost... cordial with each other. You all always used to be at each other's throats. Now you can exist together in the same room without casualties," Charlie replies. "It's kind of crazy."

I shrug. "I don't know. We've just had a change of heart, I guess. He's not actually that bad."

Now Eli laughs out loud. "That's where you're wrong. He's probably got you right where he wants you. Luring you in, pretending to be a good person until the perfect moment when he'll strike. If I were you, I'd stay far, far away from him."

"Good thing she's not you then," Grace adds, coming to defend me. "If Addison wants to talk to Noah, I don't see the big problem."

"Of course, you wouldn't," Eli growls back. "You've been trying to get them to hook up ever since you got here."

Now, Grace glowers at Eli. "Can you blame me? They'd be like a supernova together."

"I wish you would stop with that. Noah's not interested in me like that."

"Good," Eli scowls, and I glare back at him. "What? I don't mean anything by it. I think you could do better than that scumbag. He's such a freaking jerk. I can't understand how anyone would want to be friends with him."

Eli's words unsettle me, and I spear a piece of pasta with my fork. I don't bother telling him I consider Noah one of my friends now. Heaven forbid I do that, and he turns on me too. Not to mention the fact that Eli and I are not together anymore. He shouldn't have any say in who I date. Or who I don't date, for that matter. I certainly have said nothing to him about who he's making out with in between classes.

I somehow manage to keep my cool for the rest of the day after the intervention at lunch. My friends continue to make brief comments here and there about me hanging out with Noah, 'the enemy,' but I don't let it phase me. Grace is all aboard the Noah/Addison train, but Charlie and Eli both greatly oppose the notion.

I stick to my guns, saying the idea is ridiculous, and leave it at that.

After a day like today, relief courses through my muscles when the last bell rings, releasing us for the afternoon. I pack up my things and say a quick goodbye to my friends before leaving campus and going directly to my parents' café.

"Hey, Dad!" I call out when I enter the café through the back.

"Hey, Sweet Pea!" he answers back. "I'm in the front."

I wander from the back storeroom to the front counter where my dad is restocking the coffee cups and lids. A grin lights up his face when he sees me and sets everything down to wrap me in a hug. My arms tighten around his waist, and I breathe him in—he smells like coffee and caramel, the perfect blend.

"How was school?" he asks, letting me go to resume his task.

I hop up onto the counter and watch him. "It was fine, just another school day. I only have a little homework to do tonight."

My dad looks up at me and smiles again. His eyes crinkle at the corners, proof of a life full of laughter. "Well, you better get to it then, chop-chop!"

I laugh at him and then get down off the counter, grabbing my backpack and walking over to one table near the counter so I can still be close if he needs my help.

The café is quiet today. There aren't any customers, which makes it the perfect time to knock out the rest of my assignments. I settle into my seat and get to work. Almost thirty minutes pass without interruption, but it's short-lived.

"Addison, maybe you should go in the back," my dad's deep voice pulls me from the chapter I'm reading. I look up at him and find his attention on something out the window. Following his gaze, I notice the powerful figure of the mayor walking towards our café. Before I can rebut my father's request, he orders, "Now."

I gather up my homework and run behind the counter towards the back room. Confusion takes over because I've had my fair share of interactions with the mayor before. I don't know why today is so different that I can't be around. I set my stuff on the counter in the back and then tiptoe towards the doorframe so I can peek around and hear the conversation.

The bell above the door jingles, and I hear heavy footsteps on the wooden floor. "Mr. Mayor," my father's voice greets. "What can I get for you today?"

"Pretty quiet in here, Parks. I would have expected more of a crowd," the mayor responds with a snide undertone, noting the lack of customers in the café. "How is business going?"

"Just fine, sir. Is there anything I can get started for you?" my dad asks again.

I peer around the door frame and see the mayor standing in front of the counter, his hands folded behind his back as he peruses the menu. "I'm actually here to speak with you. It appears I couldn't have timed it any better as this is somewhat of a private matter."

I look at my dad, and he stiffens. "A private matter?"

The mayor reaches for a business card from the register and runs his finger over the edge. "I've heard from a little birdie that you're not the humble café owner you claim to be. I say we cut all the pleasantries and get to the point, Agent."

"Those records are private," my father growls at the mayor.

"Well, when you're a man of my level of influence, red tape is a mere nuisance more than anything. You'll understand when I say that I have men in *very high places*, Mr. Parks."

My dad responds, but I can't hear him over the blood pounding in my ears. My fight-or-flight response kicks in, and I choose to fly. I sprint towards the back door, passing through it into the alley behind the café. My feet pound against the cement as I run around the building toward the park. In the back of my mind, I remember my conversation with Noah from earlier and recall that he said he'd be at the bridge this afternoon. As I get closer, I can see his posse of three sitting on their bridge like they do almost every day and a slight sense of relief floods me. I barely register that this might be the first time I've ever felt grateful that Noah's right in front of me.

Noah sees me running towards them and stands up right away, Jordan and Caleb following his lead. I recognize the concern written across his face. "Noah!" I gasp as I close the distance between us. His arms outstretch on instinct, and he clasps his hands on my shoulders when I stop in front of him.

His alarmed eyes scan my body, checking for any injury. "What's wrong? What's happened?"

"Your father—" I gasp and bend over, trying to catch my breath from running so fast. I'm so out of shape.

Noah's hands tighten on my arms, and a thunderous expression crosses his face. "What did he do?"

"He's talking to my dad. He knows—"

"Knows what Parks?"

"FBI. He knows my dad's from the FBI," I manage to choke out.

Noah releases me, and I look up at him. Surprise colors his face as he looks at me for a moment. Then he gets himself under control and nods his head before striding away from me. "I'll be right back. Jordan?"

"Yeah, man, I got her," Jordan answers and takes my arm, wrapping it around his shoulders to hold me up. I sag against him as I watch Noah walk towards the café.

His shoulders are tight as he marches into the café as if he's on a mission. I lean against Jordan, staring at the door to the café like a hawk until I see him exit again, his father next to him.

The mayor turns to his son with a deep frown on his face, saying something to him that has Noah standing up straighter and crossing his arms over his chest. Noah replies to his father, but whatever he says has the mayor laughing in a way that makes me want to punch him in the throat. Declan continues to laugh as he turns around and heads for his shiny black SUV parked right in front of the café. Noah stands there a minute longer and then turns on his heel and stalks back to the park where we're waiting for him.

"I've got her, now, Jordan. You can go." Noah says when he gets close enough, his arm snaking around my waist. His strong muscles contract around me, taking some of my weight. Fireworks erupt in my belly, sending a flat of warmth throughout my whole body. When did Noah's arm get so strong? My body trembles in the aftermath of the adrenaline rush, but the presence of his arm against me makes me feel surrounded and safe.

He leads me over to a bench in the middle of the park. I fall into the seat, my legs unable to hold my weight up for longer than a second. Then he crouches in front of me, taking my hands in his and giving them a tight squeeze. I feel numb as my brain tries to make sense of everything that just transpired.

"You in there?" he asks carefully.

It takes a minute or two, but I muster up the strength to nod my head. "What did you say to your dad?"

"I just told him that someone needed him down at the courthouse, then we were out front. He was scolding me for interrupting business."

"Then what? You looked angry at him."

Noah's dark eyebrows pull together. "I was. He made you feel unsafe. I don't like that. Not at all. He's the mayor, he has a responsibility to this town, and he's not withholding his end of the deal."

"Thank you for going in there. He can't know about my dad. He —" I cut myself off and press my lips together.

Noah studies my face and then nods his head as if silently agreeing to not talk about it, despite me not asking him.

"You scared me, Parks," he whispers. "When you came running towards us like that, I was terrified that something had happened to you."

"I'm sorry. You were the first person I saw after I panicked. Somehow I knew you would know what to do."

"I'm glad I was here, then," he says before standing straight up. He's still holding my hands, so he brings me with him until we stand close together. "As it so happens, I tend to be pretty decent at derailing my father from his intended goals. It's something he never lets me forget."

His voice sounds bitter, likely from thinking about his strained relationship with his father. I know there's nothing Noah would like more than to be completely free of him, and I wish there was something I could do to help him achieve that. But as it is, we can't choose our family, no matter how much we sometimes wish we could.

One of his hands lets go of mine, and he raises it to my forehead, brushing a strand of hair out of my eyes. He tenderly tucks it behind my ear, and my breath hitches. His blue eyes study my face as his hand drops from my ear to the side of my neck. The skin of his hand is warm against mine, and I shiver.

"Noah?" I ask, unsure of what's about to happen.

"Just... hold still," he breathes, leaning his forehead closer to rest against mine. He observes me. Languidly, he tilts his jaw forward until our lips are touching. Shock courses through my body at the feel of our mouths fusing together.

As his lips touch mine, I instantly register that this differs from anything I've experienced before. The world stops spinning. As if I've just been living half-awake, my world sharpening into total clarity, like a sunrise barely cresting the horizon. It's as if I'm just now coming to my full senses. My world explodes into a vast, vivid color—everything brighter and more pronounced. For the first time in ages, I feel like I'm exactly where I'm supposed to be.

Noah must feel similarly because his hands wrap around my waist and pull me tighter against him as if he's trying to eliminate any distance between us, trying to get more of whatever this is. I arch my back, pressing my front closer to him, and he groans into my mouth. I gasp his name in pleasure, never wanting this moment to end.

And then, as quickly as it happens, it's over. He pulls away and lingers for a second, eyes closed, not moving before his eyes snap open, and he looks at me in alarm. It's like a bucket of cold water has splashed over his head. I watch his eyes change from a glazed expression to perfect lucency within seconds.

"Noah," I mumble his name again as he puts distance between us. His eyes are wide, and it's like he can't believe what he just did. He staggers a few steps away from me, and my fingers come up to my tingling lips, feeling where his lips were just a moment ago. Noah runs his hands through his hair, his fingers gripping the strands as a frantic look crosses his features.

"Parks, I'm sorry. I shouldn't have done that. I—"

"It's okay," I say, stepping towards him, longing coursing through my body. I want more of that, more of him. At my approach, Noah staggers back again, putting space between us.

"Give me a minute," he says breathlessly, holding up his hand to stop me from coming any closer to him.

"Noah," I repeat his name, begging him to look at me. When he finally does, I catch my breath in my throat. Somehow, his eyes are brighter than I've ever seen them before.

"I should go," he mutters. "I—I'm sorry."

With that last word, Noah turns from me and leaves. I watch him walk away from me with his head bowed and his hands stuck in his pockets. My arms cross over my midsection, and I press my lips together, still tingling from the feel of his kiss. When I can't see Noah anymore, I go back home, my mind spinning in circles.

The kiss troubles me for the rest of the night. It's all I can think about. Noah basically ran away from me after it happened. What if he's regretting it all? My relationship with Noah is better than ever, but still. What if he still sees me as his enemy? Someone who he can't trust.

Was this all just part of his game? Part of a ploy to get me to open up to him so he can strike me where it will hurt the most?

Even as I think these thoughts, I know they're not true. I recall how things have changed for us over the last year. Is now really the best time to be changing the dynamic again after how far we've come? Probably not.

With these thoughts plaguing my mind, I get in the shower and let the warm water run over my coiled muscles. When I get out, I braid my hair into pleats and fasten them with a tie before falling into bed. I do my best to clear my mind to get some sleep, but I know it's no use. Every time I close my eyes, Noah's face pops up in my mind. I toss and turn violently in bed, trying to get comfortable and clear my mind. However, even in the dead of night, I'm still wide awake, seeing his face flash repeatedly.

When I get up in the morning, I notice my eyes are bloodshot. Bright red stripes fill the whites of my eyes, exposing the restless night I had. I groan at my reflection in the mirror but decide there's nothing I can do about it now. I find my clothes for the day and do my best to cover the dark circles under my eyes with concealer and foundation. Hopefully, I can just get to school, and things will go as smoothly as they usually do.

I stop at the café to grab breakfast and coffee on my way to school. I'm sitting at a table by the window, eating my muffin and sipping on my coffee. Something outside catches my attention, and I look out the window. Across the street, I spy Noah pacing back and forth on the sidewalk. His hands are in his pockets, and his head is bowed as if he's deep in thought about something. My eyebrows raise when he stops and looks over at the café. He looks like he's trying to decide whether to cross the street or not.

Disappointment courses through my body when he shakes his head and then turns away. I watch him walk down the sidewalk away from the café until he disappears around the corner. The pieces fall into place that I'm not the only one fretting about what happened in the park yesterday. I wonder if he was planning on coming into the café this morning to talk to me about it.

Apprehension settles in, and it occurs to me that maybe he wanted to catch me before school to tell me he didn't want me to bring it up. Perhaps Noah regrets what happened yesterday and is worried that I'll go around and tell everyone what happened. I know we're in a better place now, but what if he's still concerned that I'll ruin his reputation?

I try my best not to let thoughts of Noah distract me during my first class, but again, it's pointless. He's all I can think about. My mind keeps replaying how his eyes looked as he leaned down to press his lips against mine and how his lips tasted against mine.

A whole-body shiver passes down my spine, and I glance around to see if anyone else in my class has noticed. Thankfully, no one did.

At this moment, I decide I need to find Noah and talk to him about what happened yesterday. There's no way I can go on with my day until I address this with him. It's going to drive me crazy otherwise. I tap my pencil eraser against the desk and glance at the clock. I need to get out of this classroom.

After the third hour, I see Noah walking with his friends down the hallway at school. He catches my eye for a brief moment. Again, his eyes dart away, redirecting his attention to Caleb, who's saying something to him. The sinking pit in my stomach grows.

"Hey, I have something to do before class," I tell Charlie and Eli, walking along with me. "I'll see you in there, okay?"

I don't give them time to respond as I chase after Noah, waiting until he's just a few feet from me to say his name. He stops and turns towards me. Jordan and Caleb stop a few paces ahead of him, turning back to see the commotion.

Noah's eyes scour my face, and he raises an eyebrow. "Can I help you, Parks?"

"I need to talk to you."

He rubs the back of his neck as if he's nervous about talking to me. "Class is starting soon. Don't you think this can wait?"

I purse my lips, wrapping my arms tighter around the books I'm holding. "No, I don't think so."

Noah studies me a moment before turning back to his friends and letting them know he'll be along in a moment. They head to class, and so does most of the student body as the bell rings, indicating the fourth hour. Within a minute, Noah and I are alone in the hallways.

He crosses his arms over his chest, looking at me expectantly. I shuffle my feet and then look him in his eyes. "I wanted to talk about what happened yesterday," I say. "I let it slip about my dad, and I'm sure I don't have to tell you why it's important that no one finds out."

Surprise crosses Noah's features, and he blinks at me. "That's what you wanted to talk about?"

"Yes," I reply, my cheeks heating.

Noah steps closer to me until we're close. As if they are a shield, I grip my books tighter to my chest. I know Noah wouldn't hurt me—at least not anymore—but after what happened last night, I feel like I'm walking through a maze blindfolded.

"So you don't want to talk about the other thing?"

"What other thing?" I ask, hoping I come across as unbothered, though inside I feel the complete opposite. My lips are still burning from last night's kiss, but I'm not ready to bring it up. "I figured you'd just want to pretend it never happened."

"But it did happen."

"Yes."

"So now what do we do about it?" he asks, his voice low. He studies me with scrutinous eyes as if he can see right through me. A glimmer of hope lingers behind his cautious gaze, and my chest tightens.

My mouth feels dry as I ponder my words. "Noah, we've just become friends. I don't think pushing the boundaries of that right now is a good idea."

"I see," he responds, his shoulders stiffening. "Is it because of Monty? I thought you two lovebirds were broken up."

"We are. That's not it. I just think that—" I sigh. "Not that we *can't* ever, but not right now. I like how things are between us right now."

"You just want to keep me in your collection of boy toys," he deadpans. "I understand. You want me to be there at your beck and call and leave you alone when you're done with me?"

"No, that's not it," I argue defensively, startled by the low blow. My heartbeat is thrumming in my ears. I know I'm making a mess of this, and I'm not sure how to fix things. "I just don't want to go in a new direction and lose our chance at a good friendship."

"A good friendship," he repeats, punctuating his words with a scoff.

I shuffle my feet. "It's just... I don't know. I trust you. More than I should, given our history. And I don't want to risk ruining that because I'm sure I will. Please, just... can we forget about it?"

"Sure, Parks. Whatever you say." He takes a deep breath and looks off, his eyes glazed over. "I gotta go. I'll talk to you later, yeah?"

His closed-off tone differs significantly from how he was just minutes ago, and I flinch away from his brush-off.

He doesn't give me the chance to respond before turning and walking away from me, his shoulder bumping into mine as he brushes past. I purse my lips as I stand there by myself. Even though he agreed to what I asked of him, I still feel unsettled. In fact, I feel even more restless than I did before I talked to him. I have more questions without answers than I did this morning.

I figured talking to him and being honest would be an easy fix to my dilemma. Still, I'm realizing that nothing regarding Noah is ever easy.

Chapter 25

Noah

Noah - Age 17

"Quit it, Noah. I keep messing up my math problems with you smiling at me like that," Parks protests, glancing at me before darting her eyes back down towards her homework. The frustration is evident on her face, spurring me to bother her even more. I lean against the counter towards her and give her a cheeky grin.

"Like what?"

A blush covers her cheekbones, and I find myself smiling even harder. "Nothing, it's stupid."

I lean even closer until we are face to face. Finally, Addison looks up at me fully, and a breath escapes her lips at my proximity. "Parks," I say, drawing out her name.

"Like you think I'm pretty or something," she murmurs, nervously tucking a strand of hair behind her ear.

I back off for just a second, my eyebrows raising in surprise. That wasn't what I was expecting her to say. It's unusual for me to see Parks embarrassed about something, but at this moment, she definitely is. I realize that she's not just uncomfortable but *unsure*, which is not something she's used to.

"I do think you're pretty," I tell her the truth, and her shoulders relax. "I think you're beautiful."

Her eyes find mine, and I notice a twinkle that wasn't there before. "You do?"

"Of course," I say, thinking it's probably the most genuine thing I've ever said to her.

Parks has quickly become one of my favorite people. That fact is such a night-and-day difference from a few years ago that I try not to think about it too hard. My mulling over how things have changed usually results in me developing a migraine. Still, those thoughts sneak up on me every so often, and I'm often overwhelmed with how much I realize I like her.

Addison's eyes flare, and she studies my face before shaking her head and looking down at her homework. "Don't just say that because you feel like you have to. I know what happened after the thing with the café, and your dad was just a one-off. And the kiss and everything was...well, it was good. Better than good, really. But we agreed that we shouldn't press the limits, and I think we need to stick to that."

I back off again, smirking. She's the one who brought it up, but I'll humor her. "Okay."

"Look, Noah, I get it," Parks huffs, setting down her pencil and staring at me. "This isn't easy for me either. I've never... at least not like this. But you matter to me. A lot."

"You've never what?" I prompt her, curious as to what she was going to say.

Parks presses her lips together in a thin line and looks at me, unsure. "I've never felt this way about someone. Not Eli, not anyone. Just you. And I'm scared because I like what we have, and I don't want my stupid feelings to ruin anything."

My heart shudders, and there's nothing more I want to do now than to wrap her in my arms, hold her tightly to me, and never let her go.

Unfortunately, that doesn't happen. Instead, the bell rings, indicating that our free hour is over. Before I get the chance to say anything else to her, Addison is packing her things and hurrying out the door. She won't look at me on her way out, and I can see another rosy blush covering her face.

I stare after her and take a deep breath. Her words brought something to life inside of me that I didn't know was dormant. This thing with Parks and me has been growing and evolving over the last few years. I know that the more time I spend with her, the more disappointed I become when I can't be with her.

I understand that things are tricky for Addison when it comes to me because of her friendship with Sullivan and Monty. They've been my sworn enemies for as long as I can remember. It will inevitably put her in a weird position if things heat up between us. Even though Parks and I have made up, I'm far from being buddies with the other two.

I let the moment in the lab marinate in my thoughts for the next few hours. She ran out before we really got the chance to talk about what she meant, and I'm dying to know her true motives for dropping a bomb like that and running away from me.

After school lets out for the day, I linger around, letting Jordan and Caleb know I'll catch up to them at some point later at the gym. When they're gone, I meander out to the front lobby, where I know Grace and Parks are trying to get sign-ups for their nerd competition in the next few weeks.

And sure enough, I see them sitting together when I turn the corner. Of course, Parks is working on homework, and Grace seems to be organizing and re-organizing their display table. It doesn't seem like they've gotten much traffic as there's still a whole stack of flyers and sign-up sheets lying in front of the pair. Grace looks up and nudges Addison when she sees me walking toward them. Addison glances up to see what Grace was referencing, but she quickly averts her eyes when she realizes it's me.

"Oh, look, he's coming over here," I hear Grace say to Addison, humor lacing her tone as she shuffles and stacks the piles of papers in front of her.

My heart rate picks up as I get closer. I notice that Parks doesn't grant me the privilege of looking up again. Even when I'm standing right in front of their table, she doesn't pull her attention away from what she's doing.

"Ladies," my deep voice falls over the table.

"Oh, *hi, Noah*," Grace says, pretending to be surprised that I'm standing at their table. "Are you interested in joining the decathlon team?"

"Uh," I hesitate for a moment. "That will be a no. I was wondering if I could borrow Parks here for a moment."

Finally, Parks looks up at me, and my stomach flips. She watches me guardedly with her hazel eyes, the flares standing out prominently under the fluorescent light of the lobby. Her hair is pulled into a side braid, but a few strands stray from their position, giving it a slightly messy look. I stick my hands in my pockets and clench my fists together, nerves starting to set in.

"I'm actually a little busy right now, so maybe—" she says but is cut off by Grace.

"She's not busy. No one in their right mind would join the decathlon team," her friend says. "She'll go with you."

Addison shoots Grace an exasperated look, and I can see the betrayal on her face. But despite it all, she gives a resigned sigh and stands, brushing invisible dirt off of her jeans. She crosses her arms over her chest, the movement pushing her breasts up and together, a detail accentuated by the gray v-neck shirt she's wearing today. My mouth goes dry, and I dart my eyes away from her chest to her face, meeting her blank stare. "What do you want?"

I tilt my head away from the table and toward the hallway. "Take a walk with me?"

"Is there another option?"

"Nope," I deadpan. "This is all I've got right now."

Parks rolls her eyes up to the ceiling but turns back to Grace, who is watching us with pure unadulterated amusement. "I'll be back in five minutes."

Grace waves her hand. "No rush, take your time. And I mean, *take* your *time*." Her voice is laced with innuendos, and Addison picks up on it, her cheeks turning a fiery red and worries at a hangnail on her thumb.

I catch her eyes and motion down the hallway. Parks begrudgingly follows me. When I'm finally satisfied that we're far enough away from Grace's attentive ears, I turn to Parks and ask the question that's been bothering me all day.

"What was that?"

"What?"

"Earlier, in the lab. What you said."

Parks quickly looks down at the ground, hiding her face from me as if she's embarrassed. "Nothing, I don't—I didn't mean it."

I don't respond immediately, trying to think of the best way to proceed without spooking her. I feel like I'm walking on eggshells with this whole situation. I don't want to say the wrong thing and ruin whatever chance is brewing underneath the surface.

Finally, I say, "Well, that's a shame."

Parks pulls her attention away from the tile floor and back to me. Her warm hazel gaze traces my face, searching carefully for context clues. "What?" she asks breathlessly.

I step closer to her, closing the distance between us until we're facing each other. "That you didn't mean it cause I absolutely mean what I'm about to say."

"Noah," she protests weakly, apparently not liking the husky tone my voice is taking on or my proximity. She raises a hand and presses it against my chest, stopping me from getting closer to her. I look down. Seeing her dainty hand on my chest is doing weird things to my heart, and I want to cover her hand with mine and never let it go. "Please don't. I like things how they are right now."

"But what if things could be better?" I challenge her.

"Please."

"Parks," I press on. "Just give it a chance. Give *me* a chance."

"Look, Noah, I'm sorry if I gave you the wrong impression, but I can't," she pleads with me. "I can't. Not right now."

My shoulders drop with a heavy exhale. Cutting my losses, I realize that she's not at all ready for what I want to say to her. Honestly, I want to lay it all out and put everything to rest right here and now. I want to tell her how I'm really feeling and what her slip-up in the lab meant to me. But she's not ready.

So I take a different approach, improvising on the spot with something I manage to come up with right then. The plan formulates in my head, and I go for it before I can talk myself out of it.

"Are you doing anything tomorrow?" I ask her.

She blinks at the abrupt change in subject and stares at me as if I've grown two heads for a moment, but she shakes her head. "No, I'm not."

"You don't have plans with Monty?"

Parks gives me an exasperated look as if she can't believe I'm asking that right now, given the subject matter of our last conversation. "No."

"Good. You know what tomorrow is?"

Addison looks wholly unamused. "Of course. Tomorrow is your birthday."

"And I'm going to cash in on my birthday present. I'll swing by to pick you up tomorrow at six-fifteen. Don't worry, I'll bring coffee, but you might want to dress warmly."

Finally, I have her full attention. Her hazel eyes peer at me, intrigue playing behind those golden flares. "Six-fifteen? On a Saturday morning?"

"Yep," I say, popping the end of the word. "You in or no, Parks?"

She narrows her eyes and thinks about it for a moment before giving in. "Sure, why not. I'm in."

I grin at her and dip my chin. "I'll see you tomorrow then."

We say our goodbyes after I walk her back to her table. Grace watches us with suspicious eyes, and I'm sure she will grill Addison about our conversation. I leave to hit the gym and spend the rest of the evening planning everything I will need for tomorrow morning.

When I get home, thankfully, the house is empty. My parents must be at a meeting or out to dinner. Even though I'm alone, I tread with caution as I go upstairs and head straight for the third door on the left—my father's office. I'm not usually allowed in here when my father is home, so I can only imagine the shit I'd be in if he found me snooping around while he was gone. I decide to make this quick and shuffle in, closing the door behind me.

I make my way over to the massive oak executive desk. The workspace is cluttered with an assortment of paperwork and scribbled notes. It's as if he was in the middle of working on something and got called away before he had a chance to finish his work. My feet carry me over to the big chair sitting behind the desk. I gingerly sit down, taking a moment to appreciate what it would feel like to be Declan McCoy sitting behind this regal throne.

Reaching for the pencil drawer under the main workspace of the desk, I slide it open and rummage through the sticky notes and random shit he has in there. When I don't find it there, I open up the file drawers on the right side. I want to fist pump when I see exactly what I was searching for—the spare key to the courthouse sitting in an unsealed envelope. I pull it out and stick the key in my pocket, leaving the envelope just in case my dad looks in his drawer when he gets home. I don't suspect he'll need the key until I'm done with it, so I should be safe.

I close the drawers, ensuring everything is where I found it, and then stand up from his chair. Before leaving the study, something on top of the desk catches my eye. It's a thick faux-leather bound book with gold detailing across the cover and the spine. I'm not sure why

I'm so intrigued by it, but it looks much more important than the rest of the paperwork scattered across the desk. I reach for the book, open the gold-tooled pages to the middle and scan what looks to be a ledger.

My father's handwriting is scribbled across each page in a type of ledger. My eyes zero in on some itemized sections, and I frown. Each line starts with one letter, and then on the other side of the page is the dollar amount that the item went for. Standard ledger stuff, but most concerning are a few high priced item my father has written down.

I'm talking thousands upon thousands for each item.

Flipping through the pages, I find the same pattern. Item "BH026" went for $20,000, while lower on the page, item "LG021" went for $50,000.

A sick feeling settles in my stomach. Something about what I'm seeing looks and feels all wrong, but I can't decipher what my father's ledger means. I flip through a few more pages, reading all I can but fully aware that my father could come home any minute. There are repeat items, all just identified with different combinations of letters and numbers. None of the letters are in any type of order or spell a secret word or anything. The earliest line items date back to before my father was elected mayor. Though the charges have seemed to become more frequent since then. All ranging from tens of thousands to hundreds of thousands.

My head is spinning as I finally slam the ledger book closed. Something is really not right about this, but I don't have enough information to determine what it is. I shake my head and walk out of his office, deciding that whatever it is, it isn't worth getting busted by my father for snooping.

My mind keeps spinning over the matter throughout the night, but I can't make heads or tails of it. I lay in bed, flat on my back with my eyes open, trying to figure out what is bothering me about the whole thing. When morning finally comes, I'm nowhere closer to being able to say precisely what I saw in that ledger. Knowing I need to go get Parks soon, I roll out of bed, shower, and pull on a pair of jeans and a long-sleeve thermal shirt. I quietly go down to the kitchen, brew two thermoses of coffee, and grab two fluffy blankets off of the basket in the living room. Making sure I have the spare key to the courthouse, I sneak out of the house and towards my truck and load it up before leaving the house.

I drive silently towards Parks' house, still worrying over those numbers. I park the truck and send her a quick text to let her know I'm here. When I see her at her front door, I smile, all thoughts of the ledger disappearing at my happiness to see her.

"Good morning, sunshine," I say when she opens the door to my truck and climbs into the cab. She slams the door and gives me an unimpressed look.

"I *cannot* believe you talked me into getting up this early. The sun isn't even up yet!"

"Here," I hand over a full mug of coffee towards her, amusement lacing my tone. "I think you need this."

Her attack weapons immediately lower as she accepts my offering and takes a sip. "Ah, bless you."

I chuckle to myself and shift my truck into drive, pulling away from the front of her house. Parks settles into her seat, sipping her coffee happily and humming along to the music on the radio. She perks up a little bit as we drive, even though our journey is short.

"You're taking me to Main Street?" Addison asks me incredulously, but I keep my eyes on the road, eventually pulling into one of the parking lots right across the street from her parents' café. I put my truck into park and reach behind me into the rear seat for the blanket and extra thermos of coffee I brought.

We get out of my truck and I tilt my head towards the giant clock tower that watches over Main Street, giving her a grin. "Ready?"

"I'm not sure. What are you up to?"

I offer her my hand, and she takes it without much argument. Her willingness me great satisfaction, almost as much as the feeling of her dainty hand in mine. It's a cold morning, and I pull her closer to me, so she's not freezing. With her glued to my side, I lead her toward the clock tower. I eventually have to let go of her to dig in my pocket for the spare key to the courthouse I swiped from my dad's office.

With the weight of the silver key in my hand, my thoughts return back to the ledger, and my stomach churns, thinking about it. Somehow, I manage to squash that train of thought as fast as I can, telling myself I'll worry about it later. I get to spend the first few hours of my birthday with Parks. I don't want it tainted with thoughts of whatever shady business my father is up to.

I wrestle the door open and then lead Parks in. We head up the old stairs into the maintenance room for the clock tower.

"Noah, *where* are you taking me? You're not going to murder me, are you?"

I laugh, my voice echoing off the walls. "Not this time, Parks. Sorry to disappoint you, but you're gonna be stuck with me for a while longer."

Grabbing her hand, I lead her up the stairs towards the attic door. After I wiggle the door open, I slide in, Parks following right after me. Her eyes widen when she realizes where we are. Parks steps away from me and towards the window, looking over the Main Street square.

"I didn't realize we could come up here," she says, awe lacing her tone.

"Most people can't, but that's one of the few perks about being the mayor's son, I guess. I swiped the key," I tell her with a wink. She gives me a disapproving look but wanders over towards the window anyway.

"Here, get comfortable," I instruct as I lay out one of the blankets I brought. She's still tightly clutching the mug of coffee in two hands but settles on the blanket as soon as I have it spread across the dusty floor. I pull another blanket out of my backpack and wrap it around her shoulders.

She looks up at me gratefully as I settle beside her and doesn't complain when I snuggle in under the blanket.

"Why are we up here?" she asks.

"Just wait a few more minutes, and you'll see," I say.

Only a moment or two later, the sky starts to light up. Parks gasps as her eyes take in the colorful display of bright oranges, yellows, and pinks. "It's beautiful."

The bright rays of the sun dance across her face as she stares wondrously out the window. The light brings the golden flares to life in her hazel eyes. My mouth goes dry as I watch her, realizing I never stood a chance. Not against her. I start spiraling into consuming thoughts of how I can never seem to get enough of her. Every minute I spend with Addison Parks makes me want more. I want so many more mornings like this, watching the sunrise with her. I want to fill her days with things that make her look as amazed as she does now. My chest aches at the thought of everything we could do together, all the adventures and incredible moments I could spend with her. I want all of that, and more. And hopefully someday we'll have it.

"It's amazing how something that I can cover with my thumb gives life to everything in the world," she muses, breaking me out of my daydreams of her. She's holding her thumb out and closing one eye, covering up the sun. "It's kind of crazy, isn't it?"

"What is?"

"To think that there is an entire universe out there, infinite space, and we're just here living our lives like we're the most important things in existence."

"Well, to some people, you probably are the most important thing in existence, Parks."

She looks at me then, and *finally*, I see it all click into place for her. "Are you one of those people?"

"Yeah," I tell her simply. "Yeah, you're important to me, Parks. Probably more than anyone else in my life."

"Even more than Jordan and Caleb?"

I smirk, "*Especially* more than Jordan and Caleb."

She looks away from me, a content smile covering her lips as she watches the sun rise. After another few seconds, I feel her finger start tracing a pattern on my palm. I glance away from the display in the morning sky to look down at what she's doing. She does it again and then once more.

"Infinity," I whisper, interpreting her drawing. Addison's eyes find mine, and she grins cheekily.

"Infinity," she says back and then looks out at the sun. It's almost past the horizon line, only a sliver of it still covered behind the hills. I lean towards her, resting my cheek against the side of her head. Her familiar lavender and vanilla scent fills my nose, and I close my eyes, breathing her in. She smells like comfort, like *home*.

After a few minutes, she pulls away from me but then turns to face me.

"Happy birthday, Noah," she whispers. I smile at her and lean my forehead against hers. "It's your birthday, and yet you're doing nice things for me, that's so—do you have a birthday wish? I feel like this is the perfect time to make it. The sun is seconds away from being fully risen."

I think about it for a moment but then shake my head. "No, I think I've got everything—" I pause, then pull away so I can look at her directly as something comes to mind. "Well, there is one thing...."

I know that Addison Parks has not changed her mind about where we stand since our conversation yesterday. But here in this moment, with the sun making her look like she's an angel from heaven, I kind of don't care. There's nothing I want more than her.

As I trail off, Parks' hazel eyes flare, and her lips part. Silence fills the room, and then, "You're doing it again. Staring," she whispers.

"Honestly, Parks, I don't think I've ever seen anything more beautiful than you at this moment. So yeah, I'm staring."

"It's different this time," she says.

"Different how?"

Addison swallows but doesn't take her eyes off mine. "You look like you want to kiss me."

"What if I *do* want to kiss you?"

I can see the wheels in her head-turning, quickly weighing the pros and cons. Our conversation from yesterday plays in the back of my mind, and I wonder if I'm making a mistake, pressing the issue again. Still, as I mentioned, I kind of don't care. If she says no, I'll let it be, for good. But if there's a chance, she'll say yes, I have to take it.

"Parks, just this once," I tell her. "I haven't been able to stop thinking about kissing you again."

"If I let you kiss me, I don't think it's going to be just this once," she replies, and I realize that she doesn't say no. Her eyes hold mine steady, and I see the internal battle raging within her. She *wants* me to kiss her, but at the same time, she's scared, worried that opening this door will cause irreparable damage.

"I never want to pressure you into anything, so if you don't want it, say no, and I'll never ask again."

She stares at me, blinks a few times, and then gives a hesitant nod. My mouth goes dry, and I lean forward slightly until I can taste her breath on my lips. It tastes like toothpaste and a hint of French Vanilla creamer from the coffee.

"Noah." Her voice is barely above a whisper as she leans close until her lips brush mine ever so slightly. I shiver at the sound of my name on her lips and her proximity to me.

All it would take would be for me to shift forward, to close the remaining distance between us. Then I would be kissing her, finally. Every molecule in my body is thrumming with energy, urging me to do it. Telling me to take her lips and show her how much she means to me.

But I don't.

The rational part of my brain tells me that the right time is not now. She didn't say no, but she didn't technically say yes either. I want more than just a hesitant nod of her head. I want her to want me like I want her.

Parks is right. Things will change if I do this right now—close the distance and kiss her like I want. And though that might be everything that I want, if there's a chance that she's doubting or not ready for that, I need to wait. I'm not going to be that guy. If I push her, she might turn away from me, which sounds like a fate worse than not being able to kiss her right now. I decide right then and there that Parks and I will have our time someday. Even if it takes years—which *God*, I hope it doesn't—she'd be worth the wait.

So instead of moving forward, I angle my chin back from her and close my eyes. I can feel the surprise coursing through Addison's body, and she attempts to move away from me.

"Wait, don't pull away...not yet," I whisper to her. My hand raises towards her neck, and I cup the edge of her jaw with my thumb, holding her in place. I smooth gentle circles over the skin of her cheek, falling in love with the feel of her soft skin underneath my hand. "Let's just savor this for a minute."

With great restraint, I pull my forehead away from hers and inhale through my nose, trying to let the oxygen clear my head. Her eyelids flutter open, and hazel meets blue. I can see everything that she's fighting not to say. Her breath falls against my lips, and I long to take her lips in mine and kiss her until we both forget why we shouldn't. I want to wrap my arms around her thin frame and lean her back on this blanket we brought. I've dreamt about what she would feel like against me, the warmth of her body pressed into mine. I would hold her tight, ravish her, and show her what it's like to be cherished.

I want it so bad that my gut has a hollow ache. I look back at the now risen sun and grit my teeth, holding my control tightly.

"We should probably get going before your parents notice you're missing," I tell her with a low voice. Addison rolls her lips into a thin line and nods her head.

"I'm sorry," she whispers to me, her eyes glued to the blanket we're sitting on.

I frown at her and then reach my hand to cup her chin, bringing her eyes back to mine. "Why are you sorry?"

"For not letting you—"

"Don't." I cut her off. "It's not all about me, you know. I want you to be ready for this, and I hope you will someday be. But until then, I'll back off."

"Noah, I don't want you to back off...I just—I'm scared—"

"Shh," I soothe her, rubbing my thumb along her jaw again. "It's okay. We'll be okay."

"I don't want things to change between us. I like how we are," her voice shakes with uncertainty, and I can't fight it anymore. I wrap her up in my arms and hold her to me. I tuck her head under my chin. Addison hugs me back, her cheek resting against my chest, her one free hand gripping my shirt. I hold her for just a minute too long, not wanting to let her go.

"Nothing will change. I promise."

Her eyes trace my face, searching for something. When she finds it, she nods her head. "I trust you."

Those three words make my heart soar. Her trust in me means more than I ever thought it would. More than her letting me kiss her or anything like that. Just knowing she trusts me is enough. I want to be everything she needs, and if this is how she needs me right now, I'll do precisely that.

I smile at her and then get up, offering a hand out to her to help her stand. We gather our blankets and thermos and then return to the truck. The drive back to her house is quiet but comfortable. I know she's mulling over the events of the morning as she stares out the window, and I let her. I'm perfectly content to sit in silence as long as I'm with her.

When we get to her house, she finally turns toward me. She purses her lips to the side and then gives me a shy smile. "Happy birthday again, Noah. Thanks for letting me spend the first few hours with you."

"Wouldn't want it with anyone else," I tell her, knowing she senses the double meaning in my words.

Her eyes soften, and she leans forward, pressing her lips to my cheek before pulling back. My cheek tingles with the contact, and my stomach tightens. "I'll see you later," she says before opening the door and hopping out. I watch her walk to her front door, loving how her hips sway with every step.

As soon as she's inside, I lean back against my seat, taking a few deep breaths through my nose. After this morning, I know there's no use in fighting it. I'll back off just like I promised her I would, but as for me? I'm pretty confident I'm doomed, either way, it's probably written in the stars or some shit like that—I'm going to fall for Addison Parks. It's not a matter of *if* at this point. It's a matter of *when*. I just hope she'll come to feel the same way about me.

And she will. Some day. Just not yet.

With that revelation, I shift my truck into gear and drive away. Memories of Addison gazing at the sunrise replay in my head as I drive away from her house.

"Noah, is that you?" I hear my mother's voice call from the dining room when I finally make it home. I see her and my father sitting at the grand table. My father at the head and my mother to his right. There's an extra plate for me on my father's other side. A small box with a bow sits on top of the plate. "Sit down, have breakfast with us," Mother says, smiling at me.

I hesitantly walk towards my assigned seat and settle in.

"Happy birthday, son," my father says to me with the fakest smile I've ever seen. He nudges the plate with the velvet box closer towards me, and I watch it as if it's a ticking time bomb about to go off at any second. "This is for you."

"What is it?" I ask him, my voice hesitant.

The smile on his face cracks for a second, and I know I'm testing his patience already. "Why don't you open it and find out?"

Reluctantly I reach for the box and flip open the lid. Inside is a gaudy ring bearing the McCoy family crest.

"My father gave me my own when I was turning eighteen," he tells me, puffing his chest proudly. "I thought I would carry on the tradition and get you your own."

I look over at my mother, and she's wearing a tight smile that doesn't meet her eyes. She watches me warily as I pull the ring out and slide it onto my pinky. "Thanks, Dad," I tell my father, pretending to sound enthused about it. "It's—" *awful, gaudy, ugly,* "nice."

"You come from a long line of strong McCoys, Noah," he says, his voice taking on a reverent tone. "I hope this allows you to embrace your family name. Wear it proudly."

Bile rises in the back of my throat, and I swallow thickly to keep myself from throwing up across the table. "Thank you. May I be excused?"

My father's proud expression wanes to one of confusion as he looks at me. "You don't want breakfast?"

"Uh, no. I'm supposed to meet Jordan and Caleb this morning to go over a school assignment," I lie through my teeth. Anything to get me out of this room right now. I glance over at my mother, and we share a long look. I know she sees through my façade and nods her head at me.

"Of course, have a good morning. We'll see you for dinner tonight, though, right?" she asks hopefully.

I nod my head as I scoot the chair back. "Dinner, yeah. I'll be there."

My father looks like he's about to say something else, but I don't give him a chance before hustling out of the dining room, grabbing a sweatshirt, and leaving the house.

As soon as I step outside, I hold out my hand to observe the ugly family ring sitting on my finger. I curl up my nose at the sight of it. Family pride. Right.

I slam the door to my truck and peel out of the driveway, heading straight towards Main Street again. When I make it, I wander into one of the coffee shops and order myself more coffee and a bagel. I sit for an hour or so, people-watching and mulling over the ledger situation some more. When ten o'clock hits, I toss my trash away and decide to go for a walk around the park.

The November air is still frigid, but I've got my coat and a beanie hat, so I'm warm enough. After walking a bit, I go to my favorite spot on the bridge and lean against the railing. Not long later, I hear someone calling my name.

I look up to see my favorite girl walking toward me, smiling as she waves at me. I hold my hand up in a wave and grin back at her.

"Hey," she calls out as she gets closer. Her cheeks are flushed from the cool winter air.

"Get a good nap in?"

Parks smirks at me. "Yeah, some guy made me get up at the crack-ass of dawn this morning."

"Some guy, huh?" I tease her, bumping her shoulder with mine when she leans on the railing next to me. I'm happy to find that things aren't awkward between us after this morning. I promised her I wouldn't change how I acted around her, but I didn't know if she could do the same. But as always, Parks is exceptional.

It doesn't take her long to notice the gaudy ring on my finger. She reaches for my hand and stretches my fingers out, inspecting the ring.

"What is this?" she asks me. My eyebrows knit together, and I clench my other hand into a fist at my side. The stupid ring bearing the McCoy family crest is displayed right at the knuckle of my pinky finger. "That's fancy."

I scowl even harder as I look down at it. "It's a birthday gift from my father. Apparently, It's a family tradition that the men in the family receive a family crest on their eighteenth birthday. How archaic is that, huh? I was just so lucky to get mine in the form of this god-awful ring."

"You don't like it?" she questions.

"Not if it connects me to *him*," I spit out, feeling a ball of irritation start to form in my chest. Addison's eyes soften as she looks at me, and I hate how she appears to be feeling bad for me.

I know I've been shady whenever my father comes up in conversation. She'll ask every now and then how things are going, and I don't want to worry her by telling her things are bad. My mind flits to the ledger I found on his desk yesterday, and the irritation grows. I know I could talk to her about it, and she'd listen and probably have a good way for me to proceed. But she's one of the only truly good things I have in my life. I don't want to taint her with whatever sketchy business my father is up to.

Then it suddenly occurs to me that *Addison's* father might just be the right person to talk to about this. What did she say her dad was a part of? The FBI? He would probably know exactly how to handle whatever information I stumbled across. Or, at the very least, tell me if I was being paranoid.

Addison asks me a few more questions about what my parents gifted me for my birthday, and I answer her enough to stay engaged. Still, in the back of my mind, I'm formulating a plan. I decide I need to talk to her father without her around.

We hang out for a few hours at the library before telling her I have to head home for dinner. She nods, disappointment clouding her features at the thought of me leaving, which gives me great satisfaction. If I could, I'd spend every waking moment with this girl.

The rest of the evening passes in a blur. My parents take me for a nice birthday dinner, then back home where we have ice cream sundaes for dessert. I head to bed early, my mind still busy working on the ledger situation.

I barely sleep a wink all night, running over every last bit of information I want to give to Mr. Parks. I try to make sense of it in my mind, so I don't come across as some try-hard kid, but it's no use. To be honest, I have no idea what I found. None of the numbers made sense with the charges in the ledgers. I couldn't make sense of the riddle in the brief few minutes I looked at it. All I know is that something felt really wrong about it.

At some point in the middle of the night, I can't take it anymore. I toss the covers back and get out of bed. Quietly I sneak out of my room and down the hallway to my father's office. I want to get another look at that ledger and maybe snap a few pictures to show Addison's dad tomorrow.

I'm disappointed when I get into his office and find his desk perfectly cleared off. The documents scattered around his workspace last night are now stacked neatly. Everything is in order once more, and much to my chagrin, the ledger is gone.

I scowl as I stalk back out of his office and to my bedroom again, crawling into bed and cursing everything. I doze off a few times, though it's not a restful sleep. When my alarm blares, I throw off the covers again and wander into my bathroom. I stare at my reflection and notice the dark circles under my eyes. I'm quiet as I leave the house, starting up my truck and going straight toward downtown. It's early enough that the streets are quiet, even for a Sunday morning. I part the truck and stroll up to the café. A few early risers are lingering at the tables, drinking coffee and having breakfast, but I don't stop to say good morning.

As I step into the building, I make a beeline for the front counter. Mr. Parks looks up and offers me a friendly smile. "Noah, nice to see you. Addison is still at home, I think she was going to sleep in this morning, but she'll be here later if you want to see her."

"Actually," I say hesitantly, walking towards the older man. My mind is running a mile a minute. I still have time to turn around and pretend this never happened. But instead, I stick to my guns, hoping I'm not making a terrible mistake. "I'm here to see you. I have a few questions."

"Sure, what can I do for you?" he asks, suspicion edging his tone.

I brace myself and then muster the courage. "What do you know about my father?"

If he was surprised, he hid it well. Mr. Parks' eyes harden, and his lips turn into a frown. He takes a deep breath and then nods his head once, resigned. "I think you'd better sit down."

Chapter 26

Noah

Noah - Age 18

"Okay, hit me with the next one," Parks says. I glance at her in amusement as I shuffle the flashcards in my fingers before picking the next one.

"Name the type of reaction in which the products have less energy than the reactants, causing energy to be put off during the reaction," I read off and then peek at her again.

We're camped out in the student center at school. Parks is sprawled out on her back on one of the old couches, her over-stuffed backpack serving as a pillow, and her feet on my lap. She has her eyes screwed shut as she considers the flash card I just read. Her lips mouth the words to the question as she works it out in her head.

"If energy is put off in a reaction, it must be exergonic. That's right, isn't it?" she asks me, peeking one eye open.

"You got it. Exergonic reaction. So then what's the opposite of that?" I quiz.

"Endergonic. Energy goes into the reaction, so the products have more energy than the reactants."

"Beautiful," I tell her, placing that flashcard into the 'know-it' pile.

We've been studying together for the last hour or so. Parks has her last AP biology exam before the final next week, and she wants to ensure that she's got everything down perfectly. I have no doubt in her, but ever the perfectionist, she roped me into being her study buddy.

"Okay," I say, patting my hand on her leg. "We need to take a break now. Just for a minute or two."

"Fine," she mumbles, stretching her arms above her head and arching her back. Parks has her honey-brown hair curled today, and it splays out across the surface of her backpack. I try my hardest not to look at her, but she's too beautiful that I can't peel my eyes away from her. As soon as she relaxes, I move my eyes away.

"Have you heard back from any colleges?" I ask her. A slow smile forms on her lips, and she nods. I realize she's waiting for me to ask further, so I nudge her leg. "Well?"

"I got into MIT *and* Cornell. My top two!" she exclaims, sitting up, so she's face to face with me. Her eyes sparkle as she delivers her news, and I instantly pick up on her energy.

"Parks, that's amazing! I'm so proud of you!"

"What about you? Have you heard back from any?"

A sour feeling settles in my stomach. I never actually told her that I haven't applied anywhere yet. I'm not sure what I plan to do, so I'm sure as hell not wasting money until I have a better idea. "I haven't yet."

"That's okay. There's still time," Parks chirps, smiling at me.

"Have you thought more about what you want to major in?"

Addison shakes her head. "No, I'm still leaning more towards chemistry so I can go into research. But I also started thinking that forensic science might be cool. Who knows, maybe if I do that, I could end up working at the FBI with my dad!"

"That sounds like a great gig for you," I respond.

The mention of her dad has me thinking back to my conversation with him a few months ago. I'm suddenly aware of his business card sitting in my wallet in my back pocket. After I had walked into the café that morning and asked what he knew about my father, all hell came raining down.

"You better sit down," Mr. Parks had said to me, a grim expression taking over his face.

He walked me over to one of the tables near the back of the café, and I sat across from him hesitantly. His first question was why I came to him. I told him about the ledger I had found on my father's desk and how something about it didn't sit right with me. He asked me a few more questions about what was in there, asking me to remember as much as possible about each line item and the price it was going for.

He told me I did the right thing, coming to him to talk about this, but he didn't give me many answers. He reached in his back pocket and pulled out a business card, sliding it across the table towards me. "Noah, I want you to listen to me," he started, looking at me gravely. "Your father is currently under investigation for some serious crimes. That's partly why I'm here. There's not much else I can tell you, but this is my department's business card. If it ever comes to it, call my supervisor and tell him who you are and that you've spoken with me."

I narrowed my eyes and took the card, the heavy cardstock weighing against my fingers.

"What you told me today might be able to help get this investigation rolling again, just as long as nothing compromises it. It's imperative that you don't tell anyone that we had this conversation, do you understand?" he asked me. I nodded, knowing I had no one I could talk to about this anyway.

After that, I left the café feeling only slightly better. At least someone in power knew about the ledger, so I didn't have to worry about it anymore.

"Noah?" Addison's soft voice brings me back to the present, and I look at her blankly. "You in there? I asked you a question."

"Sorry," I shake my head. "What was your question?"

"Are you going to prom?" Addison asks hesitantly. Her cheeks heat up a bit as she gauges my reaction.

"Are you?" I ask her, my brain still foggy from thoughts of my discussion with her father.

Obviously, that's not quite what she's hoping I would say. Her eyes become guarded, and I hate it. I hate it when she hides from me. "I'm not sure. No one's asked me yet."

I laugh under my breath. "That's surprising."

"Why'd you say it like that?"

I shift in my seat and frown at her. "I just figured you'd have eligible guys lining up to ask thy fair lady to the ball."

She tries to fight it, but a smile appears on her lips. "You're such a dork."

I shrug a shoulder and grin at her now. "Yeah, but you love me."

Her cheeks brighten, and she averts her eyes. "So are you? Going to prom?"

"Probably not."

"Why?" she questions, and if I didn't know any better, I'd think there was a hint of disappointment in her tone.

"I don't know, Parks. It's just not really my cup of tea, you know? Not really one for silly school dances."

"Yeah, I get it. It's dumb," Parks responds a little too quickly. She tosses her curls over her shoulder and then rests on the couch again. "Forget I asked."

Regret hits my chest like a bullet, and I watch her warily. "Parks—"

"It's fine, Noah. Let's just get back to studying. I told my parents I'd be at the café to help this afternoon."

I know she's lying. She told me she was free to hang out all day today, reinforcing my opinion that I just made a grave mistake. I acquiesce, though, and start reading off flash cards. As soon as we're done studying, she grabs her backpack, tosses me a smile that doesn't reach her eyes, and then disappears.

"I think I fucked up," I tell Caleb later that day at the gym. He's loading one of the barbells with a few plates to do a chest press. My friend shoots me a confused look and then pauses his task.

"You always fuck up, no surprise there. What was it this time?"

I grimace. "I think Parks wanted me to ask her to the prom today, and I was a total asshole about it."

Caleb's jaw falls open as he stares at me blankly for a minute. Then without any sense of confidentiality, he turns and yells across the gym, "Hey Jordy! Noah wants to go to the prom with Hurricane Addison!" I reach over and punch Caleb's shoulder just a little too hard. He flinches away from me. "Ow, what the hell!"

"Maybe don't scream my business to the entire world, yeah?" I snarl at him.

By this time, Jordan has closed the distance between us. He wipes his forehead with a towel and then looks at me curiously. "You're asking Addison to the prom?"

"No," I say too quickly.

"I thought you didn't like school dances," he says.

"I don't."

"Oooh, he's *lying*," Caleb sneers. "You *want* to go with her, don't you?"

"No. I just had a change of heart, is all," I argue back. "It's our last big dance, you know? Don't want to miss it."

"A change of heart, right," Jordan responds, looking amused now. "If that's what you want to go with.

"What's that supposed to mean?" I ask my friend accusingly.

"You tell me, man. You're the one telling Caleb that you want to go with Addison and then changing your mind on a dime. Pick a side and stay there," Jordan tells me. "Neither of us care if you like her. So if that's what you're worried about—"

"It's not," I say. It suddenly occurs to me that I'm being way too defensive. These two are my best friends. If I can't trust them, I can't trust anyone. "Fine," I say, letting my guard down. "I think there's— that is—Parks and me—"

"Oh my God, what is happening right now?" Caleb says, his eyes are wide and unbelieving. "He's rendered speechless at the thought of her."

"I told you he was crazy about her," Jordan says to Caleb. "You owe me."

"It hasn't happened yet! I don't owe you shit."

I frown at my friends, "What are you two talking about?"

"We may or may not have had a bet going to see how long it took before you finally admitted to liking her," Jordan informs me.

If possible, I frown even harder. "How long has this been going on?" Caleb and Jordan exchange glances and then look at me, both offering a nonchalant shrug. "I'm going to pretend I didn't hear whatever the hell that just was and move on. I need your guys' advice."

"So tell us what happened," Caleb says.

I do. I fill the two of them in on the entire encounter this afternoon. I told them about how we were studying together one minute, and then she asked me about prom and got pissed at me the next.

"She wanted you to ask her," Jordan states the obvious, a satisfied smirk settling on his face.

"I know that *now*," I mutter. "So yeah, I just don't know where to go from here."

"You ask her to the dance, she says yes, you get a tux and tie that matches her dress. Then you go to the dance and sweep her off her feet," Caleb tells me.

"Are you sure it's that easy?"

"As long as you're telling the truth and you didn't fuck it up any more than you say you did," he says. Jordan nods in agreement.

I press my lips into a thin line. Could it really be that easy? "So that's my plan? I'll ask her tomorrow, and hopefully, she'll say yes, and things will finally be in line that we could...I don't know; see what happens?"

Could it finally be the right time and things work out between us?

"When the hell did you become such a big romantic? I never thought I'd see the day, especially with this girl," Jordan says to me.

I glower at him. "Don't go there."

"He *likes* her, likes her," Caleb says, nudging Jordan with his elbow. My friends laugh together, and I feel my mood plummeting.

"I guess it's about time we lost you to the opposite species. It was nice knowing you, though," Jordan teases.

I roll my eyes and shove his shoulder away from me. "Whatever, go finish your workout."

I chicken out over the next few days in asking her. Jordan and Caleb give me endless shit about it, but Addison's still giving me the cold shoulder, so it's not the right time.

Finally, a few days later, I get the balls to ask her. I catch her right before lunch, grabbing her hand and stopping her in her tracks. I can hear my heartbeat in my ears. I haven't done anything like this since Rose and I were together *forever* ago. Even still, it's not comparable. Everything with Addison feels different—better.

"Hey, are you still going to prom?" I ask her in a rush. "Cause if you were still wanting to go, I thought maybe we could go together. I know I said before that I didn't want to go, but after thinking about it, I think it might be fun. With you."

"Noah, I—" she looks suddenly upset, and I backtrack, trying to think of what I said that bothered her, but I come up blank.

"What's wrong?"

Parks presses her lips together in a thin line and then huffs a breath. "Eli asked me to prom last night." My heart drops into my stomach, and I narrow my eyes at her. What in the hell? It was only a few extra days that I had to think about it. She couldn't wait before running off to Eli? "Just as friends, though," she adds in quickly, seeing my expression.

"Friends," I repeat, and she nods her head fervently.

"He made it very clear that he wasn't going to ask me, but all the other girls he wanted to go with were already taken," Addison says bitterly.

I narrow my eyes even more. "Why the hell would you say yes to him knowing that? You deserve better than that." My tone is accusatory, and she narrows her eyes back at me, gearing up for a fight.

"Well, maybe because the guy *I* wanted to go with decided he was too *good* to go to the prom!" she shoots back, her annoyance growing.

"Well, I'm not too good for it now, so what do you say, Parks? Want to go to the prom with me?"

Her shoulders fall, and she clenches her jaw, speaking her next words in a tight voice. "I already told you I'm going with Eli."

"Tell him you changed your mind."

"I can't do that. I promised," Parks says, shaking her head. "He's still my friend. I'm not going to just go back on my word because you've finally decided you want to go with me."

"Come on, Parks, throw me a line here," I plead with her.

Her shoulders droop, and she shakes her head. "I can't. We've already got plans. Maybe if you go, we can still hang out together." Her eyes spark with hope.

And as if he was summoned straight out of hell, Eli rounds the corner and finds Parks and me talking. He takes a few steps towards us and then crosses his arms, a thunderous expression setting in on his stupid face.

"Addie? Is everything okay?" he asks in his irritating voice. I roll my eyes and then look down at Parks. Her eyes are screwed shut, and she's frowning.

"Your boyfriend's calling you."

"Noah," she protests, opening those hazel eyes and looking at me imploringly. She knows I'm speaking out of frustration just as much as I do, but even when I'm upset, I can't say no to those eyes. I sigh and lean my head closer to hers until our foreheads are touching. She closes her eyes and lets out a breath.

"Just go Parks. We'll talk later," I tell her in a low tone.

"Are you sure—?"

"It's fine, Parks. I'll see you around, yeah?"

I walk away from her, wondering how this situation got so fucked up. I want to be upset at her for saying yes to someone else, but I'm not. If only I had been open to the idea of going with her from the first time she asked me. But I hadn't been, so this is my own damn fault.

It's something I kick myself over for the rest of the day. As I walk around the little park in the town square later that afternoon, I find myself slipping into a pit of frustration. Why can't I ever seem to do the right thing when it comes to her? Even when I make the right decision, it always seems to fall apart because of whatever stupid thing I did before.

Maybe this is penance for all the years I gave her so much trouble. It makes sense, karma and all that shit. Perhaps I'm destined to be chasing after Addison Parks for the rest of my life, unable to fully repent for all my wrongdoings. Though, even if that's the case, Parks is worth it.

"Hey!" a voice calls to me, and I look up, jolted out of my thoughts. I scowl right away as soon as I recognize Eli Montgomery stalking toward me. He must have seen me walking here from his father's market.

"What do you want, Monty?" I ask as soon as he's close enough.

Eli stands a few feet from me, arms crossed over his chest, attempting to appear menacing. I wager I could take him down quickly, though, if it came to it. "I want you to stay away from Addison."

I shake my head, laughing under my breath. This is classic. "Why would I do that?"

"Because I will beat you into a pulp if you don't. She's too good for you, and she deserves to have someone who actually cares about her."

"And you think I don't?" I counter back.

"All you care about is yourself, McCoy. You're just like your dad in that aspect," Eli snarls at me, and I grit my teeth. If he wanted to land a good blow, he succeeded.

"You don't know what you're talking about."

"No?" he questions snidely. "I've only known you my whole life. That's where Addison's getting confused. You've got her believing that you've changed or whatever, but I know the truth. I can see through your little game."

Now I cross my arms over my chest, not responding but hopefully conveying with my expression that I'm not impressed with his little tirade.

"Addison is *my* best friend, so it's *my* responsibility to protect her from jerks like you. You might have been able to trick her into being friends with you, but soon enough, she'll see you for what you really are," Eli continues, still trying to egg me on. "And I'll be the one right there to pick up the pieces."

I stay silent for another moment, staring at him blankly. "Are you finished?"

Eli falters but then regains whatever mojo he thinks he has. "For now."

"Great. You can leave now." On that note, I turn from him and start walking towards my bridge. Eli can run his mouth all he wants, but I won't let him get to me. I'm pleased to see that he doesn't follow me but instead turns around and stalks back towards his family's market.

I lean my elbows on the edge of the bridge and watch him walk away. He might think he knows me, but he's wrong. I'm nothing like my father, and I never will be. I might have an upward battle trying to convince everyone that even though we're related, I am not destined to turn out like him. I'm going to choose my own destiny, and Declan McCoy doesn't get to have a say.

Eli irritates the hell out of me on a good day. And today especially that he thinks that I would ever do anything to hurt Parks. He's the one running to her and asking her to the dance as a *backup* plan. But that's none of my business. All that matters now is how I'm going to move forward.

She was just telling me that she got accepted to her two top colleges. Even though they're still in the Northeast, she'll probably be leaving Willow Heights to live in the dorms. If I want to be with her, I can't risk her going without knowing how I actually feel.

Sure, there's been a few kinks in the road, but I'm confident I'll be able to set things straight. I make the decision then and now that I'm not going to let this ruin one of my last chances with Addison. We've wasted enough time skirting around each other. Slowly, a plan starts to piece itself together in my mind.

And that's how I find myself wearing a perfectly tailored tux a few weeks later. I even went out last week and bought a new tie. I decided to stick with a classic black satin tie, not knowing what color dress Addison would show up in this evening.

I stand on the edges of the ballroom, leaning against the wall and holding a cup of sparkling cider in my hand. Unfortunately, it hasn't been spiked yet, but I'm still hoping. I glance at my watch, gauging the time. I haven't seen any sign of Addison or her dynamic duo. It's not as if I'm early by any means, which means they're late. I grit my teeth, trying not to think about reasons she'd be late to dance with Eli as her date. She said they were just coming as friends, but I trust Eli as much as he trusts me.

Based on his little outburst at the park, it is not very much.

Jordan and Caleb are doing as best as they can to keep me distracted, commenting on our classmates and their dress choices for the big evening. Unfortunately, it's not enough to deter me from scanning the room every few minutes, checking to see if I've missed her walking in. But she's never there.

Where is she?

I take a sip of my drink, though my throat feels there's something lodged in it.

Then, finally, and as if out of a movie, the door opens, and she glides in. All conscious thought leaves my body as I watch her walk through those doors. She's dressed in an emerald green gown that hugs her like a second skin. The dress accentuates her figure, wide around her torso, narrow at the waist, and flaring around her hips. I notice she's complimented her green dress with a sparkly golden necklace which scoops just below her clavicles, resting delicately against her chest.

My mouth feels dry, as if I just tried to swallow a handful of sand. I can hear my heartbeat in my ears as I track her movements into the ballroom. She's got her hand looped through Eli's arm though her eyes are scanning the perimeter of the ballroom.

And then she spots me, and her eyes light up. My stomach flips like I've just been on a rollercoaster, and my vision tunnels until she's the only thing I see.

I can vaguely register Jordan and Caleb saying something next to me, but I can't decipher it. And I honestly don't care to. Everything else around me disappears.

All that matters is her.

"Your girl looks amazing," Jordan says under his breath, finally pulling me out of my stupor.

"Yeah," I agree, my chest feeling tight.

"Don't fuck it up, man."

"I'll try not to," I mutter though part of me wonders if that's possible. Given my track record, it might be a long shot.

Addison ends up staying close to Charlie and Eli for most of the evening. Dinner is served, and I sit with my friends on the other side of the room from where she is. After eating, she goes out onto the floor and dances with Charlie and Eli a few times. I keep glancing over every so often, trying to catch her when she doesn't have her bodyguards around.

Unfortunately, that doesn't come until the evening's close. She's standing over by the drinks bar when I notice Charlie turn to her and place his hand on her shoulder, leaning closer to say something. Addison nods, and then Charlie walks away, disappearing into the hallway. Not long after, Eli leaves her side too.

This is my chance. I look over to Jordan and Caleb, who give me encouraging nods. Taking a deep breath, I brace myself and walk closer to her, closing the distance between us, hopefully for the last time.

Chapter 27
Addison

Addison - Age 18

"**P**arks," a deep voice murmurs. I spin around to find Noah with his hand outstretched toward me. Relief floods through my body, I was hoping he would come over here. "Dance with me?"

I take him in standing before me, appreciating how cleaned up he is. His usually unruly dark brown hair is combed back and styled neatly. He's wearing a fitted tux with a black tie around his neck. His silver-blue eyes gaze at me, and I feel *seen* for the first time all evening. Anticipation settles in my gut, and I don't hesitate as I slide my hand in his, letting him lead me out to the dance floor. Noah spins me around so I'm facing him, his large hand snaking around to rest on the curve of my hip so he can pull me close. My arms wrap around his neck, and I trace the familiar features of his face.

"Hi," I whisper. "You look nice."

A smirk plays on his lips. "Yeah? Well, you look *beautiful*." Goosebumps break out on my arms with the way his eyes travel over my body appreciatively when he says it. I can tell he means it.

"You came. I wasn't sure if you would," I say. Noah was upset that I wouldn't go back on my plans with Eli. I should've known that he wouldn't let something so petty deter him from doing what he wanted.

And apparently, it didn't.

"I told you I wanted to spend tonight with you, Parks. That's why I'm here; I definitely don't regret it, even if it is a silly dance. You really are stunning, Addison," he says under his breath, almost in awe.

My cheeks feel warm, and I press myself closer to him. His arms wrap tighter across my lower back. "Thank you, I'm glad someone appreciates the dress. Eli said I looked like a string bean because it's such a deep green."

I almost laugh because the whole thing is comical, but I don't when Noah pulls away from me, so abruptly. His eyebrows pull together in a severe expression. He looks irritated. "He *said* that?"

I nod my head, my lips pulling wryly to the side. "Eli's never been one to keep his thoughts to himself."

Noah hums. I know he's not pleased with my attempt to make an excuse for Eli's comment, but pulls me close again anyway. We sway to the music, easily falling into a rhythm together. A new song begins, and his strong arm tightens on my back. The opening melody draws me in with a whimsical hook. The perfect song for the perfect moment. Something about being in Noah's arms feels right like this was always meant to happen. I'm not sure if I've ever felt so content. I lean my head against his shoulder, my cheek pressing into the smooth fabric of his tuxedo.

"You're quiet," I whisper. "What are you thinking about?"

Noah voice rumbles against my cheek as he says, "I'm thinking about punching Eli in the throat for saying something that absurd to you. You look lovely."

"You like the green?" I ask him hesitantly. I won't outwardly admit I picked it out because it's his favorite color, but I know he knows.

His eyes flash with something I can't place, and his gaze travels from my face down my body. He swallows thickly. "I *love* the green."

My heart flutters, and I smile, pleased with his response. "I'm so glad you came tonight, Noah. You being here makes everything feel right."

Noah's fingers trail up from my waist to my shoulder and then dance over the ridges of my spine. The feel of his hand against the bare skin of my back has me shivering. For the first time in…well, ever, I feel this is right. The whole time I was dating Eli, he would touch me or run his hands over my shoulders, but it would feel *wrong*.

I'm not sure if I ever realized how different things with Noah were until this moment. I've known that I always feel more myself with him, but even with his touch, I feel more alive than ever. His hands on my body makes me yearn for more as if we're magnets, drawn to each other.

There's just something about Noah that I can never get enough of. It's what drew me to him in that hallway and what has kept me always coming back. As we move across the dance floor, it finally starts to come together. Memories of Noah and me play back in my mind like a reel, as if to squash any type of doubt. He's everything I need, everything I could want. Noah's the one I turn to through bad days and good days. Even when we clash and go head to head—I do always come back to him, and he always comes back to me.

He's the one who challenges me when I need it but will back off when he knows I need space. He will pick me up if I've fallen and run with me when I've finally found my stride, supporting me through everything I need to accomplish. I can go off and ramble about academics and he can follow along, chiming in with his own opinions when needed. He drives me absolutely crazy sometimes, in the worst and best ways possible. I never have to be anything other than me when I'm with Noah.

I can't believe it's taken me this long to realize it, but Noah's not just my best friend. He's my other half. He understands the ins and out of who I am. The epiphany comes to me as I stare straight into his silver-blue eyes. He must be able to see something in my expression because he leans closer to me, his gaze like molten steel on me.

"I really want to kiss you right now," he whispers, his breath warm against my lips and his eyelids drooping.

His words weigh on my heart, and I make a decision that I know I won't regret. "Then do it. I want you to kiss me."

Noah stares at me, his eyes tracing my face as if looking for any sign of doubt before a small smile appears on his lips. He leans closer to me until his lips brush against mine. I close my eyes, thinking this is it, maybe the timing will finally be right, and we can do this...

Desire courses through my body when his lips press against mine. His hand splays across my back, applying slight pressure until I'm pressed flush against him. Like the last time I kissed Noah, the world explodes into vibrance, making everything more bright and meaningful. If I could kiss him forever, I would.

Noah pulls away from me all too soon, putting a slight distance between us. His attention darts around the ballroom, ensuring there are no teachers or chaperones coming to yell at us. Then his gaze is back on me exploring my face. The heat in his eyes suggests he wants to kiss me more. But he doesn't.

"Parks, there are a few things I want to talk to you about," he says in a husky voice, staying so close to me that I can still feel his lips moving against mine. His fingers continue to trace patterns against my back.

"Okay," I whisper back, my lips parting slightly.

"Everything about you is amazing to me. I've been falling for you ever since you came and sat next to me in that hallway," he tells me. He's looking right into my eyes, and I feel like he's reaching for my soul. My heart aches. "I want everything with you, Parks, and I'm hoping you want the same thing."

"Noah, I want—"

"Addison." A sharp, deep voice has me jerking away out of

Noah's arms and spinning around to face Charlie, watching us with wide, confused eyes.

"Charlie," I breathe, my hands nervously running over the lengths of my dress. I can feel Noah step up closer behind me, his hand resting on my waist.

"I was just—" Charlie looks away for a second, takes a deep breath, and then turns back to us. "I'm ready to leave if you still want a ride."

"Oh, right. Sure, let me just—"

Charlie holds up his hand, stopping me in my tracks, "I'll meet you outside in ten minutes." He turns around to leave and then has another thought, turning to face Noah and me again. "Eli left already. Just in case you were wondering."

Guilt courses through my body, but I quickly dampen it. Eli asked me to this dance, sure, but he's also the one who ditched me right after we got here. I have nothing to be guilty about. I turn back to Noah. He's observing me with a guarded expression.

"Noah," I start as he steps close to me, his hand raising to my cheek. He brushes a few strands of hair away from my face and tucks them behind my ear.

"You should go with Sullivan," he says, and surprise courses through my body.

"Why?"

"Because I think you should talk to him. I'm not running away this time, Parks," he says. "And I don't want you to run either. It's time we face whatever this is and move forward."

"What if he hates me?"

"He won't," he says, sounding almost like a promise. "He couldn't."

"What about you?" I ask.

"We'll talk later," Noah says, kissing me on my cheek. "I promise, we'll talk. I'm not letting you get away from me this time."

Anticipation settles in my stomach, and I nod my head at him. He gives me a sideways smile and then turns and walks back over to his friends who are off on the sidelines. Jordan and Caleb look between us as if unsure of what just happened. Caleb catches my eye and then waves at me. I chuckle, waving back. Noah looks at me over his shoulder and grins at me again, tossing me a wink.

Deciding that I better go catch my ride, I grab my things and then leave the ballroom. Charlie is waiting with his car in front of the hotel lobby. He's standing on the passenger side, leaning against the car's frame. When he notices me walking out, he moves to open up my car door. I settle in as he rounds to the other side, getting in and driving us away.

As Charlie drives me home, I can practically feel the tension rolling off his shoulders. I peek at him every other minute to gauge his current mind frame, and every time is the same. His hands grip the steering wheel so tightly that his knuckles appear strained. I press my lips together and then look out the window, watching the darkness pass us by.

When Charlie finally clears his throat to say what's on his mind, I don't bother looking at him. "Do you want to explain what was going on in there with Noah before I jump to conclusions?"

"What's the point?" I whisper back. "You've already jumped."

"You and McCoy?" he asks incredulously, confirming my last statement. "Really?"

"It's not like that."

"Don't lie to me, Addie. I know what I saw." Charlie swears and releases the steering wheel with one hand, running it down the side of his face in frustration. "Eli is going to lose his shit when he finds out."

"Well, maybe Eli shouldn't have asked me to the prom and then ditched me to go chase after another girl," I spit back. "And besides, it's really none of either of your business. You don't really have a whole lot of sway here, Charlie. I saw you sneak away with Wyatt tonight, so you can't sit here and act all high and mighty."

"I just asked you to explain, Addison. We're not talking about Wyatt and me. We're talking about you and Noah."

"I don't know what you want me to say. Noah's my friend, and we just—"

"What?" Charlie prompts me, glancing over at my side of the car.

I let out a long sigh. "I don't know. There's just been something *more* for a while, and the timing hasn't been right, so we haven't done anything about it."

"Until now?"

I shrug my shoulder, looking over at Charlie now. "I don't know."

"Do you want to be with him?"

I purse my lips together, my eyes starting to burn. I have been asking myself that question for months now, and every time I come up blank. "I don't know."

"Well, it definitely looked like he wants to be with you."

"He does. He's made that abundantly clear, but I've been the one holding back."

"Why?" Charlie asks me, his tone entirely different now. Instead of the aggressive approach he was taking before, now he sounds curious.

"Because I was worried about how you and Eli would take it," I whisper, my fingers knotting together in my lap. Charlie doesn't respond right away. I'm unsure if he's upset at me or trying to come up with the right thing to say. After an extended moment of silence, I look over at him. "Say something."

He shakes his head and glances at me before pulling the car off the road and onto the shoulder. He places it into park and turns towards me, taking my hands in his. Charlie stares at me with his friendly blue eyes, and his gaze is so steady and comforting that my worries slip away. Without him even saying anything, I know exactly what he's trying to tell me.

Charlie is my *friend*. He wants me to be happy.

"Addie," he says softly, "I would do anything to keep you from getting hurt. But if being with Noah is what you want, then you need to go for it."

"But what about you and Eli?"

Charlie laughs under his breath. "I'll get over it, and I'll make sure Eli gets over it. Based on how he was looking at you tonight, there's definitely something there. You know a side of Noah that I've never seen before, and if you think he's worth your time and love, then I believe you."

Love.

Do I love Noah?

I shake that thought away as quickly as it comes. There's no way. I just like him. I like being in his presence and hanging out with him. That's it.

Right?

Even as I try to rationalize it for the rest of the ride, I know I'm wrong. Noah is more than just a fling. If there's anything that I can say with one hundred percent certainty, I've been falling for him just as long as he's been falling for me. I just haven't realized it until now.

As Charlie pulls up to my house, thunder starts rolling in the distance. I lean over and give him a one-armed hug. "Thank you, Charlie."

He hugs me back, squeezing me tightly to him before letting go. "You know I'm always on your side, Addie. Always."

"Thanks," I say again and then get out of his car. As I walk towards my front door, I feel a few sprinkles fall out of the sky and land on my shoulders. I manage to make it inside before the sky completely opens up.

I shout a quick hello to my parents sitting in the living room. I hear the TV going, so they must be watching one of their shows together. They yell something back as I bound up the stairs and to my bedroom.

First, I unzip the gorgeous emerald dress and slide it down my body. It pools into a satin puddle on the floor as I step out. After removing my gold jewelry, I get into the shower, washing away all of the makeup and hairspray, holding my hair into its coiffed style. It's bittersweet watching the makeup disappear, and my hair revert to its normal style. Tonight was supposed to be perfect, and while I had a perfect moment with Noah, I wish I had gotten more.

Maybe I should've told Eli I didn't want to go with him. It would've hurt his feelings, but he didn't end up spending the evening with me anyway, so I'm sure he would've gotten over it. Instead, I put myself second as I usually do and ended up last. After the revelation I had dancing with Noah tonight, I'll never let myself do that again.

As I shampoo and condition my hair, I let my mind wander, imagining what tonight could've been like if I had said yes to Noah when he asked. Part of me wonders if things needed to play out the way they did so I could experience the difference between how I felt with Noah versus not. I'm a big believer that things work out how they're supposed to, but in hindsight, I wish I would've come to that realization earlier.

After I rinse my hair and wash the evening off, I dress quickly and then curl up underneath the comforter on my bed. I reach for the book on my nightstand, planning to read a chapter or two before bed. The rain is pelting against the window, thunder rumbling every few minutes.

I get a chapter in when I'm distracted by a pelting noise against my window. It doesn't match the rhythm of the rain. Frowning, I roll out of bed and pad over to the window, pulling open the curtains. My eyebrows raise in shock when I see Noah standing on my front lawn.

"Noah!" I gasp, opening up my window so he can hear me. "What are you doing here? You're soaked."

"I told you I would talk to you later. Well, it's later," Noah responds. His hair is dripping wet, plastered to his forehead as he looks up at me in my window. He's still got his tux on, though his tie is missing. The first few buttons of the white shirt underneath are undone.

"Go around to the backyard," I tell him. "The gate should be unlocked, and then we can talk on the porch."

He nods his head and then disappears into the darkness. I slide my window shut and look around my room, re-orienting myself. I glance down at my legs, realizing I need to put on a pair of pants or shorts. I'm sure Noah would love seeing me walk down there in my pink panties, but I still have a few reservations. I pull a pair of black sweatpants out of my drawer and slide them on before opening my bedroom door and tip-toeing down the stairs to the kitchen.

With a glance back in the direction of the living room, I push open the door to the back porch. Noah's standing there, in all his sodden glory.

"Noah, you're crazy. You're going to get sick," I scold, walking over to him and fumbling with the edges of his tuxedo jacket.

"I told you I wanted to talk to you about something," he says, chuckling.

"It could have waited until tomorrow!"

"No, it couldn't." The edge to his tone has me glancing up at him in question.

My lips part to ask what's going on, but he stops me.

"Addison," he starts, catching both of my hands in his. My heart startles at the sound of my first name on his lips, and I realize I like it a *lot*. "When I first saw you, I thought you were an absolute disaster sent to torment me." I can't help but laugh at the dismayed expression on his face. "And I was half right. You've been tormenting me from day one, though now it's because I can't get you out of my mind. You've somehow become the most important person in my life, and I can't live without you knowing how much you mean to me."

"Noah," I say, squeezing his hands.

"I know over the last year, things between us have been...different. But I think that we had to go through that to come to terms with what we could be. You are everything to me, Parks, and I've realized there's no point in me fighting this anymore. I've wanted you for a long time, and I know I'll want you forever—until infinity. So why are we wasting time?" he asks. "Just tell me you want me back. I don't want to wait anymore."

"I want you too," I whimper, stepping towards him. He anchors his hands on my waist. "I can't believe it's taken me this long to realize it, but—"

"But what?" he prompts.

I look up at him with wide eyes, reaching for his hand. My stomach clenches and I decide to just do it, admit what I've been holding onto for so long. "Noah, I think I'm falling for you, and I'm terrified because if I let myself fall for you, I know there's no coming back."

He takes a deep breath through his nose and exhales it, his eyes looking hopefully at me. "I'm right there with you, Parks. It's you and me, now. Together."

"I love the sound of that," I tell him, my cheeks warming in a blush.

"Are you sure you want this? This is your last chance to back out," he offers, his voice low. "If you say yes, I'm not letting you go."

I grin up at him. Never in my entire life have I been more sure of anything. I summon the bravery and make the jump. "I want this. I want you, Noah."

In two swift strides, Noah erases the remaining distance between us. He grasps my cheeks with both hands, pulling me toward him in a searing kiss. His first kiss is hesitant as if testing the waters. His mouth becomes more urgent when he realizes I won't push him away. I wrap my arms around his shoulders, not caring that he's soaking wet, and press into his body.

His tongue snakes against the seam of my lips, and I open for him. Noah moans in the back of his throat as he deepens our kiss, one hand moving to cup the back of my neck. I shiver against him, loving the sound of his pleasure.

He must mistake my shiver for being cold and pulls away too soon. I open my eyes and take him in. Noah's eyes are alive, the silver blue glowing with want. His hair is messed up from where I ran my fingers through it, falling in thick wet strands on his forehead. He breathes deeply and presses our foreheads together, trying to get control of himself but not wanting to let me go completely.

Even though the rain is pouring down outside, inside, I feel as if the skies are perfectly clear. Warmth travels through me straight down to my toes as if the rays of the sun peeking over the horizon are reaching through my soul.

All sense of time disappears as I kiss Noah on my back porch. Any type of worry or distraction flits away, and it's just him and me right here in this moment. Noah kisses me as if his life depends on it and is worried he'll never get the chance again.

Finally, he pulls away from me. He nuzzles the side of my nose with his before leaning in and kissing me again. Desire travels through my body, straight down to my toes. I close my eyes, basking in his presence.

"I should go," he says. "Before I take things too far."

My body burns, and I want to tell him I *want* him to take things further. I want him and everything that comes with him. I never felt inclined to explore the physical aspect of a romantic relationship with Eli, but now? After being pressed against the hard planes of Noah's chest for the better part of the last fifteen minutes?

I'm definitely interested.

Unaware of how I'm feeling, Noah, steps away. With his distance comes a chill, though I tell myself it's probably for the best. My parents are still inside and could come out any second. I wouldn't want to have to explain an awkward situation to them. Even though my dad likes Noah, I'm not sure he'd be a big fan of walking in on something like that.

"I guess this is goodnight then," I say.

A sideways smile forms on his lips, and he brushes his thumb over my cheek. His eyes soften as he gazes at me. "I guess so. I'll see you tomorrow."

"You will?"

I must have sounded surprised because he raises an eyebrow at me. "Do you not want to see me tomorrow?"

"I do. Want to come to the café for breakfast?" I offer.

He grins again and nods. "That sounds great. Tomorrow then."

Noah leans forward into my space, capturing my lips in a sweet kiss. My eyes fall shut as I savor it. Again, he pulls away too soon. He winks at me once before jumping off the stairs and hurrying away.

I stand on the porch, watching him jog out into the rain. My arms wrap around my middle, holding tightly. A giddy smile starts to form on my face. I bounce up and down in a cheerful dance as soon as he's gone.

Though it got off to a rough start, tonight was even better than I could've imagined. For once, I think everything with Noah and me will work out.

I go back to my bedroom and crawl under the covers, a delighted smile still residing on my lips. As I snuggle into my bed, I close my eyes and replay every moment of tonight. I never want to forget it.

Chapter 28
Noah

Noah - Age 18

"I'd like to take this moment to invite the class valedictorian up to the podium to give the class address," Principal Mabee informs the crowd. "Addison Parks, it's all yours."

Parks smiles at the principal as she takes her spot at the wooden podium perched on the stage. I notice her glance out at the gathered crowd and swallow. She's been working on this speech for the last few weeks since she discovered she'd be the valedictorian. Despite her preparation, I can tell by how she's shifting from her left-to-right foot that she's nervous.

Birds chirp in the distance as she takes only a second to gather her thoughts. Then inhaling, Addison looks back at the guests in the bleachers and gives a blinding smile.

"It is an honor today to deliver the commencement address for this incredible class on the night of our graduation. I just wanted to take a minute to thank you all for being incredible classmates over the last few years. And thank you to our teachers, parents, and staff who made these years everything they were. We wouldn't be here on this beautiful evening if it weren't for all of you."

Parks takes another deep breath and then launches into the body of her speech. She regales all the memories we've made over the last few years, the laughter, the tears, and everything in between. The crowd listens to her with rapt attention, and pride swells in my chest.

That's my girl up there. My girl.

"As Albert Einstein once said, 'Education is what remains after one has forgotten what one has learned in school,'" Addison says solemnly to the crowd. I fight the urge to roll my eyes. Of *course*, she would use a quote by Einstein. My little nerd. "And I think that's important to remember as we all part ways and take off into the great unknown.

"We'll forget the specifics like how to do geometry or what a conjugate verb is, but at the end of the day, we'll still have our education to see us through. What we learned here was more than just details in a textbook. While we were here, we prepared for our adventure out into the real world. We learned people skills and deductive reasoning that we'll take with us for the rest of our life. These things will last more than the information we crammed into our brains before our last few final exams."

The crowd chuckles at her little joke, and I smile at the stage. Parks is killing this speech. And to think this is the same girl who called me at ten o'clock last night in a full-blown panic about her public speaking. She had nothing to worry about, just like I told her.

"I'm excited to see where we'll all be ten years from now. I believe that our class will do great things, and I hope that at some point, we can all come back here and appreciate that this is where it all started. Even though I moved into this town, I've always felt like it was home, and I hope that never changes. Willow Heights High School will always hold a special place in my heart, and so will all of you. Thank you for the best years," Addison finishes her speech. Her eyes find mine in the crowd, and she beams at me. Our classmates clap for her, and I stand up, everyone following my lead.

The graduation ceremony continues with the presentation of our diplomas. They file us out of our seats row by row. When they call our names, we walk across the stage on the football field, accept the faux-leather cover with our diploma inside, and then file back to our seats.

Our principal gives one last brief comment, then we toss our hats into the air, and the crowd goes wild. When the ceremony dismisses, I stroll with my classmates out of our seats onto the football field. Thankfully, the weather held out for the ceremony this evening. It wouldn't have been as nice inside the stuffy auditorium of the school.

As soon as we're out of our seats, I scan the crowd, looking for Addison. She's found Eli and Charlie, each giving her hugs and congratulations. I hold back and let her chat with her friends for a moment. Her parents walk up to her, and then it's the entire process all over again. Once Eli and Charlie disperse, I take my cue to step up to the small family.

"See, I told you. You were great," I say. She spins around to look at me and gives me a gleaming smile, shrugging sheepishly.

"I guess you were right this time, don't get used to it. Congratulations!" she says, stepping forward and wrapping her arms around my neck, pressing close to me in a hug. I bury my nose in her honey brown curls, taking in her familiar scent. Too soon, I let her go and then turn to her parents. Addison still stays close to my side, and I wrap an arm around her waist, keeping her close.

Mr. Parks extends a hand to me, and I take it, giving him a firm handshake. He looks between Addison and me and smiles. After prom night, I had to have an official "sit down" with Addison's father before we went on our first official date. He asked me all about my intentions with her. As uncomfortable as the whole thing was—for both of us, based on how he kept tugging at his collar—it paid off in the end. I've grown closer to Mr. Parks, which has been beneficial in more ways than one.

Though he hasn't divulged precisely what he's investigating my father for, he's offered me a few tidbits of advice. I've stashed it away in my mental file cabinet for later.

After a few long conversations with him, I've become more interested in joining the FBI and working alongside him. I haven't made any decisions yet, but I'm considering everything. He's given me the proper resources to use if that's what I decide to do and has offered to help me out as much as possible.

"What are your celebration plans tonight, Noah?" Mr. Parks asks when he releases my hand. His wife steps forward to stand next to him, smiling at the two of us.

"I think Addie said she wanted to go get ice cream Sundaes if you want to join us," her mother says, eyes twinkling exactly how her daughter's do.

Every part of me wants to say yes, but a chill creeps up on the back of my neck before I have the chance to answer. I glance over my shoulder and see my parents walking toward us. My father stands tall, his broad shoulders stiff as he glares down at Mr. Parks. My mother's eyes are on me, an eyebrow raised inquisitively.

"Noah," my father says once they're close enough. The way his deep voice says my name has me inadvertently stiffening my muscles, immediately going on guard. His icy eyes flare when he takes in Addison standing next to me. I clench my jaw, my arm tightening against Addison's waist to keep her close to me.

Before he has the chance to say something snarky or mean, my mother steps forward toward Addison. She smiles at her and offers a hand first to Addison and then to her parents standing by. "I'm not sure if we've officially met. I'm Catherine."

Her parents introduce themselves, and Addison hesitantly takes my mother's hand, giving her a wary smile. "I'm Addison. Nice to meet you."

"Are you a friend of Noah's?" I can tell my mother knows exactly what's going on here based on the elated twinkle in her eye, but she wants to hear it officially. I don't talk to my parents much, especially not about Addison, but I know I can't avoid it at this point.

"She's my girlfriend, Mother," I tell her outright. Addison jolts next to me in surprise. Until about two seconds ago, we hadn't officially put a label on whatever this is. We've just been "dating," testing out the waters. But I decide right then and there that I'm not beating around the bush. I want Addison to be my girlfriend, and I want everyone to know it.

"Girlfriend?" my father says, surprise lacing his tone. I glare at him, only to find his attention darting between Addison and then over to her father. I've caught him off guard based on the slight slackness in his jaw and raised eyebrows. He quickly schools his features once he notices me watching him, putting on the mask of cool indifference. "Well, isn't that interesting."

"I think it's lovely," my mother says wistfully. "And the valedictorian too. I loved every second of your speech, dear. I thought it was very tasteful."

Addison's cheeks heat under my mother's praise, and she glances at me briefly. I nod my head and smile at her. "Thank you, Mrs. McCoy."

"Mr. Parks just invited me to get ice cream with them to celebrate," I say to my mother. "I wasn't sure if we had any plans for afterward."

My mother glances at my father. He seems to still be stewing over the revelation of my having a girlfriend. Then she shakes her head and grins at me. "I don't believe so. Your father told me he had to work at the courthouse just a minute ago. You go along, and I'll see you back at home." She leans forward and kisses my cheek. "Congratulations, honey. I'm so proud of you."

My father is still staring at Mr. Parks, his face hard as stone, his jaw ticking as he clenches his teeth. Mr. Parks keeps his expression neutral, focusing primarily on Addison and me. He knows my father is glaring death threats at him. I can tell by the slight twitch in the corner of his mouth, but other than that, he gives nothing away.

"Noah," he says to me while glaring at Mr. Parks. "I'll see you at home later. Don't stay out too late."

I frown at him as he turns abruptly on his heel and stalks off. I catch Mr. Parks' eyes in a quick glance, and he shakes his head, not saying a word. Once my parents are gone, I follow Addison and her family to their car, where we hop in and drive off to get our ice cream sundaes.

The evening is much better than anything I would have planned to celebrate. We stop at the Malt Shoppe in town and order ice cream and French fries. Mrs. Parks finds us an empty table to sit at, and we enjoy our dessert.

Though we're with her family, I can hardly take my eyes off Addison. She's practically glowing this evening, shrouded in the excitement of graduating and the anticipation of the summer break ahead of us. Her hazel eyes sparkle against the golden glow of the twinkle lights hung up around the Malt Shoppe patio. I think I fall even more in love with her when she tosses her head back, laughing at something her mother said.

It's a night I never want to end.

"So, Noah," her mother begins after taking a bite of her sundae with pecans. "What are you doing for school next year?"

I swallow my ice cream before looking at the Parks sheepishly. "I'm not sure yet. I think I'll take a year off, maybe try and do some internships or something to see if I can find the right fit."

Mr. Parks nods his head at me. "I think that's a great idea. You'll go far, Noah. You've got great potential."

For the first time in my life, I experience what it's like to have a male figure who is proud of me. Someone who thinks I'm more than just the name I was born with. As I sit there, I try to remember if there was ever a time when my father told me he was proud of me, and I come up blank. A ball of satisfaction centers in my chest, and I sit up straighter, looking at Mr. Parks square in the face.

"Thank you, Sir. That really means a lot to me," I tell him. My voice sounds thick. I hope he can't pick up on it, but by the understanding and pride that settles on his face, I know he has.

Addison reaches for my hand underneath the table and squeezes my fingers. Still smiling, I look over at her and squeeze her hand back. I decide right then and there that I like the feeling of having a family who supports you. It's something I've missed out on my whole life.

We stay for a bit longer, finishing our ice cream, and then the Parks drop me off at my house. Addison's eyes widen when they pull up the driveway, the large McCoy house looming over their small sedan. She's never seen firsthand the wealth that comes with my last name, and I make a note to keep it that way. If ever I have to choose between having a mansion where I've never felt more alone versus a small two-bedroom house with a family in it that loves you, I'll go with the latter option. Every time.

I wave at the Parks as they drive away from my front step and then turn to go inside. As I head to my room, my legs feel heavy with every step. As I make it to the second floor, I notice a light in my father's study, leaking underneath the door and flooding the dark hallway. I contemplate for a moment going in there and asking him what his deal was at the ceremony, but I think better of it.

Nothing my father will say is of any interest to me. So instead, I tread quietly to my bedroom, closing the door with a soft *click,* and then head to bed, ready to call it a day.

The following afternoon, I find Addison in the library—nose deep in a book called *Forensic Chemistry.* When I walk up to her, she's already got a notebook full of equations and practice problems that she's been working out. When I approach her, she looks up at me as if embarrassed but then returns to what she's doing.

I manage to sit quietly with her for half an hour. After that, the need to be closer to her takes over me. Somehow we end up sprawled out on one of the couches in the back part of the library, her underneath me, those hazel eyes staring straight up into my soul.

"You're a bad influence," she whispers right before I capture her lips in mine. Addison arches her back up, pressing her breasts against me as I kiss her deeply.

When I pull away, I smirk down at her. "Or maybe *you're* the bad influence. I can't seem to keep my hands off of you."

"What if I don't want you to keep your hands off me?" Addison asks, looking up at me from underneath her eyelashes.

A warm heat burns through my body under her gaze. Suddenly,

the weight of the moment falls heavily on me, and it hits me that I'm here with *her*. Of all the people I could be with, I have her. Finally. "You make me so incredibly happy, you know that, Parks?"

Addison hums, a smile playing on her lips as I close the distance between us again, leaning down and pressing my weight against her into the couch's cushions. Her fingers thread through my hair, gripping my head as close as she can.

Before we can get too hot and heavy, her phone rings, interrupting. The noise startles us, and we jolt away from each other. Parks groans as she reaches into the back pocket of her jean shorts and pulls her phone out, turning off the alarm. My hand trails up the length of her thigh, taking in the smooth spans of her leg.

"I've got to go," she swats at my hand that is now snaking up around her waist. "I told my parents I would help this afternoon since they're short-staffed."

"Wouldn't you much rather stay here, and we can make out some more?" I tease her, leaning forward and pressing my lips to hers. Addison opens for me, her lips parting with a sigh as I kiss her deeply. Her back arches as I wrap a hand around her waist, pulling her into me.

"That sounds much more fun than refilling coffee cups all afternoon," she murmurs against my lips. "But I told them I'd be there."

"Okay, okay," I relent, letting her go and rolling off the couch. "We'll reconvene later."

Once standing, I offer her my hand to pull her up. Parks tugs on the hem of her shirt, trying to straighten out the wrinkles, and then she grabs the rest of her things.

Together we walk out of the library and onto Main Street. Once we hit the sidewalk, I reach for her hand, interlacing our fingers. Addison glances down at our hands and then quickly refocuses on the sidewalk in front of us, fighting off a smile. Her lips are pink and slightly swollen from our makeout session up in the library. Her eyes glitter, and her cheeks are flushed, tempting me to drag her somewhere private and ravish her some more.

I spot Jordan and Caleb hanging out on the bridge when we pass the park. I turn to Addison and tug on her hand. "I'll let you go from here."

"Okay," she says, her eyes darting from my friends back to me and then nodding her head. "Will I see you later?"

I cup her cheek with my hand, tilting her jaw up before kissing her again. It's a brief kiss, but it holds the promise of more. "I'll definitely see you later."

"Bye, Noah," she waggles her fingers at me in a wave and then skips away.

I watch her as she walks the rest of the way to the café, her curls bouncing behind her. My chest aches as she gets farther from me, and I breathe deeply, trying to ease it, reminding myself that I'll spend more time with her later. As soon as she disappears into the café, I turn on my heel toward my friends.

"What's up, man?" Jordan hollers at me. "Did I see you walking out of the *library* on the first day of summer?"

"I was hanging out with Parks," I tell them, and they look at each other in amusement, muttering an insinuating "*Ooh.*"

"You're so whipped, dude," Caleb adds, reaching over and socking my shoulder. "You should've seen your face during her speech. I swear your eyeballs were popping out of your head in little heart shapes."

"We've lost you over to the dark side—*love*," Jordan adds in, crinkling up his nose at the word.

I roll my eyes and lean down on my forearms over the railing of the bridge, watching the water of the creek roil underneath us. Caleb keeps talking out of his ass, and I do my best to ignore him, instead thinking about what I want to do tomorrow with Parks. The countdown has started until she goes off to college, and I want to take full advantage of my time left with her.

Though I'm sure she would love it, I would rather not spend all my time left with her hanging out in the library, so I need to come up with more fun things for us to do together.

The guys and I spend the rest of the afternoon alternating between talking and playing a game against each other on our phones. It's a good way to hang out without having to spill our guts in conversation.

In between rounds, Caleb sniffs the air and then speculates, "The Parks must be making a whole bunch of pastries. Smells like burnt donuts."

I frown down at my phone but take a deep inhale. Then the thought crosses my mind, why would the Parks be making donuts in the middle of the afternoon? Usually, that is a task reserved for the early morning hours. Not this late in the day.

"What is that?" Jordan asks. I'm not sure if it's something about how he asks the question or if it's a realization, but I get up from my position and look around, the hairs on the back of my neck standing straight up.

"Is that...smoke?" Caleb asks, shooting up next to me in alarm and pointing his finger across the square. "Why is it so dark?"

I follow his attention and notice a thick cloud of smoke. I trace the trail back to see it pluming from the café, and my heart sinks. My feet move before my brain can catch up. Jordan and Caleb call my name as they chase after me, but I don't slow down.

I stop dead in my tracks when I get closer to the café. The entire building is in flames now. Red-orange licks of fire trail out of the front door and the windows. Cracks are already forming on the roof. I spin around and yell to Caleb, "Call 911!"

Caleb comes to a halt mid-stride and pulls his phone out of his pocket, immediately dialing. I spring into action again, and Jordan follows. "Noah, stop! What are you doing?"

I keep pumping my legs towards the café, not listening to him. A small crowd has gathered around the scene, but I break through. When I'm in front of the group, I turn around in circles, searching for those familiar honey-brown curls that belong to Addison. When I don't see her, panic seeps into my body. I only hesitate for a moment at front of the door of the café before I rip it open and run into the fire, one mantra running nonstop through my mind.

I've got to get her out.

The minute I step into the café, my skin breaks out in a sweat, and my throat begins to burn from the heavy smoke. I cough, my body's attempt to clear my airway. An idea comes to me as I spot a half-full glass of water sitting on a table nearby. I pull off my button-up shirt and douse it with the water, using it to cover my nose and mouth. Everything is dark, clouded by the smoke that's flooding the space. As I walk through the burning building, I glance uneasily up at the roof. It's cracking and popping, making sounds that threaten a cave-in. The incessant beeping of the fire alarms rips through the air ominously. It's such a stark sound that my ears start to hurt. With my shirt grasped fully against my face, I scour the café, looking for those curls and any sign of life. Somehow, I manage to discern a whimper and alter my course towards the sound.

I make it to the front counter and then jump over it, using one hand to propel myself over the edge. My feet hit the floor with a thud, and I crouch low to keep the smoke out of my eyes. And *there*.

There she is.

Relief courses through my body for a second, then I dampen it, focusing on the situation again. Addison is crumpled up underneath the fallen menu board. Her head rests next to the items listed in chalk, eyes closed, and her lips slightly parted.

"Parks!" I exclaim, crawling towards her. She's got a gash over her forehead that's trickling blood over her eyebrow and down her cheek. Her eyes open into little slits, and she stares at me, still conscious but barely.

"My arm," she murmurs so softly I almost don't recognize she's said anything. I gape at her for a moment before jolting into action. Her left arm is caught underneath the weight of the menu board. I give her shoulder a tug, seeing if I'll be able to dislodge her that way, but she only cries out in pain.

"Sorry, sorry," I tell her and then scoot back to reevaluate. More and more flames are creeping into the café from the kitchen and storeroom. I send a silent thanks to the heavens that she wasn't back there when the fire started. From the intensity of the flames I see back there, I can't imagine anyone would have survived.

I need to get her out of here *now*. Using my shirt, I wrap it around both hands to protect them from burning as I lift the sign. "Parks, can you hear me?" She moans, and I know she's still with me. "I'm going to lift this up on the count of three. I need you to move out from underneath it, then we'll get out of here, okay?" She grunts, and I take that as a 'yes.'

Positioning my covered hands on the edge of the wooden sign, I count out loud. On *three*, I grip the wood and lift the sign up. I'm relieved when I feel Addison scoot on the floor next to my legs and away. I drop the sign as soon as I think she's put enough distance and then turn to her.

Her hair is frazzled and frayed, her eyes wide and alarmed as she looks down at her left forearm. I swallow bile as I look too. Her skin is mangled and scorched, the layers of her skin destroyed in a red oozing mess.

"Noah," she says blankly, as if in shock. "My arm."

"I know. I know. We've got to get you out of here," I maneuver closer to Addison so I can pick her up, shifting her weight to carry her out of here.

I hear sirens in the distance as soon as I've got her in my arms. Carefully, I snake through the damaged café, avoiding falling rubble as I walk towards the front door. Burning pieces of the drop ceiling fall in my path, and I do my best to jolt out of the way, but a few wayward pieces singe the exposed skin of my arms. I grit my teeth, but the weight of Addison in my arms encourages me to keep moving. She rests her head on my shoulder, her sweaty forehead pressed against my neck. She's whimpering in pain against me, and I grip her tighter.

"My parents. They were in the back room," she mutters against me. A lump forms in my throat at her words. "There's no way—they were yelling for me, and then they just stopped. The door was locked, and I couldn't get in—it's never locked. It got so quiet—Noah, are they—"

"I don't know," I tell her, even though I'm pretty confident that's a lie. "Just hold onto me, Parks. I've got you."

As soon as I walk across the threshold of the café, firefighters and paramedics swarm around us. I walk down the front few stairs and then hand Parks off to one of the professionals. They get her situated on a gurney and immediately cover her mouth with an oxygen mask. Another paramedic offers me one, but I refuse it. She scowls at me and forces it over my face after checking my airway to ensure I didn't inhale too much smoke. When she's satisfied, she hands me a blanket and instructs me to sit in the back of the ambulance until the firefighters control the blaze.

I lean against the cool metal of the rig. My eyes glaze over as I stare at the flames flicking out of the windows of the café. A part of me is screaming for me to find Addison. But the adrenaline crashing in my body forces me to stay still and continue to stare.

Firefighters are spraying the fire down, trying to slow the menacing flames. The night is lit up in a mix of yellow and orange from the fire. The blue and red lights from the emergency vehicles reflect off the windows of neighboring buildings. The contrasting colors, mixed with the smoke, make my head throb.

I'm unsure how long I sit there, staring blankly into the wreckage. It may have been minutes, or it may have been hours. At some point, I register the sound of another ambulance turning on its sirens and leaving the scene—probably the paramedics taking Addison to the hospital. The fire department finally controls the fire enough for a few firefighters to run into the building. I close my eyes, press my forehead into my hands and attempt to focus on breathing.

"When the boys checked it out, they didn't see anything unusual or notice any gasoline smell. You know how old this building is, probably just an old wire sparking in the wrong place at the wrong time." I look up at two firefighters standing close to me, one stout with graying hair and the other looking fresh-faced like a rookie.

"There's nothing left of that back room, so we can't really say what was back there," the rookie says.

I take the opportunity to chime in. "The back room was where they got all their deliveries. There was a bunch of cardboard boxes back there."

The men look at each other and nod as if that was the missing piece to their puzzle. "That would make sense then. A wire probably sparked and landed on the cardboard, then before they knew it, the whole place was engulfed."

"Are you sure it wasn't arson?" I question. The men exchange another glance and face me with a look that says, '*Kid, you watch too many TV shows.*'

"Nah, just an accident. You did a good thing tonight here, kid. You should be proud of yourself," he says, leaning towards me and patting me on the shoulder before taking a few steps away, clearly done talking to me.

However, they don't walk far enough away, and I can still hear them discussing the situation. "Couldn't be arson, right?" the younger firefighter questions.

"No. The guys said the doors to the back storeroom were locked, so no one could have gotten in to set the place up. Probably just an accident. A loss, nonetheless."

I frown, gripping the edges of my blanket closer around my shoulders. An accident? That's it? Something so simple caused this disaster? I can't shake the feeling that there's more to this, but I have no proof, and my mind is too fuzzy to place a finger on what it is.

"Have you told anyone else yet? Meaning should we make a statement or—"

"Definitely not," the older fireman says bluntly. "No, until we know more, this needs to stay strictly confidential. People died in this fire. I don't want to spread anything around until we know all the facts. Might take a bit before the detectives can make it out here to say for sure."

I tune them out after that. *People died in this fire.* The firefighters didn't mention them specifically by name, but they might as well have.

Mr. Parks. Mrs. Parks. Addison's parents.

Dead.

The world spins around me, and nausea sinks into my gut. I suspected as much when Addison was mumbling about them to me. But hearing it confirmed makes me want to vomit. What is she going to do? They were her only family. Where is she going to go?

I begin to spiral, my mind mulling over this development. I was with the Parks just last night, having ice cream and laughing at her father's terrible jokes. And now they're dead, just like that.

"Hey," a familiar voice says next to me. I look up and blink at Jordan. Caleb is right behind him. Their faces are grim as Jordan sits beside me on the rig. Caleb stands right in front of us, blocking my view of the firefighters still a few feet away. I forgot my friends were here. "Did you get her out? I saw you carrying someone, but I couldn't determine who it was. Is she okay?"

"Yeah," I tell him, my voice heavy. "She was—she got burned pretty badly on her arm, so they're taking her to the hospital to check her out."

"And her parents?"

I swallow the lump forming in my throat and shake my head. Jordan sighs next to me and puts a hand on my shoulder. "I'm sorry, man."

I allow him to leave his hand there for only a minute, taking all the comfort I can. Neither of them says anything else. They just sit there with me. The weight of the situation falls over us like a heavy blanket, and there are no words.

After what feels like an eternity, a commotion down the street catches my eye. A broad figure in a black suit excuses himself past the yellow caution tape and pushes past the people standing around. The crowd makes space for him, finally letting him through. His cunning eyes take in the scene before landing on me sitting on the back of the ambulance. He stalks towards me.

"We'll leave you alone," Jordan mutters when my father gets closer, and then he and Caleb scatter as quickly as they can. I nearly laugh, *cowards.*

"Noah!" my father shouts at me. Underneath his harsh tone, I'm almost surprised to hear a hint of worry. "What the hell happened? The chief told me there was a fire, and you were running out of it. You could've been killed!"

I stare at the pavement as he continues to rant about the danger. As he goes on, my mood plummets with every word that comes out of his mouth. It might be all the smoke that I inhaled, or maybe the overall events of the evening, but suddenly, all I can think about is the way my father was watching Mr. Parks last night—calculative and threatening. I don't want it to be true. Still, the more I mull over the convenience of the events, the more I convince myself I'm right. Maybe this is what I've been feeling has been off this whole time.

I don't waste any more time as I stand up, throwing the blanket off my shoulders and grabbing my father's jacket. I pull him towards me in a surprising show of strength. "What have you done?"

If my father is surprised by my outburst, he gives nothing away. Instead, any sign of worry or concern he was showing me before slips away. "I'm not sure what you mean," he responds to me, his voice level and calm.

"I know this was you. You did this. Why?" I growl at him through my teeth. I'm sure I sound just as unhinged as I'm feeling on the inside. Depths of darkness swirl within me, and I can't contain my anger. After tonight's events, all I want to do is rage and yell.

"Son," he says, his tone condescending as if he is trying to reason with me. "I was in a council meeting all evening. Ask anyone there. I never left."

"Then how'd you know I was here?"

"I told you, Sullivan called me and told me you were involved in the fire at the Parks' café."

"How did you know that's what happened?" I snarl.

My father blinks at me as if I'm an idiot. "What are you talking about? There are fire trucks everywhere, and the building is on *fire*. Not to mention, aside from all of that, this is my town. I always know what's going on."

I recognize his deflection, and I sneer at him. "Cut the shit. You've threatened Mr. Parks before. I wouldn't put it past you to light this whole place up. It would be a good way to send a clear message, huh?"

"This is clearly an electrical fire. It was an old building. Use some sense, son," he says dryly, fingers reaching up and attempting to pry my grip off him. "I know you're upset, but you need to calm down."

"Addison's parents were trapped in there," I growl at him. "People I cared about died. How could I be calm about this?"

"When the Parks locked those storeroom doors, they couldn't have known this would happen," my father says, trying to appease me. "They blatantly ignored the fire codes."

"How would you know the doors were locked?" I growl at him. "I overheard the firemen say that information was confidential."

"Noah, what are you rambling about? Who cares about locked doors?" my father questions. "I don't see what your point is."

"Why did you do this?" I yell at him. "I know you're behind this, so just answer my damn question! What, did you find out I was getting closer to Mr. Parks? Asking too many questions? Figured that you better just get rid of him before I leaked too many of your secrets? What is it, tell me!"

My father huffs and rolls his eyes. "You've been through a lot tonight, Noah. We need to get you to the hospital and then get you home. Your mother is worried sick, and you're concerning me too."

"Your words mean nothing to me! Addison's parents are *dead* because of you!" As I say those words, my voice cracks, and I attempt to maintain my stance.

"Noah, all that smoke must have gone to your head." His voice has switched to a performative tone as onlookers stare at us. Then pulling me closer as if he was giving me a hug, he says darkly, "Now stop this. You're making a scene. I have had no part in whatever you're accusing me of. As I said, I've been at the courthouse all evening. Come on, let's get you out of here." With an exaggerated pat on my back, he pulls away and then places his hand on my shoulder with an intense grip, but I shrug him off.

"Stop lying and just admit it! This would be nothing for you to pull off. I know what you're capable of."

My father glares right back at me, seemingly reaching the end of his rope. His expression takes on a more menacing air, and he steps closer to me until only inches separate our faces. His voice is low as he says his following words so that only I can hear them. He leans forward, eyes steely and threatening. "Then you should know that crossing me might not be in your best interest. Get out of my sight, Noah, before you say something you can't take back. I need to speak with the fire chief."

My father strides away, leaving me gasping in his wake. Even with all my accusations toward him, I didn't expect him to give anything away. I have no proof, but he all but confirmed my suspicions anyway.

He did this. I'm sure of it.

"I'll tell them!" I shout after him. He's about eight feet from me, but he halts and turns on his heel to face me again.

He stares at me for a beat and then shakes his head, laughing under his breath as if I'm an amusing child. "Don't be a fool, Noah. Let this go and focus on your girlfriend."

My father doesn't say a word to me, instead turning away and walking toward where the fire chief is talking to his crew. I stare, shell-shocked, at the space where he was standing only a minute ago. Something in my heart cracks, and despair floods over me. My knees buckle, and I kneel on the pavement, staring blankly after my father.

Vaguely, I register someone calling my name. Then hands are

shaking me out of whatever trance I'm in. I look up with glazed eyes and see Charlie Sullivan leaning toward me. It's his hands on my shoulders, trying to get my attention.

"Hey, snap out of it," Sully says to me. I blink a few times, and his face entirely comes into focus. I notice Eli standing behind him, arms crossed over his chest, his jaw clenched tight. "Where's Addison? We've been looking all over for her, but no one will tell us what's happening."

"They took her to the hospital," I tell him, my tongue heavy in my mouth. "She had some burns from the fire."

Charlie turns around and says something to Eli that I don't care to interpret, and then they leave, walking away from me at a swift pace. I manage to get my brain to work enough to stand up and holler after them, "Wait!"

Charlie turns around and raises an eyebrow at me. "What?"

"Are you going to see her?" He reluctantly nods, and I take a few steps toward him. "Could you give me a ride? I need to get out of here, but I don't know where my friends and father went—" I trail off. Thankfully Charlie doesn't press the issue.

He watches me thoughtfully but then nods his head and motions for me to follow him to his car. Eli mutters something under his breath the whole drive to the hospital, but to be honest, I don't care. I'm too numb to feel anything other than shock.

Tonight was a disaster. I don't think I could have imagined anything like this happening in my wildest dreams. As I ride in the backseat toward the hospital, fear replaces the shock that's consumed me. As the distance grows between me and the wreckage, that feeling of dread only grows. I am scared shitless to see the fallout from what happened here tonight. I don't know what will happen, but I know I have to find a way to prove that my father did this. For Addison. For Mr. and Mrs. Parks.

Chapter 29

Addison

Addison - Age 18

My eyes are blurry as I blink them open. I flutter my eyelids a few times, trying to make the world around me come into focus. I'm able to make out a few figures as I regain consciousness. One of them notices me coming around and steps forward.

"Addison? Addison, can you hear me?" they ask. I register that it's a feminine voice speaking, and I blink a few more times, trying to clear the fuzzy edges of my vision. Finally, I can make her out. She has dark hair, eyes, and a kind smile as she leans toward me. "I'm Dr. Brunner. You're in the hospital, you were caught in a fire last night and had some burns, but we've treated them. We've given you some medication to help with the pain. Just try and take it easy, okay?"

I don't know what else to do but nod my head. Now that I'm aware of where I am, the panic begins. The heart monitor starts beeping faster, indicating my rising heart rate. With my vision cleared, I look around, trying to take in everything.

I was caught in a fire?

It all starts returning to me, and my horror starts to grow. Memories of flames licking up the walls of the café flash in my mind. My throat starts to feel scratchy as I visualize the thick wall of smoke which formed rapidly, making it hard to breathe. Flames erupted from the storeroom, immediately feasting on anything they could reach.

My eyes go wide as I stare out at nothing, my vision tunneling and going dark around the edges. My heart rate picks up more, the beeping from the monitor coming faster and faster. My chest heaves as I attempt to breathe, the sensation of suffocation weighing heavily on my chest as if I was still stuck in the smoke. The tube underneath my nose feels too tight, and the blanket I'm under too heavy. I reach for the tubing and attempt to pull it off my face.

I can't breathe. I need to get out of here. I need to release this constriction tightening on my lungs, suffocating me.

"No, no, no—" I whisper over and over, my voice cracking from dryness.

Then a hand slips into mine and squeezes it. The weight seems to ground me, bringing me back to the present. Though my head pounds from increased blood pressure, I find myself calming. The cool air from the tubing under my nose finally reaches my brain, giving my body the oxygen it desperately craves. As my vitals start to level out, the panic begins to ease.

"That's it," a deep voice murmurs near my ear. "Deep breaths. You're safe; you're not alone."

I do my best to listen, breathing as deeply as possible with the tube flushing air into my nose. Trying to focus on the gentle clicks and beeps of the machines around me instead of my racing thoughts. I blink a few times and am relieved to see Noah sitting by my side. He gives my hand another squeeze as I scan his face, searching and grasping onto the strength that he offers.

"Noah?" I whisper, and he scoots closer to the bed, reaching up his other hand to brush a few hairs out of my face. He offers me a small smile, and his familiar blue eyes trace over me.

"I'm here, Parks. Charlie, Eli, and Grace are out in the waiting room. We're all here for you." His voice is gentle and soothing, continuing to ease the storm inside me.

The doctor and nurses bustle around the room for another few minutes, ensuring my pupils are reactive. They then double-check my vital signs before noting them and excusing themselves from the room, leaving Noah and me in privacy.

"The café?" I croak. Noah hears the scratchiness of my voice and reaches for a cup of water on the side table, holding it up so I can take a sip. The cool water makes my throat ache, but it helps relieve some of the burn I'm experiencing.

Noah's expression is grim, his eyebrows knit together, and his lips press into a thin line. "Yeah, there was a fire at the café."

My breathing becomes heavy and exaggerated again as my heart threatens to beat out of my chest.

Noah laces our fingers together, which calms and grounds me. "Do you remember anything from last night?"

"Kind of," I whisper. I frown, trying to piece the whole story together. My head starts to hurt, and I press my left hand up to my temple to ease the ache. A white bandage on my forearm catches my eye, and I tilt my head away to get a better look at it. Most of my arm, from my hand to my elbow, is wrapped tightly. The doctor said I had some burns, but I can't determine their severity from the bandages.

"I'm sorry," Noah says softly. When I look at him, his gaze is attached to my forearm; eyes stuck on the white gauze. "I should've been there sooner, I wish—I'm sorry." The catch in his voice causes tears to threaten in his eyes, making my eyes water in response.

Pieces of it come back to me then, Noah rushing in and crouching next to me. Of him swinging me up into his arms, holding onto me tightly. I remember saying something to him as he rushed us out, but I can't piece it together.

"You came for me." My brows pinch together at what this could possibly mean.

Noah's eyes find mine, and he holds my gaze so arduously I

wonder if I might melt under the intensity. "Of course, Parks. I couldn't leave you in there."

My cheeks warm up, and I squeeze his hand. "Are my parents here? Were they able to get out?"

Noah's expression darkens, and I suddenly know without him having to say another word. I swallow the lump of melancholy in my throat and blink back tears attempting to control my emotions, but I know it's no use. I can feel the walls closing around me, and I know I will break at any moment.

"I'm sorry, Addison," Noah whispers. "I went in there to get you out, but I couldn't—I had to get you out of there."

Noah's voice trails off as my ears start to ring. I stare blankly at him, and his lips continue to move, but I can't register what he's saying to me. My cheeks feel wet, and I recognize the tears streaming down my face uncontrollably. My nose is stuffed up, blocked, and snotty, and I try to breathe through my mouth, but my chest feels like there's a fifteen-pound weight on it, pressing down against my lungs. I gasp for breath, but none will come. It only worsens the harder I try to breathe, desperate for air.

Nausea starts to swirl in my stomach, and black spots dot my vision. I press and massage the heel of my hand against my temple, trying to get the room to stop spinning, but it's no use.

Between my gasps of breaths, I manage to choke out, "I'm gonna be sick."

I don't see him move, but before I know it, there's a blue sickness bag in my hand. Within two seconds, I throw up whatever is in my stomach. I squeeze my eyes shut, tears still leaking through as I sob. My body starts shaking uncontrollably, and I throw up again, though nothing comes up this time. I dry heave into the bag a few more times before something in my brain registers there's nothing left.

With a groan, I fall back against my pillows, my eyes shut. I feel a cool cloth run against my forehead and then down against my cheeks. I open one eye and see a nurse running about. She takes the bag from my hands and brings in several more, just in case.

I can't move. I lay there, numbness sinking through every cell in my body as tears continue to stream down my face. All I can think about are my parent's faces, each flashing in the back of my mind, smiling and laughing. Images I'll never see again in this lifetime.

As I lay there in my grief, I strain to remember what happened last night, trying to put it all together. My memory is fuzzy, but it starts returning to me as I walk through the events. I remember the fire alarms going off in the café. I didn't waste time before ushering the remaining customers onto the street. Before I had the chance to join them, it hit me like a lightning strike that my parents were still in the building. I spun on my heel and ran to the storeroom, where they went just minutes before the fire alarms went off to accept a delivery.

When I got to the storeroom door, I could hear them calling for help from the other side. I gripped the door handle, pulling with all my might, but it was jammed—I couldn't open it. My hands yanked and yanked, but it wouldn't budge. I could hear my heart pounding in my ears as adrenaline rushed through my muscles, egging me to open the door. I finally had to give up because the metal handle was so hot from the flames on the other sides. My burned flesh became too sensitive, and I could no longer grip it. So I resorted to alternating between throwing my body against the door and kicking it.

I screamed for my parents, and I could still hear them, but they yelled for me to get out of there. My feet were frozen to the ground. I couldn't bring myself to move. Begging my parents to help me open the door. My father's voice boomed over the chaos, demanding I leave immediately. With tears streaking down my face, I turned away and ran back to the front door. Hating myself with each step I took.

As I passed behind the front counter, a terrible cracking noise echoed through the café. Then the massive wooden menu board fell from its spot, landing directly on me. I screamed, trying to escape the flames licking up and down the board with all our menu items scrawled neatly across it in my mother's perfect writing, but it was no use.

I've never felt more helpless in my entire life. I lay there, trapped, watching the flames devour the café my family had built, slowly accepting that this might be it for me, for us. Part of me was okay with this; I would still be with my family.

My parents' screams ceased from the back room. Looking back on it now, it was a silence that I'll never forget. A roaring silence through the smoke and the darkness, telling me that nothing would ever be the same again.

Blinking my eyes back into reality, the tears continue to come. I turn my head into my pillow, closing my eyes and letting the grief consume me. My body convulses nonstop as my pillow becomes unbearably wet with my tears. I cry for my parents and the life I had always taken for granted up until now.

I don't know how long I lay there, but finally, the tears subside a little, and I manage to take a few deep breaths. I collect myself a little and wipe my mouth and nose with the back of my hand in a most unladylike fashion that would mortify my mother. I turn back to Noah. His forearms are laid flat on the railing of my bed. His chin rests on top of his hands, watching me. His eyes are ringed in red as if the sight of my crying has finally broken his resolve, and he's been fighting off tears himself. I sniffle as I look at him and feel more tears threatening to come. A few leak out as I shift around in the bed to face him, more wholly fighting the headache pounding in my temples with each movement.

"Sorry," I whisper, and he immediately shakes his head.

"Don't be. I just wish I could take away this pain for you." His eyes sparkle in the harsh hospital lights showing a deep sincerity.

My chin trembles and I nod my head, not trusting my words yet. A few moments later, I squeak, "It doesn't feel real. Like this is a bad dream that I will wake up from, and everything will be fine. But the fire...." My voice cracks, betraying my true feelings as I choke back more sobs. "The fire keeps replaying in my mind, so I know it's real."

"What do you remember?" Noah asks, his voice hesitant as if he's scared to ask, worried that he's crossing an invisible line. That at any moment, I'll be sent into another abyss of darkness and sadness. "If you're up to talking about it."

I breathe in deeply through my nose and exhale out of my mouth before telling him what I can.

"I just remember standing there one second, and everything was fine. Then it happened so fast. Before I knew what was happening, the whole café was filled with the worst-smelling smoke. Like burning plastic."

Every other sentence, I break down into a mini fit of sobs, unable to even *think* about the whole ordeal without the pain leaking through my body. When I finish my part of the story, Noah tells me the rest, filling in some of the blanks for me. I hold his gaze, taking comfort in the familiar blue of his eyes.

"Parks, I am *so sorry* this happened to you. If I could do anything to go back in time and keep this from happening, I would. I wish I could."

"It's not your fault. At least I still have my arm," I say glumly, attempting dark humor that falls flat.

Noah's face darkens. "Yeah. That damn thing sure did a number on you."

"And you," I murmur, looking down at his hands. His hands are covered in white gauze looped between his thumb and forefinger, bandaging up the spans of his palm and wrist. Reminding me of a boxer prepping for a fight.

Noah shrugs and then drops his hands into his lap, out of my view. "They're fine. Nothing too bad."

It hits me then that I would be dead along with my parents if Noah hadn't been there. But here he is, playing off his injuries as if they're nothing. A deep, sharp pain settles in my belly, but I try my best to push it down.

"Noah," I start to protest, but he shakes his head, his blue eyes becoming fierce as he holds my gaze.

"Don't start, Parks. I'm fine. I'm not worried about a few little burns when you've been through something as terrible as this."

"Okay..." my voice trails off because I don't know what else to say. My entire body still feels numb, and I'm unsure if it's from the medication they're giving me or the realization of the events that have transpired. Or maybe a combination of both?

"Your friends are here," Noah tells me. "I rode over here with Eli and Charlie after the fire last night, and I don't think either of them has left. Grace made it here earlier this morning too."

"Are they going to come in?" My heart suddenly feels full, knowing they're all here for me. My friends are here during my darkest hour when I'm sure they would rather be doing anything else.

"They will. I can get them whenever you want me to. They just wanted to give you a chance to wake up and—" he pauses, clearing his throat. I understand what he was about to say and why he stopped. They didn't want to be the ones to share the bad news. Or maybe they thought I'd react better if Noah were the one to tell me. I don't fault them for it. "They didn't want to interrupt our time together," he finally settles on as an explanation. I press my lips together, nodding my head at his unspoken words.

"I'm glad you're here." I wouldn't want anyone else at my side right now.

Noah raises his hand and runs it over my cheek, his fingers brushing lightly against my skin. I close my eyes, settling against the pillows at the comforting gesture. My body starts to feel heavy, my middle back aching from throwing up. My eyelids grow sluggish with exhaustion from all my crying in the last few hours, but I am so uncomfortable. As if he can sense my needs, Noah runs his fingers through my hair a few times, and I sigh.

As Noah sits back in his chair, I notice my hair tie on his wrist. It's bright green and contrasts heavily against his summer-tanned skin. It's the one I was wearing yesterday before this whole ordeal happened. He catches me watching and then smirks at me.

"Where did you get it?" I question, curious as to how he got it.

"I took it from the nurse. While you were unconscious. They

were going to just throw it away and get you a new one, but I wanted to keep it. Green's my color, don't you think?"

"I thought it was *my* color," I tease him back, referring to the silky green prom dress I wore only a few weeks ago. As I say it, it's hard for me to grasp that I was blissfully dancing the night away at prom not even a month ago. Now I'm in a hospital, my parents are dead, and I have nothing. Sorrow seeps back into me, inch by inch.

As if sensing my thoughts, Noah leans forward and takes my hand in his, giving it a comforting squeeze. It doesn't stop the sadness from creeping in, but it's nice knowing he's here. "Yes, green is definitely your color. I'll never forget how amazing you looked in that dress. Like a vision."

"You didn't look too shabby yourself," I respond, a soft smile forming on my lips. I feel like a fraud, smiling and thinking about prom night when my entire life has been turned upside down, but I welcome the fleeting happy thought. My eyelids are becoming heavy again, and I can't seem to keep them open this time.

Noah's deep chuckle echoes in my ear, and I register his hand running through my hair again. I settle against my pillow, letting the rhythmic brush of his fingers calm my body. "Get some sleep, Parks. I'll be here when you wake up."

Noah is true to his word and is still holding vigil by my bedside when I blink my eyes open a few hours later. A glance at the clock tells me I slept for longer than I thought I would. Noah moves over a tray of food for me to pick at, and I send him a grateful smile. Though I hadn't thought about my hunger before, I now sense a slight rumbling in my stomach, alerting me that I should probably try to eat something. I silently pray that I won't throw it up again. *Please at least grant me not to repeat that nightmare.*

"When do you think they'll let me out of here?" I ask Noah in between bites of a turkey sandwich. I know it's not the best I've ever had, but even the dry bread tastes like the most exquisite meal.

Noah's eyes move from where they are resting on my lips up to my eyes. The color of his eyes reflects against the bright clinical light of my hospital room as he studies me. "I think they said as long as you're doing okay, they can send you home tomorrow."

I gulp down the lump that has formed in my throat. *Home.*

Picking up on my distress, Noah quickly adds, "I think Grace was saying something about you going with her for a few days. Until everything gets settled."

I nod my head wordlessly. That will be good. I've spent the night with Grace before, so this should be like any other sleepover.

Only I'll have no family to go back to. My home will feel empty without their voices and laughter filling the void.

I dampen the thought process before I can start spiraling again and turn my attention to Noah. He still looks just as ragged as before, and I frown at him. "Did you sleep too?" He gives me a rueful grin and shakes his head. "Noah, you need to rest. You've been through a lot too."

"Don't be ridiculous, Parks. I'll rest when I need to, but right now, I feel like you need me more," he says, his voice firm as he reaches and takes my hand. "Just let me take care of you as best as possible."

Despite everything, my heart swells with affection for Noah. My lips turn up into a small smile, and right now, there's nothing I want more than for him to lean forward and kiss me. I feel like it's been an eternity since I've had his lips on mine, even though I'm pretty confident it hasn't even been a day. I am so grateful that he's here with me right now.

A gentle knock on the door echoes through my room, and Noah and I look up to see who my newest visitor is. Surprise crashes through my body when I realize it's Noah's mother. She steps carefully into the room, looking between Noah and me, her gaze settling on our hands joined together.

"Hey, Mom," Noah says. His voice sounds weary at the sight of his mother.

Catherine smiles at her son and then looks at me, all her attention honing in on me as she takes in my injuries. "Hello, dear. How are you feeling?"

I'm unsure if it's the motherly way she asks or the kindness on her face, but I feel the tears threaten to start again. I don't know Catherine McCoy very well, but at the moment, I want her to step forward and wrap me in a hug and tell me that everything is going to be okay.

"I'm okay," I squeak, but it doesn't sound convincing even to me. Catherine's eyes soften, and she steps closer as if she is going to hug me, but then she stops. A myriad of emotions plays across her face as she fidgets with her fingers, clearly unsure how to handle this situation. Noah's hand tightens around my own in a comforting squeeze.

"Please don't hesitate to reach out if you need anything. I'm here for you in any way that I can be," Catherine says, and I can tell she means it. She then looks at Noah. "We should head home so you can get some rest and clean up. You've had a long night."

"Mom, I'm fine...." Noah whines, sounding exasperated. Catherine holds up her finger to cut him off and gives him that look that all mothers know, daring you to disagree with them. Noah exhales, his shoulders dropping, and he looks at me. "I'll try and come back in a few hours."

My heart aches at the thought of him leaving, but I know he needs to sleep and get some food too. "Go. I'll be fine." I try to give him a reassuring smile, but I'm certain it doesn't reach my eyes.

Noah stands but then leans down across the railing of my bed. His lips press against my forehead, and he breathes through his nose, inhaling my scent. I close my eyes, appreciating his closeness. When he pulls away, his eyes are tender.

"I'll see you soon, Parks."

"Okay," I mouth.

"I'll send in your friends on my way out, so you're not alone," He tells me solemnly.

Alone.

For the first time, the weight of that word truly sinks in, and it finally hits me. I'm alone. I have no one. My parents are gone. Their business is gone. All I have left are Noah and my friends.

As Noah steps out of the room, a single tear leaks out of the corner of my eye, tracking down my cheek. Then the floodgates open, and I let the grief take over my body.

Alone, alone, alone.

Again I find myself slowly slipping into a panic, my thoughts spiraling as it all becomes too much. What am I going to do? Where am I going to live? What about the café? From what Noah told me, it's basically destroyed, but I don't know what that means for me now. How will I pay for college? Did my parents have a will?

More sobs wrack my entire body, and I gasp, trying to get air between the tears. I vaguely register the door clicking open, and someone is beside me again. *Noah?* My heart flutters at those striking blue eyes that can calm me. But a stab of disappointment settles in my gut as I see Charlie.

"Addie, what's going on? Are you in pain? Should I call the nurse?" Charlie questions as he comes to sit right next to me. I vaguely notice Grace trailing in after him. Her dark eyes convey worry as she takes the spot on the left side of my bed. Eli stands behind Grace, shifting between his feet, arms across his chest.

I manage to shake my head. "I have nothing left. Everything is gone," I wail.

Charlie hesitates a moment before maneuvering the bed rail down so he can lean closer and wrap me in a hug. His strong arms encircle my shoulders, and he pulls me close to him. I hug him tight, my arms wrapping around his neck as I bury my face into his shoulder. I notice a hand stroking along my back, probably Grace offering comfort in the only way she can think.

He lets me cry against him, and I take the opportunity. The grief shatters through me, and the more I cry, the worse it gets until I'm hysterical. All my memories with my parents, like birthdays and Christmases, run through my mind on a loop. Then when those stop, I start thinking about all the moments they won't be around for anymore. College graduation, my wedding, my children—they will have no part of that.

As I cry, I ask myself over and over, *why me?* Why did this have to happen to me? What did I do wrong to deserve this kind of torture? It simply isn't fair.

"I'm all alone," I choke out against my friend. Charlie sits back, placing his hand on my shoulder and looking at me earnestly.

"You're not," Grace says from her post on my left side. Her warm brown eyes are wide, and I notice tears welling up along the line of her lower lid. "We're here—Eli and Charlie are here for you, and you've got Noah ready to move mountains at your word. And you'll always have me."

"I know all that," I tell her. "But I feel so empty. I'll never be able to go to my mom when I need her or ask my dad questions when I need guidance."

"We won't be able to replace them," Charlie agrees, and though it hurts to hear him say it, I appreciate the blunt truth. "But I'm not sure if you want us to replace them. Let them live in your memory as they were. There will be pain, but you can also look back and remember all the wonderful times. The ones that will one day bring back your smile and laughter at those beloved memories. I know that's going to be hard right now, and it will probably never be any less painful to think about, but they would want you to continue trying to live your life for them."

I sniffle but nod my head, looking between my three best friends. "I don't know what I would do without you. Just promise you won't leave me too."

"I promise you, Addie," Charlie starts, holding my gaze intently. "You will *never* be alone. You'll always have us, and I know Eli will tell you the same thing." I turn my gaze to Eli, who gives me a weak smile and nods. "If you need a family, let us be it. We won't let you down."

It may be the conviction in his tone or the steadiness of his gaze, but I believe him. I hold onto that, letting it be the tether that keeps me from unraveling completely. As long as I have people who love me, I'll never be alone.

Chapter 30

Noah

Noah - Age 18

"It was him," I say to my mother, my voice low as we pass through the hospital's automatic doors. I don't specify who I'm talking about because I don't think I need to. My heart aches to leave Addison behind, but the exhaustion is starting to wear on me, making my feet grow heavier with each step. I desperately need a shower and a new change of clothes.

My mother doesn't respond as we cross the parking lot to her car, but her silence is enough. I know. The tight set of her lips tells me everything she's not outwardly saying—there's no proof, but she knows my father better than I do, and by her expression, even she wouldn't put it past him.

Once I'm settled in my mom's car, I lean back in my seat. I rest the side of my head against the window, the coolness of the glass calming my rattled nerves. My mother starts the car and pulls away from the hospital parking lot. The car is quiet, aside from my mom's favorite classical music playing from the stereo and the sound of the road underneath our tires. The melodic tone of the classic piano clashes with the emotions raging inside me. Eventually, my mother breaks her silence.

"You were very brave last night," her soft voice is melodic to my ears and causes my chest to tighten. The world swims in front of my eyes. I close them tightly to stop the spinning. "You saved her life, Noah."

My stomach lurches as the events of last evening wash over me. I think the stress of finding out if Addison was going to be okay helped hold me together, but now that I know she's okay and safe, I suddenly feel like I'm spinning out of control. Nausea hits me like a tsunami, and I bend forward, grabbing onto the dashboard. "I need you to pull over," I say. My voice is muffled by my hand covering my mouth like it could prevent me from flooding my mother's pristine car with vomit.

My mother doesn't waste time pulling off the road onto a shoulder. As soon as the car slows down enough, I throw my door open and step out, throwing up all over the grass. I bend over, my hands resting on my knees as I spit out the taste of the bile in my mouth, afraid to move in case more comes up. I hear a car door open and slam, and then my mom's by my side, one hand on my shoulder and the other rubbing up and down my back.

"He did this to her," my voice breaks, my throat burning. I reach up and wipe at the tears in my eyes, evidence of the stress I've been through and a physical reaction to the violent vomiting. "Why would he do this? He took everything from her." I stand up straight, staring her in the eyes, needing to see her answer as well as hear it.

"I know, honey. I'm so sorry," my mother coos as she continues to rub my back.

"And I can't even prove that he did it! Why is he like this?" My eyes widen as the realization hits me like a ton of bricks. Stepping away from my mother, I fall to my knees and break down on the side of the road. I brace my hands on the grass, my shoulders slouching forward and my head hanging heavy. Sobs engulf my body as the world's weight crashes onto my shoulders. Memories of how Addison broke down after hearing about her parents haunt me. The sound of her heartbreak rings in my ears. I'll never be able to forget that. Her pain is my pain. And what's worse? I'm basically the one who caused it.

"Breathe, Noah," my mother says. She returns to my side and pats me on the back, speaking soothing words trying to get me to calm down. "It's okay, sweetheart."

"It's not okay. What if he goes after her again? I was stupid last night and confronted him, blamed him for the whole thing. Parks—what if he hurts her again?" Panic sets in deeper, like claws stabbing through my heart.

"We'll figure it out, Noah. Nothing will happen to her. Trust me." She wants me to have trust? My mother, I trust. My father, I don't. He's a loose cannon. Who knows what he'll do next?

My mother manages to coax me back into the car and drives us home. I fall into the seat and don't move until she parks the car again. Dragging my feet, I schlep into the house, my face downcast at the floor. Tremors take over my body as my brain still attempts to process everything that has happened in the last twenty-four hours. The taste of bile lingers in my mouth, and all I want is a hot shower and a toothbrush.

"Noah?" my father's deep voice echoes from the living room, making my heart drop to my stomach. "Catherine?"

My mother stops me with a reassuring hand on my shoulder like she can sense my anxiety from facing him. But still, I brace my shoulders and turn to face the doorway to the living room. My father steps out into the foyer, his hand wrapped around a glass of a deep amber liquid, most likely his favorite brand of scotch. My father scans over me, taking in my singed clothes and rumpled hair.

"You look like shit, son."

I sneer at him, curling my top lip up into a snarl. "And you look like a lying bastard." My father remains cool as I throw the insult at him. My mother flinches next to me at my aggressive tone and abrupt attack.

"Noah," she starts, her hand flexing against me in a subtle warning. "You've had a long day. I think you should just head up to bed and get some rest. We can all discuss this in the morning."

I turn and look at her incredulously. Her eyes are like steel as she stares me down, silently warning me to listen to her. I lower my weapons and turn back to my father once more, shooting him a sideways glance before taking another step towards the stairs. But my father decides he needs to have the last word.

"I'll be speaking at the Parks' memorial service in two days," he hums at me and takes a sip of his drink, acting like he doesn't have a care in the world.

I spin to face him again and grit through my teeth, "*What?*"

"In the face of a town tragedy, it's normal practice for the mayor to be present at the memorial," he responds matter-of-factly as if he's reading off the town bylaws word-for-word. "I figured you'd like to hear it from me first so you don't launch yourself across the stage when I get up there. I feel that's a valid concern since you seem to have lost all sense of decorum in the last forty-eight hours."

I gape at him, unsure of how to respond. My eyes flash to my mother, and I'm slightly relieved to see she looks just as dumbstruck as I am. "You have a lot of nerve," I finally growl out.

He shrugs as if the whole thing is no big deal. "I just go where they tell me. Don't be mad at me that my townspeople want their mayor to reassure them when a tragic event happens."

"So this is how you're going to play it, huh?" I say. "You're going to be the one that swoops in when people need a hero, despite knowing you're the one who caused all this pain and tragedy."

"I'm afraid I have no idea what you're talking about."

I suddenly have the greatest desire to take a few steps toward him and punch him across his smug face, but some part of my brain is coherent enough to know that's not a good idea. "I'll tell everyone, you know. And I won't stop until someone listens to me."

My father's lips twist, and his steely eyes trace over me. "No, you won't."

"And why is that?"

"Because, as I told you last night, you don't want to cross me. And besides, no one will believe you."

"They will if I shout it loud enough or if I can find proof."

He raises one dark eyebrow, takes another sip, and then turns to my mother. "Catherine, I'm sure you don't want any part of this conversation. Maybe Noah could use a glass of water or something."

My mother stiffens next to me at the blatant dismissal and raises her chin at my father in a challenge. Her voice is low and strong when she speaks, not giving any room for suggestions. "Actually, Declan, please continue. If you're going to threaten *my* son, it might as well be in front of me."

My father's gaze sharpens, and he sizes her up for a moment before visibly backing down. A part of me is pleased to see that even Declan McCoy knows when to go head-to-head with my mother and when it's best to back down.

"This isn't over," I growl at him and then turn on my heel to go upstairs, leaving my parents in their silent face-off. As I walk up the stairs, I hear them muttering to each other in low voices. I can't determine what they're saying, but I don't care anyway. I'm too exhausted.

I go to my bathroom and hop in the shower, trying to wash off the last twenty-four hours from my body. Here, in the shower, is where I realize just how sore all of my muscles are. They are so painful. I hadn't realized how tight I must have held them all day. I scrub my skin until it's red and burning, and I wash my hair, trying to get the smoky smell out. Even when I'm finished, I don't feel clean, but I'm too tired to spend any more time trying to scrub it off. I collapse in my bed after drying off and manage to fall asleep quickly.

Over the next few days, I spend most of my time with Addison. She's released from the hospital the next day, just like I told her, with a few instructions on how to care for the burns on her forearm. The defeated slump of her shoulders guts me, and I try to be supportive without being too overbearing. I go with her to Grace's house but then give her some time alone with her friend, knowing she might need a break from me. Even if it's at the risk of my own sanity, I seem to be missing when she is not around. I seem to be fraying apart at the edges, the stress looming in the background of my mind at all times.

At the end of the week, I find myself standing on the edges of the crowd gathered in the town center. Almost everyone in this town has come out to support Addison in the memorial to her parents. The wreckage from the fire still lingers, the demolished building a stark reminder of the tragedy. I notice that Addison tries her hardest to avoid looking at it. As we walk past, she grips my hand tighter in hers, keeping her gaze straight forward.

Addison stays close to my side throughout the service, her shoulders back and her head held high as people go up to the stage to pay their respects. Her hair is tied back away from her face, though a few wispy strands have escaped. Her cheeks are blotchy, and her eyes are red from the endless tears shed over the last week. My arm is wrapped around her waist, holding her close to me just in case she needs the support.

After the choir from the church sings their last song, my father takes his place at the podium on the stage. I brace myself, hoping he doesn't turn this into a disaster. He looks at all the people gathered and jumps right into his spiel.

"Today, we gather to mourn the loss of some of our own. This tragedy will leave a permanent mark and hollow spaces within our hearts for many years to come." His voice is level, hinting at a sorrow that I know doesn't exist within him. I grip Addison's waist a little tighter, pulling her closer to me and trying to breathe evenly through my nose.

Thankfully, he keeps it short. He lays on the sympathy and heartbreak, and I grit my teeth. I finally manage to breathe when he walks down the few steps from the stage. I know he kept most of the dramatics to a minimum, but I can't seem to quell the fire burning deep in my chest, knowing that he's the reason we're all here. I stamp down the frustration as much as possible and focus back on Addison standing next to me.

A slow song starts to play, and one of the main singers from the church takes the microphone, her melancholy voice traveling over the gathered crowd. The song's gravity hits harder without the background from the other choir members. The words of her song slide deep into my chest, emphasizing the hollowness within me, and my eyes start to sting. Addison reaches to my hand on her waist and laces our fingers together.

Her eyebrows raise as her thumb strokes over my wrist, and she looks down at my hand before meeting my gaze, her eyes twinkling both from amusement and unshed tears from the service. "You're still wearing my hair tie."

I look down at the green elastic wrapped around my wrist and give her a wry shrug. "Do you need it back?"

Despite everything, she fights a smile and shakes her head. "No, you can keep it. I have hundreds."

I lean over and press my lips into her hair, breathing in the familiar scent of her shampoo. Addison leans her head against my chest before looking back at the stage to wait out the rest of the service.

After the pastor finishes the service, we return to Grace's house. Her mom is hosting a little get-together for the townspeople to come to give their condolences to Addison. I stay by her side throughout the whole thing, offering her support whenever possible. She keeps it together well, accepting everyone's sympathy without shedding a tear. The entire afternoon passes by in a blur, and by the time I leave, I'm exhausted, and my patience is worn thin.

I go straight up the stairs to my father's office when I get home, knowing he'll be there. I've had enough of pretending. I throw open the door without knocking and stand in the doorway. My father glances up at me from his work with a bored expression at my boisterous entrance. One of his eyebrows arches, baiting me.

"That was quite the performance at the service this afternoon," I say to him.

My father leans back in his chair and rubs the edge of his jaw. "I thought so too."

I narrow my eyes. "Now that your precious voters aren't around, why don't we just drop the pretenses and lay it all out?"

"You're still on this, then?" my father questions, going back to his work as if I mean absolutely nothing to him.

"I won't let it go until you admit to what you've done. It was bad enough that you lied to the whole town, but Addison was there too while you were up there spewing your shit."

"And what lie would that be?" He raises his eyebrows questioningly, still not removing his gaze from the papers on his desk. "I thought I handled today's service well."

"All your fake sympathy and condolences. You really have a lot of nerve standing up there and pretending to care when you're the one who did this to her," I say darkly.

He slowly lifts his head and gives me a blank glare, seeming to ponder over his words before he says them. The room grows heavy with his silence, and the hairs on my arms stand up under the weight of his gaze. "Noah, if I were responsible for what you're accusing me of, I would think it would be in your best interest to let it go."

"And why is that?"

"Because, as you said, you've seen what I'm capable of. Do you really want to try and test me?"

"Are you threatening me, now?" I ask him, my voice dropping an octave.

"Of course not, but listen to me well, Noah. No one can bring down a McCoy, you understand? No matter who it is, they won't be able to beat me. Take the Parks' as an example. I will *always* win. I've been doing this far too long not to succeed at this game."

My body trembles as I stand there, and there's nothing that I want more than to launch at him and punch that smug expression off of his face, but somehow I restrain myself.

"And now I'm just supposed to live with that?"

My father stares down at me cooly, and then suddenly, it's as if he has a realization. Disappointment flashes over his face, and he sighs resignedly. "You're really giving me no choice here, Noah."

"What are you—?"

"I think it would be best if you leave."

He takes me off guard, and I stand there gaping at him. "We're not done talking."

"You misunderstand me," he says, his voice ominous. "I want you to leave town and don't come back."

"That's ridiculous. I can't just leave."

My father stands and takes a step towards me, the features of his face hardening into a stormy expression. "You'll find a way. This is for the best. I realize now that you'll never be able to conveniently forget what you think happened. I can't have you trying to undermine me every chance you get. I believe this is the best option for everyone."

"And how's that?"

"Because I know what's most important to you. And I'll be frank, it would take nothing for me to finish the job," he says, snapping his fingers. "It would be that easy."

My stomach churns, and I want to vomit right on his shiny black shoes. "You would hurt Addison?"

"Is that what it will take for you to understand the point I'm trying to convey?" He questions right back, seemingly unbothered about the subject matter as if we were discussing something meaningless, like the weather. "If so, then I suppose I would."

"So now you expect me to what, just leave Willow Heights and go on as if my life here never happened? As if you didn't run me out of my town and take everything from the girl I love?"

"Honestly, I think this is the best option. Leave, mind your own damn business, and no harm will come to your little girlfriend. You might think you have the upper hand here, but you couldn't be more wrong. You step one foot out of line, and I'll know, and it will all be over. Do you understand me? It's best if you just cut your losses and leave."

My jaw goes slack. I can't believe what I'm hearing right now. My own *father* is running me out of town because he doesn't want me stirring up trouble. Suddenly the world shifts underneath my feet, and I wonder if I will collapse from it all. If I stay, then I'm putting Addison in direct harm. I don't know if I'll ever see her again if I leave.

I weigh my options quickly in my head and finally conclude that I can't win here. This is a lose-lose situation. But at the heart of it, I only have one option. I have to do as he says because anything happening to Addison would destroy me. Her safety is more important than my selfish desires.

"Fine," I finally say. "I'll go. But you must *swear* that nothing will happen to Addison if I do."

My father holds my gaze steadily. "I'm a man of my word, Noah."

"Swear it."

"Fine. I swear, no harm will come to your little girlfriend."

"Alright," I say. I stare at him for another beat and then excuse myself from his office.

My body is heavy as I go to my bedroom to start packing. I can't help but feel like I've just made a deal with the devil. I'll probably regret this, but now I have no other choice.

I pass my mother in the hallway, and she gives me a concerned look as I breeze past her. "Noah? What's going on?"

"I need to leave," I say, and my mother tenses next to me. As I walk into my bedroom, I go over to my dresser and yank open the drawers, pulling all my shirts and pants out and tossing them onto the bed before finding a duffle bag in my closet.

"What? What are you doing? Stop that." she argues, trying to grab the pair of jeans I'm stuffing into the bag.

"I'm leaving. He told me to get the hell out of town and never come back. And he didn't hesitate to use her as leverage to get his point across."

"Noah, I'm not sure if that's—"

"No," I say firmly, standing up straight and scrubbing my hands over my face. I'm sure I look like a deranged animal, and honestly, that's how I feel inside. "He *threatened* her, Mom. So if this is what needs to happen to keep her safe, then so be it. I can't let him hurt her any more than he has already."

My mother stares at me, blinking a few times. I note the sadness swirling in her blue eyes, but I can't linger on it for too long. I go back to pulling all my clothes out of my dresser and then work on the clothes in my closet.

"I can talk to your father. Maybe I'll be able to talk him out of this ridiculous notion."

I shake my head. "It's no use. You know as well as I do that once he makes up his mind about something, that's it. I have to do this."

"Where will you go?" my mother asks me, her voice somber as she watches me fret around my room.

I pause for only a second, allowing her question to sink in and a sense of wariness takes over before I stamp it down, focusing back on my task. "I'm not sure, but I'll figure it out. Anywhere but here."

"What about Addison?"

My eyes fall closed, and I take a deep breath. "She has her friends. They'll take care of her."

"She needs you, Noah," my mother protests, stepping closer. "The way she was looking at you—"

"I know that," I cut her off, shaking my head. "But I need her to stay safe. And if I stick around, she'll have a giant target on her back, and I can't live with that. He won't stop. He gave me direct instructions, and he'll take it out on her if I don't do what he says. I won't let him—I can't."

Compassion floods my mother's eyes, and she closes the distance between us, wrapping me in a hug. I bury my face against her shoulder, letting her comfort me. My mother runs her hand up and down my back, but she doesn't say anything. Finally, when she lets me go, her expression is resolved.

"Okay, finish packing. I'll call my sister and see if she can let you stay with her for a while."

I raise my eyebrows in surprise. My mother doesn't talk to her family much anymore–probably because they all hate my dad. "Where does she live?"

"Further north, outside of Burlington. Hopefully, staying with her will at least give you a chance to figure out what to do next," she tells me. She runs her hand over my hair and then nods her head. "I'll call her right now, and we'll get this figured out."

Less than an hour later, arrangements are made for me to stay with my aunt for the remainder of the week. That was all she was willing to give, but it's better than living out of my car. I toss my duffel bag into the back of my truck and then turn to my mother, who came out with me.

"I guess I'll get going then. You told her I'd be there later today?" I ask her. My mother nods and then steps forward, pulling me into a hug.

"I am so sorry, Noah. We'll find a way around this. I promise you."

I wrap my arms around her, hugging her back. Part of me is grateful that my mother is optimistic. Still, my realistic side knows that my father is too cunning, too clever. I don't think beating him at his own game is going to be an easy feat.

Right before I get into the car, my father steps out of the house, standing like an ominous guard at the front of his house. His mouth is set into a firm line as he catches my gaze. I take a deep breath and dip my chin slightly at him. He nods his head at me once before disappearing back into the house. An understanding.

I turn back to my mother, whispering a goodbye and that I'll talk to her soon before I get into my truck and pull out of the driveway. As I drive away from my home for maybe the last time, I pull out my phone, dialing the one person I never thought I'd be calling, but extenuating circumstances call for sacrifices.

"What?" his voice answers, already as fed up with the phone call as I am.

"Sullivan, I need to talk to you about something. It's important," I tell him, my voice feeling thick. Charlie stays silent, waiting for me to continue. "I need to leave town, and I don't know if I'll be coming back."

He's quiet for another moment before he asks, "Where are you going?"

"I don't know," I tell him, though my mother was able to get ahold of her sister, who said I could stay with her for a few days. This should hopefully be enough for me to decide what to do moving forward. "And I need you to know because I'm about to tell Addison I'm leaving."

I hear him make a frustrated sound from the other side of the line. "You picked a shitty time to bounce, man. She'll want to go with you."

"And you need to make sure that won't happen."

"Why should I? You're the one about to rip her heart out. You can be the one to convince her not to follow you."

"Charlie," I protest, my voice tight. "Please, just—I need you to look after her."

He huffs again, and I can practically hear him rolling his eyes at my dramatics. "You know I always do that, which is why the next time I see you, I'll kick your ass for whatever bullshit you're pulling right now."

"I'm not messing around here, man," I suck in a breath and then decide to send caution to the wind. If I can tell anyone the truth, it would be Charlie. He's goody-two-shoes enough to be reliable. "I'm almost certain that my father is the one who ordered the fire to be set. He wouldn't have done it himself, but he's definitely the mastermind behind it all."

"Noah, that's—that's a big accusation," Charlie says, his voice lilting in a surprised tone. For a moment, he sounds every bit the sheriff's son he is.

"I'm not wrong," I tell him firmly. "Listen, my dad's behind a lot of shady shit, but I don't know everything. Addison's father was here to investigate him, working undercover for the FBI. It was a long-haul investigation."

"I know about that."

Now I'm the one surprised. "You do?"

"Sort of, she let it slip once that he was a cop, and that was about it, but she told me a little more about it recently. I didn't know he was investigating your dad, though."

"I talked about it a little bit with him, but he never really divulged much. But anyway, my dad caught wind of it, and I guess he just had enough and lit the place up. His version of getting rid of a problem," I tell him glumly.

"That's fucked up, man."

"You're telling me. But now he's basically given me an ultimatum: leave town, or he'll go after Addison to force me to be quiet. And I can't have him hurting her," I say. Even the thought of my father doing anything to Parks makes me see red, and I want to strangle him.

"So that's why you're leaving," Charlie says. "Are you going to tell her all of this?"

"Probably not," I respond softly. "I don't want her anywhere near him if I can help it."

"What do you need me to do?"

"Just make sure he doesn't go after her. Make sure she goes and does everything she wants to do. Promise me you'll do that."

"I'm not sure if—"

"*Promise me*," I growl at him, my patience starting to run thin. The clock is ticking, and I need to wrap things up with him. "Please, Charlie. Make sure she leaves and doesn't come back. I don't want her anywhere near him."

He sighs. "I'll try."

I realize that's the best I'm going to get out of him, so I offer him thanks, tell him I'll stay in touch, and then hang up. I'm sure he's not sad to see me go. Eli will probably throw a celebratory party as soon as he realizes I'm gone.

After texting and finding out where Addison is, I pull up to the town square and park in an open spot. My heart is throbbing in my chest as if anticipating the trauma it's about to undergo. I steel myself as I walk up towards where she's sitting and clear my throat. Addison looks up at me, her eyes brightening when she sees me standing in front of her.

"Hey!" She stumbles to her feet and looks at me with a happy expression that quickly falls when she senses my foul mood. "Is everything okay?"

Every cell in my body wants to scream that everything is okay and that everything will be fine, but that's just not the case. My soul splinters as I shake my head. Her face sobers even more as she picks up on the gravity of the situation.

"What's wrong, Noah?"

Here goes everything. "I'm leaving."

Addison stares at me as if she doesn't understand the word. "Leaving?"

I nod my head brusquely. "Yeah. I'm leaving Willow Heights. Today."

"Oh," she responds, blinking a few times. "When will you be back?"

My fingernails dig into the palms of my hands as I gear up to tell her. "I won't be."

She blinks again, her brain trying to catch up with what I'm saying to her. I feel terrible. Addison has been through so much over the last few days, and I hate that I'm adding to that load, but I have no other choice. This is for the best.

She scrunches her eyes together and then presses her non-injured hand to her forehead. "I'm sorry, I just—what? You won't be back?"

I grow nauseous, and everything starts spinning around me. "No, I won't be coming back. At least not for the foreseeable future."

Addison opens her eyes and stares at me, hurt. "Why? I thought— I thought things between us were finally—"

"Parks," I cut her off, taking a step closer and grabbing her good hand. "They are—they were. But I can't stay here. I need to go."

"Is it something I did? Just—if I hurt you, please tell me so I can fix it. We can get past it. I know I've been...needy," she struggles over the word, "the last few days, but I promise things will get better. Please, Noah. I need you. You're all—I don't have anything left."

My heart cracks in half, the strings holding me together snapping in two, but I force myself to keep it together, though the sight of her in pain does horrible things to me. All I want to do is make her happy, and fill her days with smiles and laughter. But here I am doing the exact opposite. "That's why I have to go. It's for the best. I need you to trust me."

Her eyes scour my face, searching for anything that will tell her what the hell is going on. "You know I trust you, but I don't understand."

I look up at the sky, never feeling more trapped in my entire life. I don't want this. I don't want to leave her right now, or ever. But I know my father, and I know he's not bluffing. If I don't do what he says, he'll take it out on her, and I *can't* let that happen.

Just a few days ago, I was starting to map out my whole future with her, and now I'm standing here telling her that we won't have a future together. Somehow my life has gotten twisted into this nightmare, and I'm hoping that any moment I'll wake up and things will be normal. I want to wake up in a world where Addison's parents are alive and well, and she and I are together.

As I stand there staring at her, begging me to give her answers, all I can think about is how much time we've wasted. All those years, we went back and forth, skirting around our feelings for each other. We could've been together then. I wonder if things would have been different if we hadn't been too afraid to take the leap. But I'll never know.

I wish we would've had more time. I would have liked to do everything with her.

But now...? It's over.

Addison's confusion and worry morph into frustration when I don't say anything else. I can see it on her face so clearly. She doesn't understand and *hates* not knowing what's happening. "Noah, this isn't like you. Just tell me what the hell is going on."

I shake my head. "I *can't*, Parks."

"It's your dad, isn't it? He's done something or said something to you that's scared you off." I school my features, not giving anything away, even though she's hit the nail right on the head. She exhales. "Noah, you promised."

"What?" I ask. I promised her a lot of things that I'm inherently going back on now.

"You promised me you wouldn't let him ruin your life."

I close my eyes and breathe harshly through my nose. I want so desperately to tell her that I'm doing this, so he doesn't hurt her more than he already has. That my leaving here is the only thing I can do to keep her safe.

But I don't.

"Well, I guess I lied."

I see my words' weight as they land in front of us like a pound of bricks. Her face goes slack with shock, and then slowly anger starts to form. She shakes her head vehemently at me, unaccepting.

"No. You don't get to do this. You can't just *leave* after all we've been through, everything *I've* been through. I don't want you to go."

"I have to," I tell her. "I don't have a choice."

"You *always* have a choice!" she shouts at me. A part of me is grateful she's mad. If her being angry at me is what it takes for her to accept this, then so be it. I realize that this is when I have to turn away from her and never look back.

"I don't want this. I'm sorry, but I have to go. Goodbye, Parks."

"Noah, wait."

My heart shatters into ten million pieces as I walk away from her. I hear her calling after me, telling me to stop, but I don't. I can't. The pain in her voice is like a dagger to my heart, and each step I take away from her only plunges the blade deeper. I get in my truck and start it up. Before I turn down the street, I glance in my rearview mirror, getting one last good look at her. I don't know if or when I'll ever see her again, so I take her in, appreciating her beauty.

She's standing where I left her, arms wrapped tightly around her body as if to hold herself together. The white bandage covering her burn is stark against the dark blue shirt she's wearing. Even from here, I can see the redness of her nose and the tears starting to spill down her cheeks.

My eyes burn with unshed tears, and I clench my jaw so tightly it hurts. I'm doing this for her. To keep her safe. I've already inadvertently ruined her life; I don't know if I could live with myself if anything else happened to her. I can't be selfish when it comes to this, comes to her.

The ultimatum was clear. There is only one way for me to move forward. I hope someday I'll get my chance to come back and explain everything to her, and maybe things will work out. But I can't bank on that. As long as she's happy and safe and *alive*, that's all I care about.

I drive slowly, taking my time to drink her in one last time. Then I flick on my turn signal and spin the wheel until she's out of my sight. As I drive past the city limits of Willow Heights, I note that I feel empty inside, that a piece of me is missing. I'm unsure if I'll ever be able to fill the gaping hole I've created in my heart today.

I squeeze my eyes shut once, then open them, a single tear falling down my cheeks.

I love you, Parks. I hope I'll see you again someday.

Chapter 31
Noah

Noah - Age 18

The smell of coffee and the sizzle of bacon wakes me. The intoxicating aroma beckons me to get up and indulge myself. I shift uncomfortably on the couch that is too small for my long frame, my back feels like I slept in a vice, and the crick in my neck sends shockwaves up into my head. In a swift movement, I throw the blanket off of me and sit up with a groan. I blink a few times, rubbing the sleep from my eyes. As I stretch out the achy muscles, I glance around the unfamiliar room.

Yesterday comes back to me in a rush, and I press the heel of my hand against my temple, trying to steady myself. The conversation with my father rings in my head, and I try not to think too hard about being banished from my home. And Addison...

Addison.

I left her there and didn't look back. My heart threatens to break in half the more I think about it, so instead, I get up off the couch and walk to the small bathroom in the hallway, squashing down the heartache. I turn on the faucet and splash my face with the cool water, trying to center myself.

Last night I made it to my Aunt Trish's secluded mountain home. She was waiting for me, rocking in a chair on her porch and sipping an old-fashioned. When I parked my truck in her drive, she walked down the few steps from the porch to meet me and then helped me grab my things, setting me up in the living room and promising to have the guest bedroom ready in a few days.

She left me alone to my own devices for the rest of the evening, disappearing into her own bedroom. I'm not sure if my mother told her all that was going on or if she could just sense that I wasn't in the mood to talk, but I was grateful for some alone time. I crashed on the couch and passed out in record time.

When I leave the bathroom, I'm feeling a little more refreshed. I pad into the kitchen, where I find my Aunt Trish standing at the stove. She's got the same chestnut brown hair that my mother has, but where my mom's hair is straight as a pin, Aunt Trish's is full of wild and springy curls. When she turns around, though, those same blue eyes take me in.

"Good morning, Sunshine," my aunt says to me and then motions towards the small table in the middle of the kitchen. "Sit down. Breakfast's ready."

I scoot out the chair, wincing at the sound of it scraping her hardwood. Aunt Trish turns around, pan in hand, and slides three pieces of bacon onto the plate at my seat. As soon as I'm sitting, she goes back to the stove and does the same with a pan of eggs, asking how many I want to make sure I have enough.

"Do you want toast? I thought about making pancakes, but then I decided I didn't feel like it. I can throw in a few slices of toast real easy, though, if you want."

I shake my head, smiling at her gratefully. "No, this is more than enough. Thank you."

Aunt Trish slides into the seat across from me and eyes me suspiciously. "So polite. Your mama taught you well. She ever tell you about how our parents would swat us if we were ever rude?"

"No, she never did," I respond, spooning a big bite of scrambled eggs into my mouth.

My aunt hums as she watches me eat, taking a bite out of a strip of bacon every other second. "She didn't really tell me what was going on, just that you were in trouble and needed a place to stay."

I press my lips together into a thin line and dip my chin in agreement. "Yeah, that's about the gist of it."

She narrows her eyes at me. "Trouble's not following you, is it?"

Sadness creeps into my chest at her question, and I look down at my plate. "No, it's not. I left that all behind in Willow Heights."

Aunt Trish nods her head as if she approves of my answer. Then after scrutinizing me for another minute, she asks the golden question, "This was all your father's doing, wasn't it?"

I nearly choke on the piece of bacon I'm chewing but manage to swallow it down without any casualties. "Why would you think that?"

"I've never liked that man," she spits, and I reel back at the venom lacing her voice. "I always told Catie that it was a bad idea to get roped in with him. There's just something that seems—" she waves her hand about, searching for the word, "—slimy about him. I don't know."

I don't answer but raise my eyebrows up once and then look down at my plate. Aunt Trish is on a roll now, though, and she continues to rant.

"But did she listen to me? Oh, *no*. That Declan is nothing if not charismatic. He won her over, and she didn't have a choice in the matter. Then you came along," her voice changes slightly, and her eyes return to me. "Cutest baby I ever did see, I'll tell you what."

"You've met me before?" I ask her, surprised. I have no memory of this.

She bobs her head. "Oh, yes. I came down to Willow Heights a few times while you were young. You were teeny, tiny, so I'm not surprised you don't remember." She squeezes her hands together as if to show me how small I was the last time she saw me. "But I stopped coming around after your second birthday. Your father—" she shakes her head and trails off.

"He's pretty bad."

"That's an understatement," Aunt Trish mutters, looking out the window above the sink. "When your mother called me, I was hoping she was calling me to tell me she was planning to leave him."

I frown. "I'm not sure that will ever happen."

"Well, a girl can hope," Aunt Trish says, a wry smile forming. And then she sighs wistfully. "Alright," she says, waving her hand again. "Lay it on me."

"What?" I'm quickly learning that my aunt has much more energy and moxie than I'm used to dealing with. It reminds me of Addison, and I feel a pang of guilt stab my heart.

"Tell me everything. I'm not going to be able to help you figure out what to do unless I know the whole story, so let's hear it."

I study her for a minute, trying to decide if this is a trap or not. I finally realize that she might be my best option for moving forward, so I launch into the story, not leaving a piece of it out. I tell her about the weird interaction between my father and the Parks at graduation. Then I regale the fire, telling her how I ran in there to rescue Addison, but I wasn't able to get her parents out. I tell her about my suspicions about my father, filling her in on my conversations with Mr. Parks about all of his shady business. And finally, I tell her about Addison.

I tell her all about how upset I am that I had to leave her right when things were finally starting to come together for us. It's not fair, and I make sure Aunt Trish knows exactly how I feel about all of that.

"You've really had a rough time, haven't you?" she asks though I can tell the question is rhetorical. She purses her lips and looks at me before exhaling loudly. "Alright. Here's what we're going to do. I'm going to give you this notepad," she gets up and walks towards a drawer, pulling it out. "And a pen, and you're going to sit here and come up with ideas of what your next move is going to be. I don't care if you put 'wallow in my own despair' on there, but I better see some actual ideas too."

She plops the notepad and pen down in front of me and then puts her hands on her hips. "Where are you going?"

"I'll be outside. I've got weeds that won't pull themselves, you know?"

I don't know. I've never pulled weeds in my life. My mother always hired gardeners to keep the gardens at home looking perfect.

"Come find me when you're done," she says, ruffling my hair. I watch her walk towards the front door. She pauses before pulling it open and turns back to me slowly. "And Noah? You're going to be okay. I know it feels like you've got one hell of an uphill battle, and you probably do. But I know you're going to be fine."

I offer her a small smile as she exits the house. Then I look down at the blank pad of paper sitting in front of me. Hesitant, I reach for the pen and then write down the first thing that comes to my mind.

"Wallow in despair," I say out loud as I write it down. *Hey, she said I could, right?*

After that, I run out of ideas. I honestly have no idea what I'm going to do. I didn't even know what my next plan was when I was safe at home, and now? Now I have no home, and I'm sleeping on my strange aunt's couch. I have no plan. I have no girlfriend or friends to lean on. I have nothing to return to, so what's left?

I lean back in my chair, letting out a loud sigh, never taking my eyes off the notepad. My brain spins as I try to think of something, anything.

I could go see the world. I have my truck. Hopefully, my father didn't cut off my credit card. Maybe I could hit all of the major tourist places and start a social media platform to document it.

I shake my head. No, that's not it.

There's always college. I could go to New York and start working on getting a degree. Maybe there's even the off chance that I could run into Addison while I was there. She could be working on a chemistry degree at NYU.

Honestly, working on my education is as good an idea as any. At least I'd be working towards something, at the very least. But then the question becomes, what will I major in?

There's not really anything that interests me enough to make a career out of it. Before all this bullshit with my dad, I was hoping to take a year off and test out some different ideas. I suppose I could still do that now, but I feel like now I have a looming deadline over my head.

I wish Mr. Parks were here so I could bounce ideas off of him. He was always supportive and willing to listen and give advice when needed.

With that thought process, I freeze. My mouth falls open, and I almost consider planting my palm against my forehead. It's been right in front of me this entire time.

I get up from the table and go back into the living room, walking over to where my duffle bag landed. Rummaging through it, I finally come across my old leather wallet. I flip it open and find the business card sitting safely in its slot. I pull it out and run the rough edges on the pad of my finger, my mind finally starting to come to life and putting the pieces together.

Going back into the kitchen, I sit down again and start scribbling thoughts together, coming up with a five-point plan and jotting it all down. If I have it on paper, then that's motivation. Finally, hope starts to stir in my chest, and I realize that Aunt Trish was right. I'm going to be okay.

When I've got my plan roughly drafted out, I walk out the front door. I stroll through Aunt Trish's garden towards where she's kneeling, pulling the weeds. The sun beats down, hinting at what's to come in the summer months. When I get close enough, I notice she's working around a bush with dark berries littering along the leaves. I narrow my eyes at the plant, unsure what it is.

"Are those berries?"

Aunt Trish looks up at me, one of her dark eyebrows raised. "I mean, yes. But I can't say I'd recommend eating them."

"What are they?"

A sly smirk forms on her lips, and she returns to pulling weeds. "Ever hear of deadly nightshade?" I shake my head, and her smirk grows as she leans back on her haunches, adjusting her hat as she gazes up at me, her blue eyes sparkling against the sun. "I'm sure you have. You had to read *Romeo & Juliet* in one of your English classes, didn't you?"

"We did. What does that have to do with this plant?"

"Historians suggest that this was the plant that Shakespeare had in mind when he wrote the tragic scene with Juliet faking her death."

My eyes widen as I look between her and the plant. "It's poisonous."

She nods her head. "Very much so. A few too many of these berries, and boom, you're dead. But the Old Bard thought it might do the trick to put the body into a comatose state, appearing dead to anyone who didn't look too close."

"Why do you have it?" I ask her, intrigued she would keep such a dangerous plant around.

She shrugs her shoulder and then goes back to gardening. "I like to have a little of this and a little of that. Go on, find some gloves and help me get the rest of these weeds."

I do as she says, and soon, I'm next to her, yanking at the invasive little green weeds that are trying to suck the life out of her precious plants.

"How'd your list go?" Trish asks me after a while.

I lean back and wipe off the sweat forming on my forehead with the back of my hand. "Good, that's actually why I came out here. I think I know what I want to do."

"Oh yeah?" she asks, sitting back again. "Let's hear it."

"You might think I'm crazy, but I think I want to start working towards becoming law enforcement."

Aunt Trish stares at me a moment, studying my face. Then she wipes away a stray curl. "Why would I think that's crazy?"

"Well, that's not all of it," I tell her. She raises an eyebrow, waiting for me to continue. "I want to go into law enforcement, *and* I want to be the one who brings my father to justice."

Chapter 32

Addison

Addison - Age 21

"**M**erry Christmas, Addie," Grace says, sitting next to me and offering me a paper to-go cup.

I take it gratefully and offer her a smile, the warmth from the cup seeping into my gloved hands and warming the tips of my fingers. My nose catches a whiff of the rich hot chocolate inside, and I raise it up to my lips, taking a tentative sip of the warm drink. "Thank you. Merry Christmas to you too."

"Why are you sitting over here by yourself?"

Shrugging a shoulder, I look back at the square where people are bustling about, visiting the vendors and counting down the minutes until the big moment. Willow Heights appears magical tonight, with the soft dusting of snow covering the ground and the Christmas lights twinkling on every solid surface. But despite it all, I'm not feeling in the Christmas spirit tonight. "I always kind of get a bit nostalgic when it comes to Christmas."

Grace nods her head, offering me silent support. Usually, she heads up North to visit with her grandmother for the holidays, but this year she decided to stay in town. Though I've never outwardly said it, I always get a little sad when she leaves for Christmas. We've been living together in a small apartment for the last few years, and whenever she's not there, everything feels a little dimmer. "I get it. I can't imagine how difficult it must be."

"It's never easy," I acknowledge. "But it's getting a little more manageable with every year that passes. It's just so hard to wake up during the Christmas season and think about how I used to have all these fun traditions with my parents, and now... Now it just feels like any other day."

A memory flashes in my mind of making 'Christmas Countdown Chain' every year with my mom with paper rings made out of red and green construction paper. Growing up, I would get so excited as soon as December hit, knowing that Christmas was coming soon. As each day would pass, my mom and I would end our night tearing off one of the paper rings, watching the chain get shorter and shorter as Christmas approached.

It's those little things that I miss, like waking up to the smell of freshly baked cinnamon rolls, or helping my mom decorate the giant tree in the living room, finding the perfect spot for each ornament. My mom would go all out for my favorite holiday, taking every opportunity to make the season special.

"Now you have traditions with Charlie and Eli," Grace says encouragingly, nudging my shoulder in an attempt to lighten up the mood. "And me this year, if you'll let me in on the fun."

I offer her a brisk laugh and nod my head. "Of course. But you're right. I'm just in my feelings."

"I know, and that's okay. Just let me know if there's anything I can do to help," she says. I lean towards her, pressing our shoulders together.

We sit in silence for a while, watching passersby and listening to the carolers at the end of the street. "I heard Eli might be rigging up a little mistletoe trap for you this year," Grace says after a few minutes, her dark eyes twinkling with mischief.

I feel a blush form on my cheeks, and I cover my face with one mitted hand. "Oh god, I hope not."

"Come on, sweetie. It couldn't hurt to get out there a little bit more, you know? Even if it is just a kiss under the mistletoe."

"With Eli?" I ask her, and I can't help scrunch my nose up a little. Sure, I've kissed Eli before—almost a year ago we had a moment that turned into me spending the night in his bed. Eli was gentle and sweet, knowing it was my first time, and I'll always share that experience with him. But when I think about sleeping with Eli or even just kissing him again, I don't feel any type of anticipation deep inside me or the tingle of desire that runs from my toes to the tip of my nose.

"Well," she shrugs, "he really likes you. I'd say you could do a lot worse."

I could also do a lot better, I think to myself, but I bite my tongue and look back out at the giant Christmas tree waiting to be lit up.

Maybe Grace is right. Maybe it's time I give myself a break and try and branch out a little bit. At the very worst, I could always tell Eli that I'm not looking for anything serious. It's been a long time since Noah left, and I often wonder if I'm wasting my life just waiting for him. But when I reflect on our short time together, I know I'm not.

I'll hang onto the hope that I'll see him again if it's the last thing I have.

We sit together on that bench, Grace sipping her hot chocolate and me lost in my thoughts. The lighting of the Christmas tree begins, the mayor leads the crowd in chanting down from fifteen before flipping the switch, and the square lights up even more than before. My eyes take in all the colors from the bulbs against the Christmas tree's healthy green, and I sigh.

"Are you okay if I go and say hi to a few other people?" Grace asks me hesitantly. I nod and wave her off. Grace puts her hand on my shoulder, giving me a friendly squeeze before she wanders off, leaving me alone with my hot chocolate that has gone cold and a racing mind.

As I sit on the bench, I can't help my eyes from straying over to the corner lot where the cafe used to be. Whenever I come to Main Street, I try my hardest not to look at it.

It's all cleaned up now and built back into an actual storefront. Inside one of the front windows is a *FOR LEASE* sign with a number scrawled underneath. I'm equally surprised and not surprised that it hasn't been rented out and turned into something new. It seems Willow Heights's townspeople are pretty superstitious about tragic events like what happened to my family. No one is chomping at the bit to take over the cafe and risk getting whatever bad juju my parents brought onto themselves.

It's a shame, though. I'd like to see it turned into *anything* other than just an empty lot. I can still picture exactly what the café's storefront used to look like and can almost still hear my parents laughing as they interact with customers. Maybe someday, a business will take root where the cafe once was, and I can start building new memories to ease the ache of my old ones.

Giving one last longing glance towards the empty lot, I finally get up from my bench and walk home.

Christmas comes and goes uneventfully. Just as Grace told me, Eli had planned a romantic kiss under the mistletoe for us. Thankfully, since I had a heads up, I wasn't caught completely off guard and let Eli down gently. I could tell he was upset, but he didn't press the issue of us sharing a Christmas kiss.

After Christmas, New Year's passes by in a blur. I celebrate the holidays and the beginning of a fresh new year with my friends by my side. Before I know it, it's my birthday, and January is slowly threatening to turn into February.

On the morning of my birthday, I wake up to the sun streaming in through my blinds. Blinking a few times, I eventually decide I need to get up and go for the day. When I walk out into the living room, I'm met with the grinning face of my best friend-slash-roommate.

Grace gives me a big grin and holds out a plate to me. On it rests a massive muffin that looks suspiciously like cinnamon apple, my favorite. Stuck right in the middle of the delicious cinnamon crumble mess, on top is a bright pink candle, the flame slowly dancing around.

"Happy birthday!"

I laugh at my friend, stepping forward to blow the candle out. I squeeze my eyes shut, making a quick wish before I blow it out.

"Am I the first person to wish you a happy birthday?" Grace asks, putting the plate on the counter and then turning to give me a hug.

"You are," I tell her, laughing again when she starts jumping in excitement.

"Yes! Finally!" she exclaims and then lets me go. "So, have you decided what you want for your birthday?"

I sigh and shake my head. "I don't think there's anything I need."

"It's not about *need*, girlfriend," Grace teases but doesn't press the issue. She's been asking me every day for the last two weeks what I want for my birthday, but I've come up blank every time. "Well, think about it. Your birthday doesn't end until midnight tonight!"

The rest of the day passes uneventfully. I go to my shift over at Monty's Groceries and make the most of it, striking up a conversation and making small talk when I see familiar faces come through the line. After work, I trudge back to the apartment I share with Grace on the other side of town. I'm distracted as I approach our front door, digging around in my bag and searching for the keys. Once I find them, I go to unlock the door, but I freeze as my eyes catch on something sitting on our doormat. My stomach flips as I bend down, unsure what to make of the sight in front of me. Gingerly, I pick them up, unlock the door, and head inside.

"Oh, there you are. I thought you would never get home," Grace calls from her bedroom. She steps out into the living room, fastening an earring into her ear. "Hurry up and get changed. We've got places to—what are *those*?" Her eyebrows raise as she catches sight of the massive bouquet of red roses I'm holding.

"I don't—" I shake my head, at a loss for words. "They were sitting on our door mat."

"Is there a note?" Grace asks, hurrying over to me. I set the flowers down on our table and start sifting through the soft rose buds, searching for any clue as to who sent them.

"I don't see one," I whisper, my hands dropping down to my sides in defeat. Silence falls over the room, and I share a glance with my best friend, wondering if we're thinking the same thing. Her eyes go wide, and she must be able to feel the small bubble of hope forming in my heart.

"You don't think—"

I shake my head, despite it all. No. As much as my heart might be wishing that Noah sent me these flowers, reason tells me otherwise. "He wouldn't."

Grace watches me as I reach out and stroke the satin petals. My heart aches as if a part of it is missing. I draw my hand away from the flowers and press it against my chest in an attempt to ease the hollow feeling. "I'm sure I'll figure out who sent these one way or the other," I say, taking one last longing look at the roses before turning to Grace fully. "What were you saying as I walked in?"

It takes her a beat, but Grace snaps out of whatever thought process she is stuck in. Her eyes spark with mischief as she grabs my hand and drags me toward my bedroom. "We have plans tonight, so I need you to get out of this smock and find something pretty!"

Less than an hour later, Grace and I are walking towards McKellan's Pub & Grill. It's one of my favorite places to eat, and they have pool tables and darts to keep you entertained too.

"What's going on?" I ask her suspiciously. "Why'd you make me get all fancy to come to *McKellan's*?" The pub was a jeans and t-shirt kind of place, at best.

"You'll see. Don't ask questions," Grace snaps, grabbing my hand and pulling me the rest of the way toward the door. When we get there, she pauses before we enter the restaurant. She turns to me with a gleam in her eye. "Ready?"

"Ready for what?" I ask her with a laugh.

She finally opens the door and pulls me in after her. The room is dark, but it only takes a second for the lights to flick on, displaying a room full of people all staring at me.

"HAPPY BIRTHDAY!!" They all collectively shout at me. I take a step back in surprise but slowly feel a grin form on my lips. I let out a small laugh and then turn back to Grace standing next to me, looking awfully proud of herself.

"Does it make sense now?" she asks with a wink, and I nod my head.

"Wow, you arranged all of this?"

"It's your twenty-first birthday! We've got to celebrate!" she exclaims, stepping forward and giving me a big hug. I wrap my arms around her, feeling a smile start to grow on my face. When I let her go, people start coming up and wishing me happy birthday left and right. There are so many people here it's hard to keep track. Finally, my friends make their way through the crowd and manage to find me.

"Hey, Addie, happy birthday!" Eli exclaims as he saunters up to me. He's holding a beer in one hand but wraps me up into a hug with the other.

"Thank you," I tell him back with a grin.

"Did you get your present?" he asks. I raise an eyebrow at him, waiting for him to divulge more information. Eli chuckles and shakes his head. "The roses. I figured it would be a large enough bouquet that you'd have to pay attention to them. Guess I was wrong."

Disappointment crashes through my body at his admission. Of course, I knew Noah wouldn't have sent me flowers on my birthday, but I couldn't deny that a little part of me was still hoping that he had been thinking about me.

"Oh, I didn't realize they were from you. There was no note," I tell him. "Thank you, though. They're beautiful. I love them."

Pride shines on Eli's face, and I notice he squares his shoulders a bit more. "You're welcome. I'm glad you like them. Well, what do you say, birthday girl? Should we take you to the bar for your very first 'legal' drink?"

"Sounds good to me!"

Eli leads me over to the bar and lets me order what I want. Then he says he needs to use the restroom and disappears. I step away from the bar and take in all the people who showed up for me tonight. I can't believe Grace was able to rent this whole place out—or that she *would* just for me.

"Miss Parks," a deep voice says my name. The tiny hairs on my arms stand up, and I turn.

"Mr. Mayor," I breathe in surprise.

His dark eyes survey me standing in front of him for a brief moment before he speaks again, "I was just passing through, wondering what all the commotion was about. I hear it's your birthday celebration?"

I roll my lips into a thin line and nod my head. His tall looming frame sends a stroke of unease through me.

"Well, I suppose I owe you a happy birthday then." He quickly glances over the room, his narrow eyes suspicious as if searching for something. It takes a moment, but he finally looks at me again. "Enjoy celebrating with your friends."

I don't get the chance to say anything else to him before he brushes past me and leaves the restaurant. As soon as he leaves, I let out a deep breath. I'm not sure what it is about the mayor, but he makes me uncomfortable.

"Addison," I turn towards my name and see Charlie walking over to me, a frown on his face. "Was that the mayor?" I nod my head, still at a loss for words. "What did he want?"

"I'm not sure," I finally manage with a shrug.

Charlie doesn't like that answer, his frown deepening. "Here, come with me. Eli and I have a table over here, and we just ordered pickle chips."

"Say less," I tell him with a laugh. He leads me over to the table. Eli's already sitting there, fiddling on his phone, but looks up when I walk over. A grin takes over his face as I sit down across from him. Charlie takes the seat next to me.

The boys jump into the conversation, taking turns asking me questions about how my birthday's been or how the party is going.

"Sorry you had to work today, Addie," Eli says sheepishly. "I tried to get my dad to give you the day off, but he's so short-staffed we couldn't make it happen."

I shrug and go for one of the fresh pickle chips that were just delivered to our table, dunking it in the chipotle ranch served with them. "That's okay. It was actually kind of a blessing in disguise. Helped the day pass faster."

"Well, I'm glad to hear that," Eli tells me, his blue eyes wide as they search my face. "Hey, so I was wondering; I heard there's going to be a live band here this weekend. Would you want to come with me?"

Before I can respond, Charlie's phone buzzes on the table, the screen lighting up with an *Unknown* number. He frowns at the phone as if trying to work out who it could be, letting it ring a few times before apologizing as he walks away from the table to answer it. Eli is still saying words, but my eyes are on Charlie as he takes the call. My pulse picks up when he glances over at me and then quickly turns away, avoiding my eyes. Suspicion forms, it couldn't be—

Charlie would have no other reason to hide something from me.

"So what do you say? Addie?"

My attention is brought back to Eli, who is hopefully looking at me with those big wide eyes across the table. I flounder for a second, willing my brain to recall what he was asking me, but I eventually give up. "I'm sorry. What was the question?"

Eli's face falls only slightly before he regains his momentum. "I was wondering if you'd want to come see the live band playing here this weekend with me."

I try my hardest not to grimace. "Like a date?" I ask him warily. "An actual date?"

"Uh yeah," he replies sheepishly, his cheeks turning a light pink color. "A date."

I press my lips together and try not to look over at Charlie, who's raising his voice in his conversation. "Look, Eli, I know we've been... seeing each other a little more, but I'm not sure if I'm ready for real dating. I like things how they are right now, and I don't want to commit to something I'm not ready for."

Since the mistletoe situation, Eli and I have had more than a few moments where things have gotten a little more *friendly* than before. He managed to wear me down to going out with him a few times here and there, though my heart wasn't totally in it. If he had his way, he would probably already have a ring on my finger, and that would be that, but I'm nowhere near ready for anything of that measure.

"It's still about *him*, isn't it?" Eli accuses, hurt now taking over his expression. "Addie, he's gone. It's been years now, he's probably not coming back, and we're all better off for it. Our town has enough crooked McCoys to deal with. We don't need him. You *definitely* don't need him."

I feel myself bristling as Eli gives his speech. I stare blankly at him for a moment, letting his words wash over me. Part of me is unsurprised at the outburst, and another part registers that he might be right, but I'm honestly not ready to hear it. I push my chair back away from the table. "I just remembered I have other people I need to thank for coming tonight. I'll talk to you later."

I walk away from him, ignoring the sound of his pleading for me to listen and that he's sorry. He's *always* sorry. Instead, I walk over to Charlie, who is just hanging up from his call and is running his hand across his face in frustration. I stride right over to him and plant my hands on my waist, fixing him with a stern look.

"Who was that?"

Charlie spares me a glance and then exhales. "No one, just someone from the station."

"Don't lie to me, Charlie. I saw the way you looked over at me when you picked up. Where is he?"

Charlie looks at me with frustrated desperation and lets out a long exhale, dropping his chin to his chest. "I can't tell you."

"But you do know." I don't phrase it as a question. The guilty look on my best friend's face is all I need to know the truth.

His expression contorts into one that illustrates discomfort. "I may or may not know where Noah is."

"So help me, Charlie Sullivan, if you don't tell me where Noah is right now, it will be one of your biggest regrets." I recognize the desperation seeping through my tone, but I don't care. I feel like I'm fraying apart at the edges, and the fact that Noah might be within reach is the only thing keeping me together right now.

"Fine! Fine," he shouts back at me, throwing his hands in the air. "I'll tell you, but you have to promise me you'll start applying at all those schools you've been talking about. You deserve more than this town can offer you, and you know Noah would want you to too."

I cross my arms over my chest as I glare at him. "Did Noah put you up to this? Is that what he called about?"

Charlie grimaces again. "No. Well... not all of it."

I roll my eyes. "Fine, whatever. Just tell me where he is."

"I'm not sure this is a good idea."

"The hell it isn't! Please, Charlie."

"He's going to kill me," Charlie mutters to himself, running a hand over his face. "Fine. He's in New York, but I *swear*, Addie, I wasn't supposed to tell you that, so don't go and do something dumb."

New York. Four hours away. He's only four hours from where I am right now. Before my mind can fully process this new information, my heart sets out with a plan. It's my birthday, after all, and I've finally figured out what I want this year.

Chapter 33
Noah

Noah - Age 21

"C'mon, man, it's your turn," I nudge the guy to my left, already tired of his bullshit for the night. I hate this little bar, but there's nothing else in this podunk town to do at night. I'm set to go down to Washington, D.C., tomorrow for my first official interview. I'm just killing time until checkout tomorrow morning.

"After you answer my question," the sleazy guy says. "It shouldn't be too hard. I just asked if you got a girl at home."

I roll my eyes and sneer at him. "Why does it matter?"

"Just looking out, brother. There are plenty of desperate chicks in this bar I'd be more than happy to set you up with if you need to get your rocks off tonight."

"I'm good, thanks," I say briskly, taking a swig of beer out of my mug. A tingle rises on the back of my neck, and I rub at it with my hand. "Now, take your shot."

"Hey, no need to get your panties in a twist. I'm only looking out for you," the guy says as he lines up to throw his dart at the board. "You seem to be wound up tight, man. Not to mention, this hot piece just walked in and is eyeballing you as if you're an angel from heaven. Thought I'd offer before trying to swoop in there myself."

Despite my insistence, I can't help but turn around to see who he's talking about. As my eyes roam the length of the bar, I feel my chest tighten, and my eyes widen as I meet the green-eyed gaze of the girl who haunts my every waking moment. "Parks," I breathe, unable to believe my eyes. I set my beer on the table and start heading her way, ignoring the jeering jabs of my companions.

Her eyes hold mine as I walk over to her. I don't waste time and lace her fingers through mine as I bend down and rest my forehead against hers, closing my eyes and relishing in the fact that she's *here*. Her familiar scent of warm vanilla and jasmine swirls around me, with hints of lavender ticking the edges. Even after all these years apart it's still the same. Home.

"Noah," she whispers, the sound of my name on her lips sending my heart beating into overdrive. It's a sound I never thought I would hear again. "I can't believe I found you." With my forehead still resting against hers, I open my eyes and gaze at her.

"Are you real?"

"Are you?" she teases me back, her green eyes twinkling at me. My heart squeezes, and I pull her closer to me, wrapping my arms around her until she's resting against my chest. Her arms snake around my middle, and she hugs me back tightly.

"God, Parks. How are you here? How did you know where I was?"

It's been almost two and a half years since I saw her, but it feels like no time has passed. As I hold her, the hollow part of my soul finally feels complete again, as if she's sewing me together as we stand here.

Addison tuts her tongue at me and raises an accusatory eyebrow. "Charlie got an unknown phone call last night, and based on the fact that it was my birthday and the panicked look he gave me when he answered, I put two and two together."

I shake my head. I had called Charlie to tell him about my

interview tomorrow and briefly mentioned the hotel I was staying in. Of course, I knew it was Parks' birthday, and I would be lying if I didn't admit that I was hoping Charlie would drop a line on how she was celebrating. "Charlie's going to get me killed one of these days." I reach up, run my fingers through strands of her curly honey-brown hair, and tuck a few behind her ear. "Happy Birthday, Parks."

Her eyes are wide on mine, and then she shivers when my fingers graze the skin of her neck. "Thank you."

I lean back, my eyes taking in every detail of the woman sitting in front of me. A flood of heat courses through my chest, and my heart flutters. Addison's wearing a soft blue sweater that comes down to her wrists. The neckline is a low v-shape, dipping dangerously close to her breasts. Her tight denim jeans accentuate the curve of her hips. My mouth goes dry as I take her in. She's even more beautiful than I could have ever dreamed. I let myself appreciate her for a moment longer before I let reality come crashing back. "You're not supposed to be here it could be—"

"Don't even start," she huffs, cutting me off. "I'm tired of this, Noah. I miss you."

"Parks, just trust me," I whisper. "I'm doing what needs to be done here. It might not be what we want, but it's for the best. Just trust me."

Addison stares at me, her eyes tracing my face as if she's looking for something. I expect her to press the issue even further, but she doesn't. Instead, she purses her pink lips, and I hold myself back from kissing them. She reaches up and softly scratches her fingers through the beard on my cheeks. "Fine, but I'm not leaving yet. I drove four hours just to see you, so let me enjoy tonight with you, please. As a birthday present."

I take a deep breath as I hold her eyes with mine. Finally, I give in and exhale deeply, admitting defeat. I can't say no to her when she's looking at me with those big pleading eyes. "Okay. Come on, let's get out of here."

"Where are we going?" she asks breathlessly as I take her hand and lead her toward the front door.

"Somewhere that isn't here."

We stop at the rack so we can each get our coats and then head out into the wintery New York air. I wrap my arm around her waist and direct us down the sidewalk, away from the noisy bar and toward the hotel I'm staying in right next door.

I lead her through the extravagant lobby and over to the elevators, pressing the call button. The car arrives, and we both step in. I jab my finger into the number for my floor, and the doors close, locking us in.

I'm acutely aware of where Addison is standing on the other end of the car. Glancing at her from the corner of my eye, I repeatedly attempt to convince myself that this is real and not a delusion I'm living out. Her brown hair is curled, falling gently over her shoulders, and I want to run my fingers through it. Her hands are stuffed into her coat pockets, and her eyes trained straight ahead.

It's as if there's a magnetic force between us, urging me to step closer to her, and I wonder if she can feel it too. Before I get the chance to approach her, the elevator dings, and I step out into the hallway. Parks follows closely behind me as I lead us to my hotel room.

Before I swipe my key card, I look back at her sheepishly. "I hope this is okay. It was kind of loud down there in the bar. I thought we could come up here and hang out." A rosy blush forms on Addison's cheeks, but she nods. "Have you eaten? I could order a pizza or room service or something."

"Pizza sounds great," she says, the corners of her lips turning, and I relax a bit.

I open up the door, and we step inside. After removing our coats, I fiddle around on my phone, ordering us some pizza. Then we settle on the bed, each sitting as close to the edge as possible, putting ample distance between us. I glance at her from the corners of my eyes every few minutes, trying to come up with something to say. I don't know what the hell is wrong with me. This is *Parks*. For so long, she was the one I could always talk to, but it's as if the almost three years we've been apart have driven a wedge between us.

Guilt forms in my belly, knowing I'm the one who caused this distance.

As if she can sense my discomfort, Addison takes a stab at starting up a conversation. "So, do you like New York?"

I can't help but bark an uncomfortable laugh and then look at her. "I guess. It's a lot different than quiet old Willow Heights."

"You can say that again. I was worried I would get lost and never be found."

I chuckle again. "I've felt like that the entire time I've been here."

"I'm just glad I found the right hotel," she continues, looking at me as if I'm an enigma she's struggling to understand. "I guess the stars aligned just right."

Something about that notion tugs at my heart, and I look over at her, fully taking her in since we've made it to the room. "I can't believe you're here."

"Me either," she whispers, her plump lips falling open slightly as she takes me in.

"I just don't know where to even start," I tell her. "There's so much that I want to ask, but I'm still trying to wrap my head around the fact that it's you."

"Just pick something. Ask me anything."

"How's Grace?"

Addison laughs, and the sound of it sends my heart fluttering. *God, I've missed her.* "You're really going to ask me about Grace when we haven't seen each other in years."

I laugh nervously, reaching up and rubbing the back of my neck. "I don't know, I just...I feel like I'm on a first date."

Her eyes soften, and then she turns towards me, folding her legs underneath her and facing me fully. I mirror her position until we're face to face, now sitting only a foot away from each other. "It's a little weird, isn't it? That we were so close before but now—"

"I'm sorry," I blurt out, and she raises her eyebrows at me. "I just feel like I need to say it over and over again. I'm sorry I left you like that."

"Why *did* you leave?"

I press my lips into a line and shake my head. Addison's shoulders deflate, and she exhales. "I'm sorry," I tell her again. "It's still not something I can talk about."

"Why don't you trust me enough to tell me? Or are you worried I won't be able to handle it? It's just hard for me to accept that you would just leave when everything was finally working out for us."

"It's not any of that, Parks. I didn't *want* to leave."

"Then why did you? Please, Noah, just give me something."

"I can't," I say again, pleading with her to hear me.

"Will you ever tell me?"

"I hope so." Addison's eyes trace over my face, and I notice a crease between her eyebrows.

We fall into a comfortable silence now, some of the awkwardness eased. Our pizza arrived less than half an hour later and we dig into it. Addison takes a bite of her pizza, a satisfied expression taking over her face as she chews the cheesy goodness. A bit of sauce is stuck to the corner of her mouth, and I can't help the amused smirk that pulls on my lips.

She notices and raises an eyebrow at me. "What?"

"You've got a little—" I lean forward and smudge away the pizza sauce with my thumb.

Her cheeks immediately pinken, and her eyes twinkle at me. My heart flips in my chest. I let my hand linger against the edge of her jaw for just a moment too long before pulling away and wiping my hand off on a towel.

When I glance back at her, my breath hitches, and suddenly, I wonder if coming up to my hotel room was really the best decision. All I can see is her. Her presence is everywhere, yet the cells in my body scream for more.

As if we're two magnets circling each other's orbit, I feel the urge to be closer to her tug deep in my soul. She watches me from underneath her eyelashes, her lips parting ever so slightly as I lean closer towards her. My eyes trace her face, searching for any indication that I should stop, but I see none.

The rise and fall of her chest tells me she's feeling just as affected by this moment as I am. With that thought in mind, I close the distance between us, taking her lips in mine. Parks' hands immediately come to the nape of my neck, her fingers tangling in my hair. A soft moan sounds in the back of her throat, and it spurs me on. I push the pizza box off to the side of the bed and slide closer to her.

When we're both breathless, I finally break away from her, leaning my forehead against hers as I give my heart a chance to catch up. When I look at her face, I find her watching me, her eyebrows pulled towards the center of her forehead in concern.

"What's wrong?" I ask her, my voice breathy from our kiss.

I can see the thoughts swirling in her eyes for another moment before she braces herself and opens up. "I'm afraid to blink my eyes because I'm worried you'll disappear on me again." She sighs and twists her lips downward. "I'm only getting tonight with you, aren't I?"

I pause for a moment, caught unprepared. When I realize it's no use lying, I pull entirely away from her before nodding my head regretfully. "Yeah, Parks, only tonight. I'll be leaving in the morning."

I can't tell her about the exciting prospect this interview in D.C. tomorrow will bring or that this may be the beginning of the end. She doesn't know about the *real* reason I can't go back to Willow Heights, and I plan to keep it that way for as long as I can. If I can keep her blissfully unaware of my father's deceitful game, I will.

Addison's eyes fall to the bed, and she picks at a fiber coming off of the comforter. Her cheeks are still flushed from our kiss, and I want more than anything to soothe whatever's running through her head, though I realize that might be impossible. "I thought that might be the case."

I finally reach across the distance between us, grabbing her hand and threading our fingers together. "Parks—"

She shakes her head, and I break off my sentence. When she looks back at me, her expression is resolved. "If I only get tonight, Noah, then I want *tonight*. With you."

I raise an eyebrow, unsure if I understand her correctly. "And by tonight, you mean...."

"I want you, Noah. Please."

Desire crashes through my body, and I suck in a breath in an attempt to control myself. I can't let myself get too carried away without knowing exactly what she means by that.

"I'm going to need you to be a bit more specific, Parks," I say, slightly breathless. "What do you want from me?"

She holds my gaze steady with hers, not backing down from my challenge. We've always been each other's equals, each other's other half. With that comes a level of trust and comfortability that neither of us has been able to find in another—at least, I haven't. I hold her hand tightly in mine as she stares me down.

"I want you, tonight, in every possible way," she says boldly, unashamed.

My blood thrums as I stare at her. "I don't want to risk doing something you might regret down the road. I won't do that, not with you."

"There is no way I could regret this with you. You're the only one I want."

I watch her closely as I brace myself to ask my next question, "Have you—have you done this before?"

She nods, her teeth sinking into her lower lip as if worried about how I'll react to this new development. Though a twinge of disappointment at our situation does register, I find my muscles releasing some of their tension. I take a deep breath, letting it fill my lungs and give me some clarity.

"You're sure you want to do this? It won't change anything," I caution. It guts me to see the flash of disappointment cross her face, but she dampens it almost as quickly as it came.

"I'm sure. Please, Noah, I want you."

"Well, how am I supposed to deny you when you beg me like that?" I mutter, my voice barely above a whisper. I reach out my hand, tucking a few stray pieces of her hair behind her ear. Addison leans into my touch and flutters her eyes up to me.

"You're so beautiful," I say as I scour her face, wishing I could spend time counting every single freckle that dots her nose. A small smile plays at the corners of her lips, and I can't resist her anymore. I swoop in and take her lips with mine, wasting no time and tracing the seam of her mouth with my tongue until she opens for me.

Addison's hands wrap around my shoulders, holding me tightly to her as I maneuver us across the length of the bed until I'm on top of her. Parks catches on and wraps her legs around me, ankles coming to lock against my lower back, causing us to come together in a way that makes us both groan.

I break away from her lips as I feel her center line up against the outline of my cock. *"Fuck,"* I groan as I grind my hips up into hers.

Addison whimpers and bears down against me. I'm sure we're a sight, two adults dry humping each other like teenagers, but neither of us can help ourselves. It's been too long since I've had her this close to me.

The hem of her sweater rides up, displaying the smooth contours of her belly. I pull away from her, leaning down and pressing kisses to her abdomen. The muscles bunch up underneath my touch, her fingers fisting into my hair as she writhes underneath me.

After I've tortured her enough, I pull away, pressing up with my arms and hovering above her. Her hair is splayed out across the comforter, curls everywhere. The way her cheeks flush and her breasts heave with arousal almost brings me to my knees. I've dreamed about this moment with her more times than I care to admit, and I'm not going to take any moment for granted.

My chest aches as I stare down at her, wondering if I will ever have another moment like this in my life. She's all I want and all I'll probably ever want. Unable to stand the distance much longer, I fall over her, kissing her deeply again. She opens for me without persuasion and kisses me as if this is our last time—a thought I don't wish to dwell on too hard.

My hand traces the edge of her side until I'm bunching the hem of her sweater even higher, baring her fully to me. Addison groans in my mouth when my touch trails further up and underneath the cup of her bra, locating her pebbled nipples and tracing their hardness with my fingertips. Her back arches as I pluck one, then the other.

"Noah," she gasps, pulling her face away from mine and dropping her head back with a sigh. "Noah, more."

"Shh," I soothe her, squeezing her breast in my hand. "We'll get there."

She groans at the denial but kisses me enthusiastically when I retake her mouth. While she's distracted, I move my hands to her back and pull her to sit up. Catching on to my motives, Addison swiftly removes her sweater. She then unclasps her bra, pulling it off and allowing me to see her. Without any preamble, she shimmies out of her tight jeans and drops them on the floor, leaving her only in a pair of navy panties. They're lacy with polka dots, and I lick my lips before gently guiding her back onto the bed.

"Lift your hips," I encourage her as I hook my thumbs into the edges of the lacy band. She does as she's told, and I pull her panties down her legs and toss them to the floor.

Addison takes a swift breath when I bend her knees, place her feet on the mattress, and push her knees open until she's spread open in front of me. She tangles her hands in her hair, her cheeks blushing as I look at her, with no hint of embarrassment.

"Look at you," I praise her, pressing a kiss inside her knee and trailing my lips. "You're the most beautiful thing I've ever seen."

Addison whimpers as my kisses get closer and closer to her center. She tilts her pelvis up, guiding me to where she needs me most. "*Noah.*"

"So beautiful, Parks," I murmur as I press my first kiss against her center. She bucks her hips and moans. "I've dreamt about this moment," I say before darting my tongue out and swiping against her clit. Addison cries out and spreads her legs wider than before.

With two fingers, I open her lower lips, taking a good look at her before diving in and laving my tongue against her. Addison writhes on the bed below me, her hips bucking up against my face when I slide a finger into her and slowly pump it into her. I groan when I feel her wet and tight against my hand.

"No-ahhh!"

I pull my mouth away from her but keep working her with my fingers, adding a second one shortly after. I watch them disappear deep into her before I move up her body and capture her lips, still pumping into her. I kiss her soundly, knowing she can taste herself on my lips.

"Want me to make you come, Parks?" I ask her under my breath once I pull away. I can't help but tease her. Her eyes lock on mine, glazed over from pleasure, and she nods eagerly. "Do you want to come on my fingers or in my mouth first, hm?"

She squeezes her eyes shut and undulates her hips against my fingers, rocking herself back onto them. "That's it, Parks. Fuck yourself on my fingers, good girl." The sight of her writhing under my touch causes my jeans to grow increasingly uncomfortable as I harden against them.

Addison lets out a noisy moan and starts rocking harder. I feel her gush with arousal against my hand, and my eyebrow twitches. She likes my dirty talk, such a filthy girl.

I can feel her walls tightening against my fingers. The occasional flutter of her muscles lets me know she's close. I curl the two fingers inside her and press against her walls repeatedly, hitting the spot that I know will make her see stars.

"Oh *fuuckk*," she moans, throwing her head back again. "Noah, I'm gonna, I'm gonna—"

"Yeah? You gonna come for me?" She whimpers and tilts her hips more. With two fingers in her, I maneuver my thumb to rub methodically against her clit. I bend down and capture one of her nipples in my mouth, flicking the tip of my tongue over her hardened bud. Then I lean over and pay attention to the other nipple as she climbs higher and higher.

"Come for me, Parks. That's a good girl." I instruct her when I pull away from her breasts. Her whole body tightens, and she comes around my fingers with a loud groan. I continue to work her through her orgasm until her body relaxes against me. I pull my fingers out of her, wiping away the wetness that lingers and standing up off of the bed.

She opens her gorgeous eyes to watch me as I set to work, removing my shirt and undoing my belt. I drop my jeans and boxers in one swift movement until I'm standing stark naked in front of her. My whole body comes alive as her eyes trail over every inch of me, lingering on my cock. When she licks her lips, I can't take anymore.

I move up the bed, and she spreads her legs to accommodate me on top of her. I've dreamt of our first time together since I fell in love with her all those years ago. Though neither of us has taken the plunge and admitted it, I know this means just as much to her as it does to me. I've always known that the first time we'd be together would be like this—electric, consuming. I want to see her face as we come together for the first time.

Taking my cock in my hand, I rub it up and down her slit. Addison tilts her pelvis up again to notch me into her entrance, and her hand cups my cheek. I meet her eyes with mine and then slide home.

Addison's breath hitches as I enter her, and I slow my movements to give her time to adjust. I lean down and kiss her. Her fingers scrape through my hair. I kiss her for a while, letting her get used to me inside her. I know this isn't her first time having sex, but I want to allow her whatever time she needs to be comfortable. The feeling of being inside her is incredible; it takes everything in me not to start thrusting up and into her.

After a minute, she pulls away from my lips and nods, "Please, Noah, fuck me."

I drop my head with a groan and pull out of her slightly before thrusting back in, feeling her walls clench tightly around my length. I repeat the movement, reaching for her knee and hiking her leg around my hips to drive deeper. She throws her head back at the new angle, "Oh my *God*, Noah, *Yes*."

"Fuck, you feel so good around me, Parks," I tell her, my breath hitching with the exertion. "I can't wait to feel you coming around my cock like this. You're so good, so beautiful."

I keep talking to her, saying whatever filthy words I can come up with. When I feel her tighten around me, I keep up the pace, knowing she's close.

"Noah, I'm gonna come, don't stop—ah, feels so good."

"That's it, Parks, you're taking me so well. Let go. I know you're right there. Come for me, Parks." I repeatedly drive into her until I feel her shatter with a cry. I don't have the willpower to keep going once I know what it feels like to have her come around me, and I follow her right over the edge, finding my release inside of her.

My body slumps against hers, my chest heaving. Addison's hands wrap around my back, her nails tracing patterns against my skin as we both try and catch our breaths. I stay inside her for as long as possible before I finally slide out and roll off her.

Her sleepy eyes meet mine, and she smiles, "That was perfect."

I grin back and bend over, pressing a kiss to her forehead. "You're perfect. Come on, let's take a bath."

She groans but accepts the hand I offer her, wobbling slightly as she stands to her feet. I brace my arm around her hips and lead her to the ensuite.

Addison uses the toilet while I set to work filling up the tub, making sure the water isn't too hot. I pour some fancy hotel soap into the water as it fills, watching as the bubbles start to form. Addison wraps her arms around my waist when she stands behind me, and I place my hand over hers.

"Thank you," she whispers, pressing a kiss to my spine. I close my eyes and drop my head, taking a deep breath before turning around to face her. My hands come up to cup her cheeks, and I press my lips to hers.

When I pull away, I lean my forehead on hers, holding her gaze. "It was my *pleasure*. You're amazing, Parks. Come on. The bath is ready."

I hold her hand as she steps into the tub and sinks into the water. Once she's in, I settle behind her, spreading my legs along the edges of the big tub so that she can rest against my chest. She nestles in against me and turns her head, so her cheek is against my chest. I kiss her hair, wrapping my arms around her and pulling her closer to me.

After a moment, I hear her mutter, "I usually can't finish."

"Hmm?"

"I usually can't finish when I'm having sex. Like actual sex," Addison says softly. "But you were hitting something so perfectly that I couldn't help it."

I press my lips into her hair again and smile. Further proof that we are made for each other. "Well, I'm glad to have been of service to you."

Addison sighs happily against me. "I've missed you so much, Noah. You have no idea."

"I do," I tell her. "I've missed you too, Parks. It's always been you. You know that."

She goes quiet for a moment, and I hear her sniffle. "I wish things were different. I wish you could come home."

"Maybe someday," I say wistfully, then I brace myself. "But Parks, I don't want you to wait for me."

She stiffens against me and then sits up in the tub, turning around so that she can look at me. She brings her knees up to her chest as her eyes meet mine. "What? How can you say that?"

"I don't want you to wait for *someday*. You deserve better than that, Parks."

"But, Noah, I do—"

I lean forward and catch her lips, effectively cutting her off. It's not the right time for that yet. "I know, Parks. Me too."

She pulls away from me and swipes at a tear that has snuck from the corner of her eye. Seeing her do that guts me, but I know this is for the best. "Why? Why shouldn't I wait for you?"

I sigh and run my hands over her hair. "Because I don't know when *someday* is going to be. It could be a year from now, or it could be ten years. I don't want to make promises I can't keep."

"Noah—"

"Please, Addison, just listen to me." Her mouth snaps shut when I call her by her first name. "It's not too late; you can still apply to those big universities you wanted to attend. Get your chemistry degree, and become a scientist like you've always wanted to. Win all the awards, and change science as we know it. You can do *anything* you want. I'm not holding you back."

"But I want you, Noah."

I look at my girl sadly, "I know. I want you too. But I can't offer you more than what I have tonight. You have to move on. And if someday does roll around, I'll find you, and hopefully, you'll be married, maybe with a few kids. You'll be happy. And I'll be happy for you."

"And if I'm not?" she asks me softly.

"Then we'll reevaluate," I tell her with a rueful smile. "But I want you to leave Willow Heights. Get away from that shitty town and start a new life. Charlie will help you as much as he can. I know he will."

"This sucks," Parks says, swiping at another tear. "Why does it have to be this way? If you want me to leave so badly, why can't I just come be with you?"

I reach for her, pulling her against my chest again and wrapping my arms tightly around her. I could die a happy man just knowing I've gotten to hold her like this. "It's just how it needs to be right now, sweetheart. I wish it were different. I wish I could keep you."

She doesn't say anything more on the subject. She just lets me hold her until the bath water runs cold. I drain the tub and let her dry off before scooping her into my arms again and taking her back to bed. We lay on our sides facing each other, and I hitch her leg over my hip before sliding into her again, finding her wet and ready for me. A groan escapes me as I seat myself fully inside her, going as deep as possible until I feel the deepest part of her. I take her gently this time, kissing away the tears that slide down her cheeks and knowing this might very well be the last time I see her—all the while hoping it's not.

When we both find our releases, we snuggle closer together, basking in each other's closeness. I wrap my arm around her waist and pull her flush against me, tucking one of my legs between hers. Our embrace is intimate, one that lovers find themselves in.

She falls asleep shortly after that, and I doze until the sun rises, and then I untangle myself from her. I wander around the room, pulling my discarded clothes on and locating the little notepad that the hotel provides. My heart hurts, and my stomach twists as I scrawl out a note. I keep telling myself that this is the best for her. I want her to have everything her heart desires, even though I can't find it in myself to give myself to her entirely. Not yet. There are still things I need to do, things I need to set into motion before we can live our lives without constantly looking over our shoulders.

Someday, when all is said and done, I'll hopefully be able to give her everything, my heart and soul, and everything I have. Lord knows she already owns me. Once I'm done writing my note, I lean over the edge of the bed and pull the comforter over her shoulder before pressing a kiss to her temple. I leave my note on the table next to her and pray that someday comes soon.

Dear Parks,

When I tell you that last night was the best night of my life, I hope you believe me. There is nothing that

I want more than for you to have everything you want, but unfortunately, that can't be me. Not yet. Please, do what I ask and go chase your dreams. Do everything you ever wanted, and don't let me hold you back.

I left you some cash to get you home, and the hotel checkout is at eleven. It guts me to leave you like this, but this is the way things have to be. For the time being.

We'll meet again someday, and until then, know that I'll be thinking about you. I love everything about you, from the freckles that line your nose to the amber flares in your pretty hazel eyes. You are everything to me. Never forget that. I'll never forget you. That's all I can promise for now.

Until infinity, Addison Parks.

X, Noah

Chapter 34

Addison

Addison - Age 24

I'm not sure if it's the frigid air biting at my cheeks and seeping deep into my chest or the way the house looks empty as I stand in front of it. But as soon as I step out of my car in Willow Heights after visiting New York, I decide that it is time for me to do something with my life. Noah was right; I can't waste my days wondering when he will return. It is time for me to move on.

Once I settle on that, everything starts falling into place.

It's a crisp spring morning when the idea finally comes to me. I'm out for a run, jogging around the main square as I usually try to do in the early mornings. My muscles scream out in protest as I push through my last mile. As soon as my watch vibrates on my wrist, I am hungry for breath, so I stop in front of the empty storefront that used to be my parents' cafe. I gaze at the *FOR LEASE* sign still boldly displayed in the window. The building has remained empty all these years after the fire, empty and hollow. It would seem no one wanted to move into a building with which something so horrible had happened. Can't say I blame them.

I can still picture it the way it was—*before.* The light emanating from the business every morning when my mother would flip the sign on the door from *Closed* to *Come on In!* The town square has never quite been the same since the scent of freshly baked pastries disappeared along with the cafe. I know I've missed it when I go on my run in the early mornings. A part of my soul burned away that night the cafe disappeared, and I'm not sure I'll ever get that part of me back.

As I stand there, lost in my memories, the idea strikes me like a flash of lightning. The clouds above my head clear, giving me a brief glimpse of potential.

Peering into the empty store, I can picture it all then, every piece coming together in a perfect display. A sense of peace washes over me as I imagine the atmosphere of a cozy diner that is welcoming and comfortable. I can see it all, clear as day—from the layout to the color scheme. I start playing around with names as I stand there, still lost in my daydreams.

When I finally come back to my senses, I run back to Grace's house, rejuvenated from the idea, and sprint into the kitchen, finding her making a cup of coffee. She glances at me mid-pour, taking in my sweaty and flushed appearance she has grown accustomed to over the years. But the wild look in my eyes causes her alarm as she knows something big has happened.

"What's up with you?" she asks suspiciously.

"You might want to sit down," I tell her, taking a step towards her.

Wariness crosses her face, but she does as I ask, sliding into one of the chairs at our small kitchen table. After sitting across from her, I dive into my brilliant plan.

Once I'm finished, Grace purses her lips, thoughtfully. "Are you *sure* this is what you want? I mean it's your *parents'* store."

I frown. "And?"

"And all I'm saying is that it might be hard for you to go in and revamp everything in there, given the history."

A stab in my chest tells me that my best friend might be onto something. I damper down my excitement for a moment, considering her words. Will it be too hard to start a new business where my parents were killed? Maybe. But I can't help but feel like this is what I'm meant to do, as if my parents are right beside me, nudging me forward. There is something deep within me telling me to go full steam ahead with this plan.

"I think I'm supposed to do this," I whisper. Grace raises her eyebrows at me. "I can't put my finger on it, but it's like there's some outer force screaming inside my head that *I'm* the one who is supposed to restore what that storefront used to be. I know that sounds dumb," I say, looking down at the table.

Grace reaches over and takes my hands, her dark skin contrasting with mine. When I look up, I see her eyes shining with warmth. "Addison, if this is what you want, then I'm here to support you all the way. I just wanted to make sure you knew what you were getting into."

"I do. I want this."

Grace's soft smile now morphs into a wide grin. "Well, okay then. I'm in."

And that's how Grace and I become business partners.

She is gracious enough to go in on the business loan with me, signing me over as the primary business owner but taking a seat as a partner. Then we devise a business plan on how best to succeed in a small town such as Willow Heights, and from there, everything starts coming together. I get to work on the process of renovating the cookie-cutter storefront exactly how I want it to be.

I find a fantastic architect on social media who I reach out to. She's from out of state, but after reading her reviews and perusing her portfolio, I know I have to reach out and set up a consultation. Surprisingly, though she mostly does corporate architecture, she loves my pitch so much that she agrees to take me on as a client immediately, with little effort on my end.

"I like doing pet projects like this," she says on one particular call. "It rejuvenates my passion for creating things when I get to do smaller projects from the heart. I like building things that last, and I feel this project will be one of those."

Her drawings come through only a few weeks later, and the real fun begins. As I go through the process of watching my future be built right before my eyes, I decide that I should probably get some experience under my belt. I begin working with Marjorie Taylor, who owns a little restaurant on the other side of town, just to see how she runs things. I also join the local community college and start taking classes online toward a business degree, just to say I have one. Is it necessary? Probably not, but knowing that I'll have a degree by the end of the ordeal somehow keeps my motivation strong.

It takes almost two years for everything to come together fully, the cafe not officially opening until the fall, a few months before my twenty-fourth birthday.

The night before the big opening day, I stand in the middle of my new diner, taking it all in. The furniture has been bought to meet the aesthetic I dreamed of—more of an old-style diner with red-leather booths and dark oak tables. We have plenty of seating scattered across the floor to allow visitors to dine in and the counter up front just in case people want to take out. The hardwood floors are shiny and spotless after being waxed a few days ago. The finish I chose is a warm walnut that gives the area an even more welcoming feeling.

The diner is dark as I look around, though I know tomorrow it will be bustling with all my friends, excited to join me on this new journey. As excited as I am for this next chapter, a part of me still feels nostalgic for what my life used to be. With everything in me, I wish that my parents could be here to see this. Granted, if my parents were still with me, I probably wouldn't be opening a diner in *this* location, but who knows where I would be? Despite them not being here in person, I know deep down that they're proud of me and everything I've worked to accomplish.

I'm thankful that Charlie, Eli, and Grace have all stood by my side throughout this endeavor. Each one of them has shown up and gone the distance to assist in pulling everything together. Still, a part of me feels like I'm missing something–or someone.

I haven't heard a word from Noah since I met him in New York two years ago. Even Charlie hasn't heard anything, giving me a rueful smile every time I ask him, as if he's sorry he can't give me better news.

It's as if Noah has dropped off the face of the Earth.

But what am I supposed to do? He told me not to wait on him, to live my life and continue on the path I want. And so that's exactly what I did; this is it.

Noah may have urged me to leave Willow Heights, but no matter how much I wanted to do as he asked, I couldn't. Without fully realizing it was happening, Willow Heights became my home. I couldn't fathom leaving, especially now when the only family I have left is right here.

As I stand here appreciating the fruition of all my hard work over the last few years, I have no regrets. For the first time in a long time, I know this is precisely where I'm supposed to be and what I'm supposed to be doing. Will it be easy? No, opening a new business never is. But I'm hoping all the extra work I've put in will pay off.

With one last anticipatory sigh, I leave the diner floor and walk upstairs to the loft I claimed as my new home. It's a small one-bedroom apartment, just big enough for me. With this new chapter of my life taking off, I feel a mixture of sadness and excitement. I'm sad because with this new chapter, I know I'm getting ready to close the last one, and excitement because I'm ready to be free.

This is my life, and I'm taking it back.

The following morning, I'm awake as soon as my alarm goes off. I quickly shower and then get dressed, pulling on a pair of dark wash jeans and a long sleeve thermal shirt. I tie my hair up into a ponytail, knowing I'll need it out of my way today. After brushing a bit of makeup on my face, I grin in the mirror.

"Let's do this," I tell my reflection and then don't give myself any opportunity to back out. Today's the day.

I go downstairs, wasting no time before hurrying and getting things ready to open.

"Good morning, my love!" I'm rattled out of my thoughts when Grace announces herself as she steps into the diner. As she enters, the doorbell jingles above her. She sashays into the diner, holding up a cup of specialty coffee.

I give her a wry look and tease her, "You know we're trying to sell coffee here, right? How does it look if the co-owner is walking in the door with coffee from another place?"

Grace rolls her eyes and hands me the coffee, which I begrudgingly accept. "No one will know. Plus, we've got a long ass day and probably need the espresso to pull us through, so drink up."

I chuckle but follow her advice, taking a sip of the hot coffee and sighing in relief as the bitter taste of the espresso hits my tongue. As soon as I swallow it down, I look at her and nod gratefully. "Okay, this was a good idea."

Grace gives me a dramatic bow. "Thank you. What needs to be done before we open 'er up?"

I delegate a few tasks to Grace, each of us getting to work and ensuring we're ready for the big day. Seven o'clock rolls around far too quickly. Grace and I put the finishing touches on everything, making sure the tables are fully stocked with condiments and napkins and the chairs perfectly aligned. Once we're satisfied, we turn to look at each other. Grace offers me her hand, and I take it, giving it an appreciative squeeze.

"Ready?"

"Let's do it," I tell her before pulling her into a big hug.

When I release her, we both walk to the front door and open it. There is a small crowd awaiting us outside, and my face splits into a grin when I see everyone. They break out in a small round of applause as soon as we step out, and I hold up my hand to settle them.

"Good morning, everyone!" I say, and they sound off a round of *hellos*. My cheeks are already hurting from smiling so much, so I don't waste any time. "Thank you all for coming out to the grand opening of Sunny Side Up Diner!" More applause ensues. "Grace and I have worked hard to ensure this diner is everything this small town needs and exactly what you all want. Starting tomorrow, we'll be open at our new regular hours." I give them a few more details of what all that entails, what kind of food will be served, and what not. Finally, the good part comes. "And without further ado, Grace?"

Grace hands me a pair of shiny silver scissors we bought yesterday from the pharmacy down the road. I take them in my hand before leaning over and cutting the ceremonial red satin ribbon in front of the front door.

"Sunny Side Up Diner is open for business!"

Before I know it, my diner is full of people excited to order their first meals. Grace and I man the counter, letting the small staff we hired to take care of bussing tables and refilling coffees. The morning doesn't slow down from the second those front doors open. For the next few hours, it seems as if there is a constant stream of familiar faces stopping in to say good morning and to get a coffee as they peek around, getting a feel for the place.

My heart is full as I say hello to everyone, thanking them individually for coming out and supporting us. If there were ever a moment that fully assured me that I was meant to stay here in Willow Heights, this would be it. I would never have imagined receiving this level of attendance and outpouring of love.

Finally, a little after noon, I see my two best friends enter the diner. They both look impressed as they glance around, taking in the result of all my laser-beamed focus over the last few months. I haven't given any sneak previews in these final days before the grand opening. The only ones who had any idea of what the diner was like were Grace and me. Charlie and Eli both played along like the good sports they are. I'm sure I was a terror to be around at times, as I sometimes get when I'm trying to meet a deadline, but hopefully, it has all paid off now that they can see the outcome.

When Charlie and Eli reach the front counter where I'm posted,

I notice a third person accompanying them. I gasp out loud. "Oh my god, Wyatt?"

The blond standing next to Charlie lets out a deep laugh at my reaction and nods his head. "Good to see you again too, Addison."

I glance at Charlie quickly to notice he's grinning from ear to ear. "When did you get back into town?"

"Just the other night. I'm all graduated and certified as a financial advisor now," Wyatt Bradford tells me. "After so many years gone, I was missing home."

He and Charlie share a brief tender look, and suddenly I realize that *home* might have more than one meaning for Wyatt. My chest aches as I watch Charlie's eyes soften as he gazes at Wyatt. Honestly, I feel nothing but joy for my friend. Charlie deserves everything in the world, but my heart pangs slightly, realizing that I may have had that kind of love too, and I'd give anything to go back in time.

Wyatt and Charlie sit down at the counter, Eli shortly following suit. They each pay me a round of compliments as I get them some coffee and chocolate chip cookies. I give them a grateful smile before leaving them to their breakfast and returning to work to ensure everything is running smoothly.

"You look stressed," Eli says lowly to me the next time I stop by the counter. I'm in the middle of reaching around him to take his empty plate away. I notice that Charlie and Wyatt have already taken off. Charlie must have needed to get back to the station, Wyatt going with him. Eli, it seems, chose to stay behind.

I look up at my friend and huff out a laugh, hoping I don't sound too frazzled as my first lunchtime rush is dwindling. "Is it that obvious? We were supposed to have at least one more staff member here today, but she didn't show up for her interview last week, and I couldn't find anyone else in time."

"What do you need me to do?" he asks. I raise my eyebrows at him, but he doesn't give me a chance to protest. "Come on, Addie put me to work. I've got the rest of the afternoon off, and you need the help."

I debate it for a second, gazing into those baby blue eyes imploring me to take him up on his offer. I wonder if this is really a good idea, but the need for assistance wins out. "Okay, here," I tell him, handing over the big tray of dishes I was carrying around on my hip. "Take these to the back for Sadie to wash and start doing more rounds, making sure everything is stocked and dirty dishes are picked up."

Eli nods, shooting me a wink before accepting the tray and disappearing into the back of the diner. I sigh with relief from not having that burden to carry around. I do a quick once-over of the dining area, deciding that there are waters that need to be refilled.

My eyes stop short on two men sitting at one of the booths by the window. I narrow my eyes, wondering if I'm seeing things incorrectly, but nope. Sitting here, in my diner, are Caleb Lauder and Jordan Coldwell—Noah's two best friends growing up. My mouth goes dry as I realize they came up here fully knowing that this is *my* diner.

It hasn't really been a secret that Sunny Side Up is mine, given the tons of advertising I've done around town over the last few months—we're talking radio ads, short TV spots, and flyers on every doorstep. I dolled out a lot of advertising, but I was hopeful that it would pay off for me in the long run.

I'm not sure how they slipped in without me noticing them. I'm usually acutely aware of anyone having to do with my life before Noah left. I walk over to the booth where the two men are sitting. They watch me warily as I get closer, carrying the water pitcher. My mouth feels dry. It's been a long time since I've spoken to either of them—years, probably. My skin starts to crawl with the weight of their eyes on me, and a part of me wonders what they're thinking. Do they feel sorry for me? Knowing that their buddy left me behind without looking back? Could they possibly be checking in, planning to report back to home base after finding out that I'm doing okay on my own? The intrusive thoughts are endless, thinking up all the possibilities of why they could be here.

"How are you guys today?" I ask the pair as soon as I'm at their table, trying not to make our encounter too awkward but likely failing miserably.

"Good, good. Nice place you got here," Jordan tells me, his eyes darting around my diner before settling back on me.

"Thank you, is there anything I can get either of you?" I ask. I notice that they have two well-picked over plates on the table. There's still a handful of lingering fries, but no evidence of the hamburgers I suspect inhabited the plates before.

"No, I think we're okay. We've got everything we need," Caleb tells me. He glances at Jordan for a brief moment, something passing between them wordlessly, and then stands up. I take a step back, worried I'm in his way. "I'm just gonna run to the restroom."

I point him in the right direction, and then it's just me and Jordan. I don't know much about Jordan Coldwell other than that he is—was?—Noah's best friend. As far as I know, Noah hasn't been in touch with anyone other than Charlie since he left—and even that seems to have reduced to nothing—but I could be wrong. Maybe it's just *me*, who Noah hasn't wanted to be in touch with.

Offering Jordan a tight smile, I step closer to the table to refill their water glasses. "So...how have you been?" I ask him, hoping that the awkwardness that I'm feeling inside doesn't lace over into my tone.

Jordan watches silently until he whispers a *thank you* as soon as I finish pouring his water. "Fine. Uh—and you?"

"Yep, good."

He stares at me with his warm brown eyes, studying my face. Finally, he exhales and glances over his shoulder to see if Caleb is lingering around. "I probably shouldn't be saying anything, but he's okay, you know?"

A thick lump forms in my throat, and I can't manage to get words out. With wide eyes, I nod my head once, twice, letting Jordan know that I know who he's talking about. Jordan reaches for his water, bringing it closer and taking a sip from the straw.

I stand there, gaping like a fish at him, just long enough for the moment to feel uncomfortable. Then I shake it off and hesitantly ask, "Do you—"

Jordan cuts me off. "No. I don't know anything other than that he's doing okay."

"Oh."

"I'm sorry, Addison."

I nod my head again a little. "It's okay. You won't...tell him that you talked to me, will you?"

"Not if you don't want me to," he says, watching me thoughtfully.

I am considering my options. Has Jordan actively been keeping in touch with Noah these last few years? He knows he's okay but claims that's all he knows. I could push the issue further and see if Jordan would be willing to open up a little bit more or—

My throat goes dry again, and I swallow thickly. I glance around my surroundings, taking in the impressive turnout for my first day of business. It's at that moment that I make another life-altering decision. I've spent many hours putting my blood, sweat, and tears into building this place. It would be foolish of me to throw it all away for something that's in the past, for something that has no guarantee of ever working out.

And that's precisely what Noah is now. He's my past. This diner, my life now, is my future.

"No. Please don't tell him anything," I say firmly, my voice unwavering.

Jordan narrows his eyes just slightly but then dips his chin at me. "Of course."

Out of my peripheral vision, I notice Caleb walking back to the table from the restroom. I give him a forced smile. "Just let me know if you guys need anything else. Thank you so much for stopping by today. I appreciate your support."

I don't give the men a chance to answer before I turn away and scurry back to the counter. As soon as I've crossed the line from the dining room to the back, I set my pitcher down on the counter and brace my hands against the hard surface. My head drops between my arms, and I focus on taking deep breaths.

My brain knows I made the right decision just now, telling Jordan not to bring Noah into the equation. But my heart still aches, wondering about the *what if.* I could probably sit here all day and play each and every scenario over and over in my mind, working out the finer details to give us all the happy ending in every possibility. That would be a waste of time, though, because life hardly ever works out how we want it. All we can do is roll with the punches and try to make the best of the hand we're dealt.

After a few cleansing inhales, I stand up straight, square my shoulders, and put it all behind me. What's in the past is in the past. I have no reason to worry about it now. All that matters is what I do moving forward.

And so, with my head held high, I step back onto the floor and see the rest of my opening day through. The next handful of hours is a whirlwind of activity, allowing me no time to slip back into my previous thoughts. There's simply no time to get lost in my memories until Noah's mother makes her appearance.

Things are finally starting to quiet down after the dinner rush when I notice Catherine McCoy walking up the stairs and opening the door, the bell above jingling at her entrance. I groan to myself when I see her. It seems like I'm just running out of luck today to avoid the past I'm trying so hard to move on from. When she steps into the diner, she stops right in the middle of the floor, taking a second to look around. Her keen blue eyes take in every detail before settling on me. I catch my breath as I gaze into the same eyes her son has.

Catherine offers me a kind smile. "Addison, dear, this is amazing."

I quickly glance behind her, ensuring her husband isn't trailing along in her wake. I've only encountered Declan McCoy a handful of times since Noah left. The mayor always manages to give me a polite word and then leave as soon as possible. Which is, of course, fine with me. There's something about that man that has always felt off to me.

"Thank you, can I get you a hot tea or a decaf coffee?" I ask her, stepping into her outstretched arms and accepting the hug she's offering.

As soon as Catherine lets me go, her attention darts to the display case behind me. There's not much as far as baked goods go—only a small selection of muffins, cookies, and pastries.

"I think I'll take one of those chocolate chip cookies if you don't mind. And a tea to go would be lovely, thank you," she says, her voice light.

I get to work, bagging up her cookie and pouring a cup of steaming hot water. I dunk an English Breakfast teabag into the cup and then slide it across the counter toward her. "Do you need any sugar or cream for that?"

"No, thank you. Sorry I didn't get a chance to swing by earlier," Catherine says, taking a moment to look around again. "You've done a marvelous job, my dear. I'm so proud to see something made of this storefront, and you are just the right person to have done it."

A warmth blooms in my chest at her high praise. Catherine and I aren't close by any means. However, despite everything that happened between Noah and me, I still appreciate her tenderheartedness toward me. I'm not sure how much she knows about the whole situation—honestly, I'm not even sure how much *I* know about the situation—but I'll always be grateful for her kindness.

She stays for a minute to make small talk, asking about the details of our first day and asking open-ended questions to get me to talk. I resist the whole way through, still slightly uncomfortable with interacting with her.

"Congratulations, Addison," she says to me as she moves toward the door, her dark brown curls swaying as she turns her head. "You should be very proud of all you've accomplished with this little diner. I think it will be a huge success here in Willow Heights."

Again, the warmth inside my chest expands outward, and I grin, feeling elated. "Thank you, Catherine. That really means a lot to me."

She observes me another beat before curving her lips upward, giving a slight wave of her hand, and disappearing into the night, just as stealthily as she came.

The remaining few customers linger, give their compliments about the diner, and then head home. When the dining room is empty for the night, I let out a big sigh of relief. I turn to my closing staff and give them a big, beaming smile.

"We did it!" Though only a handful of them, they offer a small round of applause. I laugh and join in. "Now you all go home and get some rest so we can do it again tomorrow!"

They disperse, giving me high-fives or small side-hugs on their way out. I breathe deeply before starting the closing responsibilities when it's just me again. My staff has taken care of just about everything. I just need to take the trash bags out back and lock up.

I reach for the packed bags, slinging them over my shoulder, and go out the back door. As soon as I'm outside, I drop the bags on the ground, lock the door, and pick them up again before heading to the dumpster.

"Hey," I hear a voice say. I glance over as soon as the dumpster lid clangs shut behind the bags I just tossed in. Eli walks towards me, his hands stuck in his jacket pockets.

I give him a wane smile, feeling the exhaustion from the day creep up on me. "Hey. Where'd you disappear to? You didn't say goodbye before you left."

"I took off right around four. You were running around like a crazy person, and I didn't want to mess your flow up. Besides, I figured you had everything under control by that time. Just needed to get the feel of the helm beneath you, I think."

I look at my friend fondly. "Thanks for helping out today, Eli. I really, really appreciate it."

"Of course, Addie. I wouldn't have wanted to be anywhere else."

The night is brisk, and I wrap my jacket tighter around my shoulders. I don't really want to be standing out here in the dark. I'd much rather go upstairs and put my feet up. However, I also don't want just to dismiss Eli after he took time out of his day to help me out in my moment of need.

I study Eli for a moment, weighing over the idea in my mind. Finally, I gear up and ask him, "Want to come upstairs and watch a movie or something? I'm exhausted, but I don't feel like being alone."

Eli blinks at me, his eyebrows rising in surprise and his eyes brightening. It takes him only a moment's hesitation before he nods his head and steps closer to me, accepting the metaphorical olive branch I'm extending. "Yeah, Addie. I'd love that."

I motion for him to follow me upstairs to my apartment, and he doesn't hesitate. Together we walk up. Today was all about new beginnings, and somehow I feel like this choice I just made to invite Eli upstairs is another fresh start.

Chapter 35
Noah & Addison

Noah - Age 25

For what feels like the millionth time, I roll over in my bed and reach for my phone resting on the nightstand. My eyes squint as I press the power button, lighting up the screen so I can see the time. A groan nearly escapes me when I realize it's only been half an hour since I last checked. My arm drapes over my forehead as I lean back against my pillow.

I blink my eyes against the darkness, willing sleep to come, but my brain is in overdrive. Tomorrow is the day I've been working toward for the last year or so. I've searched and dug for every bit of information I could scrounge together, filing it all away in a folder until I was confident I had everything I needed to present a solid case.

The last aspect of my whole case came today in the mail. When I pulled out the letter informing me that the name change was official, I think my heart might have stopped for a second.

Noah Lockwood.

It has a nice ring to it, but it will take some getting used to.

For the first fifteen years of my life, I was under the impression that I was born into significant privilege just because of my last name. The McCoys were the ones who had everything figured out, and everyone else was simply inferior. My father is mostly to blame for that ideology; he holds high esteem for the family name and set a certain standard for my mother and me to follow in his shadow. There was no going back once I discovered how wrong I was about my father and the whole belief system he brought me into.

It wasn't until I was employed by the FBI two years ago and began looking deeper into my father that I realized the depth and severity of the lies I was told. As I dug, I noticed the patterns, and if I looked close enough, I could easily see my father's involvement in several offenses. However, the problem was that there was no definitive proof. If my father was anything, it was good at covering his tracks. But the more I searched, the more the list just kept growing, and with it, my despair that I had even been involved with him.

Changing my name was one of the easiest decisions I've ever made. Ever since I was fifteen and started to question the integrity of the McCoy legacy, I've found myself drifting further and further from it. After calling my mother and telling her what I planned to do, she insisted I take her maiden name. As I said, it has a nice ring, and I don't regret it.

Not to say I don't have regrets. I have lots of them. But in this case, I find the shedding of my last name almost ceremonial. It's time for all of this to come to an end.

Realizing that sleep isn't coming to me tonight, I throw off the blankets and roll out of bed. I run another hot shower, trying to clear my mind. Once I'm toweled off, I set up camp on my couch and start flipping through everything I've compiled together. I've looked over this more times than I can count. The words have a permanent place in my brain, and I could probably recite my proposition from memory.

I run my hand over my face again, looking at a page outlining my father's suspected crimes from seven years ago. Still, this is one of the more difficult sections for me. I still have no definitive proof that my father was behind the fire at the Parks' café, but deep in my heart, I know.

My finger runs over the names of Addison's parents, noting their cause of death and the details of the autopsy report I received from Charlie a while back. A hollow ache forms in my chest, and my fist moves to my sternum, trying to rub away the discomfort.

This is why.

It's been years since I've seen her, but there isn't a day that goes by that I don't think about how her eyes would sparkle with joy or the curve of her lips as she grinned at me when I was being stupid. I miss her more than words can describe. Even all these years later, I can't help but feel cheated out of the time that I could've spent with her.

I still think my leaving was the best thing for her. It was important to me that Addison get a chance to live her best life; at the time, I wasn't sure if that included me. My father was clear with his threat; if I wanted to keep her safe, my best choice was to leave.

Hopefully, someday, once this is over, I'll be able to find her and do my best to explain everything. A large part of me is hopeful that she left Willow Heights and went away to a big fancy university. Maybe she's working on a master's or a doctorate. Addison Parks has the potential to run this entire world if she wants.

But no matter where she is, once I've put my father away where he belongs and I no longer have him lingering in the back of my mind, I'll find her. And I'll never let her go again.

It takes a few hours, but finally, I doze off on the couch, getting an hour or two of much-needed sleep. In the morning, I stop first at my favorite coffee shop on the way to the Bureau. Coffee is non-negotiable this morning. After not getting hardly any sleep last night, my nerves already feel on edge, and the dark circles under my eyes prove my rough night.

When I have my black coffee in my hand, I make my way to my desk, saying good morning to a few of the other agents on my way.

After Addison came to visit me in New York, I moved down here to interview for a dispatching position for the Metropolitan Police

Department. It was a decent job that gave me some experience. I also worked on getting my master's degree online to kill time on days I wasn't working. Luck happened to be on my side with this position, too, one of my managers had a brother who worked for the FBI, and he was able to put a good word in for me as soon as I sent in my application.

I applied to the Bureau as soon as I turned twenty-three and went through the lengthy interview process, which involved interviews, written exams, and physical fitness tests. The whole process took months, but finally, I got the job. It's been a journey, but now that I'm where I'm supposed to be, it's been worth it.

Once I'm settled at my workstation, I pull up my computer and emails, sifting through them to see if I have any new messages or assignments. After working through that, I reach for my file again, giving it one *last* look.

When I'm finally satisfied that I have enough to go on, I take my file to my supervisor's office, practicing my presentation the whole way there. My knuckles rap gently against the wooden door, and I hear a muffled "Come in" from behind it. I push into his space and stand in the doorway.

Vincent looks up from whatever he's working on and stares at me for a moment. "Noah, to what do I owe the pleasure?"

"I've got something to show you," I tell him as I step further into the office. He's got two chairs set up in front of his desk. I settle down into one of them, pushing the manilla folder I've brought with me toward him.

Vin eyes me curiously but takes the folder, flipping it open and thumbing through all the files I've compiled. I gauge the reactions on his face as he works his way through everything. I see the full range from intrigue to shock, anger, and confusion. When he reaches the end of the file, he closes the manilla folder. He folds his hands on top, eyeing me curiously as if expecting me to speak up for myself.

"Listen, I know this probably breaks a hundred different rules, but I would like to reopen the investigation on Declan McCoy," I tell him. My boss looks at me from beneath his glasses and narrows his eyes.

"That was closed almost seven years ago. Not to mention the conflict of interest it would pose. It would put me in a sticky situation if some of the higher-ups found out I was having the *son* of a POI lead the investigation. You're lucky you even got this job being related to him."

"All due respect, sir, I need to be the one to do this. I'll write another proposal or meet with whomever I need to ensure this goes through."

"Why is it so important to you, Noah?" Vincent asks me, rubbing his jaw as he watches me thoughtfully. "Why not just let me assign this to someone else on the team?"

My mouth is dry as I consider my answer. The air in the room is thick. "Closure."

Vincent taps his fingers against the folder and exhales loudly. "I really shouldn't even be humoring you on this. The FBI has policies for a reason." I gear up to protest again when Vin continues. "*But,* I've been pleased with your work since you were assigned to my department. I'll see what I can do, but I can't guarantee that you'll be allowed to proceed with this."

I nod my head at him, giving a brief thank you as I'm dismissed. My nerves are fraying even further as I return to my desk. He didn't say yes, but that also wasn't a no. Falling into my seat, I turn on my computer and return to the current case I've been working on, trying and failing to soothe my wild heart rate.

The anxiety of the prospective case doesn't ease until almost a week later when Vincent pulls me back into his office. He's leaning against the edge of his desk, arms crossed over his chest. His face is stern as he watches me walk into his office, nodding his head behind me as a hint to close the door.

When I face him, he lets out a sigh through his nose. "Well, after much pleading and convincing on your behalf, the case is yours. I just want to warn you that you will be watched meticulously. One wrong move, Noah, and they're going to pull you. They're breaking protocol, but based on everything you've put together, they admit that it's about time we shut down his business. Begrudgingly, they agree that you should be the one to do it."

I run my tongue over my teeth, letting his words sink into me. With a nod, I say, "Thank you, sir. I promise I won't let you down."

With a spin on my heel, I exit his office and close the door behind me. Relief reverberates in my chest.

I did it.

But now the real work begins. I had sketched out a timeline of how I'd like to proceed with my investigation, and now that I have the green light, it's time to get started.

As my father told me, no one could ever take down a McCoy. That may be true, but I don't think he was banking on another McCoy being the one to try it. Though I no longer legally own that last name, I still possess the drive and determination I was raised with. McCoys don't fail. And even though I may be a Lockwood now, I still have no intention of failing.

* * *

Addison - Age 27

The blare of my alarm jolts me out of a restless sleep. My hand reaches for it, feeling around on my nightstand, trying to find the device. With a click of a button, the sound disappears, and I roll flat onto my back against my pillows.

A roll of thunder echoes throughout my tiny apartment, and I frown. If it's raining, I won't be able to go for a run this morning. I scurry out from underneath my duvet and over to my windows, drawing my blinds up so I can see. It's still dark outside, given that I rise before the sun almost every morning these days. I recognize the twist of the trees outside, indicating a storm rolling in. A few stay raindrops patter against the window, and I sigh.

It's good, we've needed rain, but I always feel a little off-kilter when I don't get to start my morning with a run. Instead, I pull on some workout clothes and put up a full-body pilates circuit on my TV, following along on my purple yoga mat. Once I'm covered in a slight sheen of sweat and feeling rejuvenated, I make myself some coffee and hop in the shower.

The rest of my morning routine goes smoothly, not affected by the stormy weather outside. Once I'm dressed in my favorite pair of dark wash jeans and a long sleeve flannel, I hurry downstairs to the diner to get things rolling for the day.

Over the last few years, I've put most of my energy into my business, spending long days and nights making sure it's successful. I've been dating Eli casually ever since the night of our grand opening, and it's been good. Eli is no Prince Charming by any means, but he's a good man. He's one of my best friends, and I enjoy spending time with him one-on-one. It's also nice knowing I have someone there to take the edge off after a long day. Though truth be told, while Eli is good in the bedroom, I can't help but compare it to the singular mind-blowing night I spent with Noah.

He ruined me for anyone else in more ways than one.

I find my thoughts straying to him more often than I'd like to admit. Though on the surface, I've moved on, a part of me still yearns for him.

Each anniversary of my parent's death brings along the anniversary of Noah leaving. As the years pass, my hope that Noah will return becomes less and less. Instead of wasting energy on hoping that he'll come back, I put most of my focus on the people who chose to stay in my life and master running my business.

Several guests are already hanging out in the lobby of the diner, waiting on their coffee or breakfast sandwiches. I give a quick hello to my staff already here, patting my leading manager, Jack, on the shoulder. He shoots me a wink, and I grin to myself. Grabbing a tray, I make my rounds across the dining room, picking up any leftover coffee mugs or plates.

We open in the mornings at six, which means the first round of early-morning guests have come and gone by six-thirty. I'm in the middle of rushing a plate of dirty dishes toward the back when I spin around too quickly, almost tripping over someone standing right behind me.

I gasp as his arms shoot out to steady me, big strong hands grabbing onto my upper arms. I mumble an apology, barely registering the deep response. When I look at him, my mouth falls open with a gasp, and I can hardly believe what I see. I wonder if I'm living in a dream because this is too good for reality.

At the sight of him standing before me, all the memories and heartache seeps into me. He looks the same but so different, almost— weathered. Time stands still as I take a moment to absorb every feature of his face, lingering on the silver-blue eyes that often haunt my dreams. The long unruly dark hair gives him an edgier appearance than the last time I saw him. The man standing in front of me seems different, but every molecule in my body comes alive, telling me that it's *him*. He's *here*.

It's almost as if the wind is knocked out of me at his nearness, but I manage to squeak out, "Noah."

Part Three
Now

They slipped briskly into an intimacy from which they never recovered.
- F. Scott Fitzgerald

* * *

Chapter 36
Addison

"Noah? Can you hear me?" I ask softly. The beeping from the hospital machines echoes in my ears, and I try my best to drown it out. "It's me. I'm here. You're okay now. Just open your eyes, please, Noah."

When Noah doesn't respond to me, my heart deflates. I squeeze his hand again, wishing with everything in me that he'd just wake up.

I've been here for what feels like days, though I know it's only been a few hours. As soon as I got the call from Charlie that they found Noah stranded in the middle of the woods, I rushed over here, waiting for them to haul him in. He was barely conscious enough to tell the doctors that I was here with him and that they could share his medical records with me. Before passing out again, he gave me a weak grin, his eyes sparkling as they looked me over.

After checking him over, they decided he has a concussion from his car wreck and a compound fracture of his wrist. Before I even had the chance to process what was happening, they wheeled him out of the ER and into surgery so they could set the wrist before any permanent damage was done.

It was a few hours between when I last spoke to him on the

phone and when they found him. In that time, I frantically did exactly as Noah asked me. I called Charlie and had him reach out to whoever this Vincent person was. Charlie knew exactly who to call and didn't ask any questions, just as Noah said he would. After all that was done, all I could do was wait.

The hospital staff let me wait in one of the family waiting rooms until Noah came out of surgery. It took almost two hours before his surgeon walked out to find me. I immediately stood up, clutching my hands in front of me.

"Noah's doing very well. We have him out of the OR in recovery; you should be able to see him soon."

I breathed a sigh of relief and nodded my head. The surgeon continued, "Noah had a complete fracture to the end of his radius bone," he pointed to his forearm just under his thumb, showing me exactly where. "After x-raying it, we determined that it wasn't stable enough without this surgery, so we went in and put a plate and screws in to hold it together. He'll have to do some physical therapy, but I'm hopeful that he'll get most of his full function back in that hand."

After the doctor gave the all-clear, I could go into Noah's room and haven't left since. I've held vigil next to his bed, just waiting and waiting for him to wake up. They told me it wouldn't take long, but with still no sign of him coming to even a few hours later, it still isn't quick enough for me. The need to see his blue eyes sparkle with reassurance, to let me know everything will be okay, consumes me.

A nurse steps into the room and gives me a gentle smile. "How are we doing in here?"

I shift in my chair and glimpse up at her. "Why hasn't he woken up yet?"

"His general anesthesia should have worn off by now, but he's had a rough night. His body might just be taking the extra time it needs to get back to tip-top shape," she explains. "I bet you'll see him coming around here within the next half hour."

"The doctor said he'll need to spend the night?"

The nurse nods her head, regarding me sympathetically. "At least, just to make sure that he clears all of the concussion protocols once he wakes up."

I let out a heavy breath, my shoulders falling as I look back at Noah. His hair is unruly, and I reach over to brush a few strands off of his forehead. I run the backs of my fingers against the slope of his jaw, feeling the prickly stubble starting to form. His skin is still warm beneath my touch, reminding me he's still with me. Seeing him lying here, unconscious, just makes me want to curl up in a ball and cry.

This is *Noah*. Though we haven't had much time together since he returned, I know this man. And seeing him incapacitated in such a manner is jarring. He's not supposed to be here like this.

Despite everything the nurse told me, I cannot help but feel my chest tighten with worry. What if he doesn't wake up? What if the doctors missed something serious like a brain bleed? I've seen all the medical shows, and I know that things can go wrong quickly and without rhyme or reason. I don't want us to be the next case study that is used for prime-time TV.

My chin quivers as that thought comes and goes. Noah's chest's steady rise and fall does soothe some of my worries. The heart monitor beeping next to me assures me that he's still here with me, just sleeping. He'll wake up and give me that crooked smirk, telling me with a sparkle in his eyes that I worry too much.

I'll roll my eyes and shove his shoulder before leaning over and capturing his lips in a kiss that will leave both of us breathless. Then he'll walk right out of this hospital and take me home to our bed, where he'll get rid of every worry I've ever had in my life.

Everything will be fine. Right?

It's going to be fine.

"Hey," I hear a deep voice say, pulling me out of my spiral, then a big hand rests on my shoulder. I glance at Charlie standing over me, his azure eyes concerned as he looks me over. He's wearing a dark blue polo with khaki pants. His black duty belt is slung across his hips. "Maybe you should go home and get some rest."

I shake my head vehemently. "I want to be here when he wakes up."

"Addie—" Charlie starts and then pauses. "Look, you've had a long few hours and an even longer night before this. Just go home, take a hot shower and relax a little bit."

"I can't."

Charlie doesn't like that answer, apparently. Before I know what's happening, he's got his hand hooked under my armpit and is dragging me away from Noah's bedside. I squirm against him as he leads me closer to the doorway.

"Charlie!" I protest.

"Just calm down. You're fine," he tells me. Something in his tone has me believing him, and I stop my struggle. When I peer up at him, he's frowning at me, the expression causing deep lines to form on his forehead. "Listen to me, Addison. I want you to take an hour or so and get out of here. I think you need a break."

I shake my head again. "I don't want to."

Charlie exhales heavily and extends his arm to pull me into a hug. I rest my cheek against his chest, feeling the thick material of the bulletproof vest he's wearing underneath his polo.

"I promise I'll call you as soon as anything happens, but you really need to take some time for yourself. Get a coffee or whatever, please. You've been here all night, and I'm worried about you."

With my cheek resting against him, I let his words sink in. Maybe he's right. I don't want to leave Noah's side, but a part of me can recognize that Charlie is coming from a place of love and concern for me.

"The nurses said he should be waking up soon."

"Fine," Charlie says with a sigh, his hand rubbing my back. "Head down to the cafeteria for a few minutes at least." His hand's gentle movement and pressure suddenly bring to light the reminder that I *have* been up all night. My body aches with all the stress I've put it under the last few hours, and my eyes feel like they're being held open with strips of Scotch tape.

"Okay, coffee does sound like a good idea," I say. "You'll call me if he wakes up?"

"I promise," Charlie responds.

I give Noah one last lingering look before excusing myself into the hallway. A nurse passes by me and gives me a small wave.

My shoes echo through the hallways as I walk toward the elevator. As soon as it dings and the doors open, I step inside and lean against the side of the car, taking a few deep breaths. There's a pressure against my chest that I just can't get rid of. My nerves have been on edge ever since my phone call with Noah last night, and I just haven't been able to settle them. I'm hoping Charlie was right, and a few minutes away from Noah's room might help me get a grip.

The cafeteria is slim pickings, but I finally settle on a banana and a cup of hot black coffee. I grab a few small cups of creamer and a sweetener package and then find a table off to the side. The cafeteria eating area is bare, with only a few groups lingering about. I sit by myself and pull out my phone to check my messages.

I see one from Eli asking if everything's going okay and to let him know if I need anything. Same from Grace, though hers has a bunch of heart emojis attached to the message. After taking a bite of my banana, I type out a response to both of them. Then I lean back in my chair, taking a few sips of my coffee and trying not to grimace at the bitter taste.

And I thought *I* made lousy coffee.

The break is helpful, and I feel the unease settle slightly. I focus on people watching, seeing families come, grab their snacks, and then return to go see their loved ones. I'm only down there for half an hour before my phone buzzes incessantly on the table.

As soon as I see Charlie's name pop across the screen, I reach for it, swiping to answer the call immediately. "Charlie?"

"Addie, you should get back up here. Noah's awake."

Relief crashes through my entire body, and it's as if the world's weight is finally off my shoulders. I tell Charlie I'll be right up and return to the elevators. My heart rate increases the closer I get to his room, and I think I might pass out from happiness when I make it back and see Noah sitting up in bed, talking to Charlie.

"Hey, Parks," Noah croaks as soon as I enter the door frame. The sound of his pet name in his gruff voice reduces me to tears once more. Closing the distance between us, I throw myself at him—gently—and wrap my arms around his neck, burying my face into his skin. Noah repeatedly rubs his good hand up and down my back, murmuring, "Shh, it's okay. I'm here," to me until I manage to get ahold of myself.

When I finally blink away my tears, I pull back and shoot a glare over at Charlie. "I can't believe you made me leave."

My best friend holds his hands up in surrender. "Yeah, I'll admit I shouldn't have pushed you. I didn't realize he would be waking up that soon."

"I actually liked it," Noah chimes in. His voice is scratchy, but when I look at him, I notice the mischievous gleam in his eye that is so *Noah*. "Want to come home with us and be my nurse, Sully? You might have missed your calling. We could even get you one of those cute white dresses they wear in the movies."

"I'll pass," Charlie grumbles. "Thanks for the offer, though."

I can't help the laugh that bubbles out of me. The last few hours have been so intense that watching Charlie and Noah banter like they've always had feels like a breath of fresh air. I'm aware of Noah's gaze on me, and I turn to see him beaming, a gentle smile on his face.

"I'm so glad you're awake," I tell him softly.

"Me too," he says, his eyes warm as they roam over my face. "I'm sorry."

My eyes start to burn again as I sit next to him. Intertwining our hands, I raise his up and press a kiss to the back of it before pressing it to my cheek. "Please don't do that to me again."

"I'll try. I love you, Parks," he says, his eyes gleaming. "I'm sorry I couldn't say it last night."

A tear slips out of the corner of my eye, and I cup the side of Noah's jaw. "You were a little busy, trying not to die. I love you too, Noah. More than I could have ever possibly imagined."

Noah's lips turn up, and then he leans forward. I catch onto what he wants and close the distance between us, pressing my lips to his for the second time since he's woken up. Fireworks explode behind my eyes, and I lean further into the kiss.

Charlie clears his throat behind us, and I pull away to stare at my friend, annoyed. "Sorry to interrupt this super disgusting moment," Charlie starts, shooting me a sympathetic look. "But I need to talk to Noah for a few minutes. Alone."

"Okay," I whisper, glancing over at Noah, watching me with observant eyes. "How long is it going to take?"

"Not very long, but why don't you go home and get some rest?" Charlie asks.

I open my mouth to protest, but Noah stops me with a hand on my forearm. I dart my eyes down to him, and he gives me an encouraging smile. "It's okay, Parks. I'll still be here when you get back. I don't think they will let me bust out of here anytime soon."

A long breath leaves my lungs, and I nod, knowing deep down that I *should* get out of here for an hour or two. I'm starting to get a little stir-crazy from the white sterile surfaces and harsh cleaning agents.

Leaving the hospital feels like leaving a part of my soul behind. Now that I've got Noah back, I can't imagine my life without him. It's crazy how quickly and easily he could slide back in.

It will be a long time before I forget the fear I felt when I heard the car crash into Noah over the phone. That sickening sound of metal hitting metal still rings in my ears; Noah's swears like daggers to my heart. Maybe I can admit it now, knowing that Noah's alive, but I was worried I would never see him again.

When I get home, I stop by the diner for a moment, saying *hi* to

Jack and ensuring everything is running smoothly. He gives me a big hug but tells me not to worry and take as much time as I need and that he'll handle everything. I wave at a few familiar guests before disappearing upstairs towards my home.

My apartment feels empty, the silence like a thick blanket covering my surroundings. I glance around, taking everything in as I set my keys on the stand near the door. Taking a shaky breath, I walk into the apartment, overwhelmed by the idea that just last night, I was moving Noah's things into my bedroom as a surprise. I was hoping we would be moving into the next phase of our relationship together.

Hopefully, that will still be the case, but there will need to be some conversations before then. I'm done being kept in the dark, especially given the events of last night. It's time for everyone to come clean so we can move forward together.

Even though I know I should take a nap or a hot shower, I have too much energy running through my body. Instead, I pull on a pair of running leggings and a long sleeve shirt. I slip on my tennis shoes and grab my phone and keys, locking my door behind me.

When I make it outside, I pause for a second, noticing one of Charlie's deputy's cars sitting across the street from me. The officer inside looks up at me as I stand there, straightening my hair in my ponytail, but he doesn't make a move other than dipping his chin at me.

I grumble under my breath and decide I need to talk to Charlie later and inform him I don't need babysitting.

As soon as my feet hit the concrete of the sidewalk in front of the diner, I take off. The muscles in my legs pump as I propel myself forward, trying to run away from my problems.

Noah might be awake and coherent now, but I still can't shake the overwhelming feeling that something still isn't *right*. I need to sit down and talk to him and make him tell me everything that's going on. After finding his badge in his things last night before the shit hit the fan, I kind of have a pretty good idea of the situation, but I need him to tell me.

The weight of everything crashes into me with every strike of my heel against the pavement. I push my muscles harder and harder, trying to erase the images of the EMTs rolling Noah into the ER on a gurney, his skin almost blue. My breathing becomes more labored the harder I run, and I see black spots in my vision.

The world is closing in on me, and my chest feels like I have a 50-ton weight pressing against it. I wonder if I'll ever be able to breathe normally again.

I finally reach a screeching halt on the pavement, hunching over my knees and letting out a soul-wracking sob. My eyes squeeze shut to block the images from flooding my brain, but it almost makes it worse. My ears are ringing as the world spins around me. I take shallow breaths in and out, unable to catch a full breath.

Noah could've *died* last night.

My life has held a lot of loss, but that might have been the thing that would've broken me. I just got Noah back, thinking I could have lost him forever? It's unfathomable.

It feels like I'm going to split in half from the pain emanating from within me. A sense of dread threatens to consume my entire being.

And then...

A hand on my middle back and a voice mumbling, "Hey, it's okay."

Another sob hits my body, and I start shivering. My eyes manage to focus enough so I can see who's found me.

When I see Jordan standing before me, my chest starts to ache again. "I can't go any further," is all I manage to get out. My eyes are probably red and puffy, my nose dripping from the severity of the tears pouring from within me.

"Okay," he says softly. "Want me to help you back to your place?" I nod my head weakly, and then he takes a step closer. "Do you think you can walk?" Again I nod my head. Jordan reaches for my arm and then wraps it around his waist, giving me a chance to lean on him for support if I need it. I do, taking advantage of his strength when I have none. He wraps his arm across my shoulders, holding onto me, so I don't disappear into nothingness.

"Come on, let's get you home."

We start to take a slow pace back to the diner. The tears have subsided slightly, possibly the effect of having the presence of another human close. My nose is still horrendously stuffy, and I try to breathe without seeming too gross.

"Did you hear what happened?" I finally manage to ask Jordan. His arm tightens across my shoulders, and he exhales a heavy breath.

"I did."

"It was terrible, Jordan," I whisper softly, wondering if he hears me. "It could have been *really bad.*"

"Hey," his gruff voice manages to rattle me out of my spiraling thoughts. "It wasn't, though. I heard from Charlie that he's awake now."

I swipe at my eyes with my free hand, more traitorous tears leaking out of my eyes. "Yeah, but—"

"No buts, Addison," Jordan cuts me off. "Just take it day by day, okay?"

Jordan gets me home, and I immediately go into my bathroom, dropping my running gear on the way. With a few taps on my phone, I find my favorite playlist and ramp the volume up. I hop into the shower, turning it as high as possible until the water scalds my skin. I scrub away all the evidence from the last 24 hours with my loofa. I'm not the one who was covered in leaves and dirt when we arrived at the hospital, but somehow I still feel dirtier. As if I have a layer of stress and anxiety just sitting on my skin's surface. I let the scent of lavender from my body wash seep into my skin and nose, soothing away the worries.

By the time I get out and towel off, I'm feeling refreshed. I drink some water and find a snack out of my pantry before lounging on my couch for an hour or so. It's a nice break from the monotony of sitting in a hospital room and watching the nurses come and go.

When I return back to the hospital that evening, Noah is in the middle of spooning chocolate pudding into his mouth. He peeks up at me sheepishly as I enter his room and move to sit by him.

"Hey," he says, giving me a shy smile.

"Hi. How's that pudding?"

Noah sits back a little and looks down at the pudding cup with a wry expression. "Not going to lie, it's pretty damn good. I can't remember the last time I had pudding."

"It was probably when we were back in middle school," I laugh. "And it likely ended up all over my shirt at some point."

Noah's eyes go wide as he turns to me, alarmed. "I never did that, did I?"

The heart monitor beside Noah's bed starts beeping at an increased rate, and I snicker again, resting a hand on his shoulder. "Calm down, big guy. No, you never dropped pudding on me."

Noah exhales sharply. "There's so much I don't remember from when we were younger. And I was such a little asshole to you in those early days. I don't think I would've put it past me."

"Your weapon of choice tended to be your words," I tell him, my voice light and teasing. "I don't think you ever resorted to food fighting."

Noah groans. "Honestly, I don't know which one is worse."

I give a light laugh, then silence falls over us, and I worry at my fingers tied together in my lap. Noah notices and raises an eyebrow at me, waiting for me to tell him what's on my mind.

"I um..." I pause, thinking over my words. Noah dips his spoon into his chocolate pudding again, bringing another bite towards his mouth and eyeing me expectantly. "I was moving your stuff into my bedroom while you were at your dad's."

"Okay," he says, trailing off the word as if he's unsure where I'm going with this.

I purse my lips, gazing at the man I love so much and wondering if this will change things for us again. Will he run away? There's only one way to find out. Just like ripping a bandaid off. "Noah, I found your badge."

His steely eyes go wide, and he sets his spoon down on the tray in front of him, clearing his throat. "Oh."

"I didn't mean to. It just fell out," I tell him. "But I want you to tell me what's going on. And no more of this 'I promise I'll tell you eventually' crap. I want you to tell me *now*."

Noah nods as if he agrees that it's time. "I work for the FBI."

"I know that. I saw your badge, remember? My dad had an identical one."

"Yeah," Noah says fondly at the mention of my dad. "I'm finishing his investigation."

I sit back from him, my eyebrows furrowing together. "What?"

"Your father was here investigating my father," Noah informs me. "And after I left, I eventually joined up with the FBI and reopened his investigation."

The world begins buzzing around me, and a slight ringing in my ears begins. I'm almost afraid to ask, but I know I have to. "What has your father done?"

I don't know much about Declan McCoy besides that he's a grade-A asshole. Generally, I do my best to stay out of his way, keeping any interaction with him as short as possible. He's just an unpleasant human.

Noah gives a humorless laugh. "Where do I start?"

"You said the case was closed? Was it because of my dad—?"

"Yes," Noah says, sobering up. "After your dad died, they had nothing else to go on because if my father is good at anything, it's making himself look innocent. So the case was closed until I got there and reopened it. But...listen, there's something I have to tell you about that."

The ground beneath me feels shaky, like an earthquake roiling underneath us. Somehow I know that whatever Noah's about to tell me isn't going to be good. I'm feeling a little lightheaded as I say, "Okay."

He takes a deep breath and straightens his shoulders as much as possible in his bed. With a dip of his chin, he looks me straight in the eyes and says, "Parks, I'm certain my father ordered that fire to be set. He's the one responsible for your parents' deaths."

My vision tunnels, and the ground swallows me whole, my world slipping into blackness.

Chapter 37

Noah

My room is a flurry with activity as they try to revive Addison. As soon as I saw the color wash out of her face and her sway in her chair, I hit the call button to get the nurses in my room. They hurried in and were able to get her into a safe position on the floor so she wouldn't fall over and crack her head open.

A sinking pit of worry settles into my stomach. I lean over the edge of my bed, watching helplessly as the nurses hover around her on the ground. Her curls splay around her head, starkly contrasting with the pale white tile floors. One of the nurses rubs her fist against Addison's sternum, trying to bring her back to the present.

I wasn't expecting the news to go over well, but I wasn't expecting her to pass out. Usually, Addison is steadfast no matter what obstacle comes up. The nurses have a cool compress pressed against her forehead as she comes around. Addison's face is pale. Her eyes glaze as she finally regains consciousness, her eyelids fluttering as her vision refocuses on the scene around her.

"What happened?" She asks, her voice weak. Her gaze darts between the two nurses crouched beside her before they bounce up to where I'm still stuck in my bed.

"You just fainted, honey," the nurse closest to her says. "Have you had anything to eat today?"

"A coffee and banana," Addison responds, and my stomach twists. "And I hadn't eaten anything before that since lunch yesterday."

The nurses all share a glance, and they help get her up. "We'll get you a granola bar and some water, okay? Don't get up too quickly. Your blood sugar is probably a little low."

Addison nods as they get her back into a sitting position in the chair next to me. Addison meets my gaze, and she frowns. "I'm sorry," she says, a sheepish undertone lacing her voice.

"Don't be," I tell her. Regret settles deep into my gut, knowing I'm partly to blame for her intense reaction. It's been a crazy twenty-four hours. I should've waited to drop that bomb on her until things were a little more settled.

She presses a hand to her head and squeezes her eyes shut. The nurse runs into the room, carrying three granola bars and a water bottle. Addison takes them gratefully and opens one up, taking a tender bite out of the snack.

Her eyes avoid mine as she picks at her granola bar. Finally, she mutters a soft, "I'm embarrassed."

"Why? It's not like you could control it," I tell her back, reaching my left hand across the bed toward her. She eyes it warily but finally slips her smaller hand into mine, tangling our fingers together.

"I've never fainted before," she says as if that's enough explanation.

"Well, I guess if you were going to faint, the best place to do it would be in a hospital full of medical professionals," I try to tease her. She offers me a forced smile, and I squeeze her hand. "Hey, it's not anything you can control. Things have been crazy lately, and your body probably just had enough. Your brain needed to reboot. It's nothing to be embarrassed about." She takes another bite of her granola bar. "If anything, I should be apologizing to you. I shouldn't have dropped that on you given everything you've gone through."

"I guess so. I just feel so stupid." She presses her hand against her temple. "And I'm so tired."

I watch her for a moment taking in the dark circles underneath her eyes and how her vision glazes over slightly as she stares at me. I'm not sure I've ever seen her look wearier. I make a snap decision and let go of her hand. I shuffle around in the hospital bed, scooting further away from her until I'm close to the opposite edge. She watches me with drowsy eyes but doesn't move.

"Come here, come lay with me," I tell her, raising my arm in invitation. When I notice the alarmed look on her face, I grin, "I promise you won't hurt me."

Addison hesitates for only a moment but finally gives in. After setting her remaining two granola bars down on the table next to the bed, she crawls on top of the bed, curling into my side and resting her head on my shoulder. My arm falls around her waist, and she snuggles in closer.

"Get some rest," I whisper, pressing a kiss to the top of her head.

"You're sure this is okay?"

"It's better than okay," I mumble into her hair. She presses closer into me as if trying to eliminate any possible space between us and lets out a big sigh.

"I love you, Noah."

* * *

"Alright, now, you have your discharge papers?" the nurse asks me the following morning as she clicks through my medical record on the computer.

"I do," Addison says, holding them up. She's standing behind the wheelchair I'm currently trapped in. Apparently, it's hospital policy that patients must be wheeled out of the hospital to avoid liability.

I've never felt more humiliated.

But it's okay. I keep reminding myself that this is my ticket out of here. All I have to do is put up with one measly wheelchair ride, and then I get to go home. With Parks. I feel like that's a pretty decent trade-off.

"Well then, it looks like everything else is in order. You two should be good to go. Noah, if you have any questions, don't hesitate to call the nurse line, okay? And you're all scheduled for your follow-up visit in a few weeks."

I nod my head, itching to get out of here. I'm not sure how much longer I can put up with this.

The nurses all wave as we walk down the hallway to the elevators. They act like I'm some big celebrity, but I have to wonder if it's because they know who my father is. In a small town, you can never entirely escape the history you're born into. I might have a different last name, but at the heart of it all, I'm still Declan McCoy's son, and just about everyone in this town knows it.

Addison holds the wheelchair steady for me once we pass through the front sliding doors of the hospital, and then she puts it off to the side. She reaches for my hand, and we walk together to her car.

"Do you mind stopping at Monty's so I can pick up your prescriptions? I just got a text that they were ready," she explains.

I settle in the car and rest my head against the seat. "Could you just take me home? I feel like I could use a nap." Addison pauses and glances over at me, a smile playing on her lips as she starts the car. I raise an eyebrow at her. "What?"

"I just like the way you said that—home."

I smile back at her. "It is home. Our home."

If possible, Addison beams even brighter as she pulls out of the hospital parking lot and drives us away.

She walks me up to the apartment, ensuring I don't pass out as I take the stairs to our front door. As soon as we're inside, she sets the folder containing my medical notes down on the counter and then turns to me.

"Do you need anything else while I'm at the store?"

I shake my head and stumble over to the couch. As soon as I fall against the cushions, I look up at her, reconsidering. "Actually, could you get me some blue Gatorade and some Cheetos?"

She wrinkles her nose but nods her head. "Odd request, but of course. Anything else?"

"No, thanks."

Addison watches my attempt to get comfortable on the couch before she takes pity on me, walking over to help me settle underneath the fluffy plaid blanket. I groan as I lean back, feeling the ache begin in my wrist. She ensures I'm all tucked in before pressing a kiss to my forehead and saying she'll be back in a few minutes. I close my eyes as soon as she's gone, falling asleep almost immediately.

I'm awoken when she comes back, her keys jingling as she unlocks the door. I blink a few times and turn my head toward her. She has two white plastic grocery bags that she takes into the kitchen, whispering a quick "sorry" to me for all the noise.

I close my eyes again and turn away from her, willing more sleep to come. She rustles around in the kitchen, and I hear her run the sink. The next thing I know, the couch is dipping under her weight as she settles next to me. I peek at her, and she's got a glass of water and a few pills sitting in the palm of her hand.

She looks at me with sympathetic eyes and holds them out. Groaning, I remove my good arm from underneath the blanket and take the pills, popping them onto my tongue before taking the water to wash them down.

Addison runs her hand through my hair and over the side of my face. "Will you be okay if I run downstairs for a bit?" she asks gently.

I nod my head, "That's fine. I'll probably just rest some more."

"Okay," she whispers, leaning down to press her lips to mine before she gets up and gathers her things again. "I'll be home a little bit later."

"No rush," I tell her. "I'm not going anywhere."

Something makes her smile, and she blows me another kiss before disappearing through the front door. I reach for the remote with my good hand and click through the channels in an attempt to find something. I finally settled on an animal rescue show—not really my first choice. Still, I don't feel cognizant enough to handle anything else. I relax back into the pillows and get sucked into the program.

I must doze off again because the next thing I know, I'm jolting awake to the sound of a loud Magic Eraser ad. Grumbling, I reach for the remote and hit the mute button. The apartment feels very quiet and still without Parks here. She said she'd only be gone for a while, so I try to ignore the anxious feelings trying to well up at the back of my chest.

The pain medication Parks gave me earlier must have kicked in because I feel rejuvenated. I barely register that I just had surgery on my wrist, and I'm feeling much perkier than I was when I first got home.

Rolling off the couch, I pad into the bedroom and rummage through my new set of drawers that Addison assigned me. I find the little black notebook tucked under some of my other personal items and pull it out, flipping to a page filled with scribbled notes.

Yesterday right after I woke up, Charlie informed me that he had taken it upon himself to investigate the Witch House. Without me.

"There was nothing there," he had told me. "It was just an abandoned old shack like we figured it was."

"Are you sure? Nothing weird or out of the ordinary?"

"No, man, just a bunch of junk. A few boxes full of garbage and this nasty orange couch stained by Lord knows what. I looked in every room and in every corner. I'm sorry, but it was just a dead end," Charlie had said.

I was still a little loopy from the drugs to really worry too much about what he told me then, but now that my head is a little clearer, I need to get back to work. My father may have managed to knock me off course with this accident, but he has another thing coming if he thinks that a little broken wrist will deter me from taking him down once and for all.

My eyes scan over the notes I had jotted down about my concerns with the Witch House. Charlie may have scoured around, but a part of me still wants to go out there myself and see if I can find him. I appreciate the Sheriff's help, but he's not on the same level as me regarding this investigation. I might be able to spot something that he wasn't.

I spend over half an hour flipping through the pages and making new voice memos on my phone since I can't write with my wrist busted. As I dig into my notes, I still can't help the feeling that I'm missing something *big*. I have that niggling feeling at the back of my neck that there's something major right in front of my face, and I'm just too jaded to see it.

With a frustrated sigh, I run my hand through my hair a few times. I tell myself that it will work out one way or the other. Still, it is disheartening to think I've been running around in circles without solid leads for an eternity. Next time I see Charlie, I'll need to ask him if he had any luck with the bank information I found while snooping around my father's office.

At the very least, that will flag something in the system, and we can get this rolling again. There's nothing I hate more than feeling like I've stalled, and at the moment, that's precisely where I am.

I know there's not much else I can do at this time. It's not like I can go out guns blazing to catch the bad guy—I can't even hold my gun right now anyway. I'll likely have to do a round of physical therapy to get the strength back in my hand, even to carry my weapon properly. After that, I need to worry about my shot. Who knows if I'll even have the same type of accuracy that I did before I busted my wrist?

There are a lot of unknowns right now, and the more I think about it, the more I start spiraling into a wreck of nervous energy. Finally, I flip the notebook closed, realizing that worrying about this isn't doing me any good. I put it back where I found it and reclaim my spot on the couch, flipping on the TV to try and get myself to relax again.

I only watch through two episode breaks before someone pounds on my front door. I look over my shoulder, immediately going on guard. Slowly, I get up and walk over, in no hurry to see who the visitor is. I peer through the peephole and exhale sharply when I see my boss standing at my door.

He turns to me with a tight smile as I swing the door open. "Noah."

"Vincent," I respond. I figured I would be getting a visit from him at some point. It was inevitable once Charlie gave him the call that I had been in an accident. He was elusive, though. I was never sure when or where Vincent would drop in.

"How are you feeling?"

"Can't say I haven't been better," I tell him, pushing the door open further so he can come in. Vincent accepts the invitation, walks into my home, and looks around.

"This is a cute place," he states.

"Thank you, it's my girlfriend's." The word feels weird coming out of my mouth, but I can't deny that I like the sound. It's been a long time since I've said that.

Vincent turns toward me and raises an eyebrow as his lips press into a thin line. "Girlfriend, huh?"

I cross my arms over my chest, careful not to jostle my wrist too much. I don't bother responding to his probing question. "What can I do for you? I assume you're not here to chit-chat?"

Vin looks at me through his thick-rimmed glasses for a moment too long and then shakes his head. "I'm afraid not."

"Well, then, I guess we better get to it then. Can I get you anything, water? Shot of vodka?"

Despite the conversation I know we're about to have, Vincent, laughs. "A water will be fine, thank you."

I motion for him to sit at the kitchen's little table while I get us both a glass of water. It's a little uncomfortable. I'm still getting used to doing everyday tasks with only one usable hand at the moment. Still, I manage to hand him his glass without any significant casualties happening.

After I take my seat across from him, I motion for him to get on with it.

Vincent breathes in deeply, his shoulders rising. "You know I really, really don't want to do this, but I'm going to need you to turn over your badge and weapon." Though I figured that's precisely why he's here, I open my mouth to protest. Vincent effectively shuts me up with a wave of his hand. "You knew the deal, Noah. The order is coming from higher up; unfortunately, I have to follow it. I'm sorry, but you're done."

"So what does this mean for the case, then?" I ask him between gritted teeth.

Vincent studies my face. Then he gives a noncommittal shrug and diverts his gaze. "I don't know. They'll probably reassign it to another agent."

"But it's *my case*," I growl at him. "I've done all the work and pulled everything together. I need more time, and I think I can finally catch him."

"My hands are tied, Lockwood," Vincent tells me. "Your badge, please."

I grumble under my breath as I push the wooden chair back away from the table. I storm into the bedroom and find my badge and gun inside the drawer. Stomping back out, I set them on the table in front of Vincent.

"I think this is a mistake," I tell him.

He sighs. "I think you're right, but there's nothing I can do right now. If I find a way to get you back on the case, you'll be the first to know."

I clench my teeth, feeling the muscle in my jaw spasm from the force. "Is that all?"

"I'm afraid so," he says, getting up from his seat and pocketing my badge. He puts my holstered gun inside his briefcase after ensuring the safety mechanism is on and then turns to me. He extends his hand, and I begrudgingly take it.

Despite him completely ruining my day, I respect Vincent enough to shake his hand when he offers.

"I hope you heal up quickly, Noah. We'll be in touch once you've been cleared by your doctors to return to work. We'll need to set up a time to meet and discuss what happens next."

I follow him out, giving him a nod of my head as he waves before disappearing. As soon as he's gone, I close the door and rest my forehead against the cool wood. This has just put a major wrench in all of my plans. Without the government's backup, there's not much else I can do. At this point, my best bet would be to join up with Charlie and try and catch him committing a crime around town, but my father isn't that dumb.

His crimes range more on the national and global scale than sticking to petty small-town misdemeanors, and yet he always finds a way to keep his hands clean of any involvement.

A sense of apprehension rolls over me. I'm not sure what this means for the future, but there's nothing I can do at this point. I've been stripped of any and all power I had. I just have to hope that everything will work out, one way or another.

Chapter 38
Addison

The following few days are quiet. Noah spends a lot of time resting, letting his body heal from the accident. His pain has been getting better over the last few days too, and he's been able to use regular over-the-counter medicine instead of the heavy prescription stuff. It's such a relief seeing him get better each and every day that passes.

I've been spending most of my time at home, trusting Jack and Grace to handle everything at the diner downstairs. I only have Grace for a Noah's fully capable of taking care of himself, but something deep inside me tells me I need to stick close to him when I can. Something about him has been off since he came home from the hospital. He told me about how his boss visited him that first day he was home, but he didn't go into many details. I can only assume that it wasn't for a friendly chat.

We're sitting at the table now, Noah reading a book and me working on the weekly crossword puzzle. He hasn't bothered shaving since he got home; the dark stubble there before is now much longer and thicker. He keeps his dark hair pulled back into a low ponytail at the back of his neck to keep it out of his eyes.

This morning when he woke up, I could tell that he was really starting to feel better because the gleam was back in his eyes. We've spent a lot of time together the last few days, just the two of us, but we haven't really taken advantage of it. I still have many questions burning in the back of my mind but I didn't want to cause him any extra stress by asking. Maybe today, he'll be feeling up to getting out a bit.

I relentlessly tap my pen against the table, trying to get his attention. Finally, Noah looks up, arching an eyebrow at me.

"Is there something you need?" he asks, amusement hinting in his tone.

"How do you feel about going for a walk?"

Noah raises an eyebrow at me. "It's freezing outside, Parks."

I shrug my shoulders and grin. "And? We have coats. I just think that getting up and moving around will be good for you."

"Well then I guess we're going for a walk," Noah says, his eyes gleaming. "I better be a good patient and do as my nurse tells me."

A blush forms on my cheeks, and I smile at him. We gather our coats, gloves, and hats and then go downstairs.

I take my place on Noah's left side as soon as we hit the sidewalk. He looks down at me, a soft smile playing on his lips as I gaze back up at him. He reaches for my hand and I thread my fingers through his, giving his good hand a little squeeze.

We walk down the block together. The town is a little quiet today; only a few people are out and about running errands. They wave to us when they pass, and I smile at them.

"So—" I start after we've been walking for a bit. Noah looks down at me questioningly.

"Yes?"

"I was wondering if we could talk," I say hesitantly.

Noah chuckles, his hot breath swirling around in the air in front of him, making him look like a dragon. "That doesn't sound good. Are you breaking up with me?"

I shove him with my shoulder. "*No.* I was wondering if we could talk about what you told me at the hospital."

He bobs his head and looks straightforward. "Yeah, I was wondering when you'd bring it up again."

"I was waiting for you to start feeling better," I explain. "But I do have a lot of questions.

"As I assume you would," he says lightly. "By all means, Parks. Ask away."

I think for a moment. Of course, now that I have the opportunity to ask him anything I want, I can't think of anything to ask. Finally, I settle on a simple icebreaker, "Your dad was responsible for the fire?"

"Yes."

"Why wasn't that reported in the investigation? If he did it, why isn't he paying for it?"

Noah exhales. "Because my father is incredibly good at what he does. He has a network of people who do all the dirty work for him, so he can, theoretically, keep his hands clean."

I shake my head, not understanding. "Then how do you know he's the one who did it?"

Noah is quiet and then says, "Because I know my father. And I confronted him about it right after it happened, and he all but confirmed it."

I press my lips together, my heart rate picking up and causing my chest to ache. "The night of the fire? You've known since then?"

I can't help but feel a little betrayed. My parents weren't the only ones trapped in that fire. If Noah has known all this time, he's let me walk around in the same town with the man who tried to kill me.

As if sensing the direction of my thoughts, he squeezes my hand, pulling me back into the present. "Listen to me. My father is a dangerous man. He has resources that you and I can't even begin to understand. So yes, I confronted him about it. And in response, he threatened me, and he threatened *you.*"

"What does that mean?" I ask, already confused by the politics of whatever transpired when we were eighteen.

Noah breathes deeply through his nose. "That's why I left. When I confronted him about the fire and told him that I would tell everyone, he threatened you and said the only way I could keep you safe was to forget everything and leave."

I shake my head, my eyebrows pulling in tight.

Noah continues, "I was eighteen, Parks. I loved you, and you had just been through a horrible, horrible tragedy at the hands of my father. I felt trapped, so I did the only thing I thought was best. I listened to him and left."

"Was there proof?" I ask him. "If you had stayed, could you have gotten him arrested?"

Noah shakes his head. "No. There's no proof other than his actions when I asked him about it."

"I'm trying to follow along, Noah, but you're losing me. How have you been investigating your father when there isn't any proof?"

"Because sometimes there *are* loose ends that he forgets about or doesn't consider a threat. And I've tracked every one of them down—disgruntled employees, business partners gone wrong, a mistress he did wrong—you name it."

"So all this time, you've been chasing him, waiting for him to slip up?"

Noah nods now. "Pretty much. There have been different levels to the investigation. I've gone deep undercover a time or two to get information on how his organization is running."

I narrow my eyes and focus on the sidewalk in front of us. "When you say *organization*, what does that mean?"

"A lot of bad stuff, Parks. Pretty much anything nefarious you could dream up, he's probably done it."

"Oh," I respond, unsure what to do with this information. It's not lost on me that Noah's still being vague. But if the things his father has done are indeed that bad, I'm not sure I really want to know. "I wish you would've just told me all of this before you left."

He sighs. "Yeah, in hindsight, I wish I would've too. Probably would've spared us a lot of heartbreak. But I did what I thought was best at the time. I'm sorry that I hurt you."

I turn my head and give him a smile. "I forgive you. I just want to be able to support you, and I can't do that if you don't let me in."

"I know. There are things that I can't tell you still, just because of the nature of the case. Even though I'm not on assignment anymore, I still have a responsibility to keep things confidential. But I promise I'll do my best to keep you in the loop from now on if it comes down to it."

"Thank you," I whisper. "I appreciate that."

We finally round the corner, and my diner comes into view. I'm fully chilled to the bone now. I look up at Noah, hopeful that he'll be game for my next idea. "How do you feel about stopping in and getting a hot chocolate or a coffee?"

"Is that what the doctor ordered?"

I laugh and nod my head. "As your nurse, I must insist that we listen to the prescribed recommendations."

"Then I suppose we're making a pit stop."

Noah and I walk the rest of the way toward the diner. As soon as we're inside, my staff all offer us *hellos*. We go up to the counter and take a seat at the barstools. Jack saunters over and gives us a grin.

"Hey lovebirds, you just popping in?"

"Could you get us each a hot chocolate please?" I ask my friend. "It's freezing outside."

"Absolutely," Jack taps the countertop twice with a flat hand. "Coming right up."

While we wait, a few of my employees swing by our table. I check in with them, asking how their day has been. They also say *hi* to Noah, asking how he's been feeling.

Our drinks come just a few minutes later, and we both take grateful sips. I'm still reeling from our conversation on our walk, my brain processing all that Noah both told me and didn't tell me. He stays quiet next to me, stacking the sweetener packets, knocking them over, and starting the process again.

"Hey, Addie," I'm pulled out of my thoughts by Jack, standing in front of me, giving me a sheepish smile. "I was wondering if you could help me with submitting payroll. I think I have it all finished but I want to make sure it all looks right before I submit it."

I glance at Noah, and he gives me a smile, silently telling me he'll be fine without me.

"I think I'm going to head back upstairs and rest for a bit," Noah tells me as soon as I make it back to the counter where he's sitting. I glance at him and do a double-take. He's gone completely pale, the pallor of his skin contrasting with the dark circles under his eyes. Suddenly Noah looks as if he hasn't gotten good sleep in weeks.

"Are you feeling okay?" I ask him, concern seeping through my whole body. I thought he was doing better today, but maybe I pushed him too hard.

He nods weakly, and I can tell he's trying to ease my worries. "I think so. I just think I need to lie down for a while."

"Do you want me to go with you?"

He shakes his head, "No, it's okay you can stay down here if you want. I'm just going to sleep."

"Okay," I say, leaning toward him and pressing a kiss against his cheek. "Give me a call if you need anything."

Noah smiles at me and then disappears upstairs.

I spend the next few hours working. Grace pops in for her shift and fills me in on the updates surrounding her new endeavor. I can't lie and say I'm *not* happy for her—her whole face lights up with excitement when she tells me about it—but still, deep down, I'm a little salty about her abandoning me with such short notice. Things will be fine, and I'll continue to support her, but it does sting a little.

For a few hours, it feels like everything is back to normal. It's just Grace, Jack, and me running the show. I don't think about how our mayor is apparently a high-level criminal out to get his son, and I don't worry about what that means for our future. All I focus on is doing what I do best.

Since Noah's accident, I haven't been down in the diner as much as I usually am. Getting the time to be here now is lovely. My regular customers are happy to see me, each asking how Noah and I are doing and if there's anything they can do for us. I get a few offers for casseroles which I gratefully decline, but it's always the thought that counts.

After a while, I decide to head back home to check on Noah. I trek upstairs and reach for my keys, stopping short when I see my front door cracked open slightly. I hear a deep voice booming from inside my home. Quietly, I take a few steps closer, listening to see if I can discern who it is.

"And to lose your job on top of everything," the voice tuts. "What a shame. You must really feel like a winner right now."

"Yes, Father. I can really see your sympathy is really shining through," a voice I recognize as Noah responds stiffly. I wonder how Declan found that out when Noah hasn't even told *me* he lost his job.

"Well, sometimes things work out better than you imagined. Trust me, it wasn't my intention, but I won't look a gift horse in the mouth." With this last sentence, it all seems to click into place now. Declan McCoy is inside my apartment. A shiver runs through my whole body, and I clench my teeth. Everything Noah told me about his father earlier is now coming to light. I've always known something was off about the mayor, but now that I'm experiencing this side of him in person, there is no going back.

"I'm sure you won't," Noah's voice still sounds tired, and I wonder if he even got the chance to rest before his father came and accosted him.

"Maybe this is the best solution," Declan starts, sounding bored. In my mind's eye, I can almost picture him examining his cuticles as he says this. "Now that you're *officially* off the case, you have nothing left keeping you here."

"Is that so?"

"I would imagine. Perhaps we can revisit our previous arrangement. I really would hate for you to suffer more than you already have, but I'll admit, you're a loose cannon. I can't have you wandering around my town threatening to go off any minute. I'll give you til the end of the week to leave my town. Now that your mother is gone, I trust this time will be permanent. The original ultimatum still stands. It's time to move past your ridiculous notion and get on with our lives."

I decide I've heard enough, and I push through the door. Both men turn to face me. My eyes instantly find Noah, and his shoulders stiffen as soon as he sees me enter the room. He takes a step towards me but doesn't come any closer.

My eyes travel over to Declan, and I scowl at him. His lips pull up into a sardonic smile at the sight of me. "Ah, Ms. Parks. Wonderful for you to join us."

"What are you doing here?" I ask him, my voice tight.

Declan spares a glance at Noah before turning back to me. "I was just checking up on my son. I was concerned after I heard about the accident."

Based on what I just heard, Declan was doing everything *but* checking up on his son's wellbeing.

"I think you should leave," I say to Noah's father, standing tall. I tilt my chip up at him, though I'm a good foot shorter than him at best.

Noah's father stares down his nose at me and gives me an amused glare as if I'm a little bug on his windshield. "As you wish, Ms. Parks."

I glance at Noah and see him practically vibrating with anger. His good hand is gripped into a tight fist at his side. Declan turns to give him one last withering look before he opens the front door and steps outside.

As he steps outside, a heavy silence falls over the apartment. Noah is seething next to me, and I'm hesitant to say anything.

Then as if the timer has finally ticked all the way down, Noah explodes. In one swift movement, he reaches for the water glass on the table next to him and picks it up before chucking it at the wall opposite where we're standing.

The glass shatters into a thousand pieces, falling to the floor. I wince from the impact and look to Noah in concern. His shoulders rise and fall rapidly with his increased breaths, and then he slumps down onto the closest chair to him, burying his face in his left hand.

Noah has taken a lot of blows in the last few days, and it seems this one was the last straw. I don't know what Declan said to him, but whatever it was, it really hurt Noah.

The man I love so desperately breaks right in front of me, and there is nothing I can do.

I stand there in the aftermath for a second too long before I kick into gear. I take two quick strides over to him and take a seat. Noah's uninjured fist moves into his hair and clenches at the strands. His eyes are screwed shut as he attempts to get control of his breathing. His other hand rests against his knees.

My hand gently rests on his shoulders, his tight muscles bunching together underneath my touch. He's so warm as if his fight-or-flight mechanism is running off the charts. Sweat seeps through the thin cotton of his shirt.

I won't lie and say that seeing Declan McCoy in my home wasn't alarming—especially knowing what I know now. I can't imagine what it felt like for Noah. All of his life, he's struggled with his father seeming to be the villain of his story, and he can't ever seem to catch a break. Declan McCoy has an incredible knack for knowing when Noah is the weakest and taking that opportunity to strike.

"Noah?" I ask softly, carefully. "Do you want to talk about it?"

It takes a moment, but then the floodgates open.

"What is there to talk about, Parks? It won't change anything. Nothing I do matters! I can run away, and toss everything I care about to the side, so he doesn't try to destroy them. I can change my name, but it doesn't matter. He'll always be a part of me and in my life in one way or another, and it infuriates me!" Noah says softly at first and then raises his voice as he finishes, "I just want to be free!"

I stay right by his side and weather the storm. Noah's anger doesn't frighten me. I know that nothing in this world could push him to the point of hurting me.

But right now, he's the one hurting. Noah has shattered into a million pieces, just like the glass he threw at the wall.

Chapter 39
Noah

My heart thuds against my chest, each beat ringing in my ears. My lungs feel tight as if I can't breathe in a full breath, no matter how deeply I try to inhale. I'm breaking out in a cool sweat, the beads of perspiration making my skin clammy as I sit on our couch, all the negative and dark thoughts swirling around me like a tornado.

I feel like I'm drowning. In regret, in anger, in everything.

Since I was in that stupid accident, I've been fighting off the sense of failure lingering in my mind. Vincent taking my badge the other day only amplified that, and my father coming by to rub it in my face and threaten me was the breaking point. And now it's consuming me. The failure that everything I set out to do all those years ago is now pointless. Everything I worked toward has crumbled. I'm wondering what I was thinking, wasting all my time and energy on this when I was destined to hit this point anyway.

I've failed. That's all there is to it.

"Noah," Addison whispers, her hand coming up to cup my cheek. The whisper of my name, sounding so hopeless, breaks me even further, and I lean my head into her touch. "What happened?"

I let out a shaky exhale and close my eyes. "I'm fine."

Addison is quiet for a moment before I hear her say, "No, you're not." I don't respond to her; I just let the weight of my head rest against her palm. I know her eyes are on me as she searches my face for all my secrets. "Tell me."

I squeeze my eyes closed tighter. "Nothing. I've failed."

"No," she says firmly. "I don't believe that. You've just hit a block in the road, and you're hurting. What can I do?"

"This is enough," I say, finally opening my eyes to gaze at her. "I feel like it's been a lifetime since I've been happy. Since I've felt like myself. But ever since I've been back home with you...."

A soft smile forms on Addison's pink lips, the edges curving up. "I know. I feel the same."

"I need you to save me like you did before."

"You don't need saving, Noah. You're strong enough to save yourself."

I shake my head, and her palm falls from my cheek. I look up at the sky, my chest tight. There are grey rolling clouds forming, signaling rain soon. "I don't feel strong."

"You're the strongest person I know."

"You don't know me. Not anymore," I tell her, letting the hardness in my tone cut.

Addison takes a step back from me and covers her arms over her chest. "I do. I know you probably better than I know myself. But if you need a break, take one. Let me be strong for the both of us for once."

"I just don't know what to do from here," I breathe. "I don't know what to do."

Addison comes to sit by me again, her eyes watching me closely. She appears to think over her words for a minute or two, the silence between us almost deafening. Finally, she asks, "You lost your job?"

I nod my head once. Embarrassment sparks in my chest, but I dampen it. There's nothing I can do about it now. "Sort of. They took me off the assignment. Took my badge. I'll get it back eventually after they do an investigation and sit me through a performance review, but until then—"

"Why?"

"I fucked up, Parks. I got too comfortable and let my guard down."

"It was an accident," she protests. "How were you to know your father would go after you like that?"

"It's not that. It's—" I hesitate, thinking of the best way to phrase it. "It's a conflict of interest. Now more than ever. He figured me out, and that's dangerous."

She considers my words. "Your father referenced your 'previous arrangement.' He was talking about when you left, wasn't he?"

I put my forehead in my hand again. "He was."

"He wants you to leave?" I nod, and she presses her lips together before asking, "And what if you don't?"

"There will be consequences."

"You mean me, right? He's going to come after me?" She asks, though her voice doesn't waver. You'd think that any person would be wary when their life has been threatened, but not Addison. She appears cool, calm and collected, despite being the focus of my father's threats.

"You're my Achilles heel, Parks. He will use whatever or whomever to get his point across, and it seems like he's chosen you again." I shake my head. "I'm not perfect, not by a long shot. But I've done everything to keep you safe. I left the first time and didn't look back, all to play his game, but even still. It's not enough. When will it be enough?"

Addison is silent, waiting for me to say everything coursing through my mind. I squeeze my eyes shut.

"I don't want to keep playing this game. But it's like I'm stuck playing the same level over and over, but I never win."

"Noah—" she whispers finally, but I continue.

"I'm running out of lives, Parks. How much longer can I keep doing this? Expecting things to work out and then coming to the harsh conclusion that they can't? I don't want to do this anymore."

"Then end it," she says so bluntly that I have to look up at her.

"What?"

"If you don't want to keep playing his game, then end it."

I make a face at her. "I don't think it's just that easy, Parks."

"Why not?" She pushes. "If you know his game and what to expect, why couldn't you just not participate."

"Because he has a knack for ensuring that his messages get across. And I'm not willing to risk that."

"It's my decision, don't you think?" I frown, but I don't answer. She continues, "It should be. If I'm the one being threatened, I should be able to decide what to do about it. And I don't want you to leave again."

"I don't want to leave either," I tell her. "I'm not even sure if I could. It's just irritating."

"What is?" She asks.

I rub my hand over my face again. "I've done everything in my power to keep you safe, and even still, it's not enough. Why am I never enough?"

"Noah—" her voice breaks off. Addison scoots closer to me, pressing the side of her body against mine. Her hand comes up to my chin, and she turns my head until I'm facing her. "You are *more* than enough."

I pull my head away from her, close my eyes, and breathe deeply. "It doesn't feel like it."

Another silence falls over us. I can hear her breathing next to me as if she's taking in measured breaths, trying to come up with the correct thing to say. The clock on the wall in the kitchen ticks ominously in the silence.

"I'm afraid of being forgotten," she eventually says softly. I turn my head to look at her, waiting for her to continue. She gives me a tight smile. "All I have left are the people here in this town. That's partly why I put so much energy into my diner and relationships here. If that's all I have left, I might as well make sure my legacy remains."

"You think that's all people will remember you for?" I ask her, unsure if I understand correctly. This woman sitting beside me is incredible in so many ways. I'm not sure how she could think that people wouldn't remember her for all her other attributes. "Parks, you're so much more than just that diner."

Her eyes soften. "And you're more than your career."

I shake my head. "It's not really the same. I've spent almost the last decade working toward this, only to fail and have it rubbed in my face."

"So?" she shoots back. "Maybe you're just meant to succeed differently."

"Like what, Parks? I don't have a secret weapon sitting in my back pocket. I don't have anything."

"Great things don't just happen overnight, you know? Maybe this is just a necessary obstacle you must overcome so the real end point makes itself clear."

I force a smile at her. "I appreciate your optimism."

"Well, someone's got to balance you out when you get all gloomy like this," she says. There's a teasing lilt to her voice, but underneath it, I note that she's halfway serious.

I rub the heel of my hand against my eyebrow, trying to ease the headache that's starting to bloom behind my eyes. The last few days have been a rollercoaster of emotions. It seems to have been one thing after another, and I haven't gotten the chance to sit down and work through each of the blows before the next one comes.

The deep-seated feelings of failure and regret are still roiling in my stomach, but having Parks sitting next to me, attempting to shoulder some of the brunt, helps. I turn to her, giving her a grateful look. Her eyes scrutinize my face, and she runs her fingers through my hair. I close my eyes at the feeling of her fingernails against my scalp. Something is soothing about her motions, and I note my heart rate finally settling.

After a few quiet moments, Addison whispers. "I wish you would let me in. It kills me to see you broken like this."

I slowly open my eyes and take her in. I'm struck with the realization of how lucky I am that she's here with me. For so long, I wondered if I would ever get to have moments like this again with her. When I would lie down in my bed all alone at night, I'd dream up quiet instances like this one—the good, the bad, and all the in-between.

"I don't know what I'd be without you," I tell her, leaning toward her until our foreheads are touching. "You're the best thing that's ever happened to me."

"I feel the same way about you," she says back, the corners of her mouth pulling up into a smile.

"Really, I can't fathom the idea of my life without you in it anymore," I say, my voice low. "I don't think I could bear it if something happened to you."

"You'll never have to worry about that," she says back, leaning closer to me, so I get a hint of her shampoo.

I squeeze my eyes closed and take a deep breath, worrying over her words. Even though I've told her about my father's threats, I get the sense that they haven't sunk in, that she doesn't understand the severity. Even though she's here at home, safe with me right now, the mere thought of him hurting her makes my skin prick.

I fall silent, letting her closeness seep into my body and trying to control all these negative thoughts coursing through me. Deep down inside of myself, I know it's no use fretting over this. The threat is real, but at this point, I have no control over anything that happens. I focus on Addison sitting next to me and feel myself begin to relax the longer we sit together.

Her hand continues rubbing up and down my back muscles, occasionally kneading out a tight spot. She's humming under her breath; so softly I wonder if she knows she's doing it.

I'm struck with such intense deja vu from when she sat with me in the hallway of our high school after I just found out my father won the mayoral vote. She always seems to be saving me when I need her the most.

Addison has one of the most tender hearts of anyone I know. She'd no sooner put herself in the line of fire to protect people she cares about than let any harm come to them. Tonight she offered me her strength, and I know with every fiber of my being that she meant every word. If there was a way for me to let her take some of the pressure off of me, I would, but I'm not sure if that's possible.

It seems I'm destined to continue on this merry-go-round with my father. I'll win a round, and he'll win a round, but will it ever actually come to an end?

Like I said to her before, all I want is to be free. Free from him and free from this stupid game I got myself stuck in.

"Hey," Addison says, resting the palm of her hand against my cheek and turning me toward her again as if she can sense the tumultuous turn of my thoughts. "I think we should do something fun tonight. Get your mind off of everything going on."

I laugh humorlessly. "I'm not sure that's possible, but what did you have in mind?"

She purses her lips off to the side, thinking about it. "I haven't gotten that far yet. I guess it depends on what you're feeling up to. Maybe we could go down to Jordan and Caleb's bar, hang out for a bit, and get out of the house."

Giving her an appreciative smile, I consider the offer. I feel exhausted in more ways than one. My body aches from the stress of the afternoon, and my head is still throbbing from the emotional turmoil. I lean back against the couch's cushions and exhale all the air out of my lungs.

"If it's okay, I think I'd like to just stay in tonight," I tell her, not offering any explanation because I don't need to. As soon as the words leave my mouth, Addison is leaning back against the couch next to me.

"Of course. Want to order something in?"

I scrunch my nose up. Food doesn't sound particularly good to me right now. "Maybe we could just make breakfast for dinner later. I'm not terribly hungry."

"But pancakes fix everything," she teases.

"Absolutely," I reply. "Pancakes fix everything."

I agree with her sentiment, but even after Addison talked me down from my panic attack and comforted me in the aftermath, I still can't shake the feeling something major is brewing beneath the surface. I'm not sure what it is or when it will strike, but I'm afraid that if I let my guard down again, there will be no coming back from it.

Chapter 40
Addison

"Alright, Mrs. Macklan, here's your change," I say to the old woman waiting patiently for her check.

She offers me an appreciative smile and holds out a slightly tremorous hand for me to drop the few dollars and change into. "Thank you, Addie. The food was amazing as usual."

"Thank you," I tell her, giving her a wide grin.

Mrs. Macklan pulls out her wallet and places her change into its respective spaces. "Will you be attending the Christmas Tree Lighting tonight?" she asks.

I nod. "Yes, Jack and I will be running a hot chocolate booth. You'll have to stop by to get some."

The old woman grins at me. "Oh yes, that sounds wonderful." She gets out of her chair and pats me on the shoulder. "I will see you later this evening, then."

I wave as she exits the diner and then go back to work, closing out the rest of the tabs for the evening. Every year on December first, Willow Heights puts on the grand Christmas Tree Lighting Festival. It's a big deal for the town, and just about everyone comes out to the town center to participate.

We bring in a giant Christmas tree and display it right in the middle of the square. It's not as big as the Rockefeller tree, but it's pretty extravagant for a small town. Tonight, during the festival, we'll do a countdown, and then all of the Christmas lights in the city, including the tree, will be lit up, signifying the start of the Christmas season.

This has become one of my favorite traditions of the year. I love seeing my town come to life with sparkly white and colored lights. It gives off such an enchanting ambiance that it's hard for even the coldest of hearts not to thaw a little.

Until the big moment, different booths will be set up around the town square—crafts, games, and snacks. Many of the older ladies here in town love making custom Christmas ornaments that they sell in their booths. A few will knit together matching hat and mitten sets to buy for just a few dollars. It's not really about making money, but they've been doing it for as long as they've lived in Willow Heights. Part of the tradition is for the older generation to pass down memories to the younger.

Noah agreed to meet me at the festival later, knowing I had to help Jack get everything up and going. We're shutting down the diner a few hours early tonight, so my employees can spend the evening at the festival or with their families. Jack and I will take turns manning our booth throughout the night.

It's been a few weeks since Noah hit his breaking point. Since then, I've been paying closer attention to him, trying to sense how he's doing. Noah, after that night, has appeared to be as stoic and as put together as he can be. However, I know that those feelings of failure and fear that his father will act out are constantly in the back of his mind.

Noah is a protector at the very core of his being, and it tears him up inside to know that, at this point, he's stuck in a waiting game. I wish there were something more I could do to help him, but I know there's not. All I can do is be present and hope that he'll open up some more whenever he's ready.

As soon as my last customer leaves, I send everyone home and shut everything off inside the diner. I grab the few remaining bits of supplies that Jack left for me and walk out to the town square, wandering over to where our booth is set up.

Jack waves at me as soon as he sees me coming and rushes over the help me carry everything.

"How's it going?" I ask him once we get to the booth.

He sets the extra cups and lids down on the long table and surveys the setup. "I think we're good. I've got the hot chocolate all mixed up, and it's in the thermoses. We've got cups, lids, sleeves, and napkins."

"Did you get those mini marshmallows we talked about?" I ask, looking over everything as he points it out.

Jack nods his head. "Sure did. Bought the entire shelf out. Monty will need to do a complete restock of his marshmallow section."

I laugh, "We're going to cause a national marshmallow shortage."

"Good thing I stocked up then. Here, could you help me get the sign put up?" he asks. I help him hang our diner logo at the back of our booth. We fasten it up, ensuring it won't blow away or get knocked down too easily. As soon as it's up, we step back and observe our booth.

"Looks great, Jack," I tell him. "Great work."

"I learned from the best," he responds, nudging my shoulder with his and shooting me a grin.

We both go back behind the table and get a few more things set up. Before too long, the crowds slowly start trickling into the square. As soon as people spot our logo hung proudly at the booth, they wander over with enormous smiles, knowing we're likely offering something yummy.

Within minutes we've got a short line traveling from our booth a few yards away. Jack and I start hustling, making sure we're getting our orders out in a timely fashion. A rapid hour passes, and the rush seems to die down. Jack and I look at each other with overwhelmed grins.

I hold out a fist, and he bumps it. "Nice work, team," I say, and he laughs under his breath.

"I'm not sure what I expected, but I feel like that was crazy."

"You and me both," I tell him.

"Hey, beautiful." I hear a deep voice say, falling into the lull of Jack and my conversation. I spin around, a smile still plastered on my face.

Noah's standing before me, all bundled up to fight off the cold. He has a dark gray beanie on top of his head, covering his ears, and his puffy black coat zipped up in the front. The extra length of his dark hair pokes out beneath the hat, curling at the ends.

"Hey," I say back. "Want some hot chocolate?"

"Got marshmallows?" Noah asks, a wry smirk forming on his lips.

"Of *course*," I tell him, grinning back as I grab a cup and fill it with hot chocolatey goodness. I toss in a few extra marshmallows for good measure before slipping a lid on and handing it to him. "Careful, it's super hot."

"I thought that was implied," he teases back. I roll my eyes at him, and he chuckles. "Think you can get away for a few minutes?"

I turn to Jack, and he waves me off. "You two lovebirds, go walk around and find some mistletoe or some shit."

I laugh at my friend and grab my mittens from underneath our table. "Alright, let's go."

Noah and I walk hand in hand, me still taking the place on his left side. Though it's been almost a month since the accident, Noah is still wearing a brace on his right hand. Luckily he can take it off when he needs to shower, but otherwise, he tries to abide by the rules his doctor gave him. He's started physical therapy, working on building up the fine muscles in his hand so he can regain all of his function.

I wrap my right hand into his left hand, and we walk along the square, mostly small-talking with some of our friends who made an appearance.

Charlie and Eli wave at us as we pass by them. They're sitting at a picnic table, each with a beer in their hand. I'm happy to see

Charlie was able to get off duty for tonight. He's been working almost nonstop lately, and I know he's been feeling a little worn out. As we watch, his husband Wyatt walks over with a beer of his own and takes his seat next to Charlie, across from Eli.

I look around for Grace's familiar wild spirit, but I don't see her. She's also been swamped with all of the renovations at her new coffee shop. She had been gracious and stuck around to help at the diner after Noah's accident. It had put her a little bit behind with her plans for her storefront, but as far as I know, she's getting back on track with her new schedule. I haven't seen much of her in the last week or so because she's been running all over the place.

As soon as the sun sets, everyone gathers around Town Hall. Mayor McCoy steps up to the podium set up in front of the massive Christmas tree. As he takes his spot behind the microphone, he pulls on the lapels of his black suit coat and straightens his bright red tie. A few people clap for him, and he puts on a beaming smile, holding his hand to quiet down the crowd. As soon as he has everyone's rapt attention, he beings his presentation.

"Every year, we gather around to celebrate the Christmas season. It's an honor to be here tonight to participate with you all. Christmas is a time of happiness and cheer, and there is no better way to kick it off than by lighting up the city with everyone here to see it. So, without further ado, join me in the countdown!"

Declan starts the countdown off, "Fifteen, fourteen, thirteen—"

As soon as he gets to ten, the crowd joins in, getting louder and louder with each number that passes.

Noah's hand wraps around my waist, and I look up at him, a smile playing on my lips. He grins back at me as he mouths along with the countdown.

"Seven, six, five—"

He waggles his eyebrows at me, and the anticipation starts to well up in my chest.

"Three, two, one!"

The crowd erupts in cheers as the massive Christmas tree lights up right before our eyes. Thousands of tiny colored lightbulbs adorn the enormous pine, blending together into a mess of holiday cheer. On top of the tree, the elegant golden star lights up, emitting a ray of bright yellow light.

My breath catches in my throat, and I feel the sting of tears beginning in the corners of my eyes. Noah's hand tightens on my waist as if he can feel the emotion welling inside me.

"It's so beautiful," I whisper to no one in particular.

A sound rumbles deep in Noah's chest and I look up at him. He's watching me with an expression that I can't place. "It's alright, but I've seen better."

My cheeks heat up with the insinuation behind his words, and I press myself closer to his side. All around us, each business is turning on its Christmas lights too. The decorations range from the average white light silhouette outlining and full-blown Christmas town. As I lean my cheek against Noah's chest, I take it all in, letting myself be filled with the excitement that always surrounds the Christmas season.

"Want to go look around some more?" Noah asks me, and I glance up at him, nodding my head.

As soon as I pull away from him, Noah reaches for my hand, entwining our fingers together. I squeeze his hand and let him lead me out of the crowd and to the side to look at more of the Christmas booths.

The rest of the evening passes in a blur. Noah and I stop at every booth and look at every little thing they have displayed. I pick up a few gifts for my friends, making sure none of them are lurking around as I make my purchases.

Noah watches me in amusement each time I find a new treasure at a booth, with a smile playing on his lips as I get more excited with each discovery.

"I think you were born to be a Sugarplum fairy," he says to me after we finish at a booth selling custom-made pottery.

I bark out a laugh. "What does that mean?"

"I don't know. It's just been a while since I've seen you this excited and happy."

I raise a shoulder up toward my ear. "I just really, really love Christmas."

"I can tell," he says with a wink.

"And I love it more that you're home," I say, lowering my voice.

"Me too," he says. He's looking at me now with that same expression from earlier.

"What?" I ask him.

His lips pull up. "You're being all cute and sweet tonight. It's making me want to kiss you, then take you home and do impossibly dirty things to you."

My body flushes at his words, and my breath hitches. "I like the sound of that."

Noah arches one of his dark eyebrows at me, his eyes darkening. "Yeah?" I nod my head, bobbing my chin up and down. Noah steps closer and cups the side of my jaw, tilting my lips toward his so he can kiss them. When he pulls away, he winks at me. "Well, then I think we better do something about that, hm?"

I agree, and we make quick work of walking across the square back toward home, not wanting to waste any time. As soon as I flip on the lights in the apartment, I freeze. My eyes dance around the room, taking in the mess of red and green rings made of construction paper strung up along the walls. My jaw falls open, and I raise a hand to my mouth.

"Are you surprised?" Noah whispers in my ear, his husky voice causing goosebumps to pop up along my arms.

"Noah," I gasp, shaking my head as I turn to look at him. "How did you know?"

"You told me," he shrugs. "A long time ago, you mentioned that one of your favorite Christmas traditions was making a countdown to Christmas paper chain with your mom."

"And you just remembered that? After all these years?"

Noah grins. "I remember everything you told me, Parks. You're one of my favorite humans in the world. How could I not?"

Dropping my bags on the floor, I throw my arms around his neck, pressing my body to his. Noah wraps his arms around my waist, holding me tighter to him. He leans down and presses his lips to mine. My eyes close, and I melt against him, the feel of his kiss causing heat to bloom deep in my belly.

He kisses me senselessly, and I lose track of time. Finally, he pulls away. Both of us are breathing heavily. His eyes gleam as he stares down at me, his lips swollen from kissing me so hard.

"Would you like to do the first one tonight? Then maybe we can pick this up again in the bedroom?" he asks, his voice low and sultry.

I nod, untangling myself from him and going over to where the paper chain ends. The first ring is made up of green construction paper. I hook my finger against it and meet Noah's eyes. He gives me an encouraging grin, and I rip it in two.

There's something so satisfying about ripping apart the rings each day, counting down until Christmas. Even though I'm fully grown, Christmas is still one of my favorite holidays. There's something so magical about waking up early in the morning when the sky is still dark and seeing the Christmas Tree in my living room fully lit up.

I watch the paper ring fall elegantly to the floor. When I look up, Noah's standing close to me, his eyes glittering as he watches me. With two steps, I move closer to him and wrap my arms around his neck again. Noah's hands trace over my back, coming to settle on my waist. He pushes me back just an inch away to look down at me.

"Thank you, Noah. This was," I shake my head, "a perfect surprise. I can't believe you did this for me."

He leans toward me until our foreheads are touching. A sideways smirk appears on his lips as he whispers, "It's only construction paper, Parks. And even if I had to construct this chain out of titanium, I would, just to see you smile like that."

I close my eyes and breath him in, appreciating his specific blend of cedar wood and a swirl of green apple. All Noah. All mine.

Before I'm fully aware of what I'm doing, I tilt my chin toward him. Noah meets me halfway, closing the distance between us until there is none at all. His kiss is hot as he presses me closer to him. His hands around my waist pull at me until our hips are flushed together. My hands trail up the back of his neck and into his hair, gripping the strands.

Noah makes a guttural groan at the sensation of me tugging at his hair, and somehow his fingers hold me even tighter. He pulls away from my mouth, his lips moving down to my neck. I tilt my head away, giving his hot mouth more access to my flushed skin.

"God, Parks. You're so—" his voice breaks as I moan from the sound of his husky voice, heavy with passion.

"Noah," I whisper as he laves his tongue over the pulse in my neck. "Noah, I need you."

Before I get to ask him twice, Noah is sweeping me up in his arms. I gasp out loud, my arms gripping around his neck, so I don't lose my balance. As soon as he's got a good hold of me, Noah walks us straight out of the living room and into my bedroom. He kicks the door behind him and walks me right over to the bed, where he dumps me on my mattress.

As I settle onto the bed, Noah steps away from me. His eyes are dark as he surveys me. I stretch my arms above my head and arch my back, thrusting my breasts toward him as if to help entice him further.

Noah's chest rises and falls with his breath. He lets out a low rumble and then moves toward me. Leaning over the edge of the mattress, he claims my lips and devours me. A hot spark of arousal shoots straight from where his lips touch mine to my core. I writhe underneath him, my hands coming up and circling around his neck, pulling him in closer to me.

Noah's hand slips under the hem of my shirt. The feel of his skin on mine ramps up my need for him tenfold. I arch against him again, moving my hands down toward the edge of his top. Before I get the chance to rip it off of him, he's pulling away from me. I feel the sudden loss of his contact, and I whimper.

"Easy, baby. Let's take it slow," he whispers, gruff and gravelly. "I want to enjoy this."

I wiggle on the bed and grip the hem of my shirt, whipping it over my head and reaching behind myself to unclip the band of my bra. As soon as it's released, I fling the undergarment away from me, baring myself to him.

Noah's eyes dilate as he watches me, his pupils blowing out until his blue eyes are almost black. As his gaze is locked on me, I slide my hands onto my breasts, plucking at my nipples once, then twice, then circling around the sensitive skin until my skin breaks out in goose-bumps. Noah's attention is glued to me, waiting to see what I'll do next.

My hands move down from my breasts to the button of my jeans. As smoothly as I can, I undo the button and the zipper, sliding the waistband down around my hips. Noah finally steps in to help, hooking his fingers through the loops and yanking the denim down my legs. He tosses the restrictive clothing onto the floor and then turns his attention back to me.

Slowly, he leans down until his lips are hovering over my breast. At an agonizing pace, he sticks his tongue out. He runs a circle around my nipple, tracing the shape of my areola until I'm shivering beneath him.

I gasp out his name, arching my back and thrusting my breasts toward him, silently telling him what I want. Noah flattens his tongue and presses it to my right nipple, laving against it and then moving away so he can latch his mouth to my breast. His tongue flicks over my sensitive nipple a few times until I'm about ready to scream. Then he moves to the other side, performing the same type of delicious torture.

When he's satisfied that I've melted into a puddle, he moves down from my breasts to my abdomen.

"Look at you, so eager," Noah teases me, his tongue tracing

patterns against the sensitive skin of my belly and dipping into the divot of my belly button. "You're breathtaking. I could stare at you all day. I don't think I've ever seen anything as beautiful as you."

"I want you," I breathe out, my stomach tensing as he torments me with his tongue.

"Hmm," his voice vibrates against my abdomen. "And I want you to touch yourself for me."

My body breaks out in goosebumps at his order and how his voice rumbles in my ear. "Wh-what?"

Noah pulls away from me slightly so he can look down into my eyes. "Make yourself come for me. I want to see how you do it." My heart rate picks up, and I bite my lip. Noah's eyes are dark as he watches me with a devilish smirk on his lips. "Do you want me to help get you started?"

The offer sends another course of tingles throughout my body, from the tip of my nose all the way down through my toes, and I nod at him.

Noah laughs a low, warm laugh. "I'll take that as a yes. Come on then, sweetheart." Noah maneuvers down from where he was perched at my side until he's level with my hips. He spreads my thighs apart with one large hand, baring me to him.

His tongue darts out to wet his lips, and I whimper at the thought of his mouth on me. My hips involuntarily buck up toward him, and Noah chuckles to himself. His hand splays across my belly, right above my pubic bone, holding me down.

With his other hand, he reaches for mine, slowly trailing my own fingers down my sides and toward my center. I close my eyes, letting myself get lost in the sensation. Guiding me, he dips our fingers down lower, sliding them around and collecting some of the wetness that has pooled there.

A rumble sounds from his chest, and I snap my eyes open. He's watching our fingers in between my legs raptly as if nothing in this world could tear his attention away from the show being put on before him.

Slowly, Noah lets me take over until he's removing his fingers from my center. My fingers part my folds, slipping through my arousal and circling along my opening. I moan softly once my pointer finger brushes over my swollen clit. I do it again and again, desire pooling deep in my belly.

"Does that feel good, baby?" Noah asks in my ear. His teeth nip at the lobe, and I moan out loud. Noah captures the moan with his mouth, kissing me deeply as I continue to roll my clit between my fingers.

On and on, it goes until my legs are shaking. My tempo gets faster, and I rub harder, now chasing the release.

"Noah!" I gasp, my fingers circling my clit faster and faster until I'm rubbing furiously at the bundle of nerves. "Noah, I'm going to come!"

I hear his voice catch in his throat. "Oh fuck, don't stop. That's a good girl. Come for me, Parks. Show me how you come for me."

With a scream, my body convulses, and I come hard. The waves of arousal pour over me, and my body twitches with each pass. Before my orgasm has the chance to ease, Noah's crawling over me. The feel of his skin, hot against mine, has me ramping up again. He must have shimmied out of his clothes while I was in the throes of my orgasm.

Noah positions himself between my legs, rubbing the head of his cock between my folds and coating himself with me. He leans down and presses a hot kiss to my lips, pushing his tongue into my mouth and fully tasting me.

"You ready, Parks? I'm going to fuck you so slowly until you're falling apart and begging me for more, and then I won't quit until you beg me to stop. Think you can handle that?"

I shiver at his low husky tone and nod my head fervently. "Yes. God, yes, please."

As soon as I give him my consent, Noah slides deep inside of me, the both of us groaning at the feeling of finally finding home.

Chapter 41
Noah

Addison is so hot and wet around me that I almost come undone the second I'm inside her. I rear in the pleasure, focusing on bringing her to the brink before I unravel us both.

"Always so fucking tight around me," I grunt as I move inside her. It's like her body was made for mine.

Addison cries out as I ram into her deeper and deeper with every stroke. She grabs underneath her knees, holding her legs up and out for me to have better access to her. I thread my fingers through her hair, holding her head in place as I lean down to kiss her.

"I was made to love you, Parks," I say to her. I'm feeling overwhelmed. Her tight heat around my cock sends my head spiraling, and I feel myself falling deeper under her spell.

Addison comes around my cock without warning and tosses her head back against the pillows. Her walls spasm around me rhythmically, clenching and unclenching.

I bury my face into her neck, groaning at the feel of her falling apart around me. Her skin is moistened with sweat, her scent heady and intoxicating. I'm unraveling at the edges. I growl against her, trying to keep it all together.

I pump into her a few more times before I realize I'm fighting a losing battle.

"I can't hold back anymore," I grunt, the pleasure becoming too much for me to control. The need to come is desperately growing, and I notice a pressure forming at the base of my spine.

"Then don't," she whimpers.

That's all the permission I needed. I slam into Addison, loving how she falls apart from underneath me once more. Her fingernails claw at my back, pulling me closer to her.

I ram against the deepest part of her, over and over, until she's coming again. With a loud moan, I push myself as deeply as possible and hold against her. Pleasure courses up and down my spine as I pump into her and try to catch my breath.

As we descend from the height of our sex, I let my arms give way from underneath me. Careful not to crush her, I press my weight into hers and bury my face against her hair again.

Her chest is rising and falling, her heart pattering against mine rapidly. "I don't know how that keeps getting better," she says, breathless.

Pride swells in my chest, and I tilt my jaw so I can press a kiss to her sweaty skin. Her fingers thread into my hair, her nails scratching lightly against my scalp. With a long sigh, I push myself closer to her, basking in the closeness.

When I catch my breath, I pull away and gaze down at her. The sight of her splayed out against the pillows has my heart rate picking up once more. Her hair is messy, and her cheeks sport a rosy blush that travels down her neck and dusts the top of her breasts. Her chest rises and falls with her breath as she comes down from the high of our lovemaking.

Rolling onto my side, I prop my head up with my hand. "That was a good way to end a day."

She smiles, and my chest tightens. "I'll say. I'm not sure I can even move at this point."

"Want me to draw you a bath or get a shower going?" I ask.

Addison hums as she considers my offer. "Maybe a shower would be good."

I roll over and give her a quick peck on the cheek before crawling out of bed and padding into our bathroom to get the shower running. Addison loves the water to be as hot as she can stand it, so I crank the dial almost all the way up, knowing it probably won't be hot enough. Once the water is going, I dig around in her closet, looking for some of those shower fizzies she bought online. She was so excited when they came, bouncing up and down and letting me sniff each scent.

I pick out the lavender one, which reminds me of her, and toss it into the bottom of the tub, letting the shower's stream do its magic.

Addison sneaks into the bathroom a few minutes later, still not wearing a stitch of clothing. I look her up and down, appreciating her curves. She steps closer to me and wraps her arms around my neck, pressing our bodies together as she kisses me deeply.

My body lights up at her touch, and I pull back. "Careful, Parks. Unless you're ready for round two, you may want to get that cute little ass of yours in the shower and then into a pair of PJs."

She looks over at me with sparkling eyes and swats my hand that is inching around to get a handful of her backside. "I think I'm tapping out for tonight."

I pretend to pout at her. "Party pooper."

"You're telling me you could go again? Already?"

I lean down and take her lips in mine, parting her mouth open with my tongue and devouring her. She moans into my mouth as she arches her back against me, trying to get closer.

I pull away from her, appreciating how her cheeks are flushed and her lips swollen. I could spend the rest of my life kissing her senselessly. Giving her a devilish grin, I ask, "You warmed up to another round yet?" She emits an unsure whimper and I laugh. "Alright, you little minx, go take your shower."

Stepping away from her, I reach over and pat her ass and she yips, turning back to shoot me a playful glare before she disappears behind the shower curtain.

Still laughing, I exit the bathroom, giving her some privacy to get cleaned up. I find a pair of sweatpants and pull them, then climb into bed to wait for her.

She emerges almost half an hour later, looking fully refreshed. Her hair is still wet, trailing down her back. Her face is glowing from her face wash and the post-coital glow. She tiptoes out of the bathroom and over to her closet, where she finds the pajamas she wants to wear tonight. As she unwraps the towel, shielding herself from me, she glances over her shoulder, shooting me a sultry glance.

I pull my lower lip between my teeth, watching her give me another little show. God, this woman is too much for me sometimes. I can't believe I was able to stay away from her for as long as I did.

She's ruined me for anyone else.

"Come here, sweetheart," I tell her in a low voice. Addison's cheeks flush a rosy pink, and then she drops the towel completely from her body. She crawls up the bed and settles herself against me. I drop my arm around her waist pulling her closer to me.

The feel of her bare skin against mine does something to my head, sending it spinning and swirling in my overwhelming love for her. I lean closer to her and capture her lips in mine. I kiss her tenderly, and she moans. Her back arches, pressing her breasts harder into my bare chest.

When I pull away from her she sticks out her lower lip, and I can't help but laugh. "I thought we weren't ready for round two?" I tease.

Addison rolls her eyes but snuggles in closer. "You're right. This is much better."

"Snuggles and kisses?" I ask, holding her tighter and pressing my lips to her temple. She laughs and nods her head.

"Exactly like that."

A comfortable silence falls over us. I lean back against the pillow, closing my eyes and focusing on the sound of Addison's breathing. She shifts a little, and I feel her fingers dance over my skin. Goosebumps break out on my arms at her ministrations, but I don't stop her.

Addison begins to hum quietly to herself as her fingers trace over the hidden infinity symbol in my tattoo. I got the ink a few years ago to remind me of her, even though there was so much space and distance between us. The compass points North, at the map scrawled over my skin, to remind me to keep a weather eye towards my goals, where I'm trying to end up.

"I would've found you, you know?" I tell her as she continues to tickle my skin, drawing along the thick tattoo lines.

She lifts her cheek off my chest and stares me in the eye curiously.

"If you had left Willow Heights. I would've found you eventually."

A smile plays on the corners of her lips, "You think?"

"I would go to the ends of the earth for you. I know we've had a lot to face, but I believe in everything in me that we're destined to be together."

"For now until infinity?" she murmurs, leaning closer until our noses are brushing.

I tilt her chin and claim her lips, opening her up to me as I kiss her deeply. When I pull away, her eyes are sparkling with arousal, and her cheeks are flushed.

"Until infinity," I whisper back before giving her another tender kiss, sealing my promise.

The two of us fall into a restful sleep, tangled up in each other. When sunlight streams through the windows, we try to hold on to the little haven we've made for as long as possible.

Addison and I spend the morning in bed, kissing and touching, which naturally progresses into more passionate lovemaking. As soon as I finish inside her for the third time within the last three hours, we slump together against the mattress.

She wiggles closer to me, throwing a hand across my abdomen. "I love you, Noah," she whispers, kissing my sweaty skin.

I run my hand up and down her back, loving how her smooth skin feels against the roughness of my hand. "I love you more."

She gasps and pulls away from me, a twinkle forming in her hazel eyes. "Impossible!"

With a quick shift of my hips, I roll her over onto her back and hover above her. She shifts slightly underneath me while looking up at me with hooded eyes. Slowly I lower myself down and kiss her again.

If I were to die today, I would die a happy man, knowing I got the chance to experience all these small moments with her. It's moments like these that I wished and yearned for so fiercely while I was gone.

"You're so beautiful," I tell her.

Addison preens under my attention, shifting again to bring my weight back onto her. "I don't think I will ever get tired of you saying that."

I chuckle, "Good, 'cause I have no intentions of ever stopping."

She laughs, too, and runs her fingers through my hair. Silence falls over us for a few minutes before she takes a deep breath and pushes me off her. "We should probably get going for the day."

I groan in protest but roll off the bed to get ready.

"What do you have going on today?" Addison asks when I meet her out in the living room. She's got a mug of something in her hands —tea, I notice when she dunks the tea bag in and out of the steaming water.

I walk over to the front door and grab my shoes. "I have a physical therapy session. Hopefully, my last of this round, and then they can put me into more of a regimen geared toward getting me back to work."

"Do you know when they'll let you off this probation?"

I shake my head. "I haven't heard anything. I need to call Vincent and see if he has a date for me to go back in. I'm sure it will be a few days of meetings and debriefings, and then they'll decide if I'm well enough to get back in the field."

Addison hums as she takes another sip. I know she's worried

about what's going to happen. Hell, I am too. But until I meet with my bosses it's out of my hands. All I can do is focus on building up the strength in my hand so I can get back to the whole reason I came back here.

Or...well, most of the reason.

I realize as I watch Addison wash her breakfast dishes that I must have been fooling myself by thinking I could come back to Willow Heights for any reason *other* than her. No matter what I try and tell myself, she was at the forefront of my decision-making.

"Well I better get downstairs," she says to me, crossing the distance between us and standing up on her tip toes to press a kiss to my cheek. "Will you stop by later?"

"Of course," I reply, giving her a little pat on her ass as if to seal the promise.

She grins and grabs the rest of her things before disappearing downstairs to the diner. I put around the apartment for a while until it's time for me to head to PT.

I go through the rehab regimen, doing all the reps of each exercise, hoping that one of these days, I'll finally start to feel the strength return to my hand. All my therapists and assistants at the office are friendly and understanding, encouraging me as I continue to see minimal improvement. I appreciate their positive attitudes, but I'm getting frustrated with the process. I would like to be further along than I am currently, but I know there's not much else they can do.

Therapy takes a few hours. When I return to town, I decide to take a walk and get some fresh air to clear my head. Addison still has an hour or two before she gets finished at the diner, so I have some time to kill. I stop in at the diner to give Addison a kiss and get a hot coffee, telling her I'll see her at home later. Then I go back out to the street and start walking.

It's a dreary day. The sun has gone into hibernation with the winter. A low layer of gloomy, gray clouds takes its place, hovering over the town like a blanket that has lost all of its heat. The Christmas decorations are still up, though they are attempting to emanate some cheer.

I take a sip of my coffee, glancing around my little town and wondering for a moment what it would be like to stay here for the rest of my life. I promised Addison I would never leave her again, so now the possibility of me becoming a permanent resident of Willow Heights has increased exponentially. The risk of my father is still looming in the background, but all I can do is hope that what goes around will come back around in his case.

"Noah," a voice calls to me, and I stop mid-stride, turning around to see Charlie leaning out the window of his patrol car and waving me over.

I grumble under my breath but make my way over to him. "What do you want?"

He tilts his head toward the passenger side door, and I roll my eyes. I round the car in a few strides and get into his car. He studies me closely, eyes zeroing in on the hickey I know Addison gave me last night. Thankfully, he chooses to let it slide.

"I needed to talk to you," he finally says, pressing his lips into a thin line.

"Okay, well, you've got me. Get to it then."

He taps his hand against the steering wheel a few times, gazing out the front windshield. "I'm not comfortable with how things are currently with your father."

I narrow my eyes. "What does that mean?"

"It means he's been baiting me on purpose. I don't know. All last night he would make a point to make a snide remark every time I was around. There's just something not sitting right with me."

I place my coffee in his cupholder so I can turn and look at him more head-on. "Give me specifics, Charlie. What did he say?"

The sheriff rubs at the back of his neck. "Just stupid bullshit like how he hopes nothing terrible happens again to our town or that he has faith in our police department to prevent any more serious crimes. Then came the routine insult that I don't know how to do my job."

"That's it?"

Charlie grimaces. "And he brought up Addison."

The hair on the back of my neck stands straight up, and my body goes rigid. "What?"

"Nothing major," he says quickly as if to ease the storm he can see brewing inside me. "He just made sure to say something about her. It was along the lines of 'I'm so glad Ms. Parks has a small army standing at the ready to protect her.' Or something dumb like that. He was commenting on the fact that she has you, me, *and* Eli all keeping an eye on her."

"I don't like that he brought her up at all," I mutter. My brain buzzes as I work to piece it all together. He would have known Charlie would relay this message, so what was he trying to say?

"I don't either. As I said, there were no specifics, but something about his demeanor doesn't sit well with me. Slimy snake. I don't know what he's up to but I don't like it."

I lean my head back against the seat rest. "What should I do?"

"There's nothing to do right now, Noah. Maybe I shouldn't have told you, but I felt you needed to know I'm concerned."

I shake my head. "No, I'm glad you told me. Just keep me posted, and if anything changes, call me."

"You'll be the first to know," he says, then rethinks. "Well, after my crew." I nod, grateful that Charlie is still keeping me in the loop. "Just take it easy until then, yeah?"

I laugh under my breath. "I'll try. See you later, Sully."

I get out of his car and start trekking toward home. My coffee is now cold and so is my desire to be out and about any more than necessary at this point.

Ever since my father paid me a visit, I've been barely able to keep ahold of the anxiety bubbling inside me. After hearing what Charlie told me today, I'm losing that battle even further. All I know is that I feel unmoored, and even the slightest wind or aggravation could send me into a downward spiral.

It's one thing to be able to face my foes when I have the necessary resources, but an entirely different thing to face them, knowing that I have nothing. That I am nothing. It's something I'm going not to have to come to terms with, but it still stings.

All that matters is that Addison is safe, and even though I may not have the FBI behind me currently, I'll still do whatever it takes to ensure my father doesn't get to her. It's too easy for me to get lost in the *what-ifs*.

A hollow feeling forms in my gut as my mind flashes to past cases I've worked on. It was easy to compartmentalize the horrific details when I was alone, away from home and from Parks. But now that I'm back and the risk of all I could lose is staring at me right in the face, it's becoming more and more challenging to manage the anxiety.

I can feel myself starting to fray at the edges with worry, with fear that something is going to happen and I'm not going to be able to do anything about it.

I've seen the horrors that a person can endure too many times, and I'd rather die than have anything like that happen to Addison. I'll be damned if it even comes close.

Chapter 42
Addison

The door jingles as a family of four walks in, two parents, an older girl, and a young boy. Jack looks at me desperately, "Do you think you could take care of them? I'm swamped."

"Of course," I nod my head at him and reach for a notepad before making my way toward the family standing at the diner's door.

"Hey guys, would you like a table or a booth?" I ask them. Though the diner is usually first come, first serve as far as seating goes, I like to personally welcome new customers when I get the chance. I haven't seen this family around town, so I conclude they're visiting from out of town.

Roll out the red carpet. I love taking care of out-of-towners.

The man looks at his wife, and they silently communicate with each other before he looks back at me with an appreciative grin. "We'll take a table."

"Sure thing." I lead them to one of the free tables and get them situated, handing out menus, placing utensils, and taking drink orders. When I bring back their drinks, the man's phone starts buzzing on the table, the name *JOSIE* flashing across the screen.

He reaches for it and then glances at his wife apologetically. "I should probably get this." His wife waves him off, and he walks away from the table to answer the phone, "Something better be burning down Jo—"

I look after him with an eyebrow raised and then look back at the wife. She rolls her eyes and shrugs. I smile at her sheepishly. "It's not really any of my business."

"No, it's fine. I would be intrigued too. You never know what's going on in Josie's world."

I offer her a smile, unsure of what to say. "Should we wait for him to get back to order, or do you want to put something in right away?"

The woman looks at her kids, and they glance up at me shyly. "I think they'll each take an order of chicken strips, and I'll do the chicken club sandwich, and my husband will take a cheeseburger with bacon on it."

I scribble down everything she says and ask, "Fries for all of you okay?"

The woman snaps the menu closed and starts stacking the others on top. "Definitely, thank you."

"My pleasure," I say, taking the menus she offers me. "My name is Addie. If you need anything, just give me a holler."

The little boy sitting across the table holds up his now empty water cup, and his mom laughs. "Looks like he was thirsty."

I chuckle with her and crouch down so I'm at eye level with the boy. He's got sandy blonde hair and bright blue eyes like his mother. "I'll bring you another water. How does that sound?"

The little boy nods his head, his eyes darting down bashfully. I look back at his mom with a smile, and she watches her son with an adoring expression on her face.

"Danny, can you tell her thank you?"

His cheeks turn pink, and he whispers, "Thank you."

I grin again. "I'll be right back with that water."

Hurrying toward the counter, I grin at Jack, who has been enjoying the exchange. "They seem like a nice family. Where are they from?" He asks and hands me a freshly filled pitcher of water.

"Oh, I'm not sure. I haven't asked yet."

He raises his eyebrows. "Those kids are so stinking cute. I wonder if they're on vacation."

"I'll find out," I tell him. This is one of his favorite parts of the job too. It's hard not to get sucked into the excitement of meeting new people. Willow Heights is so small that I usually see the same crowd every day, depending on their preferred schedule to go out and eat. It's always fun and exciting when newcomers wander in.

It's a good reminder that there's an entire world out there aside from Willow Heights. Our small town has the habit of sucking you in and never letting go—though I honestly wouldn't have it any other way. The change to the routine is fun for me, though.

"So, what brings you folks to Willow Heights?" I ask the woman as I refill their waters.

She looks at me with her big blue eyes and tilts her head at her daughter. "Amy here learned all about Niagara Falls in her geography class last fall, and we told her we would go check it out over Christmas break, so here we are."

"Where are you all from?"

"Cedar Ridge, Tennessee," she tells me. "I'm Izabel. That's my husband Ryan out on the phone, my daughter Amy, and my son Danny."

"You have a beautiful family," I say, bending down so I'm face-to-face with the young boy. His cheeks heat up again, but he manages to hold my gaze this time. "Hi Danny, I'm Addie. How old are you?"

He looks at me with wide blue eyes and leans closer to his mom.

"I'm nine!" Amy informs me from across the table, her green eyes lighting up as she speaks to me. Her light brown curls sway on the sides of her shoulders as she bounces in her seat. "Danny's seven, but he's kind of shy."

"Are you shy?" I ask her, amused.

"Nope!" She replies, popping her lips on the 'p.'

"I didn't think so," I say, laughing.

At that moment, Izabel's husband returns and slides back into his seat, shooting her a sideways grin. "Heya Bells."

I notice her cheeks pinken as she smiles back at him, her blue eyes sparkling. "Hey there, Ryno. Everything okay at home?"

"Oh yeah, just Josie being Josie. I told her we were passing through Willow Heights. She said she was actually the one to draw up the plans for your diner?"

"Oh, Josie Reynolds? You know her?" I ask, surprise seeping through my voice. I had worked closely with her when coming up with the design for the diner, but I lost contact after all was said and done. I found her online, perusing her portfolio, and hiring her was one of the best business decisions I had ever made.

"She's my business partner," he tells me.

His wife rolls her eyes. "She's one of our closest friends."

"Huh," I mutter, all of a sudden getting that uncomfortable feeling that I'm part of something much more significant. "Small world."

"I'm so glad we stopped by here," Izabel says. "Ryan, did you know Josie worked on the plans for this diner?"

Ryan rubs the back of his neck, pondering. "I mean, I knew she worked on *a* diner at some point, but I don't always keep track of her projects unless I'm working on them too."

His wife scoffs and shoots me a look that just screams *men, what are you gonna do with them?* I fight off a smile. I like this family.

"Your food should be out any minute," I tell them, tapping the table and then getting out of their way so they can spend their family time together.

I wander back and tell Jack everything I learned. His mouth falls open when I tell him they work with the woman who helped me design the diner.

"Wow, I mean...how?"

I shake my head. "I have no idea. I'm a little speechless. I can't wait to tell Noah about this tonight."

"It's definitely crazy. It's not like it's a short trip from here to Tennessee by any means," he says and picks up a stack of quarters, unrolling them and sticking them into the cash register. "Makes you feel insignificant, huh?."

I scrunch my nose up. "I'm not sure I would go that far."

He shrugs and continues to unroll his quarters.

When the family's food is ready, I drop it by their table and chat a bit more with them. The kids start to open up more, telling me about all the cool things they've seen on their trip.

"Did you guys see our big Christmas tree out there?" I ask them, and they nod, their eyes wide. "Well, we turn it on at night, and it lights up the entire town."

They look at their parents, their little mouths falling open with wonder. "Are we going to get to see it, Daddy?" the little girl asks.

The man looks at his daughter with warm eyes and nods his head. "Yes, we'll stay the night here and finish the trip tomorrow." Then he turns back to me. "Is there anything else we should check out while we're here?"

I think about it and then rattle off a few other places the kids might enjoy checking out. We have a small toy store down the road specializing in custom puzzles and a few other sites I recommend.

As soon as the family finishes their meals, they pay their tab and get up to leave.

"Bye, Addie! Thanks for the chicken strips!" the little girl, Amy, calls to me, waving her hand as they move toward the door. Her little brother follows her lead, waving and yelling goodbye to me too.

I wave back, a massive grin on my face as I watch the cute family walk out of my diner. As soon as they're gone, the place feels a little quiet. I wrap my arms around my middle and watch as they regroup on the sidewalk. Amy takes off toward the giant Christmas tree, and the rest of them follow after her in her wake.

As I watch them, I can't help but imagine what my family might look like. Will Noah and I ever get the chance to have that? Does Noah even want kids? I can't say that it has come up since he's been home. Before he left, I always imagined that we'd go off to college, get married, and have babies together, but that didn't work out after all.

Would he be open to having a little family like that one? I decide that that is something I'll need to talk to him about. I'm not yet thirty, so there's still time to decide, but it is something that we should be on the same page about.

I spend the rest of the afternoon worrying about that. Noah and I have said many fancy words to each other, confessing our deep love and affection, but we've never really talked about what comes *next*. It's not that I've never considered getting married—I just figured I'd marry Eli at some point and start a family like we were expected to.

But now that's passed, I can only imagine myself being with Noah. I don't know what our future will look like, but the more I think about it, the more at ease I become. I have concluded that I'll be happy as long as I can be with him. We spent our time apart, and now all that matters to me is that we're together.

I manage to calm my thoughts long enough to focus on my tasks and get them done efficiently. As soon as possible, I leave and go back upstairs and home to Noah.

"You'll never guess who wandered through the diner this afternoon," I tell Noah as soon as I'm through the door. I drop my bag and coat off and then pad over to where he's lounging on the couch, watching a football game.

"Who?"

"The business partner of the woman I hired to design the diner!"

Noah raises an eyebrow at me but doesn't say anything. "Come on, Noah, act excited for me."

"Wow! That's amazing! Tell me more!" He matches my energy with an amused smirk.

"I know, right? They're from Tennessee, which is obviously where the architect lives too, since, you know, she works with this guy. But what are the chances that they would come through our little town, and I'd happen to be working at the same time?"

Noah shakes his head, still watching me in amusement. "Probably slim to none. I guess the odds are in your favor today. Maybe you should go out and buy a Powerball ticket."

I roll my eyes and shove his shoulder. "I don't gamble."

"I'm just saying, maybe you should. You could win the lottery, and we could buy one of those big fancy houses on the edge of town."

I gaze at him and cross my arms, pretending to pout. "Oh, I'm sorry, is my little apartment not enough for you, rich boy?"

Now Noah throws his head back and laughs. When his amusement dies, he looks at me and pretends to wipe away a tear. "But seriously, I don't care where we live as long as we're together." His words echo some of my thoughts from earlier, and I drop my arms. I must be looking at him strangely because he raises an eyebrow at me. "What is it?"

"Noah, do you want kids?"

Surprise crosses his face, and he stares at me for a moment before swallowing thickly and asking, "Do you?"

I shrug my shoulder. "I think so. Maybe? I don't know. We've just never really talked about it."

Before he gets the chance to respond, his phone starts to ring. I glance down at his device sitting on the table and see Charlie's name flash across the screen. Surprise courses through my body, but I don't say anything. I thought they weren't working with each other anymore since Noah lost his assignment. Even though Noah told me they were working together closely on the investigation, I wouldn't have guessed they would be friends at this point.

Reaching for his phone, Noah swipes the screen and puts it to his ear. He shoots me a tight smile that doesn't reach his eyes and holds up one finger before he steps out of the room. He goes out the front door into the hallway, closing the door behind him. It doesn't close all the way, though, and I can hear his deep voice rumbling as he talks to Charlie.

I reach for my book on the side table and pretend to pick up on the next chapter. I'm doing my best not to eavesdrop, but Noah's voice keeps getting louder.

"What? When?" He almost shouts into the phone. He waits for a beat before asking, "More than one?"

Silence.

Then Noah swears, and the next thing I know, he's storming back into the living room. His face is thunderous as he stops mid-stride right in front of me. He pauses for a moment and then turns to walk into our bedroom without another word.

I stare after him for a moment, confused as to what is happening. Finally, when I hear him rustling around and making a bunch of noise in there, my curiosity wins out. I hop off of the couch and hurry into the bedroom, my jaw falling open when I see the mess he's made.

Noah has his duffle bag and my suitcase lying on the bed. He's going through my drawers, scooping everything up, and then dumping it inside my suitcase. He presses his hands down on the pile of clothes to level it out and then goes to do the same thing with my next drawer.

"Noah, what the hell are you doing?" I ask him. Anxiety starts to well up in my chest. What is happening right now?"

"We're leaving. I'm packing you a bag."

"What? I can't just leave."

Noah turns around and levels me with a dark look. "It wasn't a request, Addison. So either you can help me pack, or I'll do it for you. But we're leaving. End of discussion."

I let his words wash over me as I plant my hands on my hips. He watches me take my stance but doesn't change his expression. "You want to try that again? Maybe with an explanation as to why you've completely lost your mind suddenly?"

"Because I told you, and I would appreciate it if you would just listen to me for once in your damn life."

I recoil, and Noah's words fall flat in front of us like a brick. The room goes eerily silent to the point where I can hear both of our ragged breaths. Finally, in a low voice, knowing that we're gearing up for a fight, I ask, "What the *fuck* is that supposed to mean?"

Chapter 43
Noah

The second she recoils from me and snarls, "What the *fuck* is that supposed to mean?" I know I've just dug my own grave.

I back down as much as possible, trying to let the frantic energy coursing through my body dissipate. Rubbing my hand down my face, I turn away from her. "Nothing."

"No, by all means, Noah, get it off your chest."

I can't ignore the bait. The fear and frustration engulf me again, and I whirl around to face her. "You were supposed to leave! You were supposed to leave Willow Heights and never look back, but you didn't. I didn't want you to stay here. It's dangerous, Parks. Don't you get that?"

"Well, I did."

"I'm aware."

"And I built my life here, Noah. Everything that I am is *here*. My work, my friends—the only family I have. They're here," she tells me, her voice firm. "I'm not just going to pack up my life and leave in the middle of the night without explanation. So why don't you just tell me what the hell is going on."

I grit my teeth. "I *can't*."

She scoffs and shakes her head, looking away from me. "So we're back to this then? I thought we had gotten past all the secrets and shit."

"You don't understand, Addison. We can't stay here."

Something about that rubs her the wrong way because her temper flares again. "You know what? Fuck you, Noah. I can't believe that you'd think that, after all this time, you have any say in anything I do. You effectively gave up that privilege when you walked away from me and didn't look back."

"Parks, I—"

"I waited for you, you know," she laughs humorlessly. "Oh god, I was pathetic just *waiting*. It took me years to figure out that you weren't coming back, that you had no interest in me or anything this town had to offer you."

"That wasn't the reason I left, and you know it," I growl back at her, my muscles tightening.

"No? Well, it sure felt like it. Forgive me for not catching onto your macho-hero story without you telling me anything."

"I told you I was sorry. I don't know what else you want from me. And now I'm trying to fix it. We can't stay here, but I'm not going just to leave you behind again." I exhale and pinch the bridge of my nose to fight off the headache I feel brewing behind my eyes. "I don't have a backup to keep you safe anymore. Do you understand that? They took me off the case, took my badge, and everything. And without their resources, I don't want to risk anything going wrong where you're concerned."

"Despite what you think, Noah, I am completely capable of taking care of myself. I've done it for the last ten years while you were out playing cops and robbers."

"This isn't something to joke about, Addison. It isn't *safe* here. What about that aren't you understanding?"

"I don't understand because you don't *tell* me anything!" she shouts at me. I flinch back. It's been a long time since she's flat-out yelled at me. "I've said it before, and I'm saying it again. Maybe this time you'll fucking *hear* me. I don't like being kept in the dark. I love you, Noah, but you just expect me to blindly follow whatever you tell me to do, and that is not me. I don't know what else I have to do to get you to understand that."

Regret blooms in my chest, and I drop my weapons, backing down. "Listen, Parks, I'm sorry, I—"

"No." She turns away from me. "I'm done talking about this tonight. Please leave."

My eyebrows raise up in shock. "You want me to leave?"

"Just go take a walk. I need to cool down, and I can't do that with you here," she says softly to the wall. I stay frozen in my spot for one minute, then two, wondering if she'll change her mind. When she doesn't, I let out a frustrated sigh and leave the bedroom, leaving the mess of clothes and personal items on our bed. She still doesn't look at me as I approach the front door. I reach for the doorknob and open it.

Before I leave the apartment, I pause and look back at her. "I love you, Parks."

She doesn't respond, but I can hear her sniffle, and it's like a knife straight through my chest. Without another look back, I step out of our home and into the main hallway outside. As soon as the door is closed, I lean my back against it, sliding down until I'm crouched on the floor.

I cover my face with my hands and let out a shaky sigh. How did everything get so out of hand just now? Most of the blame rests on my shoulders, but even still, a bubble of irritation settles low in my gut.

I've asked a lot of Addison over the last few weeks—hell, even the last decade. I've asked her to trust me to know that I was making the best decision for us, and for the most part, she did. So why is it now too much to ask the same?

She's tired. I know that, and so am I. I want nothing more than for this all to end, but until it does, all the responsibility still falls on me.

I let myself sit there and stew in the aftermath of our argument for a while longer before I push myself up and stretch my shoulders out.

It's a snap decision, but I decide to go to the sheriff's station. Charlie is probably out and about or at home already. I suppose I could go see if I could crash with Jordan or Caleb, but I don't feel like putting up with their questions about why Addison kicked me out. At worst, Charlie would give me a disapproving look but leave it at that. Addison may be his best friend, but Charlie doesn't stick his nose into relationship troubles that don't concern him.

Hopefully, though it's a long shot, he will be at the station, and I can ask him more about the phone call he gave me earlier. That damn phone call is why everything exploded tonight. The least I could do is get more information.

I decide to walk over to the station, though it's a good mile and a half away. After the accident, the insurance companies totaled my car, and I haven't gotten around to getting another one. I could take Addison's vehicle, but I think the fresh air will do me good.

The night is freezing. We're stuck in the middle of Northeastern December, so the night is frigid and dry. I stick my hands in the pockets of my coat and start my trek over to the sheriff's department.

The entire way, I fall deeper and deeper into my thoughts, worrying over everything Addison yelled at me tonight. By the time I make it to the police department, I've decided that this all needs to end tonight. Tomorrow I'll fill Addison in on everything as long as she's willing to listen.

It will require me to share one of my deeper secrets, one only a few people are clued in on, but if I'm going to trust anyone, it might as well be Addison. And she deserves to know the magnitude of the game we're playing.

Enough is enough, and it's time to call it.

I'm not surprised when I walk into the station and am met with a mess of activity. Detectives and cops are everywhere, running around like chickens with their heads cut off. Likely because of the call I got from Charlie.

Two more women went missing, and it's got my father's name written all over it.

I don't say a word to anyone as I walk into Charlie's office and collapse onto his couch, throwing my arm over my eyes. Taking a shaky breath in and out, I prepare myself for a long night of torturous thoughts.

I stay at the station for no more than an hour before I can't take it anymore. My anxiety is running off the charts, given everything that's happened this evening. I don't like the thought of Addison being home alone.

Giving up, I trudge back out of Charlie's office to a few confused faces. I wave them off and leave the station just as Charlie pulls up in his cruiser. He pauses mid-stride, giving me a confused look. I'm struck by how exhausted he looks, the lines on his forehead seeming more pronounced, and the bags under his eyes a dark purple. He's been running himself ragged.

Charlie doesn't stop; instead just shakes his head and walks into the station muttering, "I don't want to know."

I must look as shitty as I'm feeling too.

I go back home, fully realizing that I've wasted hours of my life, and settle in front of our front door in the hallway. I stay awake all night, watching the blackness of night fade into the breaking dawn.

Finally, when it's a respectable enough hour, I go back into the apartment and brew a pot of coffee. I'm home for barely ten minutes before I hear the bedroom door click open. I glance over my shoulder and see Addison standing in the doorframe.

"Morning," I say, eyeing her warily. Her hair is a mess, piled into a topknot on the crown of her head. Her eyes are a little red and puffy, leftover from her crying last night. I can't lie and say that the sight of her still broken up doesn't slay me inside.

"Hi," she whispers back as she shuffles on her feet.

I reach into the back pocket of my jeans and whip out a white handkerchief, waving it around in front of me and then looking around at her with one eyebrow raised. "Truce?"

A laugh slips out of her, and she wraps her arms around her middle, giving me an unenthusiastic nod. "Truce."

My body deflates at her acknowledgment. My muscles seem to lose their tension, and my shoulders seem to retreat away from my ears. Over the last ten hours or so, I've realized that I *really* don't like fighting with Parks anymore. I replayed every moment last night, every shot that was fired, and it gutted me each time I thought about us aiming to hurt each other.

That's when I came up with my plan for today.

"Do you have anywhere you need to be today?" Parks shakes her head, and my lips pull up to one side. "Okay, would you want to go somewhere with me?"

Addison looks at me, and I can see the wheels turning in her head. She appears as if she's unsure if she likes the sound of going anywhere with me. "Where?"

"I can't tell you," I say with a grimace, and her face falls. "But it might help you understand why I got so worked up last night. It's more of a 'showing is better than telling' type situation."

She exhales as if she's exhausted. "How far is it?"

Relief pours through me at her agreement, and I lean back against the counter. "Just a little over two hours. We'll be going into upstate New York."

"Can I shower first?" she asks, her voice bland.

"Of course. We can leave whenever you're ready."

Addison nods and then disappears into our bedroom again without another word. I watch her go and then turn around to pour myself a cup of coffee while I wait for her.

She takes her time, but I don't try and rush her. As she's blow-drying her hair, I resume my packing from last night, a little less crazed this time. I ensure I have enough personal items to last me a few nights and then do the same for her, asking permission before I put something in the bag.

Addison watches me with curious eyes, following me as I carry our bags down to her car. As soon as they're in the trunk, I turn to her and ask, "Do you need to let anyone inside know you'll be gone for a few days?"

She crosses her arms and looks down her nose at me. "Is that all? A few days? I don't want to tell Jack one thing and then disappear for an entire week."

I press my lips together into a line. "Just a few days, and then we'll be back. This isn't a vacation."

"You're telling me," she mutters to herself, disappearing into the diner to inform Jack of all that's going on. When she comes back out, she's got two coffee to-go cups in her mittened hands, and she shoots me a dry look, so I don't ask any questions.

It's been a long time since I've gone to battle with Addison, and with each minute that passes, I remember why I don't particularly like to do this. She can be tough to crack once she shuts down.

We both get into the car, me behind the wheel and Addison riding shotgun. She buckles in wordlessly, crossing her arms over her chest as soon as she's settled. I spare her one glance, clenching my jaw and then pulling away from the diner.

As soon as we hit the highway, she turns away from me and looks out the window, watching the scenery pass. The silence in the car is deafening, but I don't want to risk turning on the radio and forcing her to withdraw from me even further, so I bear the silence.

I've hurt her, I'm aware of that. I've misjudged and underestimated her, and she's upset. More than upset; I think she's actually thoroughly pissed at me.

At this point, though, I'm unsure what to say to improve it. I'm worried that no matter what comes out of my mouth will only worsen the situation.

Finally, after almost an hour of that suffocating quiet passes, I swallow thickly and decide to test the waters. I've been pondering how I'm going to phrase this the entire time we've been on the road, though I know it won't matter as soon as I start speaking, but I give it a go anyway.

"I promised I would keep you in the loop," I tell her, keeping my eyes trained on the road. "And I'm sorry I didn't tell you what was going on last night, but I think the severity of the situation overwhelmed me."

I can feel her eyes on me, but she doesn't say anything. The silence continues to emanate throughout the cabin of her car, and I clear my throat.

"Charlie called me last night to inform me that two women have gone missing within the last 72 hours. It was partly his idea for me to get you out of town last night. It didn't take much convincing, though," I say honestly, feeling chagrined. "I was quick to agree to take you away from Willow Heights, which is partly to explain for that manic episode you had to witness."

"What does it have to do with us?" She finally asks, and I nearly breathe a sigh of relief at the sound of her voice. "I don't understand why *we* have to leave whenever something terrible happens."

"You remember a few weeks ago when my father came by and brought up the deal we had made before I left Willow Heights?" I ask her, glancing over at her for a quick second before putting my eyes back on the road.

"The deal where you leave, and he doesn't hurt me?"

I nod my head. "That's the one. Charlie and I both think these disappearances have something to do with that."

"You think he took those girls to send a message?" she asks me, her tone incredulous. "That's ridiculous. He's the mayor. He wouldn't risk doing something like that when his entire livelihood is on the line."

I press my lips into a thin line, letting her say her piece. When she finishes, I glance over at her again. "I don't think he *took* them personally, but I do think he is involved somehow. He said some cryptic things to Charlie yesterday, and then later that evening, those girls went missing. I don't think it's a coincidence."

I notice Addison shaking her head out of the corner of my eye. "Noah, that is a serious allegation. If you think he's involved, call the FBI, call the CIA, or whoever you have connections to."

"I can't," I tell her, my voice becoming frustrated. I reel it in before things get escalated again. "I know I've told you this before, but my father is incredibly good at making it appear that he's not involved."

She exhales next to me. "I hate to be Devil's advocate here, but if you keep chasing him and chasing him and keep coming up empty-handed, don't you think that maybe you're chasing something that's not actually there?"

"I can respect that you'd feel that way," I tell her, keeping my voice level. "But I'm not the only one doing the chasing, you know? Charlie is the one who called me to tell me about this. Charlie's the one who read those missing persons' reports, and he's the one who decided it looked like my father's MO, and given the threat which came from my father directly, he thought it was enough to suggest that I get out out of town."

"Has your father done something like this before?" she asks, and I catch the hesitant note in her voice as if she's afraid to ask that question.

I don't answer her immediately, pondering the best way to respond. Finally, I say, "Yes, and it has to do with where I'm taking you today. I realize that I've left a lot of questions unanswered, and part of that reason is because there are some things that I just can't explain without you thinking I've gone crazy. I'm hoping that I'll be able to answer your questions by showing you instead."

She doesn't ask any more questions, and I'm grateful. I'm unsure how much more I can explain without having in-the-flesh evidence. Finally, I allow myself to turn on the radio, the soft, comforting sound of oldies surrounds the cabin of the SUV, and I let myself relax just a hair. Today isn't going to be an easy day. I'm not sure how Parks will react to everything I tell her, but I'm hoping she'll be open to my explanation.

We continue driving into upstate New York, deep into the Silver Lake Wilderness. Addison takes in the surroundings more as we continue deeper and deeper into the forest. I take her down a windy, old gravel road, and she holds onto the handlebars in her SUV as the car rocks and skirts over the rough terrain.

Finally, we get to the driveway to our destination. The gate is open, and I drive the car onto the property and park. As soon as we stop, Addison hops out and looks around. I follow after her, watching warily.

We're at a residential cabin with blue paneling adorning the exterior. Around the front wraps a wooden porch, a few rocking chairs sitting all alone at one end. Addison puts her hands into her pockets and then gives me an inquiring look.

"Where are we?"

I nod my head toward the front door, and we walk up together. I rap my fist against the wooden door once, twice, then three times. I can vaguely hear footsteps from inside the home, and my pulse picks up at the thought of what's really about to happen, but I do my best to level it.

This is what *needs* to happen now.

Addison's head whips around toward me as soon as the front door flies open, her eyes flashing with confusion. I dip my chin at her once, acknowledging her unspoken question, and then turn back to my mother, who is physically standing in front of us and not six feet under the ground back in the Willow Heights Cemetery.

My mother's blue eyes soften when she sees me standing in front of her, then her expression lights up as soon as she recognizes Addison by my side.

Clearing my throat, I glance back at Addison. "Parks, you remember my mother, Catherine?"

Chapter 44
Addison

"I thought you were dead," I blurt. My hand flies up to my mouth, and my eyes widen. *I can't believe I just said that.*

"Oh no, dear," Noah's mother looks at me amused, her bright blue eyes twinkling with something I can't place. "Catherine McCoy is dead. I, however, am very much alive."

I shake my head, my hand covering my mouth, moving to rub at my temple. "I don't understand."

"I'm sure Noah will fill you in on everything, but let's get out of the cold. Come on inside." She waves us in and then turns away, not leaving any room for questions.

I glance at Noah, and he nods his head toward the door. We follow her inside the quaint house. I stop short as soon as I make it to the living room. Seated on the chairs and couches are several young women. The TV is on in front of the sofa, and a few watch whatever reality show is playing. The others busy themselves with books, or a puzzle spread out across the coffee table.

They all stop what they're doing and look up at us as they enter. Their eyes are all trained on me, specifically. No one seems to pay any attention to Noah standing next to me as if they're used to him walking in unannounced. An uncomfortable feeling roils around in my stomach.

What the hell is going on here?

"Well, come on, then," Catherine says, pulling me out of my trance. "Let's get you two a warm drink."

Noah's hand rests lightly on my lower back, applying a little pressure, pulling me back into the present. I look over my shoulder at him, my eyebrows raising in question, and he shakes his head brusquely. "I'll explain later."

I frown at him but bite my tongue, allowing him to lead me out of the living room and into the kitchen. Catherine is standing at the stove and pouring hot water from a bright red kettle into two ceramic coffee mugs. She looks up as we walk in and gives us a smile.

"Have a seat. I'll get you two a snack or something too. I know it was a bit of a drive."

I fall into the seat Noah pulls out for me as I watch Catherine fly around the kitchen. I can't wrap my head around what reality shows me and what I've been led to believe.

If Catherine McCoy is standing right here in front of me, *alive*, then that means that not only did Noah lie about it, but *Charlie* did too. And that fact is almost too much for me to contemplate. I shove whatever life-altering problem deep down inside me, deciding to get the full story before jumping to conclusions.

Catherine floats over to the table carrying two cups of steaming black tea, the strings from the bags hanging limply over the sides. She sets them down in front of us and then hurries into the pantry, producing a package of grocery store brand cookies.

Placing them on the table, too, she sits across from me. She folds her hands delicately on the table, watching me with a penetrating gaze.

That's one thing I haven't forgotten about Noah's mother—how she looks at a situation and can see it for what it is. Her striking blue eyes hold depths behind them that hint at her cunningness. She's easily one of the most beautiful women I've seen. Her features are sharp and defined, though elegant. Her dark hair is pulled away from her face, a few strands loose and angling around her jawline.

"I'm sure you have lots of questions," she starts, her voice like a gentle melody breaking through the ringing in my ears.

I laugh under my breath and shake my head. "I think that's probably an understatement."

She opens her palms toward me. "Well, ask away. Now that you're here, there's no point in hiding anything anymore."

"Mom—" Noah interrupts, but she holds up a hand, effectively shushing her son. I look at him in amusement, and he scowls at his mother.

"Dear, based on how Addison here looks like she's talking with a ghost, I figure you haven't told her a damn thing. So instead of skirting around the elephant in the room, let's just call it what it is and get the uncomfortable part over with."

"You are a ghost," I say to her.

She has the decency to laugh. "Perhaps that wasn't the best phrasing. I assure you, I am very much a part of the realm of the living still."

I run my hand over the side of my head, rubbing the ropey tension out of my muscles. My head has started to throb ever so slightly, the earliest sign of an oncoming headache.

"Charlie said you were dead. I guess I'm confused, I thought—" I shake my head again, still trying to come to grips with what I'm trying to say. "I didn't think he was capable of lying like that."

Catherine's eyes narrow slightly, her lips pulling into a thin line as she contemplates how to answer my question or lack thereof. "Sheriff Sullivan was unfortunately roped into this mess long before we staged my death. I'm not sure he ever really wanted to be a part of it but realized that he would be doing the right thing in the long run." She pauses and exhales. "Your friend is a very noble man, but sometimes wrong things are done for the right reasons, do you understand?"

I nod. "And all of this comes back to your husband?"

Catherine's nose curls up on one side, but she is gracious not to correct me. "Unfortunately, yes. I'll leave that to Noah to discuss the details surrounding his involvement, as I'm not fully clued in on every aspect. Need-to-know and all that nonsense." Noah grunts from his seat, and Catherine shoots him a scathing look.

For whatever reason, that tidbit of information surprises me. When I saw Catherine standing in front of me in the flesh, I imagined her to be in on the joke. Maybe that's why it was such a huge shock—it felt like everyone knew what was happening *except* me.

"And I'm assuming Mr. McCoy has no idea that you're—" I wave my hand around. "Here?"

Now a sly smile forms on her face. "Absolutely not. We made sure that there would be no surrounding suspicion from my cause of untimely death. Declan is incredible at not realizing what's happening around him if it doesn't directly involve him. To be honest, I was never that important."

I lean back in my chair, hating how her statement twists at my heart. I can't imagine living with a husband who wouldn't care whether I lived or died.

"Did you get a model made or something that looked like you for the funeral?" I ask, trying to recall the details from her apparently fake funeral.

"It was a closed casket service," Noah adds, and I dart my gaze over to him. "I made sure that the casket was to be shut for the visitation and the funeral service. And thankfully, my father couldn't be bothered enough to try and go see her body before the funeral itself. That was the one wildcard we were betting on, but he held true to expectations. He's selfish, and selfish men don't usually stray from that persona."

"So the casket that was buried is—"

Noah nods his head. "Empty. There is nothing inside of it except sandbags to compensate for the body weight."

I squeeze my eyes shut, trying to fit together all the pieces of this scheme. "What about the coroner or the funeral director. Were they all in on it too?"

"FBI magic," Noah says as if that's a sufficient answer. "We were able to get some of our guys into those positions to take care of the loose ends."

"The FBI agreed to fake her death?" I ask him incredulously.

A wry smirk forms on his face, and he leans closer. "Reluctantly, but we made it work."

I fall back against the wood prongs of the chair, noting them digging into my back muscles. "This is all a lot to take in."

"Certainly," Catherine replies. "You two take some time to settle in. Did you bring luggage?" She looks over at Noah, and he nods his head. "Good, I'll put you all in the guest house for the night. There's a nice en suite and a hot tub on the back patio. Take a breather and relax."

Catherine excuses herself from the table and grabs the uneaten cookies to put them back in the pantry. I'm still sitting there, feeling overwhelmed. Before she exits the kitchen, she places her hand on my shoulder and squeezes gently. "If you have any questions or need to talk some more, Addison, please don't hesitate to find me."

I nod, and she squeezes again before disappearing, leaving Noah and me sitting silently at the table. The epiphanies I've just been forced to endure hang over me like a haze I can't break out of. The sounds of the TV echo in from the living room, and every few minutes, I'll hear a tinkling of laughter coming from the women.

"Want to go outside and get our stuff?" Noah finally asks me, breaking me out of my stupor. I glance at him, my heart melting at his hopeful yet careful expression. "We can go settle in at the guest house, and then I think we should probably talk some more."

I exhale and wrap my arms around my middle. "Yeah, I think talking might be good."

Noah scoots back from the table, offering me his hand, which I take. He pulls me up, and we walk back through the house to the front door. Again, on our way out, I pause in the living room for a moment. This time the women don't bother looking up at us. There's something about the situation that's unsettling me, but I can't put my finger on it immediately.

"Who are all those women?" I ask quietly as soon as we make it outside to the car. Noah presses his lips together as he pops open the trunk, getting our bags and then setting them on the ground, not caring about the dirt. As soon as the doors are closed, he turns to me and takes my hands in his, squeezing them tightly.

"Addison," Noah says, "these women are—" He pauses as if unsure how to continue. Then as if coming to a decision, he bobs his head once and squeezes my hands again. "My father is involved in high-level management of a trafficking ring in the North East. These women are survivors liberated from his system who have nowhere else to go."

My mouth goes dry, and my eyes widen as I trace the features of his face. I'm not sure what to do with this information. "Oh," I respond dumbly.

Noah looks at me with sympathy and squeezes my hands for the third time. "Let's get our stuff into the guest house, and then I'll tell you everything."

Bending down and grabbing our bags, Noah leads me around the side of the main house and off a little paved path. It's not a long walk, but enough to feel like wherever we're going is more private. When we make it through the clearing of trees, I gasp. Right in front of us is a tiny cottage. The exterior panels are painted blue, and the door right in the middle is a bright red. Two small lights sit on either side of the door, glowing like a beacon. Surrounding the cottage is a light oak porch with a railing spanning the perimeter.

"Oh my gosh," I whisper. "This is adorable."

Noah grins at me, and we walk the rest of the way toward the cottage. Once we're up on the porch, Noah drops the bag and punches in a four-digit code on the keypad. The door unlocks, and he swings it open.

Inside, we find an open loft-style layout. Straight ahead as we walk in is a small kitchen with a fridge, an oven, and a microwave. To the left of the front door is a king-size bed and the ensuite bathroom, and a tiny built-in seating area to the right.

Noah steps over to the bed and sets our bags on the made-up mattress. He looks around with an approving gaze. "Not bad, huh?"

I shake my head as I step further into the cottage. "No, it's... it's perfect."

I have never seen such a quaint tiny home in my entire life. If I could pick this whole place up and bring it back to Willow Heights, I think I would. It's not much, but it's cozy and charming. Everything I could want in a house.

"There's a hot tub on the back porch," Noah says, and I recognize the lilt of excitement in his tone. "I packed your swimsuit."

I can't help but laugh at him and follow him out to the screened-in porch. Sure enough, there sits a four-seater hot tub. Outside the screen porch is another small patio with a built-in fire pit. Two recliner chairs surround it, and I notice fairy lights strung up right above the patio.

"How long are we staying?" I can't help but ask as I walk over to peruse the patio.

"It's up to you," Noah says. "I don't know how long you told Jack you'd be gone. "

"I think I might love it here."

His deep voice rumbles in a chuckle. "Good. My mother and aunt have put a lot of work into this property to make it feel welcoming."

I turn to face him. "Your aunt?"

He nods. "Yes, my mother's sister. She's kind of in on the whole gig too. Hopefully, you'll get a chance to meet her while we're here. She's always in and out, though, sometimes hard to catch. Here, let's sit so we can talk some more."

Noah leads me back into the house and to the built-in seating area. I sit against the padded bench and look at him expectantly. He runs his hand along his jaw, looking pensive. "Do you have any questions about anything my mother told you?"

"I'm honestly not sure," I respond. "It's all a lot to take in, and I'm just feeling overwhelmed."

He nods understandingly. "I get it. I've probably handled this all wrong, but at this point, we might as well just lay everything out."

"Okay. Let's do it then," I say, steeling myself. "I guess I do have a question, actually. How did your mom get involved with this all in the first place?"

Noah leans over until his elbows are resting on his knees. He looks at me solemnly. "Once I started working on this case, I knew I had to get my mom out of there. Until then, I had known that my father was bad, but not *that bad*, you know? But after you find something horrible like that, there's no going back."

"So you told her everything?" I ask.

He shakes his head. "No, I couldn't, really. It was mostly confidential. I did find a loophole, though. I told her just enough so she could go snooping in the right areas to find out what she needed to know—that's what her little side comment was earlier. She still isn't fully clued in either."

"Then why are you telling me?"

Noah takes in a deep breath and steels me with a heavy gaze. "Because we're to the point where it's a detriment to your safety if I don't, and that's not something I'm not willing to risk. Also, to be perfectly frank, I fully intend to marry you one day, Addison Parks, and I don't want to start our life together built on lies and half-truths."

My mouth goes dry, and my eyes widen. Noah observes my face for a second as if gauging my reaction. He then doesn't waste any more time before jumping back into his story. "Once my mother knew just how bad my father was, she agreed that she needed to get out of there, but then the issue of *her* safety came up. My father barely paid attention to my mother on a good day, but he's the type of man that would never allow her to leave him."

"All about appearances," I mutter, and Noah agrees.

"Exactly. He would never allow her to embarrass him by leaving. Even if she ran away, he would have found her. So then that introduced the conflict of getting her out of there. I pulled some strings with the FBI, and she agreed to change her name and let Catherine McCoy die. She's not employed by the government but is associated with my department, kind of like an independent contractor. As far as the legal system is concerned, her name is Giselle Carmichael, and she's the founder of Carmichael House."

"And she lets women come here?"

"Yes, women rescued from the system are always given the option to come here until they can get their feet on the ground. It's a hard transition for many women, and this place allows them the time to figure out their next step."

I watch Noah's face as he explains what all he and his mother are doing. His expression takes on this determined look as he speaks, and I can tell this is something that is very important to him. He is proud of this aspect of his work.

"I think that's really amazing, Noah," I tell him. "I love that you and your mother have found a way to help these people heal from what you're father has done to them."

He chuckles humorlessly and rubs at the back of his neck. "And somehow, it's still not enough. I feel like no matter what I do, I'll always be paying for the sins of the father."

"I don't think so. You don't have to repent for all the evil he's done. You had no part in it."

"Maybe not," he acquiesces, but I feel he doesn't mean it. "But it's still on my shoulders for now, and it will stay there until I can see him rot in jail."

"I wish there was more that I could do," I say.

Noah shakes his head. "I don't. I want you as far away from all of this as I possibly can. Which I know seems ridiculous when I brought you right into the heart of it. But I don't want this to plague you like it does me."

I reach over and take Noah's hand, threading our fingers together. "We're a team, Noah."

I don't say anything more, letting my words hit home. Noah looks up at me, his eyes heavy as he traces the features of my face. He exhales and squeezes my hands. Then he leans forward, closing the distance between us until our foreheads rest together. I close my eyes, letting the closeness of our connection surround me.

After what feels like a thousand heartbeats have passed, I finally speak. "I don't know about you, but I could use a nap. It's been a long day."

It's barely noon, but mentally I feel like I've just run a marathon. Noah pulls away from me and nods his head, not disagreeing. We walk over to the king bed on the other side of the cottage and pull back the covers. Noah climbs onto his side while I excuse myself to the bathroom to freshen up a bit.

I toss some cool water on my face and take a few deep breaths. Noah's settled in bed when I step out of the bathroom. His eyes appear droopy as he watches me.

"Come here, sweetheart," Noah mumbles, extending his arm and inviting me to lay with him. I crawl onto the bed, snuggling into his side. With an exhale, I press my cheek to the warm skin of his chest and close my eyes. "Are you still mad at me?" he asks in a low voice.

I shake my head against him. "No. It's a lot to take in, though, and I'm still trying to process everything. I'm so tired."

His hand rests against my head, his large fingers threading through the strands of my hair and rubbing my scalp muscles. I let out a happy sigh at the comforting movements and nuzzle closer to him.

Before I'm fully aware of what's happening, I fall into a deep sleep. Hours later, I'm jolted awake by Noah's phone ringing. He swears under his breath, untangling himself from me, and reaches for his phone. The cottage is dark now, and I wonder what time it is.

Noah answers his phone with a husky, "Yeah?" The person on the other end of the line says a few words, and then Noah sits up straight in bed, running his hand over his face. "Sure. Next week? Yup, I'll be there, thank you."

As soon as he hangs up the call, he drops his phone onto the comforter and leans back against the pillows with a groan. "Who was that?" I ask, resting my hand against his chest, my fingers stroking the fine hair scattered across his skin.

"Vincent," he responds, and I pause. "He said the board wants to get together next week to discuss the next steps with my probation."

"Oh," I say. "Is that a good thing?"

Noah scrubs his hand against his face again, then shoots me a hesitant smile. "I guess I'll find out next week."

A heavy silence falls over us. I can't help but wish that we could have a normal life. A life without all the drama of whatever the hell is going on with Noah's father and a life where we could be free to be together. We have gone through so much at this point that a happy ending seems so far-fetched. I often wonder if it will ever end or if we're destined to live this way for the rest of our lives.

Finally, after what feels like another few hours, Noah extracts himself from our embrace. I look at him questioningly, and he smirks. "I thought we could go back up to the main house and see if my mom made anything for dinner. I'm famished."

I chuckle but nod my head, removing myself from the cozy confines of the bed and finding my shoes. As soon as we've got what we need, we walk hand in hand back to Catherine's house. The minute we walk through the door, I'm hit with the smell of home-style food, and my stomach grumbles.

We go into the kitchen, where Noah's mother is just pulling the casserole pans out of the oven. She glances up as we enter, and her face lights up. She finishes getting everything together and then instructs us to take a seat. A few women join us, each finding their place at the table as Catherine walks around and serves the casseroles.

The meal is quiet, aside from Catherine's questions, trying to get the conversation going. As soon as the women are finished eating, they disappear, quietly thanking Catherine for the meal.

"Noah?" a soft, timid voice asks, pulling Noah's attention away from his almost empty plate. A woman is standing next to him, looking between the two of us sheepishly. "I was wondering if I could speak to you about something?"

I observe the woman. She has ebony black hair that falls around her shoulders. She's tall and lanky, her frame thin. Noah glances at me as if asking for permission. I nod, and he gets up, ushering the woman off to the other side of the room where they can talk.

Catherine and I still sit together at the table. I can see Noah and the woman on the other end of the living room, sitting together on the couch. Noah leans toward the woman, still allowing plenty of space between them as he speaks with her. She listens to him raptly, every once in a while brushing a hand up to her cheek to wipe away a tear. I'm not sure what Noah's saying to her, but deep down, I know he's trying his best to assure her of something. The gentleness on his face and the way his lips form his words tell me that he's speaking to her with honesty.

Catherine watches Noah with a proud expression on her face. The way she holds herself is regal; her head held high, shoulders squared. Her bright blue eyes are piercing but kind. She watches everything with a sharp gaze, not missing a thing. "I think he enjoys working with them, the women," she muses. "He's got such a protective soul."

I nod my head in agreement and take a sip of my water. I am curious. I'll have to ask Noah how involved he is in his mother's work. I could easily see him finding solace in helping the survivors of his father's operation get their lives back.

"He told me about what's been going on back in Willow Heights," Catherine says, looking over at me. I furrow my brow at her, unsure what she means. "About the girls who have gone missing near town," she clarifies.

Oh. "He seems to think that Declan is behind it, trying to send him a message," I tell her.

"And you don't?"

I raise an eyebrow now and look down at my lap for a second. "I don't know, it seems far fetched. I don't see him as someone who would risk his power just to make a point."

Catherine laughs lightly and looks away. "Then I'm afraid you don't know my former husband well at all."

"What do you mean?"

She takes a moment to gather her thoughts. "Declan thrives on the mind games. His business involves the entire North East, including New York City, Boston, and Philly. You mentioned power, which was a valid point but I'll turn it back around on you. *Why would* he risk picking up his next victims so close to home, when he has so many other options, if it weren't to prove a point?"

"Should I be worried he's going to come after me if Noah doesn't comply to his terms?" I ask, my heart tightening in my chest. "Am I crazy for not being worried? I feel like if he is that much of a threat he would have done something by now."

Catherine sighs. "I can't pretend to know what Declan's plans are, but I can confidently advise you not to underestimate him. It's all part of the game to him. He gave Noah an ultimatum, Noah didn't abide, and now Declan is serving the consequences of that choice."

"How are you still so—" I pause and shake my head, "—okay with all of this?"

"I'm not," she says, turning her searing blue gaze on me. "The thought of anything happening to Noah because of Declan makes me —" now she pauses and catches her breath. "It keeps me up at night, let's leave it at that."

I don't say anything else to that. In the rush of everything happening today I forgot that this is Noah's *mother.*

Catherine clears her throat, bringing my attention back to her. "Noah said he brought you here to help close some of the gaps, to give you answers to things he couldn't rely on words to explain. Just trust that my son will do everything in his power to keep you safe. He'll stop at nothing to protect the ones he loves."

"I just am so confused," I admit. "How did it come to this?"

"Power has a way of turning even the best people into villains," Catherine says. "Declan wasn't always this man, but it is who he is now."

"What am I supposed to do with all of this?" I ask her, my voice coming out helpless. "I have responsibilities and things I can't run from. I'm not someone who runs away when the going gets tough."

"I'm afraid I can't answer that for you. But you're right, you are a strong woman. No matter what obstacle you face I know you'll be capable of coming out on top," she says, smiling at me. I press my lips together, feeling for the first time in forever what it's like to have a mother's approval.

My chest aches as I lean back in my chair, glancing back over at Noah who is still in rapt conversation with one of the women. He's leaning toward her, speaking low. Her eyes are focused on him, absorbing everything he's saying to her.

"You're good for him, you know?" Catherine says, looking over at her son fondly. "I knew from the start that you were something special, and I'm so glad that he's finally gotten his head out of his ass and come back for you."

I can't fight off the smile playing on my lips. "Me too."

"You helped him more than you'll ever know," she tells me. "Sometimes, when my thoughts get the better of me, I wonder what would have happened if Noah had not gotten the intervention you provided. His father is such a manipulative man. I imagine Noah would have been groomed to follow in his footsteps."

Catherine is probably right. I think back to the Noah I knew years before we meant anything to each other. He was so much different then than he is now. "Thankfully, I don't think we have to worry about that."

Her blue eyes flash to mine, and she smiles. "No, we don't. My son is a good man. I couldn't be prouder of him and all he's doing."

"Me too," I respond, smiling back.

"You love him, don't you?" Catherine asks me, a knowing glint forming in her eyes.

I nod my head. "More than I even know what to do with sometimes."

She sighs, and a soft smile plays on her lips. "That's all we ever want as parents. You hope you do right by your children and that they'll grow up to be decent humans and maybe have the opportunity to find someone who loves them. As I said, I am so glad he found you. I've never seen Noah so happy than when you're in his life."

"I guess it's a good thing my father moved us to Willow Heights, then," I say with a sad smile. "No matter what a mess it's turned into."

I mean it too. Time gives you perspective; though I lost a lot, I also gained much more. The ups and downs are part of the journey we must endure. Though our moving to my now beloved town ultimately tore my family apart, I wouldn't change anything.

Noah glances up from his conversation and locks eyes with me. A soft flutter forms in my stomach as he gazes at me appreciatively for a moment before returning his attention to the woman he's speaking to.

Noah and I have been through much together. There have been so many nights where I've lain awake in bed, wondering if we would make it or if all the heartache was worth it. But again, now that we are here and have made it, I know with certainty that it all paid off.

I've lost a lot in my life, but I've also gained all of it back and even more, and without a doubt, knowing what I know now, I wouldn't change a thing.

Chapter 45
Noah

Morning comes all too soon. I'm awoken by the sound of my alarm, pulling me out of my dreams. Reaching over to the nightstand, I click the button on the side of my phone, shutting it off. Addison stirs next to me, slowly waking up.

I flip over on my side and face her. Her eyes flutter open and latch onto mine, hazel green to blue. A soft smile forms on her plump lips, and my heart flips as I gaze at her. I close the distance between us, wrapping my arm over the curve of her hips and pulling her close into me as I capture her gorgeous mouth.

Addison kisses me back for a moment before pushing me away and covering her mouth with her hand. "Noah, morning breath!" she accuses behind the shield of her hand.

I laugh and then pull her hand away from her mouth, claiming her lips once more. This time I push past the seam of her lips with my tongue and kiss her deeply. Addison moans against me, arching her back and pressing her breasts against my chest. Before we get too carried away, I pull back and grin down at her.

"For the record, I don't care about your morning breath," I tell her.

"What if I care about yours?" she shoots back, and I raise an eyebrow.

"Do you?"

She pauses dramatically for a moment but then slowly shakes her head, her full lips curving up in the corners. "No."

I chuckle again, rolling over her until her back is pressing against the mattress. My hands move to cup her face as I retake her mouth. Addison's legs spread and wrap around my hips, pulling me into her as close as she can.

"Parks," I murmur in between kisses. "Don't you think we should get up and get breakfast?"

"Hmm," she says back, kissing my neck. "I actually have something better on my mind right now."

I groan out loud as she shifts her hips up against me. I grind down against her heat, my body stiffening as images of sliding deep inside her fill my mind. Without wasting time, I reach down between us, hooking my fingers under the seam of her panties and sneaking them down her thighs. Addison wiggles underneath me, helping to rid me of my boxers too. She spreads her legs wider when there's nothing left between us, allowing me to seat myself against her core.

We both groan at the contact, and I slide against her before notching at her entrance. My eyes catch hers, and she nods her head. "Please, Noah."

I reach down and make sure I'm aligned properly before I shift my hips into her and deep inside her. Addison tosses her head back with a groan and thrusts her pelvis toward me. I slide in and out of her, both of us getting lost in the pleasure of each other.

Once we're both sated and showered, we walk hand in hand back to the house. Addison's cheeks have that post-sex glow, and I grip her hand tighter, wondering if I've ever seen anything more beautiful than her.

"Good morning," my mom says as we walk into the kitchen. "You two sleep well?"

Addison ducks her head, her eyes gluing to the floor, but not before I notice a faint blush forming on her cheeks. I chuckle under my breath and answer for her. "Yeah, Mom, everything was great."

My mother had requested the cottage be built on the property for visitors. A lot of the time, my Aunt Trish would take up residence there when she and my mom would be working on a project. But in cases like this, where I paid a surprise visit, it worked out nicely to have a separate space I could stay away from the main house.

There was never any telling how many women my mother would have staying in her home at any one time, so it was safer for me not to bank on staying there. And anyway, I wouldn't ever want to make the women uncomfortable with my presence, as many are still leery of men, so keeping space was totally fine with me.

"I'm glad to hear that," Mom says and then turns back to the scrambled eggs she's whipping up. "I'll have breakfast ready for you two in a few minutes. Most of the girls have eaten already. If you need some, there's a little coffee left in the pot."

I let go of Addison's hand and walk over to the counter, grabbing two coffee cups and filling them with the dark, heavenly liquid. Then going into the fridge, I find the creamer and pass it over to Addison, who smiles at me gratefully, popping the top off and pouring a healthy amount into her coffee.

We settle into our seats at the table, and my mom serves us each a plate of breakfast. I sit next to Addison, and without wasting any more time, we all dig into our meals, scarfing down the eggs and toast.

"Knock knock. Anyone here?" A voice calls through the house. My mom looks up from her breakfast and grins at me, shaking her head.

"In the kitchen!" she calls out.

I hear something drop on the floor from the main hall and then footsteps echoing against the hardwood floors. A woman appears in the kitchen doorway, her curly dark hair a mess on her head. She looks at the three of us sitting at the table, and accusingly puts her hands on her hips.

"Didn't realize we were having a tea party. Where was my invite?"

"Hey, Aunt Trish," I say, laughing, standing up and wrapping my aunt into a hug. She hugs me right back, patting her hands on my broad shoulders.

"Alright, Kid, that's enough of that."

I step away from her and turn to Addison, who is watching the exchange with confused eyes. "Parks, this is my Aunt Trish. She's been helping out at Carmichael House here and there, working with my mom."

"She's also the one who killed me," my mom chimes in, grabbing her plate from the table to take it to the sink and shooting a wink at me.

Addison's eyes dart to me, furrowing in the middle, but Aunt Trish interjects before I can say anything. "Yep, that was *all* me. Guess all those years studying botany paid off, huh?"

Addison's attention now alternates between my mom and my aunt, who is sharing a little smirk with each other. "What are you two talking about?"

I sit down next to Addison again, draping my arm against the back of her chair. "My aunt graduated college with a botany degree. When I decided it was time to get my mom out of there, I reached out to Trish for her help. She combined a concoction that could put the body into a trance-like state, simulating death."

Addison stares at me blankly, and Trish chimes in. "You ever read *Romeo & Juliet?*"

Addison turns to her and frowns. "Of course," she replies a bit haughtily, and I have to bite back a chuckle.

"Well, it's like that."

Now Parks looks at me again, and I nod my head. "I know it's a little far-fetched, but that's why Charlie was such a crucial part of the plan. Since he was in on it, he could look past the signs of life that weren't extinguished with the mixture."

Addison closes her eyes and places her hand on her forehead as if overwhelmed. I wrap my arm around her shoulders tighter. "Hey," I say, getting her attention again. I carefully place my finger under her chin and bring her eyes back to me. "We don't have to talk about this anymore if you don't want. Just whenever you're ready or if you have questions."

She nods her head but doesn't say a word. I rub her back, looking over at my Aunt Trish, who is watching the two of us closely. When I raise an eyebrow at her, she curls her lip up in mock distaste. "Well, you two are just disgustingly in love, aren't you?"

Addison's jaw drops open, and I bark out a laugh. "Guilty," I say as I lean over and press a kiss to Addison's cheek. When I pull away, I grin at the rosy blush on the apples of her cheeks.

"I'm still a little confused," Addison says to my aunt. Aunt Trish raises an eyebrow at her expectantly. "How could you create such a concoction so easily when it could be so problematic."

"Guess that's the power of working for the government," my aunt responds bluntly. "I'm pretty confident I signed away my soul as soon as I handed that recipe card over," she says with a chuckle.

Addison still looks as though she's thinking hard about the whole thing. "I'm just surprised they were okay with it being used at all."

I shift in my seat, uncomfortable. "That might be partly because of me," I tell her. "I was able to convince my supervisors that this would be a one-time-only thing. I think there were equal amounts of trepidation and intrigue at the prospect of somebody having made the Shakespeare potion, so they let it slide."

"I can see that," Addison says, nodding her head twice. "Doctors all over have researched and tried to come up with the correct measurements, but they haven't been able to perfect it. But you," she turns to Trish again, "were able to make it just like that?"

My aunt shrugs and picks at her fingernail. "I guess so." She turns and shoots my mom a sideways grin. "Guess it's a good thing I didn't kill you, huh, Catie?"

My mother rolls her eyes, setting her glass of orange juice on the table. "Trust me. Even death would have been better than staying in that house one more day."

The room falls silent at my mother's admission, though no one challenges her.

I look over at Addison, who is watching my mom with an expression of compassion on her face. I know the two of them spent some time together last night. I can't help but be a little curious about what they were talking about.

"Well, on that lovely note," my aunt claps her hands, "how about those dishes? I've grown weary of this boring conversation. I'll wash. Your lovely girlfriend gets to dry!"

Addison laughs but agrees, grabbing empty plates and glassware and bringing them over to the large sink. I sit back, sipping my coffee and watching her and my aunt chat in hushed tones as they soap up the plates and dry them off. If I had to take a guess, I'd wager they are talking more about my aunt's concoction. The chemistry nerd deep down inside Parks is probably dying to know every little detail.

We spend the day with my mom and my aunt. Some of the women pop in and out, curious to see what we're up to. A few latch themselves onto Addison and sit close to her as we play board games or chat mindlessly about the weather. I can't help but be impressed with how Addison has so quickly immersed herself into this setting, though I shouldn't be surprised. Addison is resilient and easily adaptable.

When the sun starts to set, I head back with Addison to our tiny cabin. She holds my hand the whole way but doesn't say much. As soon as we're back, I go out the back door to the patio and turn on the propane fire pit. I find two chairs and bring them closer to the fire so we can sit and stay warm. Parks is leaning on the counter in the kitchen, watching me curiously. She hasn't taken her coat off yet, so I suspect she's onto what my suggestion will be.

"Want a glass of wine?" I ask, and she nods her head. I find a chilled bottle of Chardonnay in the fridge and pour us each a hearty amount into stemmed wine glasses. Before we go outside, I have the sense of mind to grab us each a fluffy blanket. It's still freezing, but hopefully, between the fire pit and the blankets, we'll be cozy.

The two of us huddle out on the patio, each taking a seat and settling in. The fire is already roaring with life, fueled by propane, which is sufficient enough to cast a warm bubble of heat around us.

I quickly get lost in the ambiance of the night. My eyes track the wayward movements of the fire in front of us as the smoke swirls around in the darkness. I keep chancing glances at Addison sitting next to me. Her attention is focused on the flames, looking lost in thought. The shadows dart across her face, obscuring her from the light.

"Noah?" her soft voice asks into the night. I flash my eyes over to her, letting her know she has my attention. "I was wondering if I could ask you about something you said yesterday."

My expression softens. "Of course, anything."

She fiddles with her fingers, her eyes falling to her lap as if she's embarrassed to ask what's on her mind. "You said yesterday that you intended to marry me."

A small smile plays on my lips, and I sit back in my chair, watching her. A small burst of pride swells in my chest at the thought of being able to call her my *wife* someday. "I did. Are you okay with that?"

She glances up at me before quickly looking back down at her fingers. A faint blush appears on her cheeks, and I fight off a smile. "I'm more than okay with that. It's just—"

Now I sit forward again, my eyebrows pulling in at the middle as I frown at her. "Just what, Parks?"

Addison reaches for her wine glass, swirling around the white liquid as she purses her lips. "You brought me out here to prove a point, I understand that but—" her sentence trails off, and she shakes her head.

"It wasn't to prove a point," I interject. Addison's eyes fly to me, and I hope she can see what I'm not saying as I gaze at her intently. "I realize that I went a little crazy the other night and that you deserved an explanation. This is all this is. I didn't feel like any explanation I could come up with would do the truth justice."

"I am grateful that you finally included me in this. I was talking with your mom some last night," she says, running her finger over the rim of her glass. I realize this is the first chance we've had to really talk one-on-one all day. "She seems to think that the threat your father poses is legitimate."

I nod my head. "It is. He's after me, and the easiest way to get to me would be by using you. You're only involved through me, which is...eating me up inside."

"I guess, with that in mind, I understand now why you were so frazzled the other night," Addison says, taking my hand and squeezing it.

I let out a sigh, knowing that she can't possibly understand. I appreciate her effort, though, and I offer her a tight smile. "Yeah. Still, I handled it like shit."

She chuckles and nods her head. "You did, but I forgive you. A lot has happened since you came back last month, and we're still trying to learn how to work together. But—" she trails off, and my stomach clenches at whatever she's about to add on. "I can't stay here, Noah. If you brought me here hoping that I would want to stay...."

"I didn't," I shake my head fervently, hoping she'll believe me. "That's not what this was."

"There are a lot of people counting on me at home. It's only me now at the Diner—and Jack. It's my responsibility to be there to make sure that everything is running smoothly. I can't just pick up my life willy-nilly and run off whenever you're worried something will happen to me."

"You're right. I'm sorry if I made you feel that way," I say, reaching for her hand. I twine my fingers into hers and exhale.

We both fall silent, letting my eyes study every fine detail of her beautiful face. Finally, I let go of her hand, scooting my chair closer to hers. I reach for her again, resting my large hand on the side of her delicate neck. My thumb soothes over her cheek, appreciating the feel of her warm skin under my palm. Addison's wide eyes gaze up into mine, searching for something. A soft smile plays on her lips when she finds it, and my heart swells with love for her.

No matter how manic I was the other night, I'll never be able to get over the peace that Addison is capable of bringing out in me. All these years I could have spent with her in quiet moments like this. She was made for me—my other half, the one person in this world who understands me in a way no one else does.

"Addison," I start and pause, feeling my throat get thick. "You mean the world to me, you know that?"

Her lips pull back from her teeth as she grins at me. "I do, and you mean the world to me too."

My thumb continues to trace her cheek as I contemplate my words. "I don't think I could live with myself if something happened to you. *That's* why I freaked out the other night. I was scared."

Her eyes narrow on me as if trying to figure out a puzzle. I'm not sure I've ever admitted anything so vulnerable to her before. She's seen me at my best and my worst, though vulnerability is something I try to dampen. "You don't have to be scared, Noah. I'm fine. Nothing is going to happen to me."

My hand on the side of her neck tightens as I pull her closer to me until our foreheads are resting against each other. "You can't know that, and it's hard for me to put everything aside, knowing that something could happen to you. You are *the* most important thing in my life, Parks. I've said that before but with every day we spend together, it becomes more and more true. You own me, heart and soul. I would give up anything and everything to keep you safe."

I close my eyes, letting myself bask in her presence. The tightness in my belly starts to release as her hands wrap around my neck, playing with the curls at my nape. I still feel frayed at the edges, though it's less now that I have her out of Willow Heights. I know it's something that I'm going to have to come to terms with. We'll be back home soon, and nothing will have changed. I'll just have to trust that everything will be okay. At this point, it is out of my control.

"We can head back whenever you want," I tell her. "I hear what you're saying, and I don't want to make you do something you don't want to."

She exhales, and I feel her breath against my lips. "Thank you, Noah."

"Just, *please*," my voice almost breaks. I pull away from her a bit and open my eyes to stare into hers. "Please promise me you won't write this off. I don't trust that my father won't try and do something to send home his message. He wants me gone, and he can be a heartless bastard when he's trying to get what he wants."

Her eyes dart between my own as if searching again. Slowly she nods her head. "I promise."

I breathe out a sigh through my nose and press my forehead to hers again briefly before taking her lips in mine. She kisses me back fervently, her lips parting against my own until I can taste the hint of wine on her breath.

With her kiss, my body lights up with awareness and arousal. I don't think I'll ever be able to get enough of this woman. I deepen the kiss, ravaging her as my hands slide down her shoulders to her waist. Tugging on her gently, I pull her out of her chair and over to mine. Addison comes willingly, crawling onto my lap and straddling my thighs with hers.

She kisses me again, tangling her fingers into my hair as she grinds her hips against mine. My jeans tighten at the feel of her heat rubbing against me, and I can't help but buck up against her once, loving the moan that escapes her throat at the feeling of me.

"Think we should take this inside?" I ask her, pulling away, breathless.

Her eyes find mine, and she nods her head up and down. I pick her up, setting her on her feet only so I can turn off the propane, and then I sweep her into my arms again, walking us through the screen porch and into the house.

In a few short strides, we're in the bedroom, and I'm dropping her onto the bed. Addison spreads out on the mattress, stretching her legs and arms out seductively. I fight back a growl low in my throat as I watch her. *Fuck, she's delectable.*

My fingers trace up the curve of her thighs until I make it to the waistband of her leggings. She squeals at my cold fingers slipping under the band, but I don't waste time before I strip them down her legs. Addison catches on and slides her top off, pulling her bra with it. When she's gloriously naked in front of me, I take a step back and admire her.

"You're so fucking sexy, Parks," I mumble low under my breath.

Addison preens and juts her chest out toward me, silently telling me she wants more. "I think you're a tad bit overdressed," she whispers, eyeballing my jeans.

I can't help the smirk that forms on my face as I go to unbuckle my belt. I slide it through the loops and toss it to the side, unbuttoning my jeans and kicking them off. My boxers follow shortly, and then I strip off my shirt. Slowly, I crawl over her, moaning at the feel of her body heat seeping into mine. I press my body against hers, claiming her lips with mine again. Addison arches into me, her fingers scraping down my back and down to my ass, where she grips me tightly. I buck against her again, and she moans into my mouth.

Before we get the chance to get too carried away, I pull back slightly and look down at her. Her cheeks are flushed most beautifully, and I can't help the desire from pooling low in my belly.

"What do you want, love?" I ask her, my voice thick.

Addison squirms a little underneath me, and then she whimpers, "You."

A low rumble forms in my chest as I lean over her again, claiming her lips as mine. Her mouth is swollen and flushed when I pull away, and yearning floods my body. Grabbing hold of her thighs, I pull her to the edge of the mattress, positioning her exactly how I want her.

My hand makes its way to the juncture of her legs, and I slide my fingers through her center. I moan deep in my chest when I find that she's soaked for me. "Mm, you're dripping, Parks. Is this all for me?"

She nods her head briskly, her arms raised up over her head. The movement makes her breasts stick out toward me, almost like an offering. I groan again as I lean forward, taking one of her perfect nipples in my mouth and running my tongue over the stiff peak. Addison bucks her hips up at the sensation.

My fingers between her thighs start stroking, finding that tight bundle of nerves and thrumming over it repeatedly. Switching to her other breast, I keep up the rhythm, noting the change in her breathing and how she writhes against me.

When she comes, she comes with a scream, tossing her head back and letting the waves of pleasure crash over her.

I pull away from her, bringing my hand up and observing her slickness covering my fingers. "Mmm, such a messy girl," I mutter before sticking my two fingers in my mouth and sucking them clean.

Addison whimpers and then bucks her hips up toward my hardened length. I raise an eyebrow at her and take my fingers out of my mouth. "You want more?"

"Please, Noah. I want you."

I lean over and kiss her hotly before placing my hands on her pelvis and directing her until she's standing. Addison watches me, confused, until I give her my next instructions.

"Come on, love. Bend over," I turn her around and place my hand between her shoulder blades, applying a bit of downward pressure. She catches on and leans over the mattress, sticking her perfect ass out toward me. I kick my foot between her legs. "Spread your legs for me."

She does as I ask, and when she's spread out gloriously for me, I position myself at her entrance and slide home. She cries out in ecstasy at the feeling of me between her slick folds. I groan at how she clenches against me, the contractions still present from her last orgasm.

"God, Parks," I groan, curling my body over her back and pressing my face into her neck. "You're perfect, sweetheart."

"Noah, faster, please," she mewls beneath me, wiggling her ass back and pushing me deeper inside her.

I start moving then, thrusting in and out into her wet heat. Addison thrusts back against me, taking her pleasure from me. I feel her inner walls flutter against my cock, telling me she is quickly climbing toward her peak.

With my free hand, I reach around her front and find her clit. I rapidly circle the sensitive spot with two fingers, leading her closer and closer to her climax. "That's a good girl," I tell her, and she moans at the praise. "Are you gonna come again for me?"

"Yes!" she shouts and thrusts back against me harder.

"That's it," I praise her again. "Come for me, Addison." At the sound of her name on my lips, she shutters against me, exploding all over my cock.

The sensation of her squeezing the life out of me, I quickly come after her, spilling deep inside her. I collapse against her, breathing deeply as I come down from my high. She wiggles underneath me, and I push up off of her, our sweaty skin sticking together.

As soon as I pull out of her, Addison rolls over until we face each other. My chest tightens at the sight of her like this. Her cheeks are flushed bright red, her lower lip plump and swollen from where she was likely biting it.

I run my hand over her forehead, catching stray strands damp with sweat and pushing them out of her face. Her chest rises and falls from the exertion as she runs her hands down my pecs and abdomen.

"You were perfect," I whisper, and she preens again at the words of encouragement.

"So were you," she teases back, and I chuckle. I step away from her and walk to the side of the bed, pulling back the covers.

When I return to her, I sweep her up in my arms and tuck us both under the sheets. Addison curls into my side, pressing her body against mine languidly. I press a kiss against her forehead, taking in her musky scent of sweat and sex. I'm not sure I've smelled anything better.

She yawns and nuzzles her cheek against my chest. I wrap my

arm around her hips and hold onto her tightly. "I love you, Noah," she whispers into my skin.

I smile to myself, loving that I get to be the man who gets to experience these moments with her. I want every high and every low with her. I know things are still up in the air, but as I hold her tightly to me and listen to her breathing even out, I can't help but feel like forever with her might not be that far away.

Chapter 46
Addison

It feels like no time has passed when we leave Noah's mother's home to return to Willow Heights. I know Noah isn't super happy with the idea of us going back to where his father is still at large, but he's been gracious and understanding that this is something I won't concede. I'm not going to stop living my life just because he's worried something will happen. I can't live that way, and I won't.

As we pull away from the small house, Catherine and Trish stand on the front porch waving at us. I feel my heart tighten as I wave back. Though my time with her was short, getting to spend time with Catherine again filled something I didn't know I was missing, and it hurts having to say goodbye.

The drive back to Willow Heights is just as quiet as the one leaving it the other day. I'm lost in my thoughts, thinking about everything that Noah and I discussed over the last few days. He gave me lots to ponder.

His words echo in my mind: *I fully intend to marry you one day, Addison Parks.*

I replay them over and over, paying close attention to every little thought that comes after and mentally working through how the idea of being married to Noah makes me feel.

In conclusion, amazing, though there is still so much that we have to work through and consider. I don't know how things will go with his father, but I know that Noah will do everything in his power to bring him to justice. Maybe then we can talk more about the possibility of marriage. There's really nothing I want more than to call Noah my husband and to be his wife.

As soon as we arrive home, we fall back into our little routine. Noah spends most of his time working and getting reading for his meeting next week. I get back to business, running my diner and juggling everything involved with running an entire staff and a successful restaurant.

Our time at Noah's mother's almost disappears into the back of our thoughts. At the same time, I'm not sure I'll ever be able to stop thinking about Catherine and the work she's doing out there.

Before we know it, the rest of the week flies by, and Noah's meeting is just around the corner.

"Hey, come here for a second," Noah mumbles in my ear the morning of. I look up at him with an eyebrow raised but take his outstretched hand, letting him lead me away from the counter and toward the storeroom. Traffic in the diner is starting to pick up with the breakfast rush, so I hope whatever Noah needs to talk to me about is quick.

"What's going on?" I ask him when we're alone.

Noah runs his hand over the side of my face, catching a few stray hairs which escaped from my ponytail and tucking them behind my ear. A sideways smile forms on his lips, and he leans down, kissing my mouth. When he pulls away, I feel breathless.

"You're so beautiful," he murmurs, rubbing his thumb along my bottom lip.

I can't help but grin at him. "Is that what you pulled me back here for? Not that I'm complaining," I tease.

He chuckles under his breath but shakes his head. "No, I stopped in to tell you that I'm getting ready to leave. My meeting in DC is at one, and then I'll hop right on a plane to come home so we can make it to Jordan's thing tonight."

"Do you think your meeting will be good news?" I ask him. He's been on edge about this meeting ever since he caught wind of it. He's been scrambling all over the place, putting together pieces of his case to convince his superiors that he can take it on again. Last night he got a text from his supervisor telling him to be in DC this afternoon with a link to a plane ticket.

It's last minute, but Noah has no choice if he wants to keep working for the Bureau. We had been planning on going to his friend Jordan's baby shower this evening, so hopefully, he'll be back in time to make it.

"I hope so," Noah answers my question, running his thumb over my lip again. "I guess there's only one way to find out, huh?"

I run my hands down the sides of his arms, appreciating the broadness of his muscles. "You'll do great. Go kick some FBI butt, yeah?"

He chuckles and leans down to kiss me. "I love you, Parks."

I beam up at him, "I love you too; now get out of here."

He laughs again, following my instructions after kissing me one last time. I watch him head out of the diner, waving as he gets in his car and drives off. I go back to what I was working on, thinking up all the different ways Noah's meeting could go. The morning passes by smoothly, and before I know it, lunchtime is coming around. "Addie, can I talk to you for a minute?" Jack asks. I turn around to face him, my eyes widening as soon as he's in my view. He looks like a mess, his hair all disheveled, and his eyes droopy. I notice his nose is red, and he's got a fist full of tissues in his hand.

"Jack, are you okay?" I ask him as we walk back to my office together.

He shakes his head and sniffles his nose. "I think I need to go home."

As soon as we're in my office, he sits in the chair in front of my desk, bringing his tissues up to blow his nose. I wince at the nasty noise and sit down in my chair. "I'm going out on a limb here and guessing you're sick?" I ask, a weak attempt at humor.

He plays along, giving a weak chuckle. "Yeah, I'd say so. I woke up feeling a little off this morning, but I chalked it up to not getting enough sleep. But it's just been getting worse. My whole body is starting to ache now."

"You should definitely go home then," I tell him, turning my computer on and pulling up the schedule.

"I feel terrible, though. I was supposed to close for you tonight, so you could go to your friend's baby shower."

I shake my head and wave my hand. "Don't feel bad for even a moment. You've been covering so much for me lately; it's nothing. That's probably why you're sick. I've been working you like a dog."

Jack leans back in his chair and frowns. "I like working."

"Even still," I respond and fold my hands on my desk. "I'll cover the rest of the shift tonight. You just go home and get some rest. Can I send you with anything? Soup or grilled cheese?"

"I might take some soup," Jack says. "My throat is kind of hurting, too, so that might feel good."

"Of course. Why don't you get your things together, and I'll get that ready for you."

He sighs. "Thanks for being so flexible, Addie."

"Seriously, Jack. You do so much for me; this is the least I could do."

My friend gives me a small smile. "I'd give you a hug, but I don't think you want me to pass whatever this is on to you."

I hold up my hands jokingly as if to keep him away from me. "Please don't. I've already been sick enough this year."

Jack shakes his head in amusement, and we leave the office. I let him grab his things while I put together a small bag of goodies. I make sure to spoon out three large to-go bowls of soup for him and toss in a few extra dinner rolls. I have our chef grill him up a fresh grilled cheese and wrap it up in wax paper once it's finished. Jack is waiting for me in front of my office when I walk out with his complete care package.

"Here you go," I say, handing it over to him. "I hope you feel better soon."

"Thanks, me too. Hopefully, it's just a little cold, and I'll be better before we know it."

I wrap my arms around my middle and give him a smile. "Take your time. I want you to focus on getting better, don't worry about a thing here."

"I'm not sure if that's possible, but I'll try," he says, holding up the bag. "Thanks again."

I see him out the back door, ensuring he gets to his car okay. As soon as he drives away, I hurry back inside to try and figure out where we're at for the day.

The day flies by in a flurry of madness. Running the diner short-staffed isn't the easiest of tasks, but we make it work. I find myself running orders and cleaning tables where needed. By the end of the day, my feet are aching, and my head is throbbing from the stress.

"You sure you're okay if I take off?" One of my employees asks timidly, peering into my office where I'm counting the rest of the cash taken in today.

I look up and give her a tired smile. "Of course, Emily. Head on home. Thanks for all your hard work today."

She smiles at me and gives me a little wave. Not long after, I hear the front door jingle, telling me she's gone, and the diner is quiet. I finish counting the cash and complete a few other closing duties before I'm finally ready to leave.

The idea of going over to Jordan's party tonight makes me even more exhausted. I check the time and decide I can run upstairs to the apartment and clean up before heading over there. Maybe I can even get a short cat nap in. Noah's not due for another hour and a half, maybe two hours. I can get some rest before having to head over to the bar.

I grab my things and flick off the lights in the diner before leaving through the front door.

My fingers fumble with my keys a little, frozen from the cold. "Oh, come on," I grumble as I continue to struggle. Finally, I find the right key and stick it in the lock, giving it a forceful twist. I give the knob a wiggle to ensure it's locked, and then I stick the keys in my pocket before turning around.

I come to a full stop when I see someone standing right in front of me. He's dressed in all black, a hood covering his eyes and face.

"Can I—" my voice shakes, and I clear my throat, my eyes glancing up and down the street for any bystanders, but there's no one. The street is empty. "Can I help you?"

"Are you Addison Parks?" he asks me. His voice is gravelly and rough, the deep timbre sending the. Hair on the back of my neck standing straight up.

Against my better judgment, I nod my head slightly. He has me trapped. I get the feeling that he was merely only asking for the sake of pleasantries. Why else would he be lurking behind me in the dark if I wasn't who he was looking for?

My blood thrums heavily through my body, and I steel myself to run, but he beats me to it. Before I even get the chance to take a step, he raises his arm and strikes me against the side of the head.

Sharp pain clambers through my skull, and my body stiffens as I fall to my knees. I let out a startled cry, my arms flying up to protect myself as he raises his hand once more, gearing up to strike again.

And then everything goes black.

Chapter 47
Noah

The bar bumps with loud music as I walk in. I take a minute to accustom myself before pushing through the crowds. I'm not sure what I expected from this party, but this wasn't it. Maybe I was thinking more along the lines of finger sandwiches and teacups. I should've known better. This is Jordan we're talking about, after all.

I scope out my friend standing by a table piled with gifts. Rose is standing next to him, tucked closely into his side. Her face is lit up in a smile as she talks to someone, her hand rubbing her rounded belly affectionately.

Jordan calls out my name as soon as he sees me, and I plaster on a smile as he pulls me into a hug. I clap my hand against his back. "Congratulations, man. So happy for the two of you."

He pulls away and pats my shoulder, a look of pride beaming on his face. "Thanks, Noah. I appreciate it. Thanks for coming."

"Of course. Hey, have you seen my girl around?" I ask Jordan, my voice raising slightly so he can hear me.

In turn, he gives me a confused look. "No, I thought she was coming with you. I haven't seen her."

My blood turns to ice, and I frown at him, not liking the uncomfortable feeling blooming low in my gut. "You haven't seen her? At all?"

"No, man, sorry," Jordan says, unaware of the implications of what he's telling me.

I stare at him for a second more, processing what he told me. Then I pat him on the shoulder and turn away, pulling my phone out of my back pocket and calling Charlie's number. He answers on the second ring.

"What's up?" his deep voice comes through the phone. "Where are you? A rave?"

"Have you talked to Addison?" I ask him, ignoring his question.

Silence descends along the line, and then he says, "No? Should I have?"

I pull the phone away from my ear and swear. Then I bring it back and tell him, "Are you at the station? I'm heading that way."

Charlie acknowledges and says he'll see me in a few minutes. As soon as we hang up the phone, I rush out of the bar without saying a word to anyone else.

Charlie is waiting for me at the police station. His eyebrows are furrowed in the middle of his forehead as I hurry up to him.

"What's going on?" he asks, his tone all business.

I come to a stop right in front of him, panting slightly. "Addison's missing."

If possible, his eyes narrow even more. "What do you mean, *missing?*"

Shaking my head, I brush past him and walk into the station. "I mean, she was supposed to meet me at my friend Jordan's baby shower tonight, and she wasn't there."

"And she's not at home?" Charlie asks, following after me.

"No, and she's not at the diner," I tell him. "I know what you're going to say, and under normal circumstances, I would agree with you. But trust me, Charlie, she's *gone.*"

Charlie stares at me as I round his desk and slide the mouse to his computer, booting up the screen. It takes him only a moment to process before jumping into action. "Okay, when's the last time you heard from her?"

I wince, thinking about the brief *good luck* text message she sent me before I went into my meeting. "Early afternoon, nothing since then. She was super busy today. She told me she planned to close around eight and then head to the bar to wait for me. My flight got in at 10:30." Charlie nods his head and grips the arm of his work chair, rolling me out of the way and taking his spot at his computer. "What are you doing?" I ask as he takes control of the mouse.

"I'm pulling up the location app for her phone. That will tell us the last place it pinged."

Charlie doesn't say anything else as he works to pull up the application. His eyes fly across the screen, and he logs into her account without a moment's pause. I frown at him as he does so. "How do you know her account information."

He barely spares me a glance. "I'm her best friend. And the chief of police."

I frown harder. I don't like either of those explanations, but I don't ask any more questions, knowing that Charlie has been in her good graces longer than I have.

"The tracker on her phone stopped moving as soon as it passed city limits," Charlie says, his eyes focused on the screen. I swear under my breath and move to see what he's looking at. Sure enough, the Find-My dot hasn't moved from the location right outside Willow Heights.

"They must have tossed her phone," I mutter, my voice deadpan.

"It would make sense. If they found it on her, they would want to get rid of it as soon as possible."

I swear again and run my fingers through my hair, gripping the strands as hard as I can tolerate. I pace back and forth across Charlie's office, trying to hold myself together. Ever since I realized Addison was missing, my chest has been tight, as if a forty-ton weight was sitting right on top of me. With every minute passing, it's getting harder and harder to take in a deep enough breath.

Bracing my hands behind my head, I begin to pace, covering the boundaries of Charlie's office until I know the exact dimensions. My heart rate is erratic, and my chest still aches to the point where I wonder if I might go into cardiac arrest from the stress.

"She could be anywhere by now."

I must sound as frantic as I feel because Charlie's eyes dart over to me, and concern etches across his face. "Calm down, Noah. We'll find her."

"Where would they have taken her? I don't even know how long she's been gone!" I shout at him, running my hand over my face to ease some of my stress. It doesn't work.

"Just take a deep breath and *think*," Charlie instructs me. "If your father is behind this, you're the best person to find her. You've been working on his case forever. Just take a few breaths and focus."

Surprisingly, I do what he says and feel a sense of clarity coming over me. I work through my process as if this were just another hot trail I was on for any other case other than this one. What would I do first?

I press my lips together and leave Charlie's office without a word. I hear him call my name behind me, but I don't say anything. Wordlessly I walk out to my car and pop the trunk before digging around in my backpack that I brought with me to DC. I find what I'm looking for and then walk back into the station.

Charlie's standing behind his desk, bracing his palms on the smooth wood. He's frowning at me. "What was that?"

I hold up my little notebook as if that's answer enough and then start flipping through, scouring over my chicken scratch notes and searching for anything that might be helpful. My hands shake as I flip through page after page, still coming up completely blank. I finally turn to a particular page that I scribbled out right before my accident, which has me pausing. I stare at my notes for a second before speaking the idea out loud.

"What about the Witch House?"

Charlie looks up at me from his computer and frowns. "I went out there while you were in the hospital. There was nothing there, Noah."

My stomach roils with unease. "I just have a bad feeling about that place."

Charlie leans back in his chair, watching me curiously. "What do you think it is?"

"I don't know. There's something about it that raises red flags." I run my hands through my hair and groan. "I know you said it was a dead end, but if the two of us go back together, we might find something you missed."

Charlie watches me with a steady gaze but doesn't say anything, even though I likely offended him by saying he might have missed something. But he maintains his calm stoicism, which only seems to infuriate me further.

"We have to find her," I plead with him. "We have nothing else to go on."

"Okay," he finally agrees. "We might as well start somewhere. Let's go."

A slight sense of relief explodes in my chest, and I take a deep breath. "Thank you."

Charlie logs out of his computer and grabs his duty belt, clipping it around his waist. He grabs his keys from his desk drawer and then nods toward the door. I follow after him, taking the front seat of his patrol car.

With a flip of a switch, the lights and sirens turn on, and Charlie tears away from the station. He grabs the radio and mutters a few things to dispatch, telling them where we're going.

"Are you gonna call for more units?" I ask him.

Charlie shakes his head. "Not right away. If we get out there and things look weird, I'll call out, but I don't want to pull my guys off the streets just yet."

I nod my head, letting silence descend as we race through town.

The screeching sound of Charlie's ringtone blares through the car, jolting me out of whatever stupor I was in. He pulls his phone out of the cup holder, and I catch a glimpse of the name *Eli Montgomery* flashing across the screen. Charlie glances at me, and I nod my head as he answers. He puts the call on speakerphone so he can still focus on driving with two hands.

"Hey," Charlie says.

"Hi," Eli responds. "Everything okay?"

"Why?"

"I just saw you speeding through town with full lights and sirens," Eli says. "Not usually your job to answer emergency calls."

Charlie pauses for a second as he rounds a corner. "Yeah...no, everything is not okay."

"What's going on?"

"Addison's missing," I chime in, letting him know I'm here.

Now Eli pauses. "Is that McCoy with you?"

I grit my teeth at my old last name but answer anyway. "In the flesh."

"Addison's missing?" he latches on to what I said earlier. "Where is she?"

"If I knew where she was, she wouldn't be missing, now would she, Monty?" I can't help but rib at him though I'm well aware the timing is inappropriate.

He scoffs over the phone, but then his voice grows serious. "Where was she last seen?"

I exhale and rub the back of my neck. "I don't know. The diner, maybe?"

"I'll look around town some more," Eli says. "If you guys need any more help, let me know." He hesitates and then says in a softer voice, "She's important to me too, you know?"

"Yeah," I say. "I know. We're going to the Witch House to check it out again. I feel like there's something there that we're overlooking."

"Okay. Just ring if you need me," Eli says. We say a few more words, and then Charlie hangs up the phone.

"Do you think we should call Grace and see if she's seen Addie?" Charlie asks.

I nod and pull my phone out now to call Addison's best friend. The conversation is short though Grace's voice grows shrill with alarm when I tell her that Parks is missing. She says she'll start calling around to see if anyone else has heard from her.

As soon as I end that call, Charlie steers the car onto the gravel road toward the Witch House. My chest tightens with anxiety the closer and closer we get to the run-down shack. I absentmindedly rub at my sternum, trying to ease the ache growing deeper and deeper.

It's nearly midnight by the time Charlie finally parks his car. He turns to me as soon as the vehicle is off. "Don't be a hero, Noah. If they're here, we gotta be smart about this."

I nod my head solemnly. "What's the plan?"

Charlie runs his hand through his sandy blonde hair. "We go in together. If there's someone in there, I'll handle them, and you look for Addison."

"You sure you don't want to go ahead and call backup just to be safe?"

Charlie shakes his head. "We're thirty minutes outside of town. If I call them out for nothing, that leaves no one in town to cover any calls. I promise if something does come up, I'll call right away. You got a weapon on you?"

I nod my head, my stomach churning at the prospect of having to use it. I won't hesitate. If Addison's in danger, I'd demolish the entire town to keep her safe. I just had the idea of her having to see me use it.

Charlie inhales deeply and then breathes out through his nose. "Alright then, let's go."

We both exit the car and make our way to the Witch House. The run-down shack is creepy at best in the daytime but in the dark? I fight off the chill that threatens to creep down my spine at the thought that this is where my father has been running his business. A part of me hopes I'm wrong and that he hasn't been under my nose this entire fucking time, and yet, for Addison's sake, my pride can take the hit.

I better be correct, and Addison better be here; otherwise, there's no telling what I'll do.

I cover Charlie in tactical formation as we walk up to the Witch House. He doesn't waste time, kicking open the front door to the run-down building and maneuvering inside. The house is dark and dusty, with cobwebs covering every visible surface. I cough when a few dust particles make it down into my lungs.

It appears that there hasn't been any type of human life in this place since the dawn of time. As we enter the main living area, I lower my gun, seeing no signs of any other presence besides Charlie and me.

"Well fuck," I mutter, turning to the police chief. He's lowered his weapon, too, giving an apologetic grimace.

"Sorry, man, this is exactly what it looked like the last time I was here."

I sigh and rub the back of my neck, my eyes tracing over every surface in the room. I come up mostly blank until, finally, I spot something amiss. "Wait, what's that?" I point over to the ratty orange couch positioned haphazardly in the middle of the room. There, standing out against the dark wood of the floor, are two noticeable prints in the shape of boots. The floor throughout the rest of the room is covered in a thin layer of dust, except for areas clearly denoted as footprints, now that I'm looking closer.

I flick the safety on my gun and stick it in my pants as I bend down to look closely at the footprints. Charlie comes up next to me, crouching to see better too.

"I wonder–" I trail off, my eyes traveling to the heavily worn couch. I stand up and push it out of the way, wincing at the sound of the pegs scraping against the floorboards. Charlie helps, moving the piece of furniture all the way against the far wall.

Sure as shit, as soon as the couch is moved away, a trap door remains in the floor. Charlie and I share a glance. He winces sheepishly at me. "I didn't see that the last time I came up."

"Yeah, well, you wouldn't have unless you moved that

monstrosity out of the way," I tell him, clapping my hands together to dislodge the dust and grime accumulated from the couch.

The two of us crouch down to have a closer look at the door. A black iron handle right in the middle matches two black hinges on the opposite side. I reach out a hand to grasp the handle, planning to swing it open and take a look at what's hidden underneath.

Before I have the chance to, we hear a car door slam and then the sound of deep voices. Charlie and I look at each other in panic, and then we split, scrambling to find somewhere to hide. I hop behind the couch, taking shelter. I don't know where Charlie went to hide, but his footsteps echo as he scatters away from the trap door.

The voices move closer, and then the front door flies open. The newcomers stop whatever they are discussing and come to a screeching halt as soon as they walk into the living room.

"What the fuck?" a man asks. "I swear I didn't forget to put the couch back, Boss. I was just here a few hours ago, and I *know* I moved it back."

"Really?" a low deep voice asks. The sound of his timbre sends shivers down my spine. I'd know that voice anywhere, and though I'm not surprised that my father is the Boss the other man is addressing, the reality of it still stings. "Then tell me, how did the couch get pushed against the wall? Did it walk by itself?"

"N-No," the other man replies in a shaky voice. "Probably not."

"Hmm, probably not," my father repeats. Though I'm hidden behind the couch, I can imagine the condescending expression on my father's face. I've seen it so many times I could draw it from memory. "So then, who moved it?"

"Beats me, Boss."

"Do you think that maybe, you should *figure it out?*" my father snarls at him, and I swear the other man whimpers from the venom dripping through my father's voice.

"Y-y-yes, sir."

A cell phone ping echoes throughout the room, and I want to

punch something. I recognize the tone as Charlie's, and irritation flows through me. *Of all the times to be texting.*

"Pull it away from the wall," my father's command rings out, and I scowl.

Footsteps come closer to the couch, and my body tightens at the prospect of being discovered. I reach for the gun in my waistband, preparing for the worst. But it doesn't come to that.

As the footsteps come closer, a speckle of dust enters my nose. Terror erupts in my stomach as I rub at it furiously, trying to get it out of my system. But it's no use. The dust filters into my nose, tickling the tiny hairs lining my nostrils mercilessly. I feel the tingle of a sneeze at the back of my throat, and I squeeze my eyes shut, willing it away. But luck is not on my side tonight.

I sneeze.

Loudly.

I curse under my breath as the couch is pulled away from the wall, revealing my hiding place.

The ugly man staring down at me gapes his mouth open. He hesitates for a second before gripping my shirt and yanking me from behind the furniture. "Boss, look what I found!"

"Let him go," my father says, and the man listens and takes a few steps away from me as if I'm radioactive. Silence falls over the room, and I push myself up from my knees into a standing position. I straighten my posture, facing my father in the moment we all knew was coming eventually.

My father narrows his eyes for a fraction of a second before his expression softens, and he holds his hands out. "Noah, how nice of you to join us." I raise an eyebrow, wondering what his game here is. "Lionel, have you met my son?"

My father's henchman looks at me and then back to my father. "Your son? What was he doing behind the couch?"

My father rubs at his perfectly groomed jaw. "Hm, that is a good question, isn't it? Would you like to inform the class, Noah?"

"Where's Addison?" I growl at him.

"I'm certain I don't know who you're talking about."

"Cut the shit, you know exactly who I'm talking about, and you know exactly where she is," I shout back.

My father examines his suit coat, picking off a piece of invisible lint and flicking it away. "I might. What would be in it for me, though?"

His question catches me off guard, though it shouldn't. A bubble of trepidation forms in my gut. "You want to make a deal?"

"Isn't this what this whole cat-and-mouse game has been leading up to? At some point, it has to come to an end. Either I win, you win, or we come to an agreement. Now, Noah, you know I'm reasonable, so tell me. What are you willing to give me for the safety of your sweet little girlfriend?"

I run the tip of my tongue over my teeth, considering his challenge. Experience tells me I must proceed carefully, but this situation feels like a ticking time bomb. I'm afraid I'll suffer the consequences no matter what route I take.

Different options course through my mind as I search for the right one. Nothing I can offer my father will satisfy what he's after. He wants immunity, and I can't do that. He's done too much.

Finally, I settle on the compromise that I'll try and get him a lesser sentence. If I sell it well enough, he might go for it. As I open my mouth to make my offer, Charlie comes flying into the room like a bat out of hell. He attacks Lionel first, choosing to take out the henchman as a threat.

My jaw falls open as I watch them fight. My father, in front of me, grunts at the interruption, crossing his arms over his chest, unimpressed.

I see quickly that Charlie is outmatched. Lionel fights dirty. They grapple for a few minutes until it appears Lionel has had enough. He grips his gun out of his holster and swings.

"Charlie!" I shout as Lionel strikes his gun against the side of his head. The sound of the gun slicing into his skull rings in my ears, and I want to throw up as I watch him crumple to the ground, out cold.

My father looks unamused as his henchman turns to him and gives him a thumbs up. He rolls his eyes and then turns back to me. "Sorry about that interruption. Where were we? Ah yes, our deal."

"I need to see her first," I tell him. My heart rate has started to slow back down from watching Charlie fight.

My father looks back to Lionel, who nods his head once, walking to the trap door in the floor and opening it. My father motions for me with his hand to follow him. I do, though every step I take is hesitant. As soon as we're standing in front of the trap door, I swallow thickly as I stare into the darkness lying underneath. A set of rickety old wooden stairs lead down into a dank basement. My father grabs onto my shoulders with a bruising grip, spinning me until I face him again.

"Why don't you say hello to your girlfriend, Noah?" my father sneers. Before I have the chance to catch up with what's happening, he raises his perfectly polished shoe and kicks me square in my sternum.

Gravity does what it does best and propels me downwards. As I fall down, the rickety stairs dig into my back, head, and shoulders. Each hit sends pain shooting through my body from the force of which I'm falling.

I finally hit the ground with a sickening *crunch*. Attempting to push myself up, I groan when I realize I can't gather the strength, collapsing to the ground again. The world around me is spinning. My ears feel like I've got cotton stuck inside them, my surroundings whooshing in and out like waves. I vaguely hear a woman scream from somewhere in the basement. Still, I can't focus enough to tell what's happening.

Pain rackets through me again when someone grips my hair, yanking my head backward. I stare straight into my father's cold, dark eyes, and all I see staring back is hatred and malice. "Oh, I'm sorry, did that hurt?" he asks, amusement now clouding his expression.

I blink my eyes open and closed a few times, still trying to reign in the dizziness. After what feels like an eternity, my vision clears slightly, and my gaze lands on her.

There she is.

It doesn't matter that my father has my neck impossibly wrenched back or that I'm pretty sure I cracked my skull falling down the stairs.

All that matters is that she's here. I found her.

Even if I die tonight, at least I'll have gotten to see her one last time.

My father grips my hair tighter, and I wince, letting out a growl of pain.

"Well, well," he says, looking between Addison and me, intrigued as if he's watching a reality TV show. "About time we have a little chat, don't you both think?"

Chapter 48
Addison

"Wake up," a voice whispers to me. I recognize my body being shaken, and slowly I start to come back into consciousness. "Hey, open your eyes."

I do as commanded and blink away the blurriness clouding my vision. It takes a few tries but finally, everything comes into focus. The first thing I see is a young woman crouching before me. She's younger than me, looking to be in her early twenties. Her hair is dark but matted into tangles and sticking out all over the place. Beneath her chocolate brown eyes are heavy dark circles, and a bruise resides on her left cheekbone.

She's staring at me with kindness in her weary eyes, shaking me again, bringing me fully back into consciousness. Finally, when I try to sit up, she breathes a sigh of relief. "I was worried about you for a moment there. You've been out for a while."

I look around, taking in my surroundings. Panic courses through me when memories come flooding back. I reach up and press my palm against the side of my head, hissing in pain at the tenderness. Someone struck me and knocked me out as I was leaving the diner. How long ago was that?

My heart rate picks up as I sit up straighter, my eyes darting across the room.

I'm in a dungeon...or a basement...or a cave?

Wherever I am, there are no windows, and it's poorly lit by a singular bulb hanging from a wire near the stairs. I move to my hands and knees and feel the coolness of the tile floor beneath my hands.

I look at the young woman in front of me. "Where are we?"

She shrugs her shoulders, "I wish I could tell you. I don't even know how long I've been here."

I sit back on my rear and press my hand to my forehead again, feeling a blinding headache coming on. "How did I get here?"

She shrugs again. "They brought you in a while ago and then left. I heard them yelling at each other upstairs afterward, but I couldn't make out what they were saying."

Upstairs.

So I must be in a basement, but how long have I been here. Does anyone even know I'm missing yet? Has Noah returned yet and noticed I'm not there?

I survey the room again, my eyes falling on a set of rickety wooden stairs.

"Don't bother," the girl says. "The door at the top is locked."

I pause, cursing under my breath. And turn back to the woman. "How long do you think it's been?"

She gives me an apologetic grimace. "I don't know, a few hours, maybe? Time kind of blends together down here."

I exhale heavily as I sit down next to her again. "We have to find a way to get out of here. It's not safe."

Her eyes fly up to mine and then down at her fingers. "It's no use. There are no windows down here. The only way out is through that door, but they keep it locked at all times unless they're down here too."

"Who are *they?*" I ask her, hoping she can give me any type of clue as to who our captors are.

"I don't know," she says, shaking her head. "I'm sorry I know I'm being utterly useless."

"No, it's okay. We need to be ready just in case an opportunity to escape arises," I tell her. "Do you think you can do that?"

She nods enthusiastically. "I'd do anything to sleep in a real bed again. Don't realize how much you take things for granted until they're gone."

I give her a sad smile, knowing exactly what she's talking about.

She wasn't lying. Time seemed to be non-existent down there. I have no idea if I sat in that dank basement for minutes or hours. The two of us stayed close to each other, curling up closely to preserve warmth against the cold floor.

After what felt like an eternity—though it could easily have been mere minutes—footsteps resonate against the ceiling. The two of us jump, startled by the prospect that there are other people here.

A scraping sound echoes throughout the basement. "What's that?" I ask, alarmed. It sounds as though something heavy is being dragged across the floor above.

"Quick! Get down!" the girl shouts at me, grabbing my arm and pulling me down into a squatting position next to her. "That usually means someone is coming down here."

Before I can respond to her, the sharp sound of squeaky door hinges draws my attention away. I look over to the staircase just in time to hear a deep shout and see someone tumble down onto the hard floor of the basement. The man collapses into a limp heap as soon as he hits the ground. I scream out when I recognize the man as Noah.

He tries to push himself up but fails, falling again to the ground.

Another man walks down the stairs, taking his time as if he's the guest of honor. Finally, the light catches just right, and I can identify him too. Declan McCoy. Behind him is another man who I don't recognize. He stands at the base of the stairs, crossing his arms like a guard.

"Oh, I'm sorry, did that hurt?" Declan sneers as he takes a fistful of Noah's hair, wrenching his neck back. Noah hisses out in pain but doesn't respond. He's blinking rapidly, and concern blooms in my gut. He hit his head pretty hard on his way down the stairs.

Noah's still trying to come to his senses. And then, finally, he spots me. I see the clarity come back into his vision as he stares at me, huddled against the other woman across from where he's now kneeling.

Tears spike in my eyes as I hold his gaze. I have never felt more helpless in my entire life.

Declan pulls on his hair again, and Noah audibly growls at the sharp sensation. His father is looking from Noah to me and back again. His lips curl up in wicked amusement as he finally settles his eyes on me.

"Well, well," he says. "About time we have a little chat, don't you both think?" I swallow thickly, unsure what he could *possibly* want to talk about right now.

I look between father and son, unsure of what will happen, but I remain silent. Declan watches me, and I feel like a mouse in a lab, under watchful eye following an experiment. Finally, I get the courage to squeak, "Why are you doing this?"

Declan laughs, "Because it's my *job*, Ms. Parks. I'm sure my son has been gracious enough to fill you in on all the elicit details of my business. If not, I'm sure you've at least got a suspicion of what industry I deal in."

I look at the woman sitting next to me. She's curled into herself, her knees pressed tightly against her chest, her eyes downcast. I turn back to Declan and scowl at him. "You're a monster!"

"Hardly," he chuckles, giving Noah's head another yank for good measure. "I'm simply a businessman."

"You're a criminal," Noah taunts.

Declan shrugs. "To some, it may appear that way. But in my opinion, the difference between good and bad depends on what perspective you view it from."

I frown at him. Declan catches my expression and laughs heartlessly. "Ahh, you have questions. Goody. Well, go on then." He waves his hand as if telling me to get on with it.

"How could you possibly believe that selling women into slavery could be good?" I spit at him.

Declan stares at me. "As I said, Ms. Parks, it's all about perspective. You might think I'm a villain, but the way I see it, I'm simply a good businessman. It's hard to turn down an opportunity such as this one when it's staring you right in the face."

"How did you even get wrapped up in this?" I question him. Noah shoots me a sharp look as if willing me to shut up, but I can't. The desire to know exactly how he got to this point is too strong.

"You're a curious little thing, aren't you?" Declan muses. "It was an accident, really—wrong place, right situation. I didn't start my adult life thinking I would run the largest human trafficking ring in the North East, but here we are. All it took was a little schmoozing, and a few power plays. People want someone in charge who can make tough decisions and who won't put up with insubordination. I happen to be that kind of person."

"So that's it then?" I challenge him. "You *accidentally* became the biggest slave dealer in the North East?"

Declan pauses as if to think about it and then turns to me again with a sardonic smile. "Yes, exactly like that. What can I say? It pays well, and I had a family to provide for."

"How can you be so nonchalant about this?" Noah sneers at him. Declan grips his hair tighter, his attention refocusing on his son. "These are *humans* you're selling. People's sisters and daughters! You're one sick fuck. You know that? You'll get what's coming to you."

"Unfortunately, Son, I don't think I will. See, what's going to happen here is this. I'll make you watch as Lionel, and I tie up your pretty little girlfriend here and ship her out. A feisty one like her will pay well on the market. Some people like a fighter, which makes breaking them so much more enjoyable."

My stomach drops out from underneath me, and a shiver creeps down my spine at the threat. I don't doubt for a moment that he would do it. He'd no sooner sell me to the highest bidder than shoot me right here if I resisted.

"You wouldn't dare!" Noah shouts, thrashing against his father. Declan wastes no time, lifting his foot up and kicking Noah away from him. His kick lands true right on the side of Noah's head. Noah slumps away from him, dazed again from the blow.

I scream as I finally launch myself from my position, flying towards Declan. I attack him, reaching out with my fingernails and finding hold of his face. The man shouts and tosses me away from him. I hit the ground hard, grunting from the impact.

The guard standing at the stairs hurries over to me, gripping me by the neck and hauling me into a kneeling position as his thick arms wrap around my body, holding me captive.

"You little bitch," Declan snarls at me, swiping his hand over his cheek and pulling it away. His eyes darken even further as he registers his own blood smeared across his palm. "You're going to regret that. I've had enough of this shit."

In a swift progression of moments, Declan grips a gun from a holster on his side and strikes Noah against the side of his head as he tries to push himself up. Noah's head snaps sideways, and then he falls to the ground again. I shout, struggling to get free to run to his side. Declan strides over to Noah, gripping him by the hair once more and pulling him up to his knees. He manhandles him into a position where I can see everything that's about to happen. He grips the collar of his shirt tightly in his fist, yanking Noah up until he's hanging limply in front of his father.

Declan takes the gun he just struck his son with and holds it tightly, raising his arm. Fear clenches at my throat, and I can't breathe.

Blood trickles down Noah's forehead, crossing over his eyebrows and down to his cheeks. His eyes find mine, and though I suspect he's dazed from getting struck across his head so many times, he focuses on me again as if I'm his lifeline and he's holding on with everything he has. Declan glares at his son, malice clouding his features as he raises his arm, positioning the barrel of his gun against Noah's forehead.

I scream and thrash against the man holding me, but it's no use. My strength is no match for his.

"Noah!" I cry out. "Let him go, please!"

My captor's grip on me tightens, and he covers my mouth with his grimy hand. I scream again though the sound of my voice is muffled against his palm. Tears streak down my eyes and vomit rises in my throat.

Declan, still keeping the barrel of his gun pressed against Noah's skull, turns to look at me. A sneer crosses his face as he watches me with cold eyes. "I'm afraid I can't do that, Ms. Parks. This has gone on long enough. Unfortunately, there's only one way for this to end." He turns to look at Noah and pushes the gun against him a little harder, forcing Noah's head back into extension, eliciting a sharp hiss between his teeth as he glares at his father. "Would you like to say any last words to your little girlfriend?"

Noah's blue eyes cut to me, and I whimper against the hand covering my mouth. My body breaks out into a cold sweat as I stare at him. My chest aches at the sight of him so helplessly gazing at me as if trying to commit me to memory for the last time.

I see Noah's shoulders rise and fall as he takes a deep breath. Then, without breaking eye contact, he says, "I love you, Addison. For now until infinity."

A few more tears escape the lids of my eyes as I blink, fighting against the tight hold of my captor again. Noah's eyes are heavy on mine as Declan pushes the gun even harder against Noah's forehead. I can see everything reflected in those blue eyes. Every moment Noah and I have spent together ricochets through my mind as if on replay. From those horrid moments when we were young to the quiet conversation in the hallway when I realized there was more to him than met my eye. I can feel our first kiss lingering on my lips and how my heart hammered in my chest at the idea of everything finally working out.

My life with Noah has barely begun, and now, I wonder if we even stood a chance from the start. Maybe all this time, with everything we have been through, we've been destined to make it to this moment—destined to fail.

I scream at the top of my lungs when the gunshot rings throughout the wrecked basement. Tears sting at my eyes, and my stomach roils. It takes a moment too long for me to recognize that it's Declan's body that slumps forward, falling on top of Noah.

Through tear-filled eyes, I scan the room looking for the source of the gunshot. My eyes lock on Eli, standing at the foot of the stairs, holding a gun. His eyes are wide as he watches the scene unfold before him.

"You bastard! What have you done?" the man holding me growls. He lets me go, not caring, as I fall to the ground with a thump as he stomps over toward Eli. My friend wastes no time, taking aim once more and pulling the trigger without hesitation. The bullet flies through the other man's forehead. Blood spatters all around me as he falls to the ground, dead. His heavy body weight falls on me, and I scream as I thrash around, trying to escape him.

Within minutes, the sound of a pained grunt rings through my ears, and then the unwelcome weight is gone. Before I know what's happening, I'm gathered up into someone's arms. The warm body I'm pressed against shakes almost as violently as I am, but my body responds either way. Some of the tension coiling tight in my belly eases as I press my face against their chest, not caring who it is. I just appreciate their presence and welcome the comfort.

My nose picks up mahogany and green apple hints, and I relax even more into their embrace.

Noah.

"Shh," his deep voice murmurs into my ear, low enough that only I can hear it. "I've got you, Parks. You're okay now. I've got you."

I move my hand up to my face and wipe away the lingering tears.

The world around me is muted. I can hear Noah's soft, soothing words rumbling in my ear. I try to blink away whatever fog I'm in, but it's no use. The rhythmic rocking of Noah's arms around me is the only thing keeping me grounded right now. Without him, I wonder if I would sink into nothingness.

My chest feels empty, as if having to be forced to watch Declan point a gun at Noah was enough to rip my heart into shreds. Deep down, I wonder if I'll ever leave this basement. These last few minutes are some of the most horrific moments I've ever endured. Everything that just played out could have gone so differently. It could have easily been Noah's body across the room, soaking in a puddle of his own blood rather than his father's.

But instead, he's here, holding me tightly against his broad chest. I close my eyes and press even closer to him, reminding myself that this is real. Noah's right here with me, holding me, comforting me.

"I've got you," he keeps whispering in a quivering voice over and over. "I'm here. You're safe. It's over."

I let his words seep into my soul and hope with everything in me that they're true.

It's over.

Chapter 49
Noah

My eyes are heavy as I watch Addison sleep peacefully in the ER bed. I rub my finger against my jawline, wincing as I run over a tender muscle from clenching so much. The last twenty-four hours have been an insane whirlwind of emotions, and now, I feel the adrenaline pumping through my body start to crash.

After everything with my father went down at the Witch House last night, the police and my team from the FBI were called in. It was pure madness for a few hours. Addison managed to get through it like a champ. Though the minutes ticked by, I could see the events of the night wearing on her. As soon as EMS made it out there, I got her on a gurney, ignoring their pleas for me to seek prompt medical attention. Thankfully there was only the other woman in the basement with her, who also was rushed out to get medical services. A social worker would be dispatched to reunite her with her family at some point too.

Once we got to the hospital, I caved in and let them check me over. They rushed me to the radiology department, taking pictures of my rib cage to ensure nothing was cracked. Thankfully, they didn't notice any fractures. I didn't really need a doctor to tell me that my ribs were bruised. I could have figured that much out on my own. Because of the sharp pain, whenever I moved just right, I didn't turn down the painkillers they prescribed me, downing one with a big bottle of water after they ran a few more tests on me and stitched up the laceration on my forehead.

My doctors determined I had a mild concussion. However, they didn't spot any neurological deficits, so I was clear to go home on the condition of cognitive rest. When they were finished, I hurried back to Addison's side and claimed a chair.

And I haven't left since.

Sitting here watching Addison rest, I repeatedly run over the night's events. I never thought I'd be at a point where I could say this, but I am immensely grateful for Eli Montgomery. If he hadn't come when he did, I would likely be the one with a bullet through my brain rather than my father. Instead, I'm left with a set of stitches across my forehead and more bumps and bruises than I know what to do with.

I exhale and drop my hand down onto the arm of the chair. It's a little bittersweet knowing that my father is dead. I'm glad because it means that he can't wreak any more havoc in our town, but it's disappointing knowing that there was no chance for him to be thoroughly punished for his crimes. I would have liked to see him rot in prison for the rest of his life, living out the consequences of his actions.

Thankfully though, one of his other henchmen, who had arrived shortly after everything escalated, was taken into custody by the FBI and is currently being interrogated. A quick text from one of my buddies confirmed that he was spilling all his guts without much prompting.

Because of that, we'll be able to lock down the rest of my father's operation and end his reign of terror across the Northeast.

The words I whispered to Addison last night have never been more true. It's over, for good.

Declan McCoy is never coming back. I'm free.

The hollow sensation in my gut that I've learned to live with for so long finally feels like it's easing. I know it will take some time to get used to this new reality, but maybe now, I can move on with my life.

I haven't fully come to terms with what this means for me yet, but hopefully, I'll be able to sleep better at night knowing that all the years I've spent pouring over this case paid off in the long run. Something deep inside me yearns to go in a different direction, maybe away from cases of this magnitude. I excelled at what I did because I had to, but now that it's over? Perhaps there's a better way I can use my skills.

Addison finally starts to stir in the bed, pulling me from the depths of my thoughts. I lean closer to the bed, taking her hand in mine and squeezing firmly, letting her know I'm here. She sighs, groaning from the pain, and then turns her head on the pillow. Her eyes open, and she blinks a few times, my face coming into her focus.

"Noah?" she croaks, and I squeeze her hand again.

"I'm here," I tell her. "You're safe." Addison moves to sit up, but I gently hold her back. "Take it easy, Parks. Everything's okay. We're at the hospital in Willow Heights. Your doctor will be back in shortly."

Her hazel eyes take in everything around her, and I start seeing the lucency return as everything settles back into her mind. She turns to me, alarmed. "How long have I been here?"

"A few hours," I tell her. "I rode with you in the ambulance from the Witch House, and you passed out as soon as we were on the road. You're okay, the doctors just think your mind was overwhelmed from everything, and you were severely dehydrated, so they've got you hooked up to some fluids."

"What about the other woman?" she asks, panic lacing her tone as she tries to sit up again. I apply gentle pressure to her shoulders again, preventing her from straining. "I didn't ever get her name."

I give her a soft smile, running my hand over her hair. "She's safe too. She's going to be meeting with a social worker, who is going to do her best to get her home."

Addison's body slumps against the pillows at this information. She blinks at the ceiling, and I notice tears welling against her lids.

She rolls her lips together into a tight line, her chin quivering slightly. I scoot my chair closer to her and rest my forehead against her temple.

"Hey, baby, it's okay," I whisper. "Don't cry."

She sniffles and turns her head away from me as if she's embarrassed. Gently, I hold her chin and bring her face back toward me so I can see her. "Everything's okay, Parks," I tell her. "It's all over."

One lone tear courses down her cheek, and the sight of it guts me. I swipe it away with my finger before it reaches her jawbone. Addison closes her eyes, pressing her face into the side of my hand. "I was so scared," she admits in a broken whisper. "I thought he had shot you."

"I know," I say, smoothing my other hand against her hair again. "But I'm okay. I'm here."

Slowly, I lean forward, closing the space between us as I press my lips to hers. Addison moans slightly, her body melting under my touch. I hold her tightly, aware that this is a moment that we almost might have never gotten to experience together again. Breathing her in, I let her surround me, and we get lost in each other.

As I lean away, Addison's hand moves to the back of my neck, halting me. "Wait," she whispers. "Don't pull away just yet."

I smile to myself and rest my forehead against hers. She closes her eyes and takes in a few deep breaths. Making a snap decision, I push out of my chair and slide into the bed next to her. Addison glances up at me, startled at first, but then quickly relaxes into my embrace as soon as my arms are around her.

The moment she's in my arms again, my chest lightens, and I feel like I can breathe, the weight that was pressing on my lungs easing significantly as Addison presses closer to me. I do my best to focus on the here and now, letting her weight in my arms be my anchor so I don't spiral away at the thought of how badly everything could have gone last night. Slowly, the stress ebbs from my body, and my breath changes from shallow to deep, refreshing inhales.

"Knock, knock," someone says, rapping lightly on something hard as the curtain surrounding Addison's bed is pulled back. We turn around to see who is interrupting, but I don't dare release her from my hold. Addison's doctor stands there, a sheepish grin on his face as he eyes the two of us crowding the bed. "Sorry to interrupt, just wanted to check-in. How are you feeling, Ms. Parks?"

I look back to Addison to see her shrug against her pillows. "I don't know. I have a terrible headache, and I feel sore all over."

The doctor comes closer into our bay and looks over her chart. "That's totally normal with everything you went through last night. We've got you on fluids right now, and I can put an order in for some light painkillers for you to take the edge off if you need them."

Addison shakes her head rapidly. "No, I don't need any of those. I'll be okay."

He gives an understanding smile. "Of course. We'll monitor you for a bit longer as soon as we're through this IV, but you should be ready to get out of here soon."

Addison cuddles back tight into my chest, looking relieved. I thank the doctor as he leaves our bay, and then I focus again on Addison. She's got her eyes closed, her chest rising and falling rhythmically.

"Are you sleeping?" I whisper. She peeks open one eyelid at me, and I chuckle. "I'll take that as a *no*."

"I just want to go home."

"Soon, sweetheart," I tell her. I can't fight off the feeling of helplessness that blooms in my chest again.

Addison settles into me, dozing off and on until a nurse comes by with her discharge papers. We gather up her things and leave the hospital without looking back.

She's mostly quiet on our drive home, lost in thought. I wish I knew what she was thinking so I could say the right thing. Instead, I opt for silence. We'll have plenty of time to talk later. I figure it's best to let her work through her trauma on her own right now. She'll talk to me as soon as she's ready.

Addison gasps as soon as we pull up in front of the diner. Her three best friends are sitting on the front stairs. They hop up and wait impatiently when they spot our car. Addison exits the car and falls into the arms of Charlie, Eli, and Grace. They hug her tightly, each relieved to see her up and well.

I exit the car, too, circling the vehicle and then leaning on the side as I watch them reunite. Addison pulls away from her friends, wiping her cheeks. I hear Grace sniffle and then blow her nose. Addison turns to Eli first, placing her hand on his arm and giving him a grateful smile.

"Eli, I don't even know how to thank you," she says to him. "I don't know what would have happened if you hadn't shown up."

His cheeks turn bright red under her gratitude. With an awkward shrug of his shoulders and a rub to the back of his neck, he says, "I would do it all over again. I'm just glad you're safe, Addie."

Satisfied, Addison turns to Charlie and wraps him in another hug. "And you, thank you so much for everything."

"Of course," Charlie replies before releasing her. "We just wanted to stop by and welcome you home."

Addison laughs breathily. "Thank you. I'm glad to be back, but I'm exhausted."

"We'll let you two get some rest then," Eli chimes in, shooting me an uncomfortable glance.

"And don't worry about the diner. Take as much time as you need," Grace says, pushing her way past Eli. "Me and this loser will make sure it stays up and running. Jack says he'll be right at it again, too, as soon as he's feeling better."

"Really? Guys, that's sweet of you, but—"

"Thank you, both," I cut her off, resting my arm against Addison's shoulders as I steer her toward our home. "It means a lot to know you have our backs."

I dip my chin at Eli, and he returns the gesture. I don't foresee Eli Montgomery and I becoming buddies anytime soon. Still, I sure am glad he was around in the nick of time.

Addison says her goodbyes to her friends, and then we make our way upstairs to our apartment. As soon as we're inside, Addison seems to collapse in on herself.

She shrugs off her coat, letting it fall on the floor, not bothered enough to pick it up. I watch warily as she pads into the kitchen, pouring herself a glass of water. She downs it in a few deep gulps and then sets the cup on the counter. Then, with tired eyes, she looks over at me.

"Are you going to come to bed with me? I feel like I could sleep for an eternity."

I nod and walk over to where she's standing by the counter. "I can't imagine a better way to spend the day." I've got her scooped up into my arms in a smooth motion, bridal style. Addison laughs though it doesn't reach her eyes. She rests her head against my chest as I walk us to the bedroom.

I set her on the side of the bed as I pull back the duvet and the sheets. Addison sets to work unbuttoning her jeans and pulling off her t-shirt until she's left in her bra and panties. Then wordlessly, she crawls underneath the sheets, settling herself on her side of the bed.

Following her lead, I tug off my jeans and pull my shirt over my head. I crawl into bed behind her, pulling her body as close to mine as possible. She nestles back against the heat of my chest and lets out a big sigh.

"I love you, Noah," she whispers.

I lean over and press a kiss into the juncture of her neck. "I love you too, Parks. More than you could ever know."

She makes a cute noise of appreciation, and before I can even count to ten, her breathing evens out, and she's snoring slightly. I follow soon after, letting my body get the rest it's desperately craved since everything went down.

* * *

A week later, I sneak into the bedroom in the early hours and gently shake Addison awake. The sky outside is black, and the room is covered in darkness. Addison stirs gently under my touch and groans.

"Noah?"

"Hey," I whisper, giving her a soft grin.

"What are you doing?" she asks and then glances over at her alarm clock sitting on the bedside table. "Why so early?"

"I have a surprise for you," I say. "Come on, get up. You can stay in your pajamas. Maybe just grab a sweatshirt."

Addison does as I ask, shooting me confused glances as I lead her out of the bedroom into the kitchen. I hand her a mug off the counter. She raises an eyebrow at me.

"Coffee," I say as an explanation, and she nods her head before taking a grateful sip.

As soon as she's got caffeine in her system, she looks at me sideways. "Okay, *now* are you going to tell me where we're going?"

I press my lips together to hide my smile and shake my head. I've been concocting this plan for the last few days, and I'm not about to spoil it now. I grab the bag I packed prior and lead her out of the apartment and downstairs to the street.

Ever since we got home from the hospital, Addison has felt like she's been off. She's gone down to the diner a few times but hasn't stayed past dark. She filled me in on what happened the night she was taken, and I can understand why she'd be wary of staying as soon as the sun goes down.

I haven't been able to find a way to help her, and I'm not sure if I even can. This might be something that she has to work through herself with time. The doctors gave her a list of professionals to help her work through the trauma. I think Addison is considering looking into it. I hope my surprise will help her feel more like herself, so we can move forward together.

It's not a very original idea, but I'm crossing my fingers that it will play out just as well as last time.

"Noah," Addison whines as I take her hand and drag her down Main Street.

The town is still fast asleep, aside from the few stragglers and early risers. I lead her away from the diner, past the small park, and toward the old clock tower, sitting proudly as the focal point of the town square.

The door is easy to open, practically rotted out from years of disrepair. Addison is quiet as I lead her in, and I suspect she's already guessed my secret plan—as I mentioned, it's not an *original* idea, after all.

When we reach the attic, I swing the bag off my shoulder and pull out the blanket I brought along. I toss the fuzzy thing down on the dusty floor, spreading it out close enough to the window so we can watch the show comfortably.

Like she did last time, Parks walks over to the window, looking down our town square. Once the blanket is spread out, I sit down, getting as comfortable as possible.

"Hey," I say, pulling her attention back to me. "Come here."

She does as I ask, coming to sit next to me. The warmth from her body seeps into mine, and my heart swells with adoration for this woman. I reach over to my bag and pull out a smaller, lighter blanket I brought as a spare.

I wrap it around the two of us, ensuring our shoulders are covered. Addison is now watching me as she takes a sip of her coffee. Her eyes are sparkling, and I can't help the smile that fights its way onto my face.

"You think you're pretty slick, don't you?" she asks, amusement lacing her tone.

I grin now, feeling accomplished. "Maybe just a little bit. Are you surprised?"

"I won't lie. I don't think I ever would have guessed that this was it. When's the last time we were here?"

I shrug a shoulder. "Probably when we were like seventeen or something."

She blows out a breath. "That was a *long* time ago."

"Yeah," I respond and then look at her warmly. "Nothing's changed, though. I was head over heels in love with you then, and I still am now."

Even in the low light, I see the blush warm over her cheeks, and she nudges me with her shoulder. "Slick guy," she whispers.

We fall into a comfortable silence then, each of us taking regular sips of our coffee as we wait for the big moment. Before too long, the sky lights up, the darkness fading into pastel pinks and yellows.

Addison gasps as soon as the sky starts its dance, pressing herself closer to me as if trying to get a better look. Instead of being captivated by the sky like she is, I find myself watching her. I see every moment of awe and wonder that flashes across her beautiful face as the sun rises.

I vividly remember the last time I brought her here to watch the sunrise. I was so in love with her, but I didn't know what to do with that information then. Even now, knowing what I do about what our story entailed, I don't think I would have changed my mind about her. Would I have done things differently? Abso-fucking-lutely yes. But what's done is done, and I can't change the past.

I fall even more in love with her as I watch the sunlight caress her face, highlighting every sparkle in her eyes and the freckles that dot her cheeks.

"You're staring at me," she whispers. I'm hit with a sense of deja vu as the memories of our past come flooding in.

"I want to kiss you," I tell her, and she turns her head toward me.

A soft smirk plays on her lips. "Then do it."

Without wasting any more time, I slide my hand up her body until I'm cupping her cheek. Slowly, I pull her to me, closing the distance between us as I kiss her. She sighs happily as I move my lips against hers.

"Noah," she gasps when we both come up for air. "Noah, I want you."

I find her eyes, feeling my body ignite under her heated gaze. "Here?" She nods her answer, biting her swollen lower lip.

Groaning low in my throat, I do as she asks and—after moving our coffee mugs away from the blanket—maneuver her until she's lying on the blanket. We both make quick work of our clothes, shimmying and wiggling out of them until we're both bare. I exhale with relief as soon as I feel her bare skin against mine, and then I claim her lips again.

I let myself get lost in Addison, allowing her love to consume me. She gives back with every lick and kiss enthusiastically, taking her pleasure from my body without holding back. This moment feels sacred. As the sun rises over us, I get the sense that we are unstoppable.

We may have a long ways to go until we're okay again, but as long as we do it together, I know we'll get there. I have no doubt in my mind that Addison and I are stronger together and that we can beat any challenge that comes our way.

Epilogue
Addison

One Year Later

"Okay, okay," I complain, laughing as Grace grabs my hand and practically drags me up the stairs toward town hall.

"Hurry up, slowpoke, we're going to be late!"

The two of us are dressed to the nines, all primped and polished, for the evening. It's a momentous night for many reasons. For starters, it's the first Mayor's Ball Willow Heights has hosted in over a decade in honor of the election of our new mayor. This leads to the second reason for celebration.

The one and only Charlie Sullivan has just recently taken the mayor's seat.

It's been a long year in the aftermath of the worst night of my life, but I think everything has finally settled down. Noah has been swamped ever since that night, cleaning up messes and putting out fires, all in order to shut down the horrific business his father had been running.

Only a month ago, Noah returned from a quick trip to DC, looking exhausted. As soon as he walked into the apartment, he collapsed on the couch and hung his head between his knees. I went over and sat with him until he was ready to talk. With a deep exhale and bloodshot eyes, he held my attention and said the words I'll never forget.

"It's done. We've done it."

Not even a week later, Noah turned his resignation to the FBI, choosing to take on a more quiet life as part of the police force in Willow Heights. This way, he can still devote himself to the work he loves on a smaller scale.

Charlie decided to run for mayor this past election season, taking over the interim mayor's position. The election was a landslide, with the people of Willow Heights going out and putting in their votes in support of the police chief they love and trust.

So tonight we're celebrating many things.

As soon as we reach the ballroom doors, Grace turns to me with a critical eye. "Smile. Let me make sure you don't have lipstick on your teeth." I roll my eyes but do as she asks, baring my teeth to my best friend, who nods approvingly. "Clear. Shall we?"

I decided to come tonight with Grace as Noah had to work all day. He said he would meet me here later as soon as his shift ended. It was all fine with me since Grace is about as good a wing-woman as a girl can get.

Placing my hand in Grace's, we open the doors and make our grand entrance into the ballroom. A few people look up as we pass, waving or giving us broad smiles. I spot Charlie and Eli near the bar, and we walk toward them together.

Charlie looks up as soon as we near, and he gives us a grin, setting his drink down and wrapping me in a big hug. "Hey, Addie. You look great."

I pull away from my best friend and straighten the lapels of his suit jacket, "As do you, Mr. Mayor."

Charlie grimaces and then rubs the back of his neck nervously. "It's been a week, but I'm still not fully used to it."

Chuckling, I pat his chest. "You'll get used to it soon enough.

Hey, Eli," I say, turning to my other friend, who's leaning against the bar. "You're looking very dapper as well."

He gives me an appreciative grin. "Thanks, Addie." Then he looks between Grace and me. "You both look incredible, too."

"It's nice to have an excuse to dress up," Grace chimes in, flipping her hair over her shoulder. "Now, how about a drink for the ladies?"

We share a laugh, and the guys step out of the way so we can place our orders with the bartender. As soon as I have my glass of wine in hand, I back up and look around the room, taking in all who are in attendance.

"He'll be here in a little bit," Charlie answers my unasked question. "Last I heard, he was just finishing a call and said he'd be here shortly."

I take a sip of my drink, feeling my cheeks heat up at my obviousness. "Thanks. Where's Wyatt tonight?"

Charlie winks at me, fighting back a smile as he answers, "He's over there, talking shop with a few of his other friends."

I nod, following his gesture to see Charlie's husband deep in conversation with a few other men in suits.

We spend the next hour or so catching up from the week. Though we live in a small town and see each other often, it's nice to have a chance to chat outside of our everyday social events. I can only chat so much with Charlie and Eli when they come in for breakfast, and throughout the week, I don't see Grace much with how busy her business is.

Finally, surprising us all, Eli asks Grace to dance with him. His cheeks heat up with embarrassment, but thankfully, Grace doesn't roast him too badly, surprising us again when she accepts without argument.

Charlie and I watch our two friends walk hand in hand to the center of the dance floor. He looks at me with a raised eyebrow, and I shrug. This may be the start of something new for the two of them.

"I suppose we better get out there too," Charlie says, holding his hand out.

I set my empty wine glass on the bar, slide my hand in his, and let him lead me to the dance floor. The song changes to something a little more upbeat, and Charlie and I dance across the floor. He twirls me dramatically, making me laugh out loud.

When the music starts to slow down, Charlie brings me closer to him, and we sway together. I smile softly to myself. "I don't know if I tell you this enough, Charlie, but I'm so grateful you're my friend."

"You can't just say that now that I'm the new mayor," he teases back. "But thank you, I'm glad we're friends too. You're one of my favorite people."

"Likewise," I say with a grin.

"Mind if I cut in?" a deep voice, one that I would recognize anywhere, interjects. Charlie looks over my shoulder and smiles.

"Of course," Charlie says as he lets me go. "She's all yours."

I turn around to face Noah and suck in a breath. He's standing before me all done up in a full tuxedo, and his hair, neatly cut and styled, makes him appear almost larger than life. He watches me with gentle blue eyes as he extends a hand toward me, inviting me into his hold. I take it without hesitation, loving how my skin still tingles as I slide through his.

Noah pulls me closer to him until we're flush together. I rest one hand against his broad chest, feeling the rhythmic beating of his heart. It's beating rapidly as he brings me into him.

"Hey, beautiful," he whispers as soon as we're close together.

I lean back and smile at him. "Hey there, handsome."

He gives me a lazy smile and then leans his head closer until his cheek rests against mine. His hand slides to the small of my back, applying slight pressure until our bodies are pressed against one another. Vaguely, I'm aware that the band has switched to a slower tune. Taking advantage of Noah's closeness, I rest my cheek against his chest. The delicious smell of his cologne tickles my senses, and I breathe him in—mahogany and apple.

Home.

As the melody continues, I close my eyes, letting Noah sway us together for a few minutes. When the song ends, another starts up without any interruption.

I pull back from Noah and look up into his eyes. "I'm so glad you made it."

"Wouldn't have missed it for the world," he tells me, his lips curling up in the corners.

I'm suddenly hit with a sense of déjà vu as I take in Noah in his tux, standing here in this room, dancing with me. Everything in my mind replays the scene from when we were eighteen, trying to navigate our feelings for each other. That night sparkles in my memory as one of the last nights before everything changed.

Since that night, we've battled against impossible odds, faced so many tragedies, and fought to be together through it all. It's been years, but finally, I feel like I can say that the battle is won. We've made it. Standing here, holding onto each other as we sway back and forth, everything feels like it should.

We've come full circle.

"What are you thinking about?" Noah whispers, his eyes studying me.

I shake my head and chuckle under my breath. "Just how far we've come. I finally feel like everything I've ever wanted is within reach."

"It is," Noah confirms, his voice a low rumble. "For both of us."

I give him a smile and then step forward, letting his arms wrap around me in a hug. We dance through this song, and then it gets quiet. I pull back and look up at the band, confused. At that moment, they start up their next tune, and my eyes grow wide. The few notes of the familiar melody play over the speakers as the keyboardist hits them perfectly. The singer steps up to the microphone and starts singing the lyrics I know by heart.

I turn back to Noah, my mouth falling open with a gasp. "Did you plan this?"

He gives me a casual shrug, a smirk playing over his lips. "Maybe."

"Noah," I shake my head, grinning back at him. "I can't believe you."

He makes a satisfied sound, pulling me into him as he leads me across the floor to the same song we danced to when we were eighteen. As he leads me throughout the song, I let myself get swept up in the moment.

All too soon, the closing bars of the song plays. Noah times it perfectly that he dips me right as the song ends.

I look up at him, feeling breathless. His eyes smolder over me, taking in the rise and fall of my breasts from the dance. He brings me back up and frames my face with his hands, gently holding my attention.

"Will you come with me for a few minutes?" he asks, his voice gentle. I nod my head, unsure of what to say. I wonder for a moment if he will find us somewhere private, and I press my legs together in anticipation. Noah's hands drop, and then he laces our fingers together, leading me off the dance floor and over to the doors leading outside.

"I have something important to show you," Noah says softly as he leads me out the ballroom doors and toward the courtyard.

"Okay," I respond, my stomach tightening with anticipation. *Is this it?*

As soon as we're through the doors, I gasp. The small courtyard has been done up with white lights and decorative roses. Small candles are lined up, leading the way to the pavilion in the middle of the garden. I let go of Noah's hand and walk through the pathway, taking in all of the small details that Noah must have spent so long perfecting.

My heart hammers in my chest, and my stomach erupts with butterflies. I look at Noah, who has followed me into the garden. He's got his hands folded behind his back. His expression is soft as he watches me; never in my life have I felt so loved and *seen*. This is the man I want to spend my life with, all the ups and downs and every moment in between. I've never been so sure of anything in my life. A sense of calm comes over me as I close the distance between us again, looking into his eyes and knowing I've found the person my soul was destined for.

"Addison, I love you," he whispers to me, and somehow my heart rate increases even more. "I feel your absence in everything I do alone, in every place I go without you. I can't imagine living a life without you by my side."

"It will always be you, Parks. I've known that for a long time, and finally, I get the chance to ask you to be mine forever. Will you do me the honor of being my wife?" He falls to one knee, reaching into his pocket and pulling out a box. He flips the lid open, and I gasp at the sight of the glittering diamond right in the middle. "Marry me, Addison, and make me the luckiest guy alive."

"Oh, Noah," I whisper. I take in the sight of him, bending down on one knee and holding out the sparkling expression of his love. His eyes are gleaming, a confident smile on his lips as he waits for me. I commit this moment to memory, never wanting to forget it. Slowly, I kick out the skirt of my dress, falling to my knees and holding his gaze. "Of course, I'll marry you."

Noah's grin splits wide open, and his face lights up as he closes the distance between us, capturing my lips with his in a searing kiss. My hands frame the edges of his face as I hold him to me. In the distance, I hear people cheering, and I pull away to see the source of the commotion. On the stairs, I see all of our friends present, watching and clapping as Noah asks me to spend the rest of my life with him.

I turn back to Noah, stealing his lips in another kiss. His hand wraps around my lower back, pressing our bodies together. I moan against his lips, and my body lights up with longing. Before we put on too much of a show, Noah separates us. He holds out a hand, and I place my left hand in his.

Carefully, he takes out the ring resting in the box and slides it over my fourth finger, where it will stay forever.

He takes a moment, appreciating how the adornment looks on my hand. Finally, he looks up and catches my eyes, and my heart constricts at the level of emotion he's displaying.

"I love you so much, Parks. You've made me the happiest man tonight."

I grin at him and wrap my arms around his neck. "I love you too, Noah. More than anything."

As I hold him there in the garden, with all of our friends and family cheering us on in the background, I can't help but feel like a girl in a fairy tale. We've come so far from when we were kids, antagonizing each other over the slightest transgressions.

Noah and I have overcome time and distance to be together in this moment. Though the journey has been challenging, and some moments seemed impossible, we've beat the odds.

We've spent so long chasing it, and now I know, without a doubt, that we've made it. Noah and I have each other now for infinity.

Bonus Epilogue
Noah

Another Year Later

"**D**ude, you need to calm down," Jordan says, clapping me on the shoulder.

My gaze darts to him and away before I go back to nervously fidgeting with my tie, trying to ensure it's lying perfectly against my chest. A hand comes out and swats at my fumbling fingers. I look up, aghast, to see Caleb now glaring at me.

"It's fine," he says, his voice steady. "Are you ready?"

I take a shaky breath, unsure why I'm so damn nervous and nod. This is a day I've been waiting for for what feels like an eternity.

I'm getting married today to the love of my life.

Jordan pats my back once more and then nods, silently telling me it's time. With both of my best friends at my side, I walk out of the house and find my place in front of the wedding arch set up in my mother's backyard.

I was a little concerned about getting married in May that the weather wouldn't have turned quite yet, but we lucked out. The sun is shining brightly overhead, barely a cloud in the sky. The temperature rose to a comfortable sixty degrees, where it's held steady all day.

Though I expect it will cool off once the sun disappears. But until then, it's a glorious day for an outdoor wedding.

It was Addison's idea to get married here at my mother's home. She wanted a quiet wedding, without the pomp and circumstance that would have undoubtedly come if we held the ceremony in town. I didn't put up a fight. It didn't matter where we got married as long as we were husband and wife by the end of the day.

My mother quickly jumped on the idea when Addison and I brought it to her. She fully threw herself into the wedding planning, assuring us everything would be perfect. And now that the day is here, I can confidently say she delivered.

Catherine Lockwood went all out for this wedding. I think there's a good chance she bought out her local craft store of everything white and glittery and every last string of fairy lights. Her entire backyard has been turned into a beautiful wedding scene, including the massive arch covered in tulle and white roses I'm now standing in front of.

Each chair set up has been adorned with a white satin draping with white roses. We only chose to invite our closest friends, so though there are few chairs set up, it still adds to the ambiance of the setting. Our friends and family are already seated, their faces beaming as they wait to witness one of the most significant moments of my life.

The aisle that Addison will walk down is lined with white pillar candles standing securely within a clear vase. White rose petals are already layered along the neatly trimmed grass.

I shuffle on my feet as I stand there, each minute that ticks by feeling like a decade being taken off my lifespan. Finally, after what I'm positive is an eternity, the lone violinist adjusts the melody. I faintly hear the click of the house's back door opening. A knot forms in my throat as soon as I see her, and I swallow, trying to clear it.

Addison stands proudly on my mother's back porch, Charlie standing on her right. As soon as she's in my view, her eyes find mine and a blinding smile crosses her face. My stomach flips with anticipation as she takes small steps down the aisle. Her hand is clutched in Charlie's arm, and I see him mutter something to her. Addison chances him a quick glance with a smile and then looks back at me.

She doesn't look away the entire way down the porch stairs and then the aisle. She doesn't glance at all of our friends and family in attendance, beaming at her as she walks. Her eyes are only for me.

Time stands still as if we're sucked into a black hole. I still see her moving toward me, but everything else fades away. I no longer hear the music playing or the muffled whispers of the guests. All I can seem to focus on is the love of my life walking to meet me.

I take in every little detail, trying to commit this moment to memory. Thankfully, Addison and I splurged to pay for a videographer, so we would have this moment forever. Yet I still don't think the video will do her beauty justice.

As soon as she stands in front of me, she hands Grace her bouquet. When she turns back to me, I'm hit even harder with the intimacy of this moment. Addison's dainty hands slide into mine and her glimmering eyes trace every inch of my face. Her cheeks are slightly pink, and a soft smile plays on her lips.

"Hi," she whispers to me, squeezing my hands.

I squeeze hers right back. "Hi. You look beautiful."

Her smile widens, and our officiant breaks our small moment, beginning the ceremony. Addison thought it would be a good idea for Wyatt, Charlie's husband, to be our officiant today. Instead, I tune him out, focusing on my soon-to-be wife, replaying every moment of how we got here.

If you had told me that very first day that the girl in the seventh grade, with the ratty disaster of a hairdo, would be my wife, I probably would have died from laughter.

And yet, here we are.

Without me even realizing it, Addison Parks became everything to me. And though it took us far too long to reach this point, we made it, and nothing can get in our way now. She's mine for the rest of our lifetimes, and just as equally, I'll be hers.

I continue to search her face as the officiant speaks, searching her eyes for everything we've been through and what is yet to come. I've never been so satisfied with how my life has turned out than at this moment. If I got struck by lighting standing here, I would die a happy man.

Wyatt starts to go through the processes of the ceremony. Though I hear him, I can't seem to take my eyes off her. I trail over every inch of her face. She seems to do the same, her hazel eyes growing studious as she watches me.

We each say our vows, repeating the words Wyatt says first. Then finally, it's the big moment.

"Noah Lockwood, do you take Addison Parks to be your wife? To love her, honor her, comfort and keep her in sickness and health, for as long as you both shall live?"

My throat grows thick with the heaviness of the moment—of Addison and me committing ourselves together. I swallow the emotion down and give a brisk nod of my head, squeezing Addison's hands in mine. "I do."

Wyatt grins and then turns to Addison. "Addison Parks, do you take Noah to be your husband? To love, honor, comfort, and keep him in sickness and health for as long as you both shall live?"

Addison beams at me, a blinding smile that lights up her whole face. I worry that I might be going into cardiac arrest, but she brings me back when she says, "I do."

"Then I now pronounce you husband and wife," Wyatt says. He pauses briefly before adding, "Now might be a good time to kiss."

A soft chuckle goes through our small group of friends. I step forward, closing the distance between Addison and myself. My hands frame her face, tilting her head slightly until she's staring up at me, adoration seeping through her eyes.

Slowly, so slowly, I lower my lips down to hers. I give her a gentle kiss at first, loving the tender way her mouth presses against mine. When I pull back slightly, her eyes flutter open again to meet mine.

"I love you, Addison Lockwood," I whisper, just for her.

Her eyes glitter, and she whispers, "I love you, Noah, so much."

With that confirmation, I lean down and press my lips to hers, harder this time. Sealing our new marriage with a kiss to shame all other kisses.

* * *

Six months later

"Z-I-N-K-Y," I say proudly as I lay down my Scrabble tiles, building off the N Addison laid a few plays before.

I look up at her with a satisfied smile to see her scowling at me.

"Zinky?" she asks, her voice deadpan.

"Yup," I nod proudly, giving her a shit-eating grin.

"That's not a word."

"Look it up."

Now that the gauntlet's been thrown down, she can't help herself. Addison whips out her phone faster than I would have imagined possible and types on the screen at a furious pace. Her scowl deepens as her eyes scan over whatever she finds in her search. She puts the phone back down on the table and glares at me. I give her a smirk.

"Well?"

"It's a word," she admits as her eyes narrow at me. "But I'm not happy about it."

"And it's on a triple word score spot," I point out to my wife.

"Of course it is," she grumbles. "Because why wouldn't it be?"

"I do believe that's—" I trail off, counting the points in my head. "Sixty-three points to me."

Addison glares at me and huffs but writes down my score nonetheless. She sets the pen down on the wooden table just a little too hard and then crosses her arms as she stares helplessly at her tiles. When she suggested we play a board game before dinner to celebrate my birthday, I don't think she quite expected she'd be losing so badly.

"Come on, Parks, don't be a sore loser," I tease her, unable to keep from further ribbing her.

Addison refuses to respond, instead narrowing her eyes and focusing on the task at hand. I lean my cheek against my fist and watch her in amusement. I can practically see the gears turning in her brain as she tries to develop the best comeback.

She takes freaking forever.

Finally, I see her eyes widen as an idea hits her. Her eyes dart to the board and then back to her tiles. The tiniest smirk plays on her lips as she reaches for a tile.

I help her out: "B-A?" I pause and let her lay her third letter. "Baby?" I question. "That's all you got?"

Addison leans back in her chair again, a delighted smile on her face now. "Yep, I think that's all I got for now."

I look down at the Scrabble board again, counting the tiles. "That's only eleven points, though."

"Is it?"

My eyes dart to her, and I raise an eyebrow in suspicion. She looks far too smug to have laid such a low-scoring word. "What aren't you telling me? I feel like I'm missing the joke here."

Addison chuckles and nods her head. "You are. But I just told you."

I look down at the board again. *B-A-B-Y.*

My heart drops into my stomach. Carefully I glance up at her to see her watching me with gentle eyes. "You spelled *baby.*"

She grins at me. "I did."

My chest starts to ache at the possibility of what she might be trying to convey. I push my chair back and round the table, falling to my knees in front of her. She turns to me when I hold my hands out, sliding her fingers against mine.

"A baby?" I say, barely above a whisper. As though if I say it too loudly, it might not come true.

Addison nods, her eyes glimmering with the prospect of the truth she's telling me. "I found out last week. I've been trying to come up with a clever way to tell you."

I bark out a laugh. "I think this was plenty clever. Took me long enough to catch on."

One of Addison's hands lets go of mine so she can run her fingers through my hair, then settle on my jaw. She tilts my head slightly, so I'm staring into her eyes. "Are you happy?" she questions.

I nod my head fervently. "I'm not sure if happy is an adequate word to describe how I'm feeling right now." Addison seems to let out a breath, and her shoulders relax. I stand up and pull her with me before wrapping her in a tight hug.

Addison's arms circle around my waist, and she buries her head against my chest.

"God, I love you so much," I whisper against her hair. "You're going to be an amazing mom."

"You think so?" she mumbles into my shirt.

"I know so," I kiss the crown of her head and then pull back. Resting my hands on her shoulders, I hold her at a distance so I can stare into her eyes. "This is the greatest gift you could have ever given me," I tell her before wrapping her into a big hug again.

Before today I thought I had it all, but now, knowing that Addison and I are going to be parents? I've never felt more whole.

I blink my eyes rapidly, trying to fight off the stinging sensation. A bubble of anticipation blooms low in my stomach. I close my eyes as I hold Addison against me, letting myself picture it—the two of us together, with our little family all around us. I never thought I would make it to a point where I could confidently say everything worked out. But I have. We have.

All that's left now is to live our lives together. And for once, I don't think that's too much to ask.

The End.

Acknowledgments

You made it!

Thank you so much to everyone who has been involved with making this edition of "Chasing Infinity" a real thing!

A big thanks to my husband who has supported me while chasing this dream. I can't imagine doing life without you! Thank you to all my friends and family in my life who have been around to support this dream of mine since I was young and writing nonsense. Crazy to think we made it!

Thank you to all my loyal readers who have followed along with this journey on Wattpad & Inkitt. Without all of you cheering me along, I don't know where I'd be.

Thank you to my dear friends, AnnRea Fowler and Kris Wood who provided a sounding board and editing for this book throughout this entire writing process. I'm so grateful to have made such amazing friends throughout this journey. You both were *instrumental* in telling this story and making it come alive. If you haven't already, please check out their writing!

Another big thank you to Graziana with Chris Covers for designing this beautiful cover.

And last but not least, thank you to everyone who gave "Chasing Infinity" a try. I hope you enjoyed this story and I would love to hear any feedback!

About the Author

Aria Harding is an emerging author of contemporary romance. This is Aria's first published work.

She resides in the good old Midwest, USA with her husband and two fur babies. Writing has always been an enjoyable outlet for Aria since she was a teenager, and she has found an immeasurable joy in being able to finally publish and share all her stories.

Be sure to check out Aria's social media, and don't hesitate to reach out!

Instagram: @ariaharding_author

Also by Aria Harding

Cedar Ridge Romances (Coming Soon)

Loathing Ryan Duet (Fall 2023)

Just Josie (Spring 2024)

Trusting Thalia (Summer 2024)

Falling For Amy (Fall 2024)